THE DARK ANGEL CHRONICLES
OMNIBUS

SERENITY RAYNE

BLOOD QUEEN PUBLISHING LLC

To those that have stood by me from day one thank you for always being there.

PROLOGUE

THANA

Do you know what it's like to have wings and not be allowed to fly? In the privacy of my own home and at work, I can unfurl my wings but not in public. Whose craptastic idea was this? I mean seriously, my wings are merely ornaments.

Because of my unique situation—being not quite light and not quite dark—it could be centuries before I'm invited to the Mate Trials. My best friend, Joscelyn, is barely a hundred years old, and she was invited to the first round this past winter. To be my age and not invited at least once concerns me. I'm nearly three hundred and seventy-seven years old, and I'm starting to feel like an old maid.

Stretching my wings, I look at them over my shoulder. Damn smoke gray . . . I'm not quite a Dark Nephilim but not a light one either. Running my fingers through my flight feathers, I flex my wings several more times, enjoying the brief freedom before putting them away.

Shaking my head, I dress for work, pulling my long, ash-blonde hair up into a bun—night shift, gotta love it. The demons come out to play on a nightly basis, and I'm here to send them back where they belong. I rush down the stairs and out the front door to where I parked my Challenger. I hit unlock before I reach the driver's-side door. Once inside my hellcat, I fire her up and take off toward St. Michael's Hospital.

There's nothing like banging through the gears and listening to some of my favorite songs. "Dragula" by Rob Zombie pops up in my playlist, and as the bass hits, I shift into the next gear. The roar of the engine nearly drowns out my music. Driving a stick and controlling the rpm makes the hellcat sing. I take several laps around the hospital, lost in the melody of my favorite song.

When the song finally ends, I drive into the east lot and park in my usual spot, far away from the other cars. With a small terry cloth in hand, I dust the road dust off from my pride and joy. I begin singing the next song on my playlist, "Never gonna stop," still on a Zombie kick, as the back door to the hospital opens automatically on my approach. The time clock is a few steps inside the door, so I swipe my badge and head up to the third floor in the elevator.

Once out of the elevator, I head to the locker room to get ready for my night. Affixed to the front of my locker is a fancy white envelope with gold-embossed lettering. I stand before my locker in a daze, staring at it. Joscelyn received an identical envelope when she was invited to the Mate Trials. My heart is in my throat, pounding away and drowning out all other sounds. Reaching out, my right hand trembles from nerves, but I gently grip the envelope and pull it free from my locker.

Without a second thought, I leave the locker room and go in search of my guardian, Raphael. Several turns through the hallways later, I arrive outside his office door. Pacing in the hall, I debate whether to knock, but just as I raise my left hand, the door opens. Raphael stands before me in all his celestial glory—disheveled, dirty-blonde hair and pale hazel-green eyes which see past my gun-metal gray ones and into my soul. His intense gaze steals the breath from my lungs. All I can do is raise my envelope to show it to him. His eyes move from me to the envelope, and a smile graces his full lips. "Are you excited?" His baritone voice surrounds me.

"Is it . . . ?" I can't even finish my question. Every other female I know prays for this day to come. Me? It scares the hell out of me. This invitation means Azrael and Raphael will test me to see if I'm truly worthy.

"It is. Congratulations, Thana. You have your chance to participate in the Mate Trials." He chuckles to himself. "How does that district lady say it? 'May the odds be in your favor.'" His hand moves to the back of his neck, defining his broad shoulders and muscular arms and making my core pulse in anticipation. He smiles. Raphael, my impossibly sexy, serious boss, just cracked a joke.

"Doubtful. But you never know what the big guy has planned." I crack a grin as I playfully point up. Raphael's smile is infectious, and I can't help but also smile as I shake my head on the way back out the door to start my shift. This fancy little five-by-five card might be my ticket to a better future—or death, if I'm unworthy. Only time will tell.

CHAPTER 1

THANA

St. Michael's Hospital . . .

I always chuckle a little when I walk into work at the irony that Raphael is in charge of St. Michael's Hospital as its medical director. Michael just so happens to be the police chief at the local precinct. Somehow, I manage to punch in on time and receive report from the Nephilim healer going off shift, who happens to be my other best friend, Mark.

"There are at least two patients who are close to dying today," Mark tells me as we walk the halls. His floppy brown hair moves as his head shakes. Sadness floods his hazel eyes as he looks from me to the hall we need to head down. My cat tattoo starts to itch, letting me know someone is near their time. I nudge Mark and show him the black whisps rising up from the tattoo. He nods slowly, knowing what this means.

We check the hallway twice before I stick my left arm into the room and allow my familiar to rise. The spectral cat leaps out of the tattoo, walks across the floor, and jumps up onto the bed with the patient. My cat nudges the patient's hand till the old man touches him. A serene smile crosses the man's lips as he pets the cat. Now, having had direct contact with the man, I know he has approximately an hour of life left.

Dropping my gaze to the floor, I quietly ask, "Is there anyone we should call?"

Mark sighs and runs a hand through his dark-brown hair. "He doesn't have anyone. He was found at a bus stop a few days ago, and his dementia makes him think he's a young soldier returning from war to his waiting bride."

I take a shuddering breath. Stories like his—a person facing their last moments of life without any loved ones there with them—break my heart every time I hear them. We finish up report quickly, and I text Raphael, letting him know to keep the other Nephilim out of my wing. If I'm to take this man's soul tonight, I can't expose my wings to the others before the Mate Trials.

I remain at the nurse's station until Raphael arrives to head with me to the old man's room. He's a handsome man, appearing unassuming with his glasses and unruly hair, despite being over six feet tall and a solid block of muscle. The light dusting of stubble along his jaw makes my hands ache to feel its roughness. He stops just outside the patient's door and rolls the sleeves of his dress shirt up to his elbows. I'm hypnotized by the flexing of the corded muscles of his forearms. Something about the potential strength of a man's hands gets my blood boiling. He catches me staring and grins. "Focus, Thana," he says softly. I do, however, notice the color has risen on his cheeks.

Raphael enters the room ahead of me, and I close the door behind us. His hands take on a soft white glow just before he touches the old man. His inhale is audible as he makes contact with the man's flesh. Raphael's eyes close, and he tilts his head back, letting his dirty-blonde hair fall backward. He remains perfectly still as I watch his eyes move rapidly under his closed eyelids. I wonder what it's like to see someone's life flash before your eyes.

Several minutes pass before Raphael lets go of the man and turns to me. "He's all yours, Thana. He has a place in paradise waiting for him." Raphael's voice sounds almost musical to my ears. Gently, he rests his large hand on my shoulder and gives it a squeeze before walking out of the room.

Closing the door behind him, I place my left hand on the glass. Raphael places his hand on the glass over mine and gives me a firm nod. We work in tandem when someone passes. My job is to comfort the soul and embrace it, then remove it from its earthly bonds. Raphael will accept the soul from me and allow it to pass into Heaven. My eyes remain locked with Raphael's hazel-green ones as I close the curtains. Sometimes I think I see something more in his gaze, but I'm not sure what that is.

Before I return to the side of the bed, I draw in a deep breath and unfurl my wings. Carefully, I stretch each one out before leaving them half-open. My hands caress my smoke-gray feathers, making sure they look presentable. Next, my fingers run through my long golden-blonde hair, trying to remove the tangles as best I can. My hands ghost over the fabric of my scrubs and change my outfit to a black wedding gown of my own design. Death shouldn't be scary. It should be peaceful and beautiful. Finally, I appear at the old man's side and reach out to take his cold hand. His cloudy, pale-blue eyes look up at me, and he smiles.

"It's time?" he asks me weakly, and all I can do is nod.

"Does it hurt?" he asks next. I shake my head no.

I sit with my hip next to his and bend forward to place my lips to his forehead. Gently, I lay my hands on his cheeks in a comforting caress. I offer up a silent prayer for his soul to find his loved ones when he crosses over. My wings lower and cover us gently, shielding us from view.

As I lift my lips from his forehead, the wisp of his soul follows me, rising into the air. Carefully, I cup the swirling wisp in my hands and retract my wings, returning to my human appearance. "Raphael?" I call softly, trying to contain the emotions threatening to bubble up within me.

The door opens quickly, and he stands before me. As always, a look of concern crosses his chiseled visage as he looks me over. After all this time, he still isn't used to me becoming emotional. I always cry when I take a life, which is why I'm such an anomaly. Angels cry, not Nephilim—and definitely not Dark Nephilim.

Gently, Raphael wraps his thick muscular arms around me, hugging me and giving me the comfort, I desperately need. The warmth radiating from his body cocoons me, and my hands ache to grip his waist, but I need to give him the soul I'm holding. Before I can open my mouth, though, his thumb and forefinger grasp my chin and tilt my head up. As I stare into his eyes, they take on their angelic quality, the hazel-green turning gold. While I'm lost in that swirling mass of liquid gold, he softly presses his lips to my cheek, keeping them there for a moment before releasing me.

"You'll make someone a perfect mate, Thana." His smile doesn't reach his eyes when he releases my chin. He holds his hand out for me to give him the man's soul.

Reverently, I place my precious cargo in his waiting hands. The wisp dances over his flesh for a moment before he closes his hand and it's gone. I remain staring at his closed hand for a few seconds too long. "No matter how many times I see you do that, it still amazes me." Slowly, I raise my eyes to gaze into his, and he smiles at me.

"This is precisely why you're so special, Thana. The others merely pass the soul off, never giving it a second thought." Raphael tilts his head to the side, studying me. "You still care. Thousands of souls later, you still care what happens to them before and after death. Your charges are lucky to have someone like you in the end." He lightly caresses my cheek, running his thumb over my cheekbone before turning on his heel to leave.

Remaining in place, I take a deep breath to regain my composure and smile. He stops and turns back to me. "There's a murderer who was brought in by the police up on the third floor." Raphael looks up at the ceiling, and I swear he can see the person he's talking about.

"I'm going to transfer you up to his floor. His deeds have brought him a one-way ticket to Hell. Azrael will collect his soul from you himself." The tone of Raphael's voice changes when he mentions Azrael's name. For centuries, the original Angel of Death has been trying to corrupt me and bring me to his side. But I've rejected every advance he's made, time and time again.

My eyes widen at this news. "Azrael will personally be collecting the soul?" My gaze darts around the room, then back to Raphael. "He scares the hell out of me. He takes the Dark Nephilim to Hell himself. And he wants me to join him in the darkness." I shudder with the thought of him wanting to take me away.

Raphael gives me a knowing look, then smiles. "I won't let him take you. You're too precious to me." He says the second sentence so softly, I barely hear it. My treacherous heart dares to hope I'm more than just another Nephilim to him. He remains in front of me a beat too long before taking off to make the assignment changes for the rest of the shift.

Nearly thirty minutes later, the human nurse I'm replacing comes down to my floor, and we sit down to give each other report. Her assignment is mostly prison transfers and various other criminal offenders brought in by law enforcement. I'm beginning to feel like I've gotten the short end of the stick in this swap.

I make it upstairs, and who did they assign to guard the inmate? None other than Christian, a five-foot-ten, 180-pound kung fu master. Not that the humans know that. All they see is a handsome, distinguished Japanese man with his long hair in a bun. "*Kon'nichiwa*, Christian," I say as I bow low to him, showing him the respect he deserves. He's been alive for centuries and has attended hundreds of Mate Trials. But since the passing of his first wife, he has yet to find himself a suitable mate.

His chocolate eyes light up as he brings his fist to his palm before bowing lower than I did. "*Kon'nichiwa*, Thana." He winks at me and opens his arms wide, offering me a hug. I go to him without hesitation and rest my head on his shoulder for a moment.

"How is my night angel doing today?" he says, kissing the top of my head and releasing me.

"Great. Up until I was told Azrael is coming for this one's soul himself." Hesitantly, I peek around Christian and into the room behind him. Evil radiates from this man. It looks like a black, inky mass moving over his skin, kind of like that anti-hero symbiote in *Venom*.

"Azrael will be fine. You're safe, *kichōna mono*," Christian says as he clears his throat. "This one's death should be a painful one. He killed a pregnant mother as well as her two children who were in the house with her."

My eyes flare, and my eyebrows raise in shock. The dark gift from my father begins to rise to the surface, and I battle to suppress it. I will not go dark. I've finally ascended enough to be considered worthy for the Mate Trials. Christian watches me closely as I rein in the darkness. "Sorry, I hate when innocents die. It makes my heart ache," I say as I absently rub my chest over my sternum.

He nods solemnly as he looks back into the room for a moment. "Anyone who murders children deserves to burn for eternity. Children are a gift. Life is a gift." His eyes lighten slightly as he looks into mine. He's also an angel, not as high up as Raphael, but he's much higher than I'll ever be.

I reach out and grip his muscular bicep and give it a reassuring squeeze. My hand remains on his arm as I look up into his eyes. "Someday . . . you'll be a fantastic mate and an even better father." I smile as my raven tattoo begins to itch. He smiles at my comment, then looks up toward the heavens. I hope he finds his mate this time.

As I release his arm, I move past him into the room. Azrael is already sitting in the corner, book in hand, waiting for the inmate to die. "Azrael, sir. I wasn't expecting you this soon," I say as respectfully as I can. He scares the ever-loving daylights out of me. I think I'd rather have my feathers plucked, one by one, than have to stand before him.

"I know. It's exactly why I'm here. I want to watch you take his soul," Azrael says with a growl in his voice that prompts Christian to pop the door open.

"I'm unmated. I'm not permitted to expose my wings with males present before the Mate Trials." I look frantically between Azrael and Christian.

Azrael rolls his eyes at Christian. "Please. As if he'll find his mate this millennium." Azrael motions to Christian, and pain crosses over his perfect, sun-kissed features.

"I need permission from Raphael before I can do this. This is his domain, and his law rules this building," I say, getting out my phone to text Raphael. I basically tell him to get his white-feathered ass upstairs, and that Azrael wants me to break the rules. Within seconds of hitting send, Raphael appears in a golden shimmer next to me.

"What is the meaning of this!" he bellows, his wings on full display, filling the cramped space of the patient's room.

"Settle down, golden boy. I need to watch Thana take this man's soul." He motions to the murderer before us.

"Since she's of mixed blood, I need to make sure she's in full control of her dark side before the Mate Trials." Azrael leans back and folds his hands behind his head.

"Both of you are welcome to stay and watch. Then again, I am the only mated one of the four of us," he says smugly, looking between Christian and Raphael.

My eyes dart between Raphael and Christian. I don't want to break the rules, but on the other hand, I'd love to find out if either of them is my mate. Christian lowers his eyes, not wanting to meet mine. "I'll step out. I'm sorry, Thana," he says, his heartache evident in his voice. In his gaze, I can see that he doesn't want to leave me. Honestly, I don't want him to go either. Sometimes, the rules are a bitch. As Christian leaves, I turn to Raphael.

I can see the sympathy in his eyes, the golden hue comforting me. He flexes his wings a bit, drawing my attention away from his eyes. I stare at the beautiful white, opalescent color of his feathers.

I desperately want to touch them to see if they're as soft as my own.

"Can we get this over with?" Azrael barks, jolting me from my thoughts. Raphael offers me a reassuring smile as he motions for me to proceed.

Drawing in a steadying breath, I walk between Azrael and Raphael to approach the murderer's bed. I angle my body so I can't see either of their eyes on me. Tilting my head back slowly, I focus my shift first on my clothing. My scrubs change to my beautiful black wedding gown. I pay more attention to the details of my gown, which is off the shoulder with see-through sleeves. The bodice has intricate beadwork, accentuating my figure. A thin lace belt with white pearls fastens around my waistline. The gossamer train of the gown floats effortlessly behind me, giving me an ethereal appearance.

I don't dare look at Raphael as I unfurl my wings. I give them a slight flex and hold them half-open. From the waist of my dress, I pull out my black veil and place it reverently on my head, obscuring my face from view. Slowly, like a stalking panther, I lean over the murderer and put my hands on his cheeks. His eyes open quickly, and he looks up at me with fear in his eyes. I know the visage he sees all too well. I look like a red-eyed demon with razor-sharp teeth. When a dark soul is taken, I appear to them as their worse fear, while a light soul sees only an angel.

"No! I'm not ready. I'm too young to die!" he screams as he tries to escape my grasp. I flex my wings once and pull his soul from his body almost violently. The wicked souls always try to cling to their vessels. Not once has one come willingly. The black inky mass, as usual, tries to break free of my grasp.

I cage the soul between my fingers and squeeze tightly as I turn to Azrael. My lithe hands extend out to him, and he quickly takes the soul from me. A smirk plays upon his lips as he looks at me. "You've passed my test, Thana. I'll see you at the Mate Trials." He vanishes in a wisp of smoke.

I shift back slowly, a little tired after harvesting two souls in one night. My head hangs low as I stare at the floor between my feet. Raphael hasn't said a word to me since witnessing me take the dark soul. I feel like a monster. I always do. Slowly, I turn my head to look over my shoulder at him. His golden eyes shine at me, and a new look crosses his face. I'm not sure what the look is, but it's not one I've seen from him before. He flexes his wings twice, then puts them away.

"You . . . did well, Thana." He stumbles over his words as his right hand rubs the back of his neck. I just nod and leave the room. I need to take a break and get my head back into the game.

I return to the nurses' station and find my coffee missing again. A single black feather is left behind as a calling card for the coffee thief. Every few shifts, my coffee vanishes. That delicious life-sustaining fluid is my only solace on a night like tonight. I sit down and hang my head. I never wanted anyone to watch me take a soul, especially not Raphael. Anyone other than him would have been fine, better even. The truth is I'm a half-blooded abomination. I'm sure the Mate Trials will prove to be a waste of time. Wordlessly, Mark saves my ass and drops off a new cup of coffee in front of me. Hopefully, all that I lost will be at the bottom of the cup.

CHAPTER 2

RAPHAEL

The events of tonight replay in my head in slow motion. How dare Azrael test Thana on the same night I did. She's got to be exhausted after freeing the old man from his earthly bonds. Her text sets me on edge, and I arrive at her side the fastest way possible.

The way her eyes roam over me—how I imagine a lover's caress would be—makes the hair on the back of my neck stand on end. She looks so frightened and unsure of herself; my instincts push me to protect her from whatever Azrael may be up to.

In what I'll find out to be my smartest move to date, I leave my wings on display, hanging half-open. In my head, it's more in solidarity with Thana so she doesn't feel alone, being the only one with their wings exposed.

This is my first time to see how she works, and it's captivating. Her scrubs turn to an ornate and beautiful black lace and gossamer wedding gown. But what nearly makes my heart stop is the sight of her wings. On instinct, my own wings want to flex and expand to show off their grandeur to her. A male's wings are his pride and joy. It's similar to how human males take pride in the size of their penis.

An angel's wings are almost directly indicative of the power, strength, and rank of the male. Azrael glances over at me, and I give him a bored-looking expression, hiding the excitement bubbling up in my chest.

So many nights I've prayed to the creator, yet I've only ever asked one thing for myself. Over the hundreds of centuries, I've wandered the earth, doing as the creator instructed, I've only desired one thing. Thana...

In a cruel twist of fate, I have to contain my excitement, hide how joyous this occasion actually is. All because of Azrael. If he were to discover Thana is mine before the Mate Trials, he could construct a reason to kill her. The thought of losing my mate causes my heart to constrict, nearly stealing the breath from my lungs.

There's beauty in the way she spreads her smoke-colored wings and lowers her body, the muscles of her back flexing and constricting. My hands ache to feel her muscles move under them. Her lithe hands reach out and cup the murderer's face, and I wish it was me she was holding.

His eyes suddenly open, and his look of terror makes my eyes widen. I wonder exactly what he sees through the veil that scares him so much. Thana is the most beautiful woman in the world. His reaction truly puzzles me. With a single flex of her wings, she rips his black soul from his body. To me, it looks like a black slithering mass —evil incarnate. She cages his soul in her hands and retracts her wings after offering it to Azrael like she does with me.

Her gaze seems sad, almost haunted. Yet all I feel is love and adoration for her. Her exhaustion is evident as she stares at her feet, keeping her eyes downcast. Finally, my wings allow me to retract them, and I make sure to tell Thana she did well.

Her eyes find mine for a brief moment, and I feel like a teenage boy crushing on his first love. I can't help but rub the back of my neck, trying to keep my hands busy so I don't reach for her.

I watch Thana leave the room, and all I want to do is go after her and comfort her like I did earlier. The Dark Nephilim side of Thana has always upset her, and I usually hold her afterward. I know she feels hurt after having to expose her wings.

I'm guessing she never wanted me to see this side of her, but hopefully she'll open up to me sooner rather than later. I've suspected for a while she was meant to be mine. Seeing her smoke-gray wings, and mine flexing in response, solidified my suspicions.

My chest hurts, watching her walk away, none the wiser. Thankfully, Azrael doesn't seem to suspect anything. At least, he didn't say anything to me if he did. The next week is going to be hell on my nerves. I must keep my secret to keep us both safe. Heavens forbid any of the Dark Nephilim find out an Archangel has taken a hybrid Nephilim as a mate. War may break out. Or worse, they might hunt her down and extinguish her light and thus, possibly kill me in the process.

Slowly, I draw the sheet up over the murderer, then pull out my phone. Several swipes later, I arrive at the site to fill out the death certificate for the man. For appearance's sake, I lift his wrist and pretend to look at his name band. Carefully, I walk around the room to make sure no evidence of divine intervention occurred here.

There, on the floor next to the bed, is one of Thana's soft, smoke-gray feathers. Quickly, I look around, making sure I'm alone before I bend down and pick it up. Her feather is velvety soft and slightly curled, telling me it came from close to her body. Reverently, I cup her feather and hold it close to my chest and then tuck it carefully into the interior chest pocket of my suit jacket to keep it safe.

Taking a few calming breaths, I step out of the room to find Christian waiting in the hallway. "What happened, Raph? You look dazed," he says as he comes over and grips my shoulders, trying to steady me. His eyes scan my face, then my suit, looking for any sign that I may have been injured.

Several deeper breaths escape my lips before I can compose myself. My eyes drift up and down the hallway, then back to Christian. "Not here," I say before turning on my heel, taking long strides down the hallway as quickly as possible. He follows immediately, like I knew he would. The office at the end of the hallway is open, so I head in there. Christian enters and closes the door behind him, making sure it's locked. I'll just have to pray no one from any of the realms is listening in.

"What was that all about, Raph? That's not like you," Christian says, motioning to the hall beyond the closed door.

"Thana," is all I say before sitting down in the chair closest to me. My fingers thread through my hair, and I bow my head down, holding it as I think about the implications of what just happened.

Christian drops to his knees before me and tries to get me to look at him. "Is she okay? Did she pass?" He seems as worried as I feel, his dark-brown eyes asking me for the answers I'm afraid to utter out loud.

"Yes." I rest my elbows on my knees and close my eyes. My chest feels as if someone is crushing my heart in their hand. I'm practically gasping for breath while still processing what happened.

"Then what's wrong? You're starting to worry me, man," Christian says as he rests a hand on my forearm, trying to get me to look at him.

Finally, I raise my head, and I know my eyes swirl liquid gold. "She's mine."

That simple statement just changed my existence. Until she acknowledges me as hers, I'll be in my own personal hell. Shock and then sympathy fly over Christian's face. Finally, after a myriad of emotions cross his usually serious expression, he settles on ecstatic.

"This is wonderous news!" he shouts, then silences himself just as quickly. He jumps up from where he was kneeling before me to look out the blinds on the office door. Thankfully, no one, except the janitor, often ventures down this part of the hallway.

I finally understand what purgatory must be like. It's not quite Hell because there's a light at the end of the tunnel. But that light is six days from now, and I'm not sure I can hold it together that long. My heart is pounding out of control, and my lungs feel like they're starving for air.

"What am I going to do, Christian? She's everything I've dreamed of and more." Sighing, I put my head back in my hands. "I feel like I'll die without her. Me, an Archangel. I feel powerless for once in my long life." My voice nearly cracks with pent-up emotions. I don't like feeling this weak, this out of control.

Christian turns on the coffee pot in the corner of the office and makes us both a cup of much-needed coffee. After what feels like forever, he hands me a cup and pulls a chair up in front of me and sits down. "You've been blessed beyond measure with such a sweet, caring, and thoughtful mate." A weak smile crosses his lips. "I'd give anything to find my mate and have her be half the woman Thana is." His forced smile finally falters. "My team and I will keep a close eye on her and protect her even more than we already do. You have my word, brother." Christian extends his hand to me, and we grip each other's forearms. An angel's word is his bond, and we would never break that sacred oath.

I grip his forearm tighter and look into his eyes. "I am grateful and honored by your promise of protection for Thana." I lean forward and press my forehead to his, solidifying his oath.

Slowly, I lean back and smile. "Hell must have frozen over. It's been over five centuries since an Archangel has taken a mate. This may be the Trials we both walk away with mates." Smiling broadly, my heart is full of hope for Christian.

He slowly nods his head and forces a smile. "Positivity will bring positive results. I'll be positive. Besides if a workaholic like you is gifted a mate, maybe I'm next." He smiles a little broader, poking fun at me. Shaking my head, I slowly release his forearm.

"Let's take a walk around the hospital and make sure everything is where it belongs before it gets much later." We leave our hiding place, and I resume my rounds as Christian double-checks on security for the hospital.

The morgue has come to claim the body, and I see Thana and Joscelyn huddled together behind the nurses' station. Joscelyn is running her fingers through Thana's long, blonde hair, holding her tightly. Casually, I motion with my head, indicating I'd like to speak with her. Joscelyn nods and says something to Thana before following me down the hall.

"You summoned me, your holiness?" Joscelyn says softly before looking back down the hall and then up at me.

"How's Thana? She seemed broken after taking the dark soul. I wanted to comfort her, but with Azrael lurking around, I didn't want her to attract his attention." It's harder than I imagined, asking about my mate without approaching her to see for myself. I have to check to make sure my "director" face is on and not the face of a caring mate.

Joscelyn looks between the nurse's station and me, then sighs. "Honestly, she feels like a monster. She never wanted you, or anyone for that matter, to ever see that side of her." She glances over her shoulder again, watching Thana sip her coffee.

I nod slowly—there's the root of the problem. "Thank you for your candor," I say smoothly before heading to the nurses' station.

Thana's head whips up as soon as I enter her field of vision. Apparently, all the answers to the universe are located in the bottom of her coffee cup. "Would you like to talk? You seem shaken." For the first time in my long life, I feel awkward and unsure of myself. Thana's eyes search my face longer than usual.

"It probably wouldn't hurt. That is, if you can spare the time." A half smile breaks free from her face, and I swear I hear the other angels singing.

Bowing slightly like I always do, I motion down the hallway to my office. Thana quirks a grin and moves past me. Her fingertips lightly touch the fabric of my jacket, and I feel energized. Casually, she glances at her fingertips then mutters something about static electricity.

She heads directly to my office with no hesitation. Letting herself in, she heads right to her favorite chair and sits down, pulling her legs up into the chair with her. She fiddles with her stethoscope, trying to distract herself. Without a second thought, I pour us both fresh cups of coffee and offer her one before sitting in the chair next to her.

"Are you okay, Thana? Reaping two souls so close together must be exhausting." My voice takes on more of a smooth, honey-like quality than I intended. It clearly affects Thana because a slight rosiness flushes her cheeks and her pulse increases.

She clears her throat, then takes a large gulp of her coffee. "I'm a horrible person, Raphael. The way I ripped out that man's soul was monstrous." Her voice quivers as the tears she was trying to hold back roll freely down her cheeks.

I take off my suit jacket and place it over her shoulders before I hug her to me. Direct skin contact would alert her to what I already know as truth, that she's my mate. That is, if her mother had ever educated her about the fact that the tingle or static shock she felt was our bodies trying to form the bond.

"Dark souls are always the most resistant to leave their vessels. You did everything perfectly. Though, I do have a question for you." Leaning back, I tilt my head to the side and wait for her to look at me. Once she raises her gaze and her eyes meet mine, I ask, "What did he see that struck such terror in him? You're a beautiful woman. I can't imagine seeing you up close would ever be frightening."

Sighing softly, Thana looks down briefly, then back up at me. Her normally beautiful gunmetal-gray eyes are black as pitch, and blood runs down her face from her eyes and nose. A giant crack appears in her forehead and blood begins to gush out. Utter terror fills my heart, and a cold sweat breaks out over my body. As fast as it happens, it's over and she's back to her normal visage.

"People see what they're most afraid of when I take a dark soul. Their fear becomes a reality." She glances down for a moment, then looks back up again. This time her eyes are beautiful silver orbs, and she's radiant. "A light soul sees me as a merciful angel, full of beauty and light. Because of my duality—it's my blessing and my curse." Thana blinks several times, and her eyes are back to normal.

She looks down at her now-clasped hands. "I never wanted you or anyone else to ever see me like you did tonight." Slowly, she looks back up at me, and her eyes are tearful. "What if my potential mate or mates reject me because of it?"

I offer her the tissues on my desk without hesitation before sitting back. It's nearly impossible to not tell her I'm hers and that I'd never reject her. That I've been attracted to her for years but couldn't act on it before now. Damn vow of chastity. I want to kiss her so hard she forgets her pain and fear.

While she's still wrapped in my jacket, I lean over the arm of the chair and hug her tightly. "Your mate or mates, whoever they may be, are lucky. If they're too blind to see your worth and the beauty in your heart, then they don't deserve you." I kiss the crown of her head, trying to reassure her.

She relaxes in my arms, but eventually pulls away. "I hope whoever my mate is, they're as wonderful as you, Raphael." She forces a brilliant smile before standing and handing my jacket back to me. "Thank you for always being there for me. Creator willing . . . I hope you find your mate this time." She smiles broadly, kisses me on the crown of my head, and leaves the room.

If only she knew . . . For once, I don't dread the Trials as I have in all the centuries before now. My own angel, my eternal love, just walked out the door with the other half of my heart. I lift my jacket to my nose. The lingering scent of her floral perfume clings to the fabric. It's the only solace I'll have for the next six days.

CHAPTER 3

THANA

Day in and day out, everything remains the same. Go to work, heal as many people as possible, and come home to panic all over again about the upcoming Mate Trials. Over the years, all I ever hoped for was to one day be found worthy. Year after year, I fight to resist the darkness within me. Year after year, I strive to be better than the year before.

I've watched my friends come and go, most of the females quit working to raise their babies. As happy as I am for everyone else, I have to be honest with myself. I envy the joy my friends experience when they find their mates. Laughing to myself, I think of all my nieces and nephews who I play the crazy aunt for. At least, I'm able to play with the little ones and fill a tiny bit of the void in my heart. Joscelyn returns from her break and deposits a cup of heaven-sent coffee before me, drawing me out of my inner monologue.

"Thanks, sweetie," I say, picking up the cup and taking a much-needed sip of caffeine. The sweet caramel flavor lingers on my tongue as I look from my notes to the computer. My eyes scan over the roster of the patients in our wing, making sure there's nothing that I haven't checked on. Everyone on this floor is stable for the most part, except the two who are slowly dying. Most of the people here Joscelyn or I could heal almost instantly, but we're not allowed to completely heal anyone. Free will can be a bitch at times.

"Anytime, babe. What are besties for, right?" Joscelyn says with a radiant smile. Her sun-kissed skin has a glow to it. The freckles on her cheeks stand out a little darker, and the green in her eyes is a bit brighter. I finally notice she's holding an orange juice and not her normal coffee.

Arching a brow, I motion to her stomach with my coffee, tilting it in her direction. "Something I need to know about?"

A smile creeps across her lips as her cheeks flush. She whips her head away from me, and my eyes widen. My heart stutters just before it picks up from the surge of adrenaline.

"No way!" I practically scream as I close the distance between us and hug her tightly to me.

"Shhh . . . We haven't said anything to anyone yet. It's still too early to let everyone know." Her joy is contagious as we stand in our tight hug, crying together. Gently, I tighten my grip around her and hold her carefully against me. I press my lips to her cheek, thrilled she's been blessed with a baby so soon into her union. Truthfully, I can't wait to have children of my own. But for now, I can deal with being the crazy, overprotective auntie to this precious child.

"I can't believe it. In four months, you're having a baby!" I hug her again, making sure not to squeeze too hard.

"Crazy, emotional females," a deep husky voice says from beside us as someone steals my coffee cup from my hand.

At the sound of that voice, my internal alarms immediately go off. I quickly release Joscelyn and push her behind me. I come face-to-face with a handsome male who radiates a powerful aura of darkness and malice. He's muscular and looks like he's of Middle Eastern or Mediterranean descent, with chocolate-brown eyes, and dark-brown, almost black, hair. His eyes seem to project wicked intent which increases my heart rate. If he wasn't so darkly intimidating and acting like such a dick, he'd be very attractive.

"Please give me back my coffee." I extend my hand out to him. The raven tattoo on my lower forearm catches his attention. To my dismay, black wisps rise off the wings of my raven in response to his proximity, as if it's attracted to him. My eyes move from my raven to the disturbing man before me.

"You're too nice to be like me," he says with narrowed, menacing eyes. His free hand pushes his sleeve up his thickly muscled forearm to expose a raven like mine. While I stare at his raven, he switches my coffee to his other hand and takes a sip. Slowly, I raise my eyes and watch the way his lips caress the lid of my coffee cup. Is it wrong to want to feel those lips on mine? Am I finally losing my mind? One second, I'm a little freaked out and upset he took my coffee, and the next, I want to be the coffee.

"Name's Cyrus," he says with one of those smug, bad-boy grins that makes you simultaneously want to kiss him and punch him. He watches me intently before offering me my coffee back.

"Thana." I take my cup and briefly glance at it. By the time I look back up again, he's gone. The mystery of who has been stealing my coffee has now been officially solved. Quickly, I turn and check Joscelyn over, making sure she and her new cargo are safe.

"I'm okay, Thana. Do you think you need to report this encounter to our boss?" Joscelyn looks down the hallway to Raphael's door.

Nodding, I reluctantly turn and head down the hall. I still feel self-conscious about Raphael seeing my wings. Come to think of it, things have been a little more awkward than usual since that happened. I double-check my appearance in the reflection of his office window before I knock. Why do I suddenly care what I look like before entering his office?

I feel like an idiot about being nervous around him. I've worked with Raphael for countless lifetimes, and up until Azrael made me expose my wings, everything was fine. Now, I feel on edge whenever I'm in his presence, like an unseen force is pulling me toward him. I don't understand it nor do I want to ponder it any longer. Lost in my thoughts, apparently, I don't notice Raphael open his office door.

"Are you okay? You look distraught." He places his large hand on my lower back and shuffles me into his office, guiding me to a nearby chair. The warmth of his hand penetrates my skin, going straight to my soul. Why does it feel different? He's always been concerned about my wellbeing. It's nothing out of the ordinary, right? He moves past me to sit behind his desk.

Shaking my head, I set my coffee cup down and pull my hair out of its bun, running my fingers through its length in an attempt to soothe myself. "A Dark Nephilim I've never seen before took my coffee, sipped from it, and then disappeared. It shook me up a bit because he projected his darkness in an intimidating way." I raise my gaze to meet his. His eyes are glowing golden, and I immediately feel the draw to him again. Those eyes that look like liquid gold captivate me, mesmerizing me. What in the creator's name is wrong with me? Why am I feeling this way?

He seems as lost in my gaze as I am in his. He shakes his head, then extends his hand. My coffee cup flies from the table next to me through the air to him. He focuses on the cup for a moment before gritting his teeth. "Damn. It's Cyrus. Don't worry about him. His father wants him to take over as the head reaper for the hospital," Raphael says with great finality.

He throws my coffee into his garbage can as if its very presence sickens him. Thankfully, he has his own coffee pot in his office and makes me another cup exactly how I like it. I watch him while he does this, captivated by the way the muscles of his back flex with every movement, as well as the striations of the corded muscles of his forearms. What in the world is wrong with me? I've always had a crush on him, but this is becoming ridiculous. I closely watch his every move, studying his muscle movements. I know the Mate Trials are soon, and the time I get to be near him more than likely will come to an end.

Until now, I didn't realize Raphael paid attention to how I like my coffee. Then again, he's been my guardian for as long as I can remember. Grinning, he offers me a new cup of coffee. I laugh a little at how thoughtful he's being.

"You didn't have to make me a new cup but thank you for your kindness." I smile as I look up at him before taking a sip. A pleased moan escapes my lips at the wonderful taste.

His breath hitches, and I blush at his reaction. "I should get back to work." I stand slowly and glance from him to the door. A gentle smile crosses my lips, still touched by his thoughtfulness.

"My break is nearly over." My eyes drift from the door, then back over to his again. I really don't want to leave, but I know I need to get back to work.

Biting his bottom lip as he looks at me, he walks to the door and opens it for me. "Cyrus touching your coffee bothered you. So, I felt compelled to give you a new one." A slow smile crosses his lips as he reaches up to tuck a wayward lock of hair behind my ear. His eyes focus on his movements as he admires his handiwork.

"Have a great rest of your shift, Thana. If you need anything, you know how to find me." His voice is husky and breathless at the same time. He hasn't released my hair yet, and we stand still for several moments before he realizes what he's doing. His hand shoots up to cup the back of his neck, and he gives me a goofy smile.

I can't help but smile back at him. I bounce up on my tiptoes to softly kiss his cheek. My lips tingle again, almost like static electricity charges his skin and mine. "Thank you for being so thoughtful."

I hurry out of the room but can't resist looking back over my shoulder at him. He's touching his cheek where I kissed him. I guess the static must have gotten him too. Damn carpets strike again, I guess. Maybe there's hope for me yet. A mixed-breed may actually be able to find love at some point. I'm still anxious about the Mate Trials, but at least I know not all hope is lost. After all, if I can get this type of response from an Archangel, I might just stand a chance.

I return to the desk and sit next to Joscelyn, going over the night's admissions charts. She looks me over from head to toe and cants her head to the side. "Someone is smiling. What did Director

McHottie have to say for himself?" Joscelyn gives me a knowing grin, and I blush in response.

Rolling my eyes, I hold the mug Raphael lent me tightly. "He said not to worry about Cyrus. More than likely, he's just here pestering all the single females. His dad wants him to take over being the head reaper for the hospital." An audible sigh escapes my lips as I stare down at my coffee. I really need to get over my crush. Hopefully, I'll be chosen, and I can stop pining for someone so unattainable.

"Ah. Makes sense, I guess. Still, he didn't have to be rude and take your coffee," she says as she looks from me down our hall. The usual night staff is checking the rooms, so nothing is out of the ordinary.

"True, but you know how guys are. They like to do dumb shit to get a girl's attention," I say, shrugging my shoulders as I finish the last of my coffee.

"Who did what dumb shit?" Mark asks as he rounds the corner. A brilliant smile is plastered on his face, and he waves a square white envelope at us.

I squeal, knowing full well that's his invitation to the Mate Trials. Mark seems as excited as I am about the invitation. "Unlike you, I only get one mate. You, missy, can end up with a half dozen," he says, teasing the hell out of me.

Jumping up from my seat, I move to him and hug my favorite work hubby. "I'm so excited for you. We'll go together." In my excitement for him, I forget to answer his question.

"Whoa. Settle down, Thana. Three days ago, you were dreading the Trials, but now you're excited? What changed?"

"Several things . . ." I hop up and sit on the desk at the nurses' station. "First, you'll be there with me." I smile and make a heart with my hands. "Second, two Archangels, as well as other high-ranking angels, are attending this time." I raise my eyebrows and point my thumb over my shoulder down the hall to Raphael's office. "Third, it's rare for a female to walk away from the Trials without at least one mate." I open my arms wide, smiling. "I might not be alone anymore." I've spent the last ten years alone since Joscelyn found her mates. To be honest, it sucks.

"Thana, you still haven't answered my question about what changed," Mark says, crossing his arms over his broad chest. He has a Superman sexiness to him—dark hair, light eyes, and muscles for days.

Shaking my head, I lean back, putting my hands behind me. I tilt my head back and close my eyes. "I just have a good feeling the Trials may not be as bad as I thought." I think about how certain males have been looking at me lately, and my skin tingles and heats.

"What naughty thought just crossed your mind, Thana." Raphael's voice is soft, breathy, and sweet as honey. It warms my insides instantly.

Hearing his voice so close to me, I launch myself off the desk, nearly falling flat on my face. My heart pounds, and I try to catch my breath. When I look up, his eyes are wide. He seems worried at my unfortunate landing. "Are you okay?" He reaches for me but quickly withdraws his hand as if I'm on fire. He appears to be at war with himself, his brows furrowing.

"I'm fine—just embarrassed." I stand up and adjust my scrubs. Forcing a smile, I look around before heading down the hall to double-check my patients. Room by room, I work around the ward, poking my head in and making sure everyone has what they need. I need to distract myself from the nerves that are building inside me.

The minutes tick by like hours, dragging slowly. But there are only so many times I can pace the hallway until I have to return to the nurses' station. Thankfully, by the time I wander back, only the morning nurse is waiting for me to give her report.

Avoidance—expert level . . .

CHAPTER 4
THANA

Summer Solstice – The Mate Trials . . .

Tonight, I take comfort in the fact my work hubby, Mark, will be with me, as well as Joscelyn. "Thana, I'm serious!" he says, being dramatic as he runs the flat iron through my hair.

"I swear, it won't be weird if you end up being my mate." I meet his eyes through the reflection of the mirror. Raising my eyebrows, I try to convey how serious I am about the weird factor being zero.

"Besides, it would be awesome! You already know all my favorite things. And we have the same taste in guys." We share a laugh at our own expense. It's nice having a wingman who appreciates the male form as much as I do.

"Seriously, Mark. What are the odds?" I continue to stare at him, and a series of expressions cross over his face before he settles on concerned.

"I just don't want to lose my best friend," he says on a sigh as he finishes the last section of my hair. Gently, he runs the comb through from root to tip, then sprays the finishing spray to keep my hair from frizzing.

"Oh, please!" I stand up and lightly slap his shoulder. "As if!

You're stuck with me, one way or another. No one can replace my work hubby!"

Finally, a genuine smile crosses his lips before he pulls me in for a bone-crushing hug. "Want to fly there together?" He walks to my balcony.

"Hahaha. Very funny. You know I can't fly till after I find my mate." Rolling my eyes at him, I turn to follow him outside.

Mark grins and opens his arms wide. "I'll carry you one last time." Sadness fills his voice, and I close the distance between us.

Wrapping my arms around his neck, I hang on to him, and he scoops me up like I weigh nothing. I marvel at his white feathers, which are a sharp contrast to my dark ones, although his don't have the same shimmer Raphael's do. He launches us up and into the night sky. The full moon behind us would make this romantic if I thought of Mark as anything other than a friend. The lights of the city twinkle like multi-colored stars below us.

An hour later, we arrive at our destination and say our goodbyes to each other. In the distance, a woman is being led to the marble pedestal by Gabriel. She smiles and waves as she passes people. I finally notice the hundreds of males surrounding the pedestal.

My initial excitement immediately turns to fear. The facts of our species are borne in truth here. For every ten or more males, only one female is born. Those odds are staggering for a male. Most females end up with two or more mates, so it's kind of a win for us. I think I'd like to have two, maybe three mates. That sounds like a good number. But what if I get six like that one woman did a few years ago? I shudder. They said she was blessed. But can you imagine all the issues there?

Caught up in my musings and anxiety, I jump when a hand grips my elbow. My flight or fight instinct has me ready to clock the person who scared me until I see it's Michael, the highest of the high. Immediately, I drop to my knees before him. "Please forgive my reaction. I didn't know it was you, your holiness."

His index finger comes to rest under my chin, and he forces me to raise my eyes to meet his. If Adonis and Thor had a love child, it would be Michael. "I've heard a great many things about you, Thana. We are blessed to have you in our ranks." His smile never leaves his lips as he speaks to me.

Honestly, I think this is the first time a man has rendered me speechless. The only thing I can think to say is, "Thank you, your holiness." I shuffle on my knees and try to keep my voice steady, but I can't bring myself to hold his gaze.

Michael shakes his head and offers me both of his hands. "Come with me. We need to finish getting you ready for your special night." A smile plays on his thick lips. "I have it on good authority," he points up, and my eyes widen "you will find your mate tonight. And to be a bit of a pain, I know who they are." He laughs at my expense.

"Not cool, your holiness. Not cool." I take his offered hands and stand up.

He leads me around the outskirts of men, or what I've hysterically dubbed the sausage-fest, to a tent in the back. My friend Joscelyn is there, picking out dresses for the remaining two females. "I've saved the best for last, Thana," Michael says as he hands me off to my best friend. "Gabriel and I will escort you to the pedestal. Don't leave the tent without us."

I can only nod at Michael before he ushers the other two females out. Jocelyn and I stare at each other, shocked that two of the highest-ranking Archangels will be my escorts. "Girl, I don't know what's going on, but that's scary and exciting at the same time," Joscelyn says as she pulls out a strapless golden, shimmering gown. I slip it on.

My eyes widen in wonder as the dress conforms to my every curve. The back is open to my hips, and I wonder how this dress will stay on. "It's beautiful. I don't deserve to wear something this expensive," I say sadly, looking down at the beautiful gown.

"Well, if you don't wear it, the male who left it for you will pluck me like a Thanksgiving turkey." Jocelyn unfurls and flexes her wings to accentuate her point.

I stare at her in surprise. For the second time tonight, I'm speechless. Who would have left this exquisite gown for me?

"Hold on, I want to see something." She steps outside to speak with someone, then returns with a matching blindfold for me. "Give me your phone and put this on. It's only us, and I want to see your wings with the dress." She smiles warmly at me with unshed tears in her eyes. She's thrilled for me.

Reluctantly, I hand my phone over and tie the blindfold on. Drawing in a deep breath, I unfurl my wings and hold them half-open. I hear the shutter click several times before Joscelyn touches my arm. "Take off the blindfold. You need to see yourself. You look absolutely beautiful," she says, smiling as she hands me my phone back.

My eyes fill with tears, and I carefully retract my wings to stare at the picture, barely able to recognize myself. Jocelyn blots my eyes and opens the tent flap, gesturing to my escorts to come in. Michael and Gabriel enter the tent and stop dead in their tracks.

I feel self-conscious under their scrutiny. "You are stunning, Thana," Gabriel says, in his baritone voice. He offers me his arm, and I gently place my hand on it. Michael takes his position on my other side. We walk toward the pedestal, and the whispers from the Nephilim begin. Words like "half-breed," and "hybrid," float in the air, and some idiot went all wizard on me, calling me a "mud blood."

My eyes dart between Gabriel and Michael, and they silence the crowd. The hateful Nephilim are immediately removed, never to return to the Mate Trials. "You're safe, Thana. I'll escort you to the top myself," Michael says as he takes me from Gabriel, and we climb the short staircase to the top of the pedestal.

The click of my heels sounds ten times louder to me than they probably are. For every step, it seems like three more appear. Finally, we reach the top, and in my anxiety, I feel like I've climbed Mount Everest. Michael smiles softly and caresses my cheek before pulling me in for a brief hug. "Everything will be okay, Thana. Trust me," he says softly as he slowly releases me. His eyes dart from mine to the sash in my hand. His large hands extract the gold blindfold from the death grip I have on it. As the silken fabric slips free from my grasp, my nerves kick in again.

He gently turns me to face the crowd, letting me see who is present. My eyes scan the waiting males, slowly making eye contact with those I know. I feel better seeing several males I recognize. Mark gives me a double thumbs-up, then he makes a heart with his hands, which makes me laugh. Michael kisses my cheek just before he ties the blindfold on me.

"I'll stay with you, just in case. All you have to do is reach behind you, and I'll take your hand, okay?" I nod my head slowly, and he ties the blindfold over my eyes, whispering into my ear . . . "Whenever you're ready, unfurl your wings."

It feels like a thousand eyes rake over my body at once. My heart thunders in my chest as my fear of showing my wings rises. The three most powerful Archangels are here. *I'm safe*, I say to myself as I tilt my head back to the sky. Drawing a slow, steady, cleansing breath into my lungs, I try to dispel my fears. Historically, every female who has attended the Mate Trials has found at least one mate. Taking comfort in these statistics, I make up my mind that I'll venture forth into the unknown and face my destiny with open arms.

My wings unfurl and open wide. Each feather spreads as I flex my wings. For the first time in my life, I'm comfortable in my own skin. Over the years, I've studied the wings of other angels. From what I've learned, mine are built for speed. The color of my feathers fades slowly from a dark, nearly charcoal gray all the way down to a medium steel gray at the tips.

I hear someone crying as I raise my arms up, reaching toward the heavens. *I am safe. I am home*, I say to myself before flapping my wings several times, achieving lift and testing them without removing my blindfold. I stretch them wide before letting them hang half-open. From what I've seen with the other Nephilim and the angels I know, my wings are larger than average.

"Thana, you have four mates. And two of them are quite impatient to meet you." Michael's voice is joyful as he speaks to me. There are so many questions I want to ask. Do I know any of them? Are they nice?

"You choose who I see first, your holiness. I trust your judgment and wisdom," I say to Michael as he turns me in the direction of the sounds of footsteps approaching. Here we go, the moment I've waited the over three hundred years for.

"I'm going to place your hands in his, and then I'll remove your blindfold," Michael tells me. "Open your eyes when you're ready. Remember, the first mate you see is the head mate, and you must bond with him first."

I nod and hold my hands out, waiting. I wiggle my fingers as Michael grips my wrists. The warmth radiating from my mate's hands is the first thing I feel. Anticipation is killing me. Large, strong hands encompass mine. Tears roll down my cheeks from the emotion of finally having made contact with him.

I curl my wings close to my body, trying to comfort myself. Suddenly, my mate pulls his hands free of mine only to wrap his arms and wings around me. Then it dawns on me. I know this hug, and his scent is familiar as well. My eyes fly open, and I look up. Raphael. His smile is soft and kind as he looks down at me in wonder.

I reach up and caress his cheek. He closes the distance between us and presses his velvet lips to mine. My arms shoot up and wrap around his neck, holding him tightly to me while my heart pounds erratically. All my prayers have been answered in a single moment. I cry uncontrollably as I hug him even tighter. Every one of my fears has been wiped away, knowing he'll always be with me.

A throat nearby clears and breaks the spell we're under. Reluctantly, we break apart, and slowly, I look in the direction of the noise. Christian stands beside us with his white wings on full display. Happy tears roll freely down his cheeks as he stares at me, his arms open wide. I look at Raphael, and he releases me at once.

Christian's Hakama is perfectly pressed and makes him look like an honest-to-goodness Samurai. I launch myself into his arms, and he spins us around in a circle, both of us laughing and crying tears of joy. I lean in and quickly kiss him, still smiling. We slowly let go of each other, and I look back at Michael as Raphael takes my free hand.

Two more men stand behind him. One I've never seen before, who is a heavily-muscled, Light Nephilim. The other is Cyrus, the coffee-stealing Dark Nephilim. I swallow and blink. To make an awkward situation even more so, Azrael appears and wraps his arm around Cyrus. "I see you've been blessed with my son Cyrus, Thana."

A shudder wracks my body. I'm mated to Azrael's son. My day just went to hell in a hand-basket.

I pass out from shock.

CHAPTER 5
THANA

Raphael's loft . . .

The shock from earlier replays over and over in my head, causing me to scream into my pillow when I wake up in a bed that's not mine. My gaze jumps around the room, and I clench the covers in my fists. My hands are clammy. Where have I ended up?

The door flies open, and Raphael closes the distance in an instant. Behind him, Christian is hot on his heels as they barrel into the room. They both climb onto the bed with me, wedging me between the two of them. Sighing softly, I finally relax.

"Are you okay, Thana?" Raphael asks as his hands take on their white healing glow. He ghosts his hands over my skin, checking every inch of me. The warmth of his healing light caresses my body, warming me in ways I'd only ever read about before now. His scent reminds me of the ocean—fresh and peaceful.

Nodding slowly, I gently kiss his cheek. "I'm better now that both of you are here. I have to admit, I'm scared." My eyes dart between them before I lower my gaze.

"What are you scared of, *watashi no ai*?" Christian asks as he presses his lips to my cheek. His warm, cinnamon scent washes over me.

I raise my uncertain gaze to look between them. "I'm afraid of having Azrael's son in our family group. And my other mate, I have no clue who he is." I raise my eyebrows, looking between them.

Raphael pats Christian's knee before speaking. "He," Raphael points up, "chose your mates for a reason. We have to trust in the process and have a little faith."

Christian hugs me to him as Raphael takes both of my hands in his. "Michael sent the other two home after you passed out. He wants the three of us to bond before we bring in the two males you aren't comfortable with." Color rises in Raphael's cheeks as he speaks of the bonding.

I giggle slightly and look at Christian, then back over to Raphael. "Why is the big bad Archangel blushing?" I ask lightheartedly as I grip his hands tighter.

"Well, you see . . ." Raphael trails off and looks at Christian as if seeking help.

"What our bond-mate is trying to say is . . ." Christian pauses dramatically, trying to find the right words. He glances at Raphael then back to me. "Archangels aren't permitted to fornicate outside their mated bond," Christian states the facts as if they're common knowledge. "Angels have a little more leeway than Archangels do, but not a lot." He shrugs, allowing the gravity of what he's just said to sink in.

Raphael shoots up and paces the room. His wings unfurl and flex randomly, I'm guessing with his stress. "Nephilim, like yourself, have free will, just like humans because you're half human. Or, in your case, one-third human. Either way, you have the gift of free will." He moves his hands around as if it helps with the explanation. From the way his hands wave in the air, accentuating his level of distress, I can tell he's on edge.

I move from what I guess is his bed to stand in his path. "Okay, so I have free will. What difference does that make?" I ask. His gold eyes churn, and the most innocent look crosses his face, and then it hits me. The crux of the problem has been laid out bare before me, and obtusely, I missed it. "Oh boy," I say as I look between the two men I've had crushes on forever.

"Okay, not a big deal. We're a team, right? We've got this." I nod, punctuating my affirmation.

Christian sighs and walks to me, then wraps his arms around me. "Unlike your other two mates, we're not as worldly as they are in that sense." He shrugs.

My cheeks heat as I look between the two of them. "I have an admission to make." I move to the bay window to look out over the city as the sun rises. "I've had a crush on the two of you for the past hundred or so years. Being what I am . . ." I shake my head. "I never thought I'd be allowed to take a mate, let alone four." I furrow my brows, unsure if I'm willing to accept Azrael's son into the bond.

Before they can say anything in response, I continue, "This is new to all of us. So, we take this at our own pace. If that means it takes months or years, I'm in it for the long run. Till death do we part." I'm practically baring my soul to them, wearing my heart on my sleeve. My eyes dart between the two of them as I unfurl my wings and flex them.

"I've always been ashamed of my wings." I reach out and touch the smoke-gray feathers. "They're proof of what my parents did. They went against the most high, against angelic law." I stroke my feathers as I continue, "Very few accept me because I walk the line between life and death. I almost hoped no one would be cursed to have me as a mate." Tears well up in my eyes. Biting my bottom lip, I try to stifle my groan.

The next thing I know, I'm sandwiched between Raphael and Christian, both of them deciding to comfort me at the same time. Raphael takes control and carefully grips my chin, lifting my head up so I'm looking into his golden eyes. "Never speak of yourself like that again, my beloved. It's true; you're an anomaly. You're our mate because you're perfect for us. Made for us." He kisses me as passionately as his words described his feelings for me. My body comes to life as his hands cup my face, holding me lovingly while he kisses me. Eventually, he releases me, and I pant for air. My heart thunders as I try to recover from the most passionate kiss I've ever had.

Christian caresses my wings reverently as he traces the soft feathers along the bone. "Feather color doesn't denote one's worth, *watashi no ai*. But if it did, your worth would be beyond measure." He slides his hands down my flight feathers and palms my wings, silently asking me to open them wide. Whether it's the stirrings of the mate bond or my desire to please them, I comply. At full stretch, my wingspan is much larger than the average female Nephilim's.

"These wings will allow you to reach new heights and one day carry our children during evening flights. I waited just as long as Raphael for our mate to be born. Little did we know, you were under our noses the entire time," Christian says as he steps around my wings to stand in front of me. Carefully, I lower my wings, letting them hang half-open as I look at him. His eyes drift to my lips. Reflexively, I bite my lower lip. I was never good at being stared at. That does him in immediately. He crushes my lips to his like a starving man who's finally able to eat after a long time. Devouring my mouth, it's as if his life depends on my kisses sustaining him. Raphael rests his hands on my hips, pressing his chest against my back.

I'm writhing between them as both sets of hands roam all over my body, discovering every curve and cut of muscle. Christian's lips move across my cheek to the left side of my neck while Raphael kisses the right side. I'm a moaning, panting mess. My body feels as if it's on fire and only they can quench it. I pull at both of them, my hands tracing the solid muscled bodies enveloping me. My senses are on overload between their kisses and caresses. Raphael's hands caress my wing feathers. I had no idea my wings would be an erogenous zone.

Raphael wraps his arms around me from behind and uses the force of his wings to pry me away from Christian. "Patience, brother.

Thana and I must settle our bond first. Remember what Michael said."

Christian reluctantly nods, but burning hunger lights his eyes. "I understand. I don't like it, but I understand." He kisses my cheek and caresses my jaw lightly."Tomorrow, Thana."

I nod, agreeing with him. "Tomorrow . . ." I say softly, and he gives me a weak smile before moving to the balcony and taking flight into the evening sky.

Raphael reluctantly releases me to lock the balcony doors. "I still can't believe you're here with me." His tone pulls at my heartstrings as I look up into his hazel-green eyes.

Flexing my wings, I finally ask the question that's been plaguing me. "You saw my wings when I had to take the soul of the murderer. Did you know then that I was yours?" I close the distance between us, pull my wings forward, and rest them on his shoulders, sliding them between his body and his wings.

Gently, he kisses my lips and wraps his wings around me as well. "I did. But because my wings were already out, they only tensed and attempted to flex." Raphael laughs. "It was so difficult not allowing my wings to fully open to display themselves for you. Azrael would have called for our union to be nullified on the spot." My eyebrows shoot up at his statement.

"He could do that?" I ask, resting my head on his chest.

"Definitely. And he's just enough of a bastard to do it. To top it off, his son is one of your mates. So, if you reject Cyrus, we could be immediately exposed and our mate bond nullified." Raphael's tone sounds defeated, and the gravity of the situation feels like a crushing weight on my heart.

My fingers nimbly start to open Raphael's dress shirt, fixated on each pearl button. His breath hitches as I reach the middle of his chest. Slowly, I lift my eyes to his. His eyes swirl like liquid gold as my hands continue on their mission to unfasten each of his buttons. As the last button falls and his shirt opens, he lifts his wings from around me, and I pull mine back.

Suddenly, he grips both sides of his shirt and rips it off his own body. Double blinking, my eyes roam freely over his sun-kissed flesh, seeing the scars from past wars littering his physique. My fingertips gently trace the lines and indentations, and his breathing accelerates.

"Thana, baby. You're killing me, my love . . ." His husky lust-filled voice turns my insides to liquid magma while my core clenches in anticipation.

"Am I?" I ask as innocently as I can.

Pouting, I turn away from him. My fear of rejection is long gone. I know Raphael. He'd never allow anything bad to happen to me. Drawing in a deep breath, I decide to be brave and go after what I want for the first time in my life. I've been infatuated with this man for years, and now he's mine. I can't wait for forever to begin.

Slipping my hands around to the back of my dress, I lower the zipper in a painstakingly slow motion. The gold fabric hits the floor in a crumpled mess at my feet. "Let me guess. The dress was from you?" I watch his reaction over my shoulder, and it doesn't disap-point. His eyes are wide, his wings flex, and his dress slacks don't hide his prominent erection.

He clears his throat as he unbuckles his dress slacks and lets them fall. "Yes." The corner of his mouth curls up in a sexy smile, looking at the dress pooled on the floor. "It looked beautiful on you, but I have to admit, I like it much better now that it's down there."

I turn slowly to face Raphael, my hands cupping my ample breasts and supporting their weight. His silk boxers strain to contain his length, the evidence of his arousal staining the front flap. My eyes drift to the dress on the floor. "I bet you do." Tilting my head to the side, I turn my back to him and lower my hands. Sure, catlike steps silently carry me across his bedroom, and I crawl onto his bed on all fours. Arching my back, I spread my wings wide, and within seconds, he's at my side, his hands roaming over my bare flesh.

Raphael makes short work of my barely-there thong and nudges me until I sit up on my knees to face him. I see that his boxers have now gone missing. He pulls me to him, and we crash together like waves during a storm. Our fevered kisses deepen by the second as our hands roam freely. Raphael rolls us without warning, and his wings spread out from under him. I end up sitting on his lower stomach. His length throbs teasingly against my soaked lips. Tentatively, I rock my hips, coating his length with each stroke. I'm beyond wet, and anticipation is killing me. My core pulses softly with desire.

The pull of the mate bond is maddening. My instincts are pushing me to go beyond my hesitance stemming from my first time. Maybe it's the years I've been around Raphael combined with my desire to fulfill the bond. But I feel safe with him, and I want nothing more than to be with him for eternity. Instinct drives me to nip at his neck and collarbone as his strong deft fingers explore my delicate folds, spurring me on. Occasionally, his fingertips find that sensitive bundle of nerves, causing my hips to rock of their own volition.

Just as I get him lined up, he stops me. "If we go further, we'll be bound together forever." His eyes betray him, imploring me not to leave. I have all the power here, and it's exhilarating. Bracing my hands on his chest, I push back quickly, sinking his length deep within me. I wince from the momentary sting of his intrusion. Maybe going so quickly wasn't my brightest idea. Drawing in slow, deep breaths, I wait while the initial sting becomes a dull ache. I feel so very full. His eyes burn brightly, and he stares up at me in wonder as I hesitantly start to move, setting the pace for our lovemaking.

Raphael's hands grip my hips tightly after the initial shock wears off, and he starts to meet me thrust for thrust. It nearly becomes a battle for dominance. But I know if he didn't have his wings out, he could easily overpower me. He grows bolder, and his hands roam over my body, finding that precious nub of sensitive nerves. Tentative strokes of his thumb have my core clenching, making me moan from the added stimulation. Just like a child with a new toy, he assaults my clit until I feel like I'll explode. I moan as my orgasm crashes over me. Lights burst behind my eyes, and a warmth fills my heart.

The words *"I love you"* echo in my head, and I think he's speaking to me in my mind. He soon follows me over the edge, his groans filling my ears. In the romance books I've read, they make it sound like sex is supposed to last for hours. Since our first time together lasted only minutes, I wonder if maybe we didn't do it right. But then I feel the mate bond forming between us, so I know we definitely did something right.

I flop down onto his sweat-covered chest and lay my head down on it, exhausted. A yawn escapes me as his arms curl around me. My wings lower and surround us. "I love you too," I say softly as I fall asleep in his arms, finally feeling whole.

CHAPTER 6

THANA

Raphael and I spend the better half of the day and night learning each other's bodies, enjoying the newness of the growing bond between us. I wake up the next morning alone in Raphael's big fluffy bed.

I smell coffee brewing and maybe breakfast as well. A rose-colored dress is draped over the back of the chair next to the bed, and a single red rose rests on the chair's seat. A card with a heart scrawled in the center is all he left.

I find my destroyed thong and smile, recalling how it was ripped off me in our frenzy. Carefully, I slip into the silken dress, and like the gold one, it instantly conforms to my every curve. I swear, angels have the best clothing. This dress has a fitted halter top and a low-cut back to leave room for my wings. Taking the opportunity, I unfurl my wings and stretch them. My hands ghost over the soft fabric, admiring the mid-calf length he's chosen for me. I quickly brush my hair and put it in a simple braid before following my nose toward the kitchen.

Several twists and turns later, I find myself in a spacious, modern kitchen with a white marble island where all four of my mates are sitting on stools. "Good morning, beautiful. I see you found the dress I left you," Raphael says as he approaches me. Without hesitation, I go to him and wrap my arms around his waist. I reach up, standing on my tiptoes, and kiss his full lips, sighing softly at the love I feel radiating from him.

"Gee. Do I get that kind of a greeting, sweetheart?" Cyrus asks playfully.

Arching a brow, I look over at him and tilt my head to the side. "Eventually, yes. I barely know you, other than your name and who your daddy is. And that you like stealing my coffee." I state the facts which make both Christian and the new guy almost choke on their coffee. Poor Raphael is trying his best to hold his laughter in.

"We can remedy that quickly," Cyrus says as he moves from his seat to stand beside Raphael and me. "Golden boy here may be your first mate, but I'll be your best." He flashes a smile at me, his chocolate-brown eyes twinkling with mischief while his dark hair falls into his eyes.

I look to the mystery man, who's still seated at the island. Raphael makes the connection and releases his grip on me. I brush past Cyrus to stand before the silent male. I offer my left hand to him. "I'm Thana. I'm pleased to meet you." His large hand envelopes mine, and he smiles at me. His eyes dart to Christian, which puzzles me.

Furrowing my brow, I look to Christian, confused. "His name is Gage. Unfortunately, during a skirmish many years ago, he lost his ability to speak."

Gage nods at me and smiles. Tears well in my eyes and threaten to spill. This sweet man was injured and cannot speak because of it. As my tears roll down my cheeks, I scoop them up and allow my hands to take on their healing glow. Gently, my hands grip his thick throat, and I attempt to heal him. My mouth pops open in my effort to repair what happened to him. Gage's gray eyes churn with emotion as he stares back at me, his own tears threatening to fall.

"Thana, love. You cannot heal what was done. Losing his voice was his punishment for speaking about a forbidden subject during the skirmish," Raphael's gentle voice breaks through the sadness I feel.

Reluctantly, my hands slide down from Gage's neck to rest on his chest. His strong right hand lightly cups my cheek to make me look him in the eyes. He mouths *"thank you"* to me and lightly kisses my lips, pulling a smile from me. Reluctantly, he breaks the kiss, and I open my eyes to see his large white wings open behind him. He smiles back at me and rolls his eyes self-deprecatingly. I can't help but giggle at his antics.

In the background, Cyrus is complaining that the new guy got kissed first. Gage and I turn together to look at Cyrus. "You're a dick," I say to Cyrus as I move to sit on Christian's lap, swiping his coffee from him.

The only male not laughing is Cyrus. He stares at me, his eyes turn black, and his large black wings burst free. I slide free from Christian's lap and move between Cyrus and the others. I allow the darkness I hide to surface, the black mist creeping over my pale flesh like a second skin. A sudden chill fills the room as if death itself walks the earth.

"You don't scare or impress me, Cyrus. You want to win your place in my heart? This," I motion to his current appearance, "isn't the way to do it." I pull hard at the darkness within me, forcing it to retract and go back where it came from. Embarrassed by my outburst, I leave the room and return to Raphael's bedroom.

I sit on the edge of the bed, facing the balcony doors and look outside. "*Kichōna mono*," Christian says softly as he walks around the bed to stand before me.

Smiling, I turn to face Christian. I know Raphael sent him to me, knowing he can calm me down. "I've been around you long enough to know that's a term of endearment. But what does it mean?"

Christian clears his throat and blushes. "It means 'precious one.' But little did I know when I first started calling you that, you'd be my mate." He sits on the bed next to me and takes both my hands in his.

"I watched Michael and Gabriel escort you to the pedestal, and my heart was in my throat." His eyes close, and his head leans back. He's so beautiful. His olive skin is as smooth as porcelain. His long straight black hair flows down his back.

"Raphael and I stood side by side, supporting each other through the Trials. We were terrified when it was your turn." Sighing loudly, he finally turns to face me.

"We knew days before that you were Raphael's. But we had concerns about who else would be in your nest." His smile broadens, and it reaches his eyes as joy radiates from him.

"When you looked up to the heavens, then unfurled your wings, I swear I heard the other angels sing. And then my wings ripped free from my body, flexing of their own volition." Christian smiles as he pulls me into his lap.

"I turned to face Raphael and saw his wings were practically glowing. We got to you as fast as we could." He laughs again. "Very silent high fives were passed out before Raphael was moved to stand before you first. I figured since he was the most powerful among us, he should be the first mate." Christian's carefree nature slowly dissipates as he looks down at our joined hands.

"Christian, I want you to be my next mate." I caress his cheek and lean in to kiss him.

He raises his hand and stops me from proceeding. "You honor me, *kichōna mono*. It will honor me more if you choose to take Gage next." His silken lips caress mine gently. "With the mate bond in place, he'll be able to talk to you."

I look at him. "What do you mean he'll be able to talk to me? I didn't know the mate bond could do that." My curiosity is definitely piqued.

Christian chuckles and kisses my lips. "Your innocence is refreshing. A side effect of the mate bond is being able to use telepathy within the bond. Try it. Say Raphael's name in your head. Call out to him."

"Okay." I close my eyes. Slowing my breathing, I hear my own heartbeat.

"Raphael?" I call tentatively and wait to see if he can hear me.

"Yes, love? Do you need me? Are you okay?" Raphael asks, sounding concerned that I reached out.

"Sorry for worrying you. Christian was teaching me about how this part of the bond works," I tell him.

"Excellent. I was going to broach the subject tonight. I'll leave you to it. I'm here if you need me," Raphael says, and the warmth from the bond fades.

Blinking, I open my eyes to look at Christian. "Wow. That could be useful." I glance down at our joined hands. "Send Gage to me. I need to get to know him first."

A wide smile graces Christian's face, and he leans in to kiss me. "You honor our bond greatly, *kichōna mono.*" He kisses me again before leaving the room.

CHAPTER 7

THANA

Shaking my head, I rise slowly from the bed and head out to the balcony to look over the yard. Placing my hands on the marble railing, I open my wings wide, enjoying the freedom of being allowed to show them. The sun caresses and warms my feathers while the gentle north breeze gently cools my skin as I wait.

A soft knock sounds at the door behind me, and I turn to see Gage standing there, a wide smile visible through his neatly trimmed beard. I motion him in, and immediately I take him in my arms and hug him tightly. He looks like he could be a lumberjack. His eyes search mine in wonder, gold flecks rising up in his stormy gray eyes.

Closing my eyes, I roll my head back, exposing my throat to him, making myself vulnerable to him. His full lips gently kiss me over my pulse point. I thread my fingers through his hair before lowering my head to look into his eyes. "I have so many questions for you," I say as I stand up on my tiptoes to kiss his lips softly. His stubble tickles my skin.

Gage gets a mischievous look in his eyes as he backs up and digs in his pockets. He pulls out his cell phone and wiggles it between us.

Nodding slowly, I pull my phone out and pull up a new contact. I punch in Gage's first name, then hand it to him.

He winks at me and gives me his phone. He has me listed as "Thana, love of my life." "Awe . . ." I say in response. I enter my information and hit save. Taking his hand in mine, I lead him back to the bed. I climb into the center and cross my legs, patting the area in front of me for him to sit. He quickly complies, and I smile at him, pleased he's so willing to "speak" with me.

"I think my biggest question is have you waited long to find your mate?" Part of me wants to know. But the other part really doesn't want to. Enthusiastically, he picks up his phone and furiously types out his message to me. My phone vibrates in my hand, and I open his message. Apparently, this was only his fourth time going to the Trials. He's grateful that he didn't have to wait as long as others have.

My next question almost turns my stomach, but I really need to know. "How long has it been since you last heard your own voice?" I cringe after spewing the question. Gently, his large, strong hand cups my left cheek, and he smiles.

Quickly, he types out his answer. He's been without his voice for almost two hundred years. Reflexively, my eyes widen in shock. I look between him and the message, and he smiles at me. His message reassures me that his punishment fits what he did. He knew he went against divine law, talking about what he shouldn't have.

Carefully, I climb into his lap and run my fingers through his thick brown hair. "You don't need your voice to be with me. Deep down, I know we were paired for a reason." I smile at him. I have complete faith in the system. I know the higher powers wouldn't pair me with males who won't be a good fit.

Gage leans forward and kisses my lips gently. I can't help but giggle at how gentle such a large muscular man can be. He arches his left eyebrow then types out his message. "Why did I giggle?" I smile and giggle a little more.

"That's easy. I'm not trying to stereotype, but you could be a fitness model." A gentle blush creeps across his cheeks just above his thick beard. "Oh, come on, Gage. You know you're a handsome man," I say, shaking my head in disbelief.

He shakes his head, attempting to look innocent. He looks down at his phone again, then begins typing furiously. Several messages from him pop up, each one causing me to smile. The final message makes me blush because he tells me as long as I find him handsome, that's all that matters to him. His words practically make my heart skip a beat. That was the most romantic thing anyone has ever said to me.

Gently, I nudge Gage to lean back, and he complies quickly. I feel powerful and beautiful because of the way he's looking at me with an undeniable hunger in his eyes. Arching my back, I allow my wings to unfurl again, and I spread them wide. His gray eyes scan over my feathers, and he reaches a single hand out to touch them. I lower my wings so he can reach them more easily.

His fingertips trace my long primary flight feathers, studying each one. Apparently, close to my wing, the spine of my feathers has whitened. This is a new development I'll have to ask Raphael about later. Right now, my attention is focused on this handsome, sweet man who's currently under me. Gage motions to the mattress, so I slide off him and sit beside him, waiting to see what he's up to.

Standing before me, he removes his t-shirt and tosses it onto the bed beside me. He turns his back and unfurls his wings for me. His wings are oversized like mine, including the feathers. Before I realize what I'm doing, I'm standing behind him, gently caressing them. His white feathers captivate me. They're so beautiful and pure, like a white dove. My hands come to rest on his bare shoulders, and I press a kiss in the space between where his wings emerge from his back. His skin slowly breaks out with goosebumps.

Digging deep, I find my courage and remove the dress I'm wearing and toss it on the floor before stepping out in front of him. My white lace demi-bra barely contains my breasts, and his eyes instantly lock onto them. Sighing softly, I feel my nerves getting the better of me. Unlike Raphael, I barely know Gage. We don't have the years of trust I have with Raphael and Christian.

He notices my hesitancy and grips both my hands, gently kissing my lips. Releasing one hand, he reaches down to grab his phone and types out a quick message. The short version is he's giving me an out. He understands how I must be feeling because he feels the same nerves eating at him as well.

Gage offers me his hands again, and I take them, trusting in the higher power. Gently, he pulls me onto his lap and kisses me softly. My nerves are electric as they come alive from being this close to him. His hands release mine, and he massages my lower back. Inch by inch, his strong hands learn my every curve. He cups my left breast, rubbing the pad of his thumb over the tip of my nipple. Tingles move through me, making my core pulse in anticipation. A gasp escapes my lips, and he smiles, knowing he's on the right track. His free hand cups my other breast, brushing the tip of my nipple with his thumb. The dual stimulation makes me breathy. I nuzzle his cheek and kiss his neck.

I'm more hesitant with Gage than I was with Raphael. Every touch is tentative, almost hesitant, until I'm able to see his reaction. He treats me with respect and handles me like I may shatter under his touch at any moment. Gage was once a warrior. I can tell by all the battle scars that cover his bronze flesh. I tenderly kiss his scars, and he stops touching me to watch me with an intensity I've not seen from anyone before. I sit back, and he grabs his phone to type out a message. My phone vibrates, and I read it.

"I kiss your scars because I feel compelled to acknowledge what shaped you into who you are. Your battles honed you into the man before me. Sacrificing your life so others can remain safe and alive is noble." I hope my eyes and actions convey my sincerity.

Smiling, he caresses my cheeks and kisses me reverently. Through the bond, Raphael offers his love and support. He must know how unsure I feel with Gage. Gently, he pulls back and mouths *"thank you"* to me.

Without warning, he reaches out to me and tickles my sides, making me fall to my back. I retract my wings and try to wiggle away from him, laughing. He drops his head and plants a kiss below my belly button. I freeze, watching him with rapt attention. His well-placed kiss causes my core to clench. He raises his brows as if asking permission to continue. I nod. His eyes refocus on my body as he continues traveling south. Wet kisses caress my flesh, igniting nerve endings I didn't know existed.

Gripping the sheets, I throw my head back, moaning as his lips make contact with my wet folds. A groan of appreciation escapes him, and his tongue slowly laps at my wet depths. My breaths come quickly in pants as a new sensation moves over me in slow, delicious waves. It's almost random where his tongue hits, and I never know when he'll touch my sensitive areas.

"Tell him what feels good, beloved. It's how we'll all learn you." Raphael's voice echoes in my head, coaxing me out of my shell.

As soon as that delicious coiling feeling starts to intensify, I grip his hair, holding him in place between my legs. "Right there . . . Don't stop . . ." I say between pants. He squeezes my ass, holding me firmly in place. My body starts to move of its own volition as I try to grind myself on his face, chasing the feeling.

He must sense something because without warning, he moves up my body and slides his length deep within me. The minute he bottoms out, I detonate around him. My core pulses around his length as he moves, each stroke drawing out the liquid heat unfurling deep inside me. I cry out my orgasm, holding onto him for dear life.

"That's it, baby, give it all to me. You're so beautiful when you come undone." A thick, raspy voice fills my head as Gage succumbs to his own powerful orgasm, pulsing his release in time with mine.

My eyes widen as I realize I just heard Gage for the first time. We stare deeply into each other's eyes, afraid to move. "I just heard you," I say out loud, caressing his cheeks and searching his eyes, hoping to hear him again.

"You did?" he asks, looking almost as excited as he did the night I met him.

"Yes, I did," I say, crying tears of joy and pulling him down for a sweet kiss.

We lie in bed for what seems like hours, talking the only way we're able to. A hesitant knock sounds at the door, and I know it's Raphael because of the bond. "Come in, Raph," I call, and Gage makes a face, probably wondering how I know.

"Sorry to disturb you two, but Michael has reminded me that the Bonded Ball is tonight, and all of the new bonds are expected." He shrugs. I can feel he doesn't want us to leave until all the bonds are in place.

"If we're expected to go, then we must go," I say as I look between Gage and Raphael. "I've finally elevated my standing to be allowed to have mates. I don't wish to piss off the powers that be by not showing up." Both men nod at me, and Raphael offers me his hands.

I look back at Gage and quickly kiss him before allowing Raphael to help me out of bed. He walks me across the room to the walk-in closet and opens the door for me. An entire side of the closet is filled with dresses and shoes.

"Pick whatever you want to wear tonight. Keep in mind that tonight you're allowed and expected to keep your wings on display as a mated female." He beams with pride as he looks at me.

My fingertips brush along the silken fabric. Tonight, I'll be introduced as a mate to an Archangel. There hasn't been an Archangel who took a mate since before I was born. Gentle hands rest on my bare hips. Slowly, I turn to look over my shoulder and see Christian smiling at me, his cheeks flushed a beautiful rosy color.

"Did you come to be my fashion advisor?" I ask playfully before spinning in his arms to face him. For once, I'm not shy or ashamed of my body. On the other hand, he's still trying to be respectful and keeps his eyes trained on mine.

He clears his throat before speaking. "Yes, I have." His short answer betrays the strain in his voice. Raphael, recognizing the strain of his bond-mate, offers me a soft cotton robe to slip on. Once covered, Christian breathes a little more easily, then moves deeper into the closet, looking over the selections.

"Something blue would do nicely, if you want my opinion." He holds out two different ornate blue gowns. One gown is a deep royal blue with an empire waist, and the other is a silver-blue with a fancy embroidered waist.

I reach out to the silver-blue gown and take it from him. I look over the patterns sewn into the fabric. "I'll wear this one tonight." I smile, tracing the patterns before I look up at my mates. Three of my four mates are in the bedroom. "Where's Cyrus?" Even though the thought of him in the family scares me, he's still my mate.

"He left a while ago, something about his dad needing to see him," Raphael says, looking disappointed.

"Oh . . . Okay, if he's not back in time, we'll just meet him there," I say, trying to be cheerful. Raphael and Gage can sense my false bravado. Christian smiles back at me, happy that I'm happy.

Christian and Gage leave the room, but Raphael hangs back for a moment, his eyes searching mine. "I know you can feel how I'm really feeling." I look down and away from him. "I don't know how to handle Cyrus. He's Azrael's son, for pete's sake," I say as my voice raises a few octaves higher. He tilts his head to the side for a moment, then opens his arms to me. Without a second thought, I move straight to him and into his arms, hugging him tightly. "He scares me, Raph. He honestly scares me," I say on a half sob.

"Who scares you? I'll destroy him," a voice thunders in the bedroom, and my eyes widen as I look around Raphael at who it may be.

Raphael immediately pushes me behind him and unfurls his wings, taking a defensive stance. "What are you doing in my house, Azrael?" I peek around Raphael's wing to see Azrael with his black wings on full display. Darkness radiates off him in smoke-like black tendrils.

"I came to deliver a present to my new daughter. Come here, Thana, and receive your gift from me." The command in Azrael's voice sends a chill down my spine, almost rooting me in place.

"I don't have all day, child!" His eyes blacken into fathomless orbs as he stares at me.

Hesitantly, I move out from behind Raphael and toward Azrael to stand before him. I curtsy and wait for whatever it is he plans to do. "Thana, you are a queen in the making. Hold your head high," Azrael says firmly as he uses a single finger to raise my head and make me look into his eyes.

"You are the mate of an Archangel and the son of Death himself. I am gifting you with a new familiar for your protection." I dare not look away from his face as he stares at my right shoulder.

"Pull out your right arm for me." I comply immediately. The last thing I need is his wrath descending upon us.

Raphael moves to my left side, holds my hand, and nods at Azrael. The minute Azrael's hand touches my skin, it feels like it's been set on fire. A blood-curdling scream escapes my lips as his hand moves over my flesh. His hand starts at the ball of my shoulder and winds down my arm to just above my raven. My other three mates, including Cyrus, rush into the room, all ready to do battle.

"What the fuck are you doing to her, Father? Release her at once!" Cyrus bellows. I barely hear him over the thundering of my heart and my own screams.

"Silence!" Azrael's voice thunders, shaking the contents and inhabitants of the room.

Shortly after he yells, the burning stops, and I fall limply into Raphael's arms. My other three mates join him as he pulls me over to the bed to lie down. "You gave her a wolf, Father," Cyrus practically growls at Azrael—possessive of me for the first time.

"Not just any wolf, son. A dire wolf. A descendant of Fenrir. He'll protect her when the four of you cannot be with her." Azrael approaches the bed and shoves Gage out of the way to sit next to me.

"Name him and touch his head when you do. If you're ever in danger, say his name, and he'll rise to defend you."

My eyes search Azrael's, and for a moment, I see a fatherly gaze looking back at me. Nodding slowly, I touch the wolf's head that now takes up most of my arm and probably part of my back. "I will name you in honor of your ancestor. Fenrir, rise!" I call out my new familiar's name, and the black inky mass rises from my skin and manifests before me. He's huge and vicious-looking. His eyes burn red like blood, and his fur is black as obsidian.

Slowly, I sit up, and he prowls toward me, his claws clicking on the marble floor as he moves. He lays his head in my lap, clearly being careful not to squash me under his weight, and I pet him lovingly. "My beautiful baby. Return." Fenrir looks up at me, licks my face then returns to the tattoo on my arm.

I slide my arm back into the sleeve of my robe, then stand before Azrael. Hesitantly, I move forward and hug him. "Thank you for your thoughtful gift." I lean up and kiss his cheek before moving away. For once, Azrael looks shocked, with his hand resting on his cheek as he stares at me. I lower my head to everyone before disappearing into the bathroom to get ready. It's going to be a long night.

CHAPTER 8

THANA

Hot water rains over my skin, running in rivulets down my body. Absently, I watch the water move this way and that. I've completed two of the four bonds, so far, with two left to finish before the rising of the blood moon. I use the body scrub, buffing my skin to a silky softness. Once out of the shower, I look at the varieties of moisturizers the guys must have left for me. I pop the top of the first one and smell the strong scent of cedar. This must be the scent Gage picked for me. The second is light and smells like hyacinth—I know this scent is from Christian. The third scent is similar to chocolate, warm and inviting. I pop the top on the fourth, finding it smells like evergreen.

I can't tell which is Raphael's and which is Cyrus's choice, for the life of me. After how Cyrus acted when he thought his father would do me harm, I'm wondering if perhaps I've misjudged him. Slipping into the silver-blue gown, I curl my hair and then put it up into a French twist, arranging it so the curls cascade out of the top. My eyes trace my new familiar running down my right arm. He almost looks like he's chasing my raven.

"Father shouldn't have marked you like that," Cyrus says as he leans in the doorway, watching me.

"You know I'm powerless to argue with him. I'm an abomination to divine law. The fact I've been allowed to live this long surprises me," I say on a huff before lowering my eyes. Even now, I don't feel worthy of having the mates I was gifted with.

Cyrus grips my jaw and forces me to face him. Emotion wells up in me, and tears threaten. "Never speak of yourself that way." He shakes his head as he loosens his grip on me.

Tenderly, he strokes my jaw as if trying to brush away his roughness. "You are not an abomination. You're . . ." He searches my face for answers before turning away from me.

The grip I had on my emotions slips away. "I'm what, Cy? What am I to you?" I cry, my tears falling freely. The inky blackness of my distress streaks around me. Tendrils of black smoke fill the room as Gage and Raphael arrive with Christian in tow.

The tendrils wrap around Cyrus like a warm blanket, and he looks down at them affectionately. They snake and weave around his body, caressing every inch as if they belong with him. His black eyes look up at me, and then he smiles, his irises fading back to chocolate-brown. "You're everything."

Those two words shatter the smoky tendrils and tilt my world on its axis. The anger I held in my chest dissipates instantly as I stare at his retreating back. "Cy! Don't leave!" I kick off my heels and try to go after him, but my damn gown slows me down. I pick up the hem and shove my way past my other three mates.

Cyrus spins abruptly, pinning me in place with his gaze. "I'll see you at the ball, Thana. I need . . ." He sighs and roughly runs his hands through his hair.

"I need some time to sort things out in my head." He closes the distance between us and sweeps me up in his arms. He dips me back and kisses me. My lips feel like they're on fire, and my heart pounds erratically in my chest. Slowly, he raises me back up until I'm standing erect. His gaze softens as he looks me over, and his thumb gently rubs along my bottom lip before he turns and leaves.

I touch the spot where his thumb was as I watch him head toward the balcony and launch into the sky. My heart continues to pound in my chest as he flies away. It suddenly feels like he's taking a piece of me with him.

"That was unexpected," Raphael says as he looks from the balcony back to me. "Are you okay, Thana? He didn't hurt you, did he?" Concern is etched over his features as he checks me over.

Hesitating for a moment, I look at all three of my mates. "Yeah, I'm okay. Just a little shaken up. I didn't expect that from him." Absently, I run my fingers over Fenrir as if petting him. "Let's get going. I'm sure Michael is expecting us to be on time." I force a smile, then move to each of them, straightening their ties and fixing their hair.

Christian offers me his arm to escort me to the car. I bow with my hands folded at my waist to him out of respect, placing my hand on his forearm and allowing him to lead me to the car. Once we exit the building, our driver hustles over and opens the car door for us. Gage enters first, then turns and offers me his hand to assist me into the limo. I slide over to the seat in the corner, which gives me the best view of the entire limo. Christian sits on my left and Raphael on my right. Gage laughs, sitting right in front of me. "What's so funny, Gage?" I grin, looking at him.

"Raphael is making bunny ears behind your head," Gage says through our bond, tilting his head to look affectionately at me.

I turn in time to catch Raphael pulling his arm back, acting suave while doing so. Guilt is written all over his face. "Something you want to tell me, Raph? Or should I see if Chris knows what you were up to?" Pursing my lips, I turn and give Christian my best sad eyes. He stares down at me and tries to look away to avoid ratting out his best friend.

"Well, at least I have one mate who honestly told me what was happening." I huff and move to sit on Gage's lap, wrapping an arm around his thick neck.

"Come on, Thana. It was in good fun," Raphael says in a cajoling tone.

I tilt my head to the side to see Raphael laughing.

"Oh, how the mighty have fallen." Instantly, I regret what I said because Gage decides a retaliatory smack on my ass is deserved. I squeal as I jump up, rubbing my ass. "Et tu, Gage?" I quickly move to sit by myself, rubbing my wounded butt cheek.

"We shouldn't pick on each other," Gage states through the bond, staring at Raphael and then me.

"What did he say?" Christian asks. Raphael fills him in, and he nods. "I agree. We should present a united front," he says, focusing on Raphael.

"I'm sorry for the bunny ears, Thana," Raphael extends his hands out to me.

I nod and get up when the limo stops at a light and take Raphael's hands to curl into his side. "I'm sorry I got upset over something harmless." I reach up and kiss his cheek. Gage nods, pleased with himself as he looks between us all. He pulls out his phone and watches something on the screen. Eventually, he turns his phone to face us, and we see it's a mapping program. According to the map, we're five minutes from our destination.

Reaching into my purse, I pull out my compact and make sure my makeup is perfect. Once I'm presentable, I move to each mate, making sure they are as well. The limo stops, and the driver opens the door. Gage exits first, followed by Christian and finally, Raphael. Once Raphael is out of the car, he reaches back into the limo for me.

Gently, I take hold of his hand and try to climb out of the limo as gracefully as I can to the blaring lights of the flashing cameras. Drawing in a slow, measured breath, I smile at the photographers. Raphael moves me to his left to hide my new ink from prying eyes. I wrap my arm around his and press my arm into his side as he leads me into the ballroom. Once we're away from the media, Christian moves to my other side and takes hold of that hand.

The three of us enter the ballroom, and it's like a vision from a fantasy novel. Butterflies flutter freely around the room, as well as doves and other beautiful creatures. The lights in the ceiling twinkle like stars. I don't know where to look first as my eyes dart to every beautiful thing catching my attention. Michael approaches us, and out of habit, I lower my eyes and curtsy to him.

"Your holiness," I say with as much reverence as possible.

He greets Raphael and my other mates first, then he gently caresses my jaw, urging me to raise my gaze to meet his. "Thana, you're mated to an Archangel. You no longer have to bow to me." His smile is infectious, and I can't help but smile back at him.

Michael looks like a slightly older version of Zac Efron but with shoulder-length brown hair and at least fifty pounds of additional muscle. "Thank you, your holiness."

"Thana, you may call me Michael. Gabe as well. Formal titles don't apply anymore." Michael gently takes me by my hands and leads me around the hall, introducing me to other high-ranking angels.

My heart feels like it may burst from my chest from excitement. For the first time in my existence, I don't feel like the abomination I was made to feel I was growing up. "Finally, this is Uriel. Uriel, this is Thana, the woman I've been telling you about," Michael says in a surprisingly proud tone. The heat from his large hand on my lower back is the only thing providing me support and a sense of grounding.

Hearing who I'm standing before causes me to become nervous again. The angel of divine truth can smell a lie or deception from miles away. "The honor is all mine, your holiness," I say, dropping into a curtsy out of habit.

"Lady Thana, please rise. You're our brother Raphael's mate. No need for the old tributes." Uriel offers his hand to me, and I look at

Michael, then to Raphael. Both men nod at me, and I take the offered hand to stand up.

"I have but one request, Lady Thana. Please show us your wings. I hear they're quite unique," Uriel says, smiling at me.

I move away from everyone, just far enough to safely unfurl my wings. Slowly rolling my head back, I allow my wings to spread wide, stretching them and then draw them back in to let them hang, resting half-open. I reach around and run my fingers over my smoke-gray feathers, making sure they're lying properly. Uriel and Michael walk around my wings, examining them closely. Michael and Uriel each take a wing in hand and manually extend them to look over my flight feathers.

"Raphael, did you notice the vein of your mate's feathers are white?" Michael asks as he stretches my left-wing out, pointing to my primary flight feathers. The three Archangels look at my feathers curiously. I raise my brows, worried what their interest may mean for me.

"Don't worry, the white means you're more Light Nephilim than fallen. It's a good thing," Gage says to me through the bond. I nod, listening to him as the Archangels continue examining my wings.

A throat clears behind me, and I turn to see Cyrus. "If the Archangels would allow it, I'd like to dance with my mate." Cyrus to the rescue—hopefully. He winks at me and cocks his head to the left, waiting impatiently for the Archangels' response.

"Would that please you, Lady Thana?" Uriel asks me as his eyes begin to turn gold. He examines Cyrus curiously before looking back at me.

"I would like to spend some time getting to know my mate, Uriel. If you don't mind, I'd like to be released into his care." I state all of this truthfully with no deception or hidden agenda. Uriel releases my wing, then kisses both my cheeks before sending me on my way with Cyrus.

Cyrus extends his right arm out to me, and I accept it gratefully. He leads me off and away from the scrutiny of the Archangels.

CHAPTER 9

THANA

Never in a million years would I have ever thought Cyrus, the hospital's terror, would become my knight in black armor. "Thank you for saving me. I was beginning to feel like a lab rat," I say, as he leads me out onto the dance floor. Reflexively, I grip his bicep a bit harder to punctuate my unease.

"I couldn't stand watching them treat you like a prize to be passed around." His eyes turn black for a moment, then they revert to chocolate-brown. Black tendrils snake out from his hair, denoting how stressed he was earlier. A beautiful slow song comes on, and Cyrus places a warm hand on my lower back and offers me his left hand. Blushing, I take his hand and move in close enough so we're nearly chest to chest.

We spin around the floor in time with the music, and I sigh softly. "Would you show me your wings, Cy?" I whisper into his ear. I draw my head back to look into his eyes. This close, I can really examine his olive skin and his broad, square jaw. He's handsome and easily sports the look of a bad boy.

"If it would please you, then yes." He gives me a half grin, then unfurls his jet-black wings.

I stare at them in wonder. They're so black, they don't look real. Reaching over his shoulder, I stroke his feathers. They're cool to the touch, and the veins feel hard as steel. I run my fingertips over the parts of his wing I can reach. Cyrus watches me closely as I gently caress his feathers. Hushed whispers filter through the ballroom as soon as the others notice his wings. I continue to stroke his obsidian feathers. They're as soft as mine but silky in texture.

"Miss, you should come with me." A strange man in an ostentatious beige suit offers me his hand, apparently worried about my wellbeing.

"Why?" I tilt my head to the side, pressing myself closer to Cy. Through the bond, I reach out to Raphael and Gage, alerting them to what's happening. I feel Cyrus's muscles tensing under his tux. I'm more worried for him than I'm afraid of him at the moment.

"He's a Dark Nephilim, miss. You're not safe with him," the man states, growing bolder this time and attempting to reach for me.

"He is my mate," I growl as I move in front of Cyrus. My left hand immediately lands on Fenrir's head. "Please leave us alone." I sense my other mates closing in on us. I unfurl my wings, keeping Cyrus behind me and backing us toward the balcony. If need be, he can fly to safety.

"She's been corrupted by him. Call for the Archangels!" the man shouts, pointing at Cy and me as I continue backing us up. The other angels and Nephilim whisper among themselves. We're outnumbered, and I'm beginning to become concerned.

I rest my hand on the raven on my forearm. "Raphael, Azrael, I need you!" I say loudly, summoning my guardians to me immediately. Raphael appears in a shimmer of gold, followed by Uriel and Michael. Azrael's black wisps appear, immediately followed by his presence, pulsing with rage.

Both my guardians look me over quickly, and Azrael notices his son behind my wings, knowing full well why I'm keeping him behind me. Raphael is the first to speak. "My love, why did you summon me?" Raphael raises my hand to his lips and kisses my knuckles.

"This gentleman," I say, motioning to the man who was harassing me, "thinks your bond-mate has corrupted me. He thinks I need to be rescued."

Raphael and Uriel turn on the man, questioning him. I get it. Part of this was prompted by a genuine concern for my safety. But the other part was because he clearly hates Dark Nephilim. Azrael has heard enough and herds Cyrus and me onto the balcony. "You make me proud, Thana. I know this hasn't been easy for you, given who I am."

Azrael grins, then tousles Cyrus's hair. "My son is a chip off the old block. He can be a royal asshole at times, but his heart is in the right place." Azrael reaches out and takes my hand, kissing my knuckles. "I'll always come when you call, daughter. Don't forget that." As soon as the last syllable leaves his lips, he morphs into a raven and flies off into the night.

"My dad can be intense at times," Cyrus says as he wraps me up in his arms.

It's now that the gravity of the situation we were in hits me. I curl tightly into his side, seeking his comfort. His strong arms band tighter around me as his wings lower to wrap around me. I retract my wings, making myself smaller as I take comfort in his arms. The hushed whispers of my other mate's filter through the feathers of Cyrus's wings. He catches them up on everything that's happened. Eventually, he relents and lets the others see me.

"Are you alright, Thana?" Raphael asks. I look from him to my other two mates and then to the two Archangels with him.

I nod slowly, then turn in Cyrus's arms to face everyone. "He scared me. I thought he was going to hurt Cyrus because of his wing color." I rub my raven, then look up again. "I was going to summon my new familiar at first. But after careful consideration, I decided summoning my guardians was a better idea." Sniffling, I blot my eyes, trying to rein in my emotions. My chest hurts, remembering I may have lost Cyrus tonight if the others hadn't arrived so quickly.

"Wise decision indeed, Thana. Summoning Raphael, knowing he was with us was a brilliant idea," Michael says proudly. "We handled the man and will be addressing the masses yet again about tolerance and acceptance." Michael lightly bows his head, then departs quickly to handle crowd control.

"There's darkness in that man's heart. You did what any worthy mate would do. You shielded your mate from potential harm and summoned the authorities. Enjoy the rest of your night, Lady Thana," Uriel states before turning on his heel to assist Michael.

I stand there, dumbfounded, watching the backs of the two Archangels as they walk away. My gaze drifts to Raphael. "I'm sorry I ruined the night. I didn't want Cy to be hurt." I look down at my hands resting on Cy's.

"Thana. You didn't ruin anything. Cyrus or you getting hurt would have ruined the night. Letting your wolf loose would have ruined the night." Raphael gently cups my cheek and kisses my lips softly, trying to comfort me. Slowly he withdraws and looks to Cyrus. "Take our mate home. I'm going to help wrangle the crowd." Raphael departs, leaving us standing on the balcony.

Cyrus releases me quickly, then turns to stare off into the night sky. "Let's get Thana home as quickly as possible." He doesn't turn to face us as he speaks. I watch the expressions of my other two mates morph at his abruptness.

"Are you ready to fly, *kichōna mono*?" Christian asks as he climbs onto the railing. His white wings spread wide as he leaps backward and hovers in place. My eyes dart between Cyrus and Gage, then back out to Christian.

"Yes." I say, wincing at how small and weak my voice sounds. Hesitantly, I stretch my wings and give them a tentative flap.

Cyrus growls as he looks between Gage and Christian. "Can't you two tell she's never flown before? Fuck, guys. Pay attention." Cyrus shakes his head at my other two mates. Obviously, they both forgot unmated females can't expose their wings, and therefore, can't learn to fly.

Christian falters in the air for a moment as he realizes his folly. Cyrus is frustrated, and he leaps off the balcony and takes off, disappearing into the night sky. I watch him leave with a heavy heart, wishing he'd have stayed to watch me fly for the first time.

Gage moves beside me and runs his hands over my wings. *"Put them away for now. Let me get you airborne before you unfurl them again,"* he says with a smile as he unfurls his own wings.

"Chris, Gage is going to help me learn to fly. Catch me if I fall?" I look to him, hoping he won't be upset because Gage wants to take point on teaching me to fly.

"I'll always be there to catch you." Christian launches higher into the air and begins to circle, waiting for us.

Gage stands behind me, pulling my back to his chest. His thick muscular arms band around me tightly right before he launches us into the air. *"Stretch your arms out, feel the wind,"* he says softly to me.

I spread my arms out and flatten my hands, letting the wind flow over them. Gage grabs one arm and changes the angle, letting me feel the resistance of the wind on my hand. *"Think of your hands like your wings. When you turn them, the wind will catch them differently."* He accentuates his point by moving my hands several more times.

"I think I understand," I say quietly, still uncertain how this will turn out. I know they'd never let me get hurt, but the fear of falling is a natural reaction.

"Then try to fly. We'll catch you," Christian says, moving closer to us, just in case. Gage slows down, gliding on the thermals and giving me a chance to unfurl my wings.

Drawing in a fortifying breath, I unfurl my wings. Instantly the wind's drag catches me and nearly rips me out of Gage's grip. I barely have a hold on Gage's hand as I try to right myself by adjusting the angles of my wings. Eventually, flapping my wings furiously, I straighten out and don't feel like I'm struggling to stay level.

"Thana, you're flying!" Christian shouts as he swoops around Gage and me. I notice I'm no longer holding onto Gage.

"I'm flying! This is flipping awesome!" I scream as I flap my wings several more times, testing them out. We play in the clouds on the way home, darting in and out of them, laughing the entire time.

"Thana, come back to me and retract your wings. Landing on a balcony takes a lot of practice," Gage says to me. Reluctantly, I fly closer to him and curl my wings in as I grip his hands. He pulls me flush to his chest as we get closer to Raphael's house. We make an expert landing on Raphael's balcony. Watching how Gage lands, I realize that he made a great judgment call, not letting me attempt to land independently.

Gage and Christian both kiss me gently, then decide to get cleaned up before bed. I watch them leave before getting changed. Tomorrow is another day. Hopefully, Raphael and Cyrus are safe. I pull one of Raphael's t-shirts from his dresser and put it on before I climb into his bed to go to sleep.

CHAPTER 10
THANA

The warmth from the sun caresses my cheek and slowly convinces me to wake up. Rolling over, I end up on my right side, facing the balcony doors and the warmth from the morning sun. As my eyes adjust, I see Cyrus on the bed near me but not touching me.

I take this time to study his features closely. His skin is a beautiful caramel color, set off by his dark hair. A single faded scar slices through his left eyebrow, disappearing up into his hairline. His t-shirt struggles to contain the muscles of his broad back and thick shoulders. He's lying on his stomach facing me, and for once, his face seems relaxed. My eyes drift over his features, memorizing every curve right down to how he has his beard trimmed and faded. Up until now, I didn't realize he had an undercut, and he apparently sleeps with his hair in a ponytail.

"It's creepy knowing you're studying me like a science project," Cyrus's voice is gravelly from sleep and does funny things to my insides. A grin plays on his full lips as he stares back at me.

A soft laugh escapes me as I continue to stare at him. "Almost as creepy as it is discovering a man in your bed you didn't invite to join you," I say playfully as I reach out and grab the rogue tendril of dark hair that's escaped from his ponytail. Gently and cautiously, I reach out, further pressing my luck and tuck the loose strand behind his ear. I smile at the progress we've managed to make. But then I see he's no longer smiling at me.

Without warning, he launches himself off the bed and paces by the balcony window. Black smoke radiates from his flexing wings as his pacing becomes more erratic. He glances at the balcony, then back to me several times. A myriad of emotions crosses his normally emotionless face as he looks back and forth between me and the door. "I fucking hate what you do to me." He roughly pulls at his hair as he paces.

I'm in shock from how his switch flipped. I remain frozen on the bed, watching his every move. Anxiety crushes my chest, making it hard to breathe. Apprehension and hurt radiate through my body as I watch him. I can't decide if he's angry because of me or if he wants to hurt me to end his suffering.

The vein in his throat throbs in time with the crushing in my chest. I stare at him and process his reaction. My three other mates burst into the room, ready to go to war.

"What do you mean what I do? I'm not the one yelling and looking scary." Cyrus looks like he could decimate the entire room without a second thought. We're taught from an early age that Dark Nephilim are to be feared because of the power they hold. The malice radiating from him drops the room's temperature.

My admitting the way he's scaring me stops him in his tracks. "I hate that you make me feel . . ." He pulls at the collar of his shirt. "I hate feeling like I can't live without you." He clutches his chest over his heart, then slides his hands up to his throat like he's choking. "I hate being this way. I can't do this." He throws his arms out wide, and his wings stretch to their full expanse. Without warning, he engulfs himself in darkness, then vanishes from sight.

I sit there in shock. The root of Cyrus's problems is that he's not used to feeling anything for anyone. I think it scares him to have these feelings. My heart breaks, thinking about how lost he must feel right now, and I can't fix it. I draw my legs up and wrap my arms around them, holding myself. Lightly, I touch Fenrir, and he manifests before me.

I turn my gaze to my other mates. Right now, I don't feel worthy of their affections or comfort. The massive wolf climbs up onto the mattress and curls himself around me. Eventually, I turn and lie down, placing my head on his ribcage, and fall back to sleep. I feel like Cyrus is rejecting me and our bond. And the distance he keeps putting between us feels like he's tearing out part of my heart. A broken heart is hard to heal from. Rest may do me some good. I hope he'll come back before I wake up.

Raphael

Cyrus unintentionally hurt our mate, and I feel how broken her heart is over his admission. I rub my hand down my sternum, trying to dull the ache there. That huge wolf guardian of hers engulfs her lithe frame, shielding her from the world. I reluctantly tear my eyes away from her before heading back down the hall to the kitchen.

I wish she would have turned to one of us instead of that beast. I want to pull her into my arms and make her feel safe and loved again. Let her know she's enough, and that she's the light of my life. That I will literally die without her. My own sadness constricts my chest as I stare at the coffee maker, waiting impatiently.

"What has you so deep in thought, Raphael?" Azrael sits at my dinette as if he belongs here. Coffee cup in hand, he tilts his head, studying me. For once, the Angel of Death has a look of concern on his face. I wonder what he knows that I don't.

"I'm guessing you sensed when she summoned her familiar." My eyes narrow, thinking about how that beast may be a mystical tracker on my mate. The dragging sound of metal on tile echoes in the kitchen as I pull out my favorite chair at the head of the table.

"He draws from the darkness that all Dark Nephilim call home. Why was he summoned?" Azrael looks at me, then turns back to glance down the hall leading to my bedroom. His eyes turn black as he stares, which makes me wonder exactly how much he can see.

"Cyrus hurt Thana's feelings. He said he hates how she makes him feel." I'm trying to remain calm, but the more I think about it, the angrier I'm getting. At the rate Cyrus is going, I don't know if their bond can be repaired.

Azrael shakes his head, looking pissed-off. "Stupid whelp. I'll beat his ass when I find him. A mate is a once-in-a-lifetime chance at being whole," Azrael says, growling as he stands up, pushing away from the table. "I'll handle him. Tell Thana I'm sorry." With that, he vanishes in a wisp of smoke to points unknown.

"Was that Azrael I heard?" Gage asks through the bond. He stalks slowly through the kitchen, then looks back down the hallway toward the bedroom before turning back to me again.

"Yes. He's just as angry at his son as we are." I finally turn to face both Christian and him. Christian looks between Gage and me, confused because he's not able to hear him through the bond. Quickly, Gage uses sign language to fill him in on what's been said.

"What should we do?" Christian asks as he looks down the hallway toward the master bedroom. Christian turns to face me again, his eyes golden. He's more on edge because he can't feel Thana yet.

"For now, go sit with her, Chris. One of us should be there for her when she wakes up." I feel powerless right now, and this is the only solution I have. Christian nods and heads back down the hall. My gaze lifts to the clock in the kitchen. Duty calls. I don't want to leave her like this, but one of us has to go to work tonight.

I decide to fly to work to give me time to sort through everything that's bothering me. Every flap of my wings is consumed with thoughts of Thana and the broken look Cyrus left on her face. My heart feels like it's breaking. Rejecting or damaging a mate bond is one of the biggest sins anyone can commit.

Her pain echoes through the bond to Gage and me. It feels as if it's happening to us as it happens to her. Distance does nothing to ease the pain I feel emanating from my beloved mate. Sooner than expected, I land on the hospital roof, and Thana's friend Mark meets me, offering me my lab coat and clipboard. He shifts from foot to foot, looking at me anxiously.

"Something on your mind, Mark?" I tilt my head, trying to look as friendly as possible. From experience, I know he and Thana are best friends, and more than likely, he's concerned about her wellbeing.

"Umm . . . Yes, your holiness. First, congratulations on finding your mate and bond-mates." He says with a flourished bow. "Second, how is she?" He looks genuinely worried as he raises his eyebrows and smiles.

"Thank you, Mark. Thana is doing as well as a newly mated female can be." I smile and laugh softly. "She has four very distinct personalities to wrangle now. No worries though. She's a strong and capable female. She'll make my nest her own in no time." I speak the truth as I guide Mark back into the hospital so we can start our shift for the evening. We head down the stairs, and I go to my office.

When I enter my office, I find Cyrus sitting behind my desk, holding his head in his hands.

"Why are you here?" My wings burst free of their own volition and take on the golden shimmer that only Archangels get when we rise through the ranks.

Cyrus raises his head, and his eyes immediately turn to black. "You don't know what it's like to grow up in darkness," he growls. His voice sounds stricken with pain. Perhaps he's hurting more than I realized. Black tendrils seep out of his pores and pulse around him like a symbiote.

Cyrus stands up, and the chair flies back into the wall, shattering into pieces. "You have no idea what it's like to be raised by demons and passed off to an unsuspecting family to grow up semi-normal." Sadness mars his normally stoic face as he stares me down. He's at war with himself, mostly about what he was raised to believe he's supposed to be instead of the man he wants to be.

"You're right. I don't understand. Archangels don't have childhoods like you've had. We're not human or even partially human." I shake my head and turn to look out the window on my office door. "You and the others in the bond have the best chance of understanding Thana. I can only guess how to help her with her human emotions." I'm honestly at a loss when it comes to dealing with how his actions may have damaged their bond.

"Boo-hoo. The golden boy didn't have a childhood. I'd give you mine in a heartbeat." Cyrus narrows his eyes, challenging me to react. The darkness surrounding him pulses in time with his speech. It's as if it's accentuating his inflection.

"I'd rather you speak with Thana and make things right." I narrow my eyes right back at him, crossing my arms over my chest. My wings flex open and closed as I stare at him, ready for anything.

"Fine!" Cyrus snarls, then vanishes again in a wisp of smoke from my office. It's times like this I wish I knew where he is and where he's going. I just have to hope he does the right thing before it's too late.

I text Christian and Gage, letting them know about my run-in with Cyrus. Gage asks why we even need him in the bond. It's time for me to relay how and when I knew Thana was mine. I watch my phone intently, watching the dots pop up and stop several times as Gage formulates his message.

He and Christian go back and forth several times about the night I saw Thana's wings. Rolling my eyes, I express my concern over Azrael exposing the fact he knows I saw her wings before the Trials. He can easily call to have the bonds rescinded and make Thana wait for the next trial twenty years from now. Not only would I lose my mate, but my life would also become forfeit. The short version is, we're stuck with Cyrus. We can only hope he gets his head out of his ass before it's too late.

CHAPTER 11
THANA

The deep rumbling of my wolf guardian gives me solace and comforts my breaking heart. Deep down, I know he'll give his existence to save me, only to have him rise again and again like a dark phoenix. My fingers thread through his thick fur, petting him. I know I should have sought out one of my mates instead, but right now, I just need to be alone.

"Thana, love?" Christian calls softly from the other side of the room. I raise my head, looking over my wolf's back at him. The sadness in his eyes makes my chest tighten, and it's hard to breathe. I've seen this look before from him. It usually occurred after each failed Mate Trial when he came back empty-handed. The thought that I've caused him pain makes me feel ill.

Gently, I pet Fenrir and bid him to return. His giant wolf tongue gently licks my cheek before he returns to my tattoo. I stare down at my arm, at his inked likeness, and stroke his body. A soft sigh escapes my lips. "Sorry for worrying you." I turn and look down and away from him. Guilt wracks my heart. I caused my sweet protective mate undeserved pain.

"*Kichōna mono*, don't be sorry. It's my honor to be allowed to worry about you." Christian closes the distance between us and sits beside me on the bed. His hand comes up, caressing my cheek so tenderly. "Let's get you cleaned up. You smell like a hellhound." He scrunches his nose and sticks his tongue out.

I laugh and slide off the bed. "Oh. Okay, fine . . ." Walking across the room, I feel Christians eyes on me. My confidence wavers as my steps carry me across the space. I make my way to the bathroom and flick on the light. Piece by piece, I drop my clothes on the floor.

Christian is different than Raphael. He's been one of my best friends and confidants for years. Raphael was the unattainable boss who was always just out of reach. Angels like Christian have the choice of whom they can bond with besides their destined mate. So, the fact that Christian waited all this time after his first wife died says something about the type of man he is. Me being his mate drops all the previous barriers between us. His request for me to take Gage before him makes me think he doesn't see me as anything other than his best friend and not someone he's attracted to.

I adjust the temperature of the water in the shower and try to clear my head of all the negativity. The fact that he's followed me into the bathroom hopefully is a sign that he's interested in me. My nerves start to get the better of me as I set the bathroom up for my shower. I'm second-guessing everything I've thought to be true.

"*Kichōna mono*, let me help you." His voice is soft as his hands rest lightly on my shoulders. I look over my shoulder at him. He's completely bare before me. My eyes drink in every inch of his toned and battle-hardened body. He looks like a sculpted piece of marble. His muscles are almost perfectly symmetrical, and what few scars he has look to be centuries old. His long, black hair flows like ink down his back, over his shoulder and onto his chest. An old tattoo of a tiger digging into his right ribcage is nearly faded away. My eyes roam over his taut abdomen, seeing the horizontal scar that would have gutted him if it was deep enough. Eventually, I raise my eyes and look into his dark brown ones.

He raises an eyebrow, and smiles. "You honor me by looking at me like I'm the only man in the world."

His lips descend on mine, and we step back into the hot running water of the shower, kissing as if there's no tomorrow.

Our hands roam over each other, searching and learning every curve of the other's body. Christian jacks me up against the wall without warning, using his arms to hold me in place against the tiles. As he leans into me, I feel the tentative nudges of his hot length at my entrance. I rock my hips, practically begging him to give me what I desire from him. He nuzzles my neck and slams me down on his shaft.

Within seconds, I feel the tethers of our bond snap into place, and he's now in my heart and soul. We grind and paw at each other fiercely. My core pulses and tingles with each thrust. My orgasm rips through me as I call out and cling to him. His thrusts become erratic, and he hugs me tightly to him, his orgasm crashing down on him. He buries his face in my neck and cries out.

As he starts to soften, he slows down his thrusts. We snuggle under the hot water as it washes over us. Giggles escape my lips as I slide down his body to stand on my own two feet. "I thought angels didn't fornicate before finding their mate." The smile slips from my lips as Christian's face darkens.

"Long before you were created—in a land far, far away—I once had a wife." He sticks his face under the water, letting it wash away his darkness.

An easy smile crosses his lips as he looks back down at me. "It was just after one of the last great dynasties fell. She was the youngest princess in the emperor's family." Christian spins me around, pushing my long, ash-blonde hair under the water. He threads his fingers through my hair, massaging the shampoo into my scalp.

"I helped her escape through the secret passage and then hid her for months. Over those months, we hid as man and wife." His eyes change yet again, as if the memories plague him.

"She died in labor, giving birth to my son. I believe you've met him. His name is Ben." He smiles as he washes the shampoo out of my hair and then begins applying conditioner.

My eyebrows shoot up, and I turn to stare at him. "Ben is your son? He's flipping awesome and so much fun." I laugh, watching Christian try not to laugh at my enthusiasm.

"He has always spoken highly of you, especially when he relieves you at the end of your shift." Christian caresses my cheek and kisses my forehead. "Apparently, it's in the genes to appreciate things of beauty."

I reach up and kiss him. He thinks I'm beautiful. The warmth blooms in my chest as his love joins Gage and Raphael's for me, all at once. I feel on top of the world, knowing I'm loved by my three mates. Happiness fills me as we kiss. Christian breaks the kiss and finishes washing out the conditioner from my hair.

"We should meet up with the others," Christian says softly, planting a chaste kiss on my lips before stepping out of the shower and moving out of sight, leaving me to my thoughts.

So many changes have happened in my life in the past week. It's strange to think that I've gone from being an outcast to someone who's desired. Moving through Raphael's room, I duck into the closet and pull out a silver gown that catches my eye. Once again, I'm amazed that it conforms to my body like it was made for me. I close my eyes briefly and focus on the bond with my guys and sense they're in the kitchen, waiting for me.

Silently, I walk barefoot through the house, heading toward the kitchen. I walk into a vision of perfection. All three men are around the table, passing breakfast food around. "We know you're there, Thana," Raphael says without turning to face me. He tilts his head, beckoning me to him.

I close the distance between us. Raphael and Gage pull out a chair for me. All my favorite foods are on the table—bacon, eggs, cheese Danishes and English muffins. They take turns passing a plate around, filling it for me.

Raphael pulls me down to sit in the chair between Gage and him.

Christian sits in the chair across from me, smiling. "You three crack me up."

"*Why do we crack you up?*" Gage asks as his hand rests on my upper thigh.

Shock crosses Christian's face as he hears Gage for the first time. I shake my head and smile at him. "I have before me three of the most powerful warriors. And you all dote on me like lovesick puppies."

Raphael draws me into his lap, then grips my chin, forcing me to look into his eyes as they churn in a liquid gold. "We . . . Are . . . Only . . . this gentle with our mate." He stares into my eyes, and the only thing I can focus on is him. "You are the most precious person in our lives. Some are never blessed with a mate. You are ours to treasure." Raphael leans in, kissing me deeply to drive his point home. My fingers thread through his hair as I hold him tightly to me. Reluctantly, he breaks the kiss, then presses a softer kiss to the tip of my nose.

"You are our love embodied." He kisses me once more before sitting me back on my chair. My eyes roam to Gage and Christian, who both nod, agreeing with Raphael.

"I'm eternally grateful to have all of you. I love you all so very much." Using the bond, I try to push my emotions to the three of them, letting them feel how deeply embedded into my being they are. Sadness washes over me as I look around the kitchen for Cyrus.

"He's not here, *kichōna mono*. I'm sorry." The resignation in his voice speaks volumes. He looks to Gage and then over to Raphael. "I'm sure he'll surface when he works through whatever plagues him."

I nod, listening to what he has to say. "I should get ready for my shift tonight." I slide off my seat and make my way around the table, kissing each of them.

"Have a great evening. Be safe please. Love you!" Their voices harmonize as they say goodbye to me. Work will be a lot more interesting, now that I'm not afraid of being exposed.

CHAPTER 12

THANA

Spreading my wings, I take flight to work for the evening shift at St. Michael's. The wind moving over my feathers feels incredible. The freedom flight has granted me is absolutely amazing. Then I realize I forgot I didn't learn to land. Panic floods my system as I circle the rooftop at least a dozen times. A burst of light streaks across the darkened sky on a direct trajectory to me. At the last minute, it stops before me. It's Raphael. His kind smile radiates at me.

"Forgot you didn't learn to land, my love?" he asks in a kind and joking tone as he motions to the rooftop.

I laugh as I flutter my wings, trying to hover in place like he's doing. "Can you show me how?" I motion to the rooftop and shake my head, feeling foolish for not knowing.

"You just learned how to fly two days ago. You're doing fantastic. Most females wouldn't have been able to fly the distance you just did." Raphael smiles at me with pride. "Let me help you." He extends his hands out to me, and I take them without hesitation. I know he'll never let me fall, no matter what.

"Do like I do, Thana. It's a lot easier than it appears."

I mirror each movement of his wings and through the bond, I

feel his intended movement before he does it. I release his hands and move my wings exactly the same as he does. We come in for a silent landing on the roof. I can't help but shout with joy, and then I jump into his arms. Raphael spins us in a circle, whispering praises in my ear. Giggles escape my lips just as he sets my feet on the roof.

"Great job, daughter . . ." echoes from the darkness, and I spin to face the voice I haven't heard in nearly two hundred years. I open my wings wide and do my best to shield Raphael from my birth father.

"Nyx. What could you possibly want from me? I haven't existed to you since I was a little over a hundred and fifty years old," I practically spit his name out like a curse.

Raphael teleports to stand before me in his full Archangel armor with his sword blazing to life. "How did you escape your sentence?" his voice booms, shaking the roof as he points his fiery sword tip at my father.

"Thana, your grandfather would be so disappointed in you . . ." Nyx spits out at me like a hissing cobra. His words cut me deeply, making me grab at my chest.

"Father, don't!" Fear runs through me like a raging river. The true name of my grandfather would frighten even Azrael if he heard it. Speaking of Azrael, I press on my raven and speak his name softly, summoning him to me quickly. Hopefully, he can imprison my father before he can spill the truth of my lineage.

Azrael manifests beside me, positioning me between Raphael and him. A husky laugh escapes him as he stares down at my father. He immediately silences my father, sealing his lips until such time that Azrael sees fit to free him. He presses a kiss to my temple and grins. "Thank you for making my job easier, daughter. Your father has eluded me for days. Though—" He looks between Raphael and me, then back to my father "—I'm guessing there's a deeper reason why you summoned me." I nod, then look away.

"Ah. I see . . . Nyx was playing dirty again. Come clean with the golden boy, then head to Club Dread. My wayward son is playing a show there tonight." I look back at Azrael, then nod slowly before he grabs hold of my birth father and vanishes in a wisp of smoke.

"Thana, love. What did Azrael mean?" Raphael looks worried and his eyes plead with me for the whole truth.

Sighing deeply, I pace the rooftop, trying to find the words I need to say. Before I start speaking, my other two mates arrive, looking equally as concerned. "You know how Nephilim are created? Either an angel or a child of a fallen sire with a human."

My mates nod along as I start the conversation off with common knowledge. "My father is Nyx, son of Samael. He took after my grandfather's darker rites." My tears threaten.

"Like me, my grandfather has a duality. He is considered the executioner of the most high. Depending on which faith you consult, he's considered both good and evil." I use my sleeve to wipe away my tears.

"Thana, my love," Raphael speaks softly, his gentle tone soothing my nerves. "Do you know Samael's wings are also gray like yours? He can easily overpower all the Archangels if he wishes it." I turn slowly to face my mates and sigh softly.

"You're nothing like your father or grandfather." I nod, listening to him as he kisses me on my temple before passing me off to my other mates. "Don't worry about tonight's shift. Go find our wayward number four," Raphael says with a smile. I give him a quick kiss, then run to the roof edge and jump off.

Maybe Raphael is right, and I shouldn't let my lineage affect who I want to be. The flight to Club Dread is rather short and uneventful. Once I land, I run my hands down my scrubs and change my clothing to that of my dark angel garb. The black wedding gown looks very goth and vampire-like, which seems to be the favored style here. I alter it slightly by removing the sleeves. My tattoos are on full display. The black and gray art stands out against my creamy, pale skin. As I approach the bouncer at the front door, I notice he's a Dark Nephilim. This will be easier than I expected.

The bouncer's eyes roam over my curvy form and get stuck,

staring at my ample breasts that are almost bubbling out of the top of my dress. Finally, his eyes raise to meet my pale gray ones, and I grin and change how I'm standing, so my back is to the line forming behind me. My eyes turn black immediately, and the minute he sees the darkness within me, he lets me into the club.

The music booms and vibrates through me. I move with purpose through the crowd, stopping suddenly at the sight of a familiar face. Azrael is in the club, waiting for his son's performance. Casually, I stroke the raven on my lower forearm, releasing him from my body. I send him on a mission to get Azrael's attention without me yelling. My raven perches on Azrael's shoulder, and he turns in the direction my familiar motions. Azrael waves me over, and I comply, not wanting to keep my father-in-law waiting. "I'm glad to see you here, Thana. Actually, I'm shocked your other mates let you out without a babysitter." He pokes my side playfully.

"They know who my grandfather is. I doubt they'll be so panicked from now on," I say.

"It's about time you own your legacy." His stance screams pride. A slight raise of his chin in the direction of the stage catches my attention.

I turn to watch for movement and whom do I see moving around in the darkness? My missing mate number four—Cyrus. He's doing a soundcheck, preparing to go through his band's set for the evening. Azrael hands me a flyer with the setlist, and I'm shocked to see most of the songs I love on the list. Azrael gives me a knowing wink, answering my unspoken question. Cyrus has changed the band's set to my favorite songs.

The lights blaze to life on stage, and Cyrus looks like a rock god. The leather and chains look is hot on him. A woman throws her thong onstage, and it lands at Cyrus's feet. He glances down at it before he looks back at the woman. "Sorry, love. My girl would rip you to shreds in a heartbeat." Cyrus promptly kicks the thong into the crowd.

And here, I was worried about him whoring around since he

seemed to not want anything to do with me. Instead, he's more faithful than most men in the same position of power he currently holds. The opening cords to "Familiar Taste of Poison" by Hailstorm fills the room, silencing the crowd.

Azrael smiles at me and tightly takes hold of me. We phase from where we were standing to the side of the stage. "Unfurl your wings, Thana. And trust me."

I obey him immediately just before he thrusts a microphone in my hand, then shoves me out on stage at the start of the chorus.

I belt out the power cord of the song's first chorus, and Cyrus spins to face me. He looks stunned as he walks toward me. Our voices harmonize and sound like we've done this a million times before. We caress each other's cheeks with our free hands. With each line, our faces move closer together as we sing. I spin away when we hit the part of the song where I sing that I don't want to be saved. At this point, I flex my wings, looking up into his chocolate eyes. In the last lines of the song, he grabs me around the waist and holds me flush to him. He sings the last part alone. I'm mesmerized by the amount of passion in his tone.

After the last note is uttered, he kisses me passionately, dipping me backward in a romantic embrace. He stands me up and whispers in my ear to pick the next song for them to do.

I choose "In This Moment" by The In-Between. He winks at me and directs the band to play the song as I walk forward. The crowd has no idea this song fits me perfectly. The audience sings along with me, clearly thinking my wings are a prop. I suddenly notice my other mates in the crowd. I sing the song, putting all my frustration and pain into the lyrics, leaving it all on the stage.

Every time I sing the words "in-between," I spread my wings wide to make the word pop. The darkness within me is clawing at my insides, wanting out even just for a little bit. So, when I say "hell," I let the darkness seep out of my pores to swirl around me. Toward the end of the song, I move to stand before Cyrus. As I sing, my hands move over the fabric of his shirt, and my nails slice it to ribbons. I lean forward and playfully nip at his bottom lip before walking off stage to his dad. Cyrus, on the other hand, stands dumbfounded, staring at me. I guess he didn't think I had it in me to fight for what's mine.

Next to Azrael, my other mates stand, staring at me in varying states of shock over my performance. "What?" I hug Azrael briefly before moving in to snuggle with each of my mates.

I just finish hugging Gage when I'm ripped away from him and spun to face Cyrus. There's a hunger in his eyes that matches the pounding of my heart.

"I—"

I place a single finger over his lips to silence him. "If you're going to reject me again, do it in private. I don't want to die from embarrassment tonight." I shake my head before taking a page out of Azrael's playbook and disappearing in a wisp of smoke.

CHAPTER 13

THANA

I don't bother going back to Raphael's nest after leaving everyone at the club. Instead, I go for a flight around the outskirts of the city. Raphael said I needed to pick a nest for all of us to live in at some point. He was more than happy to offer his loft, but it's not me. It's not my style, to be more accurate. It's nice, but it doesn't feel like it's my home.

After hours of flying, I happen upon a circular house on the side of the mountain, overlooking the valley below. The house is wrapped in cedar planks and left natural. Metal rails adorn each level, wrapping around the entire house's three balconies. Circling the building slowly, I land in front of the double cedar doors. As I peer through the stained glass along the side of the doors, I see realtor brochures along with business cards. On closer inspection, the house appears to be completely empty.

I take a look around, making sure the house is as isolated as I first assumed. Once I'm sure I'm alone, I phase into the house and begin to explore it. The majority of materials used in building the house are naturally sourced. Everything from the raw oak stairs to the solid marble flooring makes me feel at peace. Christian would be pleased.

The hours he spent trying to teach me about feng shui must have paid off. The geometry in this place screams feng shui. You can feel the harmony within the house. The positive energy and flow are incredible. I walk through the layout of the house and fall in love with every step I take. I found my nest. This is it!

I pull my cell phone out and call all four mates at once. One by one, they answer, and I have all four of them on video chat. "Okay, I'm sorry I vanished, but I found my nest!" I shout, bouncing up and down as I spin the camera around to show them the interior.

"Thana. I need you to stop bouncing and tell us where you are," Raphael says calmly, trying to be the voice of reason.

I walk out onto the balcony, then fly up onto the roof and show them my surroundings. "I'm honestly not sure. I followed my gut here."

Cyrus shakes his head and rolls his eyes. "I know exactly where she is. Remember the round house on Glacier Peak I showed you guys?" Cyrus keeps his arrogant grin firmly plastered on his plump lips. "Thana, is there a giant Norse raven in bronze in the center of the tiles in the middle of the house?"

Furrowing my brows, I glide down to the balcony and walk back inside to find the dead center of the house. "Yes, it's right here." I flip the camera again to show the guys the ornate raven in the tiles. Then I flip the camera back to face me.

"Can we please get it? I feel so at peace here. It called to me." My anxiety is through the roof, thinking that my other three mates will shoot the idea down because Cyrus found it first.

"Let's consider the nest Thana found. You know a nest calls to the female when her time begins to draw close," Christian says quietly with reverence in his voice. My other three mates murmur their agreements. Then the video cuts out.

I'm confused by half of that conversation. But instead of dwelling on my questions, I wander the house, checking out every room. While I'm standing in what I think should be the master bedroom, I sense the guys approaching. I run through the house and back down to the balcony to throw the doors open, letting them fly right in.

Christian's hands fly up and cover his mouth as he spins in a slow circle, looking at the house's interior layout. "*Tsuma*, it's perfect. This house is in perfect harmony." He immediately drops into a deep bow before Cyrus.

"Forgive me, brother. You were correct. This is the perfect nest for Thana." Cyrus accepts his apology.

"*Tsuma*?" I arch an eyebrow, looking at Christian. It's Cyrus who answers me.

"The literal translation is 'wife' or 'mate.'" Cyrus rolls his eyes and heads towards the balcony.

"Why do you always leave?" I ask tearfully. It hurts even more, knowing he picked this place out long before I found it. "Cy, please stay," I say, half in a sob.

"You don't need me." That harsh mask he wore at the hospital slips over his face, hiding his emotions. "You have the three light stooges to chase after you like puppies." He smirks, shaking his head. "I'm the outcast in the family. Have your sweet little angel babies. I won't darken your door anymore." A single blood tear rolls down his caramel skin just before he roughly wipes it away. Without so much as a backward glance, he runs and jumps off the balcony, taking flight into the night.

I feel sick, watching my fourth mate leave. My stomach is in knots, and my heart feels like it's being crushed in someone's hand. It's hard to breathe, and I feel lightheaded as I stare out into the night sky, hoping against hope that he'll return. I must look pathetic, staring off into the black of night. Deep down, I know he'll come back. It's just a question of when.

Cyrus

Flapping my wings, I put as much distance as I can between myself and the others. Every time I do something positive, one of those light motherfuckers gets credit for it. Thana has a darkness within her that calls to me like a siren. I've lived for hundreds of years without feeling a single thing for anyone, and now, here she is, flipping my world upside down. I remember the pain in my mother's eyes every time my dad took another female to bed because he could. I swore right then and there to never let anyone in. I don't want Thana to end up like my mom.

As the sun rises, I arrive at my destination. Landing softly under the weeping willow tree, I walk to my mother's headstone. Resting a hand on the cold black marble, I kneel beside it and lower my head. "I wish you were here. You'd tell me what to do." Exhaling slowly, I touch the raven on my forearm, calling for my father.

"Boy, you left your mate in tears again! What the hell is wrong with you?" I look up and see my father has his usual judgmental look on his face, like he thinks I'm no better than the shit on his shoe. His rage is palpable. It's nearly suffocating the way the air electrifies around him.

"What's *wrong* with me? For fuck's sake, Dad, that list is a mile long." I look at my mom's headstone. "You know, you're part of the reason I'm having issues with Thana. She's too fucking good for a wicked-hearted bastard like me." My fingertips trace mom's name cut in the marble.

"Your mother was too good for me too. But there's a huge difference." Azrael sits next to me and rests a hand on my shoulder. "Your birth mother wasn't my mate. The urge to please only her didn't exist for me." Azrael shakes his head. "I was a shit husband and an even worse father. I can't change the past, but I can save Thana from your mother's fate." He stands and walks to a nearby bench.

"What do you mean? What's the matter with Thana?" I feel defensive and more protective than usual. My heart thunders, each heartbeat hitting with the force of a sledgehammer. My skin crawls as I think about what horrible thing may be happening to Thana.

"You don't understand. She needs your darkness to balance out the light from the other three idiots. She'll eventually die without you." Azrael gives me a pitying look. "Her soul will be strangled by all of the holy light from them. In light of who her grandfather is, she needs you to bring balance to her." He adjusts his jacket. "Given who your old man is, she'll need only you as her Dark Nephilim to balance things out." Azrael sits down and leans back, studying me, his signature smile playing on his thin lips.

His statement catches me off guard. "Who's her grandfather?" My father finally has information I don't know. My insides quake with a nervous energy as I question why her grandfather is important.

"Samael," he says, dropping the mother of all bombs in my lap. He's uttered the name of the Destroyer, the one Archangel who's darkness and light embodied. The one being who could give The Almighty a run for his money. *My* mate, my dark angel—once she comes fully into her powers—can be a real threat to the balance.

"Tell me you're joking." Her bloodline alone puts Thana in danger. Which makes me think her mates weren't chosen haphazardly. The Almighty set the wheels in motion for some grand scheme that only he's privy to. Just like the overgrown child the Dark Nephilim take him for, he's playing a game of chess with our lives. I look over my shoulder toward the direction I just came from and contemplate heading back immediately.

"I wish I were. There are talks in the darkness that if you don't claim her by the blood moon, others will petition to be her mate." He shakes his head slowly. "Every bond has at least one Dark Nephilim. It's how balance is kept."

The harsh words I spewed at Thana in anguish hit me like a ton of bricks. What have I done?

"Shit . . ." Roughly, I drag my hands through my hair. The blood moon is less than a month away, and if I can't get her to forgive me, we'll be in one hell of a battle. I've been a selfish fuck. I didn't once think about how my actions could affect Thana. My gut tells me the vilest Dark Nephilim will petition to take my place at Thana's side. Consent will be the last thing they seek from her. I can imagine them attacking our nest, taking her by force, and making her their mate as painfully as possible.

"Instead of pacing around here like a fool, do something." My father urges me. "You can't let her die or be stolen." Inky blackness surrounds him and, for once, he looks like the epitome of death itself. His power rolls off him in waves. Each surge from him hits me in full force, almost knocking me off my feet.

I steel myself and tap into my powers. I finally stand fast against his raging storm. I look back at my father and shake my head. "For once, we agree on something." Without hesitation, I take off, heading back to Thana. Hopefully, she'll forgive me.

Each flap of my wings brings me one step closer to my mate's side. My mind races as I prepare myself for the amount of groveling I know is ahead of me. About three blocks away from our nest, I land and walk into the nearest coffee shop and grab a cup of Thana's favorite brew. I've been stealing her coffee for years, so I know how she takes it like the back of my hand—three shots of espresso, caramel, mocha, and almond milk, blended into one drink.

In the last hundred years, her coffee has varied only slightly—mostly because it was a happy accident to discover the blend. The aroma from the coffee instantly evokes memories of all the times I watched her during her shifts. Staring down at the cup in my hand, I'm so lost in thought I don't notice whoever it is that sneaks up on me until it's too late. An intense pain floods my system, and my head spins. The world around me becomes blurry as I stagger away from what I perceive as the source of pain. I make it into the alley beside the coffee shop and stare in disbelief at the person standing before me, then everything goes black.

CHAPTER 14

THANA

It's been two weeks since I last saw Cyrus. To be perfectly honest, I'm almost ready to give up hope of him returning to me. My other mates are trying to fill the void his absence has left. They take me flying and out to dinner at places I've never thought of going to. The biggest and best surprise happened last week. We bought the nest I wanted, and I've spent my days and nights decorating it.

The guys suggested I cut back my hours at the hospital so I can get my nest in order. They keep mentioning my time and that we need to have everything ready. I'll have to ask Joscelyn when I see her again about what they could possibly mean . . .

There are a total of five bedrooms in the house on the third floor. I find myself standing outside the door that should be Cyrus's. Every day, I enter his room and add things. I must look pathetic to my other mates. I hope that by having his room ready for him, he'll magically appear, and everything will be okay. Standing just within the threshold of his room, I look it over, trying to see if anything has been disturbed or if I need to add something.

"Thana," the rough, harsh voice of Azrael cuts through my inner monologue, causing me to turn and face him. I must look horrible given the way that Azrael's eyes widen as he looks me over.

"Have you seen Cyrus? Is he okay?" My voice trembles as I fight to keep my tears at bay.

Azrael's face morphs from sadness to alarm. "I thought he was with you." He searches the room for any sign of his son's presence.

"What do you mean you thought he was with me?" I rush to him and grip his arm firmly. Looking into Azrael's fathomless eyes, I practically bleed him for answers. "Please tell me. I feel like part of me is dying without him." Exhaustion and depression are a bitch, both whittling away at any drive and ambition I have left.

"The night you went to watch him at the club and then found your nest, he flew to his human mother's grave." He sighs as he caresses my cheek. He looks over my shoulder, then back down to me. "I wasn't a good father or husband when his mother was alive. His fear of feeling anything for you is likely because of me." He bends down and kisses my forehead.

"I'll search for my boy. You stay with your mates. I'll be back as soon as I can." With that, he vanishes in a wisp of smoke, leaving me with more questions than answers.

Strong hands grip my shoulders, and I'm drawn back against my mate's chest. "*Is there anything I can do?*" Gage asks softly through our bond. His thumbs dig into the muscles of my shoulders, massaging them and trying to comfort me.

I turn in his arms and rest my head on his chest. "I'm not sure. Azrael says Cy was on his way back to me weeks ago. But he never returned." I turn my head, so my forehead is pressed between his pecs. Slowly, I wrap my arms around his waist. I need to feel grounded. The thought that Cyrus may have changed his mind about returning to me makes my chest hurt.

Gage's strong arms surround me, pulling me flush to his body, and his wings wrap tightly around us, cocooning me in his white feathers. The hushed voices of my other mates filter through Gage's feathers. I hear him filling them in on what we know through the

bond. I feel so powerless, and then I remember who my grandfather
is.

"Raph?" I ask as I turn in Gage's arms and push his wings apart.

"Yes, my precious love?" he asks as he drops to a knee before me.
His pale eyes stare up at me. I know if I asked for the world, he'd give
it to me.

"Could Uriel or Michael locate my grandfather?" The gears are
turning a thousand miles a minute in my head as I think of ways to
locate my missing mate. If he's doing something other than hiding, I
need to know.

"Most definitely. But are you sure you wish to be brought before
him?" Raphael asks in concern as he reaches up and takes my hand,
holding it gently and rhythmically stroking his thumb along the
back of it. It's almost as if he's trying to convince me not to go that
route.

I break free of Gage's arms and walk around Cy's room.
"According to scriptures, he's the greatest hunter of all of the
Archangels. If anyone can find Cy, it's him." The hum of darkness
within me is comforting right now. It reminds me of my wayward
mate and gives me more reason to fight.

"If that's your wish, we'll depart now. It's a short jump to the
Angelic Realm to meet with Michael to find your grandfather,"
Raphael says. His words say one thing, but the look on his face says
something entirely different. Uncertainty and concern flash across
his face.

I wrap my arms around Raphael's waist, resting my head on his
chest. His wings fold tightly around me, and we shoot up at rapid
speed without the use of his wings. Squeezing my eyes shut, I
tighten my grip around his waistline. Fear bubbles in my chest.
When we come to a sudden stop, Raph starts to laugh. "I would
never let you fall, my love."

He opens his wings, and I see the Angelic Realm for the first time.
It's bright and vivid. Everything around us is stunning. I walk in a
circle around Raphael, keeping contact with his skin, afraid I might

be shot back to where we came from. "Do you like it?" Raph's normally strong and sure voice wavers with hesitance.

Smiling, I spin back to face him. "Like it? I love it." I move into his arms, and he laughs at my enthusiasm.

"Now, now. None of that here!" a voice booms behind us.

My eyes widen, seeing Michael in his full battle armor. My eyes dart around quickly at all the other angels in long-flowing robes. Panic overtakes me. "Did I die?" I whisper to Raph as I peer around cautiously, afraid to let go of him.

Raphael and Michael look at each other and laugh. "No, Thana, you haven't died. But I understand why you would think you did," Michael extends a hand to me. "This is the Angelic Realm. It's where the angels come to rest between assignments." I take Michael's offered hand, and he leads me around the realm. "What brings you here today?" His eyes take on their golden hue as he stares down at me.

I look down at our joined hands and swallow hard, mustering all my courage. "I need to find my grandfather. My mate Cyrus is missing, and I believe my grandfather may be the only one who can help me find him." I wince at the ache in my chest, thinking about Cyrus being hurt or dead. Cyrus being missing this long has started to have an ill effect on me.

Michael stops dead in his tracks, looking between Raphael and me. "Someone dared to steal your mate?" I nod slowly.

"This cannot be allowed. You need your Dark Nephilim mate to survive." My eyes widen at the bomb Michael just dropped.

"Someone is trying to kill you, Raphael, by using your mate," Michael says as he moves quickly, dragging me with him.

"I was afraid you'd say that, old friend," Raph says, looking from me to Michael as we chase him across the clouds.

"What do you mean someone wants to use me to kill Raph? How would that work? Archangels are impossible to kill." I shake my head in disbelief.

Michael stops at the edge of a cliff, then turns to look at me. His gaze softens as he cups my cheek and looks into my eyes. "If you die, Raphael dies. Being a hybrid, you need to have a balance with your mates. Too many light angels will eventually poison your Dark Nephilim side and kill you." He draws in a slow deep breath and closes his eyes for a moment before looking at me again.

"Whoever did this, knew what it would do to Raphael. Cyrus was targeted on purpose." Michael releases me, then motions to the cliff.

"You need to travel from here alone, Thana. The darkness at the bottom will hurt or possibly kill Raphael. Your grandfather is down there. If you need help, Azrael will assist you." Michael leans forward and kisses my forehead before taking flight.

Raphael's normally confident demeanor seems to lessen as he looks at the cliff. "I won't lie to you, Thana. I'm worried about you going down there alone." He abruptly scoops me up in his arms, crushing me to his firm chest. "Please come back to me."

Smiling, I caress his cheeks before I gently kiss him. "I'll always come back to you. You were my first crush and now my first mate." A smile forms across his lips as he stares at me.

"I'm not afraid of what I am anymore. I get that strength from you." I lightly kiss him one last time before breaking away from him. "See you soon," I say and dive over the cliff edge, heading toward the abyss.

CHAPTER 15

THANA

You know how the humans say it's not the fall that kills you, it's the sudden stop at the bottom that gets you? I completely understand the saying now. Blasting through the dark mist separating the Angelic Realm from the Dark Realm is a shock. Dark winged beasts fly free, breathing fire at each other, waging war in the air. Things of nightmares roam loose within the realm, held only at bay by what appears to be a thin layer of mist.

A castle stands alone in the distance, surrounded by what looks to be a river of blood. My gut tells me my grandfather will be there. After all, someone of his rank should live in a castle—or at least a really large house. I close the distance and land at the top of the stairs, not far from the front door. The skin on my arms feels like it's crawling.

I look at my tattoos, and they seem to be moving. Taking the hint, I release my three familiars. My raven has doubled in size, and he looks like something straight out of a horror novel. The black housecat is now a large panther beside me. It rubs its face on my leg, purring loudly. Fenrir has nearly tripled in size, his head even with my shoulder, and I can almost look him in the eyes. I rest a hand on his shoulder as we move toward the front door.

Just as I raise my hand to knock, the door flies open, and a huge man with smoke-gray wings stands before me. My own pale-gray eyes stare back at me. I notice he also has my same ash-blonde hair.

"Grandfather?" I ask softly, almost afraid to offend the man before me. Wincing, I brace for some kind of retaliation from him.

He smiles and nods. "Indeed. I see my useless son did something right . . . for once." He opens the door and makes room for me to pass. My familiars and I enter the castle cautiously. My eyes move constantly around the interior of my grandfather's home.

The castle is a mix of gothic and baroque in design. The ornate vaulted ceilings mixed with dark paint, offset by gold filagree, is a unique mix. The skulls of various denizens of the Dark Realm line the walls—much like a hunter would display his trophies. The next section of the hall changes in design and has dozens of different weapons on display. I feel like I'm in a chamber of horrors rather than my grandfather's home.

"What do they call you, child?" Samael stops walking and remains about ten feet behind me, although the way his voice echoes through the cavernous halls makes it seem as if his presence surrounds me.

"Thana." Pursing my lips, I tilt my head to the side, examining the weapons lining the walls. My father, Nyx, named me. "I know my name means death." I shake my head and allow my eyes to turn black before looking back at my grandfather. "I need to find my missing Dark Nephilim mate. I'm told I'll die without him." I stare into Fenrir's blood-red eyes. My wolf lowers his head, pressing into my side and offering me comfort.

To my left, there's a room bathed in darkness, and with a flourish of Samael's hand, the candles that line the walls ignite, illuminating the room in flickering fire. The floor appears to be blood-stained slate with ornate markings carved into it. Samael walks past me across the room to what appears to be a throne where he sits. I realize this room must also double as a training room with all the swords and weapons lining the walls.

"You're more like me than I could have imagined, Thana. You have my wings, eye color, and hair." He smiles at me. "Whose progeny is your mate?" he asks curiously.

I eye the additional weapons lining the alcoves above the furnishings. I guess there's always time for battle. "Azrael is Cyrus's sire." For once, mentioning Azrael doesn't raise any fear in my chest. Instead, pride blooms there.

"He has a very strong bloodline indeed—one worthy of my grandchild." Samael strokes his chin before looking over my familiars.

"If anyone here has him, it would be the demon Asmodai. He's wanted to get back at the Archangels for centuries, as well as Azrael for helping them." Samael rises from his throne and walks toward me. He grabs his sword from the wall above my head, and almost immediately, his armor manifests in place.

He raises his hands high above me. A tingle, almost a ripple of energy, rolls over me like a bucket of water being dumped over my head. Once the feeling leaves, I look down, and see I'm fitted with my very own armor. The ornate armor fits my every curve, perfectly protecting my vital organs. The color throws me off a bit. It's black and gold. It dawns on me—my armor is a female version of my grandfather's. "Am I ready, Grandfather?"

Pride fills Samael's gaze as he looks his handiwork over. "You're as ready as I can make you." He touches Fenrir, also adorning him with armor and then repeats the process with my other two familiars.

"Do not fear the darkness within you, Thana. It's the greatest weapon at your disposal. I sense that your power rivals my own, and that's saying a lot." He grins, moving past me to the front door. "Familiars return!" he booms, and immediately my familiars become tattoos again.

All these years, I never believed in myself because I was in between both species of Nephilim. Mom didn't know what to do with me because of what I could do. Dad shunned me because I wouldn't do typical Dark Nephilim things. Mom would tell me to stifle my darkness, that maybe my wings would whiten.

After nearly four hundred years of denying what I am, my grandfather sees me as a whole person. He sees the dark and the light in me and encourages me to be true to myself. We walk across the wasteland, and I can feel the darkness hugging me like a long-lost friend. "Why did we hide my familiars?" I ask softly, not wanting to anger him.

"Easy. It will look like we're going to war if they walk with you. Like this," he motions between the two of us, "it looks like we're less dangerous than we really are." Samael pulls me into his side. "One day, Thana, you'll realize just how powerful you are. And on that day, you'll truly be free." Samael looks down at me with a gleam in his eyes. He definitely knows something he's not telling me.

For once in my life, I feel as if I finally belong. With every step across the volcanic sands of the Dark Realm, I begin to understand little things about myself. My blood hums, infused with the power of this side of my nature. For so many years, I stifled this side because of my mother's warnings. But apparently, her fears were unfounded, as evidenced by my grandfather's existence. Various nightmarish creatures roam freely and steer clear of us as we cross the great desert, heading to the monolith in the distance.

"We must be ready for anything, Thana. If it's Asmodai, he'll use your mate against you, either through possession or torture," Samael states matter-of-factly.

My eyes dart to my grandfather at the mention of Cyrus being tortured, and anger bubbles up in my chest. My fingernails lengthen into claws as I clench and unclench my fists. "How familiar are you with the stories of the old gods?" Samael raises an eyebrow as we walk.

Shrugging, I tilt my head to the side, glancing at him. "A little bit. Mom didn't really take my education seriously, figuring I'd be cut down long before now." My mother wasn't exactly the most loving being in my life. She grew even colder toward me once she found her true mates. I was dumped on my ass in the streets to fend for myself. Thankfully, Joscelyn's family took me in until we were old enough to live on our own.

Samael pauses and shakes his head in disbelief at my mother's treatment of me. "First of all, you're not an abomination. Long before the current deity took the helm, Valkyrie flew wild and free. They were both divine judgment and death on the wings of a beautiful woman," Samael says. "He," Samael points up, "retired them to the tree of life in the Angelic Realm."

Double blinking, it takes me a few minutes to process what he just said. I'm not an abomination, and there are others like me. Nodding slowly, I turn back to the scorched path before us, looking between the remnants of charred trees. Beyond the river of blood on the other side of the black mist, an obsidian monolith rises up from the base of the mountain. Winged creatures fly patterns around the entire length of the structure.

"Is that where we need to go?" I motion to the monolith, and he nods slowly. A hard mask slips over what was moments ago a kind face. The years of war have forged him into a force to be reckoned with. Muscles jump all over my grandfather's arm as his grip flexes on the hilt of his sword.

"Once we enter the monolith, you may see people who claim to know you. That's where your wolf will come in handy. He can sense and reveal the true appearance of anything." Samael lightly touches Fenrir.

"Trust his reactions. He'll see the truth of everything. Your raven can investigate the route ahead of us and report back to you." Samael motions to my raven.

"Your cat can be any size she needs to be. If there's a tight spot you need to get into, she can go first and pave the way." I stare in disbelief at my grandfather's explanation.

"Do you think Azrael gave me these familiars on purpose?" I

glance at my pets, then look up at Samael.

He smiles and shakes his head. "I discussed with Azrael which familiars would be best for you. A prophecy has been foretold that one day, my successor will be born of my rib to ease my burden." An easy smile graces his lips for a second, then vanishes just as quickly.

I stop walking and stare in disbelief at him. "I'm not an Archangel. There's no way I can fill your shoes." Spreading my wings, I look them over. Being in the Dark Realm has caused the veins on some of my feathers to turn dark again.

He smiles broadly, breaking the stone-cold exterior he attempts to maintain. "You're my granddaughter, Thana. This realm obeys me. Therefore, it'll obey you once you come into your power."

"Tell me how I can save my mate." Lightly, I stroke my raven, sending it to go scout the monolith.

"Release your familiars, and let's go to war." Drawing his sword, it blazes to life, and hellfire ripples over the length of the blade.

Without touching my remaining familiars, I look at each of them. They rise of their own volition to stand beside me. My raven returns to me, and I stroke his feathers again. My eyes turn black as I stare into the abyss of his black eyes. He shows me the entire path he took around the monolith. At the very top, Cyrus is chained between two pillars with lacerations covering his body. It looks like they've tried bleeding him out. Resting my hand on my raven's back, I bow my head and concentrate on Azrael, calling him to me.

Seconds pass before a mass of inky blackness manifests beside me. Azrael rises from the darkness and looks to be as fearsome as I remember him being when we first met. "Have you found my son, Thana?" Azrael asks. I raise my eyes to look at him and pass on the information my raven revealed to me.

He backs up slightly, looking me over slowly, making sure I'm okay. "Tell me what you need, Thana."

I look at my grandfather then up the side of the monolith. "Let's go." Leaping up, I spread my wings wide and fly up the side of the monolith, heading straight to Cyrus. In my wake, my familiars claw up the side of the structure. My large wings thrust powerfully, rocketing me toward my goal.

The end is in sight, but I suddenly get a bad feeling about our approach. Changing the angle of my wings, I put the brakes on and move out and away from the monolith. It's a good thing I did because an eight-foot-tall demon stands with a scythe, circling the top of the monolith. Around Cyrus are a bunch of Ifrit, ready to torch anything coming within range of them.

"Embrace your heritage, Thana. You are death and destruction in one beautiful package. Give them the eternal death!" Samael shouts as he dives for the scythe-wielding demon.

I feel the darkness swirling within me, begging to be released. My grandfather attacks with an angelic sword and wields the darkness with equal precision. Countless demons pose a threat to my mate, who seems to be fading by the minute. My hesitation could cost Cyrus his life. I dive in. I must not fail him. Both of our lives hang in the balance.

CHAPTER 16

THANA

My name literally translates to mean "death." All this time, I've tried to be someone I'm not. Constantly trying to be perfect and good really grates on a girl's nerves. My grandfather calling for me to unleash my darkness made my blood start to boil. My mate hangs like a harpooned animal. His blood paints the top of the monolith, fueling the Ifrit in their volleys of fire. Swords clash as Samael battles the huge demon with the scythe.

Azrael approaches from the other side to get to Cyrus but to no avail. Out of nowhere, a large horned demon rises up from the smoke and attacks Azrael. That must be Asmodai. I'm torn between helping my grandfather and going to assist Azrael. But the decision is easy. I fly straight toward the demon and grab his horn to spin him off-balance.

Once the demon is far enough away, I land next to Azrael and quickly disarm him. "You need to get Cy out of here. I'll hold off Asmodai." I jab the sword tip in the direction of Asmodai. "Save my mate, Azrael. I can handle this."

Azrael, for once, doesn't argue with me. He takes off running toward Cy, but the Ifrit are waiting for him.

Voices whisper to me, feeding me thousands of years of history and knowledge. With knowledge comes power. Apparently, being what I am comes with superhero abilities. As the Ifrit charge, I raise my hand, sending them to sleep, along with the scythe-wielding demon. They fall swiftly under my power. Azrael glances at me briefly, then takes that as his cue to grab hold of his son and take flight toward the gateway to escape. I turn my gaze back to Asmodai and my grandfather, who are now engaged in battle.

I look down at Azrael's sword in my hand, then back at the battle my grandfather is in. Swooping down, I dive headfirst with my sword aimed right at the demon's black heart. Spreading my wings wide, I slow my descent and drive the sword through the demon's back. My blade ignites in hellfire, burning the demon from the inside out. I ride the ashen corpse to the ground, still screaming my battle cry.

Leaning on the sword, I look up at Samael to find him smiling at me. "You did very well, Thana. You chose the best course based on the information you had. Let's go save your mate."

I withdraw the sword from the demon's remains. "Yes. My Cyrus needs me." I take flight into the air, flapping my powerful wings. Catching up to Azrael, I grab Cyrus, stealing him from his father. I'm stronger than I realized because the size of my wings gives me strength to get my mate to safety. Moving faster than I ever have before, we break through the mist separating the Dark Realm from the Angelic Realm. Each flap of my wings drives us higher into the night sky. I sense Raphael on my heels, closely followed by Azrael and Samael. I'm going to the only place that I feel safe—my nest.

My grandfather and Raphael catch up, flying side by side with me. My heart aches, carrying my mortally injured mate back to my nest. The faster I fly, the further the distance seems to be getting. Eventually, I see our house on the skyline, and hope blooms in my chest. Salvation is within my grasp. I reach out through the bond to my other two mates, asking them to open the double doors, so I can fly directly into the house. Gage and Christian throw the doors open just as I swoop into the main part of the house and up to Cyrus's room. Christian has blankets and pillows in his arms as he rushes to my side. Gage has bandages, as well as every medical supply imaginable.

Gently, I lay Cyrus down on the blanket and pillow and step back, allowing Gage and Christian to attend to him. "You're the only one who can save him, Thana," Samael says to me. The minute he opens his mouth, Gage and Christian freeze and stare with fear in their eyes.

The tension in the room troubles me, so I move to my grandfather and embrace him briefly. "My loves, this is Samael. He's my grandfather. Without him, I wouldn't have known how to battle in the Dark Realm." Smiling, I gently kiss my grandfather's cheek before moving to kneel beside Cyrus.

I unfurl my wings, slowly taking in how much they've changed. The feathers along my wing bones have turned black as pitch like Cyrus's. My mid-feathers are a dark gray, fading down to my usual smoke gray. I look deep within myself, feeling the darkness and light simultaneously as I channel my healing power into my hands. Quickly, I lay my hands on Cyrus's worst wounds, and tears stream down my face, desperate to heal him. Lowering my wings, I rest my forehead against his as I straddle his body. Waves of healing energy wash over him as I direct all my power into him.

A large hand caresses my cheek, and I suddenly sit up. Cyrus gives me a tentative smile, and his eyes are half-open. I press a finger to his lips and shake my head. "Please rest. We can talk later." My eyes scan his body. Most of his wounds have closed from what I was able to do.

I look over my shoulder at Raphael. "Please try to finish healing him. I think I've depleted myself."

Raphael gives me a nod, and Gage comes to my side to help me stand up. The minute I do, I pass out.

When I wake, I'm snuggled in the warmest cocoon in the history of cocoons. This is the safest I've ever felt in my life. The morning gives way to early afternoon before I finally drag myself from the warmth of my nest. It's odd to wake up alone with all four of my mates under one roof. Searching my nest, I'm certain I'm completely alone. Reluctantly,

I slide out of bed and pull on shorts and a tank top before heading to the kitchen. My grandfather sits at the table with Raph and Azrael, and using the bond, I sense Christian is working and Gage is in the shower. I hesitate at the door, watching three of the most powerful men I know having coffee like it's a normal Thursday thing for them.

"Hey, sleeping beauty." Raphael says as he spins to face me. Quickly, Azrael closes the distance between us and pulls me into a bone-crushing hug. The fierce warrior from the day before is long gone. Now, a grateful father stands in his place, thanking me for saving his son.

Breaking away from Azrael, I smile. "Saving Cyrus was all Raphael's doing. I only carried him here." I'm certain of the truth of my statement.

"Thana, my granddaughter, you're wrong. Your dual nature is what saved your mate." Samael smiles and spreads his wings. "You used the darkness within you to heal your mate. Standard angelic healing would have killed him instantly," Samael says as he walks toward the balcony. Without a backward glance, he leaps into the air, taking flight back to the rift.

My eyes jump back and forth between Raphael and the direction my grandfather has gone. I'm puzzled by what Samael just said. There's no way I was able to heal something Raphael couldn't. I ponder this new information for several moments before turning and taking off down the hallway to see Cyrus for myself.

When I get to the staircase, I take the stairs two at a time, running up all three flights. I make it to the floor where the bedrooms are located and rush around the circular hall to get to Cyrus's room.

Softly, I place my hands on the door, then grip the doorknob, turning it slowly. The telltale click of the door opening sounds extremely loud to my ears in the silence of the third floor. His room is black as pitch, and I can't see a damn thing in front of my face. After several moments, my eyes start to adjust, and I enter the room, now able to see the outlines of everything before me.

Weaving my way between the furniture, I make it to the side of his bed and kick off my shoes. Carefully, I crawl on my hands and knees up the bed to lie down gently beside his sleeping form.

Reaching down to the foot of the bed, I pull a light blanket up and over us. I snuggle back in and make myself comfortable along the length of Cyrus's body. Placing my head on the pillow closest to him, I then move to rest my cheek on his shoulder blade. I feel like someone on the bomb squad as I slowly inch my arm over his waist, trying not to disturb his slumber.

With everything we've gone through up to this point, I'm terrified to leave him alone right now. I stifle a yawn as I nuzzle his shoulder. Sleep will do us both some good. At least lying here with him, I'm not afraid of something happening to him.

CHAPTER 17

CYRUS

My dreams are plagued with pain. The memories of my skin being flayed and ripped from my body haunt me. Watching the ribbons of my skin hit the floor at the top of that monolith plays over and over in my head. A beautiful angel swoops in out of nowhere and goes to war against the demons on the top of the monolith. Sword's clash and ring out, reverberating in my head. The fire demons surround me, trying to keep me from my rescuers.

Even in my dream, I black out several times during the attempted rescue. I remember seeing my dad—for once, looking concerned. Perhaps he actually cares whether I live or die. It's only taken him six hundred years to figure out that I matter to him. Asmodai, the demon who had me abducted, does battle with the infamous Samael. I owe a debt to whoever summoned The Almighty's destroyer. He's beating back Asmodai as if this greater demon is nothing but a fly in his ointment.

A sweet, angelic voice rings out, telling my father to get me out of there. Dad's arms wrapping around me and then taking flight is the last clear memory I have besides waking up to Thana crying.

Raising my hand, I wipe the sleep from my eyes, trying to get my bearings and figure out where I am. The sheets are black satin and a very high quality, reminding me of something I'd have in my room. But the scent tells me I'm not home. A thin arm rests over my upper stomach, and my skin begins to crawl. If this isn't my mate, I'll have a lot of explaining to do.

I inch myself sideways in full stealth mode to get the woman's arm off me. Once I completely slide free of the woman, I lift her ash-blonde hair to get a good look at her face. I'm relieved to see it's my Thana and that she decided to watch over me.

Gently, I run my fingers through her long hair, taking in every inch of her I can. Instinctually, Light and Dark Nephilim are enemies. I've always had fun harassing Thana and the other girls at the hospital by taking their coffees and desserts and hiding them. Who would have known this beautiful, powerful female would be mine? Though, instincts being what they are, it's difficult to shake hundreds of years of conditioning.

I now notice she's slept with her wings on display. Her feathers have changed colors since I last saw them. I wonder if it's from her time in the Dark Realm, coming after me. A third of her feathers have turned nearly the color of coal and rival the darkness of my own. My fingers gently ghost over her new black feathers, admiring them. She loved the color of mine, and now she has her own. I only hope what-ever happened to darken her feathers doesn't make her unhappy with the way she looks.

The pattern of the color on her wings is absolutely stunning. They fade from my pitch-black color down to the smoke-gray they were when I first met her. I can't help myself as my fingers roam over her soft feathers and her even softer long, ash-blonde hair.

I turn just enough to be able to press my lips to her temple. Several gentle nudges later, I roll her to her opposite side and care-fully straighten her wings back out, making them look perfect again. Once she settles into place and I'm happy with how her feathers look, I curl my body tightly around her, wrap my arm around her waist, and pull her flush to me. I'm still exhausted from what I've endured. For now, I'll sleep with my dark angel in my arms, finally feeling safe lying next to her.

There's a heavy arm draped over my abdomen, holding me tightly. As I open my eyes and look around, I realize I'm still in Cyrus's bed. I reach up to caress the thick forearm on my stomach. Gently, I turn his hand and stare at his palm and at the thick calluses covering it. You can tell a lot about a man by how callused his hands are. Raphael and Christian's hands barely have any calluses on them. Gage works as a carpenter, so his hands are covered in them.

"Something interesting you, beautiful?" Cyrus's voice is rough and deep from lack of use.

I raise my hand to cover my mouth when I yawn. "Just learning what I can about you before you run away again." My voice cracks when I mention him leaving again, and I turn my head to hide my face in the pillow. The weight in the bed shifts several times before I feel his hand caressing my cheek.

"Open your eyes, baby. Please look at me," Cyrus says in a low voice as he kisses my temple. Reluctantly, I turn my head and open my eyes. He looks concerned, and he also looks like he's still in pain from the torture he survived.

"I tried my best to rescue you." I scoot to sit up in bed before looking down at my hands in my lap. "I thought you gave up on us and left for good." Tears roll down my cheeks. He lifts his hand to use the pad of his thumb to wipe them away.

"If it wasn't for your dad saying he hadn't heard from you and that you were supposed to be with me, I'd have never known you were missing or hurt." I blurt out the short version of what ended up being one hell of a rescue mission.

Cyrus climbs up the bed to me and pulls me onto his lap. "With what happened between my parents, I didn't want to chance you being broken like my mom," he says softly as he hugs me tightly, being careful of my wings. "You've become as important as the air I breathe, and that scared me." His muted tone tells me he's having a hard time hearing the truth leave his lips. I kiss his cheek but remain silent to hear what he has to say.

"I went to sit by my mother's grave to think for a while. Dad managed to talk some sense into me while we were there." Cyrus caresses my cheek, moving so he can look into my eyes. "I was flying back to you when I was abducted." He gently rests his forehead against mine, and I can't help caressing his cheek.

"Raph went with me to the rift. He was afraid to send me in alone." I kiss the palm of his hand. "I dove into the abyss without fear. I knew my grandfather existed just outside the rift." Shrugging, I allow a small laugh to escape. "Besides, I knew if I called for your dad, he'd be right there with me." My laughter returns as I shake my head.

"So, picture me knocking on Samael's door and saying to him, 'Hi, I'm your granddaughter. Want to go attack a greater demon with me?'" I roll my eyes at myself. "Surprisingly, getting him to help was the easy part. Me harnessing my darkness and sword-fighting—that was a little harder."

His eyes widen as he looks at me, then my wings, then back at me again. "So, I didn't imagine you fighting the Ifrit as well as Asmodai?" I slowly shake my head, slide off his lap, and open my wings wide so he can get a good look. He stands and walks around me, looking my wings over. About halfway through him looking at all the changes, my other three mates and his dad enter the bedroom.

"Samael has named me as his successor. He said something about me coming into my full power." Shrugging, I fold my wings back in to turn and face my other mates. "I feel a change within me. I'm not at war with myself anymore. I'm not straining to hide my dark side." Grinning, I allow my nails to change to claws, then back again.

"I also feel like I need more fluffy blankets and warm things for my room." My eyes search my mates for answers. Only Azrael smiles and laughs.

"This is very exciting, indeed. Gentlemen, if my calculations are correct, you have till the next full moon to get her nest in order." Azrael slaps his son on the shoulder.

"Better get that bond in place if you want a chance to have a child of your own." Double blinking, I stare at Azrael. Cyrus seems to be choking on air, and my other three mates are giving each other high fives.

"I don't want to know what you five are thinking." Throwing my hands up in the air, I stalk from Cyrus's room and over to mine.

Once inside my room, I circle and pace around the concave nest of blankets. For some reason, the way the blankets are sitting aggravates me. Carefully, I climb into my nest and throw all the blankets out and onto the floor. My frustration builds until I'm shrieking because no matter how I set them, they're not right yet.

Eventually, I hear someone clear their throat, and I pop my head up out of my pile of blankets. Every male present in the house stands in my doorway, staring at me. "What do you want? Somebody needs to help me freaking fix this damn thing. It's not right." I know I sound like a harpy.

"Thana, I just had a talk with all your mates," Azrael says, holding his hands up in a placating manner.

"You're going through what's called the 'nesting' . . . It's what happens just before a female Nephilim can conceive children." Azrael moves cautiously, looking over my nest and then back to my mates. "She'll need something from each of you that smells like you. It's probably the reason why she keeps destroying her nest. Because it only smells like her."

I raise an eyebrow at Azrael, glancing down to my blankets and then back to my mates, looking each of them over . . . I'll be damned.

Azrael is right. Not having their scent here is what I'm missing. There's no scent-marking from my mates in my nest, and it's making me anxious.

"Okay, everybody in the nest. Let's go." I climb out and gently shove my mates to my nest, encouraging them to climb in and roll around in my blankets. One by one, the guys reluctantly climb in, each taking a different part of the nest to wrap themselves up in the blankets there.

I turn on Azrael. "So, the short version is when I'm fertile, I'll get a very strong nesting instinct?" I ask him, being as straightforward and blunt as I possibly can. Azrael chuckles and then smiles broadly, nodding. "You are 100 percent correct, Thana. Now that you've found your mates, your body will be driven to reproduce every so many years." He rests his hand on the edge of my nest, patting it.

"Until one of these geniuses gets you pregnant, the urge to breed will not relent. Just keep in mind that because you're Nephilim, only the men you've bonded to will be able to have a child." His eyes darken, and sadness creeps across his face as he looks over at his son. "I hope he gets his head out of his stubborn ass and does right by you." Azrael leans in and kisses my cheek before disappearing in a wisp of smoke.

Azrael has given me a lot to think about, especially when it comes to his son. All this time, I've been afraid of bonding with him, mainly because of my fear of myself. Having gotten to know my grandfather a little bit, I understand my duality isn't as bad as I first thought. "I'm gonna go grab some orange juice, guys. I'll be back in a few minutes. Don't move." They all mumble their assent and settle back in.

Joscelyn nearly ruptures my eardrums when I tell her what's going on with the guys and me. She makes arrangements to get to our house as soon as possible, which means her mate has to fly her here. I decide to stay in my room, arranging my nest for the one-millionth time.

Eventually, a soft knock echoes in my room. Soon after, Christian opens the door and leads Joscelyn in. Her eyes grow wide as she takes in the interior. Her mate Jacob is right on her heels and looks around my nest.

Something about this strange male being in my area sets my nerves on edge. My other three mates rush into my room to make sure I'm okay. Poor Cyrus has no idea why Raphael and Gage went running, he just knew he needed to follow them. Christian turns Jacob around and herds him out of my room. Once he's out of my space, I breathe easier and calm down almost immediately.

Cyrus moves to me and checks me over from head to toe. Joscelyn and I stare at him as he runs his hands all over my body, making sure there are no hidden injuries. "Sorry, love. Not being able to sense you, I just had to see for myself," Cyrus explains, falling over his own words. He brings his right hand up and rests it on the back of his neck, rubbing it slightly.

I can't help but smile at him and then lean forward to kiss him on both cheeks. "Thank you for worrying about me." I nuzzle his cheek and snuggle in close to him. He wraps his big strong arms around me and encloses me in his obsidian wings. This has become a thing between him and me. When I seek security from him, he hides me in his wings. I don't know what it is, but this simple movement soothes me.

Eventually, Cyrus and I break apart, and he kisses me softly on my lips, leaving without a word. I must have been wearing an expression showing how much I adore him.

"Is that *the* Cyrus? You know, the one who used to make our lives hell at work?" Joscelyn asks, her voice pitching higher as she finishes the sentence.

"Yes, that is my terror," I say with a smile and giggle as we walk to the sitting area in the corner.

"Never in a million years would I have thought I'd have been mate material." I unfurl my wings and spread them wide, allowing Joscelyn to finally see their colors. I look around me, beaming with pride at how beautiful my tricolor wings are. Joscelyn wears just as astonished an expression as I did when I saw them for the first time.

Hesitantly, she approaches me to get a closer look. "What does this mean, Thana? Your wing colors have changed, and you somehow managed to bag four mates."

I fold my wings up and walk with them half-opened to the balcony. As I open the door and look out over the cliff, I feel at peace. "It's simple, Joscelyn. I finally came to terms with who and what I am." I breathe in slowly, then let my breath out. "My lineage is no longer a mystery," I tell her plainly as I turn to face her.

"My father is Nyx, a Dark Nephilim and knight of the first order. My grandfather is Samael, The Almighty's Destroyer," I say both names solemnly, finally appreciating them for the power and weight they carry. "Someday, I'm to be my grandfather's successor. When that day comes, I'll lead the legions of light and dark without question." Pride blooms in my chest, and I know my three mates present in the house can feel I'm finally at peace.

"That's insane, if you think about it, Thana. You go from being shunned and mistreated for over three hundred and fifty years. But now, all of a sudden, your lineage changes everything?" she asks skeptically as she moves around my room with purpose.

"I'm not being mean or sarcastic. I just don't want you to get hurt because of everyone being jealous of who and what you are." Concern and worry etches her brow.

I study her closely because something seems slightly off with my friend. Her stomach should be bigger nor does she show any of the coloration changes that usually happens when a female of our kind has delivered.

"Are you okay, Joscelyn?" I ask, closing the distance between us.

Gently, I rest my hand upon the small swell of her stomach. Almost immediately, tears fill her eyes and roll down her cheeks. I push some of my healing properties through my hands and feel there is no life within her womb. The crux of her problem is evident. She lost the little one she'd been carrying. Without hesitation, I wrap her up in my arms and hold her tightly to me. I feel like such a bad friend, not realizing something had happened to her. "I'm so sorry, sweetheart. If I'd known—"

"I didn't tell anyone, Thana. Only my mates and I know—and now you." She sniffles slightly, then sighs.

"It's not uncommon for us to have problems carrying our babies. Being part human, we experience the same problems human females do." She breathes in deeply again as she looks up to me. Her fingers twirl my hair, as if needing something to ground her.

"There are several other females from the night of your mate Trial who also haven't conceived. The Archangels suspect they may have great difficulty." She finishes twirling my hair before she releases it and turns away.

"Hopefully, you'll be luckier than I was, and I'll get to meet my niece or nephew when they get here." She smiles, trying to be happy for me even though I have no clue how to get from point A to point B.

"Well, that's kind of the reason why I asked you here." I motion to my nest in the room.

"I have all these instincts. Make my nest, make sure it smells like my mates, keep the number of visitors to a minimum. And it must be the room that the sun breaks into first thing in the morning." I sigh, slightly frustrated and pace my room yet again.

"My mom abandoned me long before she was able to tell me about everything we endure as females. I'm over three hundred and fifty years old, only to just now find my mates with no clue beyond my instincts driving me to know what to do." A sad, knowing look falls over Jocelyn's face as she pulls me over to the bench by the balcony.

She sits down, so we're facing each other, and takes both my hands in hers. "It's really not that difficult, Thana. Your urge to reproduce is going to go into overdrive by the next full moon. When that happens, you'll be able to conceive a baby or two." She looks down at my hands before looking back up into my eyes again.

"I know it's none of my business, but I noticed you're still not bonded to Cyrus," she says.

"He's still healing from being abducted, but it's very high on our list of things to do," I say, my cheeks heating. "I think the biggest thing that frightened me about him was my fear he would make my dark side stronger." I laugh almost hysterically to myself.

"It took him being abducted and meeting my grandfather to come to terms with who and what I am." I stare down at our joined hands for a few minutes before I look up. "I am life and death in one body. I can create or destroy," I enunciate each word as I feel the truth of it through the very fibers of my being.

"Whatever the higher powers planned for me all those eons ago, I'll go willingly and do what needs to be done," I say with confidence I didn't have before and finally feel whole. I spread my wings a little bit again, taking in their beautiful colors.

"I'm the best of both worlds—darkness and light, shadows and bright. For every yin, there's a yang to bring balance between the light and the dark." I break into a broad smile as I look up into my friend's eyes. I finally feel at home, that I have a purpose, and I'm wanted.

Seconds after I finish my last sentence, Joscelyn launches herself at me. She wraps her arms tightly around my neck, hugging me to her and sharing in my happiness. We sit there, crying happy tears, wrapped in each other's arms, half laughing, half sobbing, and making a literal mess out of each other. The guys barge in, blowing the doors wide open and storming into my room to find us hugging and crying together.

"I'll never understand this!" Jacob says, flinging his arm in Joscelyn's and my direction. His harsh tone takes me by surprise, and I narrow my eyes, staring at him. Christian takes the subtle hint and removes Jacob from my nesting area again.

Raphael is the first to approach, kneeling in front of me and looking up at me with adoring eyes. "My love, do you need anything? Are you well?" It's a swoon-worthy moment for me, like a scene from a Hallmark movie where the prince is down on his knees, confessing his love to the girl before him.

I bend forward slowly and reverently place a kiss on Raphael's soft lips. I linger there for several moments, pushing all the love I have for him through our bond. His eyes are molten gold when we break apart, the color swirling. They look like polished orbs, the reflection showing me how I look to him. He turns and leaves with a single nod, gathering my other two mates with him and taking them out of the room.

"Oh, my goodness, Thana! Raphael looks at you like you're the beginning and end of all things for him. Like the sun rises and sets because you deem it so." With the amount of shock and wonder in her voice, it makes me wonder how well her mates are treating her if she doesn't get looked at like that by them.

"They're the beginning and end of all things for me as well. And when and if we're ever blessed with little ones, they'll rank higher than any of us," I say with certainty, knowing that my mates and I will put the children's health and safety above our own without question. "They'll be the future, and the sun would rise and set according to their needs."

I watch my best friend wince as she suddenly stands up and walks toward the door. "My mates want me to come home and rest." Her forced smile betrays exactly how she's feeling. Something one of her mates said to her through their bond has shaken her. I'd love to know if her bond is as safe as mine. Unfortunately, just like humans, there are good and bad Nephilim, no matter the color of their wings.

I walk Joscelyn to the door, and we find the mate who accompanied her. We say our goodbyes and watch him fly off with her. "Something about her situation doesn't sit right with me. I can't shake that feeling that all is not as it appears."

Before I can turn around and disappear into my room, Cyrus grabs hold of my wrist, giving the other guys a look and leading me into the library. "I know Gage and I have known you the least amount of time, but I can definitely tell something is bothering you." He gets right to the point, not holding back and just laying everything out for me to decide what to do with it. My heart pounds in my chest with how intensely he and Gage are watching me.

I sigh and move to sit on the edge of the desk in the library. "I don't think Joscelyn's relationship is as good as she makes it out to be," I state as my other two mates walk into the room with us.

"She lost the baby she was carrying, and she isn't allowed to tell anybody. The icing on the cake is it doesn't seem she's allowed to grieve the loss of her baby." I shake my head, feeling my anger starting to rise. I look up at my mates, pinning each one in place with just a look.

"If you can find out about her three mates and what they're actually like, I'd feel much better. To be perfectly honest, I don't think they're treating her well," I say with a growl, finally allowing some of my darkness to surface.

Cyrus has a good grip on my left hand, and Christian comes forward to grab hold of my right. My other two mates join us. Raphael immediately formulates a plan. "You two stay here and protect our mate. Christian and I will do some investigating. The way Jacob was acting, not having Joscelyn in his line of sight, makes me suspect that they may be abusing her. He didn't want her to be able to say anything to you."

Raphael's statement corroborates my gut instinct, telling me they're treating my best friend badly. "What can we do if that's true? Can we save her?" I ask quickly, looking between them. Christian and Raphael hang their heads, practically telling me there's nothing we can do. Whereas Cyrus looks angrier than I feel right now, and he and Gage keep looking between each other and using sign language.

"No, you two. We can't do that," Raphael says, watching the conversation between them. Raising an eyebrow, I concentrate on their hands, trying to figure out exactly what they were saying.

"The short version, love, is that we can challenge her mates to a duel to free her. But the downside is if we lose, they can try to take you as theirs."

My eyebrows raise at the terms of what one of these duels would be. "Yeah. That's not gonna work for me," I state plainly, sliding off the desk and pacing around in circles. "Does it say anywhere whether I can duel? Divine law has loopholes for loopholes, so I imagine it wouldn't be too shocking if there is."

Raphael appears to be deep in thought as his eyes churn gold. Several tense moments pass before he finally regains his normal hazel eye color. "From what Michael says, there's no rule that a friend cannot fight for another friend's freedom. But with that being said, your time is right around the corner, so it wouldn't be wise for you to take that chance."

Raphael looks to Christian and then back over to me. "Michael and Uriel will visit them like they do all new bonds to make sure everybody's okay. All Uriel has to do is lay his hands on Joscelyn, and the truth will be revealed to him." A sad smile crosses Raphael's face.

"According to divine law, a mate is not to be abused and instead, is to be treasured. If they're abusing her, they'll be put to death for breaking the most sacred traditions." He looks down for a moment before raising his eyes to meet mine again. "As her friend, you may be called to harvest their souls and send them straight to Hell." I nod solemnly, thinking about what that might entail.

"No. I'll do it for Thana. I don't want the blood of her friend's mates on her hands," Cyrus says with conviction as he moves to stand between Raphael and me. His black wings are spread wide as he tries to hide me behind them, protecting me.

"You know, Cyrus, I have no control over who is chosen to reap the souls. That will be between Michael and your father," Raphael says. His tone tells me he's pretty sure he already knows it'll be my duty to do it.

I move to stand between Raphael and Cyrus. Unfurling my wings, I spread them wide, separating my mates. I face Cyrus and smile softly, looking into his chocolate-brown eyes. "Thank you for trying to protect my heart from what I might be required to do." Reaching out, I half expect him to jerk away from me as I try to caress his cheek. Happiness blooms in my chest as my hand makes contact with his skin.

"If it's allowed, we can reap their souls together so I'm not alone." Cyrus smiles and nods, pleased with my compromise.

"After this," I motion around the room. "You and I need to talk," I state, placing a gentle kiss on his lips.

I close my wings, letting them hang half-open as I turn to face Raphael. Holding his face between my hands, I look up into his churning eyes. "Take Christian with you and assist Michael and Uriel." My eyes blacken as wisps of shadows ghost over my wings. "Do not let them get away with harming her." My voice is gravelly and not in the sultry sense. I sound more like a wild animal that's ready to attack. Raphael stares at me and the sudden change in my demeanor. He grabs Christian and leaves the room far faster than I'd expected.

CHAPTER 19

THANA

Two of my four mates are out of the house. I haven't bonded with one of the two remaining here yet, and it's been nearly a month since the Mate Trials. Cyrus and I have certainly had our issues up to this point. For years, he's made his disdain of anything outside the Dark Nephilim known. I now realize when I ended up with him in the same hospital as me and he harassed me, it was a situation of the mean boy having a crush and picking on the girl he likes.

Shrugging, I leave the library and head to the kitchen to find a drink and a snack. When I get there, I find Cy and Gage beat me to the kitchen and have an assortment of drinks and snacks waiting for me to choose from. I raise an eyebrow, puzzled. These two are definitely up to something. "Thank you," I say softly, grabbing a blueberry and pomegranate juice smoothie. They tell me when it's my time, it will increase the odds of me carrying a healthy baby. If something as simple as a smoothie will ease their minds, I'm more than willing to drink it.

"Thana, we need to talk," Cyrus says softly.

I turn to face him and discover Gage has up and vanished on me. "Yes, we do. But I don't know where to start," I say honestly.

Although I've seen Cyrus's vulnerabilities and we've had some intense moments which show him in a different way, my heart still fears him because he's rejected me before and because of who he is.

He's the son of the Angel of Death and there is no way that's not going to strike fear in a girl's heart. Plus, my own darkness seems to rise up and grow in reaction to him, which after a lifetime of being told my darkness is evil, scares me. Samael's words about my dual nature still resonate with me, but a lifetime of fear and shame of my dark side isn't easy to disregard.

Anxiety rolls off him in waves as he sits there, waiting for me to say more. He fiddles with his mug before pushing it away and coming to stand before me. "I know I've been a shit mate, and I'll never be as good as the golden boy." His words drip with venom and sarcasm as he stares down at his hands.

"Let's face it, I've always been painted as the bad guy." He tilts his head, then flashes his million-dollar smile. "I'll never be perfect like your other three mates, but I can promise you a few things." He reaches out and takes hold of my hands, grasping them tightly. "From now on, I'm going to be as straightforward and honest with you as I can." He draws in a deep breath before looking up at me with soulful eyes.

"There's no one else for me in this existence but you. I'm gonna suck at the smooshy shit the others excel in. But if you allow me, I'll always be your rock and foundation." He raises my hands to his lips and kisses the knuckles on both hands.

I watch him as he makes an attempt to undo the damage he's caused. Silent tears roll down my cheeks as I take his words to heart. "I've never expected you to be like the other three." I give his hands a squeeze. "I only ask you to be the best you can be. Nothing more, nothing less." I smile at him, and a brilliant smile moves across his lips in answer as my words sink in.

"You're my dark knight, the one no one will ever see coming. The one who won't hesitate to destroy everything in his path." I grin at him. "I walk in the in-between, and it's not quite comfortable for me yet. For most of my life, it was beaten into my head that I was the embodiment of blasphemy, the ultimate sin against divine law." Unfurling my wings, I spread them out behind me and look over my unique coloring.

"You and the others made me appreciate the fact that I'm different and most of the rules don't apply to me." I get up and place myself gently in his lap.

"My grandfather says that once upon a time on this earth, there were plenty of females born like me. Except for back then, the Norse called us 'Valkyrie.' Divine judgment and death embodied in one pretty package." I flex my wings slightly. "And I know one thing." I raise my hand and caress his cheek softly. "When I have to go to the Dark Realm, I won't be traveling alone." Smiling, I dip my head lightly to him before pressing my lips to his temple, hugging him to me. His strong arms band around me, pulling me flush against the solid mass of muscle of his chest.

"You know you and I have unfinished business, Thana." The way he tilts his head and narrows his eyes makes my insides start to tighten and get hot. I guess this is what Joscelyn meant when she told me about the bad-boy smolder. My heart rate picks up and my palms are sweaty just from how he's looking at me. I'm anxious and excited at the same time, not knowing what to expect from my Dark Nephilim mate.

With very little effort, he scoops me up and walks out of the kitchen with me in his arms. I laugh as he wiggles us through the corridors, trying not to catch my wings on anything. To make it a little easier on him, I pull my wings back in and snuggle closer to him.

Unlike my other three mates, Cyrus is worldly and was not bound by the divine law of chastity. Part of me is a little worried about what he has in store for me. He kicks open his bedroom door, then pushes the door shut with his ass. "You did a great job decorating this room for me. It's exactly how I'd have done it." He sets me down on the edge of the bed, then walks away slowly.

Curiously, I watch him walk around the room, examining the things I'd placed here for him. "Do you like it?" I lean back on the bed and then flop on my side, still watching him. He picks up a throw blanket and sniffs at it, then smiles at me.

"Very much so. My mate made a space just for me, even when she wasn't sure I'd return." He sets the blanket down, then leans back against the dresser.

"This," he motions around the room, "tells me that all these years, you paid attention to everything about me without realizing it." He pushes off the dresser and stalks forward, each silent step carrying him closer to me by the second.

"I'm going to show you how much I appreciate all you've done for me." He leans forward and kisses my lips, pushing me to my back.

He deepens the kiss, not letting up until my core weeps with anticipation. "And how do you plan to do that, Cy?" I punctuate every word with a kiss, half daring him to proceed.

"Challenge accepted." His eyes turn black immediately, and his wings burst free from his back. I don't know what it is about him and his black wings that sets my blood on fire, but every time he flexes his wings, my core clenches. Cyrus gently pulls my hands and helps me stand up again. We walk to the door leading to his bathroom. At the top of the frame, there's a two-handled pull-up bar anchored in place. "Hands on the bar, Thana," his voice is commanding yet gentle. Usually, I fight being told what to do. But with him, I just want to please him.

I stretch my body out, reaching up to grab the bar. His sharp intake of breath says it all. Apparently, he likes what he sees. "Like this, Cy?" My tone is breathier than I intended, and I turn my head to look at him. His black leather pants are tented in the front, bulging to the point it has to be uncomfortable.

"Perfect, Thana. Absolutely perfect." His voice is raspy with a growl, making the hairs on my arms stand on end.

Digging in the top drawer of his dresser, he pulls out several ties I bought for him and binds my hands to the bar, making it so I can't let go. He holds a third tie in front of me with a devilish grin. My eyes widen when I realize he's about to blindfold me. Before I can get a word out, the silk tie covers my eyes completely. "Consider this an exercise in trust, Thana. If it makes you feel better, I've invited Gage to be here, in case you get nervous." He leans in to kiss my cheek.

"He'll stay as long as you want. He can watch or . . ." He leaves that last thought hanging, and I feel a tingle starting to build deep inside my core.

"I'm here, Thana. What's your safe word?" Gage asks me through the bond as his hand comes to rest on my lower back, just above my ass.

"Why do I need a safe word?" I ask, moving my body to keep in contact with Gage.

"That's easy, beautiful," Cyrus says from somewhere behind me. "I'm not as vanilla as Raph and Chris. And Gage here likes some of the darker things in the bedroom." His voice moves around the room, and I tilt my head, trying to track him.

"Gage, slowly unbutton our girl's shirt for me." Cyrus's voice turns deep and sultry, his words smooth as velvet and dripping with sin. Gage leans in and nuzzles my cheek, tickling me with his thick beard. His fingers unfasten one button at a time. It's maddening how slow this man can move.

I try to press myself against him to hurry the process along. "Gage, stop there. You need to give us a safe word, Thana." As soon as the words escape Cyrus's lips, the warmth of Gage's body vanishes.

"It needs to be a word you won't randomly cry out in pleasure." Cyrus's hot minty breath washes over me as he enunciates the word "pleasure."

I squirm against my restraints as I attempt to move closer to Cyrus. "Strawberry." I pant the word out. This anticipation is killing me.

"Good girl," Cyrus says just before his hand slaps my ass. "Gage, please help Thana get that shirt out of our way," Cyrus says from somewhere in front of me. Gage gently nuzzles my face, letting me know in his own way he's going to take good care of me.

My shirt falls open, and the cool air caresses my skin. Goosebumps break out everywhere he touches, and a shiver lightly racks my body. My mouth falls open as Gage's fingers gently caress the length of my abdomen. His hand moves slowly down to the waistband of my leggings and starts inching them down my thighs.

My thong is soaked as his fingertips tease my body. His hot breath teases me over my mound. Arching my back, I pull at my bound hands, wanting to touch him. A second set of hands lands on my lower back, slowly trailing their way up my spine and heading to my bra strap. Soft kisses pepper the skin between my shoulder blades as another set of lips kisses me just above my mound. Soon enough, my bra is unfastened, and the straps are unhooked, freeing my breasts.

One of my mates' tongues finds its way within my soaking wet folds while the other begins sucking on my nipples. I'm in sensory overload, not sure which feels better at the moment. Thick fingers penetrate me and curl and pump in and out of me in long deep strokes. An appreciative groan escapes Gage's lips as his beard ghosts along my inner thigh. His tongue flattens as he starts lapping at my clit, and his fingers move in double time.

"That's enough, Gage. We want her begging for our touch," Cyrus says, biting my nipple, then dragging his tongue up my chest and neck until he's nibbling on my earlobe.

I hear fabric rustling and hitting the floor. Bare feet slap on the marble floor, one set moving away, the other circling me like a shark. "Lift your feet off the floor for a moment, Thana," Cyrus says from behind me as his hands caress my thighs. His grip tightens on the leg he wants lifted, and I quickly comply. I know Gage won't let anything happen to me, and I have to have that same trust about Cyrus. I lift and place my other leg as requested to find I'm now standing on towels. Something soft brushes along my side, then

around my back and up my spine. The slow slide of the silken material causes my skin to break out in goosebumps.

Something warm and wet runs down the length of my spine and
down between my ass cheeks. I'm not sure what it is till one of them
starts rubbing the silken fluid over my skin. Then two sets of hands
begin to caress and massage my body, making me moan and arch in
the direction of whoever touches me. How much longer can they
tease me? My core throbs in anticipation of one of them finally
granting me release. Once I think we're finally getting somewhere,
both sets of hands leave my body, and the oil begins tingling. What
are they up to?

CHAPTER 20

CYRUS

My beautiful dark angel is on full display and is very responsive to our touch. My body and soul crave her darkness like my lungs need air. Blackened wisps dance through her hair each time I get close to her. My own darkness reaches for her and wants to fully bond with her. The massage oil with peppermint and eucalyptus was a brilliant idea Gage brought into play. By now, her skin should be tingling and warm like my hands are.

Gage signs to me that I should make my move. He motions to the wetness starting to drip from Thana's core. Our mate is soaking wet for us, and my cock strains painfully hard, thinking about sinking balls deep into her. "Thana?" I call her name more reverently than I thought possible for me. I ghost the tips of my fingers over her flesh, causing her to break out in goosebumps. Her silky skin feels like my version of Heaven—warm, soft, and inviting.

"Yes?" Her voice is strained and breathy as Gage palms her large breasts. I watch his thumbs glide over her erect nipples. Her mouth opens as she arches her back, chasing his touch.

"May I?" I move behind her and slide my engorged head along her slick folds, coating me in her juices. I honestly don't think I'll last very long with how wet she is. I've got a stranglehold on my throbbing cock, hoping I don't blow my load before I'm able to sink into her depths.

"Please, Cyrus. I ache so badly." She squirms, trying to back up and impale herself on my dick. My eyes are riveted to the flexing of the muscles of her back and shoulders as she strains, trying to reach me. Most Nephilim females are lithe with little to no muscles, yet my mate looks like a virtual powerhouse. After what we've just endured, I'm not shocked that she's so beautiful and strong.

"As you wish, baby," I say before thrusting forward, burying my cock deep within her. Thana gasps at the intrusion, then moans as she adjusts to my size. I push her forward, slide my hand around her body, and glide it up her abdomen slowly. My hand slides easily between her generous breasts.

I gently grip her throat and apply pressure. As I move, I change the position of my hand to get a better grip and not hurt her. Snapping my hips, my thrusts are short and fast, increasing the friction. Gage kisses Thana with passion, his hands on her breasts, teasing the hell out of her sensitive nipples. With every thrust, I feel our bond growing until I can tell how good Gage and I are making her feel. I'm stunned to also feel her love for us.

Her orgasm hits her like an explosion. Her entire body vibrates and pulses with every throb. Her wings break free from between us and spread out wide, every feather standing on end. Then, her muscles clamp down on my cock, locking it in place. She vibrates and forces my orgasm from me long before I planned to be ready. My eyes blur from the pleasure overloading my body. I feel like I'm having a single, continuous orgasm which doesn't stop. Sweat breaks out on my body, and my legs start to feel like jelly.

The sound of ripping fabric echoes in the room along with the splintering of wood. When I can finally open my eyes, I see Thana has ripped free of the bar, and her other two mates have broken down my bedroom door, trying to get to her. My cock is still trapped inside her, and Thana is angry as hell, facing down her other two mates.

THANA

I honestly don't know what came over me. One minute, I'm on top of the world, having one of the best orgasms of my life. The next minute, my body goes haywire and takes Cyrus hostage. Then Raph and Chris break into the room. Keeping my wings spread wide, I stare down Raph and Chris.

"What in the nine hells are you two doing?" My knees buckle slightly from the continuing orgasms I can't seem to stop having. With each new set of pulses, poor Cyrus can't help but thrust forward, setting my nerve endings on fire. My greedy core continues to pulse and vibrate. If Raph and Chris hadn't busted in, I'd be damn near euphoric by now.

Raphael approaches slowly, hands up in a placating manner. "Thana, baby. I think your time started earlier than expected." His tone is soothing, and I begin to relax. "Cyrus, you need to withdraw from Thana and let her rest," Raphael says calmly while Gage makes a face like he's laughing.

"No can do, golden boy. Thana is an alpha, hence her alpha lock on my cock." I look over my shoulder to see him motion to where we're connected. Cyrus's tone is strained as several more pulses wash over the two of us.

"I'm a *what?*" I shoot a panicked look at each of my mates.

"An alpha. It's rare in females, but when it happens, she can lock a male in place when she's ready to conceive," Christian says with a ridiculous smile on his face. "Yet again, you bless and honor us, *kichōna mono.*" Christian bows deeply to me, then leaves the room practically singing to himself.

I finally begin to relax, and eventually, I release Cyrus. I wince as he slides free from my now sore muscles. "I didn't mean to hurt you, Cyrus." I furrow my brows, thinking I ruined our first time together.

"You shouldn't be apologizing, Thana. He should be the one doing that because of all the time that's been wasted." Raphael charges toward us. Thankfully, Gage jumps between us and stops Raphael in his tracks.

Without a second thought, I spin, grab hold of Cyrus, and run to the balcony with him. I leap over the edge, and spreading my wings wide, I soar, holding onto him tightly. I bank hard to the right and land swiftly on my balcony, shoving the doors open. Cyrus is weak, for some reason. I usher him into my nest and shove him into the pit of blankets.

Me. Of all people, I'm an alpha. This is the shock of the century for me. I head toward my shower and turn the water on, letting it warm up as I retract my wings. Through the bond, I call Christian to me, and he hesitantly knocks on the wooden frame of my bathroom door. "You called me, *kichōna mono*?" Christian calls softly as he smiles at me.

My brain finally kicks back in, and I try to focus on what I know about alphas. "If I remember correctly, an alpha female can control when and if she becomes pregnant, but not how often she cycles, correct?" I raise my eyebrows as I step under the hot water of the shower.

"That is correct." He sighs softly, contemplating how to phrase his question. "May I inquire why you wouldn't want our babies?" Sadness overtakes his beautiful face.

Shaking my head, I lower my gaze. "It's not that I don't want babies. I do. I want a large family, filled with laughter and children running and flying everywhere." I swallow hard, trying not to let my emotions get away from me.

"We still don't know who tried to kill me by stealing Cyrus. Your lives are tied to mine, especially Raph's," I say, expressing my deepest fear. As I look up, I see Gage and Raph in the doorway, listening to us.

"It's just not safe yet to do so. If someone stole our children, I know I'd rain hell on earth to find them."

Cyrus stumbles past the guys and hugs me tightly. One by one, they each climb into the shower to follow suit. Somehow, the five of us are crammed in a large shower stall, hugging it out.

Raphael breaks free first, and his eyes glow golden for a few moments. "As soon as we can, we need to find a female you trust to teach you how to control your cycle. Until then, Michael is bringing a tincture that'll stop your fertility cycle for at least four months, so you don't keep going through cycles. That should buy us enough time to catch whoever is responsible," he says with hesitance as he looks from Cyrus to me.

"I don't like that look, Raph. What aren't you telling me?" I narrow my eyes, looking at him. He's hiding something, I can tell by how his stance changed in the last five minutes.

Wrapping a towel around myself, we walk out into my nest area. "What my brother is afraid to tell you is that if you're already pregnant, you'll lose the child," Michael, who's apparently just appeared, tells me with his arms crossed over his chest, a golden vial held in his right hand.

My eyes widen in horror as I look at Cyrus, who stares in a state of shock. "Can you check me before I drink? I could never take the life of an innocent." My eyes fill with tears and threaten to spill down my cheeks as I turn to Raphael. The little I do know about Nephilim gestation is that we're only pregnant for four months, and the fetus is formed nearly immediately after conception. The possibility of a tiny heart and life form living within me is very real.

Solemnly, Raphael nods and leads me into his bedroom, instructing me to lie on his bed. Terrified doesn't begin to explain how I feel. Cyrus moves to my side and holds my hand while Raphael prepares to examine me. His hands take on a golden glow just before he lays them on me. I squeeze my eyes shut as tightly as I can, trying to ignore the fear of the unknown.

Warmth spreads through my abdomen as Raphael examines me,

the seconds passing slower than it seems humanly possible. Eventually, the warmth leaves me, and my eyes pop open. Raphael's face is an unreadable mask, and I can't sense anything through the bond either. "Raph?" I ask softly as tears begin to roll down my cheeks.

He inhales suddenly, then looks down at me. Shock is his initial reaction before he drops to his knees to take me in his arms. "I'm so sorry, love. There's no child. I didn't mean to scare you. You're completely healthy and should have no problems when you're ready."

Honestly, I'm not sure what I feel at the moment. Part of me is relieved, while the other part is disappointed. I break free from Raph to lunge at Cyrus and wrap him up in a huge hug. He's disappointed I'm not pregnant. My big, tough, bad guy wanted to be a daddy. I comfort Cyrus before Michael brings the vial to me.

"It will last approximately four months. But it's also only been tested on Angels." Michael paces the room before stopping in front of me. "I have no clue how long or if it will even be effective on you, Thana. Hopefully, it will buy us enough time to hunt down whoever had Cyrus abducted and find a female to teach you how to control your cycle," Michael says before bowing slightly. He disappears in a shimmer of gold back to the Angelic Realm.

CHAPTER 21
THANA

A tiny part of me is happy our first cycle together didn't result in me being pregnant. But the other part of me longs to hold a tiny life I helped create in my arms. Before my shift today, I find myself in the maternity ward, helping my friend Pattie with the new babies.

Half the ward is glamoured, so the human parents don't see the babies born with wings. All the baby Nephilim look so adorable in their cribs. One by one, I spend time feeding and holding each of the babies. I can't help it. I'm a sucker for their chubby cheeks and chunky baby thighs.

"I had a feeling I'd find you here," Gage says through the bond to me as he places a hand on my lower back. His body radiates a delicious heat that comforts me and draws me to him.

Leaning back, I rest against his chest. "Yeah. I'll be honest with you. I can't wait till we're able to have our own." I nuzzle the baby girl in my arms, then offer her the bottle I'd made for her. She has a voracious appetite, suckling hard on the bottle's nipple.

"The guys and I feel the same way. But we need to find out who abducted Cyrus first," Gage says as he reaches around me to gently

touch the baby's cheek. He rests his cheek against mine as we look down at the baby together.

"I heard my name. What's up?" Cyrus appears in a wisp of black smoke and looks at the baby in my arms. He abruptly morphs from a literal badass to a softie, making cute baby noises. He looks absolutely irresistible as he tilts his head from side to side, trying to get the baby's attention.

Raising an eyebrow, I look at Gage, who connects the dots quickly and gives me a terse nod. Within seconds, I deposit the baby and the bottle in Cyrus's arms and move to the next baby. "This is definitely a good look for you, Cy," I say to him, kissing his cheek. He looks both terrified and shocked at what I've said. It's kind of cute seeing him so flustered.

"Thana, are you torturing Cyrus again?" Raphael appears and asks wryly, grinning at the resident bad boy with a baby in his arms. Raphael's gray suit is exquisitely tailored and makes his shoulders look broader than usual. I'm a sucker for broad, muscular shoulders. Lucky for me, all my mates fit that type. His pale eyes shine with flecks of gold reflecting in the light as he looks me over, waiting for me to answer.

Pouting my lips, I turn my eyes up innocently at Raphael. "No?"

He rolls his eyes and vanishes in a wisp of golden glitter. Shaking my head, I look around the nursery once more and find Cyrus is also gone. The baby girl he was holding sleeps peacefully in her crib once more. Gage smiles at me before placing his large hand on my lower back and herding me out of the nursery. *That's enough cuteness overload for one evening. Your shift starts in twenty minutes.* He knows the only reason I've been sneaking down here is to satisfy my baby fix.

We walk slowly through the halls, heading up to my floor for the evening. Darius my normal third-floor co-worker stops dead in his tracks, staring at me. We've worked together for years in the telemetry wing, but for once, his gaze is anything but friendly. I wonder what could have changed. It's almost as if he's looking for any signs of weakness from me.

"I . . . I didn't expect to see you tonight," he says in a trembling voice, tripping over his words. His eyes dart around quickly as if double-checking the exits before looking at me again, his normal suave manner nowhere to be found.

Raising my brows, I tilt my head to the side, studying his tense body language. He opens and closes his hands. It's almost like he's about to get into a fight.

"Why wouldn't I be here tonight? I always work on Tuesdays," I say calmly and in a soft tone, trying not to escalate this situation I feel is strangely brewing. The more I study him, the more I notice Fenrir becoming itchy. Something's not right. A chill runs down my spine, and my instincts yell at me to run. I scan the hall we're in, making sure I know where every possible exit is.

Gage pats my ass and directs a smug smile at the much smaller Darius. *"I've already alerted the others about this standoff. Raph is having Uriel and Michael intercept him for questioning,"* Gage assures me through the bond. His large hand glides from my ass up to my lower back, offering me support. We both know Darius is getting ready to do something, but the question is—what?

"It's got to suck having a voiceless mate. You should have chosen me all those years ago. We could have forged a bond but no, I wasn't good enough for you," Darius says in a bitter tone, his gruff voice raising the hairs on the back of my neck. Malice, hatred, and jealousy flood his gaze just before his eyes turn black, focusing on Gage.

Gage's body tenses beside me, and I lightly grip his bicep before regarding Darius again. "It doesn't suck at all." I scrunch my nose briefly before threading my fingers through Gage's thick beard lovingly. "He knows how to put that sinful mouth of his to good use. Words are meaningless if there's no action to back it up," I say just before I turn on Darius. Spreading my fingers wide, I whip both hands forward quickly and engulf Darius in water from the River Styx.

I sense the minute the Archangels arrive, and they stare in disbelief at what I've done. "Azrael, I need you," I say softly without touching my raven. Within seconds, he arrives at my side and raises his brows at me. "I believe this male had something to do with Cyrus's abduction." This man almost cost me not only my life, but the life of two of my mates.

Remaining focused on my watery cage containing Darius, I move closer to Michael and Uriel. "He betrayed himself when he said he didn't expect me to be here on my normal night. Only someone who knew what taking Cyrus would do to me would know I should have been deathly ill." My eyes find Raphael's, and he nods solemnly at me. It's not common knowledge what the effect of a lost mate has on an Archangel.

"Release him into our custody and judgment, Thana. He will not escape us," Michael says firmly as he moves to stand behind Darius. I look between Raphael and Azrael, and both of them nod at me. I release Darius from the waters. As soon as the waters recede, Darius throws dark shards at Gage, trying to kill him.

Without hesitation, my wings burst free, and I use them to shield Gage from the darkness. I feel the shards strike my feathers, but they do no damage to me. Lunging forward, I charge Darius only to have Raphael and Azrael stop me. I'm shrieking like a banshee as I fight to get to him. My fingernails have grown long and sharp into black claws. Just as I nearly break free, Cyrus manifests before me. "Shh . . . my little hellcat. The golden boys will punish him far worse than we ever can." A sexy, sadistic smile crosses his lips, and it makes me pause in my forward motion.

I take a calming breath and allow my muscles to relax. "Alright." I back off, looking at Michael and Uriel. Both Archangels nod at me before gripping Darius and vanishing to lord knows where. I look back at my mates, and they stare back at me. I suddenly feel like a freak. "Did I do something wrong?" Fear tightens my chest.

"No, angel. Not at all," Raphael says as he wraps me in his arms. "You just shocked everyone by pulling a stunt that only high-ranking angels can do." He looks over at Azrael.

"What your mate is trying to say is that you're more like your grandfather than we realized." Azrael smiles at me. The wicked gleam in his eyes tells me he knows far more than anyone else about this.

My ah-ha moment happens shortly after Azrael's statement. I suddenly remember what my grandfather told me. The minute I stop fighting my true nature, my full potential can be reached. It's an exciting, yet frightening, concept to comprehend. I've never been one to crave power or status of any kind. My bloodline—and having an Archangel as a mate—thrust me into the spotlight where I didn't want to be.

Throwing off my old insecurities, I confidently walk over to Azrael and link my arm with his, striding down the hall. Sensing my mates, my wings unfurl and I spin, enveloping Azrael in my wings and vanishing in a wisp of black smoke. We manifest on the second-level balcony of my house on the hill. As I open my wings, Azrael looks at me in disbelief. "I'm thinking there's something you need to discuss, daughter." A sly smile plays upon his lips as he leans back against the rail.

"You know I do, and I can almost bet you already have the answer prepared." I lean back against the house, planting one foot on the cedar shingles and my back and wings against the window. "Grandfather said something about a prophecy foretelling of my birth. What exactly was foretold?"

A myriad of emotions flicker over Azrael's usually stoic face before he starts to pace. Azrael unfurls his wings and motions to them. "You know our wings turned black when we were cast out for Lucifer's rebellion," he says academically. The story of the great fall is told to all children so the past isn't repeated. I nod and tilt my head to the side, glancing at my wings. "Your wings are now the color of your grandfather's, which means you can migrate between Heaven and Hell. Neither Raphael nor I can cross into the other's domain without causing ourselves harm." He dramatically pauses, letting this information sink in. "Your grandfather and you can walk in both the Dark and the Angelic Realms without harm."

I make a face and push myself off the wall. "Azrael, father. I know you're stalling by giving me a commonly known history lesson." I step into his personal space and grip both his hands. "What are you afraid to tell me?" My eyes plead for the truth, and my heart is in my throat, thinking about the possible ramifications. A temporal shift occurs, and I spin to face Uriel. He's in full battle armor and smiling at me.

"What Azrael has been sworn to not say is that you're not only meant to be your grandfather's successor, you're also meant to help cleanse the fallen who wish to come home." Uriel wins the award for the best resting bitch face I've ever seen. Not a single drop of emotion or even a hint of humor is evident in his visage.

Staggering backward, I bump into the cedar shingles of the house and lean there. "Me? Seriously? Not that I'm not honored because I am. But why me?" I'm puzzled, and my heart rate is accelerating. Spots dance before my eyes as I become lightheaded from the information relayed to me. Within seconds, my mates manifest on the porch and surround me. Gage and Christian each catch me by an arm while Raphael and Cyrus face off with Uriel and Azrael.

"What did you say to upset Thana, Dad?" Cyrus asks as he squares off with his father. Darkness radiates from him, almost completely engulfing his form.

Raphael reaches out and rests a hand on Cyrus, attempting to calm his rage. "I believe they were filling Thana in on her inheritance from her grandfather," Raphael answers as he looks from Cyrus to me.

"That is correct, brother," Uriel says and finally smiles. "When Samael trains you, and the succession of power is complete, Thana, you'll be the soul ruler of purgatory. It's the gray area between the righteous and the damned." Uriel looks me over from head to toe. "I knew you were special when I was sent to judge you shortly after you were born." Uriel approaches me slowly and reaches out to cup my right cheek, gazing into my eyes. "I saw your inner light, Thana. Let it shine."

As he says these words, I feel warmth build inside my chest. It's as if a cage opened and something deep within me was released. Breathing in deeply, I move forward, away from Gage and Christian. In my left hand, I manifest a ball of light and in my right hand, a wisp of darkness. "Look at her eyes!" Raphael says as he moves closer to me. Gently, he grips my jaw and turns my head left, then right.

"Is something wrong?" I ask nervously, my hands shaking.

Raphael's expression is filled with sincerity. "Your eyes are pure silver like polished orbs, reflecting everything like a mirror. They're stunning, Thana," Raphael says softly before kissing me and backing off, letting the rest of my bond-mates get a good look for themselves.

I extinguish the power in my hands and look expectantly at my other mates. Christian's smile warms my soul. Gage winks at me and places his hand over his heart. Cyrus walks in a circle around me, looking me over completely. He arches a brow and smiles. "You know I'm a huge fan of your black eyes." His own eyes blacken, and his smile makes my core turn molten. "But these silver eyes . . . Yeah, they're hot too. Maybe hotter cause I can see myself clearly in your eyes." He winks, then backs away. All I can do is roll my eyes. That's till Azrael playfully smacks his son on the back of his head and tells him to behave.

Stifling a yawn, I raise my hand to cover my mouth. "How soon until we have the results from Michael's inquiry?" My eyes bounce from Uriel to Raphael, hoping one of them will cave and give me answers.

"Soon. But for now, you need rest. Pulling the waters from the River Styx is no small feat, and I can tell it exhausted you," Uriel says. "*Sleep,*" he says in my mind as he passes his hand before me in a mystical manner. As his hand completes its motion, my eyelids become heavy, and I quickly succumb to my exhaustion. "Guard her closely. She's the answer to the war that has waged for eons," Uriel says before disappearing off the porch. His departure leaves more questions than answers for everyone involved.

CHAPTER 22
MICHAEL

Shadow Realm . . .

I gained special permission to enter purgatory and received immunity from The Almighty. Darius is now in the hands of the one and only Samael. The inner sanctum of Samael's lair is what the humans imagine Hell to be like. Torture devices line the walls as well as most of the floor in the dungeon. Dank air assails my senses and water runs down the wall in rivulets, the constant flow catching my attention for moments before I continue deeper into the dungeon.

The cracking of a whip and screams guide me further into the dungeon's depths. The scent of dried blood, feces, and urine fill the air. I turn the corner and see Samael with a razor whip in his hand and a very bloody Darius chained and hanging from the ceiling.

Blood stains his exposed flesh, and what remains of his clothing is in tatters, barely hanging from his body. The hardened expression Samael wears betrays nothing as he relentlessly whips Darius. "Answer me, halfling! Why attack Cyrus? Why now?" he roars, and the foundation of his castle shakes with the force of an earthquake. Dust and fragments of stone rain down on Darius, further adding to his misery.

Coughing up blood, Darius smiles at Samael. "The abomination must die, and Cyrus is the key to her undoing," he sneers before he sniggers at a joke that only he must have heard.

"What do you mean he's the key?" I question him, stepping into the light and drawing my sword. It immediately ignites with Heaven's light and illuminates the dungeon. Darius's eyes widen, knowing this injury will be one he cannot regenerate from.

He coughs harder, spitting up several blood clots before panting to catch his breath. "Their child will ascend and be Azrael's successor. Not Cyrus . . ." he says on a rough exhale. Blood and air spurt out from a cut on the right side of his ribcage. If he was mortal, that wound would be fatal. But since he's a Nephilim, nothing short of decapitation or being burnt to ash will kill him.

Samael and I share a brief look before looking back to Darius. This is not news. Obviously, Cyrus would reign at Thana's side, here in this very castle along with her other mates. "What makes this child special?" Samael asks, holding the razor whip at the ready, prepared to strike Darius again.

"Azrael is terrifying enough, but his grandchild born of your descendant . . ." Darius narrows his eyes as he focuses on Samael. "None will be safe from that child doing its mother's bidding."

He has a point. A beloved son of powerful bloodlines would be a terror to behold.

Darius begins to laugh and choke at the same time. "Raphael's child will be just as terrifying." He smirks as his eyes blacken as he tries to gather strength. "Cut the head off the snake, and the body dies. Don't worry, others will continue my work once I'm gone." He laughs again, but before he's able to draw his next breath, I swing my sword and slice through both his arms and sever his head from his body, turning him to ash.

I look up at Samael, and he nods tersely. "I'll enhance Thana's familiars for her protection," Samael states plainly. "Increase the battle training for her other three mates and make sure Thana is never alone. I'll meet with Raphael personally to update him." His eyes turn black.

Everything around us shakes right before a portal opens, and Azrael is pulled through violently. As soon as Azrael realizes where he is, he immediately drops to one knee before Samael. "You summoned me, my lord?" For once, he sounds respectful and speaks to Samael with reverence.

"Your grandchild, born of Thana, will eventually become your successor," Samael's voice booms with authority, leaving no room for questions. "For Thana and Cyrus's protection, I am gifting your son with a wolf identical to Thana's." A blackened wisp rises up from Samael's hand taking the form of a dire wolf.

Azrael stands slowly and cages the wolf between his hands before absorbing it. "Thank you for this great boon, my lord. I shall gift it to him immediately upon my return." Azrael bows deeply, then vanishes. Both of these powerhouses are men of few words.

I see the gears turning in Samael's head as he tries to calculate the best course of action. Personally, I'd power up Thana and Cyrus as much as possible. As for her light mates, I can increase their training and give them better weapons as well. I reach out through the angelic bond to Gabriel and set him to this task. His new mission, fit Gage and Christian with angelic armor and light-based weapons.

Samael heads toward a staircase I didn't notice earlier. "We have a war ahead of us, Michael," he says as he turns a corner walking up the stairs. "Just like the old days, we need to figure out who or what we're up against and kill it before it kills us."

It's been eons since I fought at Samael's side, and part of me looks forward to it. The other part worries this may be the start of the fabled end of days.

"We will do what we must to keep the balance," I say confidently as he reaches the first floor. Samael makes a sweeping motion with his hands and several dozen bat-like creatures come flying at us from down the hall. They zoom over our heads and out the windows in the main hall.

"They will be my eyes and ears throughout the Realm. As soon as I hear anything, I will let my granddaughter know, and she can relay the information to you. For now, I have battle plans to formulate and a grandchild to visit sooner rather than later." Reaching up onto the wall, he pulls down an old sword and offers it to me. "Give this to Christian. He lost it during the battle at the breach shortly after the creation of the realms of Hell." Samael chuckles. "Lucifer had some seriously ugly creations back then. Looked like a drunk kid with clay." We share a laugh, thinking about Lucifer's first creations and how childish they appeared.

"I'll return the property to him promptly. Keep in touch, old friend." Out of respect, I bow slightly to Samael. He's probably one of the only living beings who's able to kill an Archangel. It makes me question whether Thana is able to wield the same power as well. Embracing myself in the light, I head back to the Earth Realm to put my part of this plan in motion. There are dark days ahead. I pray we make it out alive.

INNATE

CHAPTER 23

HELL

A gavel falling hard upon wood echoes within the great hall. The greater demons of hell turn to gaze upon Lucifer in awe. "Come to order you useless worms." His voice booms, and the room instantly falls silent. "We have temporarily lost our brother Asmodai, felled by Nyx's daughter no less!" Flames ignite around him, whipping wildly like a raging inferno as his rage becomes more palpable.

Murmurs fill the room, demons questioning how she was strong enough to kill Asmodai. Millions of questions of how she was capable of felling such an enormous, powerful, ancient Demon single handedly. Inconceivable. Exactly how much power does this wretched female hold? Lucifer runs his clawed hand down his face, and the flames blaze hotter. *The stupidity of those in his service.* "She is Samael's descendant!" Lucifer screams, slamming his fists onto the table, igniting it instantly. "For all we know, she could be more powerful than any of us in this room," Lucifer states, sitting down and resting his horned head in his hands.

Musical laughter fills the air as a sexy, large-breasted demoness approaches the table. The rhythmic clicking of her heels on the obsidian echoes loudly throughout the hall. She glides towards them, her large breasts swaying with every step. "You can always seduce her away from those pathetic angelic mates of hers," Lilith says as she leans on Mammon's back, twirling his hair in her fingers.

"And how do you propose we do that?" Lucifer lifts his head, his right eyebrow raised. Leaning forward, he cants his head to the side then motions with his hand for her to continue, his curiosity has been piqued.

Laughing again, Lilith saunters around the room, the clicking of her heels echoing again in the now silent halls. "You are The Prince of Lies and Deceit, The Seducer of the Fallen, The Almighty Lord of Hell." She smirks as she places both of her elbows on the table before Lucifer

with her ass in the air, her long forked tail lazily flicking back and forth behind her. "What is it you truly desire, dear brother?" Raising up, she reaches out to caress Lucifer's cheek. Serpentine eyes watch the path her hand takes.

"I desire to make that bitch fall to her knees before me and serve me for eternity," Lucifer says, striking out and grabbing Lilith by the throat hard and dragging her into his lap. His lips crash upon hers and he bites her bottom lip, hard, drawing blood. His long, forked tongue snakes out and laps at the blood rolling down her face. Without hesitation, he throws her across the great hall, causing her to impact against one of the marble pillars. Marble shards rain down. A large crack runs the length of the pillar, threatening to destroy it. Crimson ichor streaks down the white marble, painting it vermillion. The rest of the demons present stare at Lucifer in fear after his outburst.

"Study Samael's descendant and bring me any information that may be useful!" Lucifer commands. Quickly, the hall empties, having a solid plan to appease their lord. For now, he is resigned to wait. Lucifer returns to his throne surrounded by his Succubi, each willing to kill in his name.

It's all just one vast chess game, two steps forward, one step back. Patience is key in the long game. And Lucifer only ever plays to win.

CHAPTER 24

THANA

I've spent my days since Cyrus's rescue, flying back and forth between the rift and my nest. Every day I train with either my grandfather Samael or with one of the Archangels. My training has intensified over the last few weeks to prepare me for the unknown. Both sides of the veil agree that something is brewing, they just aren't sure what yet. The one thing that we are one hundred percent sure of, someone or something, is trying to get to me through my mates.

Tonight's flight brings me back to the hospital to assist Raphael, Cyrus, and Azrael with the duties of reaping souls. Several strong flaps of my wings send dust and debris flying across the roof as I touch down. I barely have time to put my wings away when Mark comes running over to me from the stairwell and beams. "Long time no see Thana. How's mated life treating you?" Mark's smile is infectious, and I can't help but laugh at the funny face he's making.

Thoughts of all the little things the guys have done with and for me flash through my mind. A soft sigh escapes my lips as the happiness that they have brought me bubbles to the surface. "I have some of the best mates a girl can ask for." I take the offered census for the floor I'm heading to work on tonight. With everything that has been happening lately, the guys are adamant that if I go to work, at least two of them would be present in the building with me. Looking over the list, I purse my lips, studying the names and the room numbers. "Who do I need to visit first tonight?" Briefly, I look up from the list and over to Mark as he holds open the door for me.

"Honestly, I'm not sure. Raphael said he would brief you himself." Mark wiggles his eyebrows.

Rolling my eyes, I head down the stairs to the third floor and head directly to my mate's office. An icy chill runs down my spine, setting my nerves on edge. The wing oozes death and malice. The brightly lit hallway and the stark white of the walls are in direct contrast to doom and gloom aura the wing has tonight. I can only suspect that the fallen ones have done some dark deed to cause this many people to be on the brink of death. The one thing that irks me is that we don't know who *they* are yet. I have my suspicions that some of the fallen have banded together to bring hell on earth.

Just before I knock on Raphael's office door, he suddenly opens it and grabs me, and I'm wrapped up in his arms, being held tightly to his chest. "Hello, my love, how was your flight?" Raphael searches my face, locking onto my eyes.

Giggling softly, I stand on my tippy toes and kiss his lips. "The winds were with me and it's a beautiful night for a flight."

He smiles down at me and presses his lips to my forehead. Love pulses through the bond, strong and sure, as he holds me against him.

"I will not lie Thana. Tonight is going to be exceptionally difficult. Someone poisoned a water source and people are in various stages of death." Raphael pulls me even closer to his body, forcing my head to rest on his chest. His lips press to the crown of my head and his hot breath washes over me. "Cyrus and Azrael need your help, both are getting tired from working all day and half the night." Raphael rests his head upon mine, offering me as much comfort as he can.

"I should probably go relieve at least one of them then." Gently, I extract myself from his tight embrace. I look up at him, pushing through the bond just how much I love him. A brilliant smile crosses his lips as his eyes become liquid pools of gold. I bounce up quickly and kiss his pillow-soft lips before making two cups of coffee. Steaming mugs in hand, I leave the room.

It doesn't take long to find Azrael in a patient's room. Sweat beads on his sun-kissed brow as he focuses on the task at hand. The spectral white wisp of the man's soul rises from his body and directly into Azrael's hand. "Good evening, father," I say, holding the cup of dark roast coffee out to him.

"Are you sure you're not an Angel, Thana?" Azrael says, joking as he stands and takes the offered coffee from me.

Unfurling my wings, I look back at them and flex them for good measure. The color fades from pitch black down to a light gray. "Safe to say I'm Switzerland when it comes to picking sides." I shrug and take a sip of the coffee that I had made specifically for Cyrus. Nodding slowly, Azrael sips at the coffee and lets an appreciative groan escape his lips. "I have to admit, you make the best coffee. I dub thee my dark angel," Azrael says, just as I sense Cyrus behind me.

Cyrus snakes his arm around my waist from behind. "Oh, no old man, she's my dark angel." Cyrus's gravelly voice and proclamation makes my insides clench with desire. My heart skips a beat, hoping beyond hope that this alternative version of Cyrus is permanent.

"Naughty Cy, here's your coffee, babe. I'm actually here to help ease the burden that's been placed on the both of you. Tell me who's next, and I'll take care of the rest," I say as cheerful as possible, even though it's a rather depressing task.

With one arm tightly banded around my waist, Cyrus holds me while he drinks his coffee. "To be honest, Thana, pick a direction and a room. Most of these poor souls will not make it to morning," Cyrus says in a rough exhale. Infused notes of irritation as well as disdain echo in his tone of voice.

Raising an eyebrow, I look over my shoulder at Cyrus, then back to his father before us.

"Sadly, my son isn't exaggerating this time. Out of the twenty humans poisoned, at least eleven or more will die tonight." Azrael looks wiped out and shockingly saddened by the news he relayed to me.

"I—"

"I'll work with Thana." Raphael strides into the room. "You two take turns so you don't burn out. Gage will be here in the morning with the car to drive us all home," he says with authority, even though his darkened expression says something else entirely. This current fiasco weighs heavily upon his heart. Emotionally, he's in agony over the loss of so many innocent lives. Occasionally, through the bond for a brief instance, I can sense his pain interwoven with anger over this travesty.

Carefully, I break free of Cyrus and wiggle my fingers, manifesting shadows as I approach Azrael. "Father, I would like to try something?" Phrasing it more like a question makes him contemplate the swirling mass of inky blackness similar to the river Styx, but not fluid.

"Ah," he says, investigating the mass of darkness in my hands. "Let's give it a shot. What's the worst that could happen? Nothing?" Azrael says as he goes and sits in the chair before me. Drawing in a measured breath like my grandfather taught me, I harness the dark energy in my hands. My focus is laser sharp as I replenish Azrael's power. Slowly, the harnessed energy

trickles into him, rejuvenating him, easing his exhaustion. His eyes widen in disbelief as his energy and strength return to him. When I can sense he's stronger than before, I cut the flow to him and sigh softly as I remove my hands and shove them in my pockets. "I hope you feel better," I say, almost wincing, feeling like a huge freak at the moment.

Raphael and Cyrus both look shocked. Apparently, I did something I shouldn't have been able to do. I shift my weight from one foot to the other, and chew my lip, waiting for the other shoe to drop. "Thana?" Azrael says softly, trying to get my attention. "Your grandfather has taught you well. You truly are Samael's descendant in every way." Azrael smiles proudly at me before kissing my cheek and departing the room.

Drawing in a deep breath, I look at both of my mates. "You're next, Cy," I whisper as I walk towards him. His dark brown eyes regard me as my steps carry me closer to my target. I can tell my eyes have blackened. His life force ebbs and flows as I search his, and they shift to match mine, and a smile creeps across my lips. My wings flex as I grip Cy's face, and breathe darkness directly into him, refueling his body the quickest way possible. Our lips crash together, battling for dominance as I pump him full of the darkness that I had harnessed for him. When I feel he's stronger, I release my grip on his face and retract my wings.

Wordlessly, I turn and leave the room. I can hear the quick clicking of Raphael's dress shoes gaining ground behind me. My cat tattoo itches, and I let my familiar free to walk down the hallway. She ducks into a room and climbs onto the first bed. The patient is a teenage boy, late high school, early college, if I had to guess. Sandy brown hair covers his youthful face, obscuring some of it from view. The chunkiness of his preteen years long gone replaced by the strong angles of a young man's face. From what my grandfather has taught me, not every soul has to be taken when the body is almost ready to give up. His baby blue eyes move in my direction, his pupils are uneven and sluggish as they attempt to focus on me. Death is on the horizon for him. Something pulls at my mind. Like an itch that needs scratching. My familiar meows. Maybe it's not too late if I act now.

Instinct rules me. I take on my dark angel persona and lean over the boy. "It's not your time yet, child." My voice is soothing as the boy's eyelids grow heavy and he falls asleep.

I reach back and touch Fenrir. "Rise," I say, loud enough to warn Raphael what I'm about to do. My wolven familiar looks at the boy and whines.

"I know, boy, I need you to find an older vessel for this illness when I pass it to you. One whose life is almost at the end, anyway. A life for a life." Fenrir nods his wolven head, so I turn back to the boy before me.

Spreading my wings wide, I pull at all the darkness in the room, gathering it to me before I lay my hands on the boy. I attract the poison to the darkness I've summoned as it works its way out of his veins in a green, slimy mass. Quickly, I trap the mass in an orb of darkness and pass it off to Fenrir. "Go quickly. I cannot hold it for too long."

Fenrir doesn't hesitate to jump out the window and into the dark of night. Raphael, and now Cyrus, are at my side, escorting me to Raphael's office. My blackened orbs appear vacant as I see through Fenrir's eyes while he searches for a worthy target.

My paws hit the pavement and the smells of the night assault my canine nose. A small animal scuttles past but I ignore, intent on my mission. Crashes, a scraping of metal on metal. Screams. An accident. I creep towards the wreck. Silent. Sirens wail and blue lights flash.

The victim's scent is all wrong. The obvious fatal wounds, combined with the massive amount of blood loss, tells me they only have a few moments left to live. Fenrir and I choose this person to receive the poison since it will not affect the individual's lifespan. Once his mission is complete, he returns to the tattoo on my arm. Leaning my head back, facing the heavens, I slowly close my eyes for a few moments, then open them. My gunmetal-gray human eyes clear and I relax. "The boy will live. Fenrir did his job well," I say, letting out a yawn, exhausted from controlling Fenrir long distance.

"You literally just pulled off a miracle, Thana," Raphael says, awe struck. His hands gently ghost over my face, and I can't help but smile.

"I couldn't let the boy die when I knew full well I could save

160

him." I huff. The room is bathed in a golden glow, and none other than Michael stands before us. My heart sinks seeing him standing there before us. Without hesitation, Raphael uses his body to shield me from Michael's gaze. Cyrus pulls me to stand and draws me flush to his chest, ready to leave at a moment's notice.

"No need to get defensive brother, I sensed what my sister Thana has done and wished to see if she is in need of my services," Michael says. The musical quality of his voice almost instantly settles my nerves.

"Thank you, Michael, for checking on me. I am well." Tilting my head, I study him further. My vision changes and I can see the colors of his aura. "I must ask. What is your true intention? I can see you're anxious and frightened of something." As I channel the power, I know my eyes are pure silver orbs.

Michael nods slowly and shoves his hands in his pockets. "We felt the shift in the balance. Whatever you just did—" he pauses as he looks at everyone present "—put things back in order somewhat."

I look at Raphael, asking a question with my eyes, which he immediately answers. Wrapping an arm around Michael's shoulder, he and leads him out of his office and away from me.

Cyrus still hasn't relaxed his hold on me when Azrael pops his head into the office. "I called Christian, and he relayed to Gage to come get you two. Whatever you did, daughter, pulled most of the poison out of the victims here. They have a much better chance at survival because of you. Go home and rest, I'll babysit Golden Boy for you," Azrael says, placing a fatherly kiss on my forehead.

As soon as I retract my wings, Cyrus scoops me up and carries me bridal style down the hall to the elevator. Somewhere on the ride down, I fell asleep. I couldn't be much safer than in the arms of my dark knight.

CHAPTER 25

RAPHAEL

My mate has pulled off Archangel level power flex. She replenished Cyrus and Azrael, then pulled the poison from most of the patients. Returning to my office, I pour myself a steaming cup of strong coffee and flop down in my chair behind my desk. My office illuminates golden, and Uriel and Gabriel stand before me, both grinning.

"Greetings brothers, to what do I owe this most unexpected visit?" I ask, sitting up in my chair.

"Wondrous news, brother. You should be most proud of Thana!" Uriel says. "Your mate has learned the highest of healing abilities and saved many lives tonight. Few Archangels can pull off the feat that she did tonight, save one. Samael."

Nodding slowly, I listen to Uriel and ponder his version of the news.

"Honestly brother, it concerned me she had taken after her grandfather too much, and that it would be an issue with the almighty," I say hesitantly as I fiddle with my coffee cup. My fear of losing my beloved mate far outweighs any obstacle I have ever faced in my existence.

Gabriel steps around the desk and rests a hand on my shoulder, giving it a gentle squeeze. "No harm shall ever befall your mate as long as any of us breathe. I swear this to you on my wings, may they pluck me bald, should I ever fail you," Gabriel says lightheartedly. A silly grin crosses his lips as he rolls his eyes.

Uriel shakes his head at Gabriel's antics. "Short version, Thana needs to train in the light realm and the shadow realm. We must make sure we maintain the balance at all costs," Uriel states very businesslike. I'm sure Thana won't mind traveling to the Angelic Realm more often. The only downside is that only myself or Christian can take her. Which leaves Gage without a special activity with Thana unless we get him special permission to make the trip with us. Somewhere in my inner monologue, Gabriel and Uriel depart. My new orders are explicit, yet I feel like I may be walking into a minefield. A strong, single knock sounds at my office door. Azrael doesn't wait for me to respond before entering. "All has been settled, only

two losses recorded after Thana's miracle." Azrael's tone screams with exhaustion as he leans on the right side of the doorjamb.

I study his posture for several moments, then stand and make him a cup of coffee. Closing the distance between us, I offer him the coffee and watch him take a healthy gulp. A hearty laugh escapes his lips as he raises the mug to me. "Your mate makes a much better cup of coffee. I'm not sure how she does it, but she does." Azrael continues to laugh to himself, looking down into the coffee cup as if it holds all the answers to the universe.

"Everything Thana does is better than anything I can do. Somehow it's exactly what I need at that moment." I shrug my shoulders as I refill my coffee mug.

"You still don't get it, do you, Golden Boy? Thana is perfect because she is the perfect blend of angelic, fallen and human blood. She has the abilities and flaws of each species." Azrael's face becomes an unreadable mask. "Protect her at all costs. If she falls, there will be hell on earth." Until Azrael says it, Thana becoming a Fallen Angel has never been a thought that crossed my mind.

I pace around my office. Azrael would be the resident expert on how, and if, Angels fall. Periodically, I glance up and look over at him as I run my fingers through my hair, stressing about the implications of what he's just suggested. "Brother, even though we have not seen eye to eye in the last two thousand plus years since the fall. I beg of you to assist me in preventing this travesty from happening."

Azrael's head suddenly whips up and his eyes are black as pitch as he stares at me with those fathomless orbs. "On my wings, I swear I will do everything within my power to prevent Thana from falling," Azrael says. He disappears in a wisp of smoke.

As soon as he departs, I'm left with more questions than answers. Why were they hunting Cyrus when obviously Thana or I are the actual target? What would they gain by taking Cyrus from us, other than killing Thana and me in the process, and how would that help them if she is the root of their desires? Racking my brain, I finally depart my office to head to the roof to fly home. Oddly enough, Mark is on the rooftop looking out over the city lights, staring off towards the impending sunrise. "Are you okay?" I ask as I move closer to him.

Mark turns around. "A lot has changed since the last trials, hasn't it?" A sadness crosses his visage before he looks away from me and back to the horizon.

"Change is inevitable, unfortunately. Humans are born, live their brief lives, then die. Their time on this planet is short and fleeting, yet they waste that time on petty things." Moving to the edge of the roof, leaning on the wall, I watch the changing hues of the impending sunrise.

"That's not what I was referring to, your holiness. I was speaking of Thana. For the centuries that I've known her, she's always been afraid of her dual nature. Now she wields it like a seasoned veteran." Mark's voice wavers as he expresses his concern over my mate and her wellbeing. It almost makes me wonder if he harbors feelings for her that now must be extinguished.

Shaking my head, I lean my back against the wall to face him when I answer him this time. "There's been a lot that has happened behind the scenes that many are not privy to. I can honestly assure you she is much happier now that she's not afraid of being who she is supposed to be." My tone hits with unwavering authority to further reassure him that what I say is the absolute truth.

His eyes search my face as if looking for the answers to the universe. His head slowly lowers, and he scuffs his toe along the ground. "All I have ever hoped for is for her to find her place in the world. We swore that if neither of us found our mates in the next hundred years we would cohabit so we wouldn't be alone anymore." A single tear rolls down his cheek, and I understand the pain he's in. I had been there myself for the last several thousand years.

Gripping his shoulder, I give him a reassuring squeeze. "Your time will come. Take a deep breath and relax. Your mate has only recently been born. She needs time to become the woman she is meant to be." Mark's stance immediately changes as hope floods his system. The biggest, broadest smile crosses his lips just before he lunges forward and hugs me tightly, thanking me profusely. I know I broke a sacred rule, but the result is harmless and brought hope. Soon as Mark releases me, I launch up into the sky to fly home. Bringing Thana's best friend hope warmed my heart and chased away some of the darkness from the day. Each flap of my powerful wings brings me one beat closer to home. The sun rises in the east, illuminating the earth in brilliant tones of orange and yellow as it peeks over the horizon. The thermals and headwind are with me, making my flight home easier than expected. Cresting the side of the mountain, I can see the top of our home in between all the old-growth cedar trees. Gage sits on the roof, watching the horizon like he does every morning, enjoying the way the earth comes alive at sunrise.

Gently, I land beside him and sit down. His head turns to me before motioning to the beautiful landscape around us. "*It never ceases to amaze me. Every morning the earth seems to be renewed just because the sun deems it so,"* he says with wonder and an innocence I don't remember hearing before from him.

"Is it the sunrise or our mate that makes us see the beauty in the world that we overlooked before her?" I pose the question to him. Personally, everything seems brighter with Thana in my life.

Gage's hand reaches up and strokes his beard, deep in thought. It takes several moments before a lovesick smile crosses his lips and he laughs to himself. *"Thana helps me to see life and this world as something other than a war-zone. She even talked me into going to work with a carpenter to give me purpose."* He suddenly stands up and launches off the roof and circles the house several times before landing on the roof again.

"I'm building Thana a table for the kitchen with matching chairs. I wanted to make something for her, I just hope she likes it." He shrugs his shoulders.

"I'm sure she'll love it just because you thought of her and us when you made it." The sun rises higher in the sky and a soft yawn escapes my lips as exhaustion catches up to me.

Gage claps me on the back and grins. *"Get some sleep brother, everyone is off tonight, and Thana wants to have a big family dinner. From what Christian told me, she's invited some Archangels, Azrael and Samael."* His smile broadens even further as he walks to the edge of the roof. He raises his fingers to his temple in a salute before leaping off the roof to head inside.

Following his lead, I leap off the roof and glide down to the third level, landing on the balcony. I open the double doors that lead to the sitting room upstairs silently, so that I don't disturb anyone that may be asleep. Gently, I shut the doors behind me and head to my room to take a fast shower before bed. A wet pink towel hangs on the bathroom rail, and Thana's natural floral scent floats throughout the room. Just in case, I wrap my towel low upon my hips as I use a second towel to dry my hair.

A low, soft whistle comes from the darkness surrounding my bed as a pair of silver orbs glows faintly. "Do you know, Raph, how many

years I wondered what was under that finely tailored suit of yours?"
she asks, her voice barely a whisper in the shadows.

"I had no idea Thana, I thought you only saw me as your boss."
My voice sounds raspy, even to me, as my heart rate picks up and my
cock twitches to life.

Thana slides off the side of my bed, and sure, cat-like steps
carry her across the room to close the distance. Her fingertips
ghost over the cut planes of my abdomen, eyes tracking her fingers
with every movement. Her silver orbs turn to her pale gray as she
smiles in appreciation of all the hard work I've put in over the
centuries.

Electric current seems to flow from her fingertips as she traces
my muscles, inching further into my personal space. "There were so
many times looking at you through the glass." Thana pauses and
raises her right hand up, like we always did when it was time to reap
a soul. Instinctually, I raise my left hand and place it flat against
hers.

"I swore so many times I saw something other than the reassuring gaze of my boss and guardian." She interlaces her fingers with
mine and pulls my hand to her chest.

A crooked grin crosses my lips. Apparently, my attempt to hide
my desire from her didn't work. "Oh, you saw correctly. My best
description is that I was smitten with you. Taken by your beauty and
your pure heart."

A beautiful rose blush crosses her cheeks as she looks up into my
eyes. "Is that so?" she says with a feral look in her eyes. She places
her palm flat on my chest and I feel her infuse me with power. Every
single nerve feels electrified as she backs me towards my bed. I
almost feel like a lamb being stalked by the wolf. She darts out her
tongue, wets her lips, and I'm hypnotized. I don't fight her when she
shoves me back onto the bed. I crawl backwards up the mattress as
she prowls on all fours towards me. As Thana crawls up my legs, she
licks my inner thigh, making my cock twitch and leak with anticipation.

"What does my beloved wish of me?" My tone comes out huskier than I had expected, and Thana visibly shivers.

She smiles as she crawls up my body the rest of the way and sits on my throbbing cock. Giggling, she leans forward and kisses my lips gently. "I possess everything I could possibly desire." Rocking her hips slightly, she lines herself up with my hot member. The sweet, warm welcoming depths of my mate caress my length and her wetness runs down my balls. A soft, pleased moan escapes her lips as she settles her full weight upon me.

Inching my hands up her thighs, I take hold of her hips and force her first stroke as I raise my hips to meet her. Her fingertips dig deep into my flesh as she grips my ribs tightly. I grunt as I thrust upward to meet the pace she's set for us. Thana's bouncing full breasts are the best distraction I could ask for. Such beauty in motion, I am counting my blessings with every stroke. Thana's muscles quiver and quake around me, pulsing rhythmically, till they crush down around me.

Growling, my orgasm rips through me like a freight train on the highway to hell. My fingertips tighten on her hips as I thrust up into her deeply with every single quivering pulse. I thought Cyrus was kidding when he said how tight her alpha lock was. I definitely owe him an apology if I survive. Every crushing pulse, my hips jerk up in response, pumping more of my seed deep within her.

Deep down, I selfishly hope this produces a child. On the flip side, I hope the elixir is working, and this is a happy, minor side effect. Thana is her most beautiful in the throes of orgasmic bliss. Her skin is radiant and dew wet. The sheer bliss I feel through the bond from her is intense. Eventually, her grip on my cock releases and she falls flat to my chest, the biggest grin plastered to her rose-colored lips. Gently, I roll us to the side and finally slide free from her welcoming depths. Thana snuggles in close, and in my head, I hear her telling me she loves me repeatedly. My heart is full to bursting looking down at my dark angel in my arms. Cyrus's nickname for our mate fits her perfectly. She's as close to being an Angel as a Nephilim can ever achieve. Her lips part slightly as her breaths soften as she succumbs to her slumber. I have never felt so blessed as I do in this moment. They have answered every single prayer of mine in one neat little package.

CHAPTER 26

THANA

No matter how you slice it, I hate mornings and I hate shopping even more. Christian and Cyrus won the rock, paper, scissors game and get to escort me to the stores this morning. Maybe it would be more fun if Joscelyn were here. She always makes the boring tasks seem fun. I shudder, remembering the look on her face the last time I saw her and her 'mate'. Maybe Michael or Uriel can find a way to make sure she's okay. We stop first at the local coffeehouse and grab large cups of that life-sustaining fluid. Sipping at our coffees, we wander into the grocery store, and I'm on edge. Something has set my nerves off and I'm not sure what it is. My skin feels like it's crawling, almost moving of its own volition.

A man in a suit is watching me, almost staring through me as I wander away from the guys. I duck quickly down an aisle and watch both directions carefully. The man follows me and my heart races and my skin crawls again. "Your beauty far exceeds what my master told me of. Perhaps I'll take you as my own?" His voice is smooth as silk and screams trouble. I shudder. His tone hits that 'don't trust me' vibe hard. He's not much taller than I am. His muscles fill out the suit he wears, making the material strain as he moves. His oily brown eyes slither across my skin, and I rub my arms to remove the taint.

"You would be a queen by my side, beautiful, worshiped by all those that stand before you." His words are almost hissed as a forked tongue escapes his lips.

Time suddenly stops, and the building goes silent. The hairs on the back of my neck stand on end, and, with no prompting, Fenrir rips free of my flesh. My guardian stands before me, growling, his hackles raised. Darkness radiates from Fenrir, whipping wildly around him as he stares the male down. Resting my hand on his back, I watch the male. "I know you must be a Demon, or demon kin. You reek of sulfur, so I bet you're from one of the nine circles." Deep down, I reach out through the bond and sense that Cyrus is gaining ground slowly. Damn this male and whatever power he has over the store. Poor Christian is immobilized and unable to render any help.

A second wolf that's almost the twin to mine flanks my left side and takes a protective stance before me. I know Cyrus sent his newest familiar to protect me while he fights his way here. "Merihem! Get away from my mate!" Cyrus growls out as inky tendrils grip me around my waist and pull me back towards him.

"Now, now, little cousin, you must learn to share. After all, she's a prize worth passing around, isn't she? You've rejected her numerous times, it's only a matter of time before you do it again." His tone is pure venom, and I can feel the rage bubbling up in Cyrus's chest.

My mind races as I ponder what to do at this moment. I can't phase out of here without touching Christian. I can't use my darkness without harming Christian. My only solution is to go the other direction. I look over my shoulder at Cyrus as I recall Fenrir. *Phase, I'm going to burn him to ash,* I say through the bond to Cyrus, allowing Christian to hear what I'm going to attempt. Cyrus grips my side briefly before he and his familiar vanish in a wisp of darkness.

"Awe my little cousin ran home with his tail between his legs,"

Merihem says with a hiss as he moves closer to me. The powerful stench of sulfur is almost suffocating and makes my stomach sour.

"Christian? How do I use holy light?" I question him through the bond. Hell, I'm not even sure if I can use it.

Christian and Raphael answer almost in unison, stressing how dangerous it may be for me to do it. Raphael relents and finally explains. *"Picture the sun's rays in a jar in your hand. Then visualize the jar opening and the sun escaping into the world."* Oddly enough, Raphael's explanation makes perfect sense.

During my distraction, Merihem has closed the distance between us and suddenly grips my throat. My eyes flair in shock as panic floods the bond. *"I've got this."*

I focus on what Raphael just explained to me, and I feel an unfamiliar tingle in my hands. Several times I lose grip of the power that has attempted to manifest in my hands. Finally, when I feel like I've got a good grip on it, Merihem's grip on my throat tightens, making it hard to breathe. Quickly, I press my hands to Merihem's chest and let whatever energy I gathered loose. It wasn't the most impressive flash of holy light, but it was enough to get him to release me and fall dead to the floor. I burned away most of the front of his rib cage and his insides burned to an indistinguishable, blackened mass. Sadly, my hands are tender and pink from the use of holy light. Apparently, I require more training.

Christian makes it to my side in a matter of seconds and wraps me up in his arms. My hands are throbbing and slightly blistered in a few places. I stare at the tender pink flesh of my hands, shocked that I used holy light. "Baby, we have to take you to the Angelic Realm where Raph is the strongest to heal you." Christian carries me out of the store like nothing happened and takes to the air immediately.

He soars straight up till we are bathed in a white light just before bursting through the clouds. The minute we land, Raphael is on us. Christian relents and passes me off to him. Raphael takes flight across the clouds, heading towards a large, lone tree.

Gabriel and Uriel are there waiting for us as we land. My nerves kick into overdrive as I panic about the implications of them being present, seeing my hands pink and slightly blistered. "Relax Thana, we understand your fear of us seeing you wounded. It's, after all, your first attempt at wielding holy light," Uriel says with understanding. His loving gaze puts me at ease and slowly my tense muscles relax.

Nodding slowly, Raphael lowers me to the ground and sits under the fabled tree of life. "Sit in front of me, love," Raphael says, smiling at me with his hands extended out.

I lower myself to the ground before him and offer him my hands. "I didn't know what else to do to keep everyone safe. Darkness would have harmed Christian and the light Cyrus, so I sent Cyrus away since he could move." Deep down I feel horrible choosing one mate over the other. The big picture is one way or the other one of them would have been harmed by my hands.

"You chose wisely, love, though trying to harness holy light without me was a little dangerous." Raphael raises his eyebrows gently, trying to get me to take the hint. Even though my intentions were pure, I really didn't think it through entirely. I really hate when I know he's right. Raphael closes his eyes and focuses on the task at hand. A soothing warmth rises from his hands and into mine. I watch the skin of my hands mend and return to a normal color versus the brilliant shade of pink that they were. Amazement is the best word I can use to describe watching my mate at work and feeling the effects of his powers firsthand. Because of my mixed lineage, I wasn't sure if he could heal me without hurting me. "Do you feel better, love?" Raphael's voice is soft, almost hesitant as he looks up at me, concerned.

I withdraw my hands from his and wiggle my fingers. "I feel like brand new again, baby, thank you." Rising onto my knees, I lean forward and kiss him chastely on the lips, being mindful of our audience.

"There's someone we would like you to meet, Thana, before you head home," Uriel says and motions to a pathway behind him.

Curiously, I look to the path he's pointed out and stare at it for several moments. The path itself seems to be made of cobblestone and lined with flowering bushes. The scent from the bushes, soft and sweet, reminds me of a combination of lavender and lilac. "Let's go." I extend my left hand to Uriel, and he takes it, giving it a comforting squeeze. I can't contain my excitement at being back in the Angelic Realm. Everything here is so beautiful and vivid I almost can't contain myself.

Uriel and Gabriel turn quickly and take off down the path. Raphael comes up along my right side and takes my free hand, squeezing it tightly as we walk together. "What you're about to see may shock you. It is believed that the old gods vanished once the Almighty took the throne." Raphael raises his eyebrows, waiting for my response, and I nod along. After all, it's common knowledge about the beginning, and the old gods vanishing. We round the corner, and my jaw literally drops at the winged female warriors. Some of the females are sparing in a small ring with bow staves while others glide on the breeze, enjoying the gentle winds. The big thing that I notice is that their wings are similar in color to the way mine are now.

One female in particular darts towards us, and instinctually my wings flair open as I shove Raphael behind me. My fingernails turn to claws and the darkness whips wildly like flames in my hands.

"Be at peace, sister. We are just like you," the strange female says to me.

Narrowing my eyes, I back up till I make physical contact with Raphael. "Sister?" I glance from the female to Raphael, then over to Uriel and Gabriel. Just my luck. Two out of three Archangels seem to be entertained by this new drama.

"My love, this is Sigrun, Queen of the Valkyries. She called you sister because you are very similar to a Valkyrie." Raphael's hands reach under my wings, and he rubs my sides, trying to get me to relax.

. . .

Lowering my wings, I let them hang half open as I assess the female in front of me. I make the darkness in my hands dissipate. "Thana." I offer a free hand to the warrior queen before me. Without hesitation, she grips my forearm tightly and smiles.

"Sigrun at your service, descendant of Samael." We clasp forearms for several beats before releasing and bowing slightly to each other. "You are the first of Samael's line to be worthy. The Valkyries are yours to command when you need us." Sigrun pulls what looks like a ferryman's coin from her waistband and presses it to my left forearm. It burns intensely before she lifts it up, revealing a new tattoo of wings on my arm. "Touch my mark or call my name and we will descend upon your target without question."

I nod, listening to her words, and take them to heart, knowing full well an ancient like herself wouldn't offer her protection if she didn't mean it.

I'm wary though, so I glance up and look at the men that surround me. Especially my mate, but Raphael is cool and collected and smiling. Gabriel looks on with curiosity as the Queen of the Valkyrie and I converse. I study the warrior queen that stands before me. Her rugged features and long wavy brown hair are captivating. She flexes her wings and looks around casually before focusing on me again. Her sisters, all seven of them, fly in lazy circles overhead. "We wish to train you in our ways just in case you need to defend yourself in the future," she states plainly as she looks between me and Raphael.

Raphael exhales loudly as he glances between me and Gabriel, then back over to Sigrun. He extends his right hand out to her, which she quickly grasps, gripping his forearm tightly. "Thank you for this great boon that you are offering my mate." He lightly bows his head and spreads his wings wide in deference to the Valkyrie queen.

My Archangel mate lowers himself before Sigrun. My eyes dart quickly to the other two Archangels present, then back over to what is going on before me. Sigrun smiles then lowers herself, spreading her wings wide in the same manner that Raphael had just done. "It is a great honor to be trusted with an Archangel's mate." They release each other's forearms and come over to stand before me again. "Your level of trust honors me. I will not take your education lightly."

Sigrun suddenly bows before me, much lower than she did with my mate. "Granddaughter of Samael, heir of the shadow realm, I Sigrun, Queen of the Valkyrie, swear fealty to you from now until eternity." She drops to one knee before me, grabs my right hand, presses her forehead to my knuckles.

In almost a panicked state, I look at Raphael to figure out what to do. He waves his free hand and motions for me to place it on the side of her head. He then points to his lips and then the crown of her head. *"Tell her thank you."*

Following Raphael's instructions, I caress her head gently with my left hand and lower myself to kiss the crown of her head. "Thank you, Sigrun," I say softly against the crown of her head before standing back up again.

She rises slowly and folds her wings to hang half open. "You know how to find me." She flashes me a quick smile, then takes flight to join her sisters.

Raphael is literally smirking at me. "What?"

"You had the Queen of the Valkyrie at your feet and have no clue how big of a moment that was." Raphael envelopes me in his arms, pulling me flush to his chest.

Raising my right eyebrow, I angle my head to look up at him. "I could feel the power radiating off her. She's one of the strongest females I've ever been around." I press my lips to the corner of Raphael's jaw in a quick kiss.

A bellowing laugh comes from behind me. Michael stands there in his full armor. "I can think of one female more powerful than Sigrun, and she's yet to tap into her full potential." A broad smile graces Michael's lips as he crosses his thick, corded arms over his armored barrel chest.

Tilting my head to the side, I look at him, clinging tighter to Raphael and scooting myself further under his arm. "She must be scary then," I whisper from under his arm. A hearty chuckle escapes his lips as he bends down to kiss me on the crown of my head.

"Especially scary when someone messes with what's hers," Raphael says as he squeezes me tight. "Let's get home and see what the others found out about Merihem and his impromptu visit to the surface." Raphael steps away from me and spreads his wings. He winks, then crosses his arms over his chest and falls backward into the clouds, vanishing from sight.

I stare a little too long at the place he fell through when Gabriel laughs. "The only reason the clouds are solid is because you will them to be. The fall through the clouds is an act of faith. Have faith that no harm will befall you and you will pass through the clouds easily." Gabriel smiles and crosses his arms over his chest and falls backward through the clouds. Seconds later, he shoots up through them to land beside me, showing how easy it is.

I can feel Raphael anxiously waiting for me on the other side, so I know he'll catch me if needed when I fall through. Crossing my arms over my chest, I curl my wings around my shoulders as I fall backward. Falling through the clouds is like passing through a cool mist. As I emerge from the other side, I quickly open my wings wide and swoop down to fly to Raphael's side. Thankfully, the trip home is uneventful, and I can focus on making dinner and hearing from my other mates about what they discovered.

CHAPTER 27

RAPHAEL

No one ever said being a mate would be easy, nor did they warn you about constantly worrying about your female. Every day Thana amazes me with what she's able to do and her level of personal growth. Each day, I watch her become more comfortable with who and what she is. Sadly, I discovered today she cannot handle the full magnitude of holy light. My brethren spoke to me privately through the connection all Archangels share, telling me that my mate may never handle holy light at full power. It's also common knowledge that her Grandfather Samael couldn't handle it well either, so it's not that big of a shock to me that Thana could have problems.

As I step out of my suite, the delicious aroma of dinner drifts up to me. I leap over the railing and spread my wings wide as I glide down to the first floor. Voices reach my ears and it's more than what is usual in our home. Before I head towards the kitchen, I catch Gage and Cyrus carrying the chairs that Gage had made for Thana's new table. "Need any assistance gentlemen?" I ask casually as I follow them into the dining room.

"Yes, the last two chairs are on the back porch. Can you grab them?" Gage asks excitedly as he sets the chair he was carrying at the table.

"Of course. Thana is going to love the gift you've made her." I smile broadly, proud of what my nest mate has done for our female. On my way out, Cyrus grabs my arm and yanks me outside quickly. Apparently, something is bothering him.

He quickly closes the double doors and points up, then flies up to the roof. I follow him and discover Azrael is up there waiting for us. "I figured I would speak to you in private before dinner, so I don't ruin the mood for the evening," Azrael says, crossing his arms over his chest and looking out over the treetops towards the sunset.

"Whatever it is, it seems to have raddled your cage old friend," I say as I look between father and son.

"It's far worse than I had imagined. Lucifer wants Thana for himself, or at least that's the rumor," Azrael says.

Cyrus audibly growls. "He can't have her!" he practically screams as his wings spread wide, radiating darkness.

Azrael shakes his head, and a sadness passes over his face that I've never witnessed before. "Even though you forged a bond with Thana, it's not as strong as the other three, Cyrus. Somewhere, deep in her heart, she's still afraid of you leaving her," Azrael says with the seriousness that only a father can achieve.

Cyrus's demeanor suddenly changes. He goes from raging to broken. His eyes dart from his father to me, then over the edge of the roof as if he's looking down at Thana. Wordlessly, he dives over the edge of the roof and vanishes from sight.

"His inability to connect to people is my fault. I was a shit father and an even worse mate. Hell, his mother was mostly human and was someone to lessen my loneliness." Azrael slumps slightly. "If the whispers are correct, they will keep trying till they get her to fall. If she falls, so shall you and the other two light mates." Azrael's statement shakes me to my core, almost to the point of bringing me to my knees. The entire safety of the family hinges on Cyrus cementing his bond with Thana.

Running my hands down my face, I sigh, then shake my head slowly. "So, the fate of the world hinges on Cyrus getting his head out of his ass." Dropping my hand to the side, I motion in the direction that Cyrus had gone.

I look back up to Azrael, and he nods his head slowly. "Sadly, yes, I'll prepare things on my end should this go south." I have a feeling he has very little faith in his son and his abilities.

I walk to the edge of the roof and leap off, gliding back down to the first floor of our home. As I open the back door, Gage is leading Thana into the formal dining room to see the new table he had made for her. Azrael and I join in following the group to the dining room. We file in and line the walls, waiting for Gage to remove his hands from Thana's eyes.

As soon as his hands drop away, her eyes pop open, and she squeals with excitement. Thana spins in his arms faster than expected and wraps her arms around his neck, hugging him tightly to her. Her lips find his and she kisses him silly to the point they are both smiling. Thana's giggles fill the room as Gage spins her around slowly before setting her down.

"This is the second best gift I've ever gotten!" Thana says excitedly as she breaks free from Gage's arms to run her fingertips over the wood of the white oak table.

Christian looks puzzled. "What was your first best gift, watashi no ai?" He smiles sweetly as he moves closer to her and takes hold of our mate.

"My absolute best gift is the four of you." Thana grins as she dances around the room, coming to each of us and kissing us.

Thana stops dead in front of Cyrus and stares up at him. Her eyes bleed silver as she smiles at him. Her hand reaches out and slides up his face till her fingertips end up in his thick black hair. Cyrus's eyes blacken as he stares down at Thana. Slowly, he bends down and tenderly kisses her lips. The room silences as we watch the tender moment. As they break apart, both are smiling broadly at each other. I have a lot of hope for those two that sooner than later they will fix whatever is blocking their bond from fully settling.

"Time to eat everyone!" Thana says cheerfully as she heads back to the kitchen with Cyrus in tow. Everyone present heads into the kitchen to grab a plate and fill it with some of the delicious food Thana has prepared for us. There is dragon fruit salad. Two kinds of roast chicken, London broil, fish and several other varieties of meat. I look around the island in the kitchen to find six different vegetables and sauces to go with the meat dishes.

For the first time in over a thousand years, Archangels, fallen and Samael are eating at the same table peacefully and it's all because of my beautiful mate.

~ LATER THAT **night**~

As an extended family, we discuss what the ramifications of Lucifer coming for Thana would mean for her, us, and the world as a whole. We also discuss the upcoming Solstice ball as well as what is expected from each of the families when they present themselves, along with the rest of the festivities and announcements. We also discuss the possibility of helping or freeing Joscelyn when Uriel judges their bond. Thana suddenly stands and starts pacing the room, flexing her fingers. With each flex, her fingertips become blackened claws, and her face takes on a feral appearance. Samael's lips tilt upward as he tracks his granddaughter across the room.

"What's got you smiling, Samael?" I ask, watching him closely. My question silences the room, and all eyes are on him. Even Thana stops pacing, still in that mid-shifted state. Samael stands slowly, chuckling to himself. His wings unfurl, and his fingers shift to be like Thana's. As he looks back up at us, his eyes are the same silver as hers are. "Lucifer cannot taint nor tempt my heir—she is every bit my blood, designed to walk in the veil to protect the Heavens and Hell." He retracts his claws and pulls Thana to him and hugs her tightly.

"You can command both armies, or turn them against themselves. Your parents were merely the vessels to create my successor." Samael gently presses his lips to Thana's temple and sighs softly.

Thana's face slowly contorts as what her grandfather said sinks in. "Vessels!" She throws her wings wide open, sending Samael flying back away from her. Energy crackles along her long flight feathers as her eyes take on an eerie glow. "My mother was an innocent! Her only poor choice was that asshole of a son of yours!" She says as she jabs a clawed finger in Samael's direction.

Her silver orbs turn on Azrael, and she shakes her head, looking at him. "You were a far better father than mine was. At least you didn't kill your child's mother in front of her." Thana's head whips around as she faces off with Samael again. "I've been scared of being myself for centuries." Her eyes drop to her claws, then raise back up to lock on Samael. "I've been terrified of becoming fallen all because of my father and his actions." Darkness bleeds from the black feathers at the tops of her wings. She grits her teeth, baring them like a wild animal.

Cyrus is the first to move to Thana's side, and she instantly curls into him and starts crying. My eyes lock with Gabriel's and then Uriel's before looking back over at Samael. "You realize you messed with, and manipulated free will, correct?" I call forth my armor and cross my arms over my barrel chest, looking at the destroyer himself.

"I know what I did is considered a crime." He smirks and points up. "Confirm with the big guy. I had his permission. We needed another like me to prevent the next uprising. One on earth, the other in the shadow realm, to even the odds for the greater good," he says confidently.

What he doesn't notice is the contorted rage on Thana's face as she barrels towards Samael, hands outstretched, filled with darkness. "I cast you out!" she screams as her hands impact his chest. The minute she makes contact, he vanishes in a wisp of black smoke. Thana is practically growling as she stares at her empty, clawed hands.

Everyone is frozen in varying states of shock. "Thana?" Uriel says calmly in a cheery tone as to not startle her.

Thana lifts her head and blinks twice as she tries to suppress the still radiating rage. "Yes Uriel?" Her head tilts to the side, questioningly.

"How did you know how to send Samael back to the shadow realm?" His smile softens as he stretches out his hands to her, and she takes them quickly.

She releases her grip on his hands and moves in to hug him around the waist. "I think his name is Meta something, he told me how. His voice was like an echo in my head repeating the instructions." Thana shrugs her shoulders.

Double blinking, I look towards the other Archangels, then over to Azrael, then back again. "Metatron?" I say the name I haven't spoken in more years than I can remember. He sits beside the almighty as a guardian, along with his twin.

"Yeah, that's it," Thana says enthusiastically. "Samael was speaking the truth. Metatron confirmed it after I sent him back to the shadow realm." Thana's eyes are back to being perfect silver orbs. "Grandfather is more shocked than angry with me; he didn't think I could do it." Thana shrugs it off and walks over to Gage and pulls him back to the kitchen to help her with dessert.

"So, she was created by divine will?" Christian states plainly, clearly just as puzzled by this revelation as the rest of us.

Uriel paces the dining area, his eyes pure golden orbs as he converses with someone in the Angelic Realm. "From what I can discern, there's more fallen than ever, as well as demons being created at an alarming rate." Uriel continues to pace the room. "Samael's powers are waning because he chose to remain in the Shadow Realm and not traverse between all three realms." Uriel's expression morphs as he looks pointedly at Cyrus. "If Samael falls... your mate at full power will be the only one strong enough to stop him. Fix the bond, do whatever you have to do it."

Azrael's expression says it all. He thinks Cyrus will fail and we all will perish. Thana's giggles alert us to her return, and we take our seats as if nothing has happened. The last thing we need is for her to feel as if she's being forced to have to fix things. Gage and Thana make several trips back and forth to the kitchen, bringing out a variety of baked goods along with tubs of ice cream. Delicately, Thana cuts the cakes and pies, placing them on ornate plates I didn't know we had. I catch Christian smiling, pointing at the plates, clearly being the one responsible for their purchase.

Looking around the dining room, I notice all the little things each mate has contributed to the house. Even Cyrus has left his mark with the Edgar Allan Poe Lithographs on the wall that Thana loves so much. It's now that I realize I haven't added a single thing to the house to leave my mark, my presence outside of my bedroom. A lithe hand rests on my shoulder, and I turn slowly to look up at Thana. A gentle, loving smile graces her rose-colored lips as her gunmetal-gray eyes search mine. "Raph, you're a giant ball of turmoil. What's bothering you? Is it how I decorated the dining room? I can change it." Her eyebrows knit in the middle as worry etches her beautiful face.

My actions have caused my mate to be insecure and I feel like such a wretch for doing it. Carefully, I pull her down into my lap and hug her tightly. "Thana, I was looking around the house, and I feel I've neglected you. All I do is work, and I haven't taken the time to make this place a home." My sadness bleeds through as I express my unhappiness with myself.

Gripping my jaw, Thana forces me to make direct eye contact with her. "Not left your mark? You paid for this house for us. You work hard so I can stay home safe, away from the dangers that may hunt me." Her silken lips caress mine in a slow, sensual kiss. I can't help but moan from the sensation of her love washing over me. Thana breaks the kiss, then ruffles my hair. "I appreciate and love the life I live, and it's all because of how hard the four of you work."

Thana giggles a little before standing up. "Of course, when the poop hits the fan, you call in the big guns." Thana points at herself and starts laughing.

Cyrus comes running around the table and Thana takes off, squealing as she tries to escape from his grasp. Shaking my head, I look back at the rest of the family gathered at the table, and a soft laugh escapes my lips. "Dig in everyone. I don't think they're coming back." A half chuckle escapes my lips as I offer a prayer that Cyrus gets his head out of his ass.

CHAPTER 28
THANA

Running through the house, Cyrus is hot on my heels, and I barely remain ahead of him. Upon reaching the third floor, I throw open the balcony doors and take flight. My large wings help me take off quickly as I dart towards the old growth forest below the house. Swooping in and out of the tree line, I finally think I've lost Cyrus, so I land at the lake's edge that's near the house. Without warning, he dive bombs me, grabbing me around the waist, and soars back up into the sky. Laughing hysterically, I gently pound on his shoulder. "Release me you heathen!" The smile on my face says it all. I'm enjoying the one-on-one attention from him.

"Never! I fully intend to corrupt you!" Cyrus says, also laughing as he nuzzles my neck. I return the nuzzle and retract my wings, making it easier for him to hold me while he's flying.

Looking around, I have no clue where we are. "Where are we going?" I ask softly, trying not to destroy the warm, loving embrace he has me in.

Cyrus squeezes me tighter as we fly in silence for a few moments. "I have someplace I want to take you." His voice is a little strained as he mentions it, and I have a gut feeling I know where he's taking me.

Wrapping my arms tightly around him, I snuggle in close, enjoying the flight. We fly for almost an hour till we cross over what looks like a field of golden wheat with a hill with a single tree on top. Cyrus lands carefully and lowers my feet to the ground.

Standing next to the tree is a black marble headstone with the name Celeste Draken carved into it. The dates of birth and death are worn away from years of the elements beating against the stone face. Staring at the headstone, I realize this must be Cyrus's mother's grave. "She died of a broken heart." Cyrus's voice wavers. "She lov—" he takes a steadying breath "—loved my father no matter what horrible thing he had done to her." Resting a hand on the top of the stone, he slowly turns to look at me. His eyes are bloodshot from trying to restrain the tears that threaten to break.

Without hesitation, I rush to him and wrap my arms tightly around his waistline. "I'm so sorry," escapes my lips as I rest my head on his chest as I fight my own demons wanting to break loose. Nuzzling his chest, I try to keep my own dark thoughts and emotions in check as I comfort my mate.

Cyrus pulls away and drops to his knees before me. "Baby, what's wrong? Tell me so I can fix it." His strong hands massage my hips as his eyes plead with me for answers.

"I'm sorry, I tried to stay strong for you." I bring my hands up to cover my face.

Cyrus stands and wraps his arms around and covers me with his wings, cocooning me in my own obsidian armor. "Talk to me Thana. Why are you sorry?" he says softly, encouraging me to open up to him.

Sniffling, I look up into his chocolate eyes and force a smile. "Seeing your mom's grave made me think about my mom. My father forced himself on my mother, and here I am. Soon as mom found her true mates, I was dumped on a pair of childless neighbors." Thana shrugs her shoulders dismissively "Joscelyn's future mom and dad took me in. I was thirteen when Mom abandoned me. Not even a year later, I ran into my mom in the park. She with her new family.

And my father, Nyx, drives his sword through her chest, killing her instantly for abandoning me." Silent tears flow freely down my cheeks as my chest constricts from the pain of the memory. Holding on tightly, I nuzzle Cyrus's chest. "She'd never win mother of the year, but she was still my mom." Cyrus's grip on me tightens as he tries to hold me together.

He presses his lips to my temple and breathes in deeply. "I guess I should be grateful that my father and mother were who they are." His soft tone is almost shocking to hear.

Sighing, I look back up at Cyrus and kiss him, savoring the spicy tingle from his lips. "I spent years being afraid of rejection, mostly because of my wings. I learned how to love from Joscelyn's family. But, there was always that lingering fear of what my mates would think of me if I was ever lucky enough to have some."

Cyrus opens his wings and his arms, and I pace around the tree. My wings unfurl and spread wide as I stretch them. Turning my head, I look over my shoulder at him and smile. "I finally feel whole, and it's because of you."

Cyrus's shocked expression says it all. Disbelief is written all over it. "How is that possible? I've been the worst out of the four of us," he says as he runs his fingers roughly through his thick black hair.

Turning to face him, I wink. "I know you better than I think you know yourself." Measured steps carry me across the soft moss to stand before Cyrus and I rest my hand on his cheek.

"The Angels would sacrifice themselves or me to save the world." Smirking, I stare up at him and allow my eyes to blacken. "You would let the world burn to ash to save me. Sometimes being the anti-hero is a good thing." Scrunching my nose, I lean in and kiss him.

Cyrus comes alive in my arms and his hands feel like they are everywhere at once. "Not here," he mumbles before taking off again, flying in a new direction. I retract my wings and hold on for dear life. It doesn't take long for us to reach his destination. Apparently, Cyrus still has his loft on the edge of the city. We land on the roof, and he ushers me through the door and into his lair. Within his personal space I'm shocked to see random black-and-white photos of me over the last several decades.

"I had a crush on you for ages. It seems like I wasn't the only one drawn to you like a moth to a flame." The first full tendrils of honesty from him hit me right in the feels. Image by image, my love for him comes into full bloom. Any fragments of doubt about his feelings or where his heart truly lies melt away.

There's a picture of me on the bookcase, smiling, with my eyes closed, taking my first sip of coffee in the morning. This image is recent and in Raphael's old house. I raise an eyebrow.

"You liked the coffee I bought from the same shop that you would normally get your coffee from before work. I went and purchased the grounds from them and stocked the closet with it," he says, shrugging his shoulders like it was no big deal.

"Do you know that out of the four of you, only you ever get my coffee right?" I wink at Cyrus and close the distance between us. "You once boasted that you would end up being my best mate." My is tone breathless as I lean in close, my lips ghosting over his as I talk.

"You alone understand the swirling darkness within me and don't shy away from it. Even though you smashed my heart into a million pieces, here you are gluing it back together again." My lips barely touch his as the whispered words escape my lips. Without him noticing, I shift my fingers to claws and shred the soft T-shirt from his body, careful not to cut him.

My hands make contact with his toned olive flesh, reveling in the heat his body radiates. Inch by glorious inch, I work the fabric free of his shoulders and down his arms till it hits the floor. A sexy smirk plays upon his full lips. "My dark angel wants something?" A single dark brow lifts just before his lips descend on me, kissing my lips roughly, stealing the very breath from my lungs. Leaping up into his arms, I wrap my thighs tightly around his waistline. We spin and I'm pressed against the wall as Cyrus frees a hand to work on removing my shirt.

Without hesitation, I raise my arms, making it easier for him to get the shirt off me. Leaning forward, I crush my breasts against the hard plains of his sculpted chest. Cyrus's powerful hands slide up my back to the clasp of my bra, and, with a snap of his fingers, it comes undone. I giggle as I grip the front of my bra and pull it free.

His eyes blacken as he looks at me, I mean really looks at me, as if he's seeing into my soul. I know my own eyes blacken as I stare back at my dark knight. I lunge forward and crash into him, kissing him deeply. Our tongues battle for dominance as they slip and slide over one another, caressing the entire length. His hands glide down my body, massaging inch by inch, till he has a grip on the hem of my leggings. The sound of fabric ripping is the only noise besides our own moans and panting.

Cyrus fumbles with the material as he pulls the halves down my thighs and out of the way. His fingers find my barely there thong and it's soaked through. He slides his finger between my wet pussy and the soaked, offending material. A quick downward yank and the spaghetti straps snap instantly, leaving me completely bare before him.

A pleased groan escapes his lips as he slides his left arm under my ass to jack me up the wall. His free hand works on the button of his jeans till I hear the material hit the floor. Cyrus bands both arms tightly around my body as he pulls me away from the wall and carries me down a dark hallway. Leaning a shoulder against the doorframe, he reaches into the dark room and flips on the light switch. Black lights illuminate the room, and it is almost an exact replica of the room I created in my nest for Cyrus.

I slide down his body and my feet land on a super soft carpet. Cyrus motions to the room, encouraging me to explore it. Just about everything within is a mirror image of what I had purchased for the room I created for him. Shocked doesn't even come close to describe how I'm feeling. I know Cyrus better than I believed I did.

Strong arms band around my ribs and I'm pulled back against his solid chest. His lips caress the shell of my ear as his husky honey voice utters the words I've been dying to hear. "I love you. In some sick sense, I always have. You're mine, Thana. Black heart and corrupted soul, I'm yours." Cyrus kisses the side of my neck, and that's not good enough, not for a moment like this.

Suddenly, I pull free from his grasp and unfurl my wings, one good flap of my wings, as I shove him back on the bed behind him. Leaping up, I land on Cyrus and crawl my way up his body till I'm looking down at him. My hands roam up his sides to his bulging biceps. Pushing with all my might, I put his arms over his head, and a wicked grin spreads over his lips. "Angel, you know I can break free, right?" A playful smirk appears on his sinful lips.

Leaning down, I inch back slightly till my silken lips tease the tip of his waiting cock. Tilting my head to the side, I smile sweetly. "Very true, but you're too curious to see what I may do next." I drop the tone in my voice as those words escape my lips. Cyrus's cock twitches in response to what I said.

"Do your worst, Angel." Cyrus's honeyed voice turns my insides molten as he gives me his patented bad-boy smolder. Reaching up into his hair, I pull his hair tie free and place it over his wrists as a restraint.

"Challenge accepted! That hair tie does not come off for any reason other than I'm in danger, or I tell you to stop." I raise up on my knees as I reach between my legs to lift his rock hard, pulsing cock. The muscles in Cyrus's arms tense as he forces himself to not reach for me. Rocking slightly, I spread my moisture over the thick head of his cock, then tease him by taking only a few inches into myself. His mouth pops open and he gasps, feeling my warm welcoming depths. His eyes plead with me to go further, but I don't want to... yet.

"Angel, you're killing me." Cyrus's voice is strained and sweat beads on his temples. His hips rock up of their own volition, and I allow him to, enjoying feeling a little more of his thick length.

With no warning I drop down, taking his entire length deep within me. My plan to torture Cyrus completely backfires as my own orgasm rips through me. I scream till my voice is almost raw as my core detonates around Cyrus. His muttered *fuck it* barely reaches my ears as the lights explode behind my eyes.

This time is completely different with Cyrus. I feel his heart beating in time with mine. His powerful hands grip my hips as he grinds up into me, chasing his own release. His strokes are long, deep and hit every spot, setting my nerve endings on fire. Cyrus pulls me down flush with his chest as his arms band tightly around me. Three more strokes and he's screaming his release, his pulsing cock dumping his seed deep within me. And then it happens... My muscles lock down on Cyrus again, trapping him deep within me. My muscles vibrate and pulse, milking every drop from him.

Panic floods the bond as the guys sense what's happening. The only voice of reason is Christian, he's of the mindset that this is divine will at work. Exhausted, I flop down onto Cyrus's chest and sigh softly. I hope the big guy has a brilliant plan, because we may have just signed my death warrant.

CHAPTER 29

RAPHAEL

The sudden pulse of power that floods the bond wakes me up from a deep sleep. I sit up, reaching my senses out as far as I can, and the first thing I sense is Thana and Cyrus's bond blazing to life. Their combined flame burns as brightly as mine and Thana's does now. This is a wonderful thing. We don't have to worry about other Dark Nephilim trying to steal Thana away from Cyrus. The only problem is, her alpha lock has him trapped again, and she hasn't learned how to keep herself from getting pregnant. We're not even sure the elixir will even work on her. All we can do is hope everything turns out for the best.

Leaping up out of bed, I grab my sweatpants and a shirt and head out my bedroom door. Just outside my room Christian and Gage are in a heated debate about what's going on. If Gage signs any faster, I think his fingers are going to fall off. "Gage, just use the bond, it's easier." My tone comes off a bit harsher than I had intended and promptly Gage flips the middle finger at me.

"We have bigger issues than me choosing to use sign instead of talking. How are we going to protect a pregnant Thana?" Gage raises the question that has my heart racing.

Just before I get the chance to answer, a serene look crosses over Christian's face and he raises a hand, stopping me. "He," Christian points up and smiles, "does everything for a reason. You know we're not privy to all of his plans. Everything happens for a reason. It is not our place to ask why." Christian says so peacefully, his tone is smooth and soothing. "Why not ask Michael or Uriel why this only has happened with Cyrus? We've each been with Thana multiple times in the last few months. But both times she was fertile has been with Cyrus." Christian walks down the hall towards the third story sitting room. Reluctantly, Gage and I follow.

Christian walks calmly over to the coffee machine and turns it on. While we wait, I reach out to Uriel, requesting his presence. Just as Christian passes the coffee out, Uriel materializes in our sitting room. "You seem vexed, brother. What seems to be the problem?" Uriel says calmly as he accepts the coffee from Christian.

"Thana alpha locked Cyrus again, and I'm sure she's pregnant this time," I say to him, trying not to express the anger that's bubbling up in my chest. "He's so irresponsible! Her life has been in danger since the trials. Adding a baby now may get her killed." Frustration ebbs out from every pore as I reach up, tugging at my hair, stressing out.

"Be at peace, brother, this is all part of the bigger picture." Uriel says just before he rests a hand on my shoulder to calm me. "We must maintain the balance at all costs. To do that, Cyrus must have a reason to not be corrupted. Thana and the baby give him something to fight for and remain on the good side of things," Uriel states before walking away from me to grab a bowl off the counter and filling it with water. Once filled, he places it on the table between all of us and waves his hand over it. "Look what would have happened if one of you fathered the first baby." As soon as the last word leaves his lips, he passes his hand over the water and it reveals an alternate future to us.

Fallen and Dark Nephilim blacken the skies engaged in battle with Light Nephilim and Angels, the end of days has begun. The vision fast forwards to Thana with a baby strapped to her chest, its white wings peeking out from under the harness. Christian lies dead behind her, and Gage is mortally wounded, leaning on the wall. She holds a hellfire sword in her hand and her eyes are black as pitch as Lucifer himself stands off with her. Their swords clash repeatedly and her baby cries louder and louder. Just as she gains the upper hand, a sword comes up through her chest from behind. The blade itself misses the baby but kills Thana instantly. The vision then pans to the fight in the air. I'm falling dead without a single visible mark on my body. My body splatters on the ground like a bug on a windshield. The last part we see is Cyrus mourning Thana, and taking her child away.

Gripping my chest, I look at Uriel as the tears roll down my cheeks freely. "Whose child was it?" I feel like I can't breathe. My hands claw at my throat as anxiety almost cripples me. In my heart, I know the child was mine, but I need to be sure.

"You already know the answer, brother. The way we've set the future now, Thana will come into her full power, and everyone will survive." Uriel grips my shoulder and presses his forehead to mine. "All will be well," he says, then vanishes in a golden mist.

I swear sometimes Uriel likes to drop the mother of all bombs, then leave. It's become a rather concerning habit of his of late, and I'm honestly not thrilled. "What do we do?" Christian looks from the bowl back over at me.

As I pace, Gage comes to stand in my path. *"We train harder and increase the security in the house. Do you think Michael has any familiars he can gift us to help protect Thana?"* Gage shrugs his shoulders.

Gage's question stops me in my tracks, and I ponder it for several moments. "Nothing like what Azrael gave Thana and Cyrus. They can outfit you two with angelic armor and better swords," I say. As soon as the words leave my mouth, I summon Michael to get Gage and Christian properly fitted with armor, just in case. He manifests in the room not far from us with a smirk playing upon his lips.

"I've been meaning to catch up with these two before the next

Solstice Ball." He motions to Gage and Christian, and they drop to their knees before him. "The first thing you need to know is that the bonds will be judged by Uriel. Secondly, all false or weak bonds will be sent to the elders for guidance. But in the meantime, just in case there's an attack, I need you two ready for battle." With a practiced flourish, Michael's sword blazes to life out of nowhere. I utter the words, *show* off, and he smirks at me. He places the flat of his angelic blade upon their shoulders one at a time, almost like a knighting ceremony. As soon as the blade contacts their body, angelic armor takes shape, fitting them perfectly. Gage is overwhelmed with emotion, seeing the stark white armor materialize upon his body. It's truly a rare event for a Nephilim to be fitted with angelic armor. The last time that happened was during the fall.

Christian remains on his knees, as a serene look passes over his face as he looks down at the armor he's wearing. "It's been ages since I've worn armor like this," he pauses, "I wish I had my katana that I lost all those years ago." Christian's eyes get that distant look to them as he remembers the last time he saw his favorite sword. Michael raises a brow and waves his hands before him, and an ancient, ornately curved katana manifests in his hands. "Does this look familiar?" Michael holds it out to Christian in traditional presentation stance.

Christian's eyes light up as he jumps to his feet. "How did you find it?" Reverently, he takes the sword from Michael and bows deeply, holding it out in front of himself.

"Samael had it in his collection and figured you would want it back," Michael says confidently as he turns to look over Gage and the way the armor fits him. Gage signs to Michael about not having a sword. Michael nods and creates a Damascus broadsword for him. Gage looks like a kid in a candy shop. The pure joy of having armor and a sword has made his day. Michael leans forward and touches Gage's throat. All movement stops, and it's so quiet you can hear a pin drop. "Say something. I have punished you long enough. Right now, you need your voice to help protect your bond-mates and mate." Michael bows briefly, then vanishes in a wisp of golden glitter.

Gage runs through the house to the living room on the first floor, Christian and I close behind. He stands before the mirror. The scar on his neck is gone, and he stares at himself in awe.

"Hey guys, we're home!" Thana calls from the main entranceway.

Reflexively Gage calls out, "In here!" He freezes and slaps both hands over his mouth as he looks between Christian and me. We're just as shocked as he is hearing his voice.

Thana comes running in and stops suddenly in the doorway, staring at all of us. I'm not sure what's more of a shock for her, the three of us in armor, or the fact she heard a voice she wasn't expecting to hear. Bashfully, Gage smiles and waves. "Welcome home, baby."

Thana's mouth pops open as she stares in disbelief at Gage's greeting.

Double blinking, she hesitantly takes several steps forward. "Did... did you?" Her bottom lip quivers as she creeps closer to Gage. All it takes is for him to nod, to have Thana close the distance between them and bury her face in his neck, crying.

"Shh... baby, please don't cry," Gage says softly as he runs his fingers through Thana's long hair, trying to soothe her.

"Wait! When the bloody hell did Gage start talking??" Cyrus asks as he enters the room. He looks like he's been put through the wringer, but then again, he was alpha locked by Thana, and I know firsthand that it's as draining as it feels good.

"Michael gave him his voice back to better be able to take care of Thana in the future," I state.

Cyrus nods, digesting what I said, then looks back over at me. "I think we fixed the bond." He shrugs his shoulders as he turns to watch Thana with Gage. His resting bitch face is on point. If I didn't know better, I'd say he didn't care. His words are hopeful, but the look on his face screams indifference. Out of the four of us, he's the family wild card that has to help us contain and protect the nuke we call our mate.

"While you were away, a lot has happened. The priority is protecting Thana at all costs. Second, training has to step up for all of us." As the head mate, it's my job to assure the safety of the nest and the mates within it. As I see it now, only two of us really have fought. Gage and Cyrus came in at the tail end of the second war between Heaven and Hell. "Azrael and Samael said they will come to the house to help train all of us. Thana needs to make trips between the three realms and train with both sides of the veil to make sure her power is balanced." Gripping my coffee mug, I take a sip, watching the reaction of the others.

Thana is walking around the room looking at the armor her mates are wearing, and then turns and smiles at me. Her wings burst free and spread wide at full extension. A wave of black smoke rolls over her body from head to toe. When the smoke clears, she's standing there in black and gold armor with the black angelic sword Daybreaker in her right hand. The sight of that weapon makes my skin crawl. We cannot heal the wounds it can inflict except by the sap from the tree of life. "Thana? Where did you get that sword from?" I ask cautiously.

At the mention of the weapon, she wills it to shrink to the size of a dagger that she places within its sheath at her hip. "Grandfather had it in his armory. He said it may save my life at some point." She walks over to Cyrus.

"This just won't do. I can't have my dark knight without armor." Thana's eyes churn silver, then take on an ethereal glow. She raises her hands high above Cyrus and blackened mist seeps out from her pores and blankets him. I assume Azrael felt the disturbance in the veil, he appears in the sitting room with us, watching Thana intently. Her wings flex randomly as she moves her hands up and down the blackened mass that has encapsulated Cyrus.

"Is she doing what I think she's doing?" Azrael asks softly as he leans closer to me, still watching Thana and Cyrus intently.

I shrug my shoulders. "I honestly have no clue. I don't believe it's within her scope of power yet. Then again, I could be completely wrong."

Christian and Gage circle around Thana and Cyrus curiously, watching her work with the mist.

Thana backs up and lowers her hands, beaming. "Come out, love, show off your new armor."

Cyrus steps out of the blackened mist, and I feel like I should be in Mordor rather than our house on the cliff side. His armor is straight out of a horror movie. It's black as pitch, its edges appear razor sharp and remind me of a mix between the witch-king and Sauromon. His helmet looks more like a spiked crown of death than a helmet. The face guard of the helmet looks to be a mix of a Viking's helm and a Roman gladiator. What really catches my attention are the gauntlets. Nightmare on elm street has nothing on the dagger like blades on his fingertips.

Thana smiles, beaming with pride over her creation. As she moves around Cyrus, she makes minor changes to the armor, manipulating it as if it's clay in her hands. "Wings please." Thana hits a commanding tone that shocks the rest of us. What is even more shocking is how fast Cyrus complies.

Cyrus unfurls his wings and spreads them wide, as they open armor moves like fluid over his wings, protecting the major bones of his wings. Smiling broadly, Thana bounces up and down. "Perfect, love, touch the wolf and put it away." Staring at his armor, I notice the wolf's head dead center of his chest. As soon as his fingers make contact, the armor retracts like blackened fluid into the wolf amulet around his neck.

Thana touches a similar mark on her own armor, and it flows like water back into the amulet she's wearing. "Samael made the armor for me and then a set for Cyrus for our training sessions and the trouble that's on the horizon. He said the armor would deteriorate with the use of holy light so it wouldn't be a good idea for the three of you." Thana pouts, and I swear it's gotten more adorable.

A yawn escapes her lips, and she lifts a hand to cover her mouth. "I need a nap. We have the Solstice Ball tonight I need to rest." Thana moves from mate to mate, kissing us before heading off to bed. She stops in front of me and grabs my hands.

"Nap with me, Raph?" Her gunmetal gray eyes practically beg me to join her, and I can't resist. Nodding slowly, I let her drag me down the hall and into her nest, shedding my armor as we go. Down into the nest we climb, and she pulls me to her. She places a gentle kiss on my lips before she lays her head on my chest and promptly falls asleep. Using my gifts, I ghost my hand over her stomach, and I sense life within her, I sense two distinct heartbeats. I reach out through the bond to the guys, alerting them to the cargo that Thana carries. Twins are an anomaly, so for our rare mate to be carrying twins, we must be extra vigilant.

CHAPTER 30

THANA

Best nap ever, by the time Raphael's alarm goes off, all my mates are in the nest with us, even Cyrus. Christian and Gage play pass the Thana to get me out of the nest, then Raphael and Cyrus take me to go shower. I've never been more pampered and felt more loved in my entire life. Every day I feel like I'm living in a fairytale, that tomorrow I'm going to wake up and it will all be over. That I'll be back in my apartment all alone, staring at the world passing me by. After my shower, I head into the sitting room that separates my nest from the rest of the house. I pull the hood of my sweatshirt up and over my head as I stare out the window, lost in my thoughts.

A gentle hand caresses my cheek and turns my face away from the window. "Where did you go just now, Tsuma?" Christian says softly, kissing my cheek, chasing away the darkness.

A soft sigh escapes my lips as I curl into Christian. Resting my head on his shoulder, I wrap my arms around his taut waistline. "I feel like I'm living a fairytale and sometimes I..." Shaking my head, I stop talking. I still feel like I don't deserve my mates because of my lineage.

"You sometimes what, Tsuma? Please talk to me. I want to

understand," Christian practically begs me. "Not long ago you told me your every dark secret and thought. Now that we're mates, you hide what upsets you. What changed? I'm still me, and you're still you." His lips caress the crown of my head and tears break free. He's right, nothing has changed other than the title, and I get to see him naked now.

Pulling away, I move to stand before him and unfurl my wings. "I live in constant fear that I'm going to wake up and be back in my apartment alone again. That the Mate Trials never happened. That I will lose all of you because this is just a dream." All my bottled-up fears break free and flow like a river out of my mouth.

My other three mates stand there, dumb struck listening to what I'm confessing. "You, Christian, I always loved you for your kindness, and I was always jealous of every Mate Trial you went to. I was jealous of the female that would be your mate."

Drawing in a deep breath, I walk over to Raphael. I raise my hand like I always did before taking a soul. Reflexively, his hand raises and rests against mine. "All these years of looking into your hazel-green eyes. I've been bewitched by you. My heart longed for the one male I knew I couldn't have because of your station. Not only because you're my boss, but an Archangel." Sadly, I smile at him, then I move on to Cyrus.

His eyes widen as I look up at him, trying not to get emotional. "Losing you may kill me. I never knew I needed you till I didn't have you. All those years of tormenting me by stealing my cookies and coffee, you learned who I really am. You probably know me the best out of all of my mates." Cyrus grips my hand and kisses my knuckles before I move away from him.

Gage is rocking back and forth from foot to foot, showing how stressed he is. "You're an unexpected gift. You taught me there's more to life than meaningless words. With or without a voice, I've always known how much you love me. Thank you for being you." I reach up and kiss his lips tenderly, allowing my love for him to wash over him in waves.

Reluctantly, I move away from Gage and head towards the closet. In the doorway, I pause and look back over my shoulder. "You four complete me, none above the other. I love you all." Closing my eyes, I focus on the tethers of the bonds with my guys and push my love towards them. As I focus on the bonds, I notice two new tendrils but cannot see where they go. Puzzled by this, I open my eyes and shift them to silver orbs and start searching the room.

I stop in the middle of the room and pout.

"What's wrong, daughter?" Azrael had arrived, and he's wearing a tux.

"I'm not sure..." My brows remain furrowed as I still look around the room.

"What do you see, Thana?" Azrael asks me as he comes over and cups my elbow and walks me over to the couch to sit.

Biting my bottom lip, I close my eyes, focusing again on the bond. "Two new faint tendrils. Cyrus's and Raphael's are glowing a little brighter than Gage's and Christian's." I open my eyes in time to watch Raphael pass out, and Cyrus is pale. "Is something wrong, Father?" Furrowing my brows, I grip Azrael's hands tightly.

A booming laugh escapes his lips as he throws his head back. "Not a damn thing is wrong Thana!" He hugs me tightly and kisses my cheek. "I'm gonna be a grandfather! This is fantastic news!" he says, then vanishes in a wisp of smoke.

My jaw drops. Raphael is waking up, and Cyrus is still pale. I didn't think a man with caramel skin could go pale, but here's Cyrus showing me it's possible. I mouth the word 'Grandfather,' then it hits me, and my hands fly to my abdomen. "Oh, fudge!" Panicked, I look over at Cyrus and he rushes over to me.

"It's okay, we've got this!" Cyrus looks back to the others and they nod along with him.

My eyes dart from mate to mate, then back to Cyrus. "Okay, we've got this." I take a deep breath. I know my mates have my back. We're going to be okay. I repeat it until it feels true. "I guess we have one heck of an announcement at the ball tonight, huh?" I kiss his forehead before standing up and walking back to the closet.

~Raphael~

I knew early this morning that Thana was pregnant, but her being able to sense the babies already drove it home. The question is, whose babies are they? I'm guessing by what she had said that they are mine and Cyrus's. She locked me and Cyrus within forty-eight hours of each other, so it's quite possible both of us will be dads. For now, I watch the closet door, trying to will Thana to appear so we can get this night over with. Christian darts over to the closet door and enters quickly, both Cyrus and I wait anxiously.

The Solstice Ball is presented to the humans as an event where the regional hospital benefactors come together for awards and donations. Much like the humans do for the politicians to raise money and awareness, though we do it to hide how we fund the hospitals. Only Angels and Nephilim from the local hospitals are invited to the awards banquets to keep the humans unaware of our world.

Eventually Thana emerges wearing a pale pink, empire waist gossamer gown. The surrounding material seems to move of its own volition, even when she's standing still. Her wolf pendant sits just above her ample chest, and I notice the dagger is even smaller now and is part of a bracelet around her left wrist. My sweet angel is armed to the teeth, and none will be the wiser. The car arrives sooner than expected and we rush out the front door to meet it. Gage is the first to enter, then Cyrus who promptly takes Thana's hand and helps her into the car. Christian and I enter last and close the door behind us. Thankfully, the ride is uneventful, and we get there only a few minutes later than we had planned. Thana fell asleep on the ride over with her head in Christian's lap. Gently he awakens her and assists her in getting her hair and makeup sorted. She does the most adorable yawn and stretch before signaling she's ready to exit the car. Christian and Gage exit first, then me. Reaching back into the car, I grip Thana's hand and steady her as she steps out. Hundreds of flashes go off at once as soon as she's visible. Gently, she waves at the crowd and tucks tightly into my side. I try to move forward, but she refuses to move till Cyrus has a firm grip on her hand to walk with us. Once we are within the building, Thana exhales, and then she laughs. "I know it's not good to hate things, but I could do without that welcoming party out front." Her lower lip sticks out in that adorable pout that makes my cock thicken. One bat of her long lashes has Cyrus and I stopping in our tracks to check her over.

"I'm okay, honestly guys, I just don't like being out of my nest right now." Her brows furrow as she looks between the four of us. The crux of her problem is her concern about being pregnant in public.

"We don't have to stay for the entire night. All things considered." Carefully, I place my hand on her stomach, cupping the area where the babies are.

Gage comes up on Thana's right side and kisses her cheek. "Anything you want, baby, I'll get it for you," he whispers in her ear, making her giggle.

The entrance to the hall is decorated with several species of ornamental flowers. Butterflies and songbirds fly freely around the interior, stopping at the perches on the tables. Thana gets a mischievous look in her eye as she grabs Cyrus's right arm, pulling up his coat sleeve and unbuttoning his dress shirt. The head of his raven is barely visible when Thana places her fingers on it. "Rise" is all she says, and the blackened wisp bursts into the air and his raven is free.

Slowly, she raises her left hand, and it lands carefully on her offered fingers. Her head turns as she raises her right arm and looks at her own raven. Uttering no words, her raven manifests and lands on her right hand. Smiling broadly, she walks with her head held high, holding both ravens. Stunned looks focus on her as her wings break free and flex behind her. Talks of her wings' coloring spread through the hall like wildfire. My mate is quickly learning to play the game, and we'll always be here to support her.

The guys and I look at each other and unfurl our wings, walking proudly behind our mate. For once in her life, she is owning who she is, and my heart swells with pride that I can witness this day. Without fear, she walks up to Uriel, who is presiding over the Solstice Ball, and she bows before him. Offering our bond to be the first to be judged is a power move on her part. I'm glad she took the suggestion I had offered her after Michael's visit. She glances between the ravens, and they return to their masters, becoming tattoos again.

Smiling, Uriel looks from Thana to us. "The first bond to be judged is Raphael's nest. Thana has offered herself and her mates to mine and Michael's first judgement." Uriel's words echo through the hall, causing everyone to fall silent and watch the first judgement.

Uriel motions to the pedestal to the right of his and Michael's seat and Thana moves there without hesitation. Cyrus and I walk forward and assist Thana kneeling on the pedestal. Once she's situated, we back away and watch what is about to happen. She places her hands on the rail before her and lowers her head to rest on her hands as instructed. Slowly she spreads her wings wide, having them stand behind her, tall and proud. As I look closer at our mate's wings, I notice silver veins on all the feathers. The light gray is almost iridescent, like my feathers. The black feathers appear to be velvet, like Cyrus's feathers.

Uriel's hands take on a white glow just before he places them on the crown of Thana's head. His eyes whiten and take on an ethereal glow as he searches for the bond. I feel him probe the bond through Thana's connection to me. He reaches out to each of us in turn, testing the strength of the bond. A brilliant smile crosses his normally stoic face as he looks down at Thana. "Lady Thana, please rise and receive my blessing," Uriel says in a soothing tone. Thana extends her hands out to Uriel, and he assists her in standing. A serene look crosses her face as she folds her wings to hang half open. Uriel bends forward and places his lips on her forehead, anointing her with his blessing, then stands up and raises both hands, silencing the crowd. "Raphael's nest has one of the strongest and purest bonds I have seen in many ages. We can only hope to achieve the oneness that they have." He gives Thana a quick wink and passes her back to us and motions to a table close to where he and Michael will judge the others.

Taking the hint, I move my family to the table indicated and we take our seats to enjoy the evening. "What did it feel like to you?" I say as I grip Thana's hand.

Her musical laughter and broad smile puts me at ease. "It was like a warmth spreading through me. He was looking for malice and corruption. This is how they plan to expose Joscelyn's bond peacefully. If they are worthy, they will be fine. If not, Cyrus and I will handle it." The peaceful tone she says it in doesn't match her blackened eyes when she mentions her and Cyrus handling it.

The matter-of-fact way Thana states it makes me believe there was much more involved than them just searching the bond. My bond-mates look from Thana to the stage and back again; they seem to suspect the same.

CHAPTER 31

THANA

It's nice to be at the ball and not be concerned about people trying to harm my mate because of his wing color. I take turns dancing with each of my mates and several of the Archangels. There's something that no one is telling me, and I'm determined to figure out what exactly everyone is up to. Like, for instance, I haven't been left alone for more than five minutes. The guys keep spacing out in the middle of conversations. Don't get me started on how they are watching me like hawks. Azrael is the next to take me dancing, and we move fluidly in silence. "I know something is going on, father," I say next to his ear not to draw attention to myself.

A barely audible chuckle escapes his lips as he presses his cheek to mine. "I figured you would, you're a smart woman. Your friend's bond is up next, and we believe there may be a Demon attack tonight to kidnap you." Azrael's blunt honesty is always as refreshing as it is terrifying.

"I see..." The words slip from my lips without hesitation.

I had a feeling something was brewing My skin is crawling. The music stops and we turn to see what is happening. Cyrus appears in a wisp of smoke at my side. "If you'll excuse us, father, we're needed up front." Azrael bows slightly, then kisses my cheek, releasing me into Cyrus's care. "Father updated you, I suspect?" His tone is playful as he tries to make the possible impending danger seem less.

Snuggling as close to Cyrus as I can, we walk back to our table to be close to the action. "Yes, I'm aware. I just hope Grandfather is correct that I can control the armies of Hell." Just as we make it back to the table, Raphael moves to flank my other side as a precaution.

The music changes, and Joscelyn and her mates line up at the end of the ornate carpet. The angelic guard stands at the end of the carpet and motions for them to proceed. Her mates nudge Joscelyn forward, and I can see the fear in every line of her body. Tears threaten to fall free. Her eyes dart from side to side, then lock with mine. I attempt to pull free from my mates when I see the level of distress my friend is in. Uriel's eyes land on me and he ever so slightly shakes his head no.

I understand now why exposing faults in their bond must be done this way. Uriel repeats his speech from earlier and it sounds like he's talking underwater compared to the pounding of my heart. His hands rest on the crown of her head and, unlike all the bonds before, his face contorts in rage. "To abuse and neglect a mate goes against angelic law. Females are a rare treasure, a gift." His voice booms, shaking the very foundation. Dust and pieces of plaster fall from the walls and ceiling.

The floor before him disperses, leaving Joscelyn's mates standing there almost defiantly. "She's ours to do with as we please!" Saul says, crossing his arms over his chest, almost daring Uriel to do something.

I look back at Gage and motion with my head for him to grab Joscelyn. The minute Gage makes contact with her, Saul and Jacob charge him. Uriel looks back at me and gives me a single nod. That's my signal. "Enough!" I yell, and my wings burst free from my back as I move between Gage and Joscelyn's mates.

Saul laughs as the Archangels take Joscelyn's other three mates prisoner. "What does a little mixed breed whore think she can do to me? I'm a Light Nephilim I can burn you to ash." His hand comes up, and I am bathed in holy light. It's warm and I feel like my skin may be turning a little pink.

My laughter catches him off guard and he stops the feed of light. "What can I do?" I smile sweetly as I take on my reaper persona, and I bring all of his nightmares to life. His greatest fear is witnessing the flesh melting off someone covered in thousands of spiders with snakes all around. Darkness whips wildly around me as I hover inches off of the ground. I float towards him. His screams are music to my ears as I weave his personal nightmare for him. At the height of his terror, I reach out with my taloned hands and grip his soul, ripping it free of its earthly bonds.

It takes me several moments before I return to my normal earthly form. Confidently, I stride over to Azrael and offer the liquid black mass that's swirling in my hand. "His soul is black as pitch, he belongs to you, father." My tone is devoid of emotion. My silver eyes rake over the other three, and a feral grin crosses my lips before I look back to Uriel and Michael.

"Judgement?" With a sweeping motion of my right hand, I point back to the last three mates standing.

"Death is the punishment for the abuse of a female. Send them to Hell." Michael says as he pulls Joscelyn to him.

Looking over my shoulder, I give Cyrus a nod and then Azrael as well. There's three of them and three of us. It makes work easier. No theatrics or being extra this time. We reach out at the same time and rip the souls from the men. I'll be honest, I'm tired and hungry. Two of the souls are blackened masses, the third is gray, not quite corrupted but riddled with guilt, probably because he didn't protect his mate. Whispers of corruption spread through the gathered guests. Most are shocked that Angels would abuse their mate. The most concerning of the whispers is the amount of fear sweeping the hall, the majority is frightened because of what I have done.

Christian is the first to notice my fatigue and rushes to my side and helps support me back to the table. Gage runs off to get some food and drink for me, while Cyrus and Azrael handle the souls. They have gathered Raphael with the other Archangels, talking to Joscelyn about what has happened and what the next steps are. It makes my heart hurt thinking about what she had gone through and how isolated her mates kept her to hide what they did. I mean, yeah, we texted back and forth, but it's not the same as how we used to be. I miss the sleepovers, movie nights and going for drinks. Maybe after some intensive therapy we can get back to how we used to be.

Soon as Cyrus can, he rejoins us at our table with his father in tow. "That was the most impressive reaping I have ever witnessed," Azrael says.

Shrugging my shoulders, I scoot over in my chair to lean against Cyrus. "It's how I've always done it, bring the fear and terror in their last moments." I raise my eyebrows and smile sweetly.

"Thana, we could see the horror-scape you put him in. It was terrifying, and fitting for the crimes he had committed," Raphael says as he comes to stand behind me and kisses the crown of my head. My eyebrows shoot up as I look between my mates and Azrael.

"He's right. We saw everything, every detail of the horror-scape you put him in. Your face melted off and spiders poured out of your eyes. Hundreds of snakes gathered at your feet, slithering towards him." Azrael tilts his head to the side, studying me. "Few reapers can do that. I'm honestly impressed." He points his glass in my direction, then raises it to his lips and sips from it.

Blushing, I turn away for a moment, then look back at him. "Thanks, dad." I reach out and take his free hand and give it a squeeze. Eventually, Raphael can remain at our table without having to leave to address other matters. His brilliant smile brightens the room and makes my heart pitter-patter a little faster.

"So, the part of the night where they announce the pregnancies is coming up. Who is going to go make the announcement?" I know who I want to send up there. I'm just curious to see who the guys pick to go.

The guys look at each other and start talking back and forth, trying to figure out who they want to send. Shaking my head, I stand up and lean on Christian's shoulders. "Might I make a suggestion?" I say softly and tilt my head to the side as I look down at Christian.

I watch the shifting expressions of my mates closely as they consider my subtle hint. "Let's do it," Gage says and beams. "Look at it this way. Christian goes up there and makes the announcement as an Angel in the nest. Everyone will assume the baby is his." Gage moves and places his hands on Raphael's and Cyrus's chairs. "If the actual fathers make the announcement, Thana becomes a bigger target." Gage's tactical thought process is sound and gives us the greatest chance at keeping me and the babies safe longer.

"Brilliant! I second Gage's plan," Azrael says as his eyes search the room.

My gut is telling me something isn't right. I still feel as on edge as when we first entered the ballroom. "Part of me wants to summon my grandfather. The other part thinks that may draw more attention to me than we need." I look between my mates before I crawl onto Raphael's lap.

The clinking of glass draws our attention back up to the podium where Michael and Uriel are sitting. Michael stands and raises his hands high above his head to focus everyone's attention on him. "It's time for nest updates. Please send one representative from each family up here." He returns to his chair and waits for the first family to approach.

Before Christian has the chance to stand up, I rush to his side and make sure his hair is perfect. Even though the top of his head isn't shaved, I help put his hair up into a traditional chonmage. Improvising, I remove the hair tie from my hair and use it to hold his topknot in place. Gently, I kiss the crown of his head and then move to stand before him and kiss his lips before sending him on his way. Proudly, he takes his place in the line and waits for his turn to be called forth. It takes several minutes between announcements before he gets his chance.

"Honored guests," Christian says, his accent still makes my heart beat a little faster. "I stand before you tonight to announce that our Tsuma," a soft laugh escapes Christian's lips, "Forgive please, I mean our mate is pregnant with our first child."

Cheers erupt around the hall, and the guys encourage me to stand. I wave like a princess on a float at everyone around us.

Time seems to move in slow motion as the glass around the hall explodes inward towards the guests. Before I can react, I am engulfed in Raphael's wings, and I can hear the glass shards bouncing off his feathers. Ear-splitting screeches fill the air, and the stench of sulfur fills the room. Azrael yells that Abishai have invaded the hall. Pushing free of Raphael's wings, I survey the scene before me. The Abishai look like gargoyles — thin, clawed reptilians with large, leathery, bat-like wings. Their tails whip around wildly behind them as they swoop and claw at the guests. "Thana, see if you can control them!" Azrael screams at me as his sword blazes to life to protect Joscelyn.

I look up at Raphael, and he gives me a single, firm nod. I search through the lessons Samael has taught me over the last few months, and I believe I know what to do. Flexing my wings, I allow my eyes to churn silver as my nails become long, sharp claws. I assume my reaper form and draw on all the darkness within the room, and it causes the Abishai to focus on me. "Return to your territory. You are not welcome here." My voice echoes in the hall, the tone sounds feral and haunted. They screech at me, their cries mixing in with those of the other guests in the room. One brave red one flies straight for me. Crimson ichor drips from his lips, and blood from another victim covers his curved claws. Fragments of flesh dangle freely from its talons.

Instinctually, I hold a hand out before me, and a mass of blackened fluid flies from my hand, impacting the creature, reducing it to ooze. As soon as the other creatures see that I've destroyed one of their own, they halt their attacks and hover in the air. "Samael, I summon thee," I say with a force I was unaware I possessed.

Within seconds, Samael, in all of his glory, stands before me in his armor with his sword burning with hell fire. A single wave of his hand, a portal opens in the middle of the hall. The hellscape beyond is foreboding, with more winged devils flying around. "Return!" I yell, and the creatures pour through the portal without hesitation. I'm not sure if they're more frightened of me or my grandfather at the moment. Either way, we returned them to where they belong with minimal damage to my family sustained. The rest of the guests weren't so lucky. Most are not warriors by nature and sustained some semblance of injury. Thankfully, there are no deaths reported this time. The healers are working overtime to patch up those that were injured during the attack.

Shifting back to my normal form is not as tiring as it was the last time. Perhaps, with practice, it will be easier every time. "You did good, descendant," Samael says proudly as he draws me in for a hug.

We really didn't want society to know who my grandfather was. I guess the cat is out of the bag now. Most of the guests watch us in stunned silence, taking in the scene before them. Michael and Uriel approach and congratulate us on ending the attack so quickly. "Your next lesson, Thana, is the creation of portals. Good call on summoning me here to assist," Samael says, more for my benefit than everyone else.

I simply nod my head at him, then look over to Michael and Uriel. "Thank you Samael, for arriving so swiftly," Michael says, the tension in the air is thick enough you can cut it with a knife.

A deep, almost feral growl escapes Samael's lips as he curls them back to expose canines. "Blood of my blood summoned me, and you know I cannot ignore its calling." Looking between Michael and Samael, I get the feeling there's an old, unsettled beef between them. I hug my grandfather tightly, then move back towards my mates.

I still have that feeling that something isn't right, and the hairs on my arms are still standing on edge.

"What's wrong, Thana?" Gage asks as he wraps his thick arms around me, pulling me flush to his firm chest.

"Remember, I said something feels off before and then we were attacked?" Gage gets my other mate's attention.

"The feeling hasn't subsided. It hasn't even dulled in the slightest." Slowly I run my hands over my familiars, all three of them feel like they want to rip free of my flesh. It reminds me of the feeling I had in the shadow realm when they set themselves free. My eyes bleed silver as I study the interior of the ballroom. Nothing seems out of place at the moment, but it still doesn't feel right. "Can we leave?" I turn to face my mates so they can see how uneasy this whole situation is making me.

My mates spring into action and gather our belongings at record speed. "It's best to listen to her warnings. Females, especially pregnant females, can sense danger before we do," Michael says, letting his authority wash over us in an all-consuming wave. My familiars bristle at the feel of his power. Cyrus and I look at each other briefly and roll our eyes at the unneeded power flex on Michael's part.

We say our goodbyes and head towards the door. My grandfather and Azrael accompany us to our limo and ride home with us just to be safe. The further away from the ballroom we get, the more I can relax, that foreboding feeling easing as the miles tick by. I inch my way across the seat and crawl into Cyrus's lap and rest my head on his shoulder. As I settle in, the guys mention that Uriel has taken Joscelyn to the Angelic Realm to get her the help she needs. I start to question them about seeing her, and I get shot down immediately. The biggest concern that they and Uriel have is if she's mentally stable, and how much damage those mates of hers have done. I wrap my arms tightly around Cyrus's arm and hold on tight, listening to the guys deduce the next steps. A yawn escapes my lips as my eyes become heavy, between Cyrus's body heat and the rocking of the car I'm losing the battle to stay awake. Sleep comes quickly for me. Hopefully, I'll wake up safe and sound.

RAPHAEL

Watching my sweet angel sleep in Cyrus's arms almost makes me jealous. I understand that because of who her grandfather is and how she raised herself that she feels more dark than light. I'm hoping the trip to the Angelic Realm tomorrow for her training with Sigrun and the other Valkyrie is fruitful. Thankfully, it's an uneventful ride home, maneuvering a sleeping Thana into the house is going to be interesting.

"Allow me." Samael smirks as he looks between me and Cyrus. With a wave of his hand, he lifts Cyrus and Thana up as if they weigh nothing and float them into our home. The clunking of Samael's boots echoes through the house. The sound is more ominous than the usual joyful sound of someone coming home. I'm uncomfortable with allowing Samael into Thana's inner sanctum. After all, it's her private space. Gage and Christian seem perfectly fine, leading him right into the heart of our home.

As they step into Thana's nest, she starts to stir and almost thrash within Cyrus's arms. A blood-curdling scream escapes her lips as she breaks free of his grasp. Fenrir and the cat rip free from her forearms and leap headfirst into her nest. The cat that used to be the size of a house cat is now the size of a panther. Thana's familiars are chasing something within the nest, causing the blankets and pillows to fly everywhere. A small Chasme breaks free of the blankets and buzzes around the room. It looks more like a gigantic demonic fly with what looks like a spear for a nose. The rhythm of its beating wings starts, causing Gage to get sleepy.

"It was sent here to kill Thana and drain her of her blood." Samael and I draw our swords, ready to attack, when Thana raises her hands and spreads her wings. The tone that escapes her lips is one that I have never heard before. By the look on Samael's, Cyrus, and Azrael's faces is something from the shadow realm. Thana's wings vibrate as the tone she's creating becomes louder. The Chasme lands close to her and lowers its head in submission.

Immediately Thana is flanked by Fenrir and her panther, both growling low in their throats, facing off with the creature. "Shhh, my precious." Thana says softly as she strokes the backs of her familiars. "He has information he can tell us, like who his master is." Thana's tone chills me to the bone, and the feral expression on her face is one I am unfamiliar with. I watch her approach the creature and extend a taloned hand out towards it. The closer her hand gets, the more darkness swirls within her palm. Her eyes become solid silver orbs that pulse with unfathomable power. Everything seems to move in slow motion until her hand contacts the creature's head. "Is the name Abaddon familiar to anyone?" She sounds detached, almost hollow, as she fishes around in the creature's head.

Samael and I look at each other, then over to Azrael. Abaddon is a name none of us have heard spoken in a very long time. He was another for the longest time that was considered a neutral in the alignment of Heaven and Hell. Something has caused him to pick a side, and I'm not sure why. I can see the gears turning in Samael's head as his eyes flicker from black to silver, then back again. Just as Samael is preparing to speak, Thana reaches out and snaps the neck of the Chasme, letting the body hit the floor before her. "He chose Lucifer because he promised him a queen to rule at his side." Darkness whips wildly through Thana's hair until Christian places a hand on her shoulder.

"Lucifer promised him a queen?" Christian tilts his head to the side. Thana curls into his side and holds on tightly. "He was promised me." She narrows her eyes and looks at each of us in turn. I can see the rage that is bubbling to the surface. Her hand slides to her stomach, and she cups where I assume she thinks the babies are resting. "I will burn this world to the ground to protect myself and the babies." Thana looks to us, and then to her grandfather and Azrael. "We need to train and then find a safe place for me to give birth when the time comes."

Thana's thought process strikes home. How will we keep her safe later in the pregnancy and during birth? Samael moves to the center of the room and starts pacing. "She won't be safe in the Shadow Realm to give birth, the demons have too much access to that plane."

"We can't bring her to the Angelic Realm. Cyrus can't go there and witness the birth of his child. His child may not survive the birth process there either," I say as I run my fingers through my hair, frustrated with the issues that we are facing.

Lithe fingers thread through my hair and turn my head in her direction. "Be at peace Raph. We will train, and when the time comes, I will summon the Valkyrie to stand guard. No one will get past them," Thana says with conviction. She turns her gaze towards Azrael, Cyrus, and Samael. "You need to train hard Cy. Go with your father and my grandfather. See if there're more familiars we can have to help protect us." Thana releases me then runs to Cyrus, jumping into his arms. They hug tightly before Cyrus leaves with his father and Samael.

"We should go back to the tree of life so you can train, Thana," I suggest softly, not wanting to anger my pregnant mate. I can see the gears turning in her head as she looks between Christian and Gage, then back to me.

"Can everyone go? I don't want to leave Christian and Gage

behind this time." Thana says with a pout as she looks up at me. "Please Raph?" She wraps her arms around my waist. She knows exactly what to do to get me to bend to her will.

Shaking my head slowly, I bend down and kiss the crown of her head. "Of course, with Cyrus in the shadow realm training, it is best for all of us to go together." I barely have the sentence out, and Thana releases me like a hot potato and goes running for the balcony doors. Her wings unfurl at record speed as she shoves the doors open and leaps off the balcony. The guys and I give chase as she uses her much larger wingspan to her advantage. Gage's are similar in size and shape to Thana's, and he speeds ahead to catch up with our wayward mate. Christian and I can't help but laugh at Thana's enthusiasm about returning to the Angelic Realm.

~Thana~

Bursting through the clouds feels like a cool mist upon my skin. I don't bother to land, instead I continue to the tree of life to seek out the Valkyrie. Darting in and out of random clouds, I cover the distance to the tree much faster than expected. Standing under the tree is an Archangel I have not seen before. The man is a mammoth, and he is heavily armored, denoting he has a very important duty. I land not far away and approach hesitantly, seeing that Sigrun is in conversation with the Angel before me. "Thana! I'm glad to see you here! I have someone I'd like to introduce you to," Sigrun says, closing the distance between us.

The man turns, and he is the most beautiful man I have ever seen in my entire life. His hair is as golden as the first rays of the morning and his eyes are as blue as the clearest sky. I study his features, and his wings twitch behind him. I continue to study him—I can't make myself look away.

"Thana, I'm glad we caught up!" I hear Raphael's voice as if he's underwater. "Lord Metatron, forgive us," Raphael says, and it breaks me from the spell that I'm under.

Quickly, I lower my eyes and drop to a knee before him. I spread my wings out wide and lower my head to rest on my hands on my raised knee. Crap on a cracker. I just ogled one of the highest-ranking Archangels like he was a male model. My breathing is erratic as I try to get my racing heart under control.

"Ah, so this is your lovely mate. Please stand, Lady Thana." His large hand comes into view, and the minute we make contact an electric current runs through my body like a live wire. I whip my head up and his eyes are pure gold orbs staring back at me. I know this feeling, this can't be happening.

"No no no no..." I say as I pull my hand away and scoot backward as fast as I can. Metatron is still standing there, staring at his hand in disbelief. Sigrun is the only person thinking straight, and she comes to my side to help me stand up. I look panicked between my mates and, apparently, mate number five. "I can't do this... Not now..." I use my hands to hide my face momentarily, it's all too much too soon to deal with.

"Come with me Thana. Girls only!" Sigrun's voice carries an unquestionable authority. The guys pause in their discussion and Sigrun leads me off to lord knows where.

We get far enough away, and she stops and spins me to face her. "What happened?" Her tone softens just for me as she looks around, making sure the coast is clear.

Looking down at my left hand, I stare at it like the traitor it is. "He's my mate too." The words fall from my lips, and I sigh, trying to keep from crying. It's not like the tears are going to change what just happened

"Ah, the wing thing... Stupid Angel mating ritual. Valkyrie choose only the strongest males to be our mates. We're not peacocks where pretty feathers matter, we need strength and power to produce the strongest daughters," she says, pounding her fist against the armor on her chest.

I can't help but laugh at Sigrun's actions. We walk down the path away from the others and out of sight. The other Valkyries sit gathered by a fire talking. "Sisters! Look who has come to join us!" Sigrun's excitement is contagious.

The other Valkyrie jump up and come over to introduce themselves to me. I have never felt like I belonged ever in my life. This new and exciting development has my heart pounding. I'm ecstatic! I have sisters! We play pass the Thana between the Valkyrie sisters. Everyone takes turns hugging me and welcoming me into the family.

"Talk to us Thana. Why would you refuse a fifth powerful mate?" Sigrun and her sister, who introduces herself as Brynhild, say in unison. Their combined power pulses over me like a warm blanket comforting me.

Flexing and spreading my wings, I motion to the color of my feathers. "I need balance within the bond. I have three light and one dark. Raphael and Cyrus are powerful and balance each other out well. To add another powerful Archangel to the bond will shift the power too much in one direction." I word vomit the information and sigh. I drop my head into my hands as the guilt overwhelms me.

A slender, powerful arm wraps around my shoulders and pulls me towards it. "Did you ever think it's because when you reach your full potential, you may be stronger than all of your light mates combined?" Sigrun says softly near my ear, just for me to hear.

Shaking my head, I look away, unable to face her. The possibility of her being correct almost haunts my thoughts. What if this is the plan for me? What if I have no choice in this

matter? What would happen if my death killed two Archangels instead of one? Too many questions flood my mind, and when I look back the Valkyrie are gone, and they left Gage sitting where Sigrun was standing.

"My love, please talk to me." The rasp of Gage's voice does funny things to my insides. How can I deny his request when, over the last six months, this is the most he's been able to speak?

Climbing into his lap, I rest my head on his shoulder, feeling as if the weight of the world is pressing down on me. Gages talented fingers massage as he tries to comfort me. "I know I shouldn't have run off, and it's probably the happiest day of his life." I heave a heavy sigh as emotions wage war within me.

"I'm afraid of causing the balance to shift and that it may harm or kill me and the babies. Too much light will poison me, too much darkness will harm you and the others." Wrapping my arms tightly around Gage, I hug him, hoping that holding on tightly will solve everything.

"What should I do, Gage? What should I do?" I ask between deep breaths as I hold him tightly, like I did with my teddy bear when I was little.

He kisses my cheek and forces me to lift my head to face him. "The Thana I know is a powerful female. One who has survived horrors most would be destroyed by." His radiant smile distracts me from my fear and turmoil.

"My mate." He points to himself, beaming with pride. "Loves with her whole heart, and I know she has room to let others in." Gently, he kisses my lips, and I lean into it. His love pours through the bond like a tidal wave washing over me, wave after wave.

I guess it's time to pull up my big girl pants and face the music. I have a fifth mate and I honestly don't know how I feel about it. "Let's head home, we'll have a family meeting and discuss what's happened and what it means for our family." I reach out through the bond to Christian and Raphael and let them know the plan.

They agree with how I want to handle this. I'm not completely rejecting him. But I really don't know what to think about everything at the moment. Winking at Gage, I unfurl my wings and trust-fall through the clouds. When I break through the other-side, I continue to free fall like a falling star. Through the bond, I feel my mates racing to catch up to me. At the very last second, before hitting terminal velocity, I spread my wings wide and almost stop my descent. I glance over my shoulder to see where my mates are, and my heart sinks. Metatron is with them. This is going to prove to be an awkward evening.

CHAPTER 33

THANA

I make it home first and land on the third-floor balcony. Shoving the double doors open, I rush into the house and head straight to my nest. Once in my safe place, I summon my familiars. I'm honestly in a panic. What am I supposed to do? Fenrir and my panther prowl my room, restlessly searching the room for anything out of place. Not long after they finish their search, we hear the balcony doors open and close. I can hear four sets of footsteps heading down the hall, past my nest, and down the stairs.

Unexpectantly Cyrus and Azrael manifest in my nest and I have to call my familiars off immediately. "Wow! Settle down, Kitten, what's got your feathers on edge?" Cyrus says as he walks towards me with his hands up in a placating manner.

I get ready to word vomit the events of my trip to the Angelic Realm, but instead choose to show him. "I need to show you." I move to stand before Cyrus and rest my palms on his freshly shaven cheeks. My eyes blacken almost immediately and his follow suit. The highlights of the events pass between us as we share a single consciousness for several moments. Cyrus's face changes expression several times before he finally pulls away.

My dark knight paces the room, working through whatever is on his mind. "So..." He holds his hands out in front of him several times, starting and stopping, acting like he's going to say something, then changes his mind. "Okay... So... Metatron is your fifth mate?" He stops and raises an eyebrow, looking for confirmation.

I lower my head, unable to keep eye contact with him. Cyrus has been my most difficult mate to have a relationship with. The idea that this event may destroy what we've repaired has my stomach in knots and my chest constricting. Several knocks sound at the door, and Azrael moves in my peripheral to go answer it. My other three mates enter and look at my familiars standing close by, watching over me. Cyrus shoves the guys out into the hall, and I can hear their raised voices within my nest.

Azrael walks over and sweeps me up in his arms and simply hugs me. His gentle, fatherly embrace soothes some of my nerves. He and I have come a long way since the trials. For hundreds of years, I felt like I was treated like a stain on society. Now I have mates, a father figure, and my grandfather in my life that make me feel what love is.

"Shh, little one, as long as you and the babies are fine, everything else can be fixed or disposed of," Azrael says, trying to be comforting in his special homicidal way.

Pulling away slightly, I look him in the eyes. "I know, but another Angel? Cyrus and I may get hurt by all the light in the bond." Furrowing my brows, I move away and start pacing again. "When they took Cyrus, remember how sick I got?" I force myself to utter the words I've buried deep in my heart. Azrael nods, and I hear the click of the door opening. Shaking my head, I walk to the double doors and look out across the valley.

"I remember all too well, little one. I remember how broken you looked when I told you Cyrus should have been with you all that time." A soft chuckle escapes Azrael's lips. "I also remember the determination on your face the moment you realized you were enough to save him." Large, warm hands gently grip my shoulders and turn me to face him. Azrael smiles as he looks down at me. "I was never easy on you because I was afraid of you Thana." Azrael's eyes blacken as he stares at me, letting his statement sink in.

The literal Angel of Death was, or possibly is, frightened of me? That cannot be. "There's no way you were afraid of me. You were the scariest man I've ever known." I furrow my brows as I search Azrael's face.

A smirk plays on his lips. "It has always been my job to protect you. If I had to make you frightened of me to do it, then so be it." He presses his lips to my forehead, then vanishes in a wisp of smoke.

I'm left standing there with one hell of an information bomb that was dropped in my lap. Slowly, I raise my eyes to look at my mates, and I sigh. I'm not sure how much they heard or what their thoughts are at this very moment. I turn my back on them and walk out onto the balcony to sit in my favorite chair. There're three truths that I know. The first, I'm much stronger than I realize. The second, everything that's been done over the last few centuries has been done to protect me. The final truth is a bitter pill to swallow. I have a fifth mate.

~Christian~

We watch Thana head outside with her familiars in tow. She's a swirling ball of emotions and it feels like a maelstrom in the bond. I've spent the better half of the last hour explaining to Metatron that it's not him and it's Thana's fear. Seeing my best friend and mate suffering because she's afraid of getting sick again is difficult. The fear is understandable. She almost died because of too much light in the bond without Cyrus.

"What can I do to help?" The bass in Metatron's voice draws me out of my inner monologue.

"All we can ask is for you to be patient with Thana. She's been through a lot, your holiness." I drop into a deep bow out of respect for the highest-ranking Archangel.

"We are brothers now, Christian, no further need for titles between us. Treat me no differently than you do, Raphael." Metatron's face brightens, and he radiates joy. "What food does our mate like? I would like the privilege of providing for her tonight." Excitedly, he looks around the room to each of us in turn.

"She loves the Tom Yum soup from the Thai restaurant near the hospital." Raphael offers.

"There's a corner stand close to here that does the traditional braised pork belly she loves," I add after Raphael.

"We can't forget the chicken shawarma from the cafe on Market Street." Cyrus says as he stares at his phone.

Gage laughs. "May as well throw in her love for barbecue ribs while we're at it."

Metatron makes note of all the different foods that the guys and I have mentioned. Staring at his list, several emotions flicker over his visage. "So, Thana likes a little bit of everything? Am I correct?" You can tell that he's trying to be the best potential mate that he can.

"That is correct, I can assist you if you wish?" I'm not sure how much of the area he's familiar with and it's going to be an interesting journey.

Nodding his head, a brilliant smile graces his lips. "That would be much appreciated. If someone could set the table, we will be back as soon as possible." Metatron says, yet no one moves. Raising a brow, he looks at the four of us.

Raphael gives us a single nod, and we divide. Cyrus goes out onto the balcony to watch over Thana. Gage heads to the kitchen, leaving Raphael with us. "Sorry brother, in a nest the first mate organizes the family duties," Raphael states gently but with authority.

Both of Metatron's eyebrows shoot up, and he laughs softly. "This will take some getting used to, brother. With your permission I would like to provide a dinner for our mate and nest." Metatron bows to Raphael, acknowledging his status in the family.

Raphael extends his hand to Metatron, and they clasp forearms and shake. "She loves her food, so that would be an excellent way to get into her good graces." Raphael smiles and leaves the room shortly after.

"Want to get going?" I ask Metatron and motion towards the

door. He nods and follows me downstairs and out into the street. We get into my car and head into the city. I watch him out of the corner of my eye, staring at the scenery.

"Their lives fascinate me," Metatron says, watching the people going about their day. He looks back over at me, smiling, then motions to the world around him. "All this amazes me. They go through life not knowing what we are." He looks back out the window as we pass the park. A soft sigh escapes his lips as we pull up to our first stop.

I get out of the car and head towards the shawarma place. Metatron catches up and walks beside me into the restaurant. "Everything smells so delicious!" he says enthusiastically as he stares up at the menu.

I step up to the counter and place the order for the chicken shawarma and a few side dishes I know Thana likes. Metatron listens and makes notes of everything that I order. Before I can hand my credit card over, he passes his to the man behind the counter.

"I wish to provide for our woman," he says low enough just for me to hear. I nod tersely at him before grabbing our bag and heading back to the car. "Have you known Thana long?" His question makes me pause and put the car back into park.

"A little over two hundred and ninety years, give or take a decade or two." I chuckle.

Metatron looks back out the window, deep in thought, then back over to me. "What's she like?" He pauses for a moment. "What I mean is that you've known her for a decent amount of time. What's her favorite thing in the world?" His question makes me stop and really think.

"It's been many things over the last few years. That blacked out challenger out in front of the house is her hellcat. She loves that car to death." I laugh as I pull back out into traffic, heading towards the Thai restaurant next. "We can hear her car from several blocks away when she drives it. Thana doesn't take it out as much as she used to because she can fly now." Shrugging my shoulders, I fall silent for a few minutes. "She's excited about the babies that are coming." My mouth quirks up in a goofy smile, thinking about the little ones fluttering around the house.

"Your nest is blessed beyond measure to conceive so soon into the bond. Many of the newly formed nests are not blessed with infants till much further into the relationship." His voice takes on a wistful tone as he stares at the sky through the sunroof.

"Thana loves children, give her time. One day I'm sure you'll have a child of your own." I say with confidence, thinking about how loving and giving my mate is.

"She seemed very distressed by my arrival." His shoulders slump, and he hangs his head.

My brow furrows as I ponder how exactly to explain my assessment of Thana's reaction. "The bond hasn't always been solid. Cyrus can be a royal pain in the neck at times. He's very difficult and hard to read." I rub my chin with my free hand, trying not to worry or stress Metatron out more than I have to.

"Cyrus has broken Thana's heart multiple times over the last six months because he didn't know how to let anyone in." Biting my bottom lip, I chew on its plumpness as I ponder what to say next. "The short version is. It's not you. She has past issues and damage to work through not only from Cyrus, but from what her father had done." I'm not sure how much of her past Thana wants a stranger in the bond to know, but I feel it will only help.

Metatron raises his right eyebrow and tilts his head to the side, looking at me. "So, daddy issues and Dark Nephilim issues?" He hits the nail on the head and all I can do is just nod and agree with him.

"Time heals all wounds. I've waited since the beginning of time for a mate. She has all the time in the world as far as I'm concerned," he states with such finality, I can't argue with his reasoning. Two more stops and we can head home and set up the surprise feast for Thana. I hope this earns him some brownie points.

CHAPTER 34
RAPHAEL

I can only hope that Christian and Metatron come up with a good idea of how to get Thana to accept him. I'd hate to think that the Almighty's protector was angry at our bond really wouldn't bode well for us. Cyrus is still being a dick and pulling pranks on Gage and stealing Thana's cookies like he used to.

Right now, I'm watching them flying around like a bunch of children playing sky paintball. Even as an innocent bystander, I have been hit no less than thirty times, either by accident or on purpose by Thana. Sadly, Gage has decided to get in on the game and I seem to be the only adult left in the house.

Rolling my eyes, I head back in and take a fast shower. As I exit the shower, I hear the chimes through the house that the front door has been opened. I hurry out of my room and look over the rail down to the first floor. Christian and Metatron walk into the house with several bags of food a piece. Leaping over the rail, I unfurl my wings and glide to the first floor. "Need any help, guys?" I ask as I take a few bags from Christian.

"Of course, that would be awesome," Christian replies with a smile, heading towards the dining room to set up. I follow behind

Christian as we weave through the house, avoiding the rooms with the windows facing where the others are playing.

"I hope we bought enough food," Metatron says as he pulls containers out of the bags and spreads them out on the table.

"Looks like you guys bought out half of downtown." I'm only half joking as I set the placemats and plates out on the table.

Metatron gets an unreadable look on his face as he slowly turns away from the table. "I just want to do right by our female... I'm new at this. Maybe I should just go home," he says, turning towards the front door.

Thana manifests out of literally nowhere and places a hand on his shoulder, stopping him almost instantly. "I..." Thana's brows furrow and she paces the dining room.

She suddenly comes to a stop in front of him and looks up. "You remind me of a giant teddy bear." Narrowing her eyes, she studies him up close. Metatron stops breathing the closer Thana gets to him. Her eyes bleed silver as she looks up at him.

"Your aura is pure light pulsing in waves, like thousands of stars dancing together." The most serene look crosses both Thana's and Metatron's faces. His eyes turn golden as he looks down at her.

"Little one, your life force is an enigma. Darkness and light swirl and embrace each other, wrapping together like a candy cane." Metatron boldly reaches out towards Thana. Just before his hand contacts her flesh, she vanishes in a wisp of shadow.

I search the room, puzzled by her disappearance. Cyrus is leaning against the counter, laughing at us. "Heh, can't even keep track of our little mate huh, Golden Boy?" The rasp in Cyrus's voice grates on my very last nerve when he's in wise ass mode.

"Obviously, you know something I don't?" I almost growl out the sentence, letting the little imp get the best of me again.

Cyrus leans back and I notice his hair doesn't move on the one side of his head and he motions with his eyes to his left shoulder. "Our beautiful mate is kind of in the same place emotionally where I was a couple of months ago. So, if you don't mind, Goldie, back off a little and let Thana adjust in her own time." The bass in Cyrus's voice makes several of the cups in the china closet rattle. It's a recent development for him as he tries to play it off like he knew it would happen.

Thana finally manifests behind Cyrus, sitting on the countertop, looking at all of us and the food that was purchased. "I'm sorry if I seem to be difficult at the moment. I've been attacked more times than I would like to count in my relatively short lifespan." Thana slides down off the counter and curls into Cyrus's side.

"Only recently has it been Dark Nephilim and demons." For a moment she looks down and away sadly. "Previously it was Angels and Light Nephilim calling me an abomination and wanting to destroy me."

Thana moves slowly around the room till she's at Christian's side. "Besides Joscelyn and Mark, Christian has been my best friend for the last almost three hundred years." She gently cups his face and kisses his cheek before moving to my side.

"Now not only was Raph my unattainable boss, but he is also the sexy older man that's totally taboo." Thana waggles her eyebrows looking at me. "Only you guys know how old you really are, compared to my three hundred and seventy something years. I'm a baby in comparison."

Double blinking, I take in what Thana said, and it hits hard. My age has never been a topic of conversation before. Metatron, who is older than I am, pales as Thana mentions ages.

Still giggling, Thana goes and stands before Cyrus. "Cy and Gage are closest in age to me. Both of my bad boys know just what to do to keep me on my toes." Gage and Cyrus high five and laugh as Thana turns on us again.

"So many nights I prayed to be saved from my own personal hell." She moves to stand within touching distance of Metatron as tears freely run down her cheeks.

"You are His voice, His recorder," she says passionately. "You know all, yet I was allowed to suffer alone." She shakes her head side to side slowly.

"You possess the Merkabah cube, you could have interceded on my behalf." Her voice cracks as she mentions the cube. For one so young, I didn't think she would know of its existence.

Metatron pales, looking at Thana, then back at me. His mouth opens and closes several times before he looks at Thana. "You must forgive me, precious one. They did not permit me to interfere with the affairs of the Nephilim. That changes today!" His eyes bleed golden as he stares down at her. He looks up at me briefly, then vanishes in a wisp of golden glitter.

Thana looks around the room quickly, then lowers her head. I move close and open my arms to her. She lifts her head briefly, then rushes to me. Her arms wrap tightly around my waist, and her forehead is buried in my pecs. Threading my fingers through her hair, I try my best to soothe her. My nest mates finish setting the table, and I bend down to pick her up. Carefully, I carry her to the table and sit in my seat. Gage makes me a plate that I can share with Thana. It takes Cyrus and me to manipulate Thana so that we can sit.

Tension rolls off of Thana like waves in the ocean. Holding on tightly, I feel the stress course through her body. She's hiding in my arms, with her face now buried against my neck. Looking up, I can see the rage twisting in Cyrus's features as the events that led up to Thana stressing out pisses him off further.

"What the actual fuck, dude! He knew and did nothing!" Cyrus screams at the top of his lungs and his wings burst free bleeding shadows. He's standing in the dining room mid-shift and honestly, I don't think he's aware of his current state.

"There're things in the Angelic Realm that not everyone is privy to," Christian says, trying to quell Cyrus's blossoming rage.

"Fuck that! She's a female!" Cyrus says as he jabs his clawed hand in mine and Thana's direction. "Females are rare, hell He knows I'm a fuckup, but she never deserved what they forced her to endure before us." Cyrus's rage has apparently drawn his father's attention. Azrael stands silently, taking in his son's tirade before speaking.

"Be careful, son. Even though all you speak of is true. One can mistakenly take that as possibly attempting another uprising." Azrael approaches Cyrus and gives him a brief hug. "I'm proud of the male you are becoming, son," Azrael says, sitting next to me.

"Daughter?" Azrael says softly near Thana's ear. Her trembles slow down, and eventually she raises her head to look at him. "Everything is not as easy as it seems. In all the millennium I have lived. It is truly rare that Metatron and his twin are allowed to interfere in Nephilim affairs."

Ever so slowly, Thana raises her head and looks at Azrael. Blood tears stain her cheeks and my shirt. The crimson streaks catch all of us off guard. "Thank you, Cy, for trying to defend me," Thana says, then sniffles. "I have a lot to think about. I will not fault Metatron for the restraints that were placed on him. He will have to earn his place." Melancholy is all we feel through the bond from her, and she looks like a hollow shell of herself.

Gage moves to sit next to us and offers Thana food, trying to draw her out of the funk she's in. Eventually, she moves from my lap to sit on Cyrus's and buries her face against his throat. Her wings burst free from her back, and she cocoons herself and Cyrus. Azrael motions for the rest of us to follow him out onto the balcony. Once outside, he sighs and shakes his head. "I am not proud to admit that I was among the ones that made her life difficult. She was a threat to everything I held as truth all these years." Azrael paces the balcony.

"What do you mean, she was a threat?" His statement puzzles me more than anything.

Azrael runs his hand down his face, then sighs. "Being of mixed lineage, we didn't expect her to have any ability worth mentioning. It shocked me when she had a talent for light and dark powers. Other than Samael, none ever possessed both life and death." Azrael shrugs his shoulders. "Lucifer is gunning for her big time. He wants to make her his." Azrael's tone sounds defeated. He looks up at me, then in the direction of his son, and forces a smile.

"I didn't think I would live to see the day that he would ever love someone other than himself. He must protect her fiercely," Azrael says, removing a pair of black orbs from his robes. "They can only use these at night or in the shadow realm. They feed off of darkness and will be quite fearsome." He sets the two orbs on the table, then vanishes in a wisp of smoke.

Thana must have felt the disturbance in the shadows, and slowly comes out onto the balcony. The orbs pulse with darkness, the one closest to Thana reaches towards her. She tilts her head to the side, studying it. Cyrus soon joins her on the balcony and studies the orbs as well. "Father left these?" Cyrus asks as he moves closer to the orbs on the table.

"He did." I watch how Thana studies the orbs.

Her gunmetal-gray eyes fall to the cat on her forearm and it rises from her flesh. The black cat leaps onto the table and touches the left orb with its nose. A soft smile plays upon Thana's lips as she reaches out and picks up the orb. The level of concentration on her face is impressive. "It's a new familiar, more powerful than the ones I already have." Thana's laughter is musical as she smiles at the orb.

"What's so funny, Thana?" Cyrus says as he goes to pick up his orb, but it burns him on contact. "What the hell?" Cyrus looks at his scorched hand, then over at Thana.

"Oops, I grabbed the wrong one." Thana offers Cyrus the one in her hand and he takes it swiftly, and this time without injury. Thana hovers her hand over the other orb, and it lifts into her palm. Her eyes churn silver as she stares at the swirling black mass. "Hello beautiful, rise." Thana whispers to the orb and it cracks open, and she offers her left arm to it. The mass slithers up her arm as if it's alive, then settles on her shoulder. When the smoke settles, the imprint of a dragon rests there. I move to her side and look down the back of her top and see the main part of the dragon's body is on her back.

I watch Thana for several seconds more as she studies her new familiar. Her focus moves to Cyrus and the orb in his hand. A smirk plays upon her lips as her index finger reaches out to touch his orb. "Rise..." she says with force, and the glass orb shatters at her command.

I glance at the other mates, and we are all just as shocked at the orb's reaction to Thana's command. The inky blackness slithers along Cyrus's arm and stops on his bicep. It takes the shape of a black phoenix mid-scream in flight. Thana ghosts her hand over the new familiar and smiles. "It's dark enough little one. Come out and play." Her pause between sentences sounds loving as she speaks to Cyrus's new familiar.

The shadow begins to culminate around Cyrus and the Phoenix bursts free into the evening sky. It's a being of nightmares, and its dark frame blackens the sky. The only person on the balcony not shocked is Thana. Eventually, she extends her left arm and the giant phoenix flies right at her. Just before it gets too close, it shrinks in size, then perches on her forearm. Her fingers drift over the smokey feathers as she looks the familiar over. "She's beautiful, Cyrus, she'll serve you well." Thana kisses the phoenix on the side of its head, sending it back to Cyrus.

Thana's right hand comes up and touches her new familiar. "Be small, and rise." Her shirt fills out and movement catches my eyes. We watch intently as a small black skull dragon emerges from under her shirt.

Looking closely at the dragon it reminds me of the description Thana read out of one of her romance books. I believe the guard's name was Marco or Marcus something like that. It gently nuzzles the side of Thana's face, then lies across her shoulders. "Meet Maelestor Rex, I'll call him Rex for short." The little dragon blows fire at the mention of his name. He then raises his head and puts his mouth near Thana's ear speaking to her, I think. She smirks and starts to laugh. "Okay, that's our secret." She leans her head closer to the dragon.

"What did he say?" Cyrus asks impatiently.

Thana starts laughing again. "Cy? What part of secret do you not understand?" Thana winks at Cyrus and pets the dragon, returning it to the tattoo. "I'm going to bed. Love you guys."

We watch Thana go back towards the table and grab several ribs off of the plate, then head out of sight. The guys and I finish eating and pack up whatever is left over. Tomorrow is Thana's first imaging at the OB-GYN.

CHAPTER 35
THANA

Why does morning have to start so blasted early? The guys have already left the nest and I see a bag packed by the door. Thankfully the doctor we have to see today is an Angel, otherwise the guys would have to choose who would pose as the father.

Reluctantly, I drag myself out of my warm, cozy nest and into the closet. I find the cutest baby doll dress I own and slip it on. It's such a beautiful shade of lavender, and it helps support my growing breasts. My baby bump is just becoming noticeable and I'm getting paranoid about going out in public. Looking on the shelves in the closet, I find a pale gray light sweater to pull on to cover the tattoos on my arms.

Emerging from the closet, my dresser is the next place I stop. The top right drawer is full of my headbands and hair ties. With as long as my hair is, it's getting too heavy to leave up in a ponytail for extended periods of time. Standing in front of the full-length mirror, I stare at the woman I've become.

Finally, I look happy, and actually am happy. For once, I don't feel the need to starve myself to appear perfect for everyone. For the first time in a long time, I am not afraid of who and what I am, and I owe it all to my mates. Digging through my drawer, I find a black and gold headband and slip it on to get my hair out of my eyes.

One last glance in the mirror and out the door I go. I have three choices of how to get to the ground level, fly, walk or manifest. Each way comes with their own level of fatigue. I look to the dark corner behind me and decide that walking through the shadows to manifest downstairs would be much less stressful on me. Shadow walking is a new skill my grandfather recently taught me as a way to evade capture. I emerge downstairs to the guys all standing around the island in the kitchen, dressed to impress.

"Wow guys. Are we going to an awards banquet or an ultrasound appointment?" I swear if I wasn't already pregnant, my ovaries would have just exploded. Christian, Gage and Raph are wearing finely tailored suits in varying shades of gray as a subtle nod to the gray in my feathers. Then there's Cyrus. He has a fitted blood red dress shirt under one of those black and gold embroidered male corset vests. The vest accentuates how broad and powerful his shoulders are, and I can feel the drool escaping the corner of my mouth.

Cyrus winks and me then smirks. "I feel like a steak on a platter before you." His teeth grip his bottom lip as he turns up that bad boy smolder. My greedy core clenches, begging to be filled, as I ogle my mates. A husky laugh escapes Cyrus's lips. "You can tear this off me later, kitten. Thank Gage for the vest, it was his idea." Cyrus kisses my cheek then smacks my ass as he heads towards the front door.

"The car is here, let's go," Raph says as he comes alongside of me to take hold of my arm to walk me out.

I'm still in a daze as Raphael walks me to the limo, out front. Samael, Azrael and Metatron have all hitched a ride to the appointment. My mates situate me between Cyrus and Raphael for the ride. Through the bond, I feel the mixed emotions flittering between excited and nervous and I have to laugh. "What's so funny descendant?" Samael asks and catches Metatron off guard.

Metatron double blinks, looking between Samael and me, and I laugh harder. "I can't help it, Grandfather. My big strong mates are nervous about the appointment. It's not them that has to push a watermelon out of a hole that normally is smaller than a dime." Raphael and Cyrus both pale, looking at me, then down to my stomach.

"Thankfully, it's twins, so they won't be that big. Maybe a pair of cantaloupes."

Gage, unfortunately, is taking a sip from his bottle of water when I make the statement and inhales some of his water. Christian is there with the assist patting his back, trying to help him clear the water from his lungs.

"Little one, you have one of the strongest healers on both sides of the veil at your disposal. Everything will be just fine," Samael says, smiling as he leans back in his seat, watching me while I rub my stomach.

Metatron smiles, watching everything going on. "I have it under good authority." Metatron closes his eyes slowly. His face takes on an angelic glow. "You and your children will be safe, healthy and happy." He sits up straight and leans forward, resting his elbow on his knees.

His muscles strain against the fabric of his dress shirt. "You have mine and my twins' protection from now till the end of time itself." Hesitantly, he extends a hand out to me and I stare at it for a few moments.

I reach out and grip his forearm and lock eyes with him and nod. "Thank you, Metatron, thank your brother for me as well." The most glorious smile graces his lips, and his eyes churn golden.

"It is my honor and privilege to be allowed to care for and provide for you, Thana." His tone rings with honesty and love. His thumb gently rubs my forearm in a soothing motion.

I slightly nod my head and watch his hand and the pattern his thumb moves. "Thank you for dinner last night. I wish you could have stayed," I whisper as I turn my head and look away. Gently, I release his arm and pull my hand back and rest it in my lap. I stare at my hand that's still tingling from touching him.

Metatron clears his throat and coughs several times as he rubs his hand on his pants. "You are most welcome, my precious one." His tone drops and does that reverberation that I heard the first time he spoke in my mind. My other mates' heads whip up at the tone that he uses. It's the tone he uses when he does His work.

The car eventually comes to a stop, and the guys look around excitedly. "The doctor has a back entrance, and he said to come in that way. His nurse said he will allow as many of us as we want into the room to see the ultrasound," Raphael says proudly as he ushers us out of the vehicle. We line up in the alleyway behind the doctor's office. Raphael knocks on the back door and eventually a kindly looking old lady answers and motions for us to enter.

I grip the back of Raphael's waistline as he weaves down the hallways of the doctor's office. The assistant stops before a door and opens it and motions for us to enter. "Miss, please change into the gown and climb onto the table. The doctor will be in with you shortly. Gentlemen, please take a seat along the wall. The images will be visible on the big screen on the left." She motions to the screen on the gigantic wall opposite the examination table. The table is separated by a screen divider from the rest of the room, to give me some semblance of privacy during the examination.

Without further ado, I walk to the other side of the room and get changed into the gown as instructed. Modesty is not included in hospital gowns just saying. Jeez, could they spare a little more fabric so that my bottom isn't hanging out for the world to see? I mean seriously! They make enough off insurance it wouldn't kill their pocket to add a bit more modesty.

My fingers have a kung-fu death grip on the back of the gown as I exit the changing room. Let's face it, I have my father-in-law, grandfather, the fifth mate the jury is out on, and my guys here. "Everyone I'm not fully bonded to please get behind the divider so I can get on the table." Thankfully, the guys comply quickly, and Raph and Gage help me get situated on the table of doom.

Once I'm settled, Raphael lets everyone know that I am all settled. I wish I could just hide in my wings till it's over. I go to turn my head away, but a hand stops me. As I turn back, the smiling face of my dark knight stares back at me.

"Kitten, what's wrong?" Cyrus asks in that low rasp of his that makes me blush.

"I don't like being alone up here," I whisper to Cyrus. A knowing smile crosses his lips as he bends down to kiss my forehead.

"Then that gives me the excuse to not leave your side." He murmurs the words against my forehead, then kisses my lips. Almost instantly, I relax and start to feel safer with him at my side.

"I don't mean to interrupt this touching moment but, we need to start the exam." the doctor says, drawing me out of my happy little bubble. Cyrus instantly straightens up and takes ahold of my hand and grips it tightly.

The doctor moves to the foot of the table and starts his cursory exam of my lady bits and I can see the hairs on the back of Cyrus's neck stand on end. Tugging on Cyrus's arm, I get him to bend down to my level.

"He needs to make sure I'm completely healthy before he checks the babies. It's normal." I try to be as reassuring as possible. He rolls his eyes and smirks trying to hide just how nervous he really is.

After several minutes, the doctor stands up and smiles. "So far so good, Thana, everything seems to be shipshape. Let's take a look at the little one, shall we?" I beam up at the doctor and nod excitedly. Little does the doctor know that he's going to find two babies in there and not just one.

The ultrasound gel is cold on my skin as he applies the wand to my belly. Anxiously, I watch as he slides all over my lower abdomen. The first baby is able to be visualized, and it's quite active. Two little arms, two little wings and two little legs can be seen. Azrael and Cyrus seem to be exceptionally excited about seeing the first baby.

As the doctor moves, the second baby comes into view, and it doesn't have wings like the other one did. This time Raphael and the other Light Nephilim are exchanging high fives and bro hugs everywhere. My brows knit together as I stare at the doctor.

"Why doesn't my baby have wings like its sibling? Is it human?" Saying my child is human leaves a bitter taste on my tongue. It would mean that the child would have to be put up for adoption, since Angels and Nephilim aren't real according to humans.

"That's a simple answer. Light Nephilim get their wings at about six months to a year old. Dark Nephilim have them immediately because of being creatures of the shadow realm and they need to be able to escape threats." The doctor tries to explain in the kindest way possible.

I ponder his response for several minutes. I can feel my lips upturn as the wide smile spreads across my lips. "Ah, that makes sense. Can you see the genders? I know my gestation period is shorter than a human." Biting my bottom lip as I look up at the doctor.

His smile reaches his eyes as he moves the wand around again. "Wait!! Don't say it out loud!" Azrael screams and runs over to the doctor. Quickly I slam the gown down covering everything shocked that Azrael ran over like he did. "Tell me, I want to do one of those reveal party things for Thana. A first birth should be a special occasion for a female." Azrael winks at me, then turns to the doctor.

His once kind looking expression falls to an unreadable mask. The doctor pales slightly, then scribbles on a piece of paper and hands it to Azrael. Azrael smiles looking at the paper then looks up at me.

"You truly are a miracle, Thana." Azrael's voice cracks as the words leave his lips. Emotions I never thought I would see flicker across his face before he hides them again. A quick peck on the cheek and Azrael is gone in a wisp of shadows.

Raphael's lips curve up into the most radiant smile I have ever seen from him. A light-golden sheen envelopes his golden tan, making him seem more ethereal than usual. "Thank you for giving us these little blessings." His tone is nothing short of reverent as his large hand cups my abdomen.

"Let's get you home." Christian's voice carries from the other side of the room. He and the rest of my mates stand there in awe, looking at the frozen image of the babies on the screen.

It's now that I notice that the doctor has left me printouts of our children. Gently, I pick up the images and press them to my chest as if I'm hugging my babies. Raphael moves swiftly and scoops me up off the exam table and carries me to get changed. I just want to go home. Raphael insists on helping me put my dress back on and carrying me back to the limo. He passes me off to Cyrus in the limo and almost instantly I fall asleep in my dark knight's arms.

CHAPTER 36

CYRUS

My beautiful, fierce dark angel is sleeping soundly in my arms. My eyes caress every soft, smooth plane of her face. The most enticing part, her plump, full lips with her pronounced Cupid's bow. There's a new feeling that bubbles up in my chest and it scares me. Could it be that I am irrevocably in love with her? Dark Nephilim are possessive by nature, selfish fucks the lot of us. She looks so innocent when she sleeps. Yet we know she's far more dangerous than this innocent face betrays. Our little powerhouse has yet to tap into her full potential, and she already has the shadow realm up in arms, ready to steal her for their own.

Carefully, I move her hair away from her face and watch her sleep. Creepy, yeah, it could be perceived that way if you didn't know the relationship that we have. "How is she?" Metatron says softly as he leans forward, looking at her in my arms.

"She's tired, but okay." The words fall quietly from my lips as I look down at the most precious person in my life. The sudden impact of something colliding with the limo sends me flying. Instinctually I wrap Thana and I in shadows and pass straight through the limo to land crouched with her in my arms. Time itself has stopped. Nothing moves, not even the birds in the sky.

My father materializes next to Thana and I and stares at this new threat in shock. "What the actual fuck is that thing? It looks like a minotaur and a wendigo had a love child," I growl out, as I set a furious Thana on her feet.

"I can't believe Lucifer stooped so low as to release Baphomet from his prison." Azrael's tone tells me this will not be an easy battle. "He's literally unstoppable once he gets moving kind of like that guy with the helmet from the comic book." Father draws his sword, ready to do battle if need be.

At the moment, Baphomet seems more interested in destroying the limo than anything else. "Basically, we've been attacked by an angry steak still on the hoof?" Thana says as she pulls a bag of jerky out of her purse and starts eating.

Before I can answer Thana, the limo explodes in holy light. Thana moves quickly and wraps my father and I up in her wings, shielding us. When the apparent threat is over, Thana looks more pissed than before.

Metatron and Raphael are attacking with their angelic swords. Christian and Gage are using the swords that were apparently given to them by the Angels. So far, so good we are not even on Baphomet's radar.

Thana finishes her bag of jerky, then looks over at my father and me. "Cover your ears." Her voice sounds disembodied as she slowly turns her focus on Baphomet.

"Do as she says, son. If she's about to do what I think she is, this is going to cause Baphomet a lot of pain if he resists her." Thana watches us out of the corner of her eye for a few moments, making sure we obey.

A deep hum starts, and the surrounding ground quakes with whatever power she's drawing on. In an instant, she bursts into her reaper form hovering in the air. The haunting tone that escapes her lips sounds like a siren's call. I slam my hands on my ears and just watch what my mate is about to do.

~Raphael~

The darkness that surrounds Thana is foreboding and sends a chill up my spine. Her voice feels like it envelops us. Baphomet stops his attack on us and turns to focus on Thana. He lowers his head to charge, and the word "rise" escapes Thana's lips.

A monstrous black skull dragon looms behind her, and I feel like my heart has stopped. She cuts the tone off and shifts back to her human form. Her wolf, as well as Cyrus's, flank her. "Think twice Baphomet, I will not show mercy," Thana states coldly as she stares at the Demon before her.

Baphomet laughs and strikes Christian with the back of his hand, sending him flying. "Demoness, you have no power over me!" His head lowers again, and this time, he charges. I'm rooted where I stand by whatever power Thana has over the situation.

"Now," Thana says, and the dragon snaps out and grips Baphomet like a grape in his taloned hand.

"I may not have power over you. But I do have power over him." She rests her hand on top of the dragon's as she looks Baphomet over.

"Who sent you?" she asks, placing a finger between his eyes on his nose plate. The smell of burned flesh fills the air, and whatever was holding the other Angels and me is released.

"My master is far scarier than you are." He spits in her direction, and I can see the shifting plates under her cheeks.

Thana's look becomes feral, then suddenly changes, and she looks completely at peace. She bids her other familiars to return, leaving only the dragon. "I've been going about this all wrong. Raphael, push angelic light directly into his thick skull." Thana's order catches us off guard. I'm used to being her sword and shield. Now she has chosen me to carry out her orders.

I jump at the chance to assist her. I'm concerned that the dragon may turn on me at any moment. "You wish light to be syphoned into his skull?" I quirk my head to the side and arch an eyebrow, looking down at my much shorter mate.

"Yes!" She nods enthusiastically as a menacing grin crosses her lips, her deep-seated rage evident in her twisted smile. "Right where my scorch mark is." She jabs her clawed finger into the wound, causing Baphomet to howl out in pain.

She twists her wrist just so, and he screams out again. "Either he talks, or he gets sent back to the shadow realm the most painful way I can think of." Thana pouts. My heart instantly melts and my cock stirs, looking at how full her lips are. I get distracted for a moment, thinking about where I'd rather see those lips later.

Several snaps of her fingers right in front of my face draw me out of my brief fantasy. Getting theatrical, I gather the holy light between my hands, hoping that this stubborn bull will talk. Baphomet's eyes widen like saucers.

"You're an Angel, they don't do this shit." Baphomet laughs. "Lucifer will have so much fun breaking your little bitch of a mate." The words barely escape his lips when Thana swings Azrael's sword and beheads him.

His head rolls off his shoulders onto the dragon's closed hand, then onto the pavement. His mouth still attempts to work, even though it's not attached to his body any longer. Thana stands there staring down at his head examining is momentarily. Suddenly, she changes her grip on Azrael's sword and drives it through his skull plate.

Thana's eyes churn like limpet pools of molten mercury as she twists the blade and ignites the hellfire. The white-hot flames burn through Baphomet's skull, reducing it to ash in a matter of moments. Her eyes lock on the charred remains and she sticks her right hand out over the ashes. A darkened wisp rises from the ashes and Thana grips it tightly.

A wicked gleam flickers in Azrael's blackened orbs as he stares at my mate a little too intensely. Thana cocks her head to the side, then pops Baphomet's soul into her mouth and devours it. I watch in horror as her eyes fade from mercury to obsidian. Her head slowly tilts back as her wings unfurl and stretch several times before she looks back at me.

"I'm okay Raph. I had to make sure he wouldn't resurrect in the shadow realm. No soul, no resurrection. Simple," Thana says, without skipping a beat. With a wave of her hand, what remains of Baphomet's body blows away in the wind. Metatron takes care of making the destroyed limo vanish from existence.

Thana looks at her skull dragon and bows her head slightly at him. Within seconds, he shifts into a wisp of smoke and returns to his place on her shoulder. "Let's go home." She glances at us and smiles before launching up into the air.

I stand there dumbfounded as I watch my pregnant mate fly away, pondering all that she's done in the last thirty minutes or so. "Amazing, isn't she?" Gage laughs as he watches Christian, Cyrus and Metatron trying to catch up to Thana.

"To think she's only going to get stronger the more she accepts her heritage." My voice is full of wonder as I watch Thana fly home. My heart swells with pride over the woman my mate is becoming.

Gage's laughter breaks me out of my train of thought. Slowly, I turn to look at him and raise an eyebrow.

"Can you imagine the first fool to mess with one of her babies? Ashes everywhere..." Gage throws his arms wide to further enunciate his statement.

"We better catch up to everyone else." It's now that I notice the further away Thana has gotten, the more things are going back to normal. The birds are flying again, and traffic has picked back up. The world moves on as if nothing has happened here. You would think after all these centuries, I would be immune to these odd occurrences.

Gage and I take flight and catch several thermals on the way home. Landing on the downstairs balcony, we push the double doors open to find Thana with both wolves and her panther walking loose around the house. Of all the odd things to find in the living room is

Cyrus's black phoenix sitting on a parrot's perch. It honestly could pass for a black peacock if I didn't know better.

"Why is that there?" I motion to the phoenix on the perch.

Thana laughs as she grabs a bamboo stick and shoves three marshmallows on the end. Thana sashays her way over to the phoenix and stands off to the side. "Cinder, mind helping Mommy out?" Thana waves the marshmallows in front of the phoenix. The bird tilts its head, studying the offering, then opens its mouth, spewing flames.

Cinder closes her mouth, and the marshmallows are partially caramelized, and the top one is slightly burned. Thana pulls the burned one off and offers it to Cinder. "I know you burn the top one on purpose." Cinder's beak is covered in marshmallow, and the tendrils of the gooey treat are slowly taking over.

Just before I can offer the bird assistance, flames spew from its beak, and the remnants of its snack are gone. Shaking my head, I eye my mate again. "You've avoided answering why most of the familiars are loose." Crossing my arms over my chest, I lean against the closest wall.

Thana pats Fenrir on the butt, and he trots off out of sight. I get ready to speak again and Thana holds up a single finger in my direction, stopping me. Gage and Cyrus laugh, then quickly try to cover it up with coughing.

Fenrir returns, dragging the mother of all beanbags into the living room. I search my memory, trying to remember if I've seen this massive beanbag before. Then I begin to question if I have been that unobservant to have overlooked it somehow. Thana flops down into the beanbag and wiggles around till she's satisfied. "No, it wasn't here earlier. Yes, it just arrived. And the familiars are loose because of having killed Baphomet." Thana hits all my key questions without skipping a beat.

"How did you do that?" Christian's curiosity kicks into high gear.

"Do what?" Thana's reply is terse and to the point, as usual.

"Answer without audible questions." Gage tosses in from the

couch.

"That's easy." Thana's lips slowly curl up, and I know she's up to something. "Raphael gets creases between his eyebrows when he's trying to figure something out. So, when his eyes locked on the beanbag, I figured he was wondering if he missed its arrival because of his duties outside of the nest." She shrugs her shoulders nonchalantly. I stand here in a state of shock at how easily our mate reads me perfectly. The others seem to be just as shocked by Thana's powers of observation. The only one unimpressed is Metatron, who lets a chuckle escape his lips.

"What's got you laughing, brother?" I throw in Metatron's direction.

He pushes his hulking form off the wall and moves to stand in the middle of the room. "As bonds grow, the females can anticipate the males' thought processes. Just like the males may or may not feel what the female feels when she's with child." The smirk on Metatron's lips irks me. It honestly almost pisses me off to the point I want to hit him. To be honest, it's his cockiness that reminds me of Cyrus.

My jaw drops thinking about the implication of what Metatron has said to us. We are so royally screwed, potentially. It's not even funny. Just before I have the chance to speak, Christian puts his hand up and motions to Thana. She's curled up in her beanbag, fast asleep, surrounded by hers and Cyrus's familiars.

Gage pulls up a chair up to the beanbag. "I'll take first watch. Last thing I want to do is disturb her sleep." Gage's words remind me of the time we woke her up moving her and she went all feral beast on us. Hell hath no fury like a tired, pregnant female. We silently agree with him, and those not on watch head off to bed. I set Metatron up with the guest room on the first floor, just in case Gage needs backup.

Tomorrow marks the halfway point for Thana's pregnancy. Hopefully, the little party we have planned for her will make her smile.

CHAPTER 37

THANA

I'm not sure which of my mates had the brilliant idea of letting me sleep in a beanbag but, damn, my body is sore. My eyes slowly open to the soft glow of the light coming through the shades in the living room. The honeyed tones make me think of the Angelic Realm and how warm and inviting it is. Christian is sound asleep in the chair next to my beanbag. His features are bathed in the soft glow of the morning light. My heart pounds like the hooves of a wild horse running across the plains.

I have loved this man since the first time I saw him, almost three hundred years ago. We were in the first colonies in America during the seven years' war. Battles over the colonies and the new territories erupted on almost a daily basis.

Christian was a soldier in the war, and they drafted me to help heal the wounded. They brought him into the tent I was working in, and immediately I was smitten with his exotic features. Once the others left the tent, I could heal him the most effective way I know. He knew what I was immediately and smiled thankfully. Since that day, every assignment he has been put on, he has made sure that I am within reach of him. I'm not sure if it's some sense of gratitude, or deep down, his subconscious knew I was his.

My baby bump is getting in the way of menial tasks, and to be honest, I don't feel as beautiful as I did before. Body positivity is not one of my strong suits. I know this is a natural process, but the way my body is changing is weighing heavily on me.

I walk silently around Christian, studying the way he's reclined in the chair. His long, thick obsidian hair flows like the branches of a weeping willow tree. The pressed white shirt he had on at dinner is unbuttoned and drapes off his shoulders, leaving his toned olive chest and abdomen exposed. The light plays its seductive tones over his rippled abdomen, casting the deep cuts in shadows. At the very edge of his slacks, a light dusting of hair peeks out.

It's time I take my inner goddess out and reclaim the confidence I once had. I remove my dress, leaving only my cheekster black lace underwear on. Unfurling my wings, I flex them, stretching them out briefly before recalling my familiars. My eyes lock with Cyrus's wolf, and I send him out of the room. Definitely don't need a wolf's nose in the wrong spot.

Careful to not disturb Christian, I stand between his spread legs. Resting my hands on the arms of the chair, I lean forward and press my lips to his. A soft, pleased moan escapes his lips and his eyes open slightly. "Kichōna mono, good morning." His heavy-lidded eyes finally take in my exposed body and widen. His pupils almost immediately dilate as his eyes caress every inch of my flesh.

Growing bold, I lean in closer and straddle his lap. Pressing my cheek against his, I press my lips to the shell of his ear and whisper, "I need you." My wings wrap around us, cocooning us in the chair.

The swell of my stomach presses against his washboard abs, and his hands move to caress my belly. "Anything you desire, Kichōna mono," Christian says reverently as his hand glides across my flesh, sending tingles straight to my core. It's something about how he worships every inch of me that takes my desire to new heights. He brushes a hand across my cheek and pulls me in for a kiss that burns with the desire and love he has for me.

As we kiss, I reach down between my legs and start working on his belt. I need to free him from the offending fabric that's keeping me from what I desire most. A soft chuckle escapes his lips as his hands slide down and under my thighs. In a single sweeping motion, he picks me up and the buckle of his belt hits the floor. Shifting from foot to foot, he frees himself of his pants then walks toward my beanbag.

I pull my wings back within me just as he bends down and carefully places me on the beanbag. "Be patient Kichōna mono, I wish to worship and savor this moment." I track every movement Christian makes as he removes his boxers. Inch by inch, he slides them down his thighs, and all I can think about is how good his hands are going to feel on me.

Christian drops to his knees before me and massages my feet and ankles. Taking away aches and pains I didn't know I even had till now. His hands slowly find their way up my calves working the knots out. The minute his hands hit my thighs, it feels like an electric jolt straight to my core. I go to reach for Christian to pull him to me, but a second set of hands grabs my wrists and pulls my hands above my head.

"Now, now, Kitten, let Christian work his magic. Be a good girl, and maybe I'll tend to your darker needs." Cyrus's deep, gravely tone and dark promise makes my core weep.

Christian's hand finally makes it to my core, and his knuckles brush over the lace of my underwear. His smile lights up, and he brings his knuckles to his mouth and sucks on them. "Soaking wet and sweet as always, Kichōna mono." Christian's smooth, soft tone embraces me, warming me differently than Cyrus's dark and dangerous one.

His smooth, light fingers slip between me and the lace as he draws the fabric down my thighs. "Give those to me." Cyrus's commanding tone makes my eyes widen. What is even more shocking is how quickly Christian complies. He hands Cyrus my underwear and Cyrus stuffs it in his pocket. "Continue," Cyrus says flatly, as his fathomless orbs move from me to Christian.

Christian immediately jumps into action and drops down, placing a kiss on my pubic bone. My breath hitches, and Cyrus's grip tightens on my wrists. I tear my gaze away from Christian and look up at Cyrus. His blackened orbs reflect my every response, and it's almost hypnotizing. He grips both of my hands with one of his and places his free hand on my throat. "You will come for me. Your orgasms belong to me," He growls out, bearing his canines at me.

I literally gush, soaking Christian's face as my orgasm rips through me. Heat spreads through my body, setting all my nerves on fire. I pull and strain against Cyrus's grip as I grind Christian's face against my pussy. "Good, Kitten, ride his face." Cyrus's grip on my throat tightens slightly as Christian's tongue flicks faster over my over sensitive clit.

My brain has gone to mush when Christian finally lets up. Panting heavily, my gaze moves from Cyrus to Christian. "When did this become a thing?" I try to catch my breath as Christian lines himself up with my engorged sex.

"About five minutes after you sat on my lap, Kichōna mono. Cyrus was concerned about the twins getting hurt." Christian's voice wavers as he slides into my heated depths. He doesn't bottom out like he usually does. Instead, his movements are slow and calculated. Every inch of Christian's length is setting my nerves off, making my muscles tingle and pulse.

Cyrus's grip on my wrists and throat are removed as he slides to lie on his stomach. His eyes shift back to his normal human brown as he stares at me. "Yours and the baby's health are my chief priority. Your pleasure and affection are paramount. A happy mother gives birth to happy healthy babies." An odd note enters Cyrus's tone of concern: I can pick up a hint of remorse.

As my next orgasm builds, I pull at Cyrus and kiss him deeply. My fingers interlace with his long hair, threading between the hair tie and his scalp. He swallows my screams as lights flash behind my eyes. My depths crush down around Christian's length, pulsing and milking him for all he's worth. Pregnancy orgasms are no joke. Christian maintains his speed and follows soon after me. Slowly, I release Cyrus and look up at Christian, his radiant smile exudes nothing but love and happiness.

Between Christian and Cyrus, they manage to get me out of the beanbag and drape Christian's shirt over me. "I'll clean up. Please take Thana to get bathed." Christian volunteers to straighten everything up and tasks Cyrus with wrangling me. He-he poor Cyrus.

One moment I'm standing in the living room, the next I'm engulfed in Cyrus's wings and moved through the shadows to the master bathroom. "Let's get you cleaned up." His low tone sets my insides aflame again as he ushers me towards the shower stall. So many soaps and loofas line the one wall I didn't notice before. Out of the corner of my eye, I watch Cyrus gather up soft towels and lotions.

I reach into the shower stall and turn on the water, trying to set it to the proper temperature. Through the bond, I reach out and check on my other mates. Everyone seems at peace with Cyrus taking the lead in my care for today. "Why does today seem different, Cy?" Using the mirror in the bathroom, I look behind me and see Cyrus studying me.

"You're very perceptive, Kitten. Metatron killed several demons last night that attempted to break into the house. They went straight for your nest, and he killed them there." I froze, eyes wide, struggling to comprehend what Cyrus just told me. Biting my bottom lip, I ponder what extent the demons will go to get to me.

Almost instantly, Cyrus is on me, his thick muscular arms wrapped around me. Wings of midnight wrap around me, bringing me comfort, protecting me from the world. The heat and strength of Cyrus's body gives me shelter and support in a way only he can provide. I rest my head on his chest, and his heart beats steady like a metronome. The steady rhythm calms my racing heart, helping me to relax quickly.

Cyrus's hand caresses my cheek, causing me to look up at him. "As much as I desire your body. Your heart and mind need my protection more." He kisses me passionately, drinking of their softness like a man thirsting for water.

My nimble fingers make quick work of his T-shirt, pulling it free from his waistband. A soft chuckle escapes his lips as he raises his arms, breaking the kiss for a mere moment to get the offending fabric out of the way. "Don't leave me," I beg him. Our home was penetrated again by demons and there's nothing we can do. To ward against demons would be to also ward against Cyrus and me both.

"I will never leave you again." His lips press against my forehead as he frees himself from his jeans. Cyrus reaches into the shower stall and shuts off the water, then guides me to the large spa tub Raphael recently had installed for me. With one arm tightly wrapped around me, he turns the water on and gets it to the proper temperature.

Wordlessly, Cyrus guides me into the tub when it is halfway full. The warm water envelopes my body, relaxing my tense muscles. Cyrus returns with three bath bombs and holds them out to me. Sandalwood, evergreen, and lavender, oddly enough. I take hold of the sandalwood and drop it into the bubbling water of the tub.

"Pay up, Golden Boy," Cyrus says out the door into the nest room.

The smirk on Cyrus's lips tells me he either won against Raph or Metatron. "Which of the Archangels did you prove wrong?" I lay back in the water as Cyrus climbs in.

"Gee... who do you think?" His bad boy smolder is in full effect as he flips his hair out of his eyes.

"Raph... It has to be Raph. He's the only one you seem in constant competition with." The bathroom door pops open, and Raphael drops a second twenty-dollar bill on the table by the door.

Shaking my head, I look between both mates. "Really guys? Let me guess, there's also a pool to see which baby is born first?" I raise my eyebrows, looking between the two of them.

"Yup." Cyrus says.

"Men, I swear..." Leaning back, I close my eyes, enjoying the massaging bubbles and the heat of the water.

I feel Cyrus scoot closer, and he places a hand over my eyes for a moment. "Sleep, Kitten, all of your mates are here to protect you," Cyrus says, and suddenly a nap seems like a wonderful idea.

CHAPTER 38
CYRUS

I use the new trick my father taught me and help Thana to fall asleep quickly. I will raze the earth to make sure my mate and baby are safe. Carefully, I move Thana in the spa tub so that her head and shoulders rest on my chest. The heated water and the feeling of weightlessness will ease some of the tension in her back. Using the bond, I call my bond mates into the bathroom. "Close the door," I say sternly.

"What about Metatron?" Christian asks.

"Fine, let him in too. Give me a thin towel to cover Thana." Gage tilts his head for a moment, then realizes what I'm trying to do. Quickly, he brings the blue towel to me and helps me cover our mate's body.

"You summoned me, son of Death?" Metatron's voice does that weird reverberation thing and echoes off of the walls. His eyes churn golden when he finally notices Thana sleeping, floating in the tub on me.

"Yeah, I need some of you to take Thana to the Angelic Realm for the day. Father and I are heading to meet up with Samael to try to put an end to these attacks." I push all the power and authority I can

258

into my voice. Christian and Gage visibly react to my voice. The Archangels tilt their heads, studying me.

"Why?" Raphael says, his voice booming in the bathroom.

The raising of his tone scares Thana awake, and all the darkness her little frame contains bleeds out into the bathroom. Acting on instinct, she spins and grabs me, and we vanish in a wisp of smoke. We manifest back in my bedroom and two of Thana's familiars burst free of her flesh and stand guard.

"Rise!" Thana screams, and my raven, wolf and phoenix obey her command. She moves like a specter across my room to grab one of my black silk dress shirts to put on.

"Kitten, we're okay, it was just Raphael." I hold my hands up in a placating manner, trying to soothe her.

She shakes her head no almost violently. "Something's here. I can feel it. Something is in my house!" Her voice shrieks like a banshee as she studies my room carefully.

The guys finally make it up to my room and stop dead in their tracks, seeing Thana in almost a feral state. "My love, what is wrong?" Gage's soft approach gets Thana to retract her claws for a moment.

"Something's here. I feel it... Get it out!" She shrieks again, looking frantically around the room. A mass of inky black fluid gathers between her hands, and she throws it against the wall. "Grandfather! Azrael, I summon thee!" The inky material swirls, then ripples, then my father and her grandfather walk through.

Without skipping a beat, my father scoops Thana up in his arms, holding her to him. "What is the..." My father doesn't even finish his sentence before he looks back at Samael and they both vanish in wisps of darkness.

From downstairs, we hear screeches and the sounds of metal on metal. "Keep Thana safe!" Raphael commands, then runs out of the room. Metatron follows him without question, and so does Christian.

"I'll stay and help protect Thana." Gage says, then touches the medallion around his neck and his angelic armor manifests. From the gauntlet on his left hand, he pulls free his sword and smirks.

"Wise ass." Rolling my eyes, I watch my pregnant mate pace the interior of my room. She pumps her hands, clenching them periodically as she looks around. The wolves and the panther follow her around the room. It looks like something straight out of the jungle book.

"Kitten?" I hit the dominant tone she loves so much. Almost immediately, her head whips around so she can face me. "Can you stop pacing? I'm just as aggravated as you are that something dared to enter your domain." I phrase it to give her a sense of power and control, so maybe she would settle down.

Her hands embrace her growing belly and rub it. "I want them gone, and I want food." Thana pouts her thick ruby lips at me, and my cock stiffens almost immediately.

"Watch her," I bark the order out at Gage, then vanish into the shadows. I emerge in the kitchen to an all-out war. Demons and other creatures are funneling into the house at a record pace. Between the overcast skies and the treetop canopy, it's dark enough for them to move about during the day.

Mostly lower-level demons move about the shadows as if they own the place. Unfurling my wings, I allow my fingertips to become claws, and I rush the closest Demon, ripping its throat out. Blackened ichor sprays across the kitchen, landing on the other demons whipping them into a frenzy. One minute the Demons are attacking the Angels, the next they're attacking the Demons that were bathed in blood.

Once Raphael and Metatron notice the shift in battle, they go for arteries, spraying blood on the other demons. I quickly retrieve food for Thana and return to her as fast as I can. I'm covered in blood and feral in appearance. Thana doesn't even bat an eye at the way I look. She takes the bucket of fried chicken from me and sits in the corner sharing her food with her familiars. "I need to help the others,

Thana, stay with your fur babies and Gage." Thana looks up at me with a chicken leg in her mouth and nods before returning to eating.

That was too easy. Before leaving my room, I lock the door and Gage helps me to push the dresser in front of it. The shadows embrace me quickly and I return to the battle that's waging downstairs. Fly-like demons invade the house, and that can only mean one of two things. The first, Lucifer, has called upon Beelzebub's army to assist him in destroying us. Or the second thought, he's coming for Thana himself.

Either answer is unacceptable, so I summon my phoenix familiar to me. Once the bird manifests, it bursts into flames and starts burning every fly-like Demon it can hit. Blackened flames flow like a flamethrower out of its mouth, cremating every Demon it touches. Ashes fill the air and cover everything in Thana's once immaculate kitchen.

Something feels off and my bond-mates are noticing it too. "This is too easy!" Raphael shouts as he drives his blade through the chest of the last insect.

"Samael and I will clean up the perimeter. If you need us, summon us sooner," My father says and raises a brow at me, checking in briefly. I nod back in his direction, and they take off on their task.

A blood-curdling scream rips through the house and we immediately feel intense physical pain. "Thana!" I scream and, without waiting for the others, I move through the shadows faster than I ever have before.

Arriving in my bedroom, Gage is on the floor bleeding out and the three beast familiars of mine and Thana's lie still as if dead on the floor. The stench of blood and sulfur is almost enough to make me want to vomit. "Ah, your pitiful Azrael wannabe mate has arrived."

Fuck, I know that tone... I look up, and my worst fear is realized. Beelzebub has Thana in his arms with the tip of a blood covered dagger to her stomach. "Release her! Take me instead!" I'd rather die so that Thana and my baby can live.

I barely have the words out of my mouth when the rest of the guys catch up. Their horrified faces match my own. Thana's eyes are locked on Gage. "Please let Raph save him. I'll go peacefully. Just let him heal him." Thana begs Beelzebub. Blood tears roll down her cheeks as she stares at her fallen mate.

"Fine..." Beelzebub says and with a flick of his wrist, Gage's almost limp body slides leaving a blood trail behind him towards Raphael. Without skipping a beat, Raphael drops to his knees and starts healing Gage.

"Puppets the lot of you, still following that pompous ass. He doesn't care about you!"

Thana cringes from the stench from Beelzebub's breath. Her eyes swirl liquid mercury as Beelzebub's grip on her shifts. His hand has slid away from her stomach and has moved up to her right shoulder and left bicep. She slowly rests her arms on her stomach, then slides her right hand to touch something on her left wrist. Metatron's eyes widen as Thana rolls her wrist to show us what she did. She summoned the Valkyrie.

Sooner than expected, battle cries fill the air and have Beelzebub looking around in panic. "I killed the last of them. How can this be?"

Crashing through the window beside us, Sigrun lands in her full battle armor and her sword blazing. "Release my sister," she says calmy, pointing her sword tip in Beelzebub's direction.

"Never! She is to be my bride!" Thana's eyes widen and I see her going for her right wrist.

"I don't think so!" Thana says as she snaps the sword charm from her bracelet.

Fuck me running. As soon as she grips the sword in her hand, it becomes full length. Just so happens the way she had it when the sword became full sized, the blade impales Beelzebub through the chest. Beelzebub tries to strike at Thana when she spins away, but Sigrun is faster and slices his arm clean off at the elbow.

Thana and Sigrun stand side by side, Thana's sword in his chest and Sigrun's at his throat. "That slow ache you feel in your muscles and the tightness in your throat..." Thana dramatically pauses as her eyes blacken to fathomless orbs.

"Daybreaker is one of the last swords meant to kill your kind either on contact or over time." The sword's name makes the rest of us back up. It was rumored to have been lost in the last war a millennium ago.

"An abomination like you shouldn't be able to handle it!" Beelzebub sputters inky ichor down his chin and onto the floor before him.

Thana laughs, and the look of absolute peace on her face is almost scary. "When you grow up being tormented, tortured and made to feel less than worthy, simple words don't hurt you anymore." Thana's smirk mirrors my own as she twists the blade in his chest. "I feel sorry for you, Beelzebub. You were tricked and then exiled because you are a sheep needing a shepherd."

Her eyes bleed silver, the liquid mercury swirls like a maelstrom. A golden glow encompasses her body, and she hovers like she does in her reaper form. "Time to go home and be given eternal rest." She releases her sword, and it falls to the floor. Thana looks like an Angel, pure white feathers and that golden glow surrounding her.

The terror on Beelzebub's face brings me joy. Apparently, the thing he fears most is being sent back into the Angelic Realm to be judged. The beautiful vision that is my mate floats even closer to him, and he's pinned by an unseen force. Thana silences his voice as she reaches out with her slender hands to caress his cheeks. "Go in peace." Her voice surrounds us all as if she is walking around the room talking. Those three words repeat over and over again causing him to open his mouth in a silent scream.

Thana's wings open wider, and with a single powerful flap, she rips his soul from his body, allowing it to fall away to ash. The tar-like mass ebbs in her hands, trying to slink away from her. Silver orbs lock on the mass as she compresses it in her hands. "Raph." Without hesitation, Raphael is at her side and places his hands above and below the orb. Together they embrace it in golden light till it's too bright to look at.

When the light fades away, Thana is back to her normal self, smiling. "Time to wake the babies," she says softly, before walking over to our familiars.

"What do you mean wake the babies?" Samael says curiously, looking at his granddaughter.

The musical laughter that escapes Thana's lips draws out a tentative smile from me. "They sleep, just like when they are ink upon my flesh. Before he could attack them, I put them into a state of torpor." She kneels and touches each of their heads. Each familiar rises slowly from their imposed nap and checks Thana over fully before returning to being tattoos.

"We need to discuss the elephant in the room," Raphael says before leaving my bedroom heading downstairs.

Thana smirks and twirls her finger in the air as if to say whoop-de-doo. Christian helps Gage to stand, and we all decide to follow Raphael downstairs. I can only imagine the level of bullshit we're going to have to endure.

CHAPTER 39

THANA

My snack was interrupted, Gage was almost killed, and now Raphael wants to call a family meeting. Seriously, I just want to eat and take a nap after all of this. Sigrun and I walk downstairs hand in hand as she gushes over how cute I look pregnant. If this was any other time, I would share in her excitement. Gage almost died, and I just pulled off some next level craziness.

I make it downstairs, and the guys are already sitting around the kitchen island that is covered in food from one end to the other. Metatron is using the vacuum to remove the last of the ashes from the kitchen floor. Most of the appliances and the cabinets have a light dusting of ash still on them. Metatron's presence still makes me feel uneasy. I know he's meant to be mine. I'm more concerned about the power shift in the nest if I add another light mate to the group.

Raphael has the larger chair at the end of the island, so I decide to go climb into his lap. As soon as I sit down, he bands his thick arms around my waist. His lips press against my cheek, and he murmurs he loves me against the shell of my ear.

"So, what's the elephant we need to talk about?" I ask as I reach out to the plate that Christian offers me piled high with French toast.

Metatron stumbles, Azrael and Samael stop in their movements and look back at me. "Well, the thing is, I'm not sure how to approach the subject." Raphael stumbles over his words, which is uncharacteristic for him.

Metatron sets the vacuum he was holding against the cabinet then moves to stand at the end of the island across from me. "What I believe my brother is trying to say is that you becoming an Angel took us all by surprise." Metatron's stance screams dominance and power. Yet his tone says he's unsure and possibly wary of the subject he's trying to broach. Or is it just because it's me?

Furrowing my brows, I meet everyone's gaze. My angelic mates look back at me in awe. Cyrus nods his head slowly, backing up what Metatron was saying. Quickly, I look over to my grandfather and Azrael, and they both nod as well. I put down my fork and fold my hands in front of me. "Beelzebub is frightened of Angels." I draw in a fortifying breath before continuing. "I figured if I reaped his soul as an Angel, it would be the ultimate penance for him." I turn in Raphael's lap and press my forehead against his neck, trying to hide.

Strong hands grip me under my arms and lift me off Raphael's lap. Wings surround me and I'm cradled in my mate's arms. The aromatic scent of sandalwood surrounds me, and I know my dark knight is trying to protect me from my own dark thoughts. "Kitten, you protected Gage the only way you knew how. You reaped a greater Demon's soul with the one form he is powerless against. I am in awe of you." Cyrus's declaration takes me by surprise.

He gently sets me on my feet and opens his wings. That signature smirk plays on his lips, and he winks at me. "You can single-handedly kick our collective asses. Never lower yourself to anyone unless you want to." His fingertips press on the underside of my chin, forcing me to raise my eyes. "You are the beginning and end of all things, as far as I'm concerned. I will kill anyone that disagrees with me." Cyrus's eyes blacken immediately, and I can't help but beam up at him.

Azrael's laughter draws me out of my little happy bubble, and I look over at him. "Daughter, you far exceed anything Samael and I ever thought you would be. Unlike your birth father, I am proud of the woman you have become." Tears well up in my eyes, threatening to break.

"Why does Thana cry blood tears now?" Gage fires off and I look at him puzzled, before wiping my eyes with a napkin. I'll be damned my tears are sanguine.

"That's a simple answer. Thana is life and death in one body," Samael says, approaching me. "Unfurl your wings, descendant." My grandfather's voice holds a command to it I've never heard before. Defiantly, I stare up at him, not buckling under the power he's testing me with.

"Unfurl. Your. Wings." I fire back at my grandfather, enunciating every word and syllable, pushing as much power behind it as I can. Things get knocked to the ground all around me as my mate's wings reveal themselves not of their own volition. Grandfather struggles, almost relenting under my power.

Metatron is the only other male in the room, still with his wings hidden. Not bending to my will immediately has earned him some of my respect. I rein in my power and head back to the table to grab a muffin. "What is so important about my wings, Grandfather?" I question as I spread cream cheese on the muffin.

"If I am correct, even your black feathers have silver veins." He states plainly as he unfurls his wings, showing there is not one silver vein on any of his feathers.

Taking my muffin with me, I walk to the far side of the room and unfurl my wings, looking at my feathers' veins. Every feather has a silver vein, even the blackest feathers closest to my body have silver veins. "Raph, Cyrus?" I call the fathers of my children to me and point out the feathers to them.

With as large as my wings are, I can hide my mates and their reactions from the rest of the room. Cyrus immediately starts turning the black feathers closest to my body over and examines them. "What does the vein color denote Samael?" Raphael steps from behind my wings as he addresses my grandfather. Meanwhile, Cyrus waves Gage and Christian over so that all my mates are on the same page.

Each mate takes a turn, moving my feathers, examining the veins. I can hear their whispers within the bond as they take turns pointing things out. I feel kinda bad leaving Metatron out of this discussion, but the jury is still out about him.

"It is fabled that a female shall be of a shade line, born to walk in the shadows and the light—" Samael motions to his wings, then over to me "—I am considered a shade because I chose to remain in the Shadow Realm to maintain order and to protect the veil. The fact my descendant transcended to be an Angel to reap a soul proves that the fable is true." He slams his fists down on the countertop as he looks for anyone to argue his statement. Obsidian orbs lock with mine as he tries to drive his point home about what I truly am.

Spinning slowly, I cross the kitchen, heading directly to Metatron. "You're the keeper of all things with knowledge beyond the common." I tilt my head several times and flex my wings, captivating Metatron. "Am I the one my grandfather speaks of?" I narrow my eyes briefly, studying him.

His eyes glaze over, bathed in an ethereal light as he tilts his head skyward. His long blonde locks flow down his back like a river of gold. I'm almost hypnotized by his beauty. "You are the one to prevent the end of days. The one to offer salvation to the damned or destroy them eternally." The reverberation in his voice causes his words to echo in the room, repeating themselves multiple times.

Pursing my lips, I walk over to the pantry, grab a lunch bag, and start packing it. "Cyrus. You, Grandfather, and Father head to the Shadow Realm see what you can learn. At the rate Lucifer is going, he's running out of generals." I hear Samael and Azrael discussing plans for the trip. Cyrus comes up and hugs me from behind, his lips press to my cheek.

"Be safe Cy, if you need me, summon me." I spin in his arms and kiss him deeply, pushing all the love and affection I have for him into the kiss. His length hardens between us, and it causes me to smile mid kiss.

"Evil female." He growls out before biting my bottom lip.

"Your evil female..." I growl right back at him. He walks away to leave with the others.

My eyes land on my other mates and Metatron. "Time to fly, boys, I need to learn more about the angelic powers I may have." Opening the balcony door wide, I throw my lunch bag over my shoulder and launch up into the sky. My large powerful wings move me swiftly through the air towards the Angelic Realm.

I burst through the mist of the cloud cover and land near the tree of life. Sigrun and the other Valkyrie spar in a ring nearby. I watch the women warriors battle among themselves, keeping their skills sharp. "Thana!" Sigrun yells as she closes the distance between us. We embrace tightly and she coos seeing my belly. "How's Aunt Sigrun's little warrior?" she says with a smile as she gently caresses my stomach.

"Warriors... There's two in there." I beam. Pride blooms in my chest, warming me from the inside.

Her eyes widen and she screams to the other Valkyrie, and all the sisters gather around us. Each female takes a turn, laying a hand on my stomach, offering me a blessing and a prayer for the babies. Oddly enough, each female offers me a single silver bead from their own hair. Sigrun has taken it upon herself to hold on to the beads till she adds the last one to the pile. Raising a brow, I look at the beads in her hand. "What are they for?"

"Kara is the best of us when it comes to braids. We offer beads to an expectant mother to lend her our strength during birth," Sigrun says as she looks at the beads, then at me. "The order you place the beads holds significance. The first bead is for the female tasked with protection of the child if you fall in battle."

My eyes widen thinking about it. My mates and Metatron lean against the tree, watching this most ancient of traditions. "I choose your bead to go first, Sigrun." As soon as the choice is made, Kara approaches and starts the braid on the right side of my temple. It's kind of like a mini French braid tight to the scalp. Mid temple, Kara takes the bead from Sigrun and braids it in place.

"The second bead is for the female to be your sword when you cannot fight because you are close to birthing your child." I look the beads over again this time I choose Brynhild, one of the strongest Valkyrie to have ever lived. She bangs the hilt of her sword against her chest armor and lowers her head to me. I nod in response, then look back at Sigrun.

"The third bead is the female tasked with teaching your daughter to fight," Sigrun says, and offers me the beads again. I pull out Gunnr's bead next, and she hoots and hollers, excited she was chosen.

I laugh at her antics and look back at Sigrun, who also looks very amused. "The final beads order isn't as important as the first three. They serve as back-ups if I should fall in battle as well."

I glance at Kara, then back to Sigrun. "Please set the best order for my children's safety." Sigrun hands Kara beads as she asks for them, and all I can do is sit here perfectly still. Once finished, she pulls the length of hair forward so I can see how the beads sit. "Thank you everyone!"

Sigrun helps me to stand up, and I make my way between all the females, hugging them and thanking them for their thoughtful gifts.

"Thana, we need to get going," Raphael says as he walks up and greets Sigrun.

"I know, I just enjoy spending time with the Valkyrie." Pouting, I give Sigrun a last hug and then follow Raphael down the trail.

I grip Raphael's hand, following him in a whole new direction. Reaching into my lunch bag, I pull out another chicken leg and start eating as we walk. I'm curious to see where he's taking me this time.

CHAPTER 40
RAPHAEL

To watch Thana interact with the Valkyrie warms my heart. Besides Joscelyn, Thana really doesn't have any female friends. What my beautiful mate doesn't know is that I'm taking her to pick up her best friend and for light training. Metatron moves up to flank Thana on her other side. She looks him up and down before refocusing on the path ahead of her.

I understand her fear and apprehension of bringing another angelic mate into the bond and possibly causing an influx of light. That very well could make her and Cyrus very sick, or possibly kill the two of them. "I have a surprise for you." My tone is light and warm. Hopefully, I can get Thana to see the benefits of having Metatron in the harem.

"You do?" She whirls on me and grips my bicep tightly, looking up at me.

I reach over and draw her to me and hug her tightly. "I do, well I should say we do." Motioning to everyone else with us to include them in the surprise.

"Thank you, everyone!" Thana's radiant smile shines brighter than the brightest star. Metatron double blinks, looking at Thana's reaction. I can see the moment her reaction hits home for him. His smile brightens and his eyes bleed golden.

"Yes, let's keep going right over here and … perfect." Once I have Thana in position, I wrap my wings around her and blind her from her surroundings.

"Oh, come on, Raph!" Thana whines at me and stares up with her silvery orbs.

Her tone almost gets me to break. Christian gives me the thumbs up, and I move my hands to cover Thana's eyes. Opening my wings, I position her so she can see her surprise. Slowly, I remove my hands from her eyes and place them over my ears. Even with my ears covered, I still can hear the shrill shriek that escapes Thana's mouth. "Joscelyn!!" She screams again and leaps into her arms. They cry and hug each other, bouncing up and down together.

I move to sit on the low wall watching Thana and her best friend hugging. "This is a very human thing they are doing, yes?" Metatron asks as he studies Thana's interaction.

"It's a very human thing. Being Nephilim, they are half human. Thana being the exception, she's only a third human." I explain it in the simplest form possible. Thana's unique heritage causes so many exceptions to the usual rules.

"So, is she more like us then?" Metatron tilts his head again, looking between Thana and me.

His question really catches me off guard, and I really have to sit here and think about it. Is she more like us? In all honesty, I don't have an answer for him.

"Raph?" Thana waves her hands in front of my face, making me refocus on her again. "Can we bring Joscelyn back home with us?" Her full lips drop into a pout, and I simply can't deny my mate anything when she looks at me like that.

Thana steps closer to me and my eyes bleed golden as my hand extends out of its own volition. Lightly, the pad of my thumb sweeps across the plumpness of her bottom lip. The silky texture is so kissably soft I almost lose myself in the moment staring at her. "Anything your heart desires, my love." Time feels like it stops as I lean forward and sip of her soft lips, eliciting a happy moan from my mate. Mission accomplished. Thana and Joscelyn bounce off and towards the Valkyrie.

"One day, I want to know what that's like." Metatron's deep tone rips me out of my blissful moment.

I sit back straight and run my hands through my hair, trying not to fully react to him. "In answer to your previous question, I believe Thana is more like us. Her emotions are all human, her reactions are all Dark Nephilim. Her ability to love and heal—that is all Angel." I tick the qualities off on my fingers, as I name them.

His gaze follows Thana and Joscelyn around the tree of life as well as the fire the Valkyrie have made. "I can see those wonderful traits in our beautiful mate. Do you think we need to return to feed her and the babies soon? It's been a few hours." Concern laces his tone as he briefly glances at me before looking back at Thana.

"We probably should." Before I have the chance to speak, panic floods the bond and Thana locks her gaze with me, then vanishes in a wisp of shadows.

"Crap on a cracker... Something happened either to Azrael or Samael for her to react like that." Christian and Gage catch up, and I fill them in as quickly as possible.

Metatron is gracious enough to carry Joscelyn through the clouds and all the way back to our house. Poor girl is still traumatized after what her mates had put her through. She still won't

show or use her wings since the night they died. We break through the cloud cover and Gage takes off like someone set his tail on fire. His wings are similar in build to Thana's, giving him the edge when it comes to speed and agility. I honestly believe that if he were to race Thana, she would win merely due to the weight to wingspan ratio.

Our house comes into view as we break free of the cloud cover, and there're flashes of light and darkness throughout the levels. Panicked, I push myself to the limits and fold my wings in, dropping like a stone from the sky. Throwing caution into the wind, I fly straight through the double doors Gage left open.

Thana is on her knees, leaning over Azrael, her hands glowing and covered in blackness over a gaping wound in his abdomen. Shadows flow through her tresses like waves on the ocean, blackening her normally pale blonde hair.

"Cyrus, what happened? Where's Samael?" I demand, as I watch our pregnant mate push herself further than what we have ever asked of her before.

"Somehow Samael's castle was breached!" Cyrus screams as his hands tear at the leather of his jacket. Clawed fingertips shred the leather like tissue paper. His blackened eyes appear hollow, almost vacant, like he's looking right through me. The look gives me a chill down my spine to the point I take a step back and decide to watch instead. Cyrus moves to kneel beside Thana and rests his shadowed hand on her back. A smile crosses Thana's lips as she leans into his touch and sighs. The power coming out of her hands increases almost tenfold. We watch the wounds on Azrael's abdomen and chest knit together. She unfurls her wings and spreads them wide and her power increases again. Soon enough she breathes in a deep breath and removes her hands from Azrael's stomach. Thana almost passes out within moments of removing her hands from him. "Get food ready for her, she overtaxed herself without eating." My tone carries the weight of my Archangel status.

Cyrus catches Thana before she hits the ground and cradles her tightly against his chest. Gage and Christian run into the kitchen to gather the food Thana needs. I'm shocked at how tender and gentle Cyrus is being with her. He's still an asshole to the rest of us, but at least his treatment of Thana has improved.

Azrael's condition has vastly improved since Thana healed him. His eyes open slightly, and he tries to look in her direction. "What happened?" His weak tone shocks me. All the years I've known him, I have never seen him this vulnerable.

"Samael's castle was attacked. Cyrus got you out and brought you to Thana." I reach down and assist Cyrus to stand so he can take Thana to the nearby couch and sit comfortably with her.

Azrael struggles to sit up on his own. I can't allow him to reopen his wounds. Gripping him by his bicep on his good side, I pull him up to stand. "It was a horrible experience, to say the least. Thousands of winged demons poured into the castle, ripping everything to shreds." Azrael grips my arm tightly and his eyes fade to the hazel of his human eyes. He pulls me down to his level and whispers in my ear, "They tried to take Samael prisoner."

My eyes widen, thinking about the implications of this event. "How?" My wings burst free of their own volition as panic rises in my chest. Looking around quickly, I wave for Metatron, Gage and Christian to come over as fast as possible.

Azrael's face pales as he thinks his answer over. Several times he tries to start talking, then breaks into a sweat and freezes all over again. It takes Cyrus walking into view for him to finally spit the answer out. "It was the Lance of Longinus. I thought we destroyed it after they killed the son with it." Azrael shakes his head and lowers it into his hands. His long black hair falls and covers his face.

My heart clenches as I think about the ramifications of the spear's existence. No wonder why they want Thana! She can go between all three realms and get close to the creator and kill him. I start to pace around the room, trying to sort my thoughts. Thana appears in my path and looks up at me with the most innocent smile playing upon her crimson lips. "Raph, we will be okay and so will Samael." She taps her temple, then I remember she can speak with him over a great distance. "He's safe."

Gage and Cyrus offer her plates of food, and she picks at both, snacking between the two. "Grandfather has confirmed the spear is in Lucifer's possession. And it is what hurt Azrael." Thana stares down at the plate of food before her, then rubs her stomach.

Quickly she stuffs loaded cheddar poppers in her mouth then looks at Metatron and me. "I need for the two of you to petition the most high for permission for Cyrus to be at the Tree of Life when I give birth. It's the safest place I can think of that the demons cannot get us." Her eyes plead with us to petition on her behalf.

Metatron looks at me, then Cyrus and Thana. "I will do everything within my power for you, even offer my life for your safety." He drops to his knees before her, and the room falls silent. Metatron, one of the strongest Archangels in existence, has lowered himself before Thana. His prostration at her feet shocks everyone. His silvery white wings unfurl and spread out wide at his sides in deference to Thana.

Sanguine tears roll down Thana's cheeks as she looks at Metatron. Cyrus leans in and whispers something in her ear, and she nods her head. Cyrus and Gage back away from Thana. As soon as they are clear of her, she unfurls her wings. Thana's eyes bleed silver as sanguine tears stream down her cheeks. Carefully, she lowers herself to the floor and hesitantly she extends her hand out and lays it on Metatron's head.

"If we survive whatever's coming for us. You and I will work on what needs to be fixed." Thana's wings spread wide as she lowers down the best she can and kisses the crown of his head.

"Go now, bring me good news." She rocks back onto her heels, keeping her wings spread wide. For an Angel or Nephilim, wide open wings shows trust or submission. Hopefully Thana has finally come to trust Metatron, it's been a long time coming.

Metatron goes into almost a push up to get off the floor. He remains in plank, taking in the beauty of Thana's wings. A single bob of his head is given before he vanishes in a flourish of golden glitter. Thana folds her hands in her lap and lowers her gaze to her hands. "I know I haven't been easy on him. He must be in his own hell watching everyone else with me." A soft sniffle can be heard and Joscelyn races to Thana with a box of tissues.

"Kitten, it's understandable. I was a royal asshole rebelling against the bond because of my mom." Cyrus smirks, then motions to Azrael. "Watching Dad with you, I see a different side of him.

Yeah, he's still the asshole that raised me. But he's a different type of asshole now." Cyrus rolls his eyes and motions to his dad.

Azrael grips his side and shakes his head from left to right. "Thanks? I think?"

"You're welcome!" Cyrus says with a smile that frightens the living daylights out of me. He's scarier when he's smiling than when he has his resting bitch face on point. The bastard gives me a wink, then escorts the women out of the living room, leaving me with Azrael, Gage, and Christian.

"So, what's the plan?" Christian asks the one question I have no answer for. Samael, one of the strongest among us, was almost taken. Thana, the only one strong enough to take him out if we have to is heavily pregnant. Our only hope at this point is that the creator allows Cyrus passage to the Tree of Life for Thana to safely give birth. I honestly think we're screwed, and not in the good sense.

CHAPTER 41
THANA

It's been ages since I've been able to spend time with Joscelyn. I can feel the pain and distress from her as Cyrus escorts us through the house. Her bastard mates did a hell of a job on her and now I don't feel bad for ripping their souls from their bodies. We enter my nest and Joscelyn stops dead in the doorway, looking around. "Cy? Can you please get us drinks and snacks?" Pouting, I blacken my eyes as I look up at him. He loves when I appear submissive to him.

"Anything your little black heart desires, Kitten." He places a chaste kiss on my cheek, then turns and leaves.

Joscelyn's face contorts between disgust and disbelief as she watches Cyrus and I interact. The minute he's out of earshot, she whirls on me and stares me down. "What the actual fuck was that?" She practically screams as her arms flail wildly.

My eyebrows raise in shock as I watch her losing her mind over Cyrus being tender with me. "What do you mean?" My hands caress my stomach, rubbing the growing orb, feeling my children moving around.

"That!" She throws her arm in the direction that Cyrus left in.

Narrowing my eyes, I wobble and rise to my feet. "If you're still mad about his role in your mates having their souls ripped out." My eyes instantly blacken as I stare at her, letting my wings unfurl. "Remember, I took your first mate's soul." Raising my taloned hand, I flex my fingers, staring at how menacing they look in the daylight.

Tears threaten to break and roll down her cheeks as she stares back at me. Her mouth opens and closes several times before the first of many tears trail down her cheeks in rivulets. My resolve for once didn't break from seeing her cry. Instead, I become angrier at the males that had damaged her to the point of being broken.

"I'm sorry, Thana. I guess I'm just jealous of what you have." Joscelyn wipes her tears on the back of the sleeve of her shirt and sniffles.

"Everything hasn't always been perfect. Nothing ever is perfect. We still have issues within the bond, just not as bad as they used to be." Cyrus just so happens to walk in as I finish my sentence and sets the try of food down then hugs me.

"We've all come a long way." His bad boy smolder is in full effect, and it makes my heart flutter looking up into his dark eyes.

A broad, proud smile graces my lips as I move to hug him. "Oof," escapes his lips as he looks down between us. "Was that the baby that just kicked?" His tone holds awe and excitement as he hesitantly places his hands on my stomach.

Motioning with my head, I call Joscelyn over and place her hands on a different area of my stomach. We stand here staring at my stomach, waiting for either baby to make a move. Through the bond, I reach out to my other mates and tell them to bring Metatron with them when he gets back. Deep down, I'm still having issues accepting him into the bond, but I know he will eventually be accepted.

The guys roll into my nest area excited to have their chance to feel the babies. Both babies decide to move at the same time, and I raise an eyebrow, looking puzzled. "Raph, how about you and Cyrus try holding my stomach?" At the moment, its pure curiosity as to if they are responding to their dads being close. The minute both men have their hands on my belly, the babies go ballistic.

My gaze shifts from Cyrus to Raphael and he's a vision of serenity. His orbs bleed golden, their mirror finish is hypnotizing as I watch myself in his eyes. "Aren't they amazing?" I say softly as they remove their hands, making room for Gage and Christian. Cyrus and Raph nod and smile as they move away from me.

Giggling, I grab Christian's hands first and place them on one of the babies' rumps. Gage, I find the other baby and place his hands there. Both males massage the body parts they feel and have the broadest smiles ever. The motions of their hands are soothing and comforting to me as I stand there waiting for the babies to do something. Gage raises a single brow as if to ask what we were waiting for. Just before I can answer, the twins start moving again as if they have a mini jungle gym in my stomach. Gage and Christian lean in at the same time and kiss my temples, then move away.

A shimmer of glitter forms in the corner of the room, Metatron has returned. Now is the time I am the most worried about. Hesitantly, he shuffles his feet across the floor until he's standing before me. "Lady Thana. I would like to start by saying I secured passage for Cyrus to the Tree of Life." He digs in his pocket and produces a medallion, then offers it to Cyrus. "He cannot take it off in the Angelic Realm, otherwise he will be destroyed utterly."

My eyebrows shoot up of their own volition as I look between Cyrus and Metatron. Cautiously, I reach out and grip his thick wrists and place his huge hands on my stomach. His hands encompass the majority of my stomach. Looking at the size of his hands on me really puts things into perspective. His brows knit together in the middle as he concentrates on my stomach.

Eventually, the babies move around and the look on Metatron's face is priceless. You would think I performed a miracle before his eyes, or like a blind man seeing for the first time. His mouth pops open and he slowly raises his eyes to meet mine. "They're amazing." The hushed words hold such reverence, it makes my stomach do that little flip-flop that inspires love's first butterflies.

All of these millennia of his existence, he has never witnessed life's creation firsthand. That in itself is a miracle to me. His feeling and seeing me change through the pregnancy, I suppose is as close to performing a miracle as I will ever get to do.

"Thank you." I raise my hand and cup his cheek, rubbing my thumb over his cheekbone. The blue of his eyes seems to almost glow of their own volition as his wings burst free of his back. Close up the edges of his glacial feathers appear to be lined in gold and catch every ray of light. This gentle giant before me has wanted nothing more than my acceptance and my love. My left hand finds its way into his long blonde hair and runs through it slowly. Metatron inches closer to me, leaning down and into my touch.

"What you did for Cyrus was no simple task. You have my eternal gratitude." Tears well up in my eyes as I think about how I would have had to have left Cyrus home during the birth.

Metatron's hands raise up instantly and he wipes the rogue tears away from my eyes. "Please, Lady Thana, don't cry." He hesitates for a moment before leaning in and kissing the last of the tears away. My eyes open wide, watching this herculean man bend down to my level. His tenderness doesn't match the bulk of muscle and strength he has. My hands still rest on his face and in his hair, his full lips inches from mine, and my heart hammers in my chest.

The entire room falls silent as Metatron and I stare at each other with our human eyes. My bonded mates push as much love and support as they can through the bond to me, trying to ease my nerves. His shoulders slump, and a defeated sigh escapes his full lips. He turns and pulls away from me and I tighten my grip on him. Metatron's eyebrows raise in question and my chest constricts at the pleading look in his eyes.

Reject him fully or accept him. Limbo is hell for an Archangel. Raphael's voice echoes in my head as I stare at Metatron. Closing my eyes, I draw a slow fortifying breath into my lungs, then unfurl my wings before him. Metatron's wings snap open to their full extension, displaying their grandeur in response.

Releasing my grip on him, I spread my wings wide for him to inspect just as I look his over. Carefully, I move towards his left side to get a closer look at his wings and their feathers. My fingertips skim over the soft under feathers near the bone, and I can feel him shiver from my touch. Archangels are a funny bunch. They love their wings inspected by their mates. Unlike Raphael, whose wings I have seen a million times, this is a very important moment for Metatron.

His hands cup my wing gently, tracing the length of my bones and the small feathers on the flight membrane. Goosebumps race across my flesh with every stroke of his fingers across my feathers. Gage moves behind me and rests his hands on my hips and starts massaging my lower back.

Metatron looks up, and something passes between him and Gage. Gage kisses the back of my neck and my shoulders, and I am instantly putty in his hands. There's something about being sandwiched between two powerful males that makes my body heat with desire. "He's a good male that's proven he's worthy time and time again." Gage advocates for Metatron and I can see the gratitude in his eyes.

Cyrus hits me with a low blow and puts on 'Centuries' by Fall Out Boy. I freeze in my tracks, listening to the lyrics. Retracting my wings, I shrug off Gage and step into Metatron's personal space. My palm flattens against his broad muscular chest as I push him backwards towards the arm of the couch behind him. Shock fills his eyes when his thighs hit the padded arm of the couch. Tilting my head to the side, I motion for him to sit.

I've never seen a man so large sit so quickly. A soft giggle escapes as I step between his spread legs. His scent reminds me of a warm blanket fresh off the clothesline on a spring day. Leaning in, I place the tip of my nose on his pulse and run it up to his ear. His body visibly stiffens, and I can hear his grip tighten on the couch. I press my lips to the shell of his. "I accept you," I say low enough that it's for his ears only. The breath he was holding escapes, and he lowers his head slightly in relief.

No sooner do the words leave my lips, Metatron's arms band tightly around my ribs, pulling me flush against him. I run the tip of my nose along his cheek bone till I am nose to nose with him. My hands slowly trace up his chest till my they rest on his thick neck. My thumbs sit over his arteries, feeling his heart rate pick up the minute we face each other. "You do?" His voice almost cracks as he utters the words softly so close to my lips.

I slide my hands up to up his strong jawline, running my thumb along the bone to up his cheek. Looking into his sapphire eyes, I've decided. I lunge forward and press my lips against his. The tethers of our bond flicker and lick at my lips as they caress each other. We become lost in the kiss we've both been craving for so long. All my fears fly out the window. I feel safe in his arms and wrap my arms around his neck.

Cheers erupt around us, and I can't help but blush and start giggling. Metatron quickly wraps us up in his wings and starts giggling right along with me. He peppers my face with kisses as his strong fingertips massage my lower back, finding aches I didn't realize I had till now. "You're going to spoil me." I say with a giggle, then gently kiss his lips again.

"Females are revered, because like the almighty, you can create life." His eyes shine and bleed golden as he looks at me. The mirrored orbs study me as a slow, easy smile reaches his eyes, causing the corners to crinkle. "So yes, I plan on worshiping you every day till the end of time as long as you allow me to." Gently, he presses his full lips against mine and I swear the silky texture is becoming addictive.

A pleased moan escapes me and I smile against his lips. "I look forward to it." I lightly bop him on the tip of his nose with my index finger. He scrunches his nose and does the same to me.

We start giggling and bopping each other on the nose till someone taps Metatron on the shoulder. He opens his wings and

Raphael is standing there smiling with his arms folded over his chest. "Congratulations, and Thana needs to eat." Raphael goes right back to his alpha first mate role. We break apart and he passes me off to Raphael to escort me into the kitchen to eat. The day just keeps getting more and more interesting.

CHAPTER 42
RAPHAEL

It's about flipping time that they came together. Part of me wants to throw a massive party to celebrate. But, on the other hand, I don't want them to feel pressured to take the next step.

I lead the way into the kitchen and start pulling out the dishes of food I had ordered for the family. I cover the table with several types of Japanese foods, Mediterranean food and barbeque. Thana's eyes light up the instant she sees the spread of food. Gage immediately moves to Thana's side, holding her plate as she piles it high with everything she wants to eat. "Is this usual?" Metatron asks curiously.

Nodding, I motion to the chair to my right for him to sit. "Each night it's a different mate's turn to take care of Thana and her needs at mealtime. Tonight, she'll sit on Gage's lap and eat her meal there." Shrugging my shoulders, I motion back to Thana, and sure enough she climbs onto Gages lap and starts eating.

Curiosity flickers over Metatron's face as he watches Thana and Gage interact with each other. One minute Thana is feeding Gage, then the next he's feeding her. Metatron's mouth opens and closes several times, looking at Thana, then back at me. "She's more powerful than all of us combined. She does not need to sit on some-

286

one's lap for protection." He tilts his head several times as he watches Thana curl into Gage several more times before going back to eating.

Cyrus laughs, and his eyes blacken. Just before he can speak, Christian rests his hand on his shoulder. An understanding passes between them and Christian stands, then bows at the waist. "Your Holiness, forgive the way I will say this. You do not know how it is to be shunned or mistreated. Many nights I held Thana as she cried, telling me about her day." A haunted look crosses over Christian's usually peaceful visage.

Shaking his head, he looks back over his shoulder at Thana and she smiles at him, seemingly unaware of the conversation we're having. Christian turns to face Metatron. "If you think in this lifetime or the next, I will ever allow her to endure that pain again. You are sadly mistaken." Christian's eyes burn molten gold in challenge as he stares Metatron down.

Glancing over at Cyrus, he's just as shocked as I am with the way Christian responded. I look back down the table, and Thana is missing off Gage's lap. Puzzled, I search the room, then notice Thana leaning on Cyrus's back, staring at us. "I seek the comfort of my mates when I eat because I grew up having food stolen from me by pure bloods on both sides of the veil. Going to bed hungry because I was afraid of being killed because of what I am was not a fun way to grow up." She practically growls out before freeing herself from Cyrus's back and curling into Gage's open embrace.

Metatron looks down, ashamed. "If I had been able to protect you, I would have. No one should have been put through what you were." His tone is full of remorse for the transgressions his mate endured before meeting him.

"At work Thana comes to eat in my office when Joscelyn isn't at work with her." I glance down the table at Joscelyn and tears threaten to spill down her cheeks. One can only assume Thana never told her friend about how hard life really was for her.

"I don't want anyone to feel sorry for me. The past is in the past."

She abruptly stands and walks out of the room without saying another word.

Cyrus rolls his eyes and shakes his head. "Bathroom break," he says flatly before locking eyes with Metatron.

"Angels and Light Nephilim have it easy. You're accepted the minute your eyes turn gold, or they see your white wings." He huffs and stands up, spreading his large ink black wings wide.

"These..." He motions to his wings. "Make me a target."

Cyrus slams his hands down flat on the table as his eyes blacken upon impact. "You want to help her..." He raises his left hand and jabs it in the direction Thana went. "You have years of hatred to reverse... Good luck..." Cyrus stands up and walks out the same door Thana did.

Shaking my head, I look between those that are left and sigh. "Well, we tried for a peaceful meal, sorry everyone." Sighing, I clear the table, pretty sure Thana will not be returning. Metatron unknowingly hit a very sore spot with Thana.

"Anything I can do?" Joscelyn's meek voice squeaks out from down the table at me.

Slowly, I turn to face her and shrug my shoulders. "Honestly, I'm not sure. So many things have piled up all at once on her, I'm shocked it took this long." Refocusing on my task, my hands grip the stacked plates before me, and I carry them over to the sink.

Out of the corner of my eye, Joscelyn appears at my right side with a dish towel in hand. We wash the dishes in silence, lost in our thoughts. "Thank you for taking me into your nest." Joscelyn's whisper-soft voice tugs at my heartstrings.

"You're Thana's best friend. Your parents took care of Thana and sheltered her for over three hundred years. We owe your family eternally for protecting her." Turning fully to face her, a gentle smile crosses my lips as I stare at her. "Our home is yours as long as you need it." I open my arms to her, and she rushes in and accepts my hug. I hold her tightly and she falls apart in my arms, crying hysterically.

It's more of a brotherly connection, I hold her to my chest and sigh softly. Thana walks back into the room and smiles, looking at the two of us. "Jos?" Thana's tone is firm yet soft. Joscelyn pulls away from me and rushes into her arms.

Thana goes all maternal on Joscelyn and starts running her fingers through Joscelyn's hair, trying to soothe her. "Raph? Do you know when the next trials are?" Thana says, then presses her lips to Joscelyn's temple.

Concentrating on Jeremiel, I request for him to arrive post haste to our home. Within a matter of moments, he arrives, and with the shift of his arrival my bond-mates walk into the room. "Everyone, I would like to introduce you to Jeremiel, for those not familiar with him. He is the Angel of Mercy and Divine Truth and Solutions." Smiling broadly, I motion to one of my oldest friends.

Joscelyn scoots away from Thana to go stand at the kitchen counter as Jeremiel approaches Thana. Dropping to his knees before my mate has my eyes widening.

"Lady Thana, thank you for allowing me into your nest during your delicate time." He bows his head, and his warm brown hair to falls down and around his face, hiding his visage from her.

Thana unfurls her wings and carefully bends forward and kisses the crown of Jeremiel's head. She offers her hands to him, and he rises to his full height before her. "Any friend of my mates is welcome here. I have a question for you, Jeremiel," Thana says, then moves to her favorite soft chair in the corner of the dining room.

Jeremiel follows her expectantly as she lounges on her dais, leaving her wings on display. "When is the next Mate Trials? And can the tethers of broken bonds be removed so my friend can find new mates?" Thana's eyes turn to pure chrome orbs, looking through Jeremiel as if seeing his very core.

Jeremiel swallows hard. "You're the Destroyer's descendant!" His voice wavers, and a feral grin crosses Thana's sanguine lips as she shifts her eyes to fathomless orbs, her eyes as black as pitch as she stares at him now. Reflexively, he shoots back, shocked at the display of her dual nature.

"I've witnessed nothing like this before." He looks back at me, then over at the other mates. By time he looks back at Thana, her eyes are back to being her human gunmetal gray.

"Can you help Joscelyn or not!" Thana's words reverberate around the room as if she was everywhere at once. Metatron cracks a smile as Thana pulls one of his tricks with Jeremiel.

Jeremiel's gaze jumps from Thana, then back to Metatron, then back to Thana again. "I can. I need you or your mate Cyrus's help, though. One light, one dark, it's how it's done. One to pull, the other to destroy." He says the words and Thana nods her head at Cyrus and he steps forward.

"Cyrus will help you, the twins are making me tired again." Thana's eyes move to Gage and he runs to the fridge to grab her a smoothie. Jeremiel turns to face me and mouths *twins?* All I can do is smile broadly at him and nod with pride.

"Jos?" Thana calls from her dais. Immediately, Joscelyn runs over and sits next to Thana. "I trust Jeremiel to sever the old bonds so you can find your mates. Cyrus will be with you every step of the way. Now go start your life over." Thana smacks Joscelyn on the ass and sends her to Cyrus and Jeremiel.

Christian, Gage, and Metatron all hover around Thana, offering her food and drink as she lies there rubbing her stomach. When in Rome... I sit on the floor in front of Thana's stomach, watching Cyrus and Jeremiel.

Both men place a hand on both of her arms, then unfurl their wings. Cyrus rests an obsidian wing on her right shoulder when Jeremiel places his on her left. They move at once, resting their wings on top of each other till a low hum fills the air. Cyrus and Jeremiel close their eyes as Jeremiel speaks the words needed, and Cyrus echoes them afterwards. Thana's fingers thread through the long hair on the top of my head, and her nails lightly scratch at my scalp.

"It's done, Thana send it into the great beyond," Cyrus says, holding a turbulent mass in his hands.

Thana pats me on the shoulder, and I move quickly and assist my pregnant mate. I swear her stomach has almost doubled in size in the last few weeks. She moves to stand before Cyrus and takes the orb from him.

She glances at her raven tattoo, and it comes to life instantly. Then she looks at Cyrus's as well, and it breaks free. Thana compresses the orb to a size the raven can carry in its mouth. "Take this to Samael, he'll know what to do with it." With her free hand, she holds the orb up and her raven takes off with it, Cyrus's familiar on its six.

"Jeremiel, come stand before me," Thana says with a curious tone as her eyes turn mercury, looking at him. A faint smile crosses her lips as she glances at Joscelyn. "After a bond has been broken, are there any laws forbidding a female from displaying her wings?" My eyebrows shoot up and damn, I think I know where Thana is going with this.

"None, Lady Thana," he says curiously, looking between Thana and Joscelyn.

"Joscelyn, it's time I repay the kindness you and your family have shown me my entire life. I was there the day you were born, and again today at your rebirth." Thana moves away from us and ushers Joscelyn out of the room and down the hall.

"What was that all about?" Gage walks over, stroking his beard, puzzled over the quick departure.

"I think I know..." Cyrus says, looking back at the door that Thana walked out of. He touches his bicep, sending his wolf to go watch over the girls.

"Mind enlightening us?" Jeremiel sounds a little irritated since we are speaking in fragmented sentences.

Smirking, Cyrus runs his fingers through his hair, pulling it up into a ponytail. "I'm not saying shit, she'll fucking gut me. Are you aware she killed Asmodeus, golden boy?" The cotton of his T-shirt barely contains his biceps as he crosses his arms over his chest. His resting bitch face is one hundred percent on point.

"She did what!?!" Jeremiel practically screeches, looking between us. The five of us nod and smile, looking at him. We have one hell of a female in our nest.

Almost an hour later, the girls come back, and Thana has put Joscelyn in one of her rose-colored gowns with matching heels. Thana has styled Josselyn's shoulder length hair and placed several ribbons in it. Joscelyn has put her full faith in Thana and her assessment of the situation. After everything she's been through, a fresh start would be a miracle at this point. Thana put herself in an empire waist gown matching Joscelyn's in color and fabric.

Thana tilts her head back like she did so many months ago and reaches towards the heavens as she unfurls her wings. Thana flaps her wings just enough to gain lift then leaves them hanging half open. She looks at Joscelyn and gives her a nod, then steps out of the way.

Joscelyn looks so unsure of herself as she looks around. Thana smiles at her and Joscelyn gives her a firm nod, then unfurls her white wings. Her flight feathers are clipped close to her wings, robbing her of flight. All of us growl at how her wings were butchered except for Jeremiel. His mouth hangs wide open, and his wings are vibrating at full extension. Thana's smirk says it all. Somehow, she knew.

Jeremiel and Joscelyn move into the sitting room to talk, and I just tilt my head, looking at Thana. "How?" I throw my hands up in question. I'm at a complete loss for words at what just happened.

Shifting her eyes to her liquid mercury orbs, she taps her temple. "I'm cute and I know things." She shrugs her shoulders before heading to the fridge. Grabbing a yogurt, she turns to look at me, smiling. "I can see the tethers of the bonds like this. Ours is a solid rope connecting us. Metatron's is like a spiderweb, it's there, just fragile."

Thana narrows her eyes and motions towards the sitting room.

"Theirs is a wisp of white smoke—kinda like an incense burner smoke. Just enough that it's there, but not strong enough to do anything." She shrugs her shoulders and walks out if the room to who knows where.

"The seer up on mount Sinai described the bonds the same way." Metatron's words hold a level of awe as he ponders Thana's new abilities. "We'd better keep this revelation to ourselves. I'll go speak to the others about what occurred to figure out what needs to be done to protect her." Without giving me a moment to speak, Metatron is gone in a blink.

Christian, Cyrus and I stare at each other before going back to what we were doing. Gage, on the other hand, follows Thana.

CHAPTER 43
THANA

Nothing is more difficult for me than to know my best friend had been tortured and her wings clipped. Seeing her wings made the rage bubble to the surface again after I had fought to contain it. My door clicks closed behind me, and I turn to see who followed.

Gage leans against the doorframe with a tub of ice cream in one hand and a spoon in the other. "Does my love need a snack?" Gage's smile is infectious, and immediately I motion for him to head to my gigantic beanbag.

Carefully, I crawl on my hands and knees into the beanbag, get situated, and wait for Gage to join me. Probably his smartest and dumbest decision. He hands me the ice cream before crawling into the beanbag with me.

Laughing hysterically, he rolls onto his back and takes the tub of ice cream away from me. "Hey!! Not nice Gage..." I pout and cross my arms above my stomach, still gripping the spoon.

Gage raises his eyebrow, then wobbles to get closer. His face hovers over mine and I feel the heat of his breath wash over me. His lips sip at mine and slowly work me into a panting mess. Just as I reach for him, he plucks the spoon out of my hand, then rolls to the other side on his back again. "Dick move, Gage, dick move."

Gage laughs again, and just before I can get the words out, he shoves a spoon full of ice cream into my mouth. "Hush that sinful mouth, beautiful." Gage's smile lights up the room as he sits the ice cream on the side. His powerful hands grip me under my arms and lift me up from my side of the beanbag.

He curls up to kiss me, using his arms to support himself. My hands roam his body, touching everywhere I can reach easily. He's playing with fire, and if I wasn't so uncomfortable, I'd ride him like the stallion he is.

Noises start to filter from upstairs, and I raise an eyebrow in question. "Azrael is throwing a party to celebrate the impending birth." He shrugs his shoulders like it's no big deal.

Sanguine tears fill my eyes, and I can't help becoming emotional. I've never had a party thrown just for me in my entire existence. "I want to go shower and get changed. I feel gross." My eyes plead with Gage and he immediately caves.

Cyrus enters the room and offers me his hands. "I hear from a reliable source that you would like to shower?" His smirk says it all. He and Gage are up to something.

"Out of all of the mates in this house, you two seem attached at the hip." I raise a questioning brow. Cyrus helps lift me out of the beanbag as Gage supports me from behind.

Cyrus's eyes blacken immediately. "So what if we are? Is that a bad thing?" A flicker of uncertainty creases his brows as his eyes move briefly to Gage.

Looking between both of my mates, I shake my head. "Not at all. Don't hide from me, that's all I ask." I smile and wink at the two of them and watch both of their faces light up. I kinda had a feeling they were involved when Cy said they both enjoy the darker side of things together.

Shrugging my shoulders, I head into my massive bathroom and start the shower. My curiosity is getting the better of me as I go about my shower routine. I take the world's fastest shower and braid my hair before walking into my nest room and go to search my closet for something comfortable to wear. The closet has nothing I want to wear, and it's getting frustrating. My dressers hold all my super soft and comfortable clothing. Sadly, I throw half the contents onto the bed till I finally find the leggings with belly support and the tank top that covers my butt.

Hysterical laughter echoes behind me and its Raphael standing at the door. His white dress shirt halfway unbuttoned and the sleeves rolled up to just below his elbows. I drink in every inch of him, right down to his fitted slacks. He's purposely wearing the pair that makes his ass look biteable. "Yum, what's got you looking like a GQ model, Raph?"

A blush creeps over his cheeks as a broad smile curves his sensual lips up. "Figured my mate would like this outfit." He does a very slow spin, letting me admire him from all different angles. "Does she approve?" He closes the distance and kisses my lips softly, lingering there, stealing the very breath from my lungs.

Giggling, I run my hands over the bare skin visible of his chest. "Yes, I definitely approve," I say as I press my lips against his. Reaching up, I straighten out his hair, then kiss him again. "I guess they sent you to retrieve me?" Raphael gives me a wink, then wraps the golden sash from the mate trials over my eyes.

So, this is how things are going to go down. I feel his arms wrap around me and then the sudden whoosh of him moving us through the house. I can hear Cyrus and Christian silencing the crowd, and instantly, I'm on edge. There're too many people in the house that I'm not familiar with. "You're safe love, there're several Archangels, and Azrael brought one of the Princes of Hell with him to sway him to our cause."

I relax a bit in Raphael's grip when I feel a much larger set of hands take my hands in his. "Lady Thana, will you do me the honor of allowing me to sit with you?" Metatron's baritone voice surges with a power that encompasses me. His desire to provide protection and comfort comes across loud and clear.

"Yes, I would like that." A rough exhale can be heard, and Metatron gives my hands a gentle squeeze. No sooner did the words leave my lips than his hands release mine and I feel him scoop me up as if I weigh nothing. Giggling, I throw my arms around his thick neck and curl into him. "As long as breath is in my lungs, I will never let you fall. You are too precious to me." He whispers next to the shell of my ear. If I wasn't already heavily pregnant, I think my ovaries would have just exploded.

In Metatron's arms I feel like a pixie, his broad, barrel chest is heavily muscled and hard as granite, yet his grip on me is nothing short of gentle. He rocks gently and sits down with me somewhere in the living room, then situates me on his lap so I can face the room. Carefully, he removes the blindfold, and I am at a loss for words.

They decorated the living room in little blue and pink angels. My eyes search the entire room, taking in every single detail. I'm in awe of how much trouble Azrael went through to do this for me. Azrael is the first to approach with a proud, fatherly smile. "I know this party doesn't make up for all the troubles you've faced. I just hope that now that you have your mates and nest, that the rest of your life is pure happiness. You deserve it, daughter."

"Thank you for this, Dad." My voice cracks at the end as my emotions get away from me. Damn pregnancy hormones. Azrael's usually stoic mask slips when I call him Dad, and a single tear escapes his eye. With Metatron's help, I stand up and hug Azrael tightly. I'm so grateful for all that he's been doing for me.

We slowly break apart, and he helps me wipe away my rogue blood tears. Clearing his throat, he helps me to sit back down on Metatron's lap. "Without further ado, let's get this party started." Cheers erupt around the room as the guys walk around, greeting everyone.

"Are you comfortable? Do you need anything?" Metatron asks as he cradles me against his chest, giving me the best view of the room.

Shrugging my shoulders, I look around. "Maybe a drink? But, I don't want to interrupt anyone." My tone softens and lowers out of habit. I honestly am not comfortable drawing attention to myself.

I look up at Metatron and his eyes churn gold as he stares off into the distance. Within moments, he's smiling down at me. "Raphael is having Christian bring you a smoothie and a snack. Never be afraid to ask for what you need, Angel. We are here to take care of you and every need you have." He presses his lips to my temple, and I have no reason to not believe what he's saying.

Christian arrives with the drink and fruit salad in hand. Pulling up a chair, he hands me the drink and feeds me the salad. "It's almost time for the gender reveals. Are you excited Tsuma?" Christian's smile is radiant and warms my heart, feeling the love he has for me through the bond.

"As long as the babies are born healthy, that all I honestly could hope for." Setting down my drink, my hands frame my stomach as I rub my belly slowly.

The clanging of a glass being hit draws my attention from Christian to where Azrael has Cyrus and Raphael standing up on an impromptu stage. "Attention everyone! Can I have your attention up here." Azrael's tone becomes commanding as he gets everyone to look at him. "We are here today to not only celebrate a new bond, but the impending birth of two babies from that bond." Azrael pauses as the guests cheer.

Raising his hands, he gets the room under control again. "As you can see, the expectant fathers are each holding a black balloon filled with either blue or pink confetti." He smiles. "I, of course, know what's in each…" Azrael smirks seeing how anxious Cyrus and Raphael are getting. The rest of my mates are getting a sick enjoyment out of watching their bond-mates squirm.

"As head of the nest, Raphael, you can pop your balloon first." No sooner do the words leave Azrael's mouth, Raphael's eyes light up like a little kid on Christmas morning. *POP* Pink confetti covers the surrounding area and Raphael is in shock. He stands there with the pink confetti all over him. A single piece of it in his hand staring at it.

"I have a daughter..." I say softly to myself. Females are rare, yet I carry one. My hand covers my mouth as I still stare at a confetti-covered Raphael. Metatron's strong hands rub my shoulders gently as I now look anxiously at Cyrus, fully expecting to see blue confetti in his.

Azrael motions to Gage to step up and collect a stunned Raphael. Once he's clear, Azrael starts again. "Congratulations on the daughter, Thana!" he shouts, and the crowd turns echoing his congratulations. "Now, son." Azrael turns to Cyrus and rests a hand on his shoulder. "Be a better father than I was. Be there and encourage your child from its first breath."

Cyrus nods then looks at me smiling. Crooking a finger, he beckons me to him.

Metatron helps me to stand again and escorts me to where Cyrus is. Taking one of my hands in his, Cyrus smiles. "You never gave up on me, even when I didn't deserve your faith. You've saved me in more ways than I can count. Pop the balloon with me?" Tilting his head to the side, he smiles, probably the sweetest smile I've seen from him.

Nodding, I grip Cyrus's hand tighter as Azrael hands us a bigger pin to hold together. We count to three together, then stab the balloon with the pin. Hundreds of little pink bats go flying everywhere. I have two daughters. Cyrus handles the news of a daughter much better than Raphael did and scoops me up gently, spinning me in a circle. I can't decide if I want to laugh or cry more.

We stop spinning suddenly, and Cyrus's wings unfurl. There's an ominous feeling coming from behind me, so I turn and look. The man standing before us looks like a stereotypical sleazy crime lord lawyer. His black hair is slicked back, and his suit screams opulence. It's the sharp angles of his face and his full-of-himself stance that curdles my stomach.

"Mammon…" Cyrus spits the man's name out as if it left a foul taste on his tongue.

Mammon, why do I know that name? Crap on a cracker, he's one of the seven Princes of Hell. "Cyrus…" He turns towards me and extends a hand, wanting to touch me. Rex manifests of his own volition and rests on my shoulder, blowing black flames in the direction of Mammon.

I kiss my skull dragon after he protects his mommy. "Good boy, Maelestor Rex." I curtsey slightly, not displaying my wings or overly lowering myself. "Pleasure to meet you, Prince Mammon." Taking a leaf out of Cyrus's playbook, I smirk and lean into Cyrus's side.

"Spirited female, aren't you? I can see why Lucifer is making a big deal out of acquiring you." His feral grin causes Rex to hiss on my shoulder. I look over at my familiar and whisper "return."

Turning my gaze back to Mammon, my eyes shift silver, and his face pales considerably. "I don't trust your intentions, Mammon. Besides, why the costume? If you truly aren't hiding anything, why not be yourself?" Before he can speak, I press my index finger to his forehead, stripping him of his glamor. Half Demon, half snake, he reminds me of a Naga or even a Marilith.

Crossing my arms under my chest, I tilt my head to the side. "You're known for wielding enchanted spears. Why should I believe you didn't aid in the attack on my grandfather, father-in-law, and mate?" My eyes blacken as I stare at him, and he knows he has signed his death warrant.

"My services go to the highest bidder." He crosses his arms and uses his coils to rise higher than me.

I raise my chin at Cyrus, and I unfurl my wings and click my claws together. "What's the cost of your immortal soul?" I open my clawed hand in his direction and pull at the darkness within him. The blackened wisps of his soul start to leak through his scaled chest, heading towards my hand.

His clawed hands fly up, trying to block his soul from leaving his body, and all I can do is laugh.

"STOP!! Okay, yes, I gave the spear to Lucifer. He threatened to burn me alive for all eternity." He sends panicked looks between me and Azrael, then back to me.

Turning my gaze to the Archangels present, "Judgement," is all I say before starting to hover several inches off the ground.

"Death." Is echoed Archangel after Archangel, none disagreeing.

A wicked grin crosses my lips as I drop two fingers down into my cleavage. Carefully, I remove the shrunken Daybreaker and palm it. "You do realize I've already killed Asmodeus, Baphomet, Merihem, and Beelzebub." I tick the names off on my fingers, using the tip of the shrunken sword.

"Impossible!" he bellows, and I watch the Archangels draw their swords, ready to intercede.

"Cyrus, my love, go stand next to Daddy." My tone is pure honey with sultry undertones. He kisses my cheek, then does as I ask. Most present haven't seen me reap a soul yet, this will get very interesting.

"Obedient dog!" Mammon screams, spit flying everywhere as his coils roll over each other, sounding like a rattlesnake's rattle.

Throwing my arms and wings wide open, light bursts in every direction as my reaper form becomes the one thing he's terrified of. Angels... White light bathes my opalescent wings, illuminating every fiber of their makeup. Gossamer fabric floats, shades of pale blue fading to white.

Mercury orbs focus on Mammon. "Death eternal is your judgement. Prepare to meet your maker." Infusing as much power as possible behind my voice causes it to reverberate, shaking everything within the house. Death eternal echoes over and over again. as if I am walking around the room repeating myself.

Daybreaker blazes to life, and as it becomes full length, black flames dance over the razor edge as I point it at Mammon. The balled spike on the end of his tail whips up, and then he rushes at me. A quick downward swipe of the sword, I cut his tail tip clean off.

Enraged, Mammon charges me again, and I shift back to my

normal form, clawed fingers extended and my sword ready. Before he can get to me, Raphael slices Mammon's head clean off. Blood spray covers me from eyebrow to elbow, blackened ichor runs in rivulets over my skin. Reaching out quickly with my clawed hand, I grasp Mammon's soul and burn it using Daybreaker's flames. Resurrection cannot happen without a soul. Thana five, Lucifer zero.

CHAPTER 44

HELL

The fires in Hell burn brighter as Lucifer goes on a rampage. Thana has destroyed three princes and two generals, and it makes his blood boil. Even the Succubi that bends to the Prince of Darkness, hides in fear of his wrath.

"Brother?" Mephistopheles's voice carries across the hallowed halls of Lucifer's lair.

"What!!!" Lucifer bellows, shaking the foundation of his hall.

"Your future bride vexes you I see..." Mephistopheles's voice is pure sarcasm, knowing full well the female in question is far stronger than expected.

Roaring at the top of his voice sends the minions running in every possible direction. Cloven hooves click on the marble floor as Lucifer approaches Mephistopheles. "She defies me at every fucking turn! She should be on her knees before me begging for my seed!" Flexing his taloned hand, he stares at the burned flesh before shifting back to a well-tailored man in a business suit.

Mephistopheles shakes his head from side to side, his disapproval clear. "You plan to make the Destroyer's descendent fall from grace? That's a rather tall order." The smirk that plays on his lips makes Lucifer want to punch him so hard his ancestors will feel it.

"Think about it..." Mephistopheles reclines against a pillar. "She single-handedly killed off five of your most faithful servants yet stands unscathed." Spreading his arms wide, he walks around the room.

"Get to the point already!" Lucifer's voice is deep and guttural, almost to the point of being animalistic.

"Take something she values above all others and use that to gain her submission," Mephistopheles says with a sadistic grin.

"Keep talking..." The words fall from Lucifer's lips like silk as he moves to sit on his throne.

Mephistopheles strolls around the room, then stops to face Lucifer. "Rumor has it Thana is pregnant. Steal her, and we run the risk of her destroying the underworld. Steal her baby, and she surrenders herself for her child's safe return." Mephistopheles pours himself a drink from the minibar in the corner before turning to face Lucifer again. "With as many light fuckers as she has in her bond, they would fight to save the child and let Thana go. Save the helpless innocent and all."

Drumming his nails on the arm of the chair, Lucifer ponders everything that has been laid out before him. Steal the mother, she decimates everything he's worked so hard for. Steal the child, the mother gives herself over to him willingly... It's honestly an easy decision. "Have my minions ready. The minute they leave the baby alone, I want it stolen and delivered to me!" Probably the easiest decision he's made since the fall. Now it's a waiting game. Lucifer is one step closer to finally seeking his revenge against that overgrown, power-hungry toddler in the sky.

BALANCE

CHAPTER 45

THANA

The Angelic Realm has always been the most beautiful place, I have never seen anything comparable in my existence. Raphael, Christian, and Gage have decided to join me for today's training session with Michael. Raphael carried me. Since I am in my final trimester, I am not to strain myself flying. Today the guy's head in a different direction than we have in the past.

In the distance stands what looks like a Greek coliseum. Tall white marble columns reach high into the clouds above. Rows of carved seats line the edges of the ring. In the middle of the ring where we land stands Michael in full armor with a broad smile on his lips.

"Thana! You are positively radiant!" Michael's booming voice echoes within the coliseum.

With a broad smile, I meet him halfway and he gently hugs me to him. "It's good to see you too, Michael. Thank you for making time for me today." I don't know what it is about the Angelic Realm, but here I always feel so jovial and more alive than I do back on earth.

"Whatever you need, never hesitate to ask. You are the mate of two of my brothers and I would never deny either of them anything."

Wincing at the mention of his brothers, I try to shake off the dread in the pit of my stomach.

Raph and my other mates move to the side and climb up into the bleachers to watch the training session. "I get the impression that everything isn't perfect with the addition of Metatron into the bond." Michael lowers his head and whispers near my ear.

Arching an eyebrow, I look up at him and shake my head slowly. "Am I that transparent?" My hushed tone only barely betrays my concern.

Michael looks towards the bleachers where my mates sit and then back down at me. "It's kind of obvious when only three out of four of your Angelic mates are with you." His tone is soft and understanding as he looks between them and me.

Roughly inhaling, I peer down at the swell of my stomach, watching the twins move about. "With all that he does. There is always balance. I am afraid by accepting Metatron, one of my light mates may fall or a new Dark Nephilim may join us." My eyes plead with Michael for understanding. "I can't handle anymore upheavals right now." My hands caress my stomach as I bring my eyes back to Michael, hoping he gets it.

I can clearly see the moment where what I said clicks. A slow single nod of his head marks the end of the discussion. "Today, we work on you manifesting light without crispy frying yourself in the process." Michael's voice projects, filling the ring with his baritone notes.

With a practiced flourish, Michael moves his hands so that they are palm up and light manifests, dancing over his fingers like flames. When I attempt to mimic him, blackened wisps rise from my fingers and move like waves on the ocean. "Hmm, this may be harder than I expected." Michael's tone is more curious than agitated. "Let's try again Thana."

"Remember to think about the sunlight in the jar Thana!" Raphael calls from the bleachers not far away.

Laughing to myself, I cup my left hand over my right, thinking about a mass of sunlight balled up in my hands. A gentle tingle moves over my flesh in waves as I concentrate on the light. A low hum surrounds me as I am filled with the urge to unfurl my wings. Releasing them, I feel an influx of power and flap quickly once before opening my eyes.

An undulating mass of light in my hands pulses with a power I have yet to learn to master. Flexing my wings, I notice that here, in the Angelic Realm, they are such a pale gray they almost pass for white. Imbued with a new level of confidence, I spin away from Michael and unleash the power in my hands.

The light flows like a flame thrower away from me and impacts the pillar on the other side of the ring. The light disintegrates the marble, turning it to ash. The pillar above topples and falls towards me. Standing there frozen in shock, I watch the mass of marble on its trajectory, headed straight for me.

Powerful arms wrap around me and I am lifted off the ground and into the air faster than I have ever risen before. Looking down, I see my mates and Michael looking up at me. Panic rises in my chest, stealing my breath as I finally gain the courage to turn and face my savior. Metatron somehow, someway, has managed to get to me before my other mates whom were with me. "How?" Is the only word I can get to escape my lips as I look up into his baby blue eyes.

"You needed me. I felt you amass the light and then the shock of what you had done hit me like a ton of bricks." Gently pressing his lips to the crown of my head. "I promised to protect you always, and I intend to do it." He guides us carefully back down to the training ring and the others rush us to check on me.

"I'm safe, thanks to Metatron's quick thinking." I turn my gaze to meet his and for the first time, true tethers of attachment pulse within the fragile bond.

Metatron's massive hands ghost over my wings and the pale gray returns to its natural colors. "Never change who you are just to fit in, my love. You are our dark angel, the light of our lives." His large hand cups my cheek, the pad of his thumb running gently over the ridge of my cheekbone.

Closing my eyes, I lean into his touch, sighing softly. Consequences be damned, turning my head I press my lips to his wrist. The pressure of his lips on my cheek sends a thrill through my body. My heart rate accelerates, and my hands move of their own volition to grip the front of his shirt. "Thank you." My voice is breathier than I intended as a smile creeps across my lips.

Cheekbone to cheekbone, we stand there frozen in place. Blossoming feelings warm my chest, giving me what is now so familiar when it comes from my other mates, love and affection. I sense the heat and presence of another of my mates at my back as hands gently rub my lower back. "Brother, there aren't words to express my gratitude for saving our mate." Raphael's husky tone echoes next to my ear.

"I would die for her." The honesty in Metatron's baritone voice hits me right in the heartstrings.

Flexing my wings, I push Raphael off of me and entwine myself fully around Metatron. His baby blues churn molten gold the minute I make eye contact with him. A tingle starts at the base of my skull and it is as though time stands still. Every movement honed in as our lips drift closer together. Upon contact, the tingle spreads across my lips and straight into my heart. Metatron's large hand grips the back of my head and tilts it back, deepening the kiss.

His grip on me tightens, pulling me as close to him as my stomach will allow. In what has to be the universe's biggest cock block to date. My water breaks...

CHAPTER 46
CYRUS

Taking over Dad's earthy duties has been no minor task. I have four hospitals and three nursing homes to visit as often as the Angels there need me to. Later today, I need to head back to the Shadow Realm and meet up with my old man as well as Samael. The hollow feeling in my chest is unsettling. Fucking Angelic veil blocking me from sensing my mate and child. What are those goodie two shoes hiding up there? So well at that it makes it impossible for me to feel my girl and child.

Turning a corner in the hospital that Raphael runs, he fucking glitter materializes before me. Jumping back, my sword manifests in my hand, prepared for an attack. "Be at ease Cyrus! We've got to go. Ahana is in labor." His clipped tone would normally set me off on a rampage. But it's about our mate and she needs me.

"Lead the way, Golden Boy." Dropping into a sweeping bow, I motion for him to proceed. He runs towards the stairwell leading to the roof and starts heading up. I give chase, taking the stairs two at a time.

"Do you have your medallion?" Raphael stops at the edge of the roof.

Pulling on the chain, I raise the medallion. Raphael takes that as his signal to take flight towards the Angelic Realm. Launching myself off the roof, I free fall for a moment before I spread my wings wide, shooting up into the sky. With each flap of my wings, my inner voice yells at me to turn around, that we're going to burn. Following Raphael, we break through the cloud cover and start heading towards a giant tree.

As we get closer to the tree, I notice the fucking Valkyrie are guarding my mate. She is leaning back against Metatron's chest while Christian and Gage are pacing around, concerned. We rush over to where the Valkyrie and Thana are. The Valkyrie are prepared to attack me until Thana calls my name, reaching for me. Raphael and I arrive at her side and grip her hands. A soft smile plays upon her full lips as she leans back, relaxing now that we are here.

Labor seems to intensify the moment Raphael and I make contact with Thana. Every scream makes the hair on the back of my neck stand on end. My inner demons scream at me to destroy whatever is hurting my mate.

"Raphael, please come here!" Sigrun's voice rings out, catching me off guard and snapping me back into reality. Thana looks between myself and Sigrun, then takes mine and Metatron's hands, pulling them to her chest. "On the next contraction, push as hard as you can." Sigrun says with a smile on her face.

Thana's eyes widen as she looks between me and now Raphael at her feet. I can tell the moment she steels herself for what is about to happen. Her eyes blacken as she looks at me. The vein in her right temple pops. and she bears down on the next contraction. An almost feral growl escapes her lips as she squeezes my hand tightly. This moment is when I realize how much power a female has when they bring a life into the world. Every scream and squeeze of my hand, I get to experience a little bit of what she's going through first hand.

Almost immediately after the next strong push, Thana sighs. I look down bewildered at her as I hear the first cries of the baby she delivered. It's a beautiful blonde-haired, gray eyed little girl who just so happens to shit black goo down her father's white pressed shirt. Snorting, I try to mask the hysterical laughter that wishes to escape my lips at the sight.

I get ready to move down Thana's body to take my place at her feet, waiting for my daughter when Metatron stops me. "Take this..." He hands me a second medallion like the one I am currently wearing. "The minute you can slip it around your child, do it. She may ignite up here."

I know Metatron means well, but I honestly wish he would not have mentioned this in Thana's presence. The look of fear on her sweet face makes me want to burn the heavens. "I've got this baby girl, I'll protect our child." I say quickly before moving forward to plant a kiss on Thana's lips.

I slip into the place vacated by Raphael and kneel at my mate's feet. I honestly was not prepared to see the swelling, blood and the crown of black hair peeking out of my favorite place on earth. My eyes widen, seeing the stretch and strain of my mate's most intimate parts and the crown of my daughter's head. A soft barely audible gasp escapes my lips as I stare.

"Son of Death..." a firm female voice says to my left, snapping me out of my thoughts. Sigrun, the literal Queen of the Valkyrie, is smiling at me with a pan of water in her hands and towels laid over her arm.

"Your highness..." escapes my lips as Thana screams again. With this push, my daughter's head is out, barely enough so that I can rest the chain carefully around her neck. Instinctually, my hand slides under her head, supporting it and the weight of the chain and the medallion.

"Her wings are stuck within her mothers channel. Thana had the same problem when she was born." Sigrun says softly as she kneels beside me. "Take your free hand and slide two fingers down your daughter's spine then out towards her wings." Sigrun demonstrates the motion down my free forearm.

"Okay. But I'm not medically qualified for this shit..." Sigrun rolls her eyes and shoves my hand at my daughter. Reluctantly, I draw my index and middle finger down my daughter's spine and out towards where her wing should be. A smile breaks out across my lips as I feel her tiny wing for the first time. Gently, I manipulate her wing so that it's not hung up anymore on her mothers pelvis. Slowly, I slide to the other side and free her other wing.

"Come on baby girl, one more push and our daughter is free." My heart hammers in my chest as I watch Thana strain and push with all she's got. Several pushes later, my daughter, the light of my life, slides free of my eternal love. Sigrun gently cuts the cord and cleans my daughter up while I hold her. I am mesmerized staring at my little girl. I see the perfect blending between Thana and I in this precious little bundle in my arms.

Metatron helps Thana to sit up and she leans over to look at our little dark angel in my arms. "Both girls are so perfect. We are so blessed." Thana's breathy tone pulls at my black heart. I smile warmly at her and nod, agreeing.

Sigrun and the other Valkyrie take Thana away to a healing pool and leave the rest of us staring at our precious little bundles. My baby girl flaps her tiny wings and coos, looking up at me. Blackening my eyes, I stare down at my little one and she coos even more. Her little gray eyes bleed chrome as she stares up at me, then blacken immediately. Double blinking, I look up at the others. "Um Raph, turn your eyes gold and see what your daughter does. I'm curious..."

Raphael raises a single eyebrow, looking at me, then looks down at his child and his eyes bleed golden. I can see the chubby little arms of his daughter reach up and he double blinks, looking at her.

"Cyrus... Did your daughter's eyes turn silver before going to your color too?" Raphael's voice wavers for a moment when he finally looks up at me.

"Yeah it did. That's why I asked you to check." Rolling my eyes, I look back down at my daughter and kiss her forehead.

Sigrun returns and smiles at us. "Fathers and mates of Thana, please follow me." Her powerful formal tone catches me off guard and I quirk an eyebrow up, waiting to see everyone else's reactions.

One by one the Angels and Gage move to follow Sigrun. "We may as well follow." I whisper to my daughter. Rocking carefully, I stand up and walk behind the group, heading towards what looks like a Greek style house on a hill.

Climbing the stone stairs up the side of the grassy hill, we finally arrive at the front door. The golden bars open, allowing us passage into the ornate house. They painted the walls with frescos depicting the various events before and after the fall. The one painting that catches my attention is my father with white wings off to the right-hand side of the almighty. It's definitely something I wasn't expecting to see. "Your father was and is treasured by the creator. He helps maintain balance in his own way." Metatron almost scares the daylights out of me.

"Yeah, but his work is feared and deemed evil. Let's face it, we're not favored." My tone is clipped and slightly venomous. Dark Nephilim and the fallen are treated like shit by most in existence.

Sympathy crosses Metatron's features as he looks at me. "I never understood the stigma myself. Death is equally as important as life. Without the balance of life and death, the time humans have on earth would hold little meaning." His view of the circle of life is a unique one and takes some of the edge off.

"I wish more Angels saw it the way you do. Our job is as important as yours. Angels can take lives as well, it's only a feather color thing I suppose." Shrugging my shoulders, I look down at the little black feathers on my daughter's wings. Lightly, I run my fingers over her wing bones, stroking the baby feather fluff that protects the bone.

"We're working on it the best we can. Nephilim have free will, which makes it hard to influence their thoughts and feelings towards the old rivalries." Metatron's sympathetic tone catches me off guard. I grew up thinking that all the Angels hated us because of being the children of the fallen.

"The Dark Nephilim are no better. We have an inbred hatred for anything with white wings because of how we're always treated. Look at poor Thana and what they have done to her, and no one saw her wings." I motion my hand in the general direction I know Thana to be in.

Nodding stiffly, Metatron motions down the hall for me to follow him. "I have been using the cube to seek out all of those that have mistreated our mate. They will atone for what they have done." The word *done* reverberates through the hallway, shaking the pictures in the frames as if an earthquake has hit.

Shifting my daughter in my arms, I rest a hand on Metatron's shoulder. "I've misjudged you. Forgive me." For once, I actually feel bad about what I've done. This man before me is trying to rectify all the crimes committed against our mate.

A brilliant smile breaks out across Metatron's face and he pulls me into a half hug, being cautious of my daughter. "There's nothing to forgive. You didn't know me and you were trying to protect Thana. You're a good man Cyrus..."

A hearty chuckle escapes my lips as we walk. "Shhh... don't let that get out. My rep will be damaged beyond repair." The chuckle turns into full on laughter as he turns the corner. Stepping into the ornate bedroom, my breath hitches seeing Thana propped up in the bed with Raphael's daughter latched to her breast.

Breaking away from Metatron, I arrive quickly at Thana's side and kiss her forehead. "You did good love. How are you feeling? Do you need anything? Anything I can do?" I fire off questions faster than she can possibly ever answer.

Thana's giggles echo in the silent bedroom as the broadest, brightest smile breaks across her ruby lips. "Everything is how it should be, Cy. The girls are both healthy and I am well. Love surrounds us and it can't get better than this. It's more than I could ever dream of." Thana's words make my chest constrict slightly. We brought her this joy and happiness. My job as a mate is complete. Thana is safe and happy.

Thana looks up and motions to Raphael and he collects his daughter quickly, before he moves off to the other side of the room to rock her to sleep. Christian, Gage and Metatron follow Raphael, leaving Thana and me alone.

Gently, I lay my daughter in her mother's arms and Thana smiles, looking down at her. "My little Nikita." Thana places her lips to our daughter's head and a glow envelopes her. The baby retracts her tiny wings and nuzzles Thana's breast before latching on and closing her eyes to feed.

"What was the glow?" I've never witnessed a baby being named before, so the sight of what happened puzzled me.

"Ah that..." Thana laughs for a moment, then looks back up at me. "Her name, Nikita, means unconquered. A mother infuses a name with power, blessing the child so that the name holds true. Or so Sigrun tells me." Thana's hand caresses Nikita's head gently.

"She is to be your father's successor far in the future, as I am to be Samael's successor sooner rather than later." Thana's even tone tells me she's at peace over what will occur in the future.

"Why is she my father's successor and not me?" The news almost aggravates me, but also takes a weight off my shoulders I didn't know I was carrying.

Shaking her head, Thana just smiles. "You are my mate..." She tilts her head, looking at me, expecting me to connect the dots.

I'm puzzled by her short answer, that is, before I really think about the implications of what she has said. As Samael's successor, she will be going back and forth between all three realms. She needs me more at her side than in my own place of power. "Oh... I get it." Once I looked past what I thought I was losing, I could truly see what I was gaining.

A knowing smile crosses her lips and she giggles. "Both of my daughters are like me. No one will treat them how I have been treated." Thana's eyes churn with molten mercury as she stares down at Nikita. "She has very little human in her, precisely the amount she needs to maintain her humanity and free will." Thana's voice is almost detached as she speaks and reverberates around the room.

Thana's voice gains Metatron's attention and he returns, looking between Thana and I. "Is everything okay? I heard you use the voice and came as soon as I heard it." Metatron looks between Thana and I, before settling his gaze on Thana.

"Everything is perfect. Nikita is Azrael's true successor, as I am Samael's. I felt I needed it to be announced so that all would hear me." Thana holds her head high, almost daring Metatron to go against what she had done.

Metatron barely has time to open his mouth when an orb of white light manifests in the center of the room, moving towards the bed. Thana's mercury orbs lock on the light sphere then darts over towards Metatron. Without a second thought, Thana summons all of her mates into the room as well as the Valkyrie. Collectively, we stare at the orb. Metatron and Raphael seem to be the only two not on edge. "What is going on?" I shout at the two Archangels in the group.

"Thana is about to receive a gift." Raphael says calmly. The baby in Raphael's arms reaches out towards Thana, wanting to go back to her.

Still staring at the orb, Thana adjusts her top and sits both babies on her lap with her. Reverently, she stretches her hands out, palms up towards the orb. In the palms of her hands she gathers light, welcoming the orb into her hands. The orb touches down and lands in her palms, and turns into two golden feathers and a gold bracelet.

Staring down at the treasures in her hands, she smiles and closes her eyes for a moment. The most serene look crosses over her visage before she smiles, looking back at us. "Cy, I need you to unfurl your wings then turn them towards me."

Without hesitation, I unfurl my wings and stretch them wide before angling myself towards Thana and offering my right wing to her. She takes the feather and touches it to one of my flight feathers. She lines the edges of my feather in gold and it spreads across all of my flight feathers on both wings. "What's this?" I stare at the color upgrade curiously.

"You have been granted free passage between earth and the Angelic Realm. Your choosing to forgive and ask for forgiveness has earned the upgrade, as you call it." Metatron says beaming at me.

My eyes jump between Thana and Raphael, then back to Thana again as she brushes the feather along my daughter's now exposed wings. "Nikita is also granted passage since this is the safest place for the babies to be." Thana kisses our daughter's head, then passes her off to me.

A very serious look crosses her face as she places the bracelet on herself then moves Raphael's daughter to sit before her. "Davina..." She bows forward and presses a kiss to her daughter's forehead while her name reverberates throughout the room. The same glow that embraced my daughter embraces Raphael's. Once the glow fades, Thana reaches out for Nikita, taking her back from me then snuggles both daughters to her, lays down to go to sleep.

"I wonder what the bracelet is for?" I say to no one in particular.

"Some things we are just not meant to know." Raphael says cryptically. Leaving us all hanging with more questions than answers. The only person who could possibly know has just gone to sleep.

CHAPTER 47
THANA

Dreams of earthquakes, hurricanes and tidal waves fill my slumber. Guns blazing innocents falling and at the center of it, what I picture the embodiment of evil to be. "Thana, it's about time I get to meet the next Queen of Hell." He oozes confidence and dark swagger. His sinful tone slithers into my mind, echoing his dark sexy intentions...

Looking him up and down, I finally notice he has me dressed in what I can only describe as a patent leather catsuit. "Interesting choice of clothing you picked for this invasion." A feral growl escapes my lips as I run my hands down my body, changing the outfit to my black wedding dress. "One thing you forget Morningstar... I am neither Fallen nor Angel. I am both as they designed me to be." I raise an eyebrow in challenge at him. I know full well he has no power unless I grant it to him.

Lucifer stifles a growl with his lip raised and with a sharp canine tooth showing. His prim and proper exterior falters, and the true face of Lucifer shows for a moment. He catches the slip and schools his features again. "I will have you by my side!" His tone rumbles and shakes the surrounding cityscape.

Smirking, I stare at him as I unfurl my wings and spread them wide. Deep in my chest, I feel something snap and a surge of power courses through my body. It's now that I truly start to understand what my grandfather was talking about. Focusing on the hellish cityscape, I bend it to my will. The world that Lucifer built starts to crumble around him and the shock on his face says plenty. He didn't expect me to understand how dreamscapes work.

The illusion falls away, leaving a sea of blackness, then rebuilds in the image I wish it to be. Paradise, the one place all pure souls can enter, manifests around us. Clouds lightly cover the grass like fog, and beautiful flowers sprout up all around us. For added effect, I make it seem as if Lucifer's suit is starting to smoke. His eyes widen as he stares at the sleeves of his Armani suit disintegrating before him. I raise my right hand palm flat and face him as light builds. "I cast you out Lucifer, out of my dream and out of Heaven once more." The blast of holy light heads straight for him and I awaken just before impact.

My eyes roam over my two sleeping daughters and then Metatron sitting in the chair watching us. "Are you okay, Thana? I felt the shift in your dreams and came to watch over you." He looks down and away for a moment before looking right at me again.

"Lucifer tried to tempt me in my dreams." Reaching up, I run my hands through my long hair as I draw in a slow, deep breath. A smirk plays upon my lips as I study Metatron. "He didn't know who he was messing with. I cast him out of my heaven-scape. Then I woke up." Shrugging my shoulders, I notice my other mates are standing by the doorway, listening.

"I can't believe he attacked her in her sleep!" Gage practically yells as he throws his arms up in the air.

"Bold move on his part... Where did he bring you to in your dream?" Raphael questions as he moves to sit on the end of the bed.

Running my fingers over my daughter's back, I ponder Raphael's question. "Luxor Park on the west side, north of the city. I noticed Jayce and Klaus' pastry shop on the corner of Tenth and Newman Ave." Glancing back down to my daughters, then up to the boys. "I can try to show everyone what happened?" I extend my hands out to them and wiggle my fingers expectantly.

Metatron grabs my right hand and smiles, Cyrus takes my left, then mate after mate takes hold of the next's hands. Once everyone is linked, I close my eyes and draw in a deep, cleansing breath. I pull all of my mates back into the memory of the hell-scape that Lucifer had drawn me into. The guys watch what transpired as if it's a huge movie. The part where I shift the dream takes them all by surprise and they stare at me when it happens.

Horrified looks cross their faces when I draw the light to me and cast Lucifer out of my version of what I think Heaven looks like. We return to the present and I release Cyrus and Metatron's hands at the same time. "That's what happened." I state matter-of-factly. Slowly, I raise my gaze to my mates and glance at each of them one at a time.

Cyrus is beaming with pride saying, *that's my girl*. Raphael and Metatron are huddled in a discussion in the room's corner, away from the rest of us. Gage and Christian are smiling and talking with Cyrus. Shaking my head at the guys, I lean back and latch both daughters on my breasts to feed them.

"Thana love?" Raphael says sweetly as he slides up next to me and starts petting the back of his daughter's head.

"Yes?" I tilt my looking at Raph, wondering what in the world he is working himself up to.

"The heaven-scape... What inspired that?" His eyes turned liquid gold as he looks at me. It's almost as if I hold all the answers to the universe.

Shrugging my shoulders, I tilt my head to the side. "Not sure... To be honest, if I had to picture what Heaven looked like, I would imagine it to look like what I created." I furrow my brows, looking at both Archangels. I'm kinda getting the impression that maybe I crossed a line I didn't know about. "I mean, I only really have the Angelic Realm to gauge what I would believe Heaven would be like."

"My love..." Raphael grips my elbow and smiles. "You envisioned Heaven perfectly. It's actually the field where pets go when they die." Raphael's face softens as he leans forward and kisses my cheek.

Changing the subject quickly. "How soon can we go home?" I say softly as I watch my children.

"I'm not sure. We should wait till you've completely healed?" Metatron says questioningly as he caresses my shoulder.

Turning my head, I look at Metatron, his blue eyes churn gold as he ghosts his fingertips over my shoulder. "Okay, but we need one-on-one time in the future." I waggle my eyebrows, looking at him and wink. He double blinks and looks around at the others quickly.

Cyrus almost drowns in his drink and then laughs. "Oh boy, you're in trouble now, Golden boy!" Cyrus keeps laughing as he and Gage high-five looking back at us.

"Be nice, Cy, or I won't play with you and Gage together anymore." Smiling sweetly, I watch the smile fall from Cyrus's lips as he realizes the implications of what I just said. His eyes dart to Gage, then back to me, confirming I mean business.

"What games do you play together Thana?" Metatron asks innocently, smiling at me. Raphael coughs and Christian is the first to hit him on the back to clear it.

I laugh to myself and arch an eyebrow in Metatron's direction. "Let me show you. Cyrus, I need to borrow your perspective for some of it." I offer Cyrus and Metatron a hand and wait for them to take it. Cyrus has that wicked gleam in his eyes as he smiles at me. Poor Metatron has no clue what's about to be shown to him.

Quickly, I sift through Cyrus's memory and find the one I want. I sort the vision I want to show Metatron out before I bring him into the dreamscape I created. The soft touches upon my flesh. The silk ties holding my hands strapped to the pull-up bar in the doorway. Cyrus and Gage teasing every inch of my exposed flesh, sending shock waves of pleasure to my core. Metatron's grip on my hand tightens as I push the feelings I was experiencing into him. The complete bliss that washed over me when finally forging a bond with Cyrus. His perspective, how I looked and felt to him, transferred from him through me to Metatron. A deep moan escapes Metatron's lips and his hand tenses around mine.

I break contact with my guys and look at Metatron. The evidence of what happened clearly stains the front of his slacks. I can't help but pull him in close for a hug after making him orgasm from a memory of mine. "How" His voice is soft as he bands his arms around me.

I press my lips to his cheek and smile against his flesh. "Grandfather taught me that one. My ability to pass my feelings onto others will only grow with time." Pulling back to study him, the radiant smile on his lips warms my heart.

"You need to be careful with that gift, my love. It's a trick of Lucifers to seduce Angels into falling from grace." Raphael states flatly. His face is contorted into a mask of what I can only assume is disappointment.

Shaking my head, I lower my eyes once more towards both of my daughters. "We should consider what we should do with the children when we have to return to Earth." Carefully, I pass my now sleeping daughters off to their fathers, then stand up and stretch.

Metatron drops to one knee before me and offers me his hands. "I would be honored if you allowed me to remain with you and the children to protect you while your other mates work." Metatron's sense of duty takes me by surprise. It's not that he desires to be by my side, he feels he needs to be my guardian and not my mate.

Crestfallen, I bow and press my lips to his forehead before unfurling my wings and taking off. My heart aches over the thought that my initial rejection has damaged the bond to the point he's resigned himself to being just a guard. I fly for what feels like forever till I reach a new area I have never seen before. Landing by what appears to be a lake of mercury, I stare at my reflection in the water.

"I come here to think too..." Michael's deep voice catches me off guard. My sadness is mirrored on Michael's face.

Lowering my wings, I pull them in tight to my shoulders as I approach Michael. Pressing my forehead against his chest, I sigh softly. "I think I accidentally damaged the bond with Metatron like

Cyrus did with me." He gently bands his arms around me, pulling me flush to his chest, offering me security and comfort.

His large, powerful hand cups the back of my head as he holds me. "There's nothing wrong with the bond between you two. He's had only brief interactions with anyone besides the Archangels and the almighty. He's more innocent than Raphael was. Be patient with him." Michael's hushed tone pulls at my heartstrings.

Pulling back slightly, I raise my gaze towards Michael. His lips gradually turn up into a smile, and I can't help but smile back at him. "Have you met my other mates? I think I deserve an award for being the most patient female in existence." I say jokingly as I stifle a laugh.

Michael releases me, then presses his lips to my forehead. "One day, when I am graced with a mate. I hope she's as wonderful as you are." His brilliant smile and hopefulness makes me smile right along with him.

"You're a good man, Michael. Any female that is lucky enough to have you as a mate is blessed." My words sing with honesty as I smile, looking at him. Tilting my head to the side, I study him closely. "Is there something I'm not aware of, Michael?" His golden skin blanches for a moment before returning to his full color.

"Yes?" He wrings his hands in front of him as he shifts his weight from foot to foot. "I'm not at liberty to say at the moment. Other things are still in play that can change the course we are all on." He furrows his brows in the middle, looking at me, hoping I won't press him further for answers.

"I suspected such." Tapping my index finger against my lips, I tilt my head in the other direction and smile. "Whichever of my children is your mate. I know they are in good hands." I say firmly, with certainty. If there's one thing I have learned over the almost four hundred years, I've been alive. Michael is the defender of the weak and honest to a fault. If he ends up being the mate to one of my daughters, then she's in the safest place possible with him.

This new perspective makes everything better, I am calmer and settled,

it's time to head back. "Come see the babies when you have a moment. I'd love to introduce you to them." I bounce up quickly and kiss his cheek before launching up into the sky to fly back to my family.

Each flap of my wings propels me across the sky much faster than most of the Angels and Nephilim that I know. I believe it has something to do with my inheritance from my grandfather, why our wings have such a unique shape. Everyone is super hush-hush about the details of how I am to become his successor. Most of the ancient tomes say succession only happens when the previous guardian or ruler dies or is defeated in battle.

I don't want my grandfather to die just so I can ascend, but on the other hand, if it keeps my children safe, I guess there's no other way. I'm so lost in my thoughts that I almost forget where I'm going. I make a hard turn and swoop down into the gardens of the house. I land in the roses and walk back into the house, seeing the boys huddled around the babies. Sneaking up behind Cyrus, I look over his shoulder looking at my daughter sleeping in his arms. "You did good Daddy." Kissing his cheek before moving over to Gage.

Gage has Raphael's daughter in his arms, snuggled in close, crooning to her. He looks perfect with the baby in his arms. I cannot wait to see him with his own baby in the future. "Hey baby, how's my little girl doing?" Kissing Gage's cheek, I rest my head on his shoulder, watching Davina sleep.

"She's magnificent. I never believed in love at first sight till I saw you and her. Nikita is just as amazing as Davina and the fact she has her wings blows my mind." The awe and sheer joy in his voice warms my heart so much. Who would have thought my two little miracles would bring the family closer together this quickly.

Cyrus slowly approaches with his bad boy swagger in full effect. All I can think about is being sandwiched between the two of them in the throes of passion. "What naughty thought crossed your mind, angel?" Cyrus drops his voice a few octaves and makes my body flush almost immediately.

"Oh, remembering the blindfold, the ties and the pull-up bar…" A blush turns my cheeks a brilliant shade of red as I turn my head down and away.

Cyrus grips my chin firmly and lifts my gaze to meet his. "Never lower yourself to anyone, my love eternal. You are Samael's successor and the mate to two Archangels." Cyrus releases my jaw and drops to his knees before me and spreads his wings wide, lowering his head to me. "My life, my sword, and my heart are yours always."

Bending down, I press my lips to the top of Cyrus's head and remain there for a few moments. "You are my dark knight, my protector from all the evils of the world." I whisper against the crown of his head. I rise slowly, and offer him my hands, assisting him while he stands up. Quickly, he sweeps me off my feet and bows me backwards, kissing me silly. The rest of my mates hoot and holler, cheering Cyrus on. They know how rough of a start we had.

CHAPTER 48

CYRUS

I am literally on top of the world with Thana in my arms. The major feather in my cap is that it seems to me that she favors me over the rest of her mates. Be it because of how poorly the Light Nephilim have treated her over the years or that I simply understand the war that wages within her. Either way, it's a huge win for me. I let a blushing Thana back up and laugh as Metatron walks over with my daughter in his arms. Yeah, I was sneaky and passed my little girl off to him to get my woman in my arms again.

Thana walks off with Nikita and sure as shit Raphael and Christian are hot on her ass, following right behind her. "Absolutely insane!" I throw my hand in the direction that they leave in.

"What is?" Metatron says curiously, watching them leave.

"This bull s……." I stop myself from finishing the sentence, remembering where I am currently. Metatron still isn't connecting the dots, and it's pissing me off.

Motioning again in the direction Thana departed in. "No matter what happens, they chase after her like she's unable to fend for herself. She could be the Queen of Hell if she so desired it!" I say, exasperated.

"If she falls, so will all of her light mates." Metatron's doom and gloom reminder squashes my anger momentarily.

Smirking, I look up at him. "What if adding you makes her sick because there's too many Angels in the bond? What then, your highness?" Sarcastically I spit out my worse fear, trying to play it off. What if this behemoth poisons Thana and me?

Metatron paces, pondering what I brought up. "One of two solutions comes to mind. She either takes another Dark Nephilim mate. Or a light mate needs to make the ultimate sacrifice and fall." Sadness washes over his face as the gravity of the situation hits him.

"Will the one that falls die?" Gages question catches me off guard and I turn quickly to face him. "They have already punished me once for going against divine law. It would be easiest for me to fall if it's needed." Gage's tone tells me he's thought about this before. Probably around the time I was abducted and Thana was dying from excessive light in the bond.

"Lets hope it doesn't come to that." I say quickly, hoping to table that conversation till a much later date.

Before Gage can argue the point further, Thana comes walking back in, following Raphael, who has a cart of food with him. They proceed to set up the food and we gather around to enjoy the meal together. Biting my bottom lip, I ponder the ramifications of Gage falling.

"What's on your mind, my love?" Thana's voice sobers me up quickly and I force a smile looking at her.

"Not much baby, just pondering our next move." Raising my shoulders, I smile again, trying to be more genuine this time. Looking at my mate and thinking about my daughter must have given me the look she was looking for, because she didn't press me for any more details.

I watch Thana move around the room and finally she comes to sit on my lap to eat her meal. Wrapping my arms tightly around her middle, I press a kiss to the back of her neck. Her giggles sound like music to my ears, making me smile broadly. Never in a million years did I ever think I would be able to sit at a table in the Angelic Realm. I watch over Thana's shoulder while she prepares plates for the two of us. "Where's the baby's beloved?" My soft words cause her to sigh before leaning back against me.

"Michael and Gabriel have taken it upon themselves to keep an eye on the babies while we eat. Neither are mated, and I'm kinda hoping one of my daughters are their mates." Thana's mischievous giggle tells me she has privy information that she's not ready to release yet.

"What precisely do you know, angel?" Metatron asks and his firm deep tone makes Thana shiver in my lap. Hmmm... is my mate secretly a submissive?

"Umm..." Thana stammers and pauses in her speech before looking back at me.

"What is it, beloved?" My honeyed voice seems to put her at ease and she presses her forehead against mine and breathes in deeply, calming herself.

Thana slides off of my lap and paces around the room slowly. "It is not written in stone, mind you." Thana says as she unfurls her wings, flexing them several times. "I suspect that one of my daughters will end up being Michael's mate."

Thana word vomits what she's been holding in, and I'm floored. One of the two daughters recently born may be the mate of an Archangel. "Are you sure?" Furrowing my brows, I need to know as much information as my mate will divulge.

"Just the way he acted when I directly questioned him. Archangels cannot lie when asked a question directly. I learned that from Raph." Thana smiles sweetly as she looks over her shoulder at Raphael. In response to her gaze, he pales considerably. I'm guessing he hoped that she would have forgotten that minor fact.

"So what you're delicately trying to say is that one of the two daughters born yesterday is going to be the mate of an Archangel?" Gritting my teeth, I spit the words out. In one sense, either daughter would be untouchable having an Archangel as a mate.

"Yes..." Thana says without any doubt.

Glancing at the other guys, then back to Thana, I can see she firmly believes what she just revealed to us is gospel. "Okay then..." Throwing my hands up into the air, my attention returns to the food on the table. I have resigned myself to accept the things that I cannot change.

"What's wrong?" Thana's soft tone, and gentle caresses of my shoulder, tell me my reaction upset her some.

Carefully, I stand up and unfurl my wings and wrap Thana up in them. She instantly relaxes in my dark embrace, and I kiss her forehead. What my dark angel doesn't realize is that the reason my wings comfort her is because of her dark side. We always feel safer in the black of night than in the light of day. "Nothing is wrong, my dark angel. Change has always been difficult for me. The possibility that my daughter may already have a mate is mind blowing."

Thana wraps her arms tightly around my waistline and hugs me tightly, resting her head on my chest. "You will rain Hell on earth if anyone stands against me or our daughter." She says softly against my chest. Tilting her head up, her eyes glow as the liquid mercury swirls wildly. "No one will stand against any of my children." Thana gently presses against my wings, getting me to open them. Her eyes lock with the rest of her mates and they immediately nod, agreeing with her.

"We are going home. I refuse to live in fear." Thana states as she grabs a sandwich off of the table before storming out of the room.

"You heard our mate, let's pack up and head home before she leaves without us." I say with zero fucks given. Right now, my daughter and mate need me to be at the top of my game and keep my eyes on the prize. I follow Thana into the gardens where the Archangels are playing with the babies.

"We're heading home, boys. Assemble whoever you need to assemble to keep an eye on me and the girls." Thana's commanding tone takes the Archangels and me by surprise. She pulls a long sash looking thing out of a bag I didn't notice her carrying. She wraps herself with it elaborately, then stuffs my daughter into it, securing her firmly to her chest.

Thana turns to face me and her eyes are glowing white, staring off in who knows what direction. Raphael, Christian, Gage and Metatron walk out and Raphael takes his place standing before her. Thana pulls out a second sash and practically mummifies Raphael with the material. Carefully, she stuffs his daughter into the cloth, then looks directly at me. "Let's go. The minute we clear the clouds, I'm summoning your father and my grandfather to flank us. I'm not taking any chances." Thana's resolve is impressive yet terrifying in the same breath.

"You heard her!" I wrap my arms over my chest and fall backwards through the clouds. Spreading my wings wide, I soar through the clouds waiting for my beloved dark angel to join me.

A gray, blurred missile shoots past me on a direct trajectory towards earth falling faster than I believed was possible. Curling my wings in close to my body, I immediately plummet, gaining fast on the blur in question. Thana has her wings tucked in tight and her head down, shielding our daughter from the wind shear. It's now that I see what she's racing towards. My father and her grandfather are flying towards us. She turns her head slightly and fucking winks at me before opening her wings wide, putting on the brakes.

Her impressive wingspan and larger flight feathers help her to practically stop on a dime. I, on the other hand, have to open my wings slowly and soar back up into the sky high above Thana. When I am finally able to catch up to her, she's flanked by my dad and Samael.

Looking up and over my shoulder, I can see the others catching up. I follow behind Thana, watching everything, hoping that our trip home is a peaceful one.

My father is the first to land, and he heads into our home to check it out. I catch up to Samael and Thana and fly past them and into the house. Teaming up with my father, we search the house from top to bottom. Thankfully, there're no surprises waiting for us at home.

Thana lands in the grand entryway of the house and flexes her wings. Almost as soon as her feet hit the floor, her wolf and cat familiars rip free of her flesh and start prowling the house. A sweeping motion is made with her hands as she dictates where her familiars are meant to go. Thana turns and looks around the interior as her other mates arrive and smiles. "Everything is in order. Gage and Christian, please set up a nursery area in my nesting room." As soon as the order is given, they take off without question to perform their tasks.

"Metatron, please acquire food for dinner, enough for eight." Thana smiles sweetly and the big guy practically preens under her attention.

I can't help the massive eye roll that I let loose watching the unquestioned obedience. "Watch yourself boy, she's finally feeling comfortable with who she is meant to be." My father's hushed tone warns me of the potential hellion I have on my hands.

Thana pops up behind my father, smiling as she undoes the sash that holds my daughter to her chest. Once Nikita is freed from the linen, Thana taps my father on his shoulder. "Father…" Thana waits until my father fully turns to face her. His normally abyssal orbs turn a human hazel as he looks down at the bundle in her arms. "Meet Nikita, your successor…" Thana offers her daughter to my father with as much reverence as possible.

I've never in my existence seen my father speechless till now. Nikita reaches up towards his face and he lowers himself to meet her hands. "She's amazing." My father's tone is full of wonder as he studies my daughter. Thana remains smiling, watching Azrael interact with his granddaughter.

Samael walks up with Raphael's daughter held at arm's length. "Descendant, take this one. It's broken. It's defecated on itself like an uncivilized beast." Thana laughs, thinking about how her grandfather is handling her Angelic daughter.

Shaking her head, Thana merely laughs. "Grandfather, you are truly being over dramatic. Babies always defecate in their diapers." Thana turns on her heels and leaves, laughing hysterically down the hallway.

Samael watches Thana walk away, then looks at my daughter. "Get her to show her wings. I would like to see their color." The tone breaks my father out of his happy bubble and he stares Samael down.

"That is a mother's job and ability, Samael. Fathers cannot force their children to reveal their wings." My dad says calmly as his eyes blacken. Unfortunately for us, Samael's tone has gained the attention of the other remaining mates in the house, and they begin to gather.

"What is a mother's job and ability?" Thana's tone is pure irritation and her eyes are black as pitch, searching everyone's faces for answers. The Angelic side of the family all look at Raphael and when he takes a step backwards, the others follow him immediately.

"Descendant, I wish to see my great-granddaughters wings." His firm tone makes the corner of Thana's right eye twitch almost uncontrollably.

Without a word from Thana, Fenrir arrives at her side and takes the wrapped up Davina from her and walks over to Raphael, offering him his daughter. Thana raises her hand in a flourish and my daughter is removed from my father's hand by an unseen force and delivered into Thana's. Narrowing her eyes, she stares up at Samael. The wing thing is a very touchy subject with Thana, and he just set her off. "Her wing color is unimportant." Thana growls out in challenge. Here's my mate, toe to toe with the Destroyer, not an ounce of fear evident.

"The color is important!" His voice booms, and that is his ultimate mistake. One raising his tone to Thana and secondly making it about wing color.

"No!" The force that comes off of Thana knocks Samael on his ass and I can see the darkness swirling off of her. "Her wings are of no consequence. They will not denote her worth." Thana's tone hits a deep primal note and Samael's color pales. I'm not sure what he sees as he stares at Thana. But, whatever it is, he vanishes from sight immediately.

"Nikita will not be treated like I was!" Thana screams, making the very foundation of the house shake from her anger and pain. Thana cradles Nikita tightly to her chest, hugging her as silent tears roll down her cheeks slowly.

Wrapping my arms and wings around Thana is the only thing I think I can do to bring her some semblance of comfort. "We will protect all the babies born into this union fiercely, my love. This I assure you." I press my lips to her forehead and hold them there, infusing my love and strength into her.

"I know Cy, I just don't want her to be miserable like I was growing up." Thana pulls back and forces a smile as she holds up Nikita between us. Her tiny feathers are just sprouting from the baby fluff. The color looks almost black, but then again, we are in the darkness of my wings and I cannot truly tell their color.

Opening my wings slowly, I take my daughter towards the bay windows to get her into the light. She's cooing up a storm and I flex my wings, watching her eyes intently watch my wings movements. Thana moves alongside of us and cups our daughters' back and runs her fingertips over her tiny wings. Nikita spreads her little wings wide, revealing her feather color in the sun. They are a dark smoke gray like the mid-feathers on her mother's wings. Thana's sadness can be felt through the bond as her heart breaks a little for the troubles she knows our daughter will face.

"She is the granddaughter of Death and the great-granddaughter of the Destroyer. No one in their right mind would dare to raise a finger to her." I say with a confidence I wasn't aware I had before. "Besides, when you ascend to the mantle of Destroyer. No one would dare go against Nikita." The growl that reverberates in my chest makes Thana's eyes widen as she looks at me.

"Yes, sir..." Thana's tone is low and sultry, making my cock stir to life. She smirks and walks over to Raphael and looks at her daughter Davina and smiles. "Growing up, I prayed my feathers would turn white." I watch her run her fingertip over Davina's shoulder blades.

"Why?" Raphael asks softly, curious where her thoughts are.

Laughing, Thana walks away to climb onto the arm of the couch and beckons me to her. Her hand ghosts over my feathers and I swear it's like she's touching my skin. "You saw how Cy was treated at the Mated Ball. Shunned and almost attacked because his wings are pure midnight." Flexing her own wings, she looks back at the fade from midnight to medium gray. Spreading her wings wide, she looks at them again. "These can get me killed just because I'm different." She raises a brow in challenge. None of the light mates dare open their mouths.

"Daughter, you know your grandfather and I will rain Hell upon the earth to protect your children without question." My father moves to stand before my mate and drops to a knee before her and spreads his wings wide. "I swear my life to protect you and your bloodline, Thana. From now till I take my last breath, my sword is yours to command."

Thana lowers to the floor before my father and hugs him one armed to her. "Thank you, father." She kisses his cheek, and he helps her to stand back up.

Thana comes straight to me and tucks my sleeping daughter into my arms. "I need a shower and a nap. Wake me when the food arrives?" Her furrowed brows and full lips do me in every time. All I can do is nod and hold my daughter close to my chest as I watch the love of my life walk out of the room.

CHAPTER 49
THANA

Something is brewing and I can't put my finger on it just yet. Heading up the stairs, my familiars flank me and I rest my hands on their backs. It's nice to have their silent support by my side through all of this. So many changes are on the horizon and I can't begin to fathom where life may lead me in the next week. With the way things have changed in the last six months, I can only really focus on today.

Reaching my room, I pass where the guys have set up the two cribs by my nest and the changing tables. Looking over the baby items, I really understand exactly how much my life has changed. I can only describe the bathroom in my room as opulent. The guys spared no expense adding every single creature comfort possible to my nest room and attached bathroom spa area.

The hot water cascades down my bare flesh and, for once, I leave my wings exposed to wash my feathers as well. "Can I help?" Gage's voice fills the shower stall and all I can do is smile, thinking about him touching my wings.

"Of course babe, you know I can't reach the feathers close to my back." I angle my body so that he can get my back easily. Reaching out, I work on the feathers I can reach with the special shampoo and conditioner I recently bought.

Gage's powerful hands caress the skin near my wing bases and I stand stock still, enjoying the intimate contact with him. To allow someone near your wings is one of the ultimate signs of trust. An Angel without wings is nothing but a human with an extremely long and lonely life. "How's that love?" He asks as his thumbs knead the muscles in my back that I didn't realize were sore. I tense for a moment, then moan in pure ecstasy, the tension melts away with every stroke of his thumb.

"Much better love. Sorry for my outburst earlier. You know how sensitive I am about the feather thing." I try to distract myself from the lust filled thoughts that are filling my head.

"Shhh, let me take care of you, Thana. You have the weight of the world on your shoulders. Just relax and breathe for me. Focus on my hands on your flesh and feathers." Gages tone soothes and excites me at the same time. His powerful hands caress my flesh, making me melt like putty in his skillful hands.

Deftly, he washes and conditions my feathers, making every movement as sensual as possible. I swear if he keeps going, I will come long before he gets where I need him most. Bracing my hands on the wall, I remain perfectly still, enjoying the feel of his hands on me. "That's perfect Gage." I softly moan, lowering my head, lost in the blissful sensation.

"Perfect, my love? I can make it even more perfect." He leans down and nibbles on my earlobe.

"Oh?" I pant, watching him finish rinsing my feathers.

"Yes, my love... I know exactly what to do to make your toes curl." Gage says, biting my shoulder, making me whine. His hands grip my hips tightly and he pulls me flush to him. Quickly, I withdraw my wings and reach back and grip his thighs as his teeth tighten on my shoulder.

When I finally open my eyes, Cyrus is standing before me, his eyes black as night and naked as the day he was born. "Ready

Kitten..." Cyrus's honey tone flows over me and straight to my core. I squirm, and Gage growls, I stop moving instantly. A soft growl escapes Cyrus's lips as he smiles. "Hmm, our girl is really receptive to command.."

"I see that..." Gage says as he releases my shoulder, then licks the marks slowly, making me squirm more.

Cyrus prowls forward, then nuzzles my throat. My head rolls back of its own volition. He slides his hand up between my breasts, then gently grips my throat. "How about a little loving Thana?" Cyrus says as he looks at Gage over my shoulder.

"Oh yes, our girl definitely needs some loving." Gage says near my ear as his hands slide down to my thighs. He hooks his arms under my knees and lifts me up effortlessly. My lady bits are on full display for Cyrus, which makes him smile. He reaches back and shuts the water off and stares down at me.

"What does my Kitten desire most in the world?" I don't know if it's just a Dark Nephilim thing or a Cyrus thing, but his voice has a growl to it when he's aroused. Like a primal beast ready to claim its quarry and assert its dominance over it.

Shivering from Cyrus's tone, I practically pant when I answer him. "You beloved, you and Gage please, my love." I practically beg as I shiver from need and anticipation.

Cyrus walks out of my field of vision and a loud crack sounds and Gage rocks forward from impact. Turning my head as far as I can, I can barely see Cyrus running his hands over Gage's body, teasing him, coming close to the vee of his lower abdomen. "I have a beautiful plan. Gage put our woman on the bed and make sure she's plenty wet enough for us." The command in Cyrus's tone makes my core weep and pulse, knowing full well that my needs will be fully met.

Gage lowers my legs to the ground for a mere moment before he scoops me back up again, cradling me to his chest. Gently I'm placed on the bed and he props a pillow under my head, leaving my thighs hanging off the bed and my feet flat on the floor. Raising an eyebrow,

I peer between Gage and now Cyrus, who has an enormous tube of lube in his hand. "Ummm… What's that for?" I'm curious and frightened at the same time. It's an odd combination of emotions to experience at the same time.

"Gage, get to work." Cyrus says before looking back at me as he climbs onto the bed next to me and rolls my nipple between his thumb and forefinger. "You see Kitten, we want to give you a night you will never forget." Just as Cyrus finishes the sentence, Gage's mouth latches onto my clit and sucks mercilessly at that sensitive nub. A loud moan escapes my lips as he slips a finger deep within me.

"Focus on me Kitten. I want to watch you fall apart." Cyrus's tone turns commanding and I can't help but focus on his abyssal orbs. Roughly I thread my fingers through Gage's hair as I try to grind on his face, chasing my orgasm. Cyrus notes the change and taps Gage on the shoulder and he withdraws the finger from my depths. Whining, I gasp at the loss of his finger. Turning to the side, I watch Cyrus cover Gage's finger with the lube, then help him place my legs over Gage's shoulder.

"Gage is about to loosen you up for the treat we have in store for you tonight. Relax and take in a deep breath, then let it out slowly." Cyrus says softly as I feel the pressure from Gage's finger massaging my rosette.

"Breathe baby, I'm going to be gentle and make you feel so good." Gage says softly between licks. If he's trying to distract me, he's doing a damn good job of it.

Between Cyrus who has decided to kiss me silly while playing with my breasts and Gage driving me literally insane licking me as slowly as humanly possible, he finally breached the barrier. In probably Gage's sneakiest move to date, he slides a second finger within my depths and I detonate around him. One finger slides in as far as it can go as the other withdraws at the same pace as his tongue, almost to the point of being removed. He alternates between the fingers as my muscles pulse around his digits. It's a new and intense form of pleasure and if it was anyone other than them, I never would have gone through with it.

"She's ready, Cy." Gage says as he stands up and walks into the bathroom to clean up. I watch him walk away then look at a very naked and hard Cyrus laying on the bed.

Crawling on my hands and knees, I nip at Cyrus's flesh along the way. Before he can attempt to protest, I maneuver myself to slide him deep within me. A soft moan escapes my lips as I adjust to his girth. "I missed this..." I practically purr as I move slightly, enjoying every inch that moves within me.

"Damn baby, so wet and tight." Cyrus says as he grips me by the back of my neck and pulls me down to kiss me deeply.

"Oooh I guess baby girl decided who she wants where, huh Cy?" Gage's voice drops several octaves to a low I haven't heard before. Raising up slightly, I look back over my shoulder at Gage. His hand is wrapped around his shaft and he's stroking it slowly. My eyes follow the motion and I feel my insides clench in anticipation.

"She enjoys watching you, Gage. Her muscles are pulsing around me with every stroke you take." Cyrus's tone hits that deep rumble, and I whip my head around to look down at him. My vision shifts and I know my eyes have blackened. "Yeah, we have her now. Her eyes are black as pitch and she's squirming." Cyrus's crooked smile and tone speaks of his dark promise to deliver.

"Focus on Cyrus and try to relax." Gage places his hand between my shoulder blades and presses me firmly to Cyrus's chest. I feel Gage starting to massage the lube into my rosette, getting me to relax a bit as Cyrus moves slightly to distract me. The pressure I feel next is unlike anything I have ever experienced before, shivering I grip onto Cyrus tightly, pressing my forehead against his chest.

"Breathe Kitten. Focus on my hands and my voice." His hands roam all over my flesh in steady pressure, helping me to relax as I feel Gage slip in slowly. He finally bottoms out and we collectively breathe a sigh of relief and I relax on Cyrus's chest, adjusting to the fullness. "Good girl... We're going to move now. So breathe slowly if you need us to stop, tell us." Cyrus reaches up and kisses my forehead before giving a look to Gage.

Inch by glorious inch, they slide in and out ever so slowly. Every movement sets my nerves on fire reaching highs I never knew I could attain. Carefully, I raise up and change the angle that they are hitting and throw myself over the edge into one of the most intense orgasms I have yet to experience. My body tingles everywhere as my muscles spasm, gripping the two of them, milking their lengths for all they are worth. Cyrus and Gage grunt in unison, gripping my ribs and hips as they thrust into me, pistoning their lengths, spurning my orgasm on.

Gage screams first, and I feel the pulsing of his cock seated deep within my ass as his fingertips dig into the soft flesh at my hips. Cyrus moves faster and all I can do is hold still with the way the Gage has me locked in place. Cyrus screams and darkness radiates from him as he thrusts up one last time. Every pulse and twitch of his cock sends me spiraling again. I grip his shoulders tightly, holding on as the three of us ride out our orgasms together.

Gently, Gage pulls out and walks off to the bathroom as I lay down on Cyrus's chest. His thick arms band around me and he rolls us off to the side, and he holds me tightly, peppering my face with kisses. "Cy, the tub is ready." Gage says from behind me. Slowly, Cyrus slips free of me and moves to kneel on the bed. Slipping his arms under me, he scoops me up and offers me to Gage.

Once in Gage's arms, he kisses my lips and remains there for a moment. I can feel all the love he has for me in his heart. "Time to take care of our girl." Gage whispers against my lips as he turns to walk into the bathroom.

The soft soothing sounds of a seascape play in the background and the sound of the whirlpool tub hums. Smiling up at Gage, I am so very grateful for the way he and Cyrus care for me. Just before lowering me into the tub, I hear the door click open, it's Raphael. He prowls across the floor like a stalking panther extruding a confidence I haven't seen from him except for when he's dealing with threats.

Cyrus and Gage lower me into the water and there seems to be an unspoken understanding between the guys. Cyrus and Gage both kiss me, then leave the room, closing the door behind them. Arching my right brow, I look up and over at Raphael. "We need to talk beautiful." He says as he slips all six feet of his sun kissed muscular frame into my massive tub.

Nodding slowly, I have a hunch about what he wishes to discuss with me. "I suspected that you would approach me soon. I know we've been back almost two weeks and I'm obviously fully healed." Sighing, I grab my loofa and start fiddling with it.

The water moves in a wave, and Raph is on his knees before me. "Bringing him into the fold will only strengthen the nest as a whole." Raphael's eyes plead with me and my heart breaks a little, seeing the slight tinge of sadness on his visage.

"I know he'll strengthen us all. But what if I get sick? What if Cyrus and Nikita get sick? I have a right to be afraid, Raph. When we almost lost Cyrus, I got sick. I have to worry about my daughters now too..." My tone is pleading as my hands shake before me. My nerves are on edge talking about this subject.

Leaning forward, Raphael kisses my forehead and sighs softly. "We will do what we need to maintain balance. The guys and I spoke about it at length when we got back from the Angelic Realm. All will work out, I promise you." He takes my hands in his and grips them tightly. An Archangel never breaks a promise, so I have to believe that the guys will do everything possible to keep all of us safe.

"Set up a dinner date for Metatron and I. Warn him we will be taking my Hellcat. I wanna drive my baby." I can tell by Raphael's reaction that my smile concerns him. My car is tuned and is race ready. Poor Metatron won't know what hit him.

"Consider it done, my love." With a wink and a smile, Raphael vanishes before my eyes. I swear sometimes he loves being dramatic.

Laying back in the tub, I close my eyes and breathe in a slow cleansing breath. "What have I done?" I say to no one in particular.

CHAPTER 50

METATRON

I know we are not supposed to have favorites in a nest, but Raphael has gone to the bat for me with our mate and managed to hit a home run. He helped me search the city for a steakhouse that Thana would love to eat at. It's a Japanese steakhouse that Christian highly recommends. He's already called the chef and asked for a special menu for us tonight.

Anxiously, I pace back and forth, waiting for my mate to be ready to leave. Cyrus and Gage sit in the corner laughing at my expense, as usual. "What's the big deal, guys?" I say, exasperated with their shenanigans.

"Well, big guy, you're dressed like you're going to a cotillon instead of a dinner date…" Cyrus says and I look down at my tux and shined shoes. Maybe he has a point. Maybe I went a bit overboard. Just as I start to rethink my choices for this evening, I see Raphael descending the stairs with his wings partially open.

At the bottom of the stairs he puts his wings away and I see Thana looking as radiant as ever, smiling at me. Tilting my head to the side, I raise my hand and index finger and motion for her to turn for me. The blood red gown caresses every inch of her body, leaving little to the imagination. From the sweetheart top to the low cut back that stops just below her hips, every inch is a masterpiece. Thana stops with her back facing me and she slowly looks over her right shoulder and I damn near lose it. My heart thunders in my chest as I stare at her full lips and prominent cupids bow painted vermillion to match the dress.

It's now that my eyes move up further and notice the ornate braids in her hair swept up into a pile of curls on top of her head. A hand rests under my chin and raises my jaw that I hadn't realized had dropped. "She's a vision, isn't she?" Christian says softly next to me. "She stressed for hours about the dress and her body, afraid that her post-baby form wouldn't be attractive. Your reaction to her was perfect."

I turn quickly and look at Christian in shock. "She is a mother, giver of life. How could anyone look at her as anything other than beautiful?" The thought is foreign to me that any would shame a mother for performing the miracle of birth.

Christian shakes his head sadly, then looks out the window. "I have no idea. Keep in mind she's very self-conscious." Christian places his hand on my shoulder briefly before walking over and kissing Thana on both cheeks, telling her how beautiful she is.

Glad that I planned ahead, I reach into the cabinet next to me and grab the orchids and the corsage that I purchased for Thana. Her gunmetal gray eyes sweep from mine to the flowers in my hand and her smile lights up the room. I drop to a knee before her and offer the flowers and corsage to her. Thana shocks me and bends down to kiss me. Her lips feel like the smoothest, softest silk. I can't help letting a pleased growl escape my lips.

"Why did you kneel, Metatron?" Thana says, catching her breath. Apparently, our kiss affected her as much as it did me.

Smiling, I rise to my full height. At six foot six, I am damn near almost a foot taller than my mate. Bending down, I kiss her lips briefly. "I kneel before you because I love you eternally. You are my mate, my love, my life. There is nothing I would not do for you."

Gently, I cup her cheek in my hand and kiss her to further make my point.

Soft giggles escape her lips as she moves forward and hugs me tightly. I stand up straight and wrap my thick arms around her lithe form. Thana rests her head on my chest and closes her eyes, smiling. "I would burn the Earth to ashes to protect what's mine." She tilts her head back and looks up at me. Polished chrome orbs stare up at me and I know deep in my heart she means what she said.

"Shall we be off, my love?" Tilting my head to the side, I look down at her and motion towards the door.

Thana goes from calm and controlled to excited, unfurling her wings, grabbing her keys and flying out the open balcony doors. Puzzled, I look at the guys and there's Cyrus holding his hand up doing a countdown. As each finger drops, I look from him to the door, then back again. As the last finger falls, the roar of her Hellcat's engine fires up and rattles the glassware off the shelves. Her car sounds like a massive beast rumbling, making its presence known. Soon enough she revs the engine vibrating plastic stemware off of the shelves closest to the front door. "That's why I call her Kitten..." Cyrus says with a dramatic sweep of his arm in the direction where the sound emanates from.

Quickly, I cross the entryway and practically run out the front door before her car shakes the house from its very foundation. I slip in on the passenger side and look at my angel, whom is wearing black wrap-around sunglasses and a five-point harness hiking her dress up so close to her sex. "Buckle up buttercup, you're about to see how I experienced flight without wings." Thana says, her voice drips with sensuality, making my heart beat a little faster. Quickly, I comply and strap myself into the harness. No sooner is that last buckle click than she shifts into first gear and I can hear the tires scream as the engine roars louder.

When the tires finally grip the pavement, I am thrown back into the seat from the sheer power of the takeoff. On the radio, Hollywood Undead Heart of a Champion blasts through the speakers, drowning out the sound of the engine. Thana sings along with the song as she shifts through the gears. She removes her sunglasses and her eyes blacken. I watch her as she nods along with whatever is going on. I can only guess by the color of her eyes Cyrus is giving her directions to our destination. We drift around a corner and I swear I think I saw the last several hundred years of my life flash before my eyes.

Thankfully, we arrive safely at our destination and Thana shuts off the car and stares blankly at the road before her. My phone rings and it's Raphael. "Get to the driver's side door and cover her eyes. Cyrus has her occupied so that you can surprise her with the destination." That explains why her eyes are still black. I hurry and get myself out of the car and over to her side and cover her eyes.

"Metatron, what are you guys up to?" Thana laughs as she reaches up to touch my hand.

"The guys helped me to keep our date location a secret. I wanted to surprise you." I watch Thana unbuckle her harness and offer me her hands. With my free hand, I help her out of the car, and tuck her in tight against my side and walk her towards the front door of the restaurant. I hold out the envelope to the maitre d and he reads the note from Christian and leads us to our private booth in the back. On three sides, the booth is surrounded by fish tanks. Slowly, I remove my hand from Thana's eyes and her hands fly up to cover her mouth as she stares at the booth. "Is this okay, my love?" I ask softly next to her ear, only for her to hear.

"Okay? This is the most incredible thing I've ever seen! We get to eat surrounded by fish!" Thana squeals before she turns and jumps into my arms excitedly.

Banding my arms around her tiny waistline, I kiss her cheek. "I'm so thrilled you like it. Christian helped me pick it out." Gently, I place her back on the ground, still smiling at her.

"I'm glad you and the guys get along so well, Cyrus can be an acquired taste." Thana's smile radiantly beams up at me and takes my breath away. I motion for her to take her place at the table. Thana scoots along the bench to sit in the center of the table to have the best view of the tanks.

I scoot along and sit next to her and offer the menu to her and open it to the first page where the appetizers are at. "What shall we start with, my love?" Thana takes the menu and starts looking over the selection carefully.

"Anything you don't eat?" She winces and lowers her head slowly, then tilts it to the side. "I wish I knew you better. I'm afraid to pick something you may not like or are allergic to." Thana's voice wavers as she looks from the menu at me.

Gently, I cup her cheek and kiss her lips softly. "I have no allergies and not much experience with earthly food. Order whatever you want. I'll try everything." Understanding crosses Thana's face and she looks back down at the menu, looking over everything.

"Alright, we'll try a few different things. Do you mind if I order for us?" She furrows her brows looking at me.

"Not at all my love, you know the food better than I do." I close my menu and lean back, running a single finger down her spine as she flips through the menu, looking things over. Christian texts me, asking how things are going. I catch him up and as I hit send, the server arrives. To my surprise, Thana's eyes turn chrome, looking at the server and his bleed golden in response. Every word that falls from her lips is perfect Japanese. The server bows at the waist then leaves with what I can assume is our order.

Thana turns, giggling, and shakes her head. Chrome orbs fade and give way to her gunmetal gray eyes. "Christian helped me order from the menu. It would seem that if you order in Japanese you get better quality and larger portions. I hope you don't mind?" Thana says just before she lays her head on my shoulder. Her arms band around my bicep and all is right in my world.

"I don't mind at all. The guys have been really helpful in helping me to adapt to life down here." I press my lips to the crown of her head and sigh, having my angel on my arm.

Thana moves and sits sideways, facing me. "Do you miss being up there?" Hesitantly, she points up and I can see the slight welling of tears.

Gently, I hold her little hands in mine and give them a squeeze. "Honestly, yes and no. Part of me I miss hanging out with my brother and the shenanigans. No, because I have you and our nest mates. I can always visit my twin and he can always visit me. If I'm needed, I can always go home for a bit." I squeeze her hands again and smile, trying to show her how sure I am of my answer.

She smiles and kisses me softly before looking back at the tank. "If there was one thing about you, you wish I knew. What would it be?" Her question, as innocent as it is, is very hard to answer.

Looking down and away briefly. "I wasn't always this calm. With what I am tasked with doing, I have to be violent. Let's face it. I'm a giant among the Archangels." Exhaling roughly, I look back over at Thana's inquisitive eyes. "I'm not as scary as I appear." My biggest fear is being rejected by Thana because I can be just as big, if not a bigger monster, as she could ever be.

The food arrives shortly after my admission and I feel knots starting in my stomach because of her silence. Thana rests a plate of food that she's selected for me, then rests a hand on my forearm. Her eyes flicker through all three colors, then return to her normal gray. "I should not exist as I am." She looks down at her hand on my arm, then back up again.

"They have hunted me, thrown stones at me and threatened my life because they were afraid of what I may become." Her lithe hand tightens on my forearm, then relaxes.

"Azrael, being the only mated male at the time of my alignment announcement, saw my wing color and his face dropped. I knew right then and there I was in for Hell on earth. I was called a veil walker." She draws in a deep breath and forces a smile. "He told me he was sorry for what he was about to do. He announced my color and said that by color I lean more towards the dark." Shaking her head, she picks up a piece of shrimp toast and takes a bite, gathering her thoughts.

"It was then that Michael silenced the crowd and assigned Raphael and Azrael to be my guardians. I had to work with one or the other for the rest of my existence." A soft forced laugh escapes her lips before she pops a pastry in my mouth.

"I have no regrets. Everything happens for a reason. I know you can see that I tell the truth." She finishes her shrimp toast and smiles, looking at me. The weight of her past has been lifted.

Carefully, I offer her a roll that appears to be stuffed and she giggles, taking a gentle bite from it. A warmth moves through me and I feel great feeding her. I continue feeding her from my plate till it's cleared, just to see her smile again. Gently, she offers me food from her plate and I feel like the King of the world. We clear both plates just in time for the main courses to arrive. There's an abundant assortment of sushi and sashimi to choose from, noodles and beef. Thana picks up the chopsticks and starts plating the food for the two of us. I watch her, amazed she can work those things with such deft precision.

"How do those work?" I'm curious to see how she'll teach me to use them.

Thana's eyes swirl chrome and then her fingers tentatively touch my temples and she locks eyes with me. She floods my mind with years of experience with all different ways to use the chopsticks. My mate never ceases to amaze me with what she knows and can do. A gentle smile graces her lips as she lowers her hands and eats. Staring at the chopsticks, I pick them up and it's now like second nature to me. I stare at my mate, now shocked that it was that easy for her to teach me how to use them.

Shoulder to shoulder we finish eating our meal, watching the fish and talking about our lives. This date has gone far better than I had ever dreamed it would. We've come so far since we first met. I went from fearing she would never accept me to being out on a date with the woman I love. I can tell when she's checking on the babies, her eyes churn mercury or black, depending on which mate she's talking to. Having her snuggle next to me is like a dream come true. After dessert, she asks if we can go home. Her tone has an edge of nervousness to it and I completely understand. Be it her concern for the babies, or just being out with me, it's completely understandable. I'm nervous about the possible next step that may or may not happen when we get home. I can only hope she will see it fit in her heart to bring me completely into the bond someday.

CHAPTER 51
THANA

Dinner went far better than I had ever expected it to go. I had a wonderful time and I'm now conflicted. My urge to draw this gentle giant into the fold grows minute by minute. His sky-blue eyes radiate love, understanding, and affection. His love for me is the purest love I believe I will ever find, and it terrifies me. Instinct drives me to feed him and take care of him like I do the others. My maternal instincts scream at me to protect myself, Nikita, and Cyrus from light poisoning. *Why does it have to be so difficult?* I ask myself, hoping that Metatron doesn't hear me.

"Why does what have to be so difficult?" Metatron asks innocently.

Crap on a cracker, he heard me. I hug his arm tighter as we walk out to my car. Ominously, the song Cry Little Sister by Gerard McMahon comes on when I fire the Hellcat up. I adjust my dress and turn sideways to face him. "I'm going to preface this entire conversation with: I am not afraid of you in any way, shape or form." Forcing a smile, I look up into his eyes.

"I'm glad to hear that beautiful." Metatron says as he reaches out and takes hold of both of my hands. "Anything you need to say I will listen to with an open heart and open mind." A gentle squeeze of my hands backs up his statement.

Squeezing his hands back, I draw in a fortifying breath. "I'm afraid of poisoning myself, my daughter, and Cyrus. It's why I have been so..." The words I need to say make me feel like I'm choking.

"Hesitant? Distant? Nervous" Metatron eloquently fills in the blanks with the perfect words and it makes my heart hurt worse.

I take back one of my hands and rub the spot in the middle of my sternum. "It kills me to keep my distance from you. I feel like I'm suffocating." Slowly, I slide my hand up my chest to my throat and grip it.

"Let me be the air you breathe, the wind under your wings lifting you up. Let me be your shield in times of danger. Let me be with you and love you the way you deserve." Metatron says, his tone much softer than I expected a man his size could ever manage. His eyes search my face as he leans forward hesitantly. Closing the distance, my lips press against his and he deepens the kiss immediately. Instinct drives me into his arms, over the center console of the car, and into his lap.

Thankfully, my car is blacked out and no one can see me straddling him like a wild stallion. Chest to chest and crotch to crotch, we paw at each other like feral animals in heat. I'm soaked and aching, half driven mad by this behemoth of a man between my legs. Panting heavily, I grind my aching sex along the solid ridge of hot steel contained by his dress pants. Slow rocks of Metatron's hips match mine, driving me insane with desire.

"We..." Thrust, thrust. "should..." he growls out just before his body tenses. His cock pulses under my sex, driving me over the edge with him.

"Stop?" I can barely think straight as my empty sex pulses gushing fluid soaking my underwear and his once pristine dress slacks. Catching my breath, I rest my head on his shoulder and break into the broadest smile I've had to date.

"Wow... It is more fun than I thought it would be." Metatron says half laughing.

Arching an eyebrow, I raise my head and look at him. "Oh?"

"Yeah, Raphael undersold how good sex with you feels." Metatron raises both eyebrows, so happy and excited.

Caressing his cheeks, I kiss his lips softly. "That wasn't sex." I kiss the tip of his nose and slide back over into the driver's seat and buckle myself in.

"It wasn't? It gets better than that?" His eyebrows raise almost to the point of reaching his hairline and I can't help but giggle looking at him.

"Yeah it does." Pulling a stunt out of Cyrus's playbook, I just wink at him, then change the playlist I'm listening to. Gemini Syndrome Die With Me is on and I smirk. Personally, I find it funny since I'm a reaper and I have one of the highest ranking Archangels in my car.

Turning the key, my baby roars to life and I can't help but smile every time I hear her purr. "You really love your car, don't you?" Metatron's deep voice drags me out of my inner sanctum.

A huffed out laugh escapes my lips before I turn to face him. "No matter how terrible life got for me, how lonely I was. My car, my beast, has always been there for me. No matter how bad things got, a quick spin in the car kept me sane." Shaking my head as I stroke the dashboard of my car. "He's always been there for me." I beam as my fingers caress the leather of the steering wheel.

Tilting his head to the side, Metatron watches me caress the wheel. Longing echoes in his gaze. "He?" Is all he says, and I raise both eyebrows in response.

"He." I state, then grip the shifter between us and wiggle it side to side before shifting into first and taking off. Redlining the gage before shifting makes the car thrust into the next gear and the meaning slowly sinks in for him.

"Oh... I get it..." Nodding his head, he turns and looks out the window. In the reflection, I can see his eyes bleed golden.

Gage fills me in that he's talking to Raphael about how much he doesn't understand about relationships and man woman dynamics. Thankfully, I can only hope that Raph teaches him the basics because damn. A man that size can destroy me in either sense. Banging through the gears, I take Metatron to my favorite place outside of the city. Parking in the lot near the cliff, I gently touch his shoulder and snap him out of his conversation with Raph. "I wanna show you something." His brilliant smile warms my heart and butterflies flutter in my chest.

The gravel crunches under my heels as I walk to the spot on the cliff with the weeping willow tree. The city below is lit up and the lights appear to be twinkling from up here. A gentle breeze blows from the east, lifting bits of my hair off of my bare shoulders. "It's beautiful up here." The low tone of Metatron's voice makes the butterflies in my belly flitter again. His thick muscular arms band around me as he pulls me back flush to his chest.

Closing my eyes, I lean my head back against his chest. "I used to come here in the middle of the night just to unfurl my wings alone to feel the wind move over my feathers. It was as close to flight as I could get till the Mate Trials." Reaching up, I hug his arms to me and sigh softly, feeling safe with him.

"I always felt it was unfair for the females to hide or wait to be chosen to go. Three hundred years is a long time to wait." He kisses my forehead and gives me a slight squeeze.

High-pitched screams pierce the night and send us both on the offensive. Without a second thought, I unleash all of my familiars. Rex I keep the size of a crocodile. My panther and Fenrir stand at my side as I send my raven to investigate. Metatron looks to his left at me and dons his Angelic armor. Smirking, I allow my black and gold armor to manifest upon my flesh. My fingernails elongate into blackened claws as we prepare to face whatever is about to breach the hill.

They launch a severed human head from behind us and it lands at my feet. Dead eyes staring back at me with its face frozen in a silent scream. Glancing quickly from Metatron to the head and back again. "Rex! Guard the babies! Go now!" Within seconds of the words leaving my mouth, Rex is airborne, heading back to the house with the others.

Feeling the panic through the bond, I know I made the right decision. "They are trying to get to my daughters!" I scream so loudly that my voice is almost raw.

"This is a diversion, Thana. Leave me and save your children. They are the most important right now!" Metatron's face says it all. He's ready to give up his life for the lives of my daughters.

"No, I will not leave you. Grandfather and Azrael are heading to the house. We will stand and fight together." Forcefully I unfurl my wings and take on my reaper persona and manifest Daybreaker. My sword blazes to life as the first of the Hellhounds and Demons can be seen coming over the hilltop.

Metatron astounds me as he takes on his full celestial glory. White light blasts out in every direction around him. Except where I am standing. He winks at me, then charges forward. What wasn't killed by his blast of holy light was definitely weakened by it. Winged Demons swoop down on a collision course with Metatron's back. I take to the air quickly and hack through the winged bastards.

Ash rains down around Metatron as I fight in the air above him. My familiars flank him, protecting him from the sides and rear. Hell rains on earth and it seems like there's no end in sight. Landing carefully next to Metatron, we stand back to back, fighting the oncoming horde.

Metatron laughs out of nowhere. "You guys are in trouble now!"

Raising a brow, I look back at him. I'm puzzled by his statement till the blinding flash of light streaks through the sky, then impacts close to where we are standing.

Sandalphon stands before us larger than life and glowing in the darkness. He is almost a carbon copy of Metatron in every way except bulk. Where Metatron is built for power, they built Sandalphon for speed. In a well-executed move, they cross their Angelic swords and a reverberating clash echoes as light blasts out in a powerful beam before them. They burn everything demonic in the light's path to ash before my eyes.

Double blinking, I gather up my familiars and check them over before looking at the two powerful Archangels before me. "We need to get back home, Metatron. The babies are in danger." My brows furrow as I look from him to his twin, then back again.

"Get to your children. We'll meet you there." He says quickly before rushing to me and planting the most passionate parting kiss I've received to date.

Swooning, I waver on my feet and spread my wings wide before pulling myself and my familiars into the shadows, vanishing from sight. I manifest to a war going on within the house and outside. Rex is wrapped around the house, engulfing the attacking horde in his blackened flames. My grandfather and Azrael are on different levels of the house fighting the winged Demons. The question I have is where are my mates and children?

Phasing through the darkness and into the house, I search it like a specter. I eventually find everyone boarded up in Cyrus's bedroom. Unleashing Fenrir and my panther, they join Cyrus's wolf in protecting the babies. "Looks like you guys have it all under control." Smirking, I walk past everyone to look at my daughters sleeping between the wolves.

"Under control? Have you seen the horde outside?" Christian states flatly. Clearly frustrated over the current situation.

Smiling, I walk over to Cyrus, then out into the hallway. The house is as silent as a tomb and all you can see out the large bay window is Rex's obsidian scales. "I have everything under control." Just as the words escape my lips, Metatron and his twin arrive in the entryway on the first floor. "Look, the cavalry has arrived." Gracefully, I motion to the twins downstairs and smile.

My mates rush to the railing and look down. Metatron and Sandalphon wave at them and then look over at me just as Samael and Azrael walk in through the double doors downstairs. I leap over the rail and glide down to the first level and check everyone over. I blacken my eyes next and see through Fenrir's eyes as well as Cyrus's wolves' eyes. I command both wolves to bring my daughters with them. "Rex has the outside under control for now." I state as I pace the entryway, looking around the downstairs level.

"Lady Thana, you must consider warding the house for yours and the children's safety." Sandalphon says before taking a knee before me.

When his gaze raises to meet mine, I shift my eye color from gray, to black, then to chrome, then back to gray again to get my point across. "Warding is out of the question. Myself, my mate..." I motion to Cyrus. "And my daughter would be blocked from the very house we are supposed to be safe in." As if on cue, Fenrir walks over with Nikita's bundle gently gripped in his mouth. Her wrap holds her securely suspended under his powerful jaws. I take hold of my daughter and Fenrir returns to being a tattoo on my arm. Carefully, I unwrap Nikita and show her to Sandalphon. Her fuzzy little dark gray wings on display.

He stands slowly to look at her then over to Raphael, whom is holding his daughter Davina. "I will personally rain Hell on earth if anything happens to my children or my mates." I allow my eyes to bleed chrome as I stare at Sandalphon.

His head whips to the side to stare at Metatron. "She's the Destroyer's heir!" His voice raises three octaves as he stares at his twin.

"Yes, she is. And I am honored to have been chosen to be her mate." Metatron moves and kisses my forehead, then motions for me to give him Nikita. I place my daughter in his giant arms. My child looks like a kitten compared to him.

Unfurling his wings, he looks back over them and plucks a tiny feather from along his wing bone. Carefully, he maneuvers Nikita in his arms so her wings are showing. He gently places the feather on her right wing and says words in the language only known by Angels. His white feather melds with her wing and sits proudly close to her body.

"She has my protection from now till the end of days. Even beyond that." He kisses her forehead once more. "Blood of my mate's blood, Azrael's heir apparent. My sword is yours from now until forever." Nikita coos and reaches for Metatron's face. He lowers his head and her tiny hands glow faintly. A brilliant smile creeps across his lips and she removes her hands. Tilting my head to the side, I watch the exchange.

Metatron starts to rock my daughter to sleep, then looks back at me. "All will be well my love." The words leave his lips and I believe him. Everything hopefully will just work out.

CHAPTER 52

GAGE

~The next day~

I've heard the stories of the end of days and what the rapture is supposed to look like. I'll be damned, I thought yesterday was going to be the last day for all of us. Walking through the house, I have one of my original bibles from several hundred years ago to research the end of days.

"What do you have there?" Christian asks as he tilts it down so he can see.

"My bible, the end of days is upon us according to this passage." I show him the section in Timothy where it mentions greed and self love and all of that fun stuff. I then flip to the parts about false idols. Christian and I shake our heads, seeing all the dots connect. "This can't be good. We need Thana at full power." Christian states flatly.

"The world needs Thana at full power. There's only two ways that can happen." Azrael manifests out of nowhere and joins in the conversation.

Almost jumping out of my skin, I hold my chest, taking in deep breaths, trying to calm down. "My understanding is that it would happen over time. Is there something more that needs to happen?" Concerned, I look over at Christian, then back to Azrael.

"Unfortunately, yes." Azrael walks over to the couch and takes a seat, staring off into the fireplace. "Samael needs to die or will Thana his power. Either way, he will die in the end. Then it will be like a freight train of power that will collide with her." Azrael's cold exterior falls briefly, he knows full well Samael is the closest to having a blood relative that Thana has had in forever.

"Does he know?" Thana's voice wavers slightly, looking at Azrael. We double blink looking back at Thana shocked that we didn't hear her arrive.

All the neglect and abuse that she's sustained over her life shows when emotions come into play. She reverts to that little girl that was left crying for her mother when she was abandoned. I walk over and wrap an arm around her and pull her to me. A shiver wracks her body, and I know she's trying to keep her emotions under control.

"We talked about it last night, little one. He's okay with what needs to happen to keep you safe." Azrael forces a smile and holds his hand out to Thana. She pulls away from me and rushes over to his side, and he hugs her to him. "I will always be here for you. You are the daughter I always wished I had." Thana hugs Azrael tightly, and it's now that I decide to leave the room and head upstairs.

My footsteps always lead me to the same place. The attraction is undeniable between us, and we know there's something there. Just as I raise my fist to knock on his door, it opens, and he stands there before me in just a towel. My eyes rake over every inch of his defined muscles. "You're always so lickable, I just want to string you up, grip your hips and fuck you till you scream my name." I say with a slight growl to my voice.

A sly smirk slithers over Cyrus's lips as he looks me up and down. "What do you have in mind?" Cyrus opens his door wide and I walk in and take a seat on his bed. The towel falls from his hips and I watch the striations in his muscles move as he walks around.

"We need to have a plan for if Thana gets poisoned by light again." I cross my arms over my chest and stare at Cyrus as his cock twitches to life.

Cyrus stops dead in his tracks and stares at me as his eyes blacken. "I know what we need to do. If needed, you need to fall and we can make it happen." A feral grin crosses his lips as he looks at me like I'm his lunch.

Raising an eyebrow, I look at him, and I can taste the desire in the air. "I bet you know exactly what we need to do to save our girl." Tilting my head to the side, I watch him closely as he smiles back at me.

"I do…" Cyrus lays back against the counter hard cock waving in the air leaking. The single rivulet of pre-cum runs down the channel on the underside of his cock. My eyes follow the rivulet down to his ball sack.

Licking my lips, I rise and prowl towards him. My hands land on either side of him on the counter. My lips hover just over his as I press my body against him, pinning him in place. "We will do what's best for the family and Thana. If I have to fall to save her and you…" My tone is breathy as my heart hammers in my chest. Roughly, I grip Cyrus's jaw, holding him so close I can almost taste his lips. His breath washes over my flesh and my cock twitches in anticipation. "I've always loved you, always will." Pulling away, I turn to leave the room before I cross the line I cannot come back from.

Cyrus's hand grips my wrist tightly, and I stop and look back at him. Dark desire and promise leak from his every pore as his eyes rake over my body. "I know… After it's all said and done we can finally be together." The corner of his lip quirks up as he forces a smile. He knows full well the fall might kill me. It's a sacrifice I am willing to make for the ones I love.

~Samael~

Walking through the halls of my castle, I peruse over the items

I've collected over the millennium. My fingertips ghost over my collection and I get lost in the memories that surround the items before me. My eyes lock on my favorite swords and I remember the battles won with them.

"What's on your mind, old friend?" I hear from behind me. Slowly, I turn and look down the hall to see Azrael standing there.

Shaking my head, I turn fully to face him. "There are a lot of things going on, Azrael. My impending death, for example." Smirking, I reach down and touch my wolf familiar and run my fingers through his fur.

"Oh, is that all?" Azrael raises an eyebrow and leans against the wall, looking at me. "Thana and the guys were having a similar conversation about what needs to happen before she can ascend. My black heart is breaking for her." Azrael's tone hardens, and I know he's serious about his emotional attachment to my descendant.

Shaking my head, I motion to adjourn to my sitting room that isn't far from the armory. Raising a hand, the fires in the room ignite and the hearth warms the room quickly. Azrael walks over to the minibar and pours us both three fingers of my finest whiskey. I take my seat by the hearth and watch my wolf lay down on the rug at my feet. Azrael hands me my glass, then sits across from me, still with that serious face on.

"Your death very well may break something within her that there's no way for anyone to fix. You are the only blood relative that she has left who is free and alive." Azrael's tone tells me there's no joking involved.

I look down at my wolf, then back up again. "It's difficult for me on this end as well. I go from having eternity to limited time because the end of days is upon us." Folding my hands in front of me, I stare down at them. "I just got Thana and my great granddaughters. I don't wish to leave them yet." There's a tightness in my chest that I am unfamiliar with. Absently, I raise my hand and rub the area, hoping it goes away.

"That discomfort you're feeling... That's emotional pain. It tells us we're still alive and that we can love. You're experiencing the pain of loss." Azrael accurately diagnoses the problem and I sit back, stunned. Never in my existence have I ever felt like this.

Arching an eyebrow, I stand up and knock back my drink. "I shall go spend what time I have left with my family then. It may ease the pain a bit." Watching Azrael, I can tell my decision has pleased him with the broad smile on his lips.

I don't bother to do anything fancy and I merely manifest in the main hall of Thana's house. My wolf came along for the trip and he stays at my heels. The musical tone of Thana's voice calls to me from the kitchen area. I follow her voice through the house and come upon the most beautiful scene my eyes have seen in centuries. Thana has her Angelic daughter on her lap and Cyrus is holding his daughter in the air, flying her around the dining room. "Hello Descendant, family." I force a smile and open my arms wide.

"Grandfather!" Thana yells and passes off the daughter she's holding to its father before running right at me and hugging me tightly. Her arms band around me, squeezing me, and I embrace her like she's my lifeline.

"My precious Descendant." Softly escapes my lips as I kiss the crown of her head.

"Metatron and Christian should be back with dinner. Will you stay with us and eat?" Thana's eyes sparkle with life and love and it makes my chest tighten all over again.

How is one so full of light and love going to be able to handle all the darkness that's required to maintain the veil between Hell and earth? Threading my fingers through her long blonde hair, I ponder my own question. "If it will make you happy, then I most certainly will stay for dinner." Thana bounces up and down in my arms till she breaks loose and pulls out her phone and walks away.

Raising a single brow, I look each of her mates over, searching for the answer as to why she left the room. Raphael smiles as he sets the table. "She's calling Metatron about dinner arrangements and picking up extra food stuff as she calls it." Raphael shrugs and smiles as he holds his daughter walking around the table.

Thana comes skipping back in and grabs her daughter from Cyrus and starts dancing with her through the kitchen singing Skillets Back from the Dead. During one spin, she unfurls her wings and gets them in on the dancing, opening one side at a time. Nikita's giggles are music to my ears and I can't help but smile, watching two of the most precious people in my life enjoying this brief moment.

"Amazing, isn't she?" Cyrus says as he motions to his mate and daughter. "They contained all the power of the universe in one being, light and darkness, life and death in one beautiful package." Cyrus's pride blooms as he speaks about my descendant. My decision has been made easier just watching her interacting with her children and mates. This moment right here needs to be preserved at all costs.

"Females are miracles to behold. Like the one in charge, they can create or destroy life. They can heal with a touch or kill when needed." My words catch the family off guard and they turn to face me to listen to what I have to say. "To birth twins and both are daughters is a miracle in itself. I don't remember a time in recent history that its happened." Shrugging my shoulders, I look back towards the front of the house, sensing Metatron's arrival.

The big guy comes in the front door with his hands full and a broad smile on his face. "I'm home!" He yells and does that reverberation thing with his voice that Thana can mimic. The guys rush to him and take the bags and set the dinner table out for everyone. Once freed from his duties, he comes over and kisses Thana soundly before offering me his hand to shake. "I hope all is well Samael." Metatron exudes confidence and poise that the other mates lack.

"All is as well as it can be, ole friend. This..." I motion towards my descendant and her children and mates. "Must be preserved at all costs. I am at peace seeing this, knowing my sacrifice will not be in vain." Forcing a smile, I look away from Metatron and watch the family hustle and bustle around the kitchen and the dining room.

Metatron wraps an arm around my shoulder and leads me towards the dining room table and motions to the chair he wants me to sit in. Once seated, Thana brings me Nikita and places her in my arms. Staring down at the little miracle, her eyes blacken then churn mercury. Raising my eyebrows, I stare down at Nikita and see myself in her chrome eyes. "When did she start doing this Descendant?"

Thana stands up and walks over to me and leans over the back of the chair, looking down at her daughter. "Soon after she was born, why?" She moves to the side and leans on the table, looking down at Nikita, whose eyes return to the same shade of gray as her mothers.

"She's going to be powerful when she gets older. It's no wonder she will take Azrael's place when he deems he's ready to retire." Leaning forward, I press my lips to Nikita's forehead and imbue her name with power. Once finished, I turn to my familiar and my descendant. "I wish to change your familiar Descendant. I will give you Skoll to match his brother Hati that Cyrus has. Maelestor Rex will be contained till Nikita comes of age. She will need him more than you will, all things considered." I watch Thana's eyes move between her daughter and then Skoll, whom sits patiently waiting to be accepted.

"I accept your gift on behalf of myself and my daughter." Thana cups her hand over Maelestor Rex and contains him in a glass orb. She then drops to her knees before Skoll and allows him to sniff her. "I accept you Skoll to be my familiar and guardian." She pulls down the shoulder of her shirt and Skoll presses his nose to her shoulder and becomes another tattoo on her body.

Thana slowly stands, then wraps her arms around me and kisses my cheek. "Thank you, grandfather. I love you." Thana's voice breaks at the end and my chest constricts, making it hard to breathe.

"I love you too, little one. Now until the days go unnumbered and my name is long forgotten." I smile, finally at peace with everything that I know needs to happen.

Smiling, Thana looks more at peace with everything than I do and I didn't think that was possible. "You will never be forgotten. If I give birth to a son, his middle name will be your name. You will live on through me and my descendants." Her eyes swirl chrome and her voice reverberates like Metatron's does. I know in this moment she has let all the Angels in heaven and on earth know her intentions. I can truly rest easy tonight.

CHAPTER 53
THANA

Last night was one to remember. I didn't realize how at peace with my grandfather passing I actually am. Staring down at my two little cherubs sleeping, my life is finally complete. Well, mostly complete. Looking over my shoulder, I see Metatron watching me, and I know I have made that man wait long enough.

"Sweetheart, can you draw me a bath in my suite?" Turning slowly, I face Metatron and start to stalk him.

"Anything your heart desires, my beloved mate." The deep rumble of his voice makes my heart rate speed up. Closing the distance between us, I look up into his blue eyes and they churn golden. I love seeing myself in his eyes. I can only imagine how he sees me.

"I desire you and me in the bath sooner than later." I trail my index finger down his chest as I lock eyes with him. He swallows hard and I watch his Adam's apple bob. He nods his head frantically, then vanishes in a wisp of golden glitter. Cyrus is standing in the hallway holding in a chuckle and I smirk right along with him.

"Don't break him, Kitten." Cyrus's tone holds a command to it that I still am not used to hearing from him. His lips turn up slowly as he creeps towards me and embraces me tightly. "Everything will be alright Kitten, Gage and I have been talking to him for the last two days. He's in better shape now than when you first met him. We've got you, babe." Cyrus punctuates his statement by sweeping me off my feet and kissing me deeply, making my core throb.

He releases me and I'm breathless. I stare after him for several moments before walking past him into my private chambers. I cross my room and into the bathroom on the other side, the short walk seems to be the longest walk of my life. Every step my heart thuds harder and louder. I cross over the threshold of my ensuite and the scent of lilacs assault my senses. Candles of every color imaginable line every available surface, their flickering light cast random shadows throughout the room. Soft instrumental music plays in the background, barely audible over the jets of the whirlpool tub.

My eyes scan the room and find a tray on a table with a bottle of wine and two glasses with an eloquently scrawled note saying, *drink me*. A soft chuckle escapes my lips, picking up on the Alice in Wonderland reference. I guess the big guy remembered it's one of my favorite movies. Carefully, I pour myself a glass of wine and sip at it slowly. Its rich, full-bodied flavor explodes on my tongue and a moan of pleasure escapes my lips.

"I remembered you liked the wine from the Angelic Realm, so I brought back a bottle for you." Metatron's voice fills the room and warms me from the inside, making the butterflies flutter like a tornado in my belly. He strides across the room with the grace of a panther stalking its prey. I'm hypnotized watching the stretch and flex of his abdominal muscles.

A blush briefly highlights his high cheekbones as he looks down at me. Slowly, he cocks his head off to the side and smirks. "Like what you see, my love?" That move right there was all Cyrus and I arch an eyebrow looking at him.

"You know I do. What are you going to do about it?" I arch my brow and move to lean back against the tub edge and watch him falter for a moment.

His wings unfurl in all of their pristine snow white glory. My eyes caress every single inch of their span like a kid looking through the window at candy. Metatron pulls a Cyrus and wraps me up in his wings. Tentatively, I reach out and touch his silky white feathers. Stroking them, I feel his length harden between us and I turn to look up into his eyes as they churn molten gold. "You're pushing me to the edge, Thana. If you do not wish to have me, please stop." His strained voice pulls at my heartstrings and I throw caution into the wind.

Gently, I push on his wings, and he opens them up, looking dejected. I turn my back to him and slowly unbutton my shirt and let it fall to the floor at my feet. Next I roll forward with my thumbs hooked in the top of my leggings and drag them down my legs inch by inch. I make sure Metatron has a good view of my ass as I bend over. Slowly, I roll back up to stand and step out of my leggings. I reach back and unclasp my bra and allow it to slide down my arms, then drop it to the floor. I can hear his breathing hitch each time I do something new. All that is left now is my blood red thong. Thankfully, it's not my favorite one. I shift my fingers into claws and slice through the material at my hips, destroying the fabric.

His eyes follow the fabric to the floor, then slowly his eyes lock with mine. Desire burns in his eyes and he closes the distance between us in a matter of seconds. His hands feel molten as they slide over my flesh, caressing every curve. My breath hitches as he presses me back behind the edge of the tub and kisses me soundly. My hands run over his solid chest and my fingers find the buttons on his crisp white shirt.

His eyes follow the trail of my fingers over his shirt, then across the hard planes of his chest. I slip my hands under the material and over his shoulders, sliding the shirt off of him. His eyes follow my hands as I grip at the muscles of his biceps, appreciating the tone and strength there. Trailing my fingers down his chest, I follow the ripples in his abdomen. Gently, I slide the tips of my fingers in between his stomach and the fabric of his dress pants. Raising my eyes, I look for consent from him before I go further.

He nods his head, then kisses me passionately on my lips, confirming he's ready for the next step. Unbuttoning his pants, I hear him inhale sharply. It's now that I discover Metatron goes commando. Double blinking, I stare at the solid length standing at attention before me. He is much longer and thicker than the others. Carefully, he steps out of the pants he was wearing that pooled at his feet and picks me up as if I weigh nothing.

Deftly, he maneuvers us into the tub and sets me to rest between his legs with my back facing him. His hands grip the muscles of my shoulders and start to massage away the tension I didn't realize I had. Soft moans escape my lips as his hands span the width of my back and ribs, making me feel like the tiniest person on earth. His lips caress the side of my neck and send shockwaves through my body, directly to my core.

Reaching out to my sides, I still his hands and I feel him stiffen behind me. Turning quickly, I see the doubt flash in his eyes and it breaks my heart. I place both of my hands on his chest and push back, getting him to recline against the back of the tub. Standing up, I motion for him to straighten his legs out for me. When he does so, I smile and lower myself onto his lap, keeping his thick member between us. I grip his thick wrists and raise his hands to rest on my breasts, in my own way of granting him permission.

His mouth pops open as he gives my breasts a tentative squeeze. Leaning forward, I kiss his lips, nipping the bottom one, trying to get him out of his headspace. I'm hoping beyond hope his instinct kicks in as I rise up on my knees and tease the tip of his cock with the lips of my pussy. Long slow strokes along his length. It's maddening how he's content with sitting still while I drive myself insane is beyond me. I open my eyes and he's just staring blankly, his eyes are bathed in an ethereal glow. My gut tells me that Raph is trying to encourage him to do something.

The next thing I know, Metatron is in motion and his hands grip my hips tightly and with a determined look on his face, he slams his length home. I gasp at the sudden fullness and stretch from him being seated deeply within me. We stare into each other's eyes and I can tell that mine are chrome by the way everything looks around me. When I am finally comfortable, I move up and down his length, splashing water out of the tub with each bounce. Several bounces later, Metatron wraps his arms around me and drives his length up into me. His arms feel like steel bands holding me securely in place as he pistons in and out of me. Every slip and slide of his thick cock sends shockwaves of pleasure and tingles to my core. The early flutters begin deep in my belly as my body tenses like a coiled up spring ready to explode.

I wrap my arms tightly around his thick neck and hold on for dear life. The man I believed had no clue about what he's doing is making me see stars. Throwing my head back, I scream as my orgasm rips through me. Every muscle tenses as my core throbs and pulses around his cock. My legs feel like jello and my greedy core continues to pulse. Apparently, Cyrus taught Metatron the trick of sustaining my orgasm. "I'm close..." Metatron pants out between thrusts.

I do the only thing that comes to mind. I bite his shoulder as hard as I can. He roars loudly as I feel his cock twitch and pulse within me. Metatron rams his length, burying it within me several times before the final thrust seating himself balls deep. Carefully, I withdraw my teeth and lick the wounds I created. The warmth I felt in my chest before has blazed to life and feels like an inferno. The bond is there and his link to me seems to be one of the strongest besides the one I have with Cyrus.

We snuggle close for several minutes till we feel him go flaccid. Showing off just a little bit, Metatron takes ahold of me and stands up. He carefully navigates us out of the tub and over to the shower stall. I feel exhausted and weak as a kitten. Who knew sex could do this?

Metatron takes the better half of an hour showering me and

massaging every muscle in my body till I feel like a huge pile of jello. The last thing I remember is him bundling me up in my towels and carrying me back to bed.

~Metatron~

The bond being fully in place makes me feel more alive than I have ever been in my life.. Carefully, I lay Thana down in her nest and tuck her in tightly. My finger tips graze over her familiars and I get the three of them to rise and lay with her in the nest.

Quietly, I leave the nest and find all the guys and the babies in the dining room. The Angelic side of the bond seems to glow, whereas Cyrus seems to be a little lackluster at the moment. Tilting my head to the side, I study everyone individually. I'm not sure if I am correct, but I think Thana's fears were warranted.

"Guys, I think we may have a problem." I state as I watch Cyrus almost sway on his feet.

Raphael is still beaming as he walks up and gives me a brow hug. "Nonsense, the bond is in place and the family is whole. What could possibly be wrong?" You know how they say never ask the question you really don't want the answer to?

Almost as if on cue Cyrus hits the floor passed out. Gage rushes to his side to try to rouse him as Raphael and I rush to Thana's side. Thana is passed out and her familiars are asleep at her side, refusing to wake up.

I do the only thing I can think of doing. "Azrael Guardian of the Veil between life and death I summon you!" My voice reverberates with power as it shakes items free of the shelves surrounding the nest.

A mass of dark shadows gathers in the center of the room, and soon Azrael is standing there. The rage evident on his face rapidly falters as he notices Thana limp in Raphael's arms. "What the fuck is the meaning of this?" He bellows at the top of his lungs as he kneels next to Thana, running his shadow filled hands over her forehead.

"We completed the bond about an hour ago. Your son also

passed out." My eyes widen as I run through the house to where Christian is.

Little Nikita is also unresponsive. I take her from Christian and order him and Gage to bring Cyrus to Thana's nest. By the time I return, Samael is in the nest, running his hands over his descendant slowly, it seems that with the aid of Azrael, he is awakening Thana. Tears form in Samael's eyes as he sees his great granddaughter is in worse shape than her mother. He gently takes the child from me and cradles her in his arms, sharing his life force with her. She eventually awakens and coos up at Samael.

Azrael, on the other hand, works on awakening his son. Cyrus's eyes eventually open and he looks pointedly at Gage. It's now that I connect the dots. They have been prepared for this event even though I was in denial that it was a possibility.

Thana's familiars return to just being tattoos on her flesh and she slowly sits up. Her eyes drift to her daughter laying on her grandfather's chest. "Take her to the Shadow Realm with you, where she can draw strength from the environment." Thana's voice screams exhaustion and she flops back against the pillows, watching Azrael work on Cyrus.

Cyrus's color is back to normal and he looks concerned down at Thana. "We suspected this may happen. Gage and I have a plan." Cyrus looks over at Gage and his sadness is all-consuming.

"I will make the sacrifice and fall to save Thana, Nikita and Cyrus." He swallows hard, then kneels at Thana's side. "I love you, and I will do anything to make sure that you are healthy and happy. If I have to give up paradise to do it, then so be it." Gage kisses Thana's forehead, then moves to Cyrus and offers him support, and they walk out of the room together.

"What are they planning to do?" Thana asks weakly. Seeing her like this breaks my heart. Apparently, I am the reason for her, Cyrus and the baby falling ill.

"Pick a sin and more than likely add three more if I know my son.

I'll stay with Thana till the problem is solved. She needs my darkness to counteract the light poisoning." Azrael confirms my worst fear.

Thana forces a smile as she looks up at me. "It's not your fault, Metatron, please don't blame yourself. Watch over Davina for me." Azrael scoops Thana up and slides her to curl up in his lap. Wings of midnight embrace my mate in a cocoon of shadows, hopefully saving her life till Cyrus and Gage do whatever it is they have planned.

CHAPTER 54

CYRUS

Fucking light mother fucker almost killed my mate daughter and I all in one fell swoop. Gage drags me to my room and lays me on my bed. We've had long discussions about when and if this day was ever going to come and what we planned to do about it if it was needed.

"Are you ready, Cy? I know we planned on you being in charge, but you're barely able to hold your head up at the moment." Gage looks down at me, concerned, as he pulls his shirt over his head and drops it to the floor.

"I'm good. How many sins can we pack into the next twenty minutes?" Smirking, I force a smile, trying to lessen his concern.

Rolling onto my side, I take the paper from Gage and note that we figured out there's at least one hundred and twenty-four sins we could commit. The question is how many and what ones would be sure to make him fall. Arching a brow, I look over to where Gage was several moments ago. And he's missing in action. Gage comes walking into the bedroom in a full harness and nothing else on but a smile. The smirk that is playing on his full lips has me mildly concerned. In his left hand a bottle of regular lube, in the right a bottle of tingling lube. I am truly in deep trouble if this noob is walking in here in Dom mode with enough lube to last a month.

"Gage, what do you think you're doing?" I ask curiously as I watch him sit the tubes down. He moves to the foot of the bed and starts untying my shoes.

"What the fuck does it look like I'm doing? I'm getting ready to fuck the man I love and fall from grace for the woman we love." The confidence Gage has is impressive. I just am getting concerned.

"Do you have a clue what you're about to do?" My voice rises several octaves higher than I had intended and Gage fucking laughs at my concern.

Smirking, he waves his phone in my direction. On the screen, the feed from one of the more popular porn websites. "Research Cyrus, research." He waggles his eyebrows at me as he sets his phone down and works on removing my pants. Both eyebrows raise in surprise as he discovers I like to wear thongs. "Damn Cy planning for tonight or am I just lucky?"

Forcing myself to sit up, I look at Gage and the boner he's sporting. "Standard equipment buddy. I enjoy keeping the boys in one place and not stuck to my thigh." My eyes drop down to the list again as Gage crawls up onto the bed with me and starts unbuttoning my shirt.

Gage takes the paper and starts pointing at sins. "We definitely can hit Adultery, chambering, clamor, defiling the body..." Gage points at the new tattoo he must have gotten today. It's a pair of wings with a heart and Thana's name in the middle.

"Ooh, my favorite. Desiring the praise of men!" I yell and we share a laugh at the list's expense. "Better yet.." I point at number forty on the list, evil concupiscence.

Gage's brows furrow as he looks at the one I'm pointing at. "What does that even mean?" I lean forward and press my lips to his and grip the back of his head, holding him to me. Moving the arm that was supporting me, we fall back onto the bed together.

"Exactly what we are planning to do. What we have, a forbidden desire for forbidden things." I reach down and cup his balls, then stroke his shaft slowly, feeling it harden under my hand.

"The things we do for love..." Gage whispers against my lips as he rocks his length against my hand.

"Lay on your side in front of me. I don't have the strength to stand at the moment." Gage does exactly as I ask and I snuggle up behind him after using my claws to cut my underwear free from my body. My hand slides over the muscle of his hip and down to his groin. My fingertips nestle in the curly hair at the base of his cock before finding the rod I seek.

Slow rocks of my hips, my cock rests between his thick, hard ass cheeks. "Pick the lube you want, Gage. I suggest regular for your ass and the tingling for your cock." I say just before biting his shoulder blade, making him moan my name.

I hear the top of the lube pop open and the bottle is wiggled in my line of sight. Smart man has taken my suggestion. Being the magnificent lover that I am, I warm the lube up before massaging his anus with it. His moans are music to my ears. Who knew Gage would be into the same carnal sins that I am?

"God, Cyrus, now please..." Breathlessly Gage begs for my cock as I continue to prepare his ass for my intrusion.

"Soon love, put the tingling lube on your cock and start stroking, I want to watch you cum." I push as much dominance into my tone as I can. To be honest, he can easily overpower me at the moment. I simply don't have the strength to fight back.

I watch the long, slow strokes of his large hands on the thick shaft of his cock. "Good boy, grip it tighter like Thana's pussy would do." I say between bites on his shoulder. His hips buck forward with each bite, and I can see the pre-cum leaking from the tip already.

Every blasphemous word that falls from his lips, my strength seems to increase. I can only hope his sacrifice saves us all. His next thrust forward, I rub the head of my cock against his anus. Gage's breath hitches and he goes deathly still. "Remember how we introduced

Thana, same theory love." He wipes his hand on the bed sheet then reaches back to rest his hand on my thigh as I start to push forward. "Nice slow even breaths, Gage. Relax the best you can." I watch his head nod and he grips my thigh a little harder as I work my way in.

Just for good measure, I draw back a moment and coat my cock and his anus again with more lube. Slow, even pressure and a lot of lube hopefully will make this easier for Gage to endure. I breach the barrier and he moans, arching back, resting this head on my chest. I take that as my cue to start rocking my hips, inching my length into him slowly. Lucky for him, I'm not as long or thick as he is. According to Thana, I'm just right.

I bottom out balls deep in his ass and stop moving immediately, letting him adjust. Reaching forward, I grip his pulsing cock and stroke it just before I move again. Gage's hand grips mine as I stroke his cock. The tingling lube makes my hand feel funny as I try to grip and thrust at the same time. Gage knocks my hand away and grips his cock roughly. "Fuck me Cy." Soon as the words leave his mouth, it's like a switch flips in me.

I grip his hips with both hands and withdraw, then slam myself home. Every stroke, every thrust, I feel my strength starting to return. Gage suddenly arcs back and I see a stream of cum shoot across the room and impact on my wall. My efforts are redoubled now that he's cum first.

It's time I focus on my orgasm. Flipping Gage to kneel with his ass in the air, I position myself behind him and sink back in like I had never left. Each thrust is long, hard, and balls deep. My fingertips grip his hips almost to the point of bruising as I slam myself to the hilt into him over and over again.

I roar as my orgasm hits me like a freight train. My entire body feels electrified as I pump Gage full of my seed. My wings unfurl on their own and spread wide. Gage cries out from his second orgasm seconds after mine. Like me, his wings burst free from his back. His once snow-white wings are black as midnight and rival my own. My hands caress his feathers as I look them over, marveling at the change.

Wood splinters fly through the room as the door to my room explodes in a million pieces. In the doorway stands a very furious, heavily armored Thana. Apparently, Gage falling healed not only me, but her as well, which means our daughter is safe. I withdraw from Gage's ass as Thana barrels straight for him. Her hands caress every inch of his face, checking him over. Blood tears stream silently down her cheeks as she finally looks at his wings.

Her hands shake as she hesitates, reaching out to touch his feathers for the first time. The armor she is wearing melts away, as does the fury we saw earlier. Her fingertips ghost over his obsidian wings. The best I can do to describe how she looks is... confused. She looks from Gage to me, then back again with her brows furrowed in the middle. Gage looks scared as he looks back at me, hoping to diffuse the Thana bomb that's in our lap.

"Kitten, we balanced the bond so that we wouldn't get sick anymore. Gage fell willingly to save us." I hold my hands up as if trying to calm a wild and rampaging beast.

"Baby, my love... I would fall a million times if only to see you smile again. You are the most precious person in my life. My heart belongs to you." Gage says as he steps off the bed towards Thana. I motion to him to wrap her in his wings, and he does so immediately. I can feel the tension in the room dissipate quite quickly by that one simple action.

Looking towards the door, the rest of the bond mates stand there staring at us as if we have five heads a piece. "Gage crossed the veil and fell to save me, Thana, and Nikita. Now if we have to battle in Hell or any of the circles, Thana will have two bond mates instead of just one."

Something must have dawned on Thana because she pushes free of Gage's wings, then moves to stand before him. The gold bracelet she was gifted glows faintly. Removing it from her wrist, she touches it to Gage's feathers, and they become lined in gold like mine. I guess in some recess of her mind; she knew exactly what it was meant for, just not when she was going to need it.

"I'm hungry..." Thana states plainly before grabbing Gage's hand and leading him out of my bedroom past the others.

With zero fucks given, I watch a very naked and lubed Gage follow behind Thana willingly. "What were you two thinking?" Raphael states as he moves further into my room.

"Gee I don't fucking know? Maybe? Not fucking dying would be nice!" I scream at Raphael, honestly not fucking caring one bit about his biased opinion at the moment. I fling my arms up into the air and simply stare at him.

"Raph, he's right. For all intents and purposes, they were dying because of me." Metatron states. "The most logical solution was to balance the bond. They did it within the bond instead of... How did Thana put it? Add another rando? Who's Rando and do I know him?" Metatron innocently states and causes Raphael to facepalm over it.

"Exactly!!!" I motion towards Metatron. "He gets it!" Raphael is turning redder than an apple as he stares at me, clearly frustrated that even Metatron gets what Gage and I did.

"I give up on you two seriously." Raphael says before vanishing in a mist of golden glitter. Shaking my head, I get up and pull on my pants after I wipe myself off. "Let's see what Gage and Thana have gotten up to." I glance at Metatron before leaving my room to find the others.

Walking through the house, I hear the musical giggles of my mate echoing through the house. Leaping over the rail, I open my wings and glide down to the first floor. There's Thana, sitting on the kitchen island with Gage between her legs, with his wings spread wide for her inspection. Somewhere between the time I saw him and now he found shorts. I'm almost jealous watching Thana's fingertips glide over the feathers.

Looking over his shoulder, Thana smiles brightly at me. "Hey baby, feeling better?" Thana was sicker than I was because of bringing Metatron into the bond and here she is worrying about me and if I'm okay.

"Much better Kitten. More importantly, how are you feeling?" Moving to the side of where she and Gage are, I take her free hand in mine and hold it, looking up into her stormy gray eyes.

A broad smile moves swiftly across her plump ruby lips. "Never better, actually. It's really weird, I feel like the power in me has been balanced. Like I don't have that lopsided feeling anymore." She furrows her brows as she formulates her explanation.

"What do you mean lop-sided *Kichōna mono?*" Christian says as he enters the kitchen along with the rest of the light side of the family.

Thana motions for Gage to move out of the way, and she slides off the countertop and onto the floor. "Okay, I think we need visuals for this explanation. Remember in the beginning, how I struggled with wielding the light and dark side of me concurrently?" We nod along and she graces us with a smile. With a practiced flourish, she extends both hands out before her. In the palms of her hands dark and light energies amass flickering like balls of fire in her hands.

"You shouldn't be able to do that." Raphael and Metatron say at the exact same time. They look at each other, shocked, then back over at Thana, who is giving them both a death glare.

"Exactly why not? Why shouldn't I be able to? I was flipping, created to be Samael's successor. Created!" She practically screams. The boom of power that comes off her almost knocks us on our collective asses.

"Kitten..." I say softly and flex my wings a little to get her attention.

Her head whips in my direction and her eyes are flickering between obsidian and chrome. The color almost pulses in time with what I would suspect is her heartbeat. "What I believe they..." I motion to Raph and Metatron. "are trying to say and failing miserably at it is that they haven't seen what you can do before. Like you said, they created you for a purpose. There's no way anyone would know what your true capabilities are." I hold my hands up in a placating manner as I attempt to approach the time-bomb we call our mate.

"Exactly my point. No one has a clue about what is or isn't normal for me except the big guy." Thana points up and raises her eyebrows at the same time.

Gage and I watch the rest of the family's emotions flicker over their faces, telegraphing their every thought. What I'm picking up loud and clear is that they are concerned, and I believe Thana hit the nail on the head about only the big guy.

CHAPTER 55

THANA

Every day seems to be a new adventure and the freak factor just keeps raising the bar. Gage fell to save us, and the rest of my light mates seem to be up in arms over it even though it was the only choice we had left. It's times like this that I really ponder the age-old feud between the fallen and the ascended.

On one side, it's quite antiquated, where everything is based on the book, not allowing for any gray areas that exist in life. On the other side, it's almost pure chaos because of the book, and they rebel against every concept. But, just like with everything, there should be a middle, and it doesn't exist.

Shaking my head, I choose an outfit for tonight's adventure. The guys and I are going to watch Cyrus's band play. Michael and Samael both agreed to take the babies for tonight so we can have a night off. It's kind of scary to think about the accelerated growth rate for my daughters. They are only a few weeks old, and as of today, they appear to be several months old. Raphael said because there's very little human in them, and that they will grow at the rate the Angels and Nephilims do. So, from what I understand, one week equals a month of growth for the first six months. It's done that way for survival more than anything.

Rolling my eyes, I pick out my favorite jeans and halter top paired with my absolute favorite timber boots. Finally dressed for the evening, I head downstairs to meet up with everyone. The guys are in various degrees of casual dress except for Cyrus and Gage. I can tell that Cyrus has revamped Gage's wardrobe because both of them are in leather. Holy hotness! Leather pants, black snug tee shirt, and combat boots. I go from one bad boy in the family to two. My heart is hammering in my chest, watching them both with their swagger on ten.

"Let's go." I let the words fall free from my lips, then head right out the front door and straight to the Hell-Cat. Slipping into the driver's seat feels like slipping into the arms of a lover. The driver's seat was specially made to conform to my body after I bought it from Dominik.

The passenger door pops open and Gage slips in and Cyrus manifests in the back seat. "Let's beat the goodie two shoes to the venue." Cyrus says with a sadistic grin. I know the others have been being dicks since Gage fell. Eventually they have to get over it or I may have to step in and say something sooner than later.

"I have a friend and her mates stopping by to watch the show. They're in town for the night and wanted something to do." Raising my eyes, I look into the rear-view mirror and watch Cyrus for a moment before looking at Gage.

Both guys nod before I fire the beast up, letting her roar to life. Before the limo can get rolling, I hammer the clutch and pop her into gear, lighting the tires up sending gravel everywhere. We're off like a shot and down the road long before the dust cloud settles. The bass thumps almost in time with the shifting of gears as we head into the city. Europe is so different than America, the Autobahn for example. It's as glorious as it is dangerous and mostly it's the tourists that think it is an Indy track that makes it scary.

I thank the import gods daily for being able to bring Dominik's

Hell-Cat here and finding a shop that was capable of the upgrades she needed. Popular Monster by Falling in Reverse blasts from the speakers as we make the trip halfway across the country. At one hundred and forty kilometers an hour, we'll make the venue in less than an hour. "Kitten, remember, drive no faster than your guardian Angel can fly." Cyrus says from the back seat and all I do is give him a thumbs up.

Gage laughs and turns to look at Cyrus. "Apparently her guardian Angel has a jet pack." Gage points at me and laughs. I can't help but join in on the laughter. Never once did I ever believe the concept of a guardian Angel. After all, where was mine when I needed them most, way back then?

We arrive at the venue, and I pull around back to the performers' parking area. Cyrus passes me his stage pass, and the VIP passes for Gage and me. When the security guard comes over, I show him all three badges, and he directs me to the proper place. Once parked, we unload Cyrus's guitar as well as his stage clothes for his performance. "Did you get a hold of my guest guitarist?" His smirk does things to my stomach, and I raise an eyebrow in response.

Pointing across the lot to the big ass black diesel. "She beat us here." I twirl my finger in the air, then pull out my phone. "Yo bitch, where are you hiding?" Her deep growl makes me laugh. "See you in a few minutes." Laughing, I hang up and look at the guys. They both look at me with raised eyebrows.

"Did she just growl at you?" Gage says, tilting his head to the side.

"Yes, yes, she did. It's all good love." I take Gage and Cyrus by the arms and walk into the club. Screams from Cyrus's fans fill the air as we walk in. They stop dead when I turn and look at them, my eyes blacken then churn chrome.

The crowd parts the minute I begin to radiate darkness. I'm finally feeling like my duality has found its balance and that now I can truly be at peace. About twenty feet before us, a mountain of a man blocks the better half of the stage and it can only be one person. "Dimitri!" I scream at the top of my lungs.

He spins quickly and meets me halfway, closing the distance between us in an instant. "How is my favorite Angel doing?" He kisses both of my cheeks before setting me back down.

"Fan-flipping-tastic! These are two of my mates." I motion back to my guys. "Cyrus who your mate will be performing with, and Gage." Both guys shake Dimitri's hand and the big guy laughs.

"Aurora is at the bar with Alaric. She told me that Klaus and Jayce saw you recently." Smiling, I send Gage to the bar to get my whisky sour.

"Yeah, I love their deserts. I'm so glad I moved closer to where you guys live." Dimitri's smile is almost as scary as his angry expression, and I'm honestly not sure which mood bothers me less.

Lithe fingers cover my eyes, and the scent of the woods fills my nostrils. I know exactly who's behind me. Pulling one of my favorite stunts, I vanish in a wisp of smoke, only to manifest standing directly before Aurora. Her eyes are liquid mercury with the dragon slits pulsing in the center. Shifting my eyes to come close to matching hers, a smile breaks out on her sanguine lips. "I missed you, Rory." Aurora cracks up and hugs me tightly to her.

"Missed you too, Ana." Aurora says, before kissing my lips passionately. We crack up laughing and look back at the guys. The men are in various states of shock as we laugh our asses off. Aurora winks at me and starts dragging me up to the stage. "We're up first. Come on pretty boy, you need to play too." She winks at Cy and we head up just as my other mates arrive.

As soon as I hear the first cords I know which song Aurora wants to do. The Evanescence version of the song The Chain. Aurora and I sing in perfect harmony throughout the song. When we hit the *damn the dark damn the light* part I unfurl my wings, spreading them wide. Aurora sings the harmony as I sing the lead vocals. We hit the part where I scream *chain* and I vanish in a wisp of shadows for several moments before manifesting back on stage for the last part of the harmony. We repeat the last lines several times, then I deliver the last lines and manifest shadows in my claws, ending the song.

The crowd erupts, cheering, wanting us to continue singing together. Aurora high five's me and then Cyrus and we huddle up to pick the next song. We decide the Daughtry song Heavy is the Crown is appropriate. Cyrus takes lead with the lyrics and I harmonize with him, dancing around with my mate. The more the lyrics escape his lips, the more the song holds meaning for me. The song is about not conforming to what society wants or deems to be status quo.

Myself, Aurora and Cyrus live our lives that way one hundred percent every day. We sing the song with heart and put power behind the lyrics. Then it happens. The mood in the room shifts and I feel something ominous is coming. We look around and I watch as Aurora's nose starts working. "I smell sulfur…" Her eyes shift to her dragonic eyes and she searches the room.

Looking back at my mates, I signal for them to separate and start to evacuate the humans out of the club. Aurora and I look at each other and I shake my head no. "There are some things that even a hybrid cannot survive, old friend. I think it's best you and your mates evacuate while there's still time." Unfurling my wings and manifesting my armor at the same time tells Aurora just how dire the situation is. Quickly, she moves in and hugs me briefly before grabbing her mates and running towards the door.

Just before the shit hits the fan, I reach out to Gage and grip him tightly. I force myself beyond my limits and manifest dark armor for him similar to mine. Without a second thought, Daybreaker blazes to life just as the shrieks of whatever is coming can be heard. Breaking through the skylight, winged Demons start attacking the occupants of the club.

Cyrus, Gage and I take to the air to meet our foes head on. Swords and claws clash in battle as we try to push the Demons back through the skylight. My other mates remain on the inside, trying to protect the patrons that didn't make it out in time. Wings of beasts blacken the evening sky blotting out what remains of the visible stars and moon. The longer and harder I fight, the stronger I seem to get. Could it be related to the ichor that is sprayed upon the armor or is it that the rumors are true? Daybreaker feeds off of the blood of its enemies and fuels the user.

I'm believing the latter since I seem to get stronger with every strike I deliver instead of getting tired. Gage and Cyrus are perfectly synchronized as they move back-and-forth blocking and striking at the Demons. It's times like this I wish Samael didn't take Maelestor Rex from me. Releasing the dragon to battle would have solved all the problems in one fell swoop.

Soon enough, the rest of my mates join the battle in the air and we knock back the Demons following them to their point of origin. On the edge of the city, what was once the site of the European witch hunts comes into view. A scythe welding crone stands on the hilltop summoning Demons from the pit. My eyes widen when she looks up and half of her face is missing and she's speaking a language that hasn't been heard since before I was born.

She moves quickly and points the scythe in my direction, shooting a stream of darkness right at me. I raise Daybreaker at the last possible moment, it deflects most of the energy and absorbs the rest. Trying to hide my shock, I fold my wings close to my body and power dive right at her. Using the scythe, she catches my ribs with the back of the rod and sends me crashing into a tree nearby. Standing slowly, I lean against the tree for support while I catch my breath. "RISE!" I yell with a force I didn't know I could muster. Both wolves, as well as my panther and raven, burst free from my flesh and go on the offensive, attacking the crone.

While she's distracted, Christian swoops in and cuts her head clean off. I watch with sadistic glee as the corpse-like head goes rolling down the hill and stops against a headstone. Fenrir walks down the hill and retrieves the head. He drops it at my feet and wags his tail. Gently, I pat the top of his head and tell him what a good boy he is. Time for him and his counterpart to go and bury the desiccated thing. Once the wolves are done, I check over my mates, making sure everyone came out of the battle relatively unscathed.

"It's odd that they vanished once Christian cut the corpse witch's head off." Gage states as he kicks the headless corpse with his boot.

"Not really. Cut off the head of the necromancer or summoner in this case and the spell is broken." Shrugging my shoulders, I look back towards the city, making sure nothing else is flying around that shouldn't be.

"What are you watching, love?" Metatron whispers near my ear as he presses his chest against my back. His hands caress my wings slowly from my back up to the bend of my wing.

"Just the skyline. I don't think it's over yet. Something feels off still." Sighing softly, I lean back against Metatron as he carefully bands his arms around me.

"I'm sure everything will be fine once the sun comes up in the morning," Raphael says as he moves to stand beside us, watching the horizon.

CHAPTER 56
CHRISTIAN

Everything wasn't fine when the sun came up. Several more uprisings of Demons happened all the way up till sunrise. The sun itself aided us in dispatching the Demons, but the damage was done. The human media was having a field day with the mass hysteria that swept through the cities that surrounded the epicenter.

Arriving home shortly after sunrise, Thana passes out on the couch, not even making it very far into the house. I find the throw blanket she hides in the footstool and throw it over her. Raphael motions for me to follow him into the kitchen with the others. "Daybreaker was fueling Thana if no one noticed." His blunt tone hits like a sledgehammer and sobers the room up quickly.

"That's just a myth. It can kill us and Demons and that's it." Crossing my arms over my chest, I stare down at Raphael.

"No, it's not. Did you see it absorb some of the power the Witch threw at Thana?" Raphael's agitation radiates through the bond and he inadvertently awakens Thana.

"Yes, Daybreaker steals energy and life force. Yes, it fueled me in battle. No, it's not dangerous to me." She lays it all out there for us, then makes eye contact with each of us.

"I'm concerned for the bond and what it might do to the rest of us." Raphael says and his tone goes from confident to almost defeated.

"Listen. I get it." Thana says as she walks around the room, touching each of us in turn. "It's the one thing that can and will defeat Lucifer. Once he's dealt with I plan on locking Daybreaker away." Thana looks me in the eye. Apparently, she listened to my concerns the other day and took it to heart. I smile at her, then look over at Raphael, whom I assume wanted me to side with him more than I did.

"We need a weapon that without a doubt will put the Morningstar down once and for all. They designed Daybreaker to destroy the Morningstar." Thana says with that strange reverberation to her voice. Metatron smiles, watching Thana make the announcement across the Angelic Realm.

"We have a fundraiser to go to tonight and tomorrow Raphael has a new telemetry wing opening up in the hospital." I say, purposely trying to change the course of conversation.

"Let's go get cleaned up and ready to sleep at least for a few hours before we have to take off running again." Raphael states as he heads towards the stairs leading to the upper levels.

Thana stands there rolling her eyes, then shifts them through their various colors. Raising an eyebrow, I watch her as she unfurls her wings and raises a single finger in my direction. Samael and Michael arrive within moments of each other. They hand Thana her daughters, kiss her cheeks then vanish as quickly as they arrived. Shaking her head, she passes Davina off to me and we head upstairs. Once in Thana's nest room, she climbs down into the fluffy blankets and reaches back out for Davina. I kiss the baby's forehead and pass her off to her mother. Thana and both daughters snuggle into the soft blankets and fall asleep almost immediately. With no warning, Thana's familiars rise from her flesh and lie around the perimeter of the nest.

"I still can't get used to seeing that." Raphael says in a low tone as to not disturb Thana.

"What's there to get used to? She's never felt safe sleeping alone. Most of the attacks happened when she was resting. I hate to admit it, but it was Light Nephilim that did it." Shrugging my shoulders, I draw in a deep breath, watching my mate and her babies resting peacefully.

Raphael runs his hand down his face, then slowly turns to face me. "It makes sense why most times she'll spend the entire night only with Cyrus. Dark Nephilim seem to comfort her more than we can." A sadness crosses his face that I never witnessed before. He shifts his weight uncomfortably as he watches me, then back down at her.

"It will get better in time, old friend. Trust the process." I smile, looking at him as I lead him out of the nest area.

"I hope so. Now that Gage has fallen, I feel as though the nest is off balance again." Raphael shrugs as we walk out of the nest and towards the common sitting room. Once there, we catch up with the rest of the guys.

"How are we going to explain Gage's change?" I ask the group. It's a subject we're going to have to broach at the fundraiser tonight. I take a relaxed stance, leaning back on the countertop behind me, letting the others map out how to handle tonight.

"I'm honestly not sure it's anyone's business." Gage states as he looks at each of us in turn. Most of us agree with him.

"They are going to ask when they sense the change in you." Raphael says, running a hand down his face, frustrated with the situation. "Can everyone please take this seriously! This could cause issues based on the fact you FELL!!" Raphael loses his cool over the situation. I can only guess it doesn't look good for someone to fall on his watch, and especially in his nest.

"So, he fell to save Thana, Nikita, and me. Isn't that what Angels do? Sacrifice themselves to save others?" Cyrus finally chimes in and smirks. He knows what he said is a fact. Angels sacrifice themselves all the time to save others. So for Gage to sacrifice his place in heaven to save others shouldn't be looked at in a negative light.

The two Archangels stare at each other for several minutes and nod slowly. "We do... Others may not see it that way." Metatron says with a dejected tone.

Our voices must have carried further than we thought because there's an exhausted Thana standing at the doorway watching us closely. "There will be no problems tonight. I will not allow it." Thana says with a strength she's never revealed before. "Anyone comes for Gage..." She raises her right hand and her fingernails turn to claws. "They will go through me." Not even giving us time to react, Thana turns on her heels and leaves the room again.

"I believe we may have to remain on our toes tonight. She's going to be on high alert." I say as calmly as possible, not wanting to set the others off long before we have to be. Turning on my heel, I pull a page out of Thana's playbook and I leave at the end of my sentence. Detouring, I head past her nest one last time and look in on her to make sure she's okay. Thana and both daughters are curled up in the mass of blankets surrounded by her wolves with the panther on the prowl.

Enroute to my room, all I can think about is the past and all that my poor mate has endured over the centuries. Every day I promise myself I will make everyday better for her, that I would erase the damage left by others of my kind. Here she is still afraid to sleep alone, yet won't sleep with any of her light mates all night because of her nightmares. She's afraid she will lash out and hurt one of us by accident.

Heading into my suite, I search my closet for something to wear tonight. Part of me wants to go traditional Japanese, the other half standard American, with a tux. Digging through my closet, I find the Hakama that Thana helped me pick out for my promotion several years ago. It's black and burgundy with an embroidered waistband. It's perfect for tonight, formal yet not stuffy. I guess I will wait and see what later brings.

~Later that night~

Samael and Uriel have taken it upon themselves to watch over the girls for tonight. Worse case the Valkyrie will take Davina. While Samael keeps Nikita in his castle with him. With everything that is going on, I am kind of shocked that Thana is comfortable with her daughter in the Shadow Realm.

Once I have my sash wrapped and tied, I head out to meet up with everyone else. The guys are all dressed in their best suits with their ties tied perfectly. Thana is in the room's corner, adjusting her hair one last time in the mirror. Raphael summons us all because the limo has arrived to take us to the fundraiser.

Thana kisses each of us before going and climbing into the limo. We follow her into the limo and take our places. She sits between Metatron and Gage with her head resting on Gage's shoulder. Her eyes flicker back and forth between gray, black, and chrome. In my heart, I know she's communicating with both Uriel and Samael, checking up on the babies.

We arrive faster than expected to flashing lights and loud music. We follow the normal procession, with Thana being escorted by Raphael. Entering the fundraiser, we can enjoy the beauty of the decorations in the entryway. Thana's hand extends out and touches the flowers as she passes and Metatron picks the orchid and offers it to her.

Those two have come such a long way. A smile graces my lips as I watch her release Raphael's hand and take hold of Metatron's. "What's making you smile, Christian?" Cyrus asks softly as he bumps my shoulder.

"Just happy that the nest is stable at the moment. Apparently it only takes two Dark Nephilim to equate two Archangels and an Angel." I smile, looking at Cyrus and I can see I had stroked his ego.

"What can I say?" Cyrus adjusts his tie, then runs his fingers down the lapels. "I'm the son of death. And the mate of the descendant of the destroyer." Cyrus's swagger is on ten, without a doubt. Thana turns and looks at him over her shoulder and smirks at him.

With a simple roll of her eyes, Cyrus's entire mood shifts and his swagger falters.

I burst out laughing as I watch the exchange, and shake my head at him. "That was impressive, son of death." I have to goad him on a bit more, as I watch the rest of the nest make their way down the carpet towards the tables, I think about how I will poke him next.

Thana stops short and looks around suddenly. Something here caused her to react, and it puts us all on high alert. Out of nowhere, a female cuts through the crowd and practically tackle hugs Thana. Joscelyn looks nothing like how I last remember seeing her. Her cheeks have filled out, and the luster has returned to her hair. The smile on her face is the biggest change of all that I notice. She's honestly happy and is radiating happiness to everyone.

The girls walk off arm in arm gushing back and forth about their mates, the houses and what life is like for them at the moment. The girls giggle and carry on as if no time has passed between them. It makes my heart swell to see that we made the right decision to help free her from her false mates. "What's on your mind, old friend?" Raphael says, startling me out of my thoughts.

Almost jumping out of my skin, I turn to look at Raphael and force myself to laugh. "Just happy that things have worked out for the best for Joscelyn. No female should know pain or mistreatment." Keeping my tone low, I lean towards Raphael when I speak.

Raphael looks up and watches Thana for a few moments, then looks back at me again. "Yes, they both have known more pain and trouble than any female should ever endure. It appears both have come out stronger on the other side. They've been blessed." Raphael says in that tone that I know means that he's done with the subject.

Raphael and Metatron move off to go speak with Michael and Gabriel before joining us at the table. Thana and Joscelyn position themselves side by side so that they can continue their conversation. Casually, I glance periodically over at Raph and Metatron, still in deep discussion with the other Archangels. Next thing I know, a lithe hand is waving in front of my face. Thana has her right eyebrow raised as she gazes at me.

"The others sense the change in Gage and the Archangels are doing their best to quell any negative reactions from those present." Thana states simply, as if it's the most natural thing ever. Shrugging her shoulder, she motions towards Raphael then taps her temple, letting me know it was Raph that had given her that information.

I simply nod, and smile at her, not questioning her further. It's times like this I wonder exactly how the bond varies between all of us. As if sensing my question or perhaps hearing my words in her mind, Thana smiles at me. "As the bond grows, I can almost expect what you desire. The look on your face says it all. You were curious about how I knew. You looked between Raph and I knowing full well he must be talking to me." She smiles and picks up her drink and sips at it.

Her logic is infallible, and I nod agreeing with her. We sit back and watch the interaction of the Archangels and the others up at the head table before Raph and Metatron return to us. They fill us in on what was being said and how popular the event seemed to be with the donors. The only concern that they have is that a few of the older Angels are not keen on the idea of Gage falling. Most suspect Raphael isn't as strong as he used to be and that the heavenly balance has shifted.

Thana rolls her eyes and stands up. "So basically it's one big pissing contest?" Shaking her head, clearly frustrated by the current subject, she leaves the table heading towards what looks like Azraels' table. Aggravation and frustration radiate through the bond as she walks further away. I notice that none dare speak to her as she passes the various tables. Is it due to fear or are they concerned about what she may become when she ascends. Her stance has changed, and she holds her shoulders with confidence. Thana walks as if she owns the room, and it's a beautiful thing to witness her coming into her own.

CHAPTER 57

THANA

All eyes are on me, and I feel their gazes burning into my skin. I'm back under a microscope with the Angelic community. To be perfectly honest, I really don't care what the others think anymore. Striding confidently across the floor, I stop in front of Azrael and the other representatives from the Shadow Realm.

"Father? Might I have this dance?" The smile that graces my lips is nothing short of feral.

Azrael arches an eyebrow at me and his answering smile is just as feral as mine. "Anything you desire, daughter." He rises up slowly and offers me his hand.

Quickly I accept his hand, then wrap my arm around his as we walk towards the dance floor. "We need to talk, father." My ominous statement makes him arch an eyebrow again. A simple nod is all that he gives me till we take our place on the far side of the dance floor.

"What's on your mind, Daughter?" We sway slowly on the dance floor and he pulls me in close. "I know that there's been a lot of changes lately. But, all will work out in the end." His tone drops several octaves as he speaks closely to my ear.

Forcing a smile, I nod my head and continue to sway in time with the music. "The others all feel the shift in the bond and the Angels seem concerned." I tilt my head to the side, looking up into his eyes. "I will protect my nest at all costs, father." I feel my eyes blacken immediately with the declaration, then shift to silver. The auras of everyone in attendance blaze to life before my very eyes. Some of the Nephilim's auras are not as bright as they should be and it concerns me.

"What do you see, daughter?" Azrael says as he leans close to my ear.

"Several Nephilim have gray streaks in their auras. I worry about them being tempted." As I utter those words, I feel Azrael's body become rigid. Tension rolls off of him in almost oppressive waves.

Azrael's eyes blacken immediately, and he tilts his head to the side further, looking at me. "Which ones?" His question is as concerning as it is demanding.

Drawing in a slow deep breath, I focus on what I have seen before when my eyes were shifted. It's easier to pass memories and visions between bond mates. Azrael is my mate's father, so the family bond should help. I slide my hand up his chest and rest my hand on his throat, my thumb on his pulse point. I force the visions from my memory and into Azrael's mind. I watch his eyes widen as he sees who I point out to him.

At the end of the dance, he kisses both of my cheeks, then walks over to some Archangels. I can tell by Azrael's stance that his conversation isn't going well. Turning slowly, I walk off of the dance floor only to be stopped by Cyrus.

"What's gotten into dad?" Cyrus spins me and we dance cheek to cheek. The warmth from his body soothes something deep within my soul. My dark knight, my constant reminder that not everything is as bad as it seems.

The bond is an absolutely beautiful thing at times. Through the bond I share with not only Cyrus but my other mates, exactly what I saw. There's at least four Light Nephilim that seem to be well on their way to being corrupted. Either way, we have to be very wary as to how and when the end of days will happen. A myriad of emotions flickers over Cyrus's face as he watches what I've shown him. "Do the others know?" He arches his brow, then ducks in and kisses me softly.

Laughing, I lean in and kiss his lips. "Of course they do, I showed them at the same time as you. We are all aware. I also showed your dad." Cyrus spins me around the dance floor when suddenly I start to not feel well. My chest constricts and panic sets in. Looking around frantically, I search for whatever it is that is making me feel this way.

"Kitten, what's wrong?" Cyrus grips the sides of my face, forcing me to look him in the eyes.

"I'm not sure..." The words feel strangled, painfully escaping my lips as the world around me spins. The hall is filled with a brilliant light. Just as I turn to see what it is, the fireball from Hell hits me, setting every nerve and fiber of my being on fire. I feel as though I am being electrocuted from the inside.

~Cyrus~

Thana writhes in my arms as that mass of power hits her. It looks like a pulsing mass of living energy, it undulates and flickers as it surrounds her and rips her free from my arms. She's thrashing, hovering almost ten feet off the ground. Her wings rip free of her body as she twists and turns. A blood-curdling scream echoes through the hall, silencing everyone and stopping their actions.

The guys gather around, watching our mate in horror as she thrashes and screams in the air. All of us are standing here helpless as that strange sphere of energy, whatever it is, tortures our mate.

"I haven't seen this in many millennia." Uriel says as he stares at Thana.

My head whips to the side and I stare at Uriel while his eyes remain locked on Thana. I study him and then I look at Raphael and Metatron, then back to Uriel. "What do you mean you haven't seen this in many millennia? What is happening to my mate? How long is this going to go on for? And for that matter when did you get here, where is Davina?" For the first time in my existence, I know fear. I am honestly afraid for Thana, afraid of what is happening to her.

"I was called here when it started and as planned I left Davina in the care of Sigurn. Don't you see? She is ascending, there're many factors that will determine the duration." Uriel states clinically. "The first and most important factor is which family member either died or willed her their power?"

Uriel paces around where Thana is hovering. "If it was Nyx, this shouldn't last very long." Uriel shrugs his shoulders as he briefly looks from me back to Thana.

"What if it was Samael?" I ask. I feel my chest tightening as I watch Thana spasm and thrash in the orb of power. We feel nothing but pain through the bond as if every fiber of her being is being ripped apart, then put back together again.

Uriel, Raphael, and Metatron stop dead and stare at me. Briefly, their eyes meet, then they look back at me. "If it was Samael, this could take all night. If they killed Samael and Nyx, I don't know what will happen. That much power, I'm not sure her body can handle it, that anyone can handle it all at once, even her." Sadness crosses his face and his shoulders sag in defeat.

The Archangels divide and start to empty the room. With the assistance of Azrael, they remove everyone that isn't family or part of the nest.

I feel so weak and powerless watching my love thrash and writhe in pain, and there's nothing I can do to help her. Gage mirrors my expression, lost in thought as to what we are able to do at the moment. My hands are tied metaphorically, and there's nothing I can do to help her. Reluctantly, Gage leans into my side and rests his head on the ball of my shoulder. Christian is in shock watching Thana.

Metatron and Raphael are leaning shoulder to shoulder, seeking comfort the only way they know how. With the next surge of power, Thana's body bows and her wings straighten behind her. One last shriek escapes her lips and the orb of power explodes, knocking us all back and to the ground. The concussive force knocks the wind from my lungs. I notice barely intime that Thana is falling to the ground. Diving quickly, I throw myself under her, sliding on my back and she falls on me.

Banding my arms tightly around her, I hold her limp form tightly to me. Her breaths are slow and labored and her body twitches almost uncontrollably. "What's wrong with her?" Forcing myself up, I cradle her tightly to my chest.

"Her body is battling the change. We need to keep her warm and safe." Metatron says softly, his voice almost quivers with a strangled emotion I've never seen him express before.

Metatron kneels down beside me and runs his fingers through her hair, offering a bit of comfort. Oddly enough, Thana's breathing seems to have stabilized a bit with his physical contact. "I have an idea. We need to get Thana home." Metatron helps me to stand up, and we quickly gather up our nest mates and head straight to the limo. In the limo, we each scoot closer to Thana and place a hand on her somehow. With each of us touching her, she seems to have calmed down and resting easily.

I order the driver to drive faster. This time the unflappable Raphael looks like he's ready to break at any moment. My dark angel seems to barely hang by a thread the minute anyone loses contact with her. I'm doing my best not to lose my temper with every whimper that crosses her lips.

We round the corner and pull into the garage. Raphael barks out orders on how to remove Thana from the car and where to take her to. Carefully, we lift and pass Thana out of the limo. Once out, we all get our hands back on her and carry her through the house.

The journey upstairs is more difficult than it really needs to be. We lower ourselves down into the nest and surround her, each of us making sure at least a hand is on her bare skin. Pressing my lips to Thana's temple, I can feel her life force steadying out. She's not at war with herself and whatever that new power was that she absorbed. Until she wakes up, we have no clue whose power she received.

We snuggle in close with each other and move enough to each keep a hand on her. Raphael sets up the order in which we are to stay up and keep watch over her. I volunteer to take the first watch, and Azrael is kind enough to stay with us volunteers to get food and drinks. I watch as the others slowly succumb to sleep. Raphael fought the longest and the hardest to remain awake with me.

Azrael eventually slides up alongside me and offers me an energy drink. "How's she holding up?" His fatherly gaze slides from me down to Thana, then back up again.

"I'm not sure Dad. I'm kinda scared, to be honest." My voice slightly wavers and I clear my throat to hide the emotions.

Nodding his head in understanding. "Something is off that her familiars are not rising to protect her in her sleep." His eyes narrow and blacken as he stares at Thana. Ghosting a shadow filled hand over her body, he tries to read her. Instead, her body starts absorbing the shadows as if starving.

"Shit!" Azrael says, and the hair on the back of my neck stands on end. He looks back and forth between all of Thana's mates, then locks eyes on me. "She needs to feed." Is all father says before he starts gathering all the shadows he can to him. With a force I didn't know was possible, dad funnels all the shadows he's gathered into Thana. Her body arches slightly off the bed, then lies dead still once more. The major change is her heart rate is steady now.

"Will light help?" Metatron asks as he holds a small orb in his hand out towards us.

"Wouldn't hurt to try." The words almost burn like acid on my tongue as they slip from my lips. Tentatively, I raise Thana's hand and hover it over the mass of light. Gentle ghost-like wisps of light reach towards Thana's outstretched hand. We decide to let her hand make contact with the light and she absorbs all that is being offered to her.

We look at each other, stunned, then over to Raphael since he's supposed to be in charge of this nest. "Let's feed her whatever energy we can. Hopefully that will help her wake up from whatever she's dealing with." Raphael leans forward, brushing a stray hair away from Thana's face.

Raphael leaves the room shortly after tending to Thana. His behavior and stiffness as he moves telegraphs how stressed this current fiasco is making him. Two of the highest-ranking Archangels have no clue as to what's happening. That cannot bode well for us.

CHAPTER 58

THANA

One minute there's a flash of light, the next thing I know, every fiber of my being is on fire. My muscles feel as though they are being cooked within my skin like a baked potato. "Baptism by fire Descendant. Awaken." Samael's words echo in my head repeatedly as I bade my body to obey me. His hand gently runs down my back, trying to soothe away the pain I'm in.

"Rise Descendant and take your rightful place." Samael's voice soothes the fires that seem to burn my very soul. The nerve endings finally begin to settle down and allow me to regain control. The muscle spasms cease and I can move with almost no pain.

I struggle to roll over and regain some semblance of balance. Falling over several times before I can finally get my legs under me. My muscles feel like they are made of jello and my bones of rubber. Weak as a kitten, I finally regain my footing and rise to my feet, only to wobble and almost fall again. Samael catches me before I hit the ground and pulls me towards him. I rub my eyes, trying to get my vision to clear, and all I see around me is smoke and ruins. "What is this place, Grandfather?" My blurry eyes scan the horizon, and the same desolate landscape greets me.

His gray eyes lower and a sadness crosses his stony visage. "It is the place between life and death, the in-between. It's where creatures and beings of great power go after their demise till they conclude their business." Samael says as he walks me over to a bench that manifests before us. We sit down, side by side, and he wraps an arm around me.

Tentatively, I lean my head on my grandfather's shoulder, snuggling in close, fearing the worse. "Did I die?" I furrow my brows, looking down at my hands, then back up to him. The only thought that crosses my mind is the fear of leaving my babies and my mates when they need me most.

"Not you, precious one. I did just a little while ago." He shakes his head side to side as he looks down at his own hands. His words are like a slap to my face, sobering me up quickly to the severity of my current situation. Jolting out of his embrace, I sit up and stare at him, ghosting a hand over the arm closest to me.

"No Grandfather! I'm not ready to take your place." My heart hurts thinking about the one family member I truly love being dead. It feels like a knife has been driven through my chest and I've been run clear through.

"It's time Descendant I've waited thousands of years to rest. You are ready to step up and take my mantle." Samael's eyes meet mine and I can see that he's completely at peace with the situation. I burn the image of his face in this moment in my mind to remember him this way forever.

"What do I need to know, Grandfather?" Furrowing my brows, I struggle to keep the unshed tears at bay. I want to cry, but I find myself more aggravated that my grandfather is dead. There's a fire that has ignited deep within me. It screams for vengeance, and I couldn't agree more.

"There's two ways we can do this. Talk through it or I can push all of my knowledge through our bloodline to teach you things even I may have forgotten." He gently cups my cheek and, by the way he's looking at me, he knows what I want. I need to know everything he does and so much more.

"Show me everything." My words are barely above a whisper as I turn to face him fully. The thought of this being one of the last interactions with him makes my chest constrict as I swallow down my grief. With a single nod of my head, I let him know that I am as ready as I'll ever be.

Both of his large battle-hardened hands frame my face as he lowers his lips to just above my forehead. "This may hurt. Forgive me, my precious

Thana." His words caress my flesh just before he presses his lips to my forehead.

The blinding light I saw just before impact at the fundraiser has nothing on the light that envelops me now. When it finally fades, we are in the Silver City, the realm where only Angels tread. Lucifer has white wings, as does Samael. All the Angels are gathered around a being in golden robes whose face I cannot see.

Lucifer strikes out at the being in the golden robes. I recognize this as the great war and the fall of Lucifer. The battle wages on in the air and on the ground. The ranks of Angels stand divided. Brother fighting brother, friend against friend and so on. Those cast out of the Silver City, their wings immediately blacken, and they fall from sight.

Time seems to go fast forward and Samael stands with the being in the golden robes. With a single touch, Samael's wings become tricolored like mine are now. They embrace one last time and Samael walks out of the golden gates of the Silver City, never to return. He was apparently hand-picked for the position of Destroyer choosing to leave the Silver City forever. His sacrifice way back then paints my grandfather in a different light. We were taught the destroyer was the most feared Archangel in history, never that he made this sacrifice, never that it was a choice born from good, we learned only to fear him. Yet all I've known is a loving, self-less man, I should have known that he gave up a comfortable existence to keep the balance, and has done so alone for millennium.

History is a fickle thing, through centuries of the stories being told, facts are always neglected. The visions continue to the use of portals, manifesting them and being able to close the ones I didn't create. He's very detailed in how my hands need to be positioned and the exact words that need to be spoken. As the Destroyer, the manifestation of portals will be tons easier than when I tried just as his descendant.

Next, he seems to give me the cliff notes on the creatures of Cell and of the Shadow Realm. Which ones I can control, the ones I can corrupt and the ones I can turn against others. This seems to be the most interesting of the lessons. We spend the most time on the lesson on the creatures. Apparently, they will help turn the tide in battle.

There's something nudging at the back of my mind and I have a feeling my grandfather is keeping something from me. The lesson continues on to the creatures of the deep and the different dialects spoken by the tribes that live in Hell. Who knew there were so many creatures and humanoids that live there. He quickly teaches me who the notable leaders are, and the customs needed to befriend them. I'm growing curious as to why the lessons are being conducted this way. It seems like he's preparing me to go to war. I know eventually I'll have to storm the gates of Hell, but is it really so soon?

He moves onto describing the circles and the princes that rule each. "You've already killed three out of the seven princes, clearing three of the seven circles." Samael says, pride rings in his tone and his grip on me temporarily tightens. He sits back after passing on all the skills and lessons he can. "The last four princes will not fall as easily as the first three. Lucifer will be the most difficult. Trust me. I've tried." He raises his eyebrows at me, making sure I realize just how difficult it will be.

"I understand Grandfather. Where is Nikita? She was with you." I feel as though my heart is being ripped out of my chest when I finally realize she's alone.

"Taken. Nyx and Lucifer came for her themselves. Your worthless father bargained for his own freedom in exchange for your daughter's life." Samael growls and I watch his canines lengthen. The bone plates in his face shift and realign before he gets it back under control.

"What else aren't you telling me?" Narrowing my eyes, I watch him shift back to the way he was before. Something in the pit of my stomach tells me there may be something more sinister behind the scenes.

"We can shift in the shadow and Hell realms. It's why the wolves obey us so well. We are considered changelings, able to manifest the form we need most. But there's a price for doing it." His ominous tone holds centuries of warning and power. His shoulders stiffen and his back straightens, the subject obviously bothers him.

"What's the cost?" Narrowing my eyes, I watch as my fingernails become claws. Raising my gaze to meet his, I wait for his answer.

Lowering his eyes, he stares at the cracked calluses of his hands. "You can never enter the gates of the Silver City after you shift, no matter how good of a life you live. One shift is all it takes, no matter what the noble reason is. There is no repenting after that." His tone becomes hollow as I see his body starting to change before my eyes.

"What happens to us?" I ask softly as I witness my answer firsthand. I lean forward, resting my hand on his knee.

His hand raises and touches the familiars on my forearms. "We serve as guardians to the next Destroyer or reaper, never to regain our human form again. We live to serve after death in the form we took the most often." He grips my hands and his eyes beg for understanding. The wolves on my flesh, the panther, the crow were all at one time like Samael and I. Sentenced to a life of protection because they shifted to save another's life.

"I promise to give you to Nikita when she becomes old enough to understand the responsibility." A forced smile crosses Samael's lips and a single nod is given. He seems pleased with my decision.

"You are my greatest gift, Thana. I am lucky to have gotten to know you. Save your daughter, return the Shadow Realm back to the way it was before the balance shifted." His voice becomes more animalistic as his face takes on its wolven form. "You hold the deadliest form out of all of us. Use it wisely." His last words leave me with more questions than answers. I realize then that something deep within me has awakened, and it wants blood.

I sit there with my hand on what used to be my grandfather, armed with yet another familiar and the knowledge of the ages at my disposal. Once his final form is achieved, I move the cat from my forearm to my ribcage and add my grandfather's wolf to my left arm. I raise my arm to my lips and kiss the tattoo of Samael's wolf.

"Thana... I have something you want..." The voice is as smooth as silk and dripping with seductive undertones. It can mean only one thing. Lucifer. I turn slowly to face him and put on the sad, broken little girl act. The rumors of his incredible pride weren't exaggerated and seeing me cry adds to his swagger. "Hand yourself over and I'll send your daughter back to her useless father. Come to my castle alone." He smiles that slimy salesman smile that makes you feel you need a shower from looking at him.

"Fine... I'll be there..." I narrow my eyes as I watch him vanish from sight. *That was entirely too easy. I focus on waking up in the real world. The crap is about to hit the fan sooner than later and the guys need to be ready.*

I blink several times, trying to clear the fog that clouds my mind. The guys all stare at me as well as Azrael. "Samael is dead..." My tone is flat and emotionless as I stare down at his wolf on my arm. "He's dead but not gone entirely." I say as I crawl out of the nest and walk over towards the mini bar to grab a drink.

"What do you mean he's not gone entirely?" Metatron is the first to question me, and all I can do is smile. My smile slowly becomes a smirk and I look down at Samael's wolf. It rises from my flesh for the first time and I can already tell he's far bigger than Fenrir and Skoll.

"When a destroyer or a reaper dies, if they were able to take another form in life, they take that form and role of guardian in death. One shift is all it takes, no matter the reason, no matter how pure the intention, the doors to Silver City close for them and they are to live on as guardians, serving and protecting." I scratch my grandfather behind his ears and wait for what I said to sink in with everyone else. The only one who seems to have gotten it is Cyrus as he looks at the familiars on his arms.

"So you mean???" He says before motioning to the animals on his arms.

Laughing, I walk over and touch the animals on his arms, telling him the names they held in life. Shock is evident on everyone's faces as they look at Cyrus and I now. "One day I will adorn Nikita's arm, or perhaps her child's arm. Either way, I will live on forever watching over my family even in death." As I look up, I shift my eyes to my chosen new form, then back to human. I don't hold the shift long. Now is not the time to educate the other side of what I know I can do now. I need the element of surprise if I have any hope of getting my daughter back.

<h1 style="text-align:center">CHAPTER 59
THANA</h1>

Without warning my mates, I walk outside and take flight towards the Angelic Realm. My massive wings propel me through the cool night air and into the upper stratosphere. It's odd that for once I fear nothing. I ponder the lack of fear as I fly directly to Michael's house and land on his front staircase. I assume he will have gone to get Davina from Uriel or Sigrun to ensure she was protected as much as possible after he saw me ascend.

Just as I raise my hand to knock, he opens the door with Davina in his arms. "Here to pick up..." The sentence dies on his lips as he looks at me differently than he ever has. "He's gone?" He asks the question I know he already has the answer to and all I do is give him a single nod of my head.

"We need to talk..." He leaps from his front door, allowing me to enter his home. Once inside, I turn to face him and sigh softly. "Lucifer and Nyx killed Samael and stole Nikita. My worthless father exchanged his life for hers." I blurt out the core of the issue at hand without even the slightest bit of emotion.

"Are you okay, Thana? Is there anything myself or any of the other Archangels can do?" His concern at any other time would have warmed my heart. Right now, the words ring hollow. What can an Archangel do when they can't go to Hell and fight?

"Guard my family. Keep Davina and the Angelic side of my bond safe and secure. Move them to the Silver City if that's best. I'm going to war." My words reverberate and shake the very foundation of Michael's house. I feel the influx of power from the other Archangels awakening and heading towards us.

Several Archangels manifest in Michael's home, most of them I have met over time, the other's eye me warily. "Lucifer and Nyx stole my daughter." I push power and dominance into my tone, making most of the Archangels back up. "Samael died trying to protect her. In his last moments he gave me his mantle and knowledge." Touching my forearm, I unleash my grandfather's wolf as proof of what I just told them.

"What would you have us do, Lady Thana?" Uriel says just as my mates catch up and enter Michael's home.

"Protect my mates and my daughter. Grant me this boon and the new Destroyer will be in your debt." Raising my fist to my chest, I touch my amulet, unleashing my armor. With the influx of my grandfather's power, it changed. My armor is now an exact copy of his, right down to the armor over my wings. At my hip, Daybreaker rests on full display for the Angels to see.

Turning to face my mates, I smile. "Raphael, Christian and Metatron do not leave the Silver City till I come for them no matter how much they beg. They cannot follow me where I need to go." I turn and lock eyes with Uriel as my mates begin to protest my command. Uriel nods his head and offers me his hand to seal the deal. I reach out and grip his forearm tightly and with a single shake, my request is accepted.

I move to stand before my Angelic mates and smile, probably the most confident at peace smile I have had in a very long time. "I love you three with all of my heart." I breathe in deeply and look into their eyes one at a time. "I cannot focus on the battle before me If I have to worry about whether you are safe or not."

Slowly, I move to stand before Raphael and I can see the undercurrents of his anger rippling. "You taught me to be strong and sure in the face of danger and to always do the right thing. Keeping you and our daughter Davina in the one place Lucifer cannot reach tactically is the best move. You know that, Raph…" I appeal to his logical side and to the tactician I know he is. He nods reluctantly, then bends down and kisses me passionately. Butterflies flutter to life in my stomach as I smile at the end of the kiss.

Christian grabs me next and doesn't give me a chance to talk. He kisses me silly, holding me tight to his chest. "You have been my friend since the beginning, my rock and my mentor. I love you Watashi no otto." I blush slightly as I catch Christian off guard calling him my husband.

Christian passes me off to Metatron, who clearly looks distraught. Framing his face with my little hands, I smile, looking up at him. "You are one of the best surprises I have ever received. I didn't know I needed you till I had you in my life. Thank you for your patience, strength and unconditional love." I kiss Metatron softly, the most gentle kiss we've probably ever shared. When I break away, tears have welled up in his eyes. "This isn't goodbye. I fully plan on bringing you Lucifer's head on a pike as a present." A feral grin crosses my lips as I allow my eyes to shift, to hint at the form I will take in Hell.

"Good choice, my dark angel." Metatron says softly before he kisses me one last time.

I move over to Davina and kiss her forehead. "Be good for your daddies and mommy will bring your grandpa's head on a pike." Davina scrunches her nose at my statement.

My eyes move to Michael and I smile. "I will return with my daughter. Hell hath no fury like a pissed off mom." I manage to get him to laugh a little before I lean in to hug him and whisper in his ear. "I will find your mate and bring her back safely, son…" I lean back and the shock on Michael's face is more than worth it.

The Archangels surround my Angelic mates and usher them

further into Michael's home. I stand there watching them as Gage and Cyrus flank me. "What's the plan?" Cyrus says with a smirk as he watches Raphael react to his question.

My eyes search the crowd until I see the person I am looking for. "Raziel, I seek your counsel." I state plainly and the Archangel moves to stand before me. "Do you have knowledge of the rings of Hell and what we may face searching for Nikita?" I state my purpose exactly how I need the information. Any deviation from what I specifically need may send us on a wild goose chase in Hell.

He bows deeply at his waist, then ushers us to the table in the kitchen. Waving his hand over the tabletop, an ancient map spreads out before us. The map shows the seven rings of Hell and the positions of the castles on each level. I don't even want to know how he obtained this knowledge, but it's useful.

"Things may have changed. This map is thousands of years old, mind you." Raziel smiles as he looks from the map to me.

"A general idea is better than the no idea we had before. I appreciate this, thank you." I say with a bow before examining the map again, memorizing every minute detail.

"What's the first order of business Thana?" Cyrus asks with that smirk on his face that I don't know if I want to smack him or kiss him.

"We need your dad. And we need to raise an army." I stare at the map again, deciding that going after Belphor on the Sloth ring may be our best bet to start with. "We'll start here and work our way in." I point to the gates of sloth and then the battlement to the west. As long as Belphor hasn't somehow moved his castle, we should be good to go.

"First things first, we take back my grandfather's castle and use that as our base of operations. Second, we seek the most powerful creatures of the Shadow Realm and we turn them to our side to gather an army, or the start of one" I tick off my list as I go along, making sure I don't miss anything.

"Raziel, do you have the map of the Shadow Realm?" Arching a brow, I look up and over at him.

Bowing his head, he waves his hand over the table again and the map of the Shadow Realm manifests before us. My grandfather's castle is in the center of the Shadow Realm, standing tall like a sentinel. The layout of the realm is similar to a clock face divided like a sliced pie. The castle is in the center of neutral territory. Each sliver has a different species of creature as the ruling faction. All I need to do is petition each species for help.

"Do you mind if I take this with me, Raziel?" I look up from the map to him and he smiles.

The map rolls up, and Raziel offers the map to me. Gently, he places the map in my hand and smiles. "Anything to assist you, Thana. You need me, call me, I am welcomed in the Destroyer's castle." He bows at his waist again, then vanishes from sight.

I stare at the rolled-up map in my hand, then up at Cyrus and Gage. "Let's head back to the nest and gather what we need from there." Turning my head, I look back at my other mates. I blow them a kiss before gripping Gage and Cyrus and moving us through the shadows.

We manifest back in the house and move into the kitchen, and I spread the map out on the tabletop. I study every tiny detail and make mental notes on where I want to go next. "Baby, you need to eat." Gage says, as he slides up alongside me.

Nodding slowly, I look between Gage and Cyrus, then back over to the fridge. "Yes, let's have something to eat. Can you do that chicken dish you did the other night?" I smile sweetly at Gage, hoping that he will make it for me.

"Anything you desire, my love." Gage kisses my cheek before raiding the fridge, as he starts to make food for us.

"You did that to distract him." Cyrus says as he slides up behind me, gripping my hips tightly. The heat of his body comforts me, and I lean back against him.

"Of course I did. He's worried, and I wanted to give him something to do." Smirking, I turn to kiss Cyrus on the cheek before looking back over the map in front of me. My grandfather's knowledge surfaces, filling in the blanks in my knowledge of the Shadow Realm. It's kinda like that game where they buy letters to form a phrase, except it's me looking at an area of the map and the region's knowledge fills in for me.

"What are you concentrating on so hard, Kitten?" Cyrus's tone drops before he nips at my jaw.

I draw in a deep breath and sigh softly as I exhale. "I feel like a supercomputer was put in my head. I look at a spot on the map and I can almost hear my grandfather's voice telling me about it. His parting gift was his knowledge, and I am well aware of that, but it's still freaky as all hell." I shrug my shoulders slightly as I drag my fingers over the map to a new location.

"That's quite useful, isn't it? I mean, you know what to expect and can plan for it." Cyrus says as he moves to stand beside me, still looking at the map.

"Quite..." I place my fingertips on the map over my grandfather's castle. "We reclaim the castle first, then gather allies and form an army." Tactically, it makes the most sense. We need a base of operations to work out of, and the castle is central to that part of Hell.

"If that's what your gut is telling you we need to do, then that's what we'll do. You're stronger than all of us combined now, Thana. We follow your lead." Cyrus says before giving me a side hug.

"That's probably the second smartest thing I've ever heard come out of your mouth, son." Azrael says from the balcony before walking into the kitchen.

I break away from Cyrus and rush into Azrael's waiting arms and hug him tightly. Part of me wants to cry and grieve over the loss of my grandfather, the other part wants to burn Hell to the ground and destroy it utterly. "I'm so sorry for your loss, little one. If I had known what was about to happen, I would have been at your grandfather's side. Maybe this wouldn't have happened and your daughter would be with you." Azrael says before pressing his lips into my hair as his arms band tighter around me.

I breathe in the scent of burned earth that is uniquely Azrael's and sigh softly. "No, father, as much as I know you would have battled at his side. If I would have lost both of you, part of me would be destroyed." I pull back slightly to look up into his brown eyes, the pain creases at the corners tells me he's hurting like I am.

"Any news of my granddaughter? Is she safe, alive?" His voice becomes strangled speaking about Nikita and tears escape from the corner of my eyes.

"Lucifer and Nyx have her. Trust me... They will die." My eyes blacken, shift to chrome, then back again to human gray. "The hunt begins after I gain control of the castle." I point to the structure in the center of the map.

"If you grant the Archangels passage, they will be able to move about within the castle. It's the only place in the Shadow Realm that is deemed a neutral space. They can come and go once we invite them in." Azrael imparts this most beneficial knowledge to me, and I search the knowledge my grandfather gave me and I confirm its validity.

"Once the castle is secure, I will summon Michael and Gabriel to me for their battle knowledge and maybe Raziel." My gaze drops back down to the map.

"Not your mates?" Azraels' shock doesn't go unnoticed.

"No... I need them and Davina safe." My tone leaves no room for argument as I focus on the map.

"Understood daughter, you honor Samael's memory." Azrael says as he looks back to Gage, who is setting the table for dinner.

"I hope so..." There's nothing left to say at this point. No amount of I'm sorry or well wishes will bring my grandfather back or return my daughter to me. I'm not a violent person by nature, honestly I'd rather be left alone. But my daughter needs me and I swear I will bring a whole new meaning to the word rage when I go to war.

<h1 style="text-align:center">CHAPTER 60
CYRUS</h1>

It's like a switch flipped within Thana, and her inner bitch has been awakened. There's a determination in her eyes that didn't exist before tonight. Be it that our daughter was abducted or her grandfather being murdered, but this is the Thana I've been waiting for. She's finally come into her own and is adjusting fantastically to the power thrust into her lap.

Gage and I stand shoulder to shoulder to shoulder watching Thana plan our attack on her grandfather's castle. Her logic is incredibly sound and father seems to agree with every step she plans to take upon entering the Shadow Realm. "We must leave soon. The Shadow Realm is in disarray without Samael there to maintain order." Azrael says as he traces the castle on the map.

"Are you sure we're ready, father? I mean, she just received the mantle. Doesn't she need to train?" I'm concerned for my mate and her wellbeing. This sudden influx of power can be a lot for her to handle.

Thana steps into my space and kisses my lips softly before looking back at my father. "Grandfather took the time to teach me about all of his powers before his final passing." Thana draws in a slow, even breath, and she smiles looking at me.

"Whatever you wish us to do, my love, we will follow your lead." I kiss her cheek and she melts into my side and hugs me to her. My lips brush her forehead next and I hug her tighter.

"We'll feed, then we'll leave." Her words leave no room for argument at this point. Gage rushes around the kitchen and passes out food to the four of us, and we gorge ourselves like there's no tomorrow.

Dinner concludes way too fast, and I can see Thana itching to leave immediately. "How do you wish to get there, daughter?" Father asks, and I can see the gleam in his eye. He already knows the answer to that question.

"Armor up, we're going in hot." Thana says as her armor embraces her form. I swear it's become more terrifying than when I first saw it. She smiles at me and Gage and raises her hands and rips the armor from our amulets.

Looking down at my now armored form, I arch an eyebrow at her. "Really Kitten?" I motion to my body and then look up at her questioningly.

"Yes." That one word answer sends a chill down my spine. Thana raises her hands and starts speaking a dialect I am unfamiliar with. Within moments, a portal opens and it seems to be in a bedroom with stone walls. "It's the guest room in the tower. Best entry point for us. We can see the entire courtyard and several levels within the castle from here." Thana says before walking through the portal and into the guestroom.

"Here we go boys..." I say before following my mate through. As soon as my feet hit the stone floor, my familiars rip free of my flesh and manifest around me.

Thana stands there with three wolves, a panther, and an incredibly large raven on her shoulder. She kisses the raven on its wing and her eyes blacken. "Go..." The raven takes flight out the window and I watch it circle the courtyard several times before flying close to the first-floor windows.

"Hmm, the majority of the forces are on the first and second floor." A feral grin crosses Thana's lips before her eyes return to human gray. "Daddy dearest is sitting on my throne. This should be fun." Thana cracks her knuckles and heads towards the door.

Much to my surprise, the door opens on its own and the lanterns in the hallway ignite the minute Thana steps out of the bedroom. My father's smirk tells me he knows something that I don't. "Okay, pops, what am I missing here?" Tilting my head to the side, I await his answer.

A muffled laugh escapes his lips as he motions to my mate leading the way. "The castle recognizes its true owner. It will bend to her will like it did the Destroyer before her. Whatever her whim is, it will obey." My father smiles as we descend the stairs. Every step Thana takes, more lanterns and candles ignite. It's magical and incredible that the building knows she's the rightful owner of the castle.

We make it to the first floor and the first wave of Demons comes charging down the hallway at us. Thana raises a hand and they stop dead, as if hitting an invisible wall. It's like a scene out of that hacker movie. Time slows down and beasts impact the invisible force. They stop and stare at Thana. A feral growl escapes her ruby lips and the beasts immediately sit, obeying her.

She glances over her shoulder at me, and her eyes have serpentine slits that expand and contract. The emerald, green color around the black slits flickers with power before she turns back to face the beasts. The first one that has six horns on its head approaches her and bumps its forehead against her hand. Thana scratches the beast behind its ears and it joins her familiars at her side.

Thana's familiars and the Demons arrive at the throne room door just before we do. We stand there with the Demons flanking us, everyone looking expectantly at my dark angel. Drawing in a deep breath, Thana yells, "FATHER!!" The walls of the castle shake and fragments of stone fall down around us. With a single move of her hand, the throne room doors fly open and are ripped clean off of the hinges. Thana's father is sitting calmly on the throne, drumming his fingernails on the arm of the throne.

"Daughter, it's nice that you've come to visit me. How do you like my new castle?" Nyx stands up from the throne and walks down the stairs. "All of this is mine because of my father's death." He spins slowly with his arms spread wide.

"Interesting..." Thana states flatly and raises a hand making a chair slide across the stone floor and stops before her. She sits down and smiles, looking at her father. "I see the castle obeys you so well." Her sarcasm is strong and her smirk is so on point, and clearly irritating her father.

Nyx raises his hands, and nothing happens. The candles fire don't even flicker at his command and none of the Demons move. "What have you done! I am his heir! This is all mine!!" Nyx rages as he throws things wildly around the throne room.

Thana watches as her nails lengthen and become claws before she looks up at her father. "Oh Daddy dearest, it is rather unbecoming someone of our bloodline to act like a childish imp. Act your age, not your shoe size, please. It's embarrassing." Her tone is as demeaning as it is sarcastic as she stands to face off with him.

Nyx charges at Thana with very little regard for his own life. His nails extended like claws but clearly no match for his daughters. At the very last moment, Thana side steps and slashes at Nyx's side, opening up wounds on his ribcage. A shocked expression crosses his lips before he turns and charges again at her, screaming like a wild beast. Thana drops low and swipes at Nyx with her armored wing, knocking him off his feet and onto the ground. With a single tilt of her head, her three wolves and my one surround Nyx, growling at him. "Tisk Tisk Daddy... You should never fight angry. You lose focus when you fight angry. Grandfather taught me that." Thana places her boot's heel on her father's throat.

He reaches up and attempts to claw at her Achilles tendon only to find the boots she's wearing are armored and his claws do no damage. "I am the Destroyer, the beginning and end of all things within this realm. Do you honestly believe your tiny kitten claws would harm me?" Thana wiggles her own talons in his direction and smiles ever so sweetly.

"Azrael, you are to obey the true ruler of the Shadow realm. I am my father's rightful heir as his only child." Nyx yells from under Thana's boot heel. "Destroy this usurper!" Nyx points up at Thana and it causes her to laugh.

Father moves forward and leans over and kisses Thana on the cheek. "The only usurper I see is under my daughter's boot already." My father smiles and bows his head lightly to Thana, then moves back over to stand with Gage and I.

I smirk at my father and realize he is exactly where I get my resting bitchface from. Thana kicks her foot out and sends Nyx flying across the throne room floor. "Where is my daughter, Nyx?" Thana's voice has a distinct animalistic growl to it when she speaks. Her words reverberate around the hall of the throne room, shaking the candles and various pieces of art off of the walls and shelves.

Blood leaks out of the corner of his lips as he forces himself to sit up. "Lucifer has her. He wants you as his bride and your daughter is his leverage." Nyx laughs and coughs up blood. What a shame, I believe my mate may have punctured his lung.

"So you put your granddaughter in the hands of a madman just to attempt to claim Samael's castle. You're much sadder than I thought." Thana's tone drips venom as she stares at her father with disgust.

"The Destroyer's legacy is mine!!" Nyx pushes himself to stand, and he charges blindly at Thana...again.

Not a single muscle moves in Thana's body as Nyx barrels towards her. His sword manifests in his hands and is aimed directly at her. I prepare to charge in and intervene, and my father stops me. "She's got this. Feel the room, feel the pull. She's going to do something massive." His hushed tone catches me off guard.

My eyes return to Thana, just before Nyx's sword can impact her armor he's ripped back by an unseen force and dangles in the air. Shaking her head, Thana raises her hands and flexes her talons in the air. Each flex matches a new cut on Nyx's flesh. His screams fill the hall as she keeps flexing her fingers, watching her father writhe in pain. Ribbons of his flesh fall to the floor in a bloody heap. All the while, Thana remains focused on him. "What have I ever done to you!" He screams and Thana freezes in her movements.

"Seriously? You killed my mother, my grandfather and stole my daughter." The pitch of her voice changes as she lists the people. By time she says daughter she down right sounds feral. Nyx's eyes widen as he stares down at Thana, and that's all he needed to do. She raised her hands and pulled them apart, quickly ripping Nyx in half, sending his body flying in two different directions. Blood sprays everywhere, painting the stone floor vermillion. The wet thunk of his body impacting the wall in two different places. Bones crack and break upon impact, if he wasn't already dead, I would say that would have hurt. The miniscule orb of power rises from Nyx's chest and Thana's hand waves dismissively at it then it poofs out of existence. She rejected his power, by the size of the orb it really wasn't much of an inheritance.

Breathing deeply, Thana moves towards me, hands bloody, as if she split his body herself. She comes in close and presses her forehead and bridge of her nose to my throat and sighs. My father motions for me to hug her and I do immediately, holding her firmly to my chest. Gage moves to press in behind Thana and we just hold her and rub her sides, trying to soothe whatever may be hurting her.

"Daughter..." My father says softly as he runs his fingers through her golden tresses. Ever so slowly, Thana moves her forehead away from my throat. My father opens his arms to her, and she breaks loose of Gage and I and dives into my father's arms. No matter how powerful she is, there's still some part of her that's a lost little girl. My father, I assume, fills that void of the parent she wished she had growing up. I watch my old man hold my woman and it's a fatherly embrace. Her wings fold in tight, then retract fully. "We have an army to build, daughter, one worthy to storm the gates of Hell itself." My father says, smiling as he looks down expectantly at Thana.

Gently, she pulls away and kisses his cheek before walking away from us and over to the throne. She stares at it for several minutes before raising her hands and the ground quakes. The throne itself falls away to dust before liquid magma rises from the ground. The throne reshapes itself to look like two large wolves as the arms of the chair. The back of the throne appears to be some sort of dragon snake hybrid, its large tooth filled head rising above the throne with its mouth open. Thana takes her place on the throne and rests her hands on the heads of the wolves. "Time to summon our neighbors…"

CHAPTER 61

THANA

Just like that, I assume control of my grandfather's castle and remake it in my image. The exterior of the castle begins to change as I shift my eyes to liquid mercury. Every stone obeys my whim as I focus on restructuring the castle to suit my needs. Azrael looks at me with pride blooming in his chest, my mates stare at me in awe. In my gut, I know what I am doing will draw Lucifer's attention. Perfect, let him know he's not messing with some unprepared whelp.

"Thana, there're creatures of all shapes and sizes out front." Cyrus says to me and I look over to my grandfather's wolf.

"Samael, bring me the alphas of the local packs. Fenrir, go with him and assist if needed. Skoll stay at my side." My wolves move once I give the orders. Skoll approaches the throne and rests his head upon my lap. My fingers find their way into his thick fur and I scratch him behind his ears, waiting for the others to arrive.

Six large wolves walk in flanked by Samael and Fenrir, each wolf looking meaner than the next. I keep my eyes shifted to my mercury orbs and I weigh and measure each wolf and its potential. The first alpha from the southern pack with the rust brown fur growls out his wishes. More territory and more hunting privileges is what he seeks

423

from the alliance. The hunting ground he wishes for is the territory of the newt like Demons to the west of his current lands. Raising a single finger, I silence him and listen to the other five alphas. Each alpha wants more range and to hunt a different species. What interests me is why my Grandfather kept them confined to such meager territories. Searching my inherited memories, I figure out that the requested prey keeps another race of Demons in line. To allow the additional hunting would throw the balance off.

I deny the rust-colored alpha his request and he growls deeply at me, threatening me. Shifting my eyes to the serpentine ones, I tap into one of the new powers that I have gained. As he leaps at me, his body turns to stone, then crashes to the ground and shatters. "Next?" I turn to the other alphas and they are quick to agree to my terms. Twenty wolves from each pack will be at my disposal as soon as tomorrow morning.

"Kitten?" Cyrus says softly.

"Hm?" Arching a brow, I don't lose eye contact with the Demons before me.

"Upgrade?" Cyrus's tone almost makes me crack a smile. I simply nod and return to negotiating with the next Demon before me.

His finger tangles in the hair at the back of my head close to my scalp while he plays with my curls. I sigh softly and lean back against his touch. "We will have the Demons from the northern regions next." I say softly before something bangs hard on the front door of the castle. Raising my hand the doors open, and a monstrous being stands in the archway.

Memory serves, it is a Balor, two and a half tons of war mongering Demon, born and bred to do battle for the strongest Demon lord it can find. He folds in his large leather wings and ducks his head. His horns barely fit in the door as he stomps his way into the throne room. His guttural language bellows roughly in the hall, setting the lesser Demons on edge. I stand up and rest my hand on the pommel of my sword. I step down the stairs and meet the twelve foot tall Balor half way. He looks down at me as if trying to size me up. Blackening my eyes, then shifting them to chrome, catches him off guard and he backs up.

The minute the Balor backs up, I have won the battle for dominance between us. I walk back over to the throne and take my seat, waiting for him to begin. He catches me up on what is happening in the abyssal region which exists between the Shadow Realm and the first circle of Hell. He wishes to take over the wrath ring due to the metals available there for weapon making. I sort through the memories from Samael and find there is no reason to deny him his request. We shake on the request, and he offers to bring his legion here for us to march together. Azrael seems pleased with this turn of events, and I agree.

In one afternoon, I solved about a quarter of the staffing problem for the legion I need to build. Demonic wolves and Balor that can fly definitely give us a slight edge. "Azrael!" A human voice yells from across the throne room and we all look towards the yelling.

Slowly, I draw Daybreaker and hold the sword at the ready. The man in the archway looks to be the mix of Archangel and dragon. Beautiful yet tortured. He has an aura of power around him that's undeniable and I want to get closer to him. The creeping feeling that runs up my spine warns me against the idea, so I hang back. "Astaroth! What are you doing here?" Azrael calls to the man, which confirms my suspicions.

Arching a brow, I sheath Daybreaker and flex my wings once. "To what do I owe the pleasure of a visit from a Duke of Hell?" I fold my arms under my chest as I look him over. His gaze sweeps over me and I feel like I need a two-hour shower just to get clean.

"The Heir of Samael may need my forty legions to take over Hell, if that is her desire?" His voice practically purrs as he tries to entice me. Rolling my eyes, I raise my hands and I am flanked by shadow beasts of my creation.

"What are you up to, Astaroth? You are going against your Lord suddenly. What is it that you truly desire?" My fingertips shift to menacing talons as I get closer to him. His eyes widen as he looks from my talons back over to my mates, then back again. Something isn't sitting right with me. For a Duke, he's not as commanding as I would imagine him to be.

"My Queen, why would I be up to something?" His tone is smooth as silk and sweet as honey. My gut tells me he's definitely up to something. Him calling me Queen proves he's in league with Lucifer, the question is how deep?

"I'm no Queen. Nor do I ever want to be one." Rolling my shoulders, I put my wings away. My gut tells me something is about to happen. I'm just not sure what. I need to make sure I am as nimble as I can possibly be.

"Consider this. You upon a blood covered throne drumming your perfect nails on the skulls of your enemies." He smiles broadly and opens his arms wide, as if inviting me in for a hug. There's a distinct nudge from his power trying to pull me towards him. Without realizing I'm doing it, I take several steps forward till I feel a shift in the room.

Throwing my hand out at Astaroth, I throw him against the far wall and the Balor chief holds him there with the edge of his sword. Spinning on my heel, I find Cyrus being held at knife point by a Demoness. "Such a yummy specimen you have here my Queen... Mind if I have a taste?" The Demoness purrs as her forked tongue slides up Cyrus's neck and stops on his cheek.

I can feel my blood boiling in response to the level of revulsion coming from Cyrus. Gage is ready to spring into action and try to help free Cyrus. Through the bond I push towards them a wave of love, and then I share with them what I know about the Demoness. "Hmm, interesting to see The Lilith here... Adam's first wife shunned and kicked out of Eden." My sickeningly sweet tone even makes my skin crawl and I watch her shutter in response.

"Ah, you do know me. Very interesting." She releases Cyrus and starts down the steps towards me. Her hips and breasts sway in time with the clicking of her heels on the stone floor. Her scent changes and it's a mix of something sweet and sex. I allow her within inches of me, her large barely contained breasts press slowly against my armor.

"What can I do for you, Thana? Kill for you? Strip for you?" Her clawed fingertips trace her cleavage before moving to the armor over my breasts. "Would you like me to fuck you?" Her forked tongue slips slowly from between her crimson lips and flickers in the air hinting at its potential. "I can be anything you desire." She backs up, and she's fisting possibly the largest cock I've ever seen in my life. She jerks off before me till she orgasms shooting cum all over her own breasts and abdomen. "Give yourself to me Thana..." Her tone changes and something in my hindbrain wants to respond to her seduction.

My jaw aches and I want to bite her and make her mine. A primitive side of me wants to mark her flesh. My fingertips ghost over the soft flesh of her abdomen as I lean in to press my nose to her throat. In that instance, I smell Nikita on her and I snap out of whatever spell she was putting me under. Pretending to remain in her thrall, I move my hands to touch the cut of muscle that extends from her bellybutton up. In the space of a heartbeat, I drive my fingertips with my claws extended up into her stomach. With another thrust, my claws break through her diaphragm, and I wrap my fingers around her beating heart.

"You made a mistake, beautiful." I lean back and observe the shock expression on her face.

I lick the side of her cheek and smile. "You smell like my daughter." I feel the warmth of her blood running down between the plates of my armor. Every beat of her heart, more blood pumps out and onto me. It dawns on her I know she had held Nikita. She begs for her life and her heart beats wildly in my hand. The darkness within me begs to be unleashed and my smile twists to be more sadistic in appearance.

"Poor, poor Succubus did the bad man's bidding and now she stands to have her heart broken... What a shame..." I whisper close to her ear as I give her heart a squeeze. "Where is my daughter?" My voice is more of a growl than human in tone and her body tenses further.

"Lust… She's being held in the lust realm with my sisters… Lucifer…" She practically chokes on his name as I squeeze her heart harder. "Lucifer wants you to come to the castle. You were never getting her back…" Her voice is strained as I squeeze harder, making sure she will not be tempted to lie to me.

"Interesting concept. If you're lying, I will slaughter every single Succubus that draws breath." I lean back and stare into her widened eyes.

"No… not my sisters…" She begs as blood tears roll down her cheeks.

"Are you lying to me?" Tilting my head to the side, I study her reaction. There're no signs she is lying to me at all. I smile at her and she starts to laugh, thinking that everything is going to be okay. When she's downright jovial, I ignite the black flames in my hand and burn her alive. The minute her heart is dust in my hand I bring my free hand forward and add to the flames, burning her to ashes.

"Any who wishes to harm a child, especially my child, I will burn you in the abyssal flames, you will be ashes. There will be no resurrection." The Demons nod along with me and agree that retribution is of the utmost importance for balance. Demon after Demon approaches me and swears their allegiance, knowing full well I just painted a target on my back, killing Lucifer's favorite Succubus.

CHAPTER 62

GAGE

My first day in the Shadow Realm and I've already seen things I cannot unsee. The Demons, the creature and the landscape alone are the things of nightmares. Thana and Cyrus seem at peace, but me, I'm nervous as all hell looking around at all the crazy shit I never thought existed till now.

The way Thana killed the Succubus was over the top, and possibly excessive. On the flip side, if it was my birth daughter, I would expect no less from her mother than to rain the fires of Hell on her enemies.

"What's on your mind, Gage?" Thana's tone is oddly soothing as she slides up alongside me and drapes her arms over my shoulders and around my neck.

"It's a lot to take in. All of this was just rumors and faerie tales till today." Shrugging my shoulders, I lean my head to the side and kiss her cheek when she rests her head on my shoulder.

Her silky soft lips press against my cheek and stay there for a moment before she pulls away slightly. "Yeah, I guess it is a lot. I'm sorry my love." Thana furrows her brows and then leans in and kisses me again. "We know where Nikita is, possibly. Knowing that

Asmodi is dead, there's no reason for us to go to his realm. It's logical to hide her there." Thana slides down, then backs up and shrugs her shoulders. In some sense, the logic is sound. Why would you go to a realm you don't need to fight in if you don't have to?

I follow Thana out of the throne room and into the parlor not far away. Several of the high-ranking Demons are sitting around drinking something that looks like blood. I stare at it for a beat too long, Thana tugs on my arm and redirects my attention to her. "Yes, it's what you think it is. No, it's not abnormal, and yes we can drink it too." Thana fires off answers just as a lesser serpent like Demon slithers over with a goblet filled with a bloody looking drink for Thana.

Half way through her glass, a second Demon approaches and whispers in her ear and her eyes light up. "Brilliant! Let the dungeon master know I will be there posthaste." Thana says excitedly to the toad looking Demon before he heads back to points unknown.

Thana whistles and grabs both Cyrus's and Azrael's attention before heading out the door. We practically chase after her through the hallways and then down a spiraling staircase. At the bottom, several women with multiple arms and snake bottom halves slither around the room. Against the back wall hanging in chains is Astaroth and a man in a tailored suit with slicked back black and blue hair. He spins on his heels and bows deeply. "Mistress... I am prepared to do your bidding." He stands up slowly, only to cautiously approach Thana and gently take both of her hands in his. Submissively, he kneels before her and presses his forehead against his knuckles.

"Rise Alvarez and proceed." Thana's tone is nothing short of dominant, with a tinge of a feral growl to it. The man bows, then unveils a tray of torture devices you would find in the next Hellraiser movie. It's to the point I'm half expecting pin-head to come out of one of the many doors. He promptly gets to work cutting away the clothes from Astaroth's body, exposing his scar littered flesh.

Alvarez pulls out two razor whips and motions for us to move a safe distance away. With each flick of his wrists, ribbons of

Astaroth's flesh are cut free of his body. Blood droplets cover the floor, wall and even us. Thana and Azrael watch him work with rapt attention and a sadistic glee in their eyes.

"There's one thing that puzzles me." I say to no one in particular. Thana motions for me to continue, so I do. "Why can't you just sense Nikita and go to her?" I direct my question to my mate and several emotions flicker over her face.

Thana unfurls her wings and flexes them several times. "I sense her throughout the rings. Lucifer is using mimics to hide Nikita's true location." Thana's eyes churn chrome. "I will locate one mimic and kill them all through that one." Her voice is monstrous, to the point where Alvarez stops his torture to observe Thana.

"Destroyer?" Alvarez gets Thana's undivided attention. A slight dip of her head is given. "The mimics will flock to the smell of your blood. Cut yourself and the mimic will come." He returns to his torturing of Astaroth. His screams fill the hall, making Thana smile.

"To the roof boys, time to lure in a mimic." The toothy grin on Thana's face concerns me. We follow her as she races towards the stairs and up to the first floor. Spreading her wings, she takes off flying. Once she gets to the foyer, she shoots straight up. To keep up Azrael, Cyrus and I spread our wings and fly after Thana. Without skipping a beat, she breaks through the skylight and into the air. She hovers for several moments before she slits her palm and flies in circles around the castle.

She comes to land on the roof and starts scanning the horizon, watching for the mimic to take the bait. Thana licks her palm, staunching the bleeding as she watches the horizon. We each take a corner of the tower, watching in four different directions. "Thana to the north!" Azrael calls to her, and we turn as one to look to the north.

I move to flank Thana's right side, Cyrus took the left next to his father as we watch the ghost-like creature approach. It shifts its form to perfectly mimic Nikita and starts screaming. I watch Thana and Cyrus both tense, hearing the Nikita copy crying. "It's not her...

Remember, it's not her..." I'm not sure if I'm saying it out loud for them or more for my benefit.

"I know... Cover me." Thana finishes the sentence and dives off the tower. She holds her wings tight to her body and power dives down the tower face before spreading her wings wide and rocketing towards the mimic. The monstrosity turns in time to see Thana gaining ground on it faster than it expected. Thana draws Daybreaker from its sheath and holds it in front of her as the blade ignites. The mimic breaks its disguise and takes to the air, trying to escape Thana.

Cyrus and I dive off the tower at the same time, followed closely by Azrael. We move in formation, making sure the mimic doesn't escape Thana. Thana seems to be picking up speed, and it's now that I realize the reason for the difference in our wings. Hers were built for speed and power, mine were built for strength. Azrael's and Cyrus were built for stealth and speed. Thana barrel rolls and grabs the mimic's wings and rips one off, then takes it to the ground.

Thana dangerously brandishes Daybreaker in the mimic's direction, speaking a language I've never heard before. Arching a brow, I look over at Azrael as he lands and he shakes his head. "Part of the mantle of Destroyer is knowing the languages of the abyssal and Hell realms. From what she found out so far, there's at least eight more mimics between here and where Nikita is." Azrael states as if it's no big deal.

"Oh, that's all?" Sarcasm has become a second language for me since being friends and lovers with Cyrus.

"Yes, that's all..." Azrael obviously missed the sarcasm in my voice and I smirk trying not to laugh.

"So what's our next move?" No sooner does the question leave Cyrus's lips,it is answered. Thana rips the head off of the mimic with her claws. She walks over to us like nothing happened covered in blackened ichor.

She examines her bloody claws for a moment before moving her shadowy power over her flesh, burning away the blood. "It's an easy solution. You guys go for Nikita and get her out of here. Azrael, I need you to meet Michael on earth and hand him Nikita. He will guard her with his life." Azrael nods, not questioning Thana's command.

"Am I the only one that's noticing the elephant in the room? Thana, where are you going?" My voice hitches at the end of my question because in my gut I know exactly where my psychotic mate is heading.

Cyrus and Azrael catch my drift and the three of us focus on Thana. "I will go to Lucifer as planned. I will not be there unarmed. After all, I have my new form hidden for an emergency." Thana shrinks Daybreaker and slips it into the scabbard on her hip, then unclips the scabbard and offers it to me. "In case of emergency, use it. Don't hesitate. Make sure my daughter makes it to Michael." Thana's brows knit together and I can see the stress she's under and the fear that she's hiding.

Closing the distance between us, I scoop Thana up quickly and hug her tightly to me. My tongue caresses the seam of her lips till her mouth opens to me and I can deepen the kiss. This isn't goodbye by any means, this was, be careful, I love you. We part ways and I watch Cyrus slide in where I once was and kiss our mate just as passionately. Thana's bottom lip quivers as she approaches Azrael and he smiles, understanding where Thana is. He knew she was going to sacrifice herself to give her daughter time to get away. He knew she was going to bring the war to Lucifer and crumble his empire from the inside. He knew something that neither Cyrus nor I were privy to and I'm not sure if I'm okay with that. Sometimes relationships depend on blind faith and trust to function. This was one of those times and it still sucked balls, no matter how you slice it.

I stand there staring as my mate walks away. She dramatically raises her arms and dozens of shadow creatures rise and walk with her. By the time she reaches the chasm to the first ring of Hell, a legion of shadow creatures are beside her. She looks back over her shoulder and gives us that megawatt smile of hers before crossing her arms over her chest and falling backwards out of sight. Creature after creature dive in after her like a shadow waterfall.

Once the last creature falls, Azrael clears his throat, causing Cyrus and I to turn to face him. "We have a mission, boys. Let's not fail Thana, she has the toughest job of all." Azrael's voice is stern, but I notice a slight waver at the end. We nod and follow behind him as he walks back towards the castle.

"Where are we going?" Tilting my head curiously, I await Azrael's answer.

"There's more than one way to get to the different rings. Some are more direct than others." His flat tone tells me he's in deep thought about the mission ahead of us. Arriving back at the castle, I'm still curious why we didn't follow Thana. But with Azrael's sudden change in demeanor, I really don't feel like pushing him for answers.

We wind through the various halls till we come to one with roman numerals over the top of the doors. Arching an eyebrow, I look over at Cyrus, who has now put on his armor. Following his lead, I touch the wolf shape pendant and my armor moves over me like liquid. Once it is in place Azrael smiles and motions towards the doors. "These are the doors to the rings. Portals if you will."

"Why didn't we just follow Thana?" Cyrus fires back at his father.

Shaking his head, looking at his son, I can see the disappointment there. "This way, Lucifer will not know where we are. I warded these portals against his sight. This one will bring us straight to the lust realm." Azrael's logic is sound. If we were to have followed Thana, he would have had a clue that we knew where Nikita is.

"If this is what you think is best, then this is what we will do, Dad." Cyrus says before walking over to the portal door to the lust realm.

"Time waits for no man. Let's go save Nikita." Azrael says as he grabs the doorknob and opens it. Within the door frame is a swirling mass that looks suspiciously like blood. Azrael steps through and we are quick to follow on his heels.

CHAPTER 63

CYRUS

I'm torn... I want to save my daughter, but I also don't want my mate to face Lucifer alone. Stepping through the portal was probably one of the single most disgusting things I have done in a long time. We step out onto more black sand under a blood red sky. The sun here appears to be a shade of red-orange and the clouds are black wisps in the sky. Several pixie looking creatures flitter around naked in the air. Some being so bold as to fuck mid-air.

Shaking my head, I look over at my dad and Gage. Neither seem phased by what's happening around them. We follow my father through the various landscapes and little villages that pop up across the land. It's not until we crest a hill and spot a city that honestly looks a lot like the Vegas strip. "How the fuck did we end up in Nevada?" I say more to myself.

Laughing, my dad turns towards me and smirks. "Vegas is called sin city for a reason boy..." He turns and looks over the skyline of sin city and laughs. "I bet Cynna will know where Nikita will be." Dad unfurls his obsidian wings and leaps over the edge to glide down to the streets below.

Waggling my eyebrows, I unfurl my wings and follow my dad

gliding towards the city. Gage catches up and keeps staring at everything around us. "Is this really Vegas?" He raises his eyebrows, seeing familiar landmarks that line the Vegas strip.

"It's the mirror image of the real Vegas. The Succubi catch their human victims in the real Vegas, then pull them here to feed. The humans are none the wiser to what's going on." Dad says, explaining the set up to him. As we walk the streets, the ghost images of the humans in the real world move around, not knowing we are here.

One lady stops and stares right at me. "Dad, can she see me?" I watch her tilt her head several times, then rub her eyes.

"See the glow around her, the slight tinge of green?" Dad steps beside me and motions to the surrounding aura.

"Yeah? What does it mean?" Curiously, I move behind her to study it further.

"She is a witch or a descendant of a witch. The Succubi's glamor won't work on her." Dad says, as if it's common knowledge. Gage and I look at each other for a beat too long, then shrug our shoulders, catching up to Dad.

He stops in front of a casino with a club. The Unholy Roller Casino and Night Club is lit up in blood red neon lights. "This is Cynna's place, if she doesn't know where Nikita is, no one will. She has eyes and ears all over the strip." Dad says her name almost reverently as he pushes the door to her club wide open.

Music booms through the speakers and the scent of sex and ambrosia fills the air. More human silhouettes flutter through the casino like moths attracted to the flame. One in particular stops dead in front of dad, its aura is black as pitch and she smiles at him and motions with her head to move off to the side. She leads us through a set of doors into a conference room. She extends a hand out and grabs dad making herself physically manifest in this plane. "You're seeking someone." She says without even a glance in my direction.

"Yes Mirra, my granddaughter Nikita. Oh, how rude of me. Mirra, this is Cyrus, my son and his bond mate Gage. Boys, this is Mirra, a veil walker. She is a descendant of a reaper. So she's able

436

to see when people are about to die and she can see the para-
normal like us." Dad says with a smile on his face before facing
Mirra.

"Pleased to meet you, boys. More pressing matters. Your descendant is up with the Succubi in their nest. If she's not removed from
their lair before the eclipse, she will become just like them." Mirra
implores us. She glances straight up as if she can see through all the
levels of the building.

"Fuck! The eclipse is in less than twelve hours." Dad says then
kisses Mirra's forehead. "Thank you for your help. I owe you." Mirra
simply bows her head and releases my father before moving on as if
nothing happened. "We need to get going. The nest is on the top
floor." Dad turns quickly and runs through the building and back
outside. Spreading his wings wide, he flies straight up the face of the
building. Gage and I are hot on his heels, flying as fast as our wings
can carry us.

We crest the top of the building and its one huge orgy going on
with a woman sitting on a throne watching the whole thing. On her
right knee sits my daughter with her little wings fluttering behind
her. Fuck, when did she get so big? She looks like she could be a two
year old instead of a baby. We step over and around the writhing
bodies and make it into the throne room.

"Welcome Gentlemen!" Cynna says, spreading her arms wide.

The minute her hand moves away, Nikita takes flight and comes
right to me. "Daddy daddy daddy..." My heart damn near explodes
hearing my daughter call for me as her little chubby body impacts
mine. My arms wrap around her tightly, holding my little girl to my
chest.

"Interesting turn of events... I was unaware she was of your line
Azrael, I was told and sensed she was of the Destroyer's line." Cynna
tilts her head to the side and stares at her crimson claws before
regarding us again. "Samael owes me so I was holding her till he
came for her." Cynna says, looking back at her claws again. "I sense
his power increased tenfold and I want some." The beautiful visage

she had before morphs to something grotesque, her mouth opens and fangs similar to a vampire drops into view.

"I guess you didn't hear... Lucifer killed Samael and stole my daughter." I kiss Nikita's temple and smirk. "The power you sense is my mate. She is Samael's successor and mother to Nikita." Cynna pales and looks around panicked, then back to us.

"Take her... Get that child out of my sight. I don't need the Destroyers' descendant to come here and wipe us out." Cynna does a shooing motion at us and we take the hint and leave.

It was way too easy to get in and out, so we suspect that there is something far more sinister going on. For a high-ranking Succubi to not put up a fight is concerning. Dad kisses Nikita's cheek, then smiles. "Succubi have a hive mind. They know Thana killed Lilith, who was the most powerful of them all. She'll eventually be reborn, but not for a long time." Dad turns and takes flight, I'm guessing back to the portal door.

Carefully, I shift out of my armor and reveal my regular clothes. I stuff Nikita into my jacket and zip it up the best I can. My little girl is stroking my chest as she lays her head against it. Nikita is happily babbling away about all sorts of little things. I wrap my arms tightly around her before I stake flight, following my father.

Gage flanks my right side and searches the surrounding sky. "Thana is going to be pissed that Nikita isn't a baby anymore." Gage voices the biggest concern I have been battling with since seeing my daughter again.

"I know... I think I'd rather set my balls on fire than face her." I smirk after saying that, and Gage and I share a chuckle over it. It's the truth, and it's going to suck facing Thana after this is all over.

"Truth. At least we accomplished our part of the mission. What do we do after we deliver her to Michael?" Gage's question haunts me. In one sense, I want to storm the gates of Hell and go get my mate back. Logically, I know I don't have the power and sway that Thana does.

Dad stops short of the portal and looks back at the three of us.

"Nikita is our primary objective. Once we deliver her to the Archangels, we return and rally the forces." Dad's face goes from stone cold, back to happy grandfather when Nikita turns her gaze on him.

"Sounds like a solid plan, dad." I kiss the crown of my daughter's head and she snuggles back down into my jacket with a death grip on it. Dad goes through the portal first, then we follow right behind him.

Once out of the portal and heading down the hallway, dad stops us in our tracks. "Go now!" He waves his hand, creating a portal behind us and shoves us towards it.

"What's happening?" Gage whisper yells as he practically runs towards the portal dad created.

"The castle has been breached. Get Nikita out of here. I'll catch up." Dad shoves Gage through first, then me.

As suddenly as we were shoved through, the portal snaps shut behind us. I turn on my heels to look behind us and see that dad isn't there. "What the fuck!" I scream as I look around for any signs of my father with us.

"Fuck!" Gage screams as he runs his fingers roughly through his hair looking around.

Two golden shimmers appear in front of us and we stare at them curiously. Michael and Gabriel appear before us smiling. "I see the mission was successful." Michael says softly as he looks at my sleeping daughter.

"Rescuing my daughter, yes. My father stayed behind so we could escape with Nikita." My voice wavers slightly. My father and mate have sacrificed themselves for the safe return of our daughter.

"Where's Thana?" Gabriel asks, concern lacing his tone.

I look down at my precious sleeping daughter and kiss the crown of her head. "She went directly into the lion's den to draw attention away from us." I look up slowly, fighting back the emotions that threaten to escape.

Gabriel reaches out and grips my shoulder tightly, offering

comfort. "We have watched Thana since the beginning. Her heart is in the right place and she will do everything possible to right the wrongs." I nod slowly, listening to Gabriel's words, then look over at Michael.

"Thana said to specifically hand Nikita over to you." Gently, I pull my sleeping daughter out of my jacket. Her little black wings fall open under her. Michael's eyes widen as his wings unfurl and spread wide to full extension.

"Oh, shit…" Gage's tone mirrors the shock I feel.

Wide eyed, I carefully fold my daughter's wings and place her in his arms. "I see why now Thana was so specific. I know I have nothing to worry about now." Michael dips his head in a bow to me.

"I will guard Nikita with my life. She is my future and my world. Thank you for trusting me with your daughter." Michael says reverently as he presses his lips to the crown of my daughter's head.

I smile softly, looking at how much love I see in Michael's gaze as he watches my daughter sleep in his arms. "Thana trusts you, so I trust you. Knowing what I know about the mate bonds. I know you will do everything in your power to protect her. Go in peace." Michael and Gabriel nod their heads at me and disappear in a golden shimmer.

"We need a plan to go help your dad." Gage says.

"I know, but I think we need to get some of my friends and bandmates to go with us as backup." In my mind, I list the close friends I know I can trust that have the skills to help in this situation. Fortunately or unfortunately, depending on your perspective, I have learned through the years exactly who I can trust and who I cannot.

"Let's go see my band and ask them if they can assist us in bringing Thana back." Pacing back and forth, my anxiety is through the roof. I can only hope my friends want to go with us on this rescue mission.

CHAPTER 64
HELL

Thunderous yells and crashes can be heard echoing throughout the castle's interior. Lucifer is in a rage and is throwing things around the throne room as if he is a child having a temper tantrum. The sharp tones of glass breaking, as well as the tones of stone crumbling, carry throughout the halls.

"My Lord..." Bael says, leaning against a stone column, watching his master lose his mind.

"She killed Lilith!" Lucifer bellows as his claws swipe at the stone pillar. His pain echoes in the ragged tone of his voice. The feel of the room is somewhere between hostile and pure undistorted pain.

"I understand, my lord, but she's vanished. I can't locate her here in Hell, the Shadow Realm, or on earth. It's like Thana ceased to exist." Bael watches as Lucifer slows his motions down, then stops to look at him.

"How is that possible? She can't just stop existing." Lucifer stares at Bael for several beats, then moves through the castle to his viewing room. His clawed hand passes over the abyssal waters of the pool as he searches for Thana.

He's able to watch the last moment she shares with her mates and Azrael, then she takes to the sky. Lucifer tracks Thana through several rings of Hell as she fights various beasts and befriends others. The emotions he tries to keep guarded flicker over his face. Some of it is fear, other parts may be excitement at the prospect of having a powerful mate at his side.

Staring intently, the crowd that is gathering presses themselves against the wall. Jaws drop as they watch Thana vanish into thin air. Everyone looks shocked at each other, then back over to Lucifer. The Lord of Hell stares at the pool and watches everything shift again as he searches the different rings.

"Boss, what are you searching for?" Bael says as he moves closer to the pool.

Lucifer stops moving time through the rings and then looks at Bael. "It's impossible for her to just have vanished!" Lucifer roars as he turns to address Bael and the rest of his generals.

"Do you think she could have made it to the Angelic Realm without us knowing?" Bael questions as he moves around the pool, looking at the scene before him.

"Impossible... We would have felt her leave the planes." Lucifer's power and pride are in question. He focuses on the pool and starts searching closer to his level in Hell. His brows furrow as he stares at the images that flash before his eyes and studies them repeatedly. He dissects the visions flashing before his eyes and drums his fingers on the edge of the viewing pool.

Lucifer is deep in thought as he flips through the time and space of the Hell universe. The Demons in the room are becoming uncomfortable with Lucifer's growing aggravation. Some Demons leave the throne room and head off to do their respective jobs.

Shadows wind and shift around the room, moving with a life of their own. Lucifer raises his eyebrow as he considers what may cause this change in the room. Adrenaline spikes in his system and he shifts to his cloven Demon form. Sanguine leather wings spread wide behind him as blackened talons extend from his fingertips. The mass of his body almost doubles in bulk, making him a formidable opponent.

"Master?" Bael backs away from Lucifer's shifted form and scans the room for anything out of place. On the mantle over the fireplace, a large raven sits with its head cocked to the side, watching them. "Master?" Bael says a little more urgently. Lucifer's great horned head turns and regards Bael. Bael slowly raises his hand and motions to the raven over the hearth before backing fully out of the throne room.

"Come out Thana! I see your familiar watching me." His rumbling tone echoes in the now empty space.

The raven simply tilts its head to the side and utters two words. "Never more..." It spreads its wings and flies to the other side of the room as Lucifer tracks its path.

"Where is she!!" Lucifer roars up at the raven perched on top of his throne.

The raven looks up towards the skylight, then back down at Lucifer again. Its fathomless orbs seem to look right through him. Is Thana watching him through the raven's eyes, or is it someone else's familiar? Suspicious, Lucifer walks around the throne room, not taking his eyes off of the raven. "Who do you belong to?" Lucifer says, more to himself than anyone else in the room.

The raven flaps its wings several times, flies back across the room and spreads its obsidian appendages wide. "Your death. Your death..." The raven calls and its voice reverberates around the hall, setting the hair on the back of Lucifer's neck on edge.

He backs up suddenly as his memory of the last time he heard that voice. Metatron's voice would reverberate like the ravens just did. Wide eyed, he looks around the hall, making sure no one else is with him after the Demons fled. At his behest, Hellhounds flood the throne room, taking up most of the great hall.

The Hellhounds turn their heads to the skylight as one and howl.

Their haunting tones puts Lucifer even more on edge. Bael returns to the throne room upon hearing the hounds mournful cry. The raven and the Hellhounds are all watching the skylight.

It's now that Bael looks up and gasps. A legion of Balor are now circling the castle, blackening the sky with their wings. "My Lord, it seems the Balor are up to something." Bael points up and directs Lucifer's attention to the skylight.

Just as Lucifer looks up, what seems to be a comet appears, streaking through the air on a collision course with the castle. He yells for everyone to clear out and barely dives out of the way before the comet crashes through the skylight.

Black flames rise high from the impact zone like a flamethrower up and through the now shattered skylight. The Hellhounds have all dropped to their bellies whining, staring at the flames. The only creature not phased is the raven. It takes flight from the mantle and straight into the inferno.

A silhouette appears in the middle of the blaze, Thana slowly steps out from the blaze in her black wedding gown. Her veil is over her face and her wings are fully extended behind her. The visage behind the veil keeps changing. All the horrors and fears that Lucifer has manifested over the years flash before his eyes. "You stole my daughter." Thana's voice thunders in the throne room, reverberating, causing things to fall off of the wall. She raises a sword and points it in Lucifer's direction. Along the edge of the blade, flames erupt. It's not just any sword.

Lucifer takes several steps backwards, trying to put as much space as possible between him and Daybreaker. A wicked smirk plays upon Thana's blood stained lips as her familiars rip free of her flesh. She's soon flanked by three wolves, a panther, and her raven.

"You summoned me here... Time to finish it." Thana's voice is sure and firm as she stands there, unwavering. The Thana of a year ago would have cowered in Lucifer's presence. The Destroyer before him stands tall and proud, the secrets of the universe at her fingertips.

. . .

DESTROYER

CHAPTER 65
THANA

Burning rage and pain battle for supremacy within me, fueling the power Samael gifted me. Through ring after ring of Hell, I battle and befriend all manner of beasts and demons, turning most to my side. Grandfather's lessons play in my mind as I fly. My singular purpose is to distract Lucifer and the princes of Hell so my mates and my father-in-law can save my daughter.

During the descent, the Balor follow me through all the rings, adding to the formidable force I am. The creature within me slithers, winding itself over its own coils, sounding like a rattlesnake's tail. It speaks to me, telling me what I can and cannot do with it and still ascend to the Silver City at the end of my days. I suspect when my mates arrive in the Lust ring, they won't be met with opposition. The focus should be on me because of the trail of bodies I'm leaving behind.

"Destroyer?" Agron, the leader of the Balor, says to me, trying not to draw attention to himself.

"Yesssss?" The "s" is a drawn-out hiss from the beast curled up in my chest.

"When will we attack Lucifer?" Agron's bloodthirsty nature suits my drive for vengeance, and I can't help unleashing a toothy, feral grin.

"Later. For now, I must keep him focused on me till my daughter is safe. After I check on her and return to the castle, we'll plan to storm the gates of Hell." Tactically, my plans are sound and hold merit. The Balor lack patience and are impetuous.

Agron nods his great horned head as he motions his legion to attack the guards Lucifer placed on the outer reaches of the Pride ring. As suspected, this is the grandest of the nine rings, evidenced by its streets lined in gold. The craftmanship here is the best I've ever seen. The devil is in the details. No expense was spared, nor was any intricate detail overlooked.

Lucifer's castle is in view as we crest the horizon, and I send the Balor ahead of me, changing my form to shadows and mist to hide from Lucifer's detection. My raven rises from the mist and flies to the castle and gains entrance. He flies around the interior, undetected, till he lands on the mantle.

Watching Lucifer lose his cool because he lost track of me three rings ago does my heart good. Through the bond, I sense my mates approaching where Nikita is, so it's time for me to do my part and distract Lucifer. Summoning the black flames of the abyss is much easier now that I've ascended. I signal the Balor to blot out the blood moon before I make my approach. The raven warns Lucifer of his impending death, and I see him panic and scramble his troops.

Shooting like a black comet across the sky is as enjoyable as it is deadly. The high-pitched crackles of the glass shattering fill the air as my fiery comet of doom destroys the ornate skylight. Landing in a crouch, I watch Lucifer stare at the flames in abject horror. His hellhounds know a far bigger beast lurks in the castle now, and they drop to their bellies in an effort to save themselves. The fire reaches for the heavens like a flamethrower set on high. On my command, my raven flies into the flames with me and lands on my shoulder before returning as a tattoo on my arm. Shifting to my reaper form, I make a grand entrance and hover several feet off the ground.

Everything Lucifer fears flashes over my face under my shroud. His face contorts in horror at the visions I reveal to him. "You . . . Stole . . . My . . . Daughter . . ." My voice reverberates, sounding like Metatron. It fills the hall as if I'm everywhere at once, moving around where he's frozen in fear. My blood-stained lips curl up in a smirk as I stare down at him, and my familiars rip free of my flesh to flank me.

Resting my hand on the back of my grandfather's wolf, I tilt my head to the side. "You summoned me here . . . It's time to finish this." I stand before Lucifer without fear, my heartbeat slow and steady, with no inclination toward fear or anxiety. The old me would have buckled and broken before the prince of lies. I have more than enough reasons to turn this place to ash, making it nothing more than a memory in the annals of time.

"How dare you! Do you not know who I am? Bow before me, bitch, and serve me for eternity!" Lucifer finds his balls and bellows, shaking the very foundation of his castle, knocking stones and glass loose from their places.

Sensing my mates and Azrael reaching my castle, I smirk again, then drop my reaper persona. My armor manifests, and I rest my hand on the pommel of my sword. I wish I hadn't given the boys Daybreaker. If I'd have kept it, I could end this all right here, right now. Needing to stall for time, I shift my hands to talons and look over the long, obsidian, hooked claws, studying the razor-sharp edges. "You and I both know that won't happen, Luci." Lucifer sputters at the shortening of his name, and my resting bitch face is on point as I walk among the hellhounds.

"How fucking dare you!" he screams as he throws his clawed hand in my direction, sending a fountain of fire at me.

Halting the flames before they get close to me, I extinguish them with a wave of my hand. "Neat parlor trick, Luci. Learn anything cool since you fell?" Rage flows over his crimson skin like the tide rising up the beach. The twitching of his left eye and the agitated flicking of his forked tail tell me I've pissed him off.

I feel the moment my castle is invaded, and the rage I suppressed bubbles up again. Lucifer must have noticed the change in my demeanor. His stance changes, and he smiles. "I can make it stop, you know? Spare your mates and Azrael." He shifts back to his human form. He's quite a handsome human.

"I bet you could . . ." I shift my hands back and concentrate on sending the wolves living around the castle, as well as several of the larger demons, to aid Azrael. The minute Michael has Nikita, I smile and start laughing, staring down at the stones beneath my feet. "Unfortunately for you, I don't need you to do anything other than be oblivious." My sanguine smile broadens as I sense my daughter reaching the Angelic Realm.

The hellhounds that were once under Lucifer's command come to stand behind me, along with several of the smaller demons who were in his employ until my arrival. "I'll be back, Luci . . ." I wink over my shoulder at him before vanishing from his castle, leaving nothing more than a wisp of smoke in my wake. I could have entered his castle the same way, but it was far more entertaining to destroy part of his domain in the process.

Minor demons besiege my castle in large numbers, and I shake my head, looking down at them. Landing on a battlement above, I throw my hands in the air, engulfing the area around the castle in flames. The scent of charred flesh and scorched earth hangs in the air as a reminder of what I've done. The wolves I summoned to Azrael's aid leave the castle as soon as the fire is extinguished. Leaping down, I glide to the front steps leading to the interior. Azrael stands in the door to the castle with his arms over his chest, grinning. "Theatrical much?" He can't keep a serious face as he looks at the scorched earth and charcoaled remains of the demons frozen in silent screams outside the castle.

Raising my hand, I hold my index finger and thumb slightly apart and wink. "The megalomaniac doesn't know who he's messing with." Shrugging, I step into my castle, and it bends to my will, reshaping itself into a fortress. The grinding sounds of the stones sliding and realigning fill the halls as Azrael and I walk toward the war room. Once inside, the door shuts behind me and locks. "Breaching Lucifer's castle was far too easy. It won't be the next time we attack." I look up at Azrael as he nods in agreement.

"True. He'll fortify his defenses and either move the castle or reshape it, like you're doing now." Tactically, it's the most sound decision to make at the moment, so it's the path I'd chosen.

"I'm going to head to the Angelic Realm and check on my family before we clean house. We must purge the rings before we cut the head off the snake." Without either of us touching them, the chess pieces representing the princes and their castles move onto the map. With only four princes left, in theory, it shouldn't be difficult. Unfortunately, they've had time to study and prepare for my attack far longer than I did. I have an ace in the hole with my grandfather's knowledge, and I don't believe they know I inherited his wisdom at my ascension.

CHAPTER 66

RAPHAEL

To say I'm stunned by how fast Davina has grown is an understatement. My daughter, who was extremely small not so long ago, is now nearly the size of a five year old. This happened in the blink of an eye. I flip through pages in some of the older books to try to understand whether this is normal. However, this is something that has never been documented. The biggest problem I'm anticipating at the moment is how Thana will react to the size of her daughters.

The thought of trying to explain this to Thana without her losing her mind concerns the ever-loving hell out of me. My mate is a dynamo who will not be at all excited to learn her daughters, who were tiny when she left, are now the size of five year olds rather than the infants she left behind. This does not bode well for the other mates or me.

As I remain in my mini-panic, considering the best way to discuss this with Thana, Michael arrives with Nikita in his arms. Nikita is also nearly the size of a five-year-old human child. How he cradles her reveals she's much more to him than we thought.

Michael stops walking and stares at me, knowing full well he's busted. He arcs his head, nodding down the hallway, and starts walking that way. I follow him into the room. In the back, lying in the bed, is my Davina. He places Nikita next to her. Both children seem to be growing more rapidly than we anticipated. He makes a shushing motion with his finger to his lips and then herds me out of the room once my other daughter is tucked in. "I know I have a lot to explain to you, old friend, but this is not the place." Moving down the hallway, we catch the attention of Christian as well as Metatron.

We follow behind Michael as we weave through his house and end up in the dining room. He reaches over and pours us glasses of angelic wine and motions for us to have a seat. The three of us stare at him as he makes his way around the table with our drinks. "I know you're all quite concerned about what's happening," he says as he stares at his hands. "I'm not sure how to explain this to you or how it affects everyone." In his nervousness, he paces around the table and then stops.

"As some of you have already figured out, Nikita is my mate." He lowers his eyes and stares at the ground, knowing full well to see his mate's wings before the Mate Trials would bar the male from taking the intended mate as his own. It goes against divine law, created as a safety measure to protect the females.

Metatron begins to say something, but I reach over and touch his shoulder to stop him. I shake my head and then turn to face Michael. "It's not the first time this has happened, old friend. It happened to Thana and me when Azrael tested her to make sure she was eligible to participate in the Mate Trials. He wanted to make sure she could contain her darkness, that her dark side wasn't stronger than the light." I look down and stare at my own hands for a few moments, pondering the fact that two of the most trusted Archangels have knowingly violated divine law.

Metatron stands up suddenly and paces around the table. "I understand where both of you are coming from. I saw Thana's wings at the Tree of Life when she landed with her wings open. That's how I knew she was mine." He bites his bottom lip, looking between

Christian, Michael, and me. "But this is an entirely new precedent." He rests his hand on my shoulder, then he looks back over at Michael.

"You're the mate of Cyrus's daughter. I don't think this will bode well for you, Michael, if Azrael catches wind of this," he says with the kind of confidence that makes clear he doesn't understand how close this family is. Shaking my head, I stand up and pat him on the shoulder, then move to stand next to Michael in solidarity.

"It won't be an issue since Thana already knows. She calls Azrael father now and not her own birth father, so I don't believe it's going to be a concern." I smile, trying to reassure Michael about the future he and his mate have. It's ironic—the highest of the high being the mate of the successor to the throne of death. Definitely a twisted turn of events.

Just as we finish up our conversation about what's to be done with the girls and how things will proceed from here, Uriel enters the room, carrying his large bowl filled with water. He sets it on the table and waves his hand over the top. Our view of the water changes, and we now see the deepest ring of Hell inside the bowl. As we watch, Thana streaks across the sky in an enormous ball of blackened fire. She lands inside the castle, and her fires burn, terrifying all within.

We were already aware this has happened, so I'm unsure why Uriel is showing it to us. We watch as Thana takes on her reaper form, and her face flickers between that of a Basilisk and an Archangel. Lucifer's terror is almost palpable in the air. Thana lets him know he's stolen her daughter. Her familiars rip free from her and take a stance, flanking her. We watch as Lucifer loses his mind and see the calm and peace moving over Thana when she realizes that Azrael and the boys have made it out of the Dark Realm.

I sputter and almost laugh when Thana calls Lucifer "Luci" and not his full first name. As if it were nothing, she blocks and extinguishes his flames roaring toward her. The demons and other beings present in the room stand motionless and awestruck. These are all moments we did not see before, and I'm still not certain why Uriel shows them to us now.

We watch everything unfold, and I'm amazed that Thana remains calm through the entire confrontation. We see the exact moment Michael receives Nikita from Cyrus and when that happens, she gains control of the room, and the creatures who were once under Lucifer's dominion are now under hers.

The scene in Uriel's bowl flashes forward to the attack on her castle and her quick obliteration of the attackers. We hear bits and pieces of the discussion of what they're getting ready to do. She looks at the moving map that was only a rumor during her grandfather's time. We're now down to four princes, which will make the rest of this campaign much easier than it was previously.

Before we're able to discuss our next moves concerning the rings, Thana, and our other plans, a knock sounds at the front door. Michael leaves the room to answer it. After hearing a bit of murmuring, two sets of footsteps sound down the hallway toward us. Entering the room with Michael is Sigrun, who smiles and bows before us, holding out two small wooden training swords.

"Your mate requested me to train her daughters for war. She wants them to have the skills they need to survive. Creator forbid, we leave them defenseless for even just a moment. She wishes for them to know how to protect themselves in all situations." Sigrun lays the two practice swords on the table, then looks up at me. "You know, I only agreed to this because she asked. No child should know the fear or the concern of war." I look down at the practice swords and then up at her again.

"Thana has a valid reason for calling you here and requesting this of you. I know you've been working with the girls and teaching them to fly. I've always believed it was an error on the part of the angels not to teach our daughters to fly at a young age. So in times of danger, despite the preference they not show their wings, they'd have a way to escape." I fold my hands and look between Uriel and Michael. "This is something we should speak to our brethren about.

454

We've lost so many females through the centuries because of that one simple thing: they haven't known how to fly. Divine law needs to be rewritten in order to keep our females safe." The female population has suffered greatly because of an ancient law written during a time of peace.

I hesitate, though, hearing the uncertainty in my voice as I look between the others gathered here. Christian stands and walks to my side and then claps me on my back. "It's about time someone higher ranking among us believes that. Too many females have been slaughtered because they have wings, yet they're forbidden from using them. They die senselessly because they don't know how to fly, nor do they have the strength to take off and remain airborne for long periods of time because their wings have remained hidden since birth." Christian asserts nothing but the truth and then moves his hand over the bowl, much as Uriel did.

Wars over the past hundreds of years play before us. We watch as female Nephilim and female Angels were slaughtered even though their wings were out. They didn't possess the strength to take off and save themselves. He glances between the Archangels gathered here and then over to Sigrun. "Do you know why the Valkyrie live?" He smiles, tilting his head to the side. "Because they don't shelter their daughters. They teach them to be the warriors they are. Women are the strongest among us. They bring life into this world and endure more pain than a man can ever imagine." He looks down at the water one last time, then over at Sigrun.

"When it comes time for me to be a father again, I will joyfully hand my daughter over to you to train and teach all the things she'll need to be a strong female. I don't want my daughter to know fear or to be a victim because of antiquated ideals." As Christian utters these words, I see the seriousness in his eyes and his stance. This is one subject he has considered, and I know deep down he will not bend in his belief. Perhaps it's time for the old ways to change. And I believe it will begin with Thana.

Thana

Standing over the map, I watch the chess pieces put themselves into play, each representative piece moving to the exact location of its prince for that ring. "Raziel, I summon thee." My booming voice reverberates through the castle as the pieces move into place. An influx of power accompanies Raziel when he arrives. The thudding of his boots echoes through the halls as he makes his way to the war room.

Dropping to a knee before me, Raziel lowers his head and spreads his wings wide. "You summoned me, Destroyer?" He looks up at me and smiles. I suspect he's getting a kick out of seeing me now that I've ascended.

Bending down, I kiss the crown of his head and offer him my hands. "Rise, Raziel. I seek your counsel." I motion back to Azrael and the map with the moving chess pieces.

His steps quicken as he approaches the table and looks over the map in awe. "I've heard rumors of Samael having an enchanted map that can locate all the princes." He glances up from the moving pieces to me, then back again to the map.

Laughing, I pick up Lucifer's pawn and hold it in my hand. "It's not the map that's enchanted. It's the pieces. Grandfather obtained blood from each of them at some point, and here we are." I motion to the piece in my hand and smile, looking at it. Memories flood my mind as the way my grandfather procured each prince's blood is revealed to me. It was through battle. After every fight, he saved and preserved the blood covering his sword until he had gathered enough.

"That's brilliant!" Raziel exclaims, looking from the map to me. I place Lucifer's pawn back on the edge of the map and it moves back to where it was on the Pride ring. Fascinated, Raziel picks the piece up again, setting it on a distinctly different part of the map and watches it move back to its place again. "With this at our disposal, what do you require of me, Destroyer?" I see a new level of confidence in Raziel's stance.

"I need you to work with Azrael to come up with several strategies to purge the rings and also for the final attack on Lucifer himself." Glancing between Azrael and Raziel, I see various emotions flicker over their visages before determination finally wins out.

"Consider it done." He extends his hand out to me, and we shake. Our firm grips on each other's forearms seal our agreement.

"Father?" I whisper.

"Yes, daughter?" Azrael closes the distance between us and hugs me. I see love and pride for me shining in his eyes.

Raising a hand, my eyes blacken as I summon a duke of Hell to me. An honest-to-goodness knight steps through a portal that opens in my war room. "Eligos, so good of you to join us on such short notice. I need you and your legions ready to march on my command. Will that be an issue?"

Removing his helm, the man behind the iron mask smiles. "Never a problem for the Destroyer. Tell me where and when and our swords will drip with the blood of your enemies." He draws his armored fist to his chest and raps it twice.

I know summoning the duke will come at a cost, so I may as well deal with that now. "I desire all sixty legions at the ready. For your payment, what is it you request?" I rest my hand on the sword at my hip, watching the duke study the map of the rings.

A twisted smile crosses over his lips as he turns to face me. "Wrath. My legions can battle to their black hearts' content. Plus, I understand the Balor will be there as well, and they are excellent blacksmiths." He leans back against the wall, staring at me and raising his chin in an attempt to dominate the conversation.

Smiling, I hover above the ground as my reaper form bursts forth. "If you and your legions can do as you claim, then we have a deal. Wrath will be yours and your legions." I extend my hand to him, waiting to see if he'll take the bait.

He paces the interior of the room, looking occasionally at the map, then back over to me as he processes what I've said. Taking a more relaxed stance, I lean against the wall, watching him move about the room. "I'll take the deal." Surging forward, he grips my forearm, and we shake on it.

As soon as we break apart, he vanishes from sight. Looking back at my father and Raziel, I announce, "I'm going to see my family and make sure my children are okay. Then, we take over Hell and set things back in order." Azrael and Raziel nod in my direction before I head out of the war room. Walking through the castle, I hear my grandfather's voice in my head, filling me in on the history of the objects I'm passing.

Stepping out on the front steps of the fortress, I scan the horizon, watching for movement. Once I'm sure nothing is coming or feels out of place within my realm, I take flight, heading toward the rift. Looking out over the Shadow Realm, I see how my will has changed the surface of the land. It's not as harsh and foreboding as it was under my grandfather's control.

Stretching my wings feels good when I'm not defending against an attack in battle. The veil of mist looks more beautiful than the last time I saw it. What may have only been a blink of the eye to me has been days, if not weeks, on Earth. And I have no idea how that time translates in the Angelic Realm. All I know is I miss my guys and my children to no end.

Closing my eyes, I reach out my senses, feeling for where everyone is in relation to my location. It's not much further to the Angelic Realm. And good news for me, Michael kept my mates and children at his house for safekeeping. When I break through the clouds, it feels like a mist of cool water washes my sins away. It's as if a great weight has lifted off my shoulders when I see the Valkyrie fly toward me to follow me to Michael's. Landing in his front yard is like coming home, and my heartbeat quickens in anticipation of seeing my babies. The door opens of its own volition, and I enter his home unannounced. I hope it isn't rude to just enter his house, but considering who he is to my daughter, he better not try to keep me out.

I find no one in the house, so I make my way to the backyard. At the stained-glass door, I pause and look out over the immaculate landscaping, seeing my mates and my two small daughters. One has nearly white hair, while the other has hair I can only describe as the color of dark smoke. It's not gray, but it's not black either. Pushing open the door, I step out into the yard, and as one, both girls turn to look at me.

My heart damn near stops beating as I stare at them. How long was I gone? How did I miss so much of their tiny lives? Multiple emotions threaten to erupt, but the main feeling is rage. My pulse pounds with anger that I missed this much of their lives because of Lucifer. "Sweetheart . . ." Raphael's soft and affectionate tone breaks through the outrage burning deep in my chest.

I turn to face him, and his smile never falters. I feel as if there's a maelstrom inside my chest, fueling the rage that wants to be set loose on Hell. I motion to the children. "How?" I can't form more of my question beyond the obvious. "How long was I gone?" I search his face and then look at the others, hoping someone answers me.

Metatron grabs my hand and holds it as Raphael takes the one closest to him, walking me to my daughters. "Because they're mostly of divine origin, their growth rate has happened more quickly than a human's would," Metatron tells me in a clinical tone.

"Nikita? Davina?" I call to my daughters and drop to my knees as they run to me. They appear to be around the size of five-year-old children. Davina breaks away from her sister and closes the distance between us as fast as she can. Her little body slams into mine, and I hug her tightly to me. Burying my nose between her shoulder and neck, I breathe in her scent, reassuring myself she's mine.

Nikita makes it to us and runs her hand over my cheek, smiling. I grab her and wrap both of them in my wings, holding them like they're the only things in the world that matter. I bury my nose between Nikita's neck and shoulder, just as I did her sister, and clasp them both to me. These are my babies, and I've missed them.

Reluctantly, I open my wings and release my girls. I glance over at the Archangels, waiting for a more complete explanation. "Nephilim grow at a faster rate than humans," Metatron states as he paces. "And a child that's mostly divine will grow faster than a Nephilim. At least that's what we've learned so far. From the information we have of your birth and childhood, you grew amazingly fast as well." I take in this information and realize it's a bitter pill to swallow. No matter how many kids I have, they'll grow faster than the average Nephilim.

Forcing a smile, I look between my angelic mates, then focus on Cyrus and Gage. Pulling on their essences, I call them to me. Honestly, I can literally pull them to me. It would take little effort to rip open a portal and pull them through. The moment they take flight, the hum in my chest increases. Looking at my other mates, a smile crosses my lips, and I close my eyes. My senses stretch out, and I know Cyrus and Gage are closing in fast. "The others will be here soon."

I look down at my daughters, and their eyes shift to chrome like mine. They each reach out and take my hands, squeezing my fingers tightly. I show them how to use their senses and pass on some of the knowledge I've gained from my grandfather to my daughters. Releasing my hand, Nikita moves in front of me, raising her palms in front of her and pointing to the sky. In one hand, a mass of black flames erupts. On the other, a tiny flickering ball of white light poofs in and out of existence.

Davina looks at both of her palms and raises them, mimicking her sister. A fountain of white light bursts from her left hand, rising to the heavens. In her right hand, a small mass of black undulates over her palm but does not rise more than a quarter inch. Curiously, I look back and forth between both of my girls and then over to my mates. The Archangels huddle in a corner as Gage and Cyrus arrive, seeing both girls with their palms up and different energies resting above them.

"When did this become a thing?" Cyrus asks as he kneels before his daughter, inspecting the black flames rising above her hand. I pace several times back and forth between my girls, watching how the different energies interact with each of them. Cyrus glances at the Archangels, who seem to be in conference with themselves rather than paying attention to what's going on over here. "This is an interesting turn of events," he says curiously. "The girls have the major talent for their designation, with a minor affinity for the other talent in their blood." I digest this information logically first. Then I begin to parse it out, trying to understand what this means for my children.

On the one hand, it looks like they'll have a tolerance for both types of power, which means, unlike my Archangel and Dark Nephilim mates, being hit with the opposing power will not affect them as strongly as their pure-blooded or half-blooded relatives. Neither power harms me because my nature is almost perfect in its duality.

Christian leaves the angel huddle and kneels before Davina, passing his hand through the white energy she's stabilized above her palm. "This alone is a miracle. For one so young to hold this power and some of the power her sister contains amazes me tremendously." Christian's reverence when he says this warms my heart. He looks at Nikita. Her dominant power, of course, is the black abyssal flames. Her secondary power is a minor bit of the white light her sister wields. "I believe neither girl will be severely harmed, as the rest of us would be, if she's hit by the opposite power. At least, this is what the Archangels and I believe." Hearing these words from Christian confirms my gut instinct and what I also believe.

With a wave of my hand, I extinguish both sets of flames from my girls' hands. They smile, looking up at me. I take several moments to praise them both for their ability to handle the power they were born with at such a young age. Davina motions for me to kneel, and I drop to her height, then sit with my legs crossed in front of her.

They immediately climb into my lap, resting their heads on my shoulders. I wrap my arms around them, gripping them tightly. "Don't worry, Mommy. Great Grandpa told us what we needed to do." Arching a brow, I look at Davina curiously.

How could Samael possibly teach them when they were just infants? This thought alone makes me wonder at the extent of the Destroyer's power. Will I also be able to teach my future infants the knowledge I've gained from my grandfather long before they're able to speak or parse out the information themselves? Will it be more of a burden than a help if they gain so much knowledge at such a young age? So many questions roll around in my head at this moment, it nearly causes a headache.

Sitting still with my daughters, I feel their little bodies go limp in my arms and see they've both fallen asleep. Motioning to the guys, they come and take the girls from my lap so I'm able to stand up. Michael motions for us to follow him through the house and into the back bedrooms. He's dedicated a bedroom for the girls with two twin beds and everything a little girl would love to have. I'm amazed at how thoughtful and loving this gentle giant is, but then I remember my little Nikita is fated to be his mate when she's older.

I smile as we tuck my daughters in for sleep. They apparently take their nap around the same time every day, which just happens to be now. Michael motions us out of the room. I have a feeling he and the others have a lot they need to share, just as I need to fill them in on all the information I've gathered on my journey. So much for a peaceful homecoming.

<h1 style="text-align:center">CHAPTER 67
THANA</h1>

Following Michael through his house, we end up in the dining room. The round table dominating the room is large and made of what appears to be mahogany. Along the edges of the table are a series of angelic runes depicting the history of Michael and his noble house. With a wave of his hand, multiple maps appear on the table along with a bunch of pewter animals. In addition, there are several other creatures depicting not only angels but also Nephilim and the fallen. He braces his hands on the edge of the table. "We need to plan for the assault on Hell."

He states this plainly, looking down at the maps before him and then up at me, apparently trying to discern whether I'll argue the point with him. Rolling my eyes, I move to stand beside him and look down at the maps on the table. Shaking my head, I wave my hand over his maps and make them disappear. "These are outdated and not close to being an accurate depiction of what's going on in each of the rings and the Shadow Realm."

Shocked doesn't describe the look on Michael's face as he looks between me and his now-missing maps. "What do you mean my maps aren't accurate? They were accurate as of a couple of weeks ago."

"Michael, you and I both know a lot can change in a couple of weeks." I arch a brow, looking at him before waving my hand over the table, creating exact replicas of the maps I have on my table in the Shadow Realm. He looks between what I'm showing him presently versus what information he had before. His eyes dart from the main map of the realms to me and then back down to the map again.

"How is this possible?" I can't tell if his agitation stems from his curiosity about *how* it happened versus how he wasn't aware of it happening.

Rolling my eyes, I move my hand over the map yet again to bring it back to the Shadow Realm. "I'm not sure whether you were aware of the level of control or the power my grandfather wielded." I look between Michael and my angelic mates. My Dark Nephilim mates know all too well how easy it is for me to reshape the realm I'm currently standing in.

Michael stares at the map, then back up at me. "What do you mean? The Destroyer is meant to only do three things. First, to keep the balance. When somebody gets out of line, as the name says, to destroy it. Second, to make sure that Hell and the Shadow Realms stay balanced." I'm guessing he's feeling his Wheaties because he raises three fingers and stares at me. "And third, to destroy any being that goes against the will of the Creator." Seemingly satisfied with himself, Michael leans on the chair behind the map and rests his weight on his forearms, waiting to see how I'll react to what he's said.

I chuckle as I walk around the table. "I think someone forgot to tell my grandfather that," I say with a slight English accent, mimicking Michael a little.

Cyrus and Gage do everything in their powers not to laugh at this exchange. "Grandfather handled the realms as he saw fit, keeping balance the best way he could, considering what he was dealing with. The fallen and the demons they created care not one bit what the Creator wants since they were cast out," I say as I stare down at the map.

"The only thing these creatures care about is their own wicked desires." I go to the sink in the other room to grab a bowl and fill it with water. Having watched Uriel do this before, I remember exactly how he did it and recall how my grandfather's memories tell me to do it. Passing my hand over the bowl, I show everyone different parts of the nine levels of Hell.

A multitude of different creatures comes into view, creatures many of them didn't even know existed until this very moment. When I get to the Shadow Realm, Michael stops me. "This is not how I remember it," he says with slight agitation in his voice.

I laugh. "You're right. It's not how you remember it." I stare down at the bowl of water, passing my hand over it and return the vision to how he must have remembered it.

"When my grandfather was in control, the land was harsh, bathed in flames and ash. It looked like something out of a horror novel. Then we have what I've made it look like today." Grinning, I glance up at him.

"This is the Shadow Realm you're familiar with." I stare down at the desolate landscape. Shaking my head, I pass my hand over it again, returning it to the vision of the current Shadow Realm over which I rule. The land is still mostly desolate, but it's not as foreboding and as much of a horror-scape as it was previously. In some spots, there are trees. Granted, they're not green. There's also grass, and no, it's not green either. It's how I envision the Middle Realm to be. It's an interesting mix of Earth and Hell, combined to maintain a balance between the three realms.

The angels in the group stare, puzzled by how I could meld the realm the way I did. I look at my Dark Nephilim mates and shake my head in disbelief at how little the angels and Archangels realized my grandfather was capable of.

"How is this possible?" Michael questions as he points at the bowl. I look down and move our view around the realm, revealing the unique landscapes I created. The wolf demons are much happier now. The Balor that visit are much happier with their section. Everyone has what they need, not what they want, which was the biggest problem with how my grandfather constructed the realm to begin with. He tried to satisfy everyone's wants and desires rather than giving them what they needed. Now the wolves have plenty of game within their territories, and they don't need to fight and go after other sections of the pie.

In a particular quarter of the map, I discovered that there were a few large wild herds of warhorses. They're heavily armored, and when they run, the frills on their legs above their hooves ignite, setting the world on fire. I'm not sure what their true name is, but I call them "Firemares." There's a huge stallion who I assume is the leader of the herd. His fur is black as pitch, and his eyes are red as blood.

Interestingly, he seems to be my new best friend. Focusing the view in the bowl on that beast and the herd he runs with, I watch them for several moments. I've taken quite a fancy to them and plan on building more of an adaptable area for them in particular. I figure they'll be of use to everyone, not just in the Shadow Realm but also in the Angelic Realm. Assuming what Michael said was previously true, that I can help things ascend, there's no reason I can't bring some of the Firemares to heaven, or at least to the Angelic Realm.

"So what does this all mean?" Michael questions, drawing me out of my line of thought.

I move around the table again and stand next to him. "This means Lucifer has no clue what he's gotten himself into this time. When I bring the war to him, nothing will be left standing." My voice reverberates around the interior of the house, shaking everything, including the foundation of the building itself.

Metatron beams with pride at how powerful his mate has become. Raphael and Christian look at each other and nod their heads, agreeing with my statement. I look to Cyrus and Gage, and both my Dark Nephilim mates give me a thumbs up, grinning smugly at how uneasy the angelic faction seems.

"Raziel and Azrael are reviewing the maps of the rings we still need to purge. My armies are ready and waiting for me to call for them." Moving to the bowl again, I show them the armies I gathered during my time distracting Lucifer.

Drawing in a deep breath, I cup one hand over the other and manifest several glowing orbs in between my hands. "Just as the Creator blessed my Dark Nephilim mates with passage to the Angelic Realm, I can grant my angelic mates passage into the Shadow Realm and the rings." Obsidian rings form and rest on the palm of my hand.

"Your beautiful angelic armor will not protect you where we're going." Glancing between the angels before me, I sigh softly, knowing full well the danger associated with this journey.

Picking up the first ring, it expands as I move to stand before Metatron. "I offer you the armor of the general of one of my legions. With this ring, I grant you passage to my realm and the nine rings beyond." Holding the ring out, I wait for him to accept it.

His eyes flash golden as he stares at the large, bracelet-sized ring. "I freely accept your protection and command of your legion, my dark angel." He slides his left hand through the ring, and it shrinks to fit his wrist. He stares at it in wonder, then presses the carved wolf at his inner wrist. Black and gold armor, like my grandfather's and mine, blankets his form. His eyebrows shoot up as he bangs on the metal, testing its strength. "Thank you for this boon, my love." My gentle giant bends down and kisses my cheek before making room for the others.

Raphael is next to stand before me, and I can't hold back my smile. "I know this is a strange and difficult thing I'm asking you to endure, but if any of the other angels become injured, I need you to be there to heal them." Holding out the ring, it expands to the size of a bracelet.

Raphael stares at the ring, then hesitantly slides his arm through it. The ring shrinks to fit snug around his wrist. He inspects the band circling his wrist and touches the wolf, just as Metatron did. The black and gold armor moves over his body like water, blanketing every inch of his muscular form in the Shadow Realm armor. Gently, I touch the bracelet. "With this ring, I grant you passage to the Shadow Realm and the nine rings beyond in Hell." As I did with Metatron, I infuse the bracelet with power.

Raphael drops to one knee and looks up at me with his golden eyes. "I accept the role of healer to serve and protect my brothers in arms as we battle alongside you." Bending down, I kiss him firmly on the lips. I know for him to not be in charge as the first mate is a bitter pill to swallow. That, coupled with the fact his mate, the mother of his daughter, is leading the attack on Hell must weigh heavily on him. I push all my love and appreciation for him through the bond. I feel the tension balled up in him slowly diminish. He stands and draws me flush to him and hugs me tightly. He kisses me passionately, and my heart thunders in my chest with excitement. At moments like this, I know how blessed I am.

Christian, the most willing of my three angelic mates, takes me from Raphael. Gently, he kisses both my cheeks and then drops to his knees before me. "My love. Whatever you need from me, I will do without hesitation for you. If you need me to lead a legion, then I will do it. If you need me to fight alongside you, I'll do that too. My love, my heart, and my soul are yours." He extends his arm out to me, offering it for the ring to be placed around it.

Carefully, I pick up the obsidian ring, and it expands to the size of a bracelet. I slide it onto his wrist and smile down at him. "With this ring, I grant you safety within the Shadow and the Hell Realms so you can traverse between all nine rings and the realms I rule." The bracelet conforms to the size of his wrist and then blankets him in the same black and gold armor. He stands and hugs me tightly, kissing me soundly on the lips and making my heartbeat flutter.

Love from my three angelic mates floods the bond, warming my heart from the inside. Both my Dark Nephilim mates appear to be just as proud. I look at Michael and Gabriel. "Michael, I ask you to undertake the hardest part of this entire mission."

I approach him and offer him one of the obsidian bands. "I offer you this in goodwill, granting you access to the entire Shadow Realm but nothing beyond that. Your job will be to provide safety to both my daughters. They will be your top priority and nothing else. You may remain within my castle in the Shadow Realm with them. It will move and bend to your will in order to protect my daughters. Or you may remain here if that is your preference."

I glance at Raziel and Gabriel and hold up two bands for them, which they accept quickly. "Your job, if you agree to accept it, is to accompany me and my mates as we battle through the rings heading to Hell. Lucifer will be the ultimate conquest. When we storm the gates of Hell, there will be no force that will stand against me." For once, I'm completely comfortable and confident in my abilities. and I let my power stretch out and reverberate throughout all the Angelic Realms. They need to know I mean business and will return the Dark Realm to its intended place and purpose.

CHAPTER 68
THANA

In my heart, I know it's difficult for the Archangels and the others in the group to accept that I've come into my full power. I also know it will be hard for them to deal with the fact that I'm leading this charge and none of them are above me. I don't know what the grand scheme of things is, nor do I care. Vengeance is mine.

I head into my daughters' room and sit beside them, watching them sleep peacefully. Part of Nikita's future is certain, and I know at least one of her mates will be very good to her. But in another sense, I fear who else she might end up with in her bond.

As for Davina, we have no idea who'll be her mates. And to be honest, they better be good to her. Otherwise, I'll burn them to ash without a second thought. The moment Raphael enters the room, a familiar hum and buzz warms me from the inside out. He situates himself behind me on the floor, placing his legs beside mine and pulling me flush to his chest. I lean back, resting against him, and watch my daughters sleep while nestled in his arms.

"What's on your mind, sweetheart?" He kisses my cheek.

Looking down at the band I placed on his arm, I lightly touch the top arch of it. "I know this is difficult for you," I say gently and turn to face him.

When he doesn't respond, I continue, "As an Archangel and our first mate, I know you're used to being in control, to being the one who gives the orders for the rest of us to follow so you can keep us safe. This entire situation can't be easy for you, and I'm sorry." I run my fingers along his strong jawline and caress his cheek, rubbing my thumb over his cheekbone just below his right eye.

"I know how things have to be. Doesn't mean I have to like it." His eyes drop to my hand on his face. "And you're right. It's difficult for me to sit back and watch you take control, knowing I've been in thousands of battles since the day of my creation." He closes his eyes and breathes in deeply.

He continues, "After all the horrors I've seen, I only hoped to shield you from them, so you wouldn't know or carry that pain with you for the rest of eternity." A single tear breaks loose from his left eye and rolls down his cheek.

Reflexively, I lean forward and kiss the tear away. "You're the best mate I could have ever hoped for. And you protect me from everything within your power," I say softly as I smile, trying to coax him to open his eyes and look at me. When he finally does, I see his unshed tears. Through the bond, I feel his belief he's failed as a mate. He thinks he's let everyone down because he wasn't the one powerful force to protect us. He also feels he failed because they stole Nikita from my grandfather after they killed him in the Shadow Realm.

Everything he's feeling floods my system, and my own tears flow down my cheeks. He's not shielding me from his emotions as much as he thought he was. "Baby, please don't cry," Raphael says as he kisses away my tears, trying to soothe the raw edges of my nerves.

"My love, I don't cry from pain. I'm crying because of how you're feeling. You haven't failed us." I spread my arms wide, motioning to the room where my daughters sleep.

"You couldn't have foreseen the lengths Lucifer would go to in order to take over the helm of the Destroyer." Tilting my head, I stare into his hazel eyes. I force myself to move past the negative feelings in my chest. "No one could have foreseen what I was meant to be."

My mind drifts back to a more chaotic time of my life. I figure now is a good time as any to bring up a secret I've held for over three hundred years. "All those years ago, the first time you met me, when I was brought before Azrael and you, there was no way you would have known I was to be yours." I kiss his forehead and then sit back.

"Only two beings knew what I was meant to be." I fiddle with the edge of my shirt, trying to regain my confidence from earlier.

Raphael gently pulls my chin toward him, using his index finger and his thumb. "Look at me, Thana." His hazel eyes plead with me to stay focused on him.

"There has never been one moment between then and now that I've ever regretted being in your presence." His velvety-soft lips gently ghost over my mouth just enough to make me center all my attention on him.

"Besides our daughter, you're the single greatest gift I've received in my entire existence." He quirks a brow, then laughs to himself. "There's only one other thing that comes even remotely close to having you and Davina in my life." He tilts his head to the side, waiting to see if I'll know what he's talking about.

Curious, I shake my head and his hand drops from my chin. "The only other thing that comes close was when I ascended to become an Archangel." Double-blinking, my heart stutters in my chest, realizing his ascension pales in comparison to having our daughter and me in his life.

The warmth of the love he has for us blossoms in my chest, burning like an inferno. I'm stunned speechless at what he just said. All I can do is smile and nod at him. I reach up and run my fingers through the longer hair on the top of his head, then frame his face with my hands.

"I've been in love with you from the first moment I laid eyes on you. That was the day my designation was pronounced. The way the

Light Nephilim reacted, I was sure it would be my last day on Earth." I glance down for a moment before making eye contact with him again.

"It was when you stepped forward, with your armor blazing to life and shining like a star in the heavens, that I knew I was safe." Looking into his eyes, I remember that day fondly, allowing my own eyes to turn chrome to show him exactly how I saw him at that moment. To me, he appeared brighter than the North Star and more precious than the largest gemstone to be found. The only two beings more precious to me than my mates are my daughters. I make sure he sees this clearly through my eyes.

In response to what I've shown him, he wraps his arms tightly around me. Pulling a Cyrus, his white wings burst open and he cocoons me within them. Something about finding the safety within my mate's wings puts my heart and mind at ease and gives me the comfort I desperately need. Even as powerful as I am as the Destroyer, all living beings—even me—experience moments of weakness. I've come to terms with the fact that not everything in my life has been rosy or perfect. I've also learned to accept the things that I cannot change. The only thing within my power is to rid the world of some of the evil within it. That's within my grasp.

Raphael leans forward and kisses me, drawing me out of my inner monologue. When we break apart, his eyes are glowing almost white from the power within him. "Remember what your grandfather told you. You're able to command the legions of Heaven and Hell. In this existence and the next, there is no time you'll ever walk alone again." Tapping his finger on his chin, he thinks about his statement for several moments.

"I think you need to assemble more of an army up here before we head back down to the Shadow Realm." Raphael's tactical mind has always amazed me. He thinks of so many things outside the box I'd never have considered.

I extract myself from his lap and begin to pace the room, moving back and forth between my daughters and looking them over, making sure that they're fine while also thinking about what he's said. Once my mind is made up, I motion for him to follow me out of the room. Stepping into the main part of the house again, we head back to the dining room. While we were gone, the guys made food and fed everyone. "Gabriel, Uriel, I need you to assemble the strongest warriors you can find up here."

I glance over next to Metatron. "My love, my teddy bear. I need you to go to Sigrun and enlist her and the Valkyrie. I need them here in the gardens tonight."

I motion to Raphael as I grab a bagel from a plate on the table. "My brilliant mate brought something to my attention that I'd overlooked." With my free hand, I reach to Raphael and pull him to my side. "I will grant passage to a legion of angels and Valkyrie to accompany us. Any who follow me to the Shadow Realm and beyond, to all who follow me through the nine rings of Hell, I will grant them safe passage when we bring the last war to Lucifer."

Michael nearly chokes on his drink as he stares at me. "What you're proposing has never been done before. There is no way you're strong enough to maintain all of us going into Hell's bowels." Narrowing my eyes, I stare at Michael, ready to fire back at him.

Before I can say anything, from out of nowhere, Metatron's twin, Sandalphon, manifests in the middle of the dining room. "Thana speaks the truth." He looks between me and the Archangels. For him to come down from the Creator's throne to confirm what I said means a lot to me.

One of two things has occurred. Either I've pleased the Creator by taking the mantle of Destroyer and going forth to do his work, or he needed the other Archangels to believe in my mission so we could accomplish everything we've set out to do. This is one of those moments where blind faith is what will see this through to the victory at the end.

Ignoring the elephant in the room, I return my focus to breakfast. I'll let Michael question Sandalphon if he feels the need to. But right now, he's not questioning what he said.

Stepping forward, I hug Sandalphon, then step back to the table and spread the cream cheese on my bagel. "Join us for breakfast?" I motion to the spread the guys set out. He nods and makes his way around the table.

I hear my daughters waking up and head down the hallway to check on them. Davina is sitting up in her bed and stretching her wings. Her opalescent feathers shimmer in the morning light. I'm almost jealous of the gorgeous color of her feathers. Pale gray feathers lining the inner part of her wings are framed by her white flight feathers. Moving into her space, I sit on the bed next to her and run my fingers through her smokey-gray hair.

"Mommy?" Davina's soft voice wavers slightly. I stop playing with her hair and draw her into my lap as she puts her wings away.

"Yes, baby?" Kissing her brow, I hug her to me, trying to comfort her.

Davina plays with a length of my hair, speaking hesitantly. "Are you and Daddy leaving again?" She pouts, looking up at me, and I watch her lips quiver.

Drawing in a deep breath, I think over my response several times before I kiss the top of her head again. "Your Daddies and I love you very, very much." I rest my head on top of hers and breathe in her scent, calming myself. "Forces are at work in Hell that I need to take care of before you get much older. I don't want the darkness to strike out at my children and harm one of you to get to me." Exhaling roughly, I leave the bond open to let my mates know what's happening here in the back bedroom.

Raphael leans in the door frame, listening in on the conversation. "But you just got back, Mommy." My chest clenches, hearing my daughter's words. Raising my gaze, I silently plead with Raphael to step in as my heart breaks.

"Little one . . ." Raphael comes to kneel before us, and Davina dives into his arms, crying.

I thought my heart was breaking before, but watching her cry makes my chest constrict. "Mommy and I love you and your sister very much. The task given to us is difficult, but it's not more than we can handle." Raphael rocks Davina as my other mates file into the room.

Nikita awakens and moves to comfort her sister. Davina eventually pulls away from Raphael, and both girls look at me. It's time for the girls to see what their mother has become. "Girls." I say gently, gaining their attention.

I step away from everyone and unfurl my wings. The armor of the Destroyer manifests on my body, heeding my call. Gage steps forward and hands me Daybreaker. "Little ones, they created me to right millenniums of wrongs." Sadly, I look down at the sword in my hand. "Eventually, Davina, you will ascend to take your father's place in the hospital." Her eyes flair to life, looking between her dad and me.

"Nikita will ascend to take Azrael's place as Death eternal." Nikita bows her head slightly, accepting what I say with a grace beyond her years.

"We battle," I say, motioning to all my mates and our gathered friends, "to give you and the world the best possible future." Drawing in a deep breath, I look from one daughter to the other.

They both nod their understanding. "Will you be back?" Davina and Nikita say at the same time, and I beam.

All my familiars rip free from my flesh and surround me. Extending both my hands out before me, I ignite both powers within the palms of my hands. Light in one hand and darkness in the other. "I will burn Hell to ash to make it back to you, my daughters. Then I will rebuild it how it was meant to be before they twisted it into what it is." Extinguishing the powers in my hands, my armor returns to the amulet, and I drop to my knees when my daughters approach. Leaving my wings on display, both girls run their fingers over my feathers, looking at the differences for themselves.

Motioning to my mates, I watch as they remove everyone who isn't family from the room and shut the door. I smile broadly as I look at my daughters. "Unfurl your wings and see the similarities between you and your parents."

The girls do as they're told and compare the wing shapes and colors between us. Davina has her father's wings, 100 percent, except for the pale gray feathers on the underside close to her body. Nikita's wings are a blend of Cyrus's and mine. Her feathers are closer in color to my mid-feathers—not quite black but not gray either. We devote the better part of the next hour to giving the girls the opportunity to inspect all of our wings and ask questions about them. What began as an emotional minefield turned into a great learning experience.

CHAPTER 69

THANA

Darkness descends on the Angelic Realm, and we put the girls down to sleep for the night. Out of habit, Cyrus and I release our familiars to sleep in the room with the girls. Creeping down the hallway, I head back into the living room where everyone else is gathered. Out of habit, I pace the room, trying to decide exactly what I want to say. Half of me does not want the angelic side of the bond to go into the rift with me. The other half wants to leave Raphael here, at least, so the girls would have one parent left should the worst happen.

"Babe?" Cyrus calls for the fourth time, trying to draw my attention back to him. I stop pacing in the middle of the room.

"Yes, love?" I glance over my shoulder and look at him before turning fully to face everyone. I apparently caught all their attention when I didn't initially respond to him.

"What's bothering you?" Cyrus asks as he steps forward with Christian hot on his heels. They each take a hand and draw me over to the couch. Once seated, I fiddle with the edge of my shirt again, which is a major tell that I'm stressed.

"I'll be honest," I whisper, staring down at my hands.

Out of habit, I flex my fingers, elongating my nails into claws and then back again. "I'm concerned about all of us going through the rings and leaving the girls here without at least one parent. I don't want them to be orphans should the worst happen to us." I stare down, still flexing my fingers.

Christian grabs both my hands and kneels before me to stop me from shifting them back into claws again. "You're the most important person in our lives besides the girls. And if you feel one of us needs to remain with them just in case, then let it be me." His eyes shine as I stare down at him. He's always been willing to sacrifice himself for others to keep them safe in times of trouble, all the way back to his life in Japan.

"As much as I'd like to agree to what you're offering, Christian, I believe Gage would be a better choice to leave with the girls." Biting my bottom lip, I smile at him.

"You have not lived as a Dark Nephilim. Gage, on the other hand, has been both dark and light. I think he would best understand both girls and their natures," I say with regret in my voice. It's not that I discount the knowledge Christian has, it's just that he lacks the understanding of the duality of my daughters. Never having experienced the power of the shadows in his blood. He couldn't possibly understand anything Nikita would go through as she gets older and her power manifests at full strength.

Drawing in a deep breath, I glance at my other mates, and they nod, agreeing with me. Michael comes forward and rests a hand on Christian's shoulder. "Why not leave both Christian and Gage with the girls? That way, they can both help them with their unique abilities."

He moves over and rests his hand on top of Gage's shoulder. "As much as Gage spent most of his life as a Light Nephilim, now he can't manifest light. And in order to help Davina as she grows, he would need to have that ability." Michael's counsel makes sense.

I turn to Raphael, and he nods in agreement. I stand up slowly and draw both my mates to me. "If you two agree to this, I'd be in your debt from now until the end of time." Gage and Christian both kiss a cheek and hug me tightly between them.

"We'd do anything for you and the girls, you know that," Gage says forcefully. I guess he's slightly irritated I'd think they wouldn't be willing to make this sacrifice for the girls and me.

"Our hearts are yours to do with as you please. And to be of service to your daughters is the greatest honor I've ever achieved," Christian says as he rests my head on his shoulder, snuggling me into his side.

"Then it's settled," I say with great finality before looking at my other mates.

"I'm gonna take Christian and Gage back to our nest for tonight." I waggle my eyebrows, looking over at Cyrus as he chokes on his drink. He knows exactly what I have planned for the two of them. He laughs and excuses himself from the room in order to not spill my little secret. Gage looks quickly at Cyrus, then back at me, and his eyes light up. He's caught my drift and is now anticipating what's to come.

Poor Christian sits there with no idea what I'm planning tonight. I move around the room after I break away from Christian and Gage to hug and kiss my other mates, making sure they each know how much I love them. Samael's wolf returns to the room since I summoned him to come with us back to the house. He presses his nose to my thigh and then returns to the tattoo on my arm. The only other familiar with me is my raven, which remains on my rib cage.

Once all the goodbyes are over with, we take flight and leave the Angelic Realm. Flying through the night over the city, the twinkling lights below us are a beautiful sight. As I look down at the hustle and bustle of the world below us as we glide on the thermals, I realize just how small our own personal world is.

Breaching the mountain north of our home, I catch a good up current and then dive straight down, running my fingertips over the tops of the trees as I pass them before shooting back up to our house in the distance. Breaching the incline, I land on the third story rail. The doors to the house open on their own before me.

Stepping through the double doors on the third-story balcony is a bittersweet homecoming. When we originally purchased this house, I thought I would come home to my family, to the laughter and giggles inside this beautiful home, for our lifetimes. Not prepare for war and spend what is possibly my last night with my two gentlest mates. As much as I'd prefer to have Gage with me in the Shadow Realm, I know my daughter Nikita needs someone of the darkness to be with her in a parental role should anything happen to Cyrus and me.

We walk through the halls in silence. The only noise is the clicking of my heels on the tile floor. The boys know better than to interrupt me as I prowl through the house, double-checking to make sure it's safe. I extend my senses out, making sure nothing except my familiars and us are the only beings present.

In some sense, I still feel the essences of my other mates inside the house. Part of me mourns the fact that my children didn't get to spend their early days of life here like we'd planned. I swear on everything that I am, when I sink my claws into Lucifer's flesh, he'll feel every ounce of pain I've experienced from the day Nikita was taken till now. He not only stole my grandfather from me, but he also stole the early days of my children while they were still babies.

I missed seeing their first steps, hearing their first words, and experiencing their first everything. This last thought makes the entire house rumble. Pictures and glassware vibrate off the shelves, hitting the floor and shattering into pieces. Christian stands back, staring at me, studying me, and trying to understand exactly where my thoughts are.

Gage, being the braver of the two, moves forward and gently caresses my cheeks. "What's on your mind? What caused the mini-earthquake?" He tilts his head to the side and grins cockily, trying to play the part of Cyrus.

Shaking my head and rolling my eyes, I step away from him and allow my wings to flex several times. Drawing in several cleansing breaths, I think about how to explain what I'm feeling to them. Part of me is afraid of crushing the mood for the evening, but the other part knows if I'm not honest with them now, I'll probably never be able to tell them how I'm feeling about all this.

"Well, it's like this . . ." I pace the third floor, literally walking in a circle around the upper level.

"I wish I hadn't sent Nikita with my grandfather into the Shadow Realm, even though she needed it. If he didn't feel the need to be there alone with her, she might not have been stolen and he might not have been killed." I know more than likely my assessment is incorrect, and it was bound to happen, whether Nikita was there or not. But my guilt is real.

"Also, if I hadn't ascended to the level of Destroyer, we wouldn't be in this debacle that we're in now. We're getting ready to storm the gates of Hell. I wouldn't have to divide my family in order to provide the safest possible environment for my children." I keep pacing, trying to parse this all out in the most digestible form for them. I'm not great at expressing my emotions. Half the time, I cry when I'm angry.

Before my ascension, everybody took my tears as weakness and not as the frustration they really were. I may have been called moody. Some may have called me unstable or weak because I cried. But really I cried because I was afraid of what I could do to others, knowing the power that was deep within me. Fearing my dark side has never been a secret. Part of me still fears it. The other part of me has come to terms with it and is ready to unleash it and rend the flesh from Lucifer's body.

The storm brewing in my chest as I think about everything I have to do feels like I'm being ripped apart from the inside. Then suddenly, Gage and Christian are both in front of me, and I smile at them. "I love you both with all I am and all I'll ever be." I reach out and take a hand from both of them.

"I won't go lightly into the darkness when we leave to storm the different rings of Hell to seek our revenge and purge the shadows." Biting my lower lip. I study both men's reactions to everything I've said.

Where Gage is an open book and able to be read, Christian is guarded. His features don't give any signs of where his head's at. I tilt my head and stare pointedly at Christian, waiting to see if he says anything. He forces a smile and then leans forward and kisses my cheek. "*Washi no ai*, I've loved you since the first day I saw you. It might not have been the romantic love it is now, but part of my heart has always belonged to you." He kisses the knuckles on my hand before continuing.

"If you wished it of me, I'd follow you into the bowels of Hell. I'd battle beside you and destroy everything that stands in your way." He pulls my fist to his chest and lays my hand flat over his heart.

I feel the familiar beat of his heart against the palm of my hand. "Do you feel my heart, *watashi no ai*?" he asks, calling me his wife or "precious one."

I nod, not wanting to break him from his train of thought. "My heart beats for you and our children alone. Yes, I love my bond brothers like a brother would love his siblings. But you and the girls hold my heart alone." I smile, feeling everything is just about right in the world.

Slowly, my gaze slips over to Gage, and he laughs. "Listen, beautiful. I'm not good at this romantic shit like loverboy here. But I can tell you a few things." He places my hand against his throat in a semi-choke-hold.

I can't help but laugh a little when he does this. "My life is yours to extinguish when you see fit. I'd lay down my life and die for you a thousand times if it meant you could live and be free and happy. Your daughters are my daughters. I don't care who their father is. They're mine, just as they're yours." His words make me smile, and I feel the warmth blossom in my heart as the rest of the bond floods me with the love and security I need.

"Now, not saying that I don't love Cyrus, 'cause I do. He's a sexy bastard," Gage says bluntly, and Christian nearly chokes on his spit.

Gage looks at Christian and slaps him on the back. "Oh, come on. If you weren't afraid of falling, you'd go after him too," he says in that sarcastic tone of his I love so much.

Christian is taken aback by what Gage has said, and his shock has rendered him speechless. Laughing, I walk past both boys. "I'm going to shower. I suggest you both do the same, then meet me in the master bedroom." Before either can say anything, I vanish in a wisp of shadows.

CHAPTER 70

THANA

Manifesting in my bedroom, my nerves have hit an all-time high. Gage is accustomed to doing the menage thing, whereas Christian is very traditional and one-on-one when it comes to his lovemaking. In opposition to that, you've got Gage and Cyrus who give it their all the entire time.

Christian is slow and methodical, and it's pure poetry in motion. I'm guessing it's almost a cultural thing as to how things are done in the bedroom, but I'm not 100 percent sure of that at this point. With as passionate as Christian is with certain aspects of his life, I can almost imagine he could go off the rails and unleash that passion if the moment presented itself.

But then I wonder if he'll have problems having Gage in the room with us. I walk around my bedroom, picking out clothes I'm not afraid of shredding. Why am I bothering to get dressed, only to be undressed the minute the boys show up?

Rolling my eyes, I head into the shower and adjust the water to the temperature I'm most comfortable with—scalding hot. I laugh, thinking about the temperature of my water and the fact that I'm getting ready to storm the gates of Hell. Maybe this is a warm-up for

485

that. I may very well be putting myself into my own personal hell when I try to combine the two men I love into one brief scene in my bedroom tonight. Neither male is dominant, so this will be interesting. I'm almost curious to see which one will take charge and start the shenanigans off tonight.

My hands glide over my wet flesh, caressing every inch of my body. Closing my eyes, I lean back against the cool tiles of the shower, allowing the hot water to cascade down my curves. Rivulets of water run over and between my breasts, and the impact of the shower on the tips of my erect nipples sends jolts down to my greedy core.

My thoughts drift to the last time I had shower sex and the feel of my mate's powerful fingers gripping me. Sliding my hands up my body, I grip my full breasts. The full, heavy globes flow over my hands, and I lift them, testing their weight.

The soft click of the door unlatching barely phases me. Squeezing my legs together, I roll my nipples between my fingers. "Beautiful, you keep that up. I'm gonna come before I touch you." Gage's husky voice sends a shiver through me.

Opening my eyes, I lock on a very naked and very hard Gage. His cock bounces in time with the beating of his heart. The tip glistens with the evidence of his arousal. Not far behind him is Christian, also naked and hard as a rock. Cradling both breasts with one hand, I slide my free hand down my abdomen to trace along my folds. Their eyes follow my fingers, scorching their way to my pussy.

Christian's mouth pops open as his hand grips his length tightly, holding on to it and trying not to stroke it. My eyes rake over both their bodies as my fingertip finds my sensitive nub. A soft gasp escapes my lips as I gently stroke it, while watching them move their hands in time with mine. Christian, usually the shy one, strokes his length nearly as fast as Gage.

"*Watashi no ai*, let us take care of you. Watching you is killing me." Christian's voice is strained as he occasionally stops and squeezes his shaft tightly to prevent himself from finishing.

"Hmm . . . Maybe . . ." The words come out as a purr as Gage shoots his load all over the bathroom floor. The guttural roar that escapes him is music to my ears. I did that to him. I made him feel the need to ease the pressure within himself.

"Gage, baby. Come clean up." I push the glass door to the shower open, and he quickly enters, turning on the second showerhead.

A wicked grin crosses my lips as I dip two fingers inside myself, stroking at my core, my fingers curled just enough to stroke my g-spot. My eyes blacken as I stare at Christian and bite my bottom lip. "Come for me. Let me see what I do to you." My voice sounds breathy even to my ears, and Christian can't help but do as I ask.

It's almost a chain reaction when my core pulses and grip at my fingers. I cry out as my knees buckle, and I slide slightly down the tiles. Gage reaches over, playing with my nipples and drawing out my pleasure. Christian curses in Japanese as his come shoots out over the bench and towels.

I finally withdraw my fingers, turn to Gage, and then shove them in his mouth to suck clean. That simple act has him hard as a rock again. Without skipping a beat, he scoops me up and carries me out of the shower to the massage table. He lays me down and adjusts the table's height to suit him. Before I know what's happening, he grips my hips and slams his length home, sending shock waves through my body.

I try to hold on to the table as his thrusts send me up the sheet. Christian approaches, then sucks and nibbles my nipples, driving me insane. "Aw, baby girl, why don't you help Christian out? He's hard, and his cock looks lonely." Gage's gravelly tone holds a hint of command to it. Then I notice his eyes are black. Cyrus is probably telling him what to do.

Running my fingers through Christian's thick black hair, I pull at it till he looks up at me. "Want me to take care of this for you?" I reach down, palm his cock, and give it several strokes. Blushing, he nods as he sort of tells me what he wants. Poor baby, we've got to break him out of his shell.

As soon as Gage sees Christian agree, he flips me onto my stomach. Squealing, I extend my claws and dig into the tabletop to stabilize myself. The next thing I know, Gage is directing Christian to kneel on the table in front of me. Looking over my shoulder, Gage grins smugly at me and motions for me to turn to face Christian. "Hold your cock steady for our girl," Gage fires over my shoulder at Christian.

He looks down at me with his eyes churning gold. "Is this alright, *watashi no ai?*" Christian asks softly, looking at me in concern as he holds his cock in front of me.

Winking, I shift my tongue to my Basilisk's and coil its forked length around his shaft, drawing it into my mouth. Sucking hard on him, I draw him to the back of my throat. My tongue coils and uncoils around his length as I move in time with Gage's thrusts. Bracing my hands on his thighs, I bob along with Gage's forward motion.

Christian moans softly every time I suck him to the back of my throat. The slapping of skin and the deep thrusts have my senses on overload. When I arch up quickly, Christian's cock pops free from my mouth as my orgasm rips through me. My alpha-lock takes Gage hostage, ripping his orgasm from him as well. Thankfully, with the memories inherited from my grandfather, I know how to prevent pregnancy now.

Somewhere between Gage's and my never-ending orgasm, Christian came all over the table and floor. Panting heavily between contractions, I attempt to laugh at the mess in front of me. Gage is still stuck and spasming with every pulse of my muscles. I can only assume he's regretting his decision to stand while he fucks me. Christian is the first who's able to move and walk around the room. He heads into the bathroom, and I hear the water running.

After several minutes, he returns to the massage room, carrying a pair of wet washcloths and some towels for Gage and me to clean ourselves up with. It takes a little while, but finally my alpha-lock releases Gage, and he's able to withdraw, crashing to the floor like a newborn. It's kind of funny to me to see this big muscular man sitting on the floor, unable to stand on his own.

After I accept the towel from Christian, I attempt to stand after taking a few minutes to get my feet underneath me. I move to find my clothes and dress quickly.

Slowly, I turn and look back at the guys. "Tomorrow will be one of the hardest days of my life, second only to the day I left to hunt down my daughter."

Gage forces himself to sit up and smiles, looking at me. "You have given Christian and me the most difficult duty of all. We are to protect your daughters. There's no power on heaven or earth that will save us from your wrath if anything should happen to them."

Christian shakes his head, then moves to rests a hand on Gage's shoulders. "I, for one, am doing everything in my power not to anger our mate. After all, at some point in the future, I'd like to have children of my own." He smiles happily, probably having made the smartest statement of the day.

"Come on, boys. Let's go get some dinner, then come back home to chill out and enjoy our last night on Earth together until I return." They agree, and we all break, heading to our individual rooms to grab clean clothes.

We gather in the main hall of the house downstairs, waiting to leave. Christian is the last to enter, and he's on the phone, speaking with someone I'm not familiar with. Just as I'm about to question him, he holds up a single finger, stopping me in my tracks. And all I can do is arch an eyebrow at him, questioning why he shushed me.

When he's finally off the phone, he smiles broadly, proud of himself. "I just secured us spots at the hot new Sushi Palace that opened up over on Martin Boulevard."

We stop and stare at him because that's a place I've been waiting to open for weeks. Christian links his arm with mine, dragging us to the door. "Tonight is opening night. We're one of the first customers who'll be allowed in. And you have a full run of the menu because the chef is a good friend of mine. He wishes for you to try a little bit of everything."

Smiling as he bows slightly at me. "He wishes for you to give him suggestions as to what female Nephilim may prefer."

Squealing with excitement, I practically drag Christian the rest of the way down the driveway to my car. A soft *"Oh no"* escapes Gage's lips, and he thinks I didn't hear him. I laugh softly and unlock the doors. Climbing into the driver's seat, Christian and Gage play rock-paper-scissors for their position in the car.

Lucky for Gage, he's better at it than Christian is and wins the passenger seat. Turning the ignition, my beast roars to life. I swear, she sounds louder than she did before. I slide my hand across the top of the dashboard as if petting a favorite animal. Just as I hear the final click of the seatbelts being locked in place, I slam my foot to the gas and pop her into first gear. We launch off like a rocket, heading down the road at top speed.

Christian is praying in the back seat. Gage is laughing like a lunatic in excitement right beside me. He flips through the channels and stops on Eminem's "Rap God." Of all the songs he could have picked, this is the most interesting one to shift through the gears to. Not that I don't like the song, but I usually play a lot of hard rock and heavy metal. Only Gage knows I dabble into hip-hop and hard rock.

Before we know it, we arrive at the restaurant and find a parking space in the front. Gage gets out first and opens the door wide so Christian can climb out.

Everything appears normal at first when we enter the restaurant, but I keep getting a nagging feeling that something is about to happen. Knowing my mannerisms, Christian stares at me without blinking for several moments. "What's wrong," he says bluntly rather than posing it as a question.

Looking around the restaurant, I can't put my finger on what's out of place. "I'm not sure." I continue searching the surroundings, watching everyone as they move about, continuing on with the first service of the day within the new establishment.

The feeling that something doesn't seem right keeps bugging me. We're halfway through the meal when time suddenly stops. The server who was falling with the tray is frozen mid-fall. All the items that were about to crash to the floor are suspended in midair. Gage and I seem to be the only ones in the restaurant who can move.

"This is the work of one of the dark ones." I move from my seat, extending my wings and plucking a feather from close to my body. I take it and wrap it several times around Christian's ring finger and speak the ancient words my grandfather taught me. My feather morphs into an obsidian ring, and Christian becomes unfrozen. He looks around in shock, staring at everything suspended in air that shouldn't be.

"What's happening?" he asks, looking around the room in wonder.

I touched the amulet above my breast, and my armor covers me quickly. "I'm not sure, but I'm ready for whatever it is." My voice is steady and full of confidence. For once, I'm okay with who I am.

CHAPTER 71

THANA

The scent of rotten eggs and sulfur fills the room. My eyes scan the interior of the restaurant, searching for what's causing the stench. Christian and Gage quickly don their own armor and stand at the ready.

"Now, now, my queen. Put down your sword. Let's have a conversation." The silken words wrap around me, trying to seduce me to succumb to his will.

Rolling my eyes, I tap the sword on my hip. Bael doesn't know I have Daybreaker back from Gage. And I have no issues using it in the middle of a public establishment. "Why would I have a conversation with Lucifer's right-hand man?" My words flow like venom from my lips as I stare into the abyssal orbs of the sharply dressed man before me.

He looks like a quintessential Mafia prince with his silken hand-kerchief perfectly folded in his pocket, ostentatious diamond cuff-links at the edge of his sleeves, and the impeccably tailored Armani suit accentuating his broad shoulders and narrow waistline. If he wasn't a minion of my enemy, he'd almost be attractive.

"My queen, all I want is what's best for the Realm. And you're the one who could temper Lucifer's rage," Bael says as he motions to the table next to him.

Rolling my eyes, I motion for my mates to retake their seats on the bench as I place myself between Bael and them. "What you say may be true. But why would I want to be his queen when I already have five kings at my side?" I say, patting Christian's shoulder.

"They are no kings," he exclaims at the top of his voice, causing the glassware in the restaurant to shake and shatter. At the booming of his voice, several people who were balanced in precarious positions fall over onto the floor. It appears he's not strong enough to both hold the room and express his rage. Something else must be distracting him if he's unable to hold the room the way he was before.

"I'm guessing boss man's not happy, is he?" I walk around the room, making sure the other patrons are safe. I watch Bael's right eye tick when I mention his boss not being happy. I must have hit the nail on the head with that one.

"I've been sent here to collect you and bring you to my master, and that's what I intend to do." His voice is deep and guttural, with a growl to it that is all too familiar of the demons of the underworld. His face morphs and shifts from the handsome man to the demon he truly is. He loses his glamor for only a split second, but I see his wickedness underneath the façade.

Glancing back at my mates, I speak to them through the mate bond and tell them what I'm planning. I'm about to remove Bael and us from the middle of the restaurant.

I wouldn't want any innocent bystanders harmed because of the little tantrum he's throwing. With a wave of my hand, I open a portal and then, by sheer force of will, I throw everybody through it.

Once everyone is on the other side, I walk calmly in behind them. Christian stutters when he realizes where he is. "I've thrown us into the Shadow Realm," I state matter-of-factly.

Bael looks around, shocked. He wasn't expecting me to throw us here. The minute my feet hit the blood-red sand, shadow creatures rise up around me and flank us. My most favorite beings are the demon wolves that come out of the woods. All three species of wolves come together and surround us. Each of their heads nearly reaches my shoulders as I stare at Bael.

His eyes widen, and he assumes his demonic form. As I watch him, I start to notice a few things. It looks like he's a crossbreed between three different demons. And it's obvious his mother was a succubus, or at least one of his parents was either a succubus or an incubus. Even with his red skin, his features are beautiful.

"Why are we here, my queen?" he questions as he frantically looks around. At that moment, I feel the power shift slightly as he tries to leave the Shadow Realm. But my will keeps him from departing.

"What have you done?" he bellows, and my realm does not react to him. My eyes roam over the creatures at my command before I look back at him.

"I took you from an area where you have control, and I put you in a place where you have none. Sucks to be powerless, doesn't it?" I walk around the interior of the circle my wolves have created. "My will alone controls this realm, and with that thought in mind . . ." I shift the surrounding sands and a great coliseum rises from the ashes. It looks exactly like the coliseum in the Angelic Realm where I trained.

Bael's eyes widen in concern as he stares at our surroundings. "What are you doing?" His voice is panicked as he sees the stark white marble columns rising. They gleam as if bathed in celestial light.

Christian stares at the coliseum in wonder, knowing full well he's seen this before in the Angelic Realm. He glances back at me, then spreads his white wings. He flies around the interior of the coliseum, and Bael can't help but watch him.

I growl to the wolf standing next to me, and the rest of the wolves and other demonic creatures quickly pour out of the coliseum. Gage steps just outside the coliseum but remains close by.

Now I invite the Archangels into the Shadow Realm. One by one, they manifest within the coliseum and surround us. Raphael, Metatron, Uriel, Michael, Gabriel, and several others, including Raziel, all manifest upon the pure white marble.

I look for my mates, the other Archangels, and then back over to Bael. "I may not be your queen. But this is my realm, and these are my people. And what you are attempting to do on Earth? That won't be tolerated."

The Archangels each move and position themselves before a pillar. I search my grandfather's memories for what they're getting ready to do. Apparently, each pillar is marked with their angelic rune, thus amplifying their powers.

There's one particular pillar in the coliseum with no marking. I move to it and place my hand on it. An elaborate, scrolled mark appears on it, and I conclude this one is my angelic rune. I do as the Archangels do, and I put my back to the pillar, spreading my wings wide.

In the middle of the coliseum, Bael becomes panicked, but he can't move outside the circle I've put him in. On Michael's command, we all begin to gather the holy light in our hands.

When Michael gives the order, we let loose with a volley of angelic power. Bael is struck and disintegrated on contact. The wisp of his soul floats within the circle, trapped, but unable to leave because of my power.

I walk to the orb, and then, with a flourish of my hand, I capture it.

"Such a paltry amount of power for the right hand of the devil himself." I consider the size of the orb and the amount of magic within it.

Its relatively small size really causes me to wonder how much power Lucifer actually holds. If this is the size of his right-hand man, he probably can't be much more powerful than this because it wouldn't take much to control somebody with this little power. So many thoughts are running through my head at this moment, I just can't focus on them all at once.

A large hand encompasses my shoulder, and I look up and see Metatron. His blue eyes sparkle with his inner light as he stares down at me. "What's troubling you, love?" he whispers to me as he bends down and presses his lips to my forehead.

"Total swoon moment," I say softly and then turn into him and wrap my arms around his waist, resting my head on his massive chest. I take a moment to listen to his heart thudding away.

"I'm wondering about the extent of Lucifer's true strength. So far, all I've seen is a lot of deception. Tricks with smoke and mirrors, and nothing genuinely omnipotent. You'd think the first fallen one would be a lot more powerful than he is." Shrugging, I look up at Metatron.

"Seriously though, instead of doing the dirty work himself, he's sending out these low-level minions, who I'm guessing are more disposable than anything else." Stepping out of his hold, I begin to pace.

"Lilith wasn't all that impressive by herself either," I say, as I return to him to snuggle and rub my face against his pecs. I sigh, holding on tight to him and feeling comforted for a little while.

"What do you mean, Lilith wasn't a big deal?" Raphael asks from behind me.

I turn in Metatron's arms, continuing to rest my back against his chest as I look at my other mates. "To be perfectly honest, it wasn't that hard to kill her," I say as I shrug my shoulders, still surprised about that myself.

"She was always a formidable opponent. I wonder what changed," Michael says from the side as he brings Gage back within the coliseum walls.

"Not sure what changed, but she's diminished. Or should I say they diminished her before I destroyed her?" I roll my eyes and shrug again.

"Samael could never defeat her," Uriel says as he steps closer to the rest of us.

"That's interesting." I tap my finger on my chin. "She didn't pose much of a threat to me." I nibble on my bottom lip as I think about that. "I can't decide what's different." Based on my grandfather's memories, I expected an all-powerful being when I faced Lilith. But she was nothing more than a whore with claws and an attitude.

Gabriel moves forward but stops several paces away. "I'm gonna broach the subject nobody else wants to touch." He looks at me and motions for Uriel to step forward and place a hand on me.

"How are we all here?" he asks his question plainly, making his intention clear so he receives the answer he desires.

I look at him, then over at Uriel. "You are here by my will alone. I created a place within my realm that's safe for all of you to be. If you step outside the columns, you'll be fried," I tell them plainly.

"Now, I can do for you what I did for Christian and give you each a ring which will grant you passage through my realm. But I'd have to infuse it further for you to be able to go into the Hell Realm." I look deep into Uriel's eyes, letting him see I speak truthfully and am not hiding anything from him.

He studies me for several moments, then smiles. "What Thana says is completely true. She's the one who granted us passage, and she's who is safely keeping us here." He walks away from me and puts his hand on one column, then looks out beyond at the marble border. Plucking a single feather from his wing, he tosses it out between the columns into the Shadow Realm. The minute it leaves the marble border, it immediately disintegrates.

"I'm not sure how she's capable of doing this, but she is, and I trust her." Uriel moves and kneels before me.

"Please grant me passage into your realm so I can be of assistance to you when you need me," he requests with reverence as he looks up and offers me his hand. I reach back to my wing, pulling out a curled feather close to the bone and wrap it around his ring finger. As I speak the words

I did earlier for Christian, the feather becomes an obsidian ring marked with the same rune on the marble. Smiling, I motion for him to pass between the marble columns and out into the Shadow Realm. With blind faith, he walks between the columns and steps out onto the blood-red sand. He flexes his wings several times, still safe and in one piece.

"It's the dawning of a new era, Gabriel. And I intend, with the Archangels' and your help, to bring all those who wish to ascend back home." As I say the words, they reverberate around the coliseum, imitating Metatron almost perfectly.

My big softie smiles broadly, proud of what I'm doing. The only one not smiling is Gabriel, who stares at me with narrowed eyes. "How are you able to do that? You've been doing it since before you bonded with Metatron, and he could speak to you before there was even a bond in place."

I shrug. "Honestly, I have no clue. Perhaps Sandalphon knows. Perhaps Metatron was preordained to be my mate long before they created me. Maybe it was written in the stars by the big guy." I raise my hands in the *who knows?* pose. "Maybe he needs a speaker in Heaven and Hell." I laugh at myself and look at my wings, flexing them several times.

"Let's face it, we're not privy to his divine plan. For all we know, this was written in the stars eons ago. It just wasn't time for me to be here yet," I say with a calmness and peace in my heart. I feel the rightness of my words.

"For once, I can genuinely accept the path they put me on. With all the trials and hardships I've dealt with and all the damage I've sustained, I know everything happened with a purpose and a lesson behind it. I've learned to have temperance and patience. I've learned to forgive. I've also learned the full level of my internal strength." Flexing my wings, I move around the interior of the coliseum, looking at each of the angelic runes closely.

"On one side, it was good for all the bad things to have happened to me because it gives me a sense of justice so I won't allow those things to happen to anyone else. But on the other side, I realize part

498

of me is broken, and it's okay to not be perfect." I smile at the Archangels as I pull feathers from my wing and offer it to them.

They each step forward, including my mates, and I speak the words over the feathers, granting them passage into the Shadow Realm. "For now, please return home and make sure my daughters are safe. I'll be back shortly, and then we'll begin our assault." As the last word falls from my lips, everyone except my mates vanishes.

Stepping forward, I make sure to kiss Raphael as well as Christian soundly on the lips, pushing my love to them. The only one who remains behind is Gage, who looks out over the burned blood-red sands of the Shadow Realm. "Lucifer has no clue what he's started, does he?" he asks, arching a brow. Finally, he's getting his bad-boy swagger on.

"He has no bloody clue what he's started," I say with the utmost confidence, for once. Then I grip Gage's hand, bringing us back to the Angelic Realm.

CHAPTER 72

THANA

I follow the angels back to the Angelic Realm with Gage in tow, and Cyrus and the girls run to me, welcoming me back to our temporary home. I reach down and pick up Davina first, hugging and kissing her. Then I hold her tightly to me, telling her how much I missed her. Next, I scoop up Nikita and repeat the process, snuggling my little girl to me, and hug and kiss her and then, also tell her how much I missed her. I gently sit her down, trying to be mindful to not favor one daughter over the other. I suspect I feel closer to Nikita because of our wing color versus the fact that she's my child.

I make a mental note to make sure to be conscious about spreading my affection more evenly between them in the future and to find something special I can do with Davina daily, such as practicing with the holy light. Sigrun shows up at the house and takes both girls out for the afternoon. Because of where the Valkyrie live, it's far enough away, and it's a place where the angels dare not tread. So she's taking the girls for the day for their flying lessons.

Sooner than later, they'll be adults, and against my better judgment, they'll be entering the Mate Trials. Sadly, it'll likely be within the next three to five years, many years before I'm ready. Drawing everyone to the dining room, we gather around Michael's round table. I run my fingers over the ornate carvings of the edge of the table again. They mystify me every time I see them. But when I only study them for a brief time, they look different, and I see the translation for once, which is kind of odd.

Michael taps me on the shoulder and smiles. "Your eyes are chrome. What are you staring at so hard?" Double-blinking, my eyes return to normal, and I look back at the table again.

"The carvings on the edge of your table are interesting. The runes previously could not be read. Although now, I can read them but only when my eyes are chrome, not like this." Motioning to my human eyes, I say this more with curiosity than anything else.

He smiles and begins to laugh. "Well, they are angelic runes, after all. Neither humans nor demons can read them."

Then I realize the eyes of the Destroyer can see both the angelic and the demonic. "That's why I'm able to read them." Nodding my understanding, I take a seat at the table.

Uriel, sensing my intention, brings over the large metal bowl he uses for divination. He places the bowl in the center of the table, then fills it with two large pitchers of water. Once it's filled, he passes his hand over the water, and the furthest he can see into the lower realms comes into view. It now reaches to the Shadow Realm, where I've granted him passage.

"I'll need your help with this next part." He smiles and motions to the bowl in front of him. Understanding what he's getting at, I stand up and move over to the bowl.

I speak the words, opening our view to the Sloth realm, where Abaddon rules. This ring is horrid. There are pits of snakes where they force people to dance, torturing them with constant movement in punishment for their damnation.

We watch Abaddon mulling through the pathways between the pits, kicking the sinners deeper into the pits when they struggle to get to the edge. The snakes writhe and coil around their victims, pulling them back to the center of the pit, nearly drowning them in their scaled bodies. It's interesting that in Abaddon's realm, he's surrounded by snakes, yet he walks around on two legs.

When I furrow my brows, Michael catches onto what I'm staring at. "His true form is like that of a Marilith, half-snake and half-human. He chooses to walk around on two legs because it's easier to kick the sinners back into the pits." I digest this information and stare at him.

I pass my hand over the bowl again, investigating deeper into his realm. On the far side of the realm, where his castle is, his people move around in snake-like bodies with four arms and heads like Gorgons made of snakes. "This won't be a simple task, will it?" I pose my question to the group, not just one individual.

"No, it won't," Raziel says as he arrives in the room. "If you're not careful, their gaze can turn you to stone."

I see patterns in the snakes' movements on the top of their heads. "Think about the Greek and Roman myth of Medusa when you look at them." I hum to myself as I walk around the table, continuing to watch the creatures as they move about. "Only one creature is immune to them." The words fall from my lips as I stare at the water, watching the Mariliths slither around the interior of his castle.

"Yes, but where will we get a Basilisk?" Raphael asks, throwing his hands up in the air. Frustration radiates from him, pulsing off him in waves, almost knocking me to the ground with its oppression. A sense of hopelessness rolls off Christian. He's worried and concerned that those of us who go into that castle might never come back out again. Cyrus and Gage stand shoulder to shoulder, worry etching their brows as they stare at me and then occasionally glance at each other, their eyes pulsing black as they converse telepathically.

Metatron sits with a sly grin on his face, knowing full well I've got a trick up my sleeve I've yet to expose. "I know where to get a Basilisk," I tell them flatly and turn my eyes to that of the beast coiled deep inside my chest.

Gabriel drops the glass in his hand the minute he sees my eyes. Michael grips the edge of his table in shock and stares. Uriel simply nods, looking at me and knowing what this means for me.

"But you'll never ascend," Raphael says, gripping both my shoulders and shaking me.

Weakly, I smile at him and then kiss his lips softly, trying to push all the love I have for him through the bond. "I know." I bite my bottom lip and rest my forehead against his. "You angels and Archangels have taught me one thing. Sacrifice one for the good of all. Gage taught me that self-sacrifice for those who you love is the greatest way to show you love them. He sacrificed his chance at Elysium to keep Cyrus, Nikita, and me alive. So, if I have to sacrifice walking through the pearly gates to keep you and my children safe, I will."

I grip the sides of Raphael's face and stare up into his eyes, turning mine back to their pale-gray color. "I'd do it a thousand times over to make sure that you, my other mates, and my children will be safe for eternity. No one should have to worry about being hunted their entire lives."

Breaking away from a stunned Raphael, I move to stand before the bowl again. "If Grandfather's memories serve me, there is a demonic sabbath coming up on the thirteenth. It's a full moon. It's also called a 'blood moon,'" I say as I think about what day would be the best day to strike.

I keep moving the vision around the Sloth realm, looking for any points of weakness, and the only one I see is the north tower of the castle. It seems to be barricaded shut. And as I search further, breaking through the barrier on the north tower, I find a treasure trove of weapons. I suspect these are weapons Abaddon seized from his generals to make sure no one stabs him in the back.

"One thing about Gorgons is, even though they're poisonous, they're not poisonous to each other. So it seems that disarming them of physical weapons would remove the only thing they'd have to use against each other." Moving the vision around the interior of the weapons cache, I'm impressed with what I find there.

"What are your thoughts on this, Raziel?" I glance up and over the bowl at him, waiting for him to impart some great knowledge.

He stares at the castle as I move it around, showing him every potential entry point. Then I move it around the realm as a whole, showing him how wide open it is, with little to no cover. Shaking his head, he stands and begins pacing the room with me. "I hate to say it, Thana, but you're gonna have to go in hot and cause a distraction. Then the rest of us will follow in behind you."

Gage, Cyrus, and Christian all yell "No!" at the same time. I raise a hand and silence them for a moment.

"Unfortunately, for the safety of everyone," I stop my pacing and turn to face them, "I need to go in first. The armor of the Basilisk is unrivaled. There is no single weapon out there, besides possibly Daybreaker, that can break through the thickness of its scales." Grinning smugly, I lean on the wall behind me.

"The minute I use the Basilisk's stone gaze, the battle is over. No one will be able to stand before me, not even the Gorgon," I continue with the utmost confidence as I fish through my grandfather's memories.

"I never planned to walk through the pearly gates. Not with Nikita, Cyrus, and Gage being in my life. It wouldn't be fair to them for me to leave them behind to enter the Silver City." Smiling, I push off the wall to lean against the table.

"I'm sure if the Creator wishes an audience with me, he'll meet me at the gates. Or grant me passage for the day," I say as the words tumble out of my lips. I think about the ramifications of what I'm planning to do. To assume this form blocks me from the pearly gates forever. The dark side of me is like, *yeah, whatever.* The light side is like *no, we need to have that option.* I shrug to myself at the internal battle I'm having. It really doesn't matter what I want. It's what needs to be done.

I gather a mix of light and shadows in my hands. The orb seems to have a life of its own, pulsing almost perfectly in time with my heartbeat as it stretches out, intertwining the light and the shadows as it enlarges enough for a human to step through. Once it's the same height as me, I touch my hand to the center of it, and a portal into my castle in the Shadow Realm opens wide. Looking between my mates and the Archangels, I motion for everybody to move forward and pass through before me.

"This has never been done," Michael states flatly as he motions to the portal before him. "Not even your grandfather could achieve this. Most times, he would have to travel to the Earthly Realm and pass through the portal from there to his realm." Shrugging, I just motion to it again.

"Well, I'm a quick study, and apparently a lot stronger than we originally thought. But if you'd be so kind as to pass through now, since I'm straining to hold it open here, that would be greatly appreciated." Sarcasm drips from every word I speak, and the other guys laugh softly.

Michael doesn't like things that are outside of what he considers appropriate. And evidently, a hybrid like myself, a manufactured Destroyer created by his boss and apparently my grandfather, is another thing that's not high on the list of things he's comfortable having power. Gabriel, Uriel, Raziel, and my mates pass through. I watch them gather in the war room and take their seats at the table. I motion to Michael again, and reluctantly, he passes through next. Shaking my head, I follow through last and then shut the portal directly behind me.

"Now that we're all here," I say as I round the table, "let's plot our next move."

I'm calm, and my voice is slow and measured. In this realm, I'm more powerful than everyone standing before me. Several demons walk in, carrying trays of refreshments. Three of the pitchers contain only water, and two contain blood. I remove the pitchers from the trays and set them on top of the table and then send my demons back for the plates. Being the wonderful hostess I am, I pour the water into the glasses and slide them across the table to the Archangels and the angels gathered before me. For Cyrus, Gage, and myself, I pour goblets of blood. Gage is still adjusting to the idea of having blood in his glass and that it's something he's able to drink.

"So, my love, what's your plan?" Raphael asks as he stands up, raising his glass of water to me.

I motion my hand over the slate of the table in front of us, and the stone rises up, forming an intricate map in three dimensions before us. I pull aside my grandfather's maps, the ones I can put those unique little chess pieces on and watch the princes move around in their realm. I reach over to the side and grab the piece specifically for Abbadon, prince of the Sloth realm. Carefully, I set his chess piece on the stone map and watch it slide across the tabletop to the precise place he's currently located. He moves within his castle between the upper floor and the rooftop, as if he's watching for something to come to him.

I motion and move the map to focus on the construction of the castle. As he switches between layers of the castle, the map changes so we can see precisely where he's at. He moves between an impressive library and what looks to be a telescope on the rooftop. "I wonder what he's looking for," I say to no one in particular.

When I look up and around, I crack up. All the Archangels stand there, stupefied and staring at the map as it keeps manipulating itself to follow the princes of Hell. "I can only suspect he's looking for one thing," Metatron says as he motions to the piece moving between the library and the telescope on the rooftop.

"He's watching for you." Metatron drops that bomb, then leans back against the wall, waiting for it to sink in.

CHAPTER 73
METATRON

As the realization hits me that Abbadon is watching and waiting for my mate, the hairs on the back of my neck stand on edge, and the urge to become more protective than I already am grows fiercely, like a burning inferno in my chest. Flexing my shoulders, I try to relieve the tension I'm feeling about not being able to be at my mate's side at all times. I pace the room, staring at the map in the center of the table, trying to parse out the best course of action to deal with Abbadon.

This creature was once with us up in the Silver city behind the gates, and now, he serves in the darkness down below, in the deepest depths. His tactical mind is likely so twisted there's no returning to the man that he once was. It irritates the hell out of me, thinking that someone who was once amongst us now serves with Lucifer. I watch him moving between his rooftop telescope back down into the library. He circles one section in the library's corner. That makes me wonder what books he has stored there and which ones he's using to figure out exactly what's going on up here.

What I said before about him watching and waiting for Thana was 100 percent accurate. If I were him, and I knew there was one person in particular coming after me to kill me, I'd keep a weather eye on the horizon and watch for their arrival, so I could hopefully send my legions out to meet them before they could get to me. Tactically, it's the best idea to sit there and keep an eye out, watching for your enemy to arrive.

My only thought beyond that is what other securities he could have in place within his castle to protect him from anyone invading his realm. Or is he so egotistical he believes his strength within his domain alone is enough to protect him from what's possibly coming after him?

Lithe hands rest on my lower back and then slide up both my shoulders. They move across the tops of my shoulder blades and over the ball of my right shoulder. Then Thana is finally standing before me. She reaches out and takes both my hands into hers and stares up into my eyes, her pale gray ones glittering and shining like the edge of a finely polished sword. There's a great depth of knowledge behind those eyes. Years of infinite wisdom I'll never understand because no one knows exactly what the former Destroyer, her grandfather Samael, knew before his passing.

In the many millennia since Samael last stepped foot inside the Silver City, none of us truly knew exactly what was going on with him or in his mind. It's one of those things you wonder about. Then you realize, at one time, you all were really close. But then, because of time and the wear and tear on the world, and because jobs and responsibilities changed for everybody, suddenly, those who used to be very close to you are not close anymore.

Her hand slides and moves up to the top of my chest and up my throat, finally resting on my cheek and directing my attention down to her. I feel a gentle tug on my beard and can't help but smile down at the little powerhouse before me. "You're in deep thought again. What's bothering you right now? Talk to me," she whispers as she tries to caress my cheek, running her thumb over my cheekbone.

I can't help but sigh and melt into her touch, loving and enjoying the fact that my mate is fully focused on me right now. "There's a lot

I don't want to worry you about, but there's also a lot I know you need to know," I say in my habitually rhythmic way.

Thana giggles that musical laugh of hers as she stares at me and then tilts her head to the side. "I know exactly what you mean. Everyone always wonders what I know and don't know because nobody knows exactly what Grandfather knew all those years. But I'll tell you right now, any wisdom you want to impart to me, anything that would keep any of us and all of us safe, I want to hear. It's because I have infinite cosmic powers." She steps back from me and flexes her little arms.

Her biceps may be the size of my wrist. This makes me laugh, thinking here's this little female who has the power of the Destroyer, light and dark at her fingertips, who could easily smite everyone in this room. Here she is, quoting a line from a Disney movie she'd seen as a young woman. That genie, by the way, is absolutely hysterical, if I'm honest. "Yes, O' Destroyer almighty," I say and then bow to her with a flourishing sweep of my arms and grin at her. She laughs and ruffles my hair, which she knows I dislike her doing.

Thana smiles and bounces up on her tiptoes, pulling me down for a kiss. Her lips gently caress my bottom lip, sucking it slowly into her mouth. She giggles softly and then ends it with a light nip on the fattest part of my lip. I can't hold back my smile, loving and enjoying the level of attention and affection I'm receiving from her right now.

"All will be well, Metatron. Have faith," she says with a smile and then unfurls her wings, spreading them wide, flexing them several times before folding them back up again to rest against her back.

"No one knew what I'd become when I was born, except maybe you-know-who." She points up, indicating the Creator, and she smiles sweetly.

"I thought they'd have cut me down hundreds of years before now." She stares down at the ground for a few moments, making me wonder exactly how horrible her life had been. I'd seen, from using the cube, a lot of the atrocities done to her by not only the light but also the Dark Nephilim. This poor girl endured more in just shy of four hundred years than most do in thousands.

Reaching out, I pull her to me and hold her tightly to my chest. "I have to believe everything will happen the way it's supposed to. I know that's not always how things work out, but you can't blame a guy for hoping for the best outcome for his family," I say before pressing my lips to the top of her head and just resting there for several moments, hoping my words are heard. That someone greater than myself is listening and wills it to be so.

Thana wraps her arms tightly around my waist and gives it a good squeeze. "I have full faith we'll set everything right. It's just a matter of time."

I can't believe the grace my mate has shown with the weight of the world and the fate of humanity thrust upon her shoulders at such a young and tender age. She's closing in on three hundred and seventy-five years old, but that's just a blink of the eye compared to the rest of us. Our ages are beyond thousands of years.

I get a front-row seat to watch as she grows into herself and her powers day by day. And she never ceases to amaze me. Yes, she's had her moments when her emotions got out of control because she was overwhelmed and stressed and those who could have made her life easier only made it more horrendous.

She didn't exactly have the greatest parents, but I guess they were chosen for that specific reason. Something within their DNA was exactly what the Creator wanted to be passed on to attain the power she's been given.

It's a shame her grandfather passed on so early in their relationship. She didn't really have the time to get to know him as a person beyond just knowing that she was his descendant and that he was the progenitor of her entire bloodline. It almost breaks my heart to think she barely had any time to get to know him. Especially when what little time she had with her father, Nyx, was nothing but negative and horrible.

I wonder exactly what events shaped my mate into the woman

she is now, a woman who is loving and caring and giving, despite everyone in her life being horrible to her and mistreating her. Perhaps the old adage is true—that you put out what you wish to receive most. All she ever shows is unconditional love, faithfulness, and understanding.

I pass this knowledge on to the other mates within the bond, and they all have their own little *a-ha* moment over it. Everything Thana does is what she, in her little heart, wishes for the most. She wishes for love and understanding. She wishes for compassion, and she wishes for all of us to love with our whole hearts and show that love just as easily as she does.

By divine will, what is probably the perfect family for her has been created. And then it was equaled out by the falling of Gage. For that man to give up his chance at the Silver City truly shows the quality of the man he is. He gave up his eternity of peace to keep his mate, her daughter, and his lover alive. If that isn't the meaning of sacrifice, then I don't know what is.

Taking a page out of Gage's playbook, Thana is similarly willing to sacrifice herself to keep all of humanity and her family safe. So, if that's not the definition of an angel, then again, I don't know what is.

CHAPTER 74

THANA

After listening to Metatron tell me I'm being watched over and we take a few moments to snuggle, I start pacing the room again, trying to formulate a better plan. A tower sits across from where Abbadon has his telescope. I look at all those gathered here, then back down to the moving map. The prince of the Sloth Realm continues to move back and forth between his library and the telescope. Suddenly, I stop dead in the middle of the room and look at the guys. "I have a plan."

When I move my hand over the map, it changes. It now focuses on the tower across from Abbadon. I swipe my hand over the top of the tower a second time, and it shows the inside of the armory. "I'm gonna open a rift right here for you guys. That's where you're gonna enter from."

Before I can say my next sentence, Michael leans on the table to stare at the map, and then he looks up at me. "And where will you be?"

I moved my hand over the map again, and it shows the castle from an aerial view. "I'll fly in from here by opening a rift dead center in the sky. If I draw Abaddon's attention to me, the rest of you can make your entry into the tower without being noticed." I motion between the two places and how much distance I'll be keeping between us.

"Between him and his forces, they'll definitely come after me." I expand the map further. "Using my abilities, I'll summon the larger creatures of his realm to come to my aid. Once I summon them., we'll attack the castle's walls, keeping him distracted."

Running my fingertips over the outlying walls of the castle, I point to where I plan to focus my attack. "Your job is to go in and clean house." I resume focusing on the tower and raise it up again from the surface of the table. Running my hand over the side of the tower, I remove the bricks so they can see the interior and the layout of the entire side of the tower. They can see the pathways and how to get into the castle.

As they study how to move through the tower and down into the castle, I move my hand over the side of the building, raising it up so they can look at the interior of the second floor. Then, moving my hand over the top, the roof is removed, giving them the layout of the interior. Several places within the castle look like they hold small caches of weapons and torture chambers.

One torture chamber seems to be surrounded by white marble, which tells me one thing. Someone of angelic descent is being held hostage in there. "Your job, guys . . . I want you to focus here." The marble prison has a top that I move my finger over. "I don't know who or how they put an angel here, but somehow one is being held there, and we need to free him." My voice is a growling mess.

"I wonder who it is." Gabriel focuses his attention on that marble prison.

Moving around the table, Uriel stares at it. "Several brothers and sisters didn't make it back when we went to war to banish Lucifer to Hell. It could be any number of our brethren within that cage." He paces around the table, looking at the prison as if willing it to reveal its secrets.

"Especially since it's the first ring of Hell. It wouldn't be shocking to discover one of them survived long enough to be captured." Uriel taps his chin with his index finger as he studies the cage further and says, "I wish we could see inside there."

I wonder if I can see in there. I wonder if there's a creature prowling on that floor that I can focus on and use its eyes to see who's within the cage.

The marble prison is located in the room that I hover my hands over. As I focus on it, I can almost see clearly. Several creatures live in the room close to the chamber. Large abyssal bats hang in the far corner, resting and waiting for nightfall to take flight. I focus on the largest bat and push my influence on him to make him open his eyes and turn his head.

His head turns, and I have a clear vision of the room before me. I motion with my hand for the bowl containing the water to slide to me and get rid of the map. Once the bowl is in front of me, I pass my hand over it and dip my fingers into the water. Whatever I'm seeing now, everyone in the room also sees as I transfer my vision to the water before us.

I bade the bat to fly and get closer to the marble pillars. Reluctantly, the creature moves and then hangs just above the person. As he looks down, I see an Archangel. He has his head resting on his arms on his knees. His wings have been plucked nearly bald, and he looks to be skin and bones. I make the bat squeak and make noise and rustle its wings, trying to get the Archangel to look up.

When he does, I feel the shock through the bond when Metatron and Raphael recognize who it is. "It's Zadkiel. We lost him at the Battle of the Rift. They must have taken him prisoner and put him in there. But who would go through the problem of creating a marble prison for him?" Metatron asks, his voice filled with distress.

Just as I'm about to move the bat, I feel intense pain. The bat looks down, and I see it has a spear through its chest, then it looks back across the room. Abaddon has thrown the spear and harpooned the bat.

"I know it's you, Destroyer. Come and get me," he says just before a blackened mass steals my sight within the realm.

Blinking, I breathe deeply, trying to catch my breath and rub my chest, easing the pain of the impalement. "So let's review what we know. He's holding an Archangel prisoner." I raise a finger before pacing. I make a lap around the table before stopping again, looking down at the bowl. "Apparently, he has the castle warded to sense when someone spies on him." I hold up a second finger, then pace again.

Staring at the water, I pass my hand over it again. Scanning the realm, I focus on the creatures there. At that moment, I decide to give Rex to Gage for the rest of our attacks on the rings, since he doesn't have a familiar of his own. "We need to head to my castle. I need to outfit Gage with a familiar." I smile, looking at him. The utter joy on his face warms my heart.

"We thought you were leaving him with Christian," Metatron says as he looks back to the Sloth Realm, then up at me.

"I was . . ." My eyes blacken and then bleed chrome as I turn my gaze on Gage. "But I need you."

Gage moves to me without hesitation and hugs me tightly. Canting his head to the side, he smiles, looking down at me. "What does my angel desire?" His tone becomes husky with a slight growl to it.

"You and Cyrus cannot leave the Archangels' sides during the assault. I have a present for you when we return to my castle." Kissing his cheek, I step away from him and move to stand before Christian.

"Christian, *watashi no otto*, I need you to protect my most precious treasures. But Gage will return to assist you if you need him before we go into Hell." Gripping Christian's hands, I stare up into his dark-brown eyes.

"No, love. He needs to be at your side through the rings. Your mates will guard you more fiercely than anyone else." He releases my hand and caresses my cheek. "You are the most precious. They created you for a reason. They gifted us with you for a reason." His sincerity warms my heart and makes it skip a beat.

Christian is always the rational one and the planner of the group, not allowing his emotions to cloud his judgment. If he's agreeing that Gage needs to be with me as we go through the rings, then there's an excellent reason for it.

I look at the others and close my eyes for several seconds, and when I reopen them, they're chrome. "Let's go back to my castle. It's time to plan."

Moving my arms in a circular motion, I rip open a portal in the Angelic Realm leading to the war room inside my castle. The Archangels are the first to step through, and I hesitate, watching them head into my domain. Each one arrives safely and heads straight to the table with the moving map on it.

Just as Raphael is about to walk through, Davina and Nikita run into the room, crying and not wanting us to leave. Raphael, Cyrus, and I embrace our daughters, hugging them, kissing them, and reassuring them we'll return and that this has to be done to secure the future for them. They understand, but they still want to be by our sides. Unfortunately, as unstable as the Shadow Realm and the rings of Hell are right now, it's not safe for our daughters to traverse into the dark world.

Keeping my eyes chrome, I touch both my daughters' foreheads and share with them the knowledge of what's coming. I show them their ascended forms and bits of their future that I've figured out. I don't reveal to Nikita who her mate is, but I do show her working in the Dark Realms with me. Then Davina sees she'll be working with her father in the hospital. It's always been that someone has to replace him every so many years, so his infinite lifespan goes unnoticed. It's only right for his daughter to be the one to take his place next.

As I flip through the images, the girls gain a sense of understanding of the level of the importance of this mission. "Now, girls. I know it's tough. Mommy loves you so very much, and what I do, I do in the safest way possible for all of us," I say just before I kiss them both on their foreheads.

"Stay with Daddy Christian. Listen to everything he says. Spend your time with Aunt Sigrun. Learn to fly, and learn to battle from the Valkyrie. You're going to need it. And if I can, I'll make it so you'll be able to walk into a world that's safe and stable, hopefully, for the rest of your existence." I imbue my words with as much power and confidence as I can.

Even though my sight has extended far further than it ever has before, I don't know everything. There are still four princes left, and one of them is Lucifer. There's no way to tell what the outcome will be at this point because there are too many variables still at play. Maybe if I get two out of the four princes out of the way, then I'll know which way the tide of the battle is going and have a better idea of what needs to be done.

The girls launch themselves at me at the same time and hug me tightly around my neck. They tell me they'll miss me and beg me to be safe, and if I need them, to call. What can you say to that? The girls want me to summon them to assist. "I'll think about it, little ones. But for now, Daddy Gage is going to borrow your familiar, Nikita, that I will give you when you come of age." I manifest the black orb in my hand and hold it out before her.

"This is Maelestor Rex." Smiling, I look at the orb and the small dragon coiled in it.

"It's Rex. He'll be the one to protect Daddy Gage in the Dark Realm." Nikita smiles and nods, then kisses the orb. "Take good care of our daddies." The orb pulses with power for several seconds after Nikita speaks to it. Arching a brow, I stare at this. Perhaps my daughter is more powerful than initially expected. One last time, I kiss the girls' foreheads and push the last of my mates through the portal. I stand in the opening with my back facing my realm as I look at my daughters snuggling closely with Christian. I blow them all a kiss and then step backward, shutting the portal behind me.

CHAPTER 75

THANA

The portal shuts, and I stare entirely too long at the spot where I last saw my daughters. My thoughts are bouncing all over the place. One minute, I'm questioning whether what we're doing is the right thing to do, and the next, I want to get this over with and send whoever needs to go into oblivion there, while helping those I can save to ascend. Sadly, I don't think many will want to ascend. But I have to give them the choice.

Walking back to the table, I see the guys all staring at me, sensing I'm a maelstrom of emotions. Clearing my throat, I force a smile, then hold up the orb in front of me. "There's business I need to attend to before we can finish this meeting," I state clinically.

I watch the orb in my hand pulse with life and power. Maelestor Rex is one of the strongest dragons known to exist besides my niece Tiamat. And here he is in my hand as an itty-bitty orb. How this all will play out remains a mystery to me. But one thing I do know is I need to outfit Gage with him now to make sure my children have a future worth living. "Follow me, gentlemen. This will be something you'll want to see." I say as I grab Gage's hand and lead him out the door.

At the end of the hallway is the spiraling staircase leading to the top of the tower and a door outside. It seems like the stairs go on forever. Maybe it's because this is a pivotal moment for Gage, or maybe this is the moment that will change the tide in the history of the Dark Realms. Opening the door to the outside, we see many creatures flying in circles around the castle, each waiting for the opportunity to serve me, each one wanting and waiting to go to war and taste the blood of my enemies.

The Archangels are now getting a taste of the power of the Destroyer. But unlike my grandfather before me, I treat everyone and everything with respect and care. More species than not will fight at my side compared to how many did during my grandfather's time. Back then, they were reluctant to become involved in the Destroyer's plans. I don't know what changed him during the centuries he lived down here, but to me, it seems he forgot that at one point he'd been an Archangel.

My wings unfurl and spread wide, and the creatures all land along the stone walls at the top of the castle, watching and waiting to see what I'm about to do. "Gage, I need you to step forward and away from everyone else. Gentlemen, you might want to watch from the lower roof because this will be explosive." I wait for the Archangels and my mates to land on the lower level. The only one who remains up top with us is Cyrus.

"Gage, I won't lie to you. This will hurt. It's going to burn, and it'll feel like your insides are on fire." Wincing at the memory, I attempt to smile.

"What's the old saying? Baptism by fire." I raise my hand high, and the orb hovers over the palm of my clawed hand.

"As the Destroyer, I'm about to gift you Maelestor Rex. He's a skull dragon of great power and strength. During his time, his reign was undefeated."

Gage stares at the orb in wonder. "But then, how is he in there?" he asks. And I agree, it's a valid question.

"From what I understand, he sacrificed his life to save his people.

In exchange for his life in service to the next Destroyer, his kind have immunity and have been hidden away from the human world." Drawing in a fortifying breath, I steel myself for what I'm about to do next.

Passing my hand over Gage's armor, it disappears from his right arm. I look over the muscle and the striations in it as he flexes it several times before me. I find the perfect spot mid-bicep, where the muscles cross over each other, and I press the orb into his flesh. A blood-curdling scream rips from his lips as he drops to his knees, holding his hand over the spot where I pressed the orb into his arm.

I watch him writhe on the floor on the top of the tower as the blackened mass moves over his flesh, encapsulating it. With every beat of his heart, the ink spreads further until his entire arm is covered. Rex's head begins on the knuckles of Gage's fist, and his form spreads up his arm and over his shoulder. The outline of the dragon's body is immense. I pass my hand over the armor of Gage's upper body, exposing his broad muscular back to me. The bulk of the body of the dragon rests between his shoulder blades and down his spine. His wings wrap around Gage's rib cage, holding onto it and looking like the embrace of a lover. The tail of the dragon and the rest of its body disappear down Gage's back and into his pants.

For Gage's sake, I don't bother stripping him of the rest of his armor to explore how far down his body Rex has gone. I raise his arm up and run my hand over the scaled neck of the dragon. My hand then slides down and caresses the head, and I see the horns are pressed tight against his body. I step back and motion for Gage to raise his hand a little. "Rex, rise."

The power behind my words shakes the foundation of my fortress, and Rex rises from Gage's flesh in a black mist. The mist slowly manifests over the top of the fortress and takes the form of the dragon. Here, in the Dark Realm, Rex can assume his true size. The massive beast lands beside the fortress. His head rests on the top of the tower that's over five stories high. Walking over slowly, I caress the scales of his face and use my claws to groom them, removing the dead scales from around his eyes.

"Rex, this is Gage." I motion to my mate in front of him. "Gage, this is Rex," I say, motioning back to the dragon standing beside me. His huge horns look like a ram's horn with the deadly points facing forward, sharpened and honed like the killing machine he is.

"For now, Rex, Gage is your master. Once this war is over, you can rest again. Then, when my daughter is of age, I will gift you to her." Rex raises his massive head and looks down at me, giving me a single nod. I look back at my mate to see he's shocked at how sentient the giant dragon is.

"Rex is a wyrm dragon. He's the largest and oldest of his kind. At last count, he's several thousand years old. He traded his freedom for the protection and the continuation of his species." I run my hands over the scales next to me.

"In return, as the Destroyer, I provide him with safety and a place to be. His life is directly tied to the fact that a Destroyer lives, as do the rest of the familiars Cyrus and I possess." Gage stares in wonder at me and then up at the giant dragon beside me. "We have a war to plan, and Rex will help us take three out of the four circles."

Without warning. Metatron lands beside me. "Why only three?" He looks between the giant beast and me. Rex cants his head to the side, regarding my angelic mate next to me and not thrilled with the idea of an Archangel being in the Shadow Realm.

Reaching over and running my clawed hand over Rex's scales again, my eyes blacken to abyssal orbs as I scan the horizon. A wicked grin crosses my lips as I look up at my new giant baby. "Rex, love. There are blood worms in the northern quadrant of the Shadow Realm. Will you be a dear and go destroy them for Mommy? Eat as many as you want and bring me back the alpha's head. I have plans for it," I say as sickeningly sweet as possible.

Rex's giant, forked tongue reaches out and licks along the side of my body before he backs up and takes flight. The downdraft from the force of his wings nearly knocks everyone off their feet. Fortunately, I was prepared and held onto the wall when I saw he was about to take flight. The size of Rex blacks out the blood sun in the sky for several moments. And when he passes it, the light returns, shining back down on my fortress.

"Well, now that's out of the way," I say cheerily as I head back toward the door to head inside. "Let's finish planning how we'll storm the castle, take over the Sloth Realm, and then move down to the next one." I'm practically dancing as I move through the halls of the tower. The winding staircase is fun for me, so I skip down the stairs. I'm excited about being able to unleash a giant dragon in the world.

"Thana?" Uriel calls my name, and it sounds more like a question.

I stop at the bottom of the stairs and move out into the hallway to lean against the wall and wait for him to catch up to me. "What do you need?" Arching both eyebrows, I waggle them slightly before smiling.

It's interesting to see the Archangels out of their element. In the Angelic Realm, I have very little power or control. But here, the world bends to my will, and everything I deem becomes so. "You've just unleashed a titan in your realm. How do you plan on controlling it?"

"Your question has some merit." But again, I don't think he understands the full extent of the mantle of the Destroyer.

I motion for him and the others to follow me, and we walk back into the war room. I remove the prince pawns from the table and move my hand over the map to show the Shadow Realm. When I create the map this time, we see the giant dragon moving over the landscape. Everywhere Rex flies, we can watch him. Glancing over at Uriel, I motion to the map. "Any familiar controlled by Cyrus, Gage, Azrael, or me can be seen on the map if we've unleashed them." The Archangels stare at the map in wonder.

Being the asshole he is, Cyrus unleashes his raven and sends it out the window. Within moments, it appears on the map. It goes out, then it comes back. The thing goes out and comes back again. Rinse and repeat at least a half dozen times before it returns as a tattoo back on his arm again. "Now, *that* was cool," Cyrus says, watching the motion of the ghost tracings where his raven had gone.

The guys then notice there are ghost tracings remaining in the path Rex has taken. It's similar to the map from that wizard movie where you could see the footprints on it. We see dragon prints where the dragon was and feathers where the raven had been. And I assume there'd be paw prints where the wolves would have gone. I haven't tested the theory myself yet, but seeing what's happening with these familiars, I can only assume it would be the same with the wolves.

"This is certainly an interesting turn of events," Uriel says as he stares down, watching Rex. "You could do this at any time?" He says this more like a half question rather than an actual question, and I grin at him.

I try with all my might to keep my attitude to a minimum. "Well, yeah. This is my realm. I can do whatever I want here. The darkness fuels my dark side. The lightness fuels my light side. So if I'm in darkness, wouldn't it stand to reason that it would fuel me?" Despite my efforts, my last few words come out as a sarcastic question.

I don't know how much the Archangels are aware my grandfather has taught me, and at this point, I'm not ready to divulge how much I know. It's not that I don't trust them, but it seems I can go from zero to hero almost overnight. I feel like that genie in that children's movie with infinite cosmic powers. But thankfully, I'm not smashed into the itty-bitty living space.

THANA

After the meeting with the guys, I move down to the lower part of the castle. In what was once my grandfather's throne room, I stare at all his mementos lining the walls. I can only imagine the great battles he considered in this very room and the number of dignitaries and monarchs who visited him here over the centuries.

My mates and the Archangels follow me and slowly file into the room, taking positions along the walls. We all stare at the tile floor in the center of the room and specifically at the likeness of a giant raven, much like the one on the floor in the house we purchased in the Earth Realm. I'm always amazed at these coincidences. This one isn't as much of a shock as it would have been six months ago. I can only assume, at some point, a Destroyer or a reaper previously owned that house, hence the construction of the Celtic raven in the foyer.

"I'm planning to open the rift for you guys. It'll lead right into the weapons storage room, like we discussed. Once the last of you are through, I'll follow." I scan everyone present, making sure they're all in agreement about this plan.

"I still don't like you going by yourself," Raphael says with more force than I think he intended. I shrug, looking at him and then smile.

"I know. But there are a lot of things in this world we don't enjoy doing. Unfortunately, we still have to do them. Each of us has our own special abilities, our own piece in this puzzle, and are a separate cog in this machine." I walk to Gage and touch his arm. Within seconds, Rex is back where he belongs. I cause Gage's armor to manifest back on his body, protecting my mate.

I move before all the Archangels and raise my hands, opening up the rift before them. It ebbs and flows, pulsing to life. Then they see the armory before them. "I need you to go now. I won't be able to hold this open long." The Archangels move past me, heading into the rift and into the storage area.

I look back over to Cyrus and Gage and see them both shaking their heads and staring at me. I give them a single nod, accepting the fact my two Dark Nephilim mates won't let me go into this alone. Before the Archangels can argue, I close the rift behind them, sealing them in the hidden weapons chamber and the tower of the castle.

"It's time to go, boys." Once again, I open my hands, sliding them in a counterclockwise position, and another rift opens. We have a view of nothing but blood-red skies, clouds, and winged bestiary flying around us.

"Let's go make history," I say, looking back between Cyrus and Gage. Unfurling my wings, I launch myself through the rift and take to the skies. The moment I sense my two mates on my heel, I close the rift behind them so no one can gain entrance to my home. We fly on a straight path, heading directly toward the center of the castle. Suddenly, winged beasts launch from inside the castle walls, heading straight for us. Most are blowing flames of blackened mist. If I recall, these creatures have a flame similar to Rex's acid breath, and it will scorch the skin right off our bodies.

Without hesitation, I throw my hands forward and project the water of the River Styx directly at them, killing three on contact. The remaining five flying toward us stop and hover, waiting and watching to see what I'll do next. I growl loudly at them, allowing the eyes of the beast coiled tightly within my chest to become visible. Of the five, another three fall like stones to the earth. I say "like stones" because they're now made of granite, and they disintegrate upon contact with the ground.

The last two break off and take flight, disappearing into the darkness. Gage and Cyrus stay on my six as we fly toward the castle. All kinds of shadow beasts rise from the dirt and head toward the castle in time with my mates and me.

Landing about a hundred yards from the castle walls, the impact of my feet hitting the soil sends up a large plume of dust and dirt debris. Flapping my wings, I increase the size of the dust cloud to where it looks like a rolling storm on the blood-sand sea. The flap of my wings increases the mass of the cloud, nearly doubling it with every downdraft. The second volley of winged creatures emerges from the castle, trying to attack us, but they're taken down by the sandstorm I've created.

Gage and Cyrus flap their wings in time with mine, increasing the size and speed of the storm heading directly toward the castle. Several species of demons escape through the front door, heading directly for us. I can barely see them through the dust as it moves. Just before they reach striking distance, the bloodworms, like the ones I sent Rex after, rise up and eat their quarry whole.

I stop flapping my wings and allow the sand storm to die down and settle before us so I can assess the situation. They constructed the castle walls of bloodstone, one of the hardest materials in the realm of Sloth. I stare at it for several minutes, thinking about the best thing to attack it with, and then it comes to me. I don't need to attack it at all.

Being who I am, it should bend to my will. I extend my taloned hand out before me and begin turning it slowly, with my fingers fully outstretched. On the side of the castle wall, the stones move and reform themselves, and I've created a giant circular window through which to look into the castle.

The moment the hole opens, wayward spirits that were trapped in the serpentine pit fall out of the hole. The spirits of the dammed begin clawing their way across the sand, no longer able to stand on their own from all the years of being supported by the weight of the serpents' bodies. They writhe and scream upon the sand as they're almost scorched to death by the blood-red sun hanging above us. Their skin is ghostly white and devoid of coloration other than the darkness of the partial decay they've already become victim to.

Thousands of demonic serpents slide out upon the sand, coiling themselves around their previous victims, attempting to take them hostage a second time. Gage, Cyrus, and I stand and watch as the serpents reclaim their victims. The serpents team up to drag them back into what were their pits within the castle. Taking our cue, we stride across the sand to the hole I created. Raising my hands again, I create stone pillars resembling steps leading up and into the castle.

As we climb the steps, more snakes pour out as their ghostly victims continue trying to escape. "Don't let them touch you," I say to Cyrus, as one hand stretches toward him.

"Why? What will happen?" He moves his leg out of the way and draws his sword to slice off the arm reaching for him.

"That's easy. You'll begin to decay like they are. They'll try to drain your life, then take your place, and place you where they once were. It's how it's done." I manifest flames in my hands, burning and clearing a path before us so we'll be able to make it into the castle without being taken prisoner and swapped out with one of the lost souls.

Once inside, we face a maze of catacombs containing pits filled with snakes and multiple tortured beings, all screaming, reaching and writhing, trying to escape their eternal torment. Most of these beings have been here for tens or hundreds of years. Their time on this plane is infinite at this point. Carefully, we maneuver ourselves between the pits, keeping to the center of the walkway so the creatures trying to escape can't touch us.

Looking up, I see demons descending down the walls as if they're giant tarantulas. Some of them actually look like they're part arachnid. As they come closer to us, the boys draw their swords which blaze to life, and they fend off the attack coming at us from all different directions. For every demon slain, three more rise. It's a never-ending battle. I know Abbadon set this trap for us, knowing full well we'd go directly for the Archangel to release him from his interminable captivity.

If memory serves me, he's been down here close to a thousand years, maybe longer, depending on what part of the war they captured him in. Either way, he's been here too many years, too long for someone of angelic blood.

I reach over to Cyrus and let him know he needs to release his familiars. As he does, mine rip free. Gage looks at me questioningly, and I shake my head no. We're not ready to reveal the fact that we have Rex in this world. It would give away our ace in the hole when it comes time to escape. I'm not about to give away that secret. We battle forward, slicing through demons as we go and making sure none are left standing.

When I motion to the guys, they move to stand behind me as I spread my wings wide, gathering the angelic light in my hands. I unleash it upon the room, decimating the demons the moment the light hits them. Ash fills the air and falls heavily to the surrounding ground. Trudging forward, we make it to the marble columns, and I stare into the prison, studying the Archangel.

Behind us, I hear the rest of the Archangels arriving in the room we're in. "Secure the room. I'll get Zadkiel out of here safely." Looking over my shoulder, I see the guys approaching rapidly.

Metatron reaches out, touching the marble, and the palm of his hand is scorched. Raphael quickly reaches out and heals his injury. "What have they done to the marble?" Metatron asks as he looks at his healed hand.

My eyes churn into chrome as I stare at the pillars. "Demonic carvings are hidden under the marble." But when I place my hand on the marble, nothing happens.

Retracting my wings, I slide between the pillars and enter the prison. Zadkiel is weak and barely able to hold himself up. "I'm here to rescue you," I whisper as I kneel before him.

He raises his head slowly, and turquoise eyes bore into mine. He simply nods and lowers his head again. Unfurling my wings, I wrap them around him, infusing him with holy light and hopefully reinvigorating him. Raising my hand, I rip open a portal directly to the Angelic Realm. Sandalphon stands at the edge of the portal and frowns. "Is that Zadkiel?" His tone betrays his sadness.

"Yes," is all I say as I assist Zadkiel to stand and help him wobble over to Sandalphon. I pass the Archangel over to him, and he forces a smile. I watch them as they shuffle into the room beyond the portal.

Quickly, I close the portal and turn back to the guys. "Time to cut the head off the snake." I leave the words hanging in the air as I turn and unleash the full magnitude of the power within me. I bathe the room in a cyclone of shadow and light. Everywhere my power touches is cleansed of the evil and taint from eons of torture. I feel for the inhabitants of the castle, and I know exactly where my target is. Raising my arms, a table rises from the floor. The map of the floor above us is on it. Then it happens. Abbadon abruptly vanishes from the castle. Biting my bottom lip, a low rumbling growl escapes my lips. "Clear the castle. We hunt Abbadon next." The guys take off running, leaving me to my thoughts.

CHAPTER 77

THANA

Interestingly enough, I stand in the middle of the floor that held the Archangel as I stare at the map of the rest of the castle. I know exactly what I'm doing and that it makes me a prime target. Being down here by myself, I pretend to not be aware of my surroundings, but everything with eyes I've unleashed in this room since the guys have left enables me to see the room from every angle. My fingers trace the map, studying every room within the castle.

I hear the faint movement of rubble. I don't move, nor do I acknowledge the fact that I heard the stone move behind me. I know exactly what's happening. Abaddon has returned to the castle and is sneaking in from a secret passageway the Archangels were unaware of. It doesn't shock me that he faked his escape in order to kill me, since I'm the leader of our group. I listen and wait as I feel his presence creeping close to me.

One thing he's forgotten about the Destroyer is I can sense and feel all the darkness in the room. Every time it shifts even slightly, it sends out shock waves to me, making me even more aware of my surroundings than an Archangel. I understand now why my grandfather was considered the ultimate hunter since, like me, he was able to feel everything he's responsible for within his realm.

I stand poised and know that he's within striking distance now. His every movement is telegraphed through the air long before he makes it. The metallic slide of the blade sliding out of the scabbard at his side sounds eerie, like claws on a chalkboard. I don't bother moving. I know exactly what he's planning, either running me through or slicing straight down, trying to cleave my body in half. Just before he swings, he screams, his voice echoing through the room. Just as quickly, I vanish in a wisp of smoke. His blade comes down and fractures the table in half. The two halves crash down to the floor.

He looks around, confused, not knowing where I've gone. "Come out, Destroyer. You're nothing but a scared little girl," he yells as he turns in circles, trying to monitor the entire room.

His pets, the vipers, are long gone, and nothing else remains. The pits are empty, so he walks through the room, double-checking all the holes to make sure that I'm not crouched down in one. The mistake he made was not looking up. I hang suspended from the ceiling by my claws, staring down at him, using the strength of the shadows within me to cling to the stone above him. When he's finished searching the room, and he thinks he's in a safe place, I silently drop behind him and place my talons against his throat.

"Now, now, little fallen one. Is this any way to greet a guest in your home?" I whisper next to the shell of his ear, digging the tips of my talons into the flesh of his throat.

The sharp tang of copper fills the air as I smell his blood. It flows over the edges of my talons. "Do you not know who I am?" His baritone voice reverberates in his chest, vibrating mine.

If I wasn't so enamored with the idea of watching his blood run over my talons, I'd probably start laughing. "I know exactly who you are. You're Abaddon, the demon prince of the Sloth realm, a once fallen angel from the service of the Creator." I say the words mockingly.

As I hold on to him with the talons of my right hand, the talons of my left hand dig into his side just about where his kidney is, slowly adding pressure till the tip breaks the skin and blood begins to flow down his darkened flesh. "You know, killing me will stain your soul, and you'll never pass through the golden gates."

I laugh as I give him a little more of a squeeze with my talons at his throat and his side. "It's funny you say that," I whisper as I slide my head to the side of his, keeping my lips at the edge of the shell of his ear. "I have no desire to enter the Silver City and leave behind two of my mates and children. There will be no Elysium for me. I will walk in the in-between from now until the end of time. One day, I'll serve as my grandfather does now. Even after death, the Destroyer still walks." I leave those words hanging in an ominous tone.

I slide myself back and withdraw my talons from his throat and side. Casually, I walk around to stand in front of him and stare up, looking into his dark hazel eyes. "I assume at one time you were quite beautiful, like most of the angels. You can be beautiful again, and you can repent. They have given me the gift of absolution." Even in this ring of Hell, I'm able to manifest the holy light within my hands as it pulses with a life of its own.

"I can help you repent for all you've done and your transgressions against your brothers. And I can allow you to return to the Silver City, or I can smite you, here and now. And realize there is no resurrection for you." My eyes change from gray to black, then to chrome as I stare at him, seeing several slivers of light within his soul but not much beyond that. It might be just enough to cultivate for his ascension. Only time will tell if he asks for forgiveness.

I watch his resolve waver at the offer I've presented to him. Those two little slivers that I can see in his soul pulse, attempting to grow, but are stifled by whatever strangling darkness is within him. Unfurling my wings, I stretch them out and flex them several times. "The choice is yours. You can rise, or you can fall. All you have to do is take my hand." As the words leave my mouth, I extend my hand out to him while still holding holy light in the other.

"Ask me to absolve all your sins, then I can send you back." I stare into his eyes as I watch his resolve waver.

He looks frantically around the room, then back over at me. The sword falls from his hand and clatters on the floor, and he reaches out and places a hand in mine. "This is not the eternity they promised me. They promised me power. And they promised me a place to rule. This was not how I pictured it would be," Abaddon says as he looks down at his much larger hand engulfing mine.

"I wish to be forgiven for my part in the rising. I wish to return home and see my brother Jophiel again." Nodding my head slowly, once the holy flames extinguish, I place my other hand on his forehead.

The words I speak seem to reverberate in my ears and around the room, shaking free loose stone and mortar from between the bricks. When I utter the last word, his skin changes from its nearly dirty appearance back to what looks like a healthy olive tone. His blackened hair returns to a light brown. On his wings, the black melts away, bleached back to white again. The only difference between his wings and those of the Archangels is the border of black on the edge of all of his feathers, placed there to remind him this is his last chance.

Once done, I rip open a portal back to the Angelic Realm. "I cannot promise you Elysium, nor can I promise you the Silver City. You must repent for yourself. I can only open the gateway and give you the chance. Keep in mind you may still be smited on the spot." He gives me a solemn nod, then lowers his head and spreads his wings wide to me, showing his gratitude for this chance.

Several angels wait for him on the other side, shocked to see what the Sloth realm looks like through the portal. When he passes through, unfortunately for him, the moment his feet hit the clouds, he's incinerated immediately. Apparently, there was too much darkness in his heart. At least he tried. I close the portal, somewhat disappointed because it didn't work. On the other hand, at least I now know I can change them back to their angelic form. But it's up to them whether they can ascend. I can only imagine the hidden machinations going on in his head. He probably had plans to storm the gates and try to take over.

Shrugging, I turn to see my mates standing nearby and staring at me. Most of them wear a mask of shock. The only one who looks amazed by what I did was Metatron. He smiles broadly and crosses the room to engulf me in a hug. "You did well, beautiful. He was just not meant to return." He kisses my forehead once more and releases me to my other mates so they can hug and embrace me, making sure I'm fine.

"What's our next move?" Michael questions me, and I'm kind of shocked. One of the greatest generals of the Archangels is asking me, a baby compared to him, what we should do next.

I look around the room, then back over to him. "Part of me wants to return to my castle to plan from there because we still don't know what else is loose and able to get us here. But the other part of me wants to continue on to the next ring," I say as I consider our options, knowing there are still three princes left and three rings to cleanse.

Michael moves to me and takes a knee before me, looking up. "I suggest we return to your fortress. Tactically, they'll expect us to move forward into the next realm, so they'll be preparing for us. If we return to your fortress and plan our next move from there, they'll likely drop their guard, suspecting we might have given up. Or that we're planning for a different type of attack." Listening to Michael's words, I think about our options.

Charge forward with no intel, or go back and use the maps at my disposal. Study the next realm, then attack. Putting it that way and being able to lay all the puzzle pieces out on the table and study them, returning to my fortress seems like the most logical and safest path to choose. Without hesitation, I rip open a portal back to my war room. Silently, they all file through. I'm the last to step through, and I prepare to close the portal behind us. But just as the portal starts to close, I turn back to look at what was Abaddon's castle. In his impeccable suit, Lucifer stands where I just was, looking perfectly groomed, and smiling viciously at me. Taunting me yet again. I close the portal and raised the wards around the castle to make sure he doesn't attempt to follow us.

CHAPTER 78

THANA

I stand in my war room, staring blankly where the portal once was. Knowing full well I saw Lucifer on the other side. Large warm hands cup my shoulders and slowly turn me.

I look up into Metatron's eyes as he stares down at me, concerned. "What did you see, beautiful?" he whispers as he gently kisses my lips and then pulls me in for a bone-crushing hug.

I exhale loudly as I melt into his arms, wrapping mine around his waistline and holding onto my giant teddy bear. "Lucifer was in the Sloth Realm just as I was closing the portal." The words tumble from my mouth, and I still can't believe it. He was able to move between realms without me sensing him, which by itself concerns me.

Everyone clamors around, firing off a million questions at once. As if I'll be able to answer them succinctly and in rapid succession. I press my forehead against Metatron's chest and feel the thudding of his heart against my skin. Trying to use its rhythmic beat to center myself and calm the waves of emotions washing over me.

A part of me is inclined to go into rage mode and destroy everything in my path. But the logical part of me knows we need to be extremely careful and use precise timing and action so we don't harm ourselves or cause excessive casualties on our side. We have a clear-cut mission. With three more rings to take over, the end doesn't seem as close as we initially thought it would be.

Sloth was not as difficult as we expected, which by itself concerns me. I'm wondering if they sent Abbadon as a sacrificial pawn, handing him over to see what my true intentions and abilities are. Now that Lucifer has lost his guinea pig, he knows how to prepare in theory.

In future battles, he knows I'll attempt to cleanse the fallen and return them back to paradise. This may or may not have been a stroke of genius for him. Now that he's already shown his hand by showing up, in the future, I know what not to do. I won't be questioning anyone if they wish to ascend. I'll just go in, seek and destroy my targets, and that's it.

"We must cleanse the rings. We will return the rings to how they were. I'll put a new ruler in each of the castles in each of the rings, making sure that they're loyal only to me." As I voice these thoughts out loud, I feel Metatron's fingers running through my hair, trying to soothe me. This guy really gets me. Although my Dark Nephilim mates soothe the darkness within me, it seems he knows what to do to soothe the light that urges me to do the best at all times.

I am creation and destruction in one body. It's kind of tough sometimes to separate the two and take care of both sides equally. Right now, I'm hell-bent on revenge because of my grandfather being taken from me and my daughter having been abducted. But the creation side doesn't want to destroy everything. Instead, it's inclined to focus on the intended targets and nothing else.

Raphael gently extracts me from Metatron's arms and draws me to him. His white wings slowly wrap around me, and he holds me close, resting my head on his chest. He lightly presses his lips against my forehead and simply holds me. I need no words at this point. Raphael knows I'm at war with myself at the moment. Part of me wishes Christian was here with us, but the other part of me is happy because my daughters are in his care.

"I miss my babies," I whisper as I nuzzle my face against Raphael's.

"I know. I miss them too," he says as he threads his fingers through my hair. "The sooner we get this done, the sooner we can go home and see them." Always businesslike, Raphael puts everything in the simplest form possible.

Take care of what we need to take care of, and then we can go home. It's kind of like when I take him grocery shopping. He's in and out within a moment because he only hits the aisles he absolutely needs to. Shaking my head, I laugh and push against his feathers so he opens his wings.

"You are so silly, Raph," I say to him, tapping his nose with the tip of my finger.

"Why am I silly?" he questions with both brows furrowed, puzzled by my statement.

"You're handling this as if I sent you grocery shopping. There's a list in front of you. You just need to check the boxes off, get done, and get out. But nothing ever goes completely according to plan when you go to war, you know that," I say, smiling as I walk around the room.

Next to steal me is Gage, who pulls me back against his chest so I can still face the others. Cyrus moves to us and offers me a glass of what looks like blood, and I drink it, refueling myself for the battle ahead. "Only three things are certain while we're here," I say as I make eye contact with all the Archangels in the room.

"The first thing . . ." I hold my thumb up as I face them. "We know Lucifer is orchestrating this entire thing." The guys nod along with my statement because it's 100 percent true.

"Number two," I say as I raise my index finger and lean back a little further into Gage's embrace. "I have the most brilliant strategic military minds with me. So I'm sure if I go off script, one of you will reel me back in and put me back to task." The Archangels turn and high-five each other, acknowledging yet again another factual statement.

"Number three," I say as my middle finger rises, and I make eye contact with each of them. "If everything goes to hell in a handbasket, who you gonna call?" The minute I say that, I put both my thumbs to my chest, tilt my head and smile broadly. "Cause when in doubt, pull out the big guns."

My Dark Nephilim mates laugh, and Cyrus smacks my ass. "Settle down, lady. Settle down."

Grinning smugly, I look back at Cyrus and roll my eyes. His sarcasm game is completely on point today. To be perfectly honest, I'm not sure how to respond to him when he tells me to settle down. Walking back over to the planning board, I process exactly what's been done and what's left to do.

With three circles left, countless unnameable horrors have yet to be faced. We can't go into this blind. Every facet of this trip needs to be planned out with the utmost caution, right? Cyrus wraps an arm around me and holds on tight as he draws me back against his chest. "Whatever we need to do. We'll get done. Don't worry about it," he whispers softly against the shell of my ear.

All I can do at this point is simply nod and hope his assessment is correct. The next few circles will not be as easy as Sloth was. As we go further down, each ring will become more difficult. It may get to the point where I have to tell the Archangels to retreat. Mostly because I'm not sure if they can handle the darkness as we go further in.

This is not a subject I want to broach at this point. We achieved something minor today by taking down the Sloth Ring. But the further in we go, the less sure I am of what we'll face. I know I can handle whatever the circles will throw at me. I also know Cyrus and Gage can handle it as well. My concern is for the Archangels who are with us. For now, I need to table that idea and get everyone settled for the night. Plucking several feathers from close to my body, I hand them out.

"Pick a room and touch my feather to the door. It will become what you need." The Archangels leave to find their rooms.

I turn next to Cyrus and Gage. "Pick a room and enjoy tonight together." I wink at them as they head off.

I look now at Metatron and Raphael. "Bedtime," I say and take off, walking to the back of the war room with Metatron and Raphael until I reach the wall and press my hands against the stones. When I do, they move to reveal a staircase leading to parts unknown. They both arch a brow at me, questioning whether the staircase has always been there.

I smile mysteriously at them and remind them gently through our mate bond, *This is my castle and my home, and it will be what I need when I need it.* They nod, acknowledging what I've said.

We climb up the stairs, which wind and twist, almost like we're heading toward a tower. At the top of the stairs, a massive master bedroom sprawls out before us. I watch the guys as, before their eyes, a bed rises from the floor. Curtains drop from the ceiling, and the vaulted rococo design catches their eyes. It's almost an engineering masterpiece, what I pulled off in the few moments I've been standing here staring at the room, trying to figure out what to do with it. When the room is complete, I motion to the bathroom in the far corner. "Go get cleaned up. When you return, we'll go to bed." Short, sweet, and to the point.

Both of them run to get cleaned up as quickly as possible, not knowing what I have in store for them. To be perfectly honest, I'm not 100 percent sure myself. I move through the room, putting the final touches on everything, making sure it's fit for what I want it to be tonight. The bed is much larger than a California king. It's probably the size of two California kings put together.

The soft duvet on the bed reminds me of the blankets in Heaven, warm and inviting. I put the finishing masterpieces on and order room service to be brought up to us. Then, keeping in mind my angelic mates can't consume everything here, I open a rift to the

Angelic Realm and rush in quickly to grab several bottles of the angelic wine and fruits they can eat. After all, I don't want my mates to suffer on my account. After tonight, the journey becomes more perilous. If we're to die tomorrow, I at least want my angelic mates to know how loved they truly are.

CHAPTER 79

THANA

Walking around the interior of the newly created master bedroom, I move to the closet on the far side and swing open the double doors. I let my imagination go wild, and tons of new clothing appear inside the closet. I stretch out my arm and pull a blood-red nightgown from the rack. The fluffy ostrich feathers on the edge seem to dance on their own with the slightest breeze. The nightgown is a wrap, so with one pull of the sash around my waist, it'll fall wide-open. It's the perfect outfit for tonight. I shed my clothing and slip into the nightgown. I pull out the matching robe with the ostrich feathers also lining its edges and slip it on.

Quickly, I pull my hair into an up-twist and bobby pin it in place so my hair won't be in the way. I don't bother with the matching slippers 'cause they'll only end up annoying the crap out of me. By the time I step out of the closet, Raphael's already in the bedroom. He looks around, slightly unsure of his surroundings, with a towel wrapped around his waistline. A wicked grin curls on my lips, and I arch an eyebrow at him.

"What are you thinking, Thana?" he asks as I watch him tighten his grip on the towel around his waist.

A soft laugh escapes my lips as I lean against the post of the bed. "Gee, I don't know. Maybe that you're a little overdressed," I say as my voice drops to a sultry, almost breathy tone.

Raphael's jaw drops as he stares at me. Metatron then comes out of the bathroom behind him, also with a towel around his waist. "Why do I think we're in trouble, brother?" Metatron asks as he looks at me for a moment, then over to Raphael and then back at me again.

"If I didn't know better, I'd think trouble is her middle name," Raphael says as he motions to me, making the mistake of taking his hand off the towel. I practically sit there and start laughing as I raise my hand and snap my fingers, Thanos-ing the towel so it disappears from his body.

Raphael's eyes widen as his hands fly down to cover his crotch, and Metatron can't help but laugh at the predicament his brother is in. Rolling my eyes, I look at Metatron and start laughing too. "So, you think you're safe?" I ask him as I watch both of his hands move to tightly grip the edge of his towel.

"Yes, I think I am," he says with wavering confidence. He looks down at his towel and up at me with pleading eyes, practically begging me not to make his towel disappear too.

Shaking my head, I move to sit on the edge of the bed at the foot and watch them both. "What makes you think you're safe, Metatron? Raphael is the first mate, and he's not even safe from me," I say as I sway slightly back and forth, trying to look as innocent as humanly possible.

Sadly for him, he buys into the cutesy routine I'm putting on and relaxes his grip on the towel. And for the sake of theatrics, I raise my hand again and snap my fingers. In a matter of seconds, his towel disappears just like Raphael's did.

"Now, this really isn't fair," Raphael says as Metatron looks down at his nakedness, then shrugs , not caring about his state of undress.

I look at the difference in their stances, and honestly, it's not shocking. Raphael is the prim and proper one, the one who keeps everyone in line and tries to remind us all what's right and wrong.

Metatron accepts the existence of free will for those of us who are not Archangels. He's probably considering this is one of those situations where I'm exercising my free will. I chose to remove my mate's towel. Therefore, it is my free will to wish to see him in all his naked, celestial glory.

I smile as I look both my naked mates over, and I celebrate the fact that I'm a very lucky girl. Metatron's cock is in direct proportion to the size of his body. The thing is massive and definitely a world-ender if not used properly. Raphael's is also proportionate for his body size—just right, and a little on the thick side. That is, when he's not covering it with his hands.

Rolling my eyes, I stride across the room to stand before both my mates and place my hands on their chests. "We don't know what we'll be walking into tomorrow, or what we'll face in the days after as we hunt our prey. I'd like for us to enjoy tonight together. Because tomorrow is always uncertain."

Even though it's a rather grim topic to address when we're mostly naked, I'd rather throw it out there and let the chips fall where they may. I'd like to have a night together with them where we're not worried about what tomorrow brings. Where we're only worried about pleasing each other instead of worrying whether blood will stain our swords in the morning.

Metatron is the first to move, and he bends down to kiss my temple. "Angel, whatever you desire, I will do it for you. Be it my body, my heart, or my soul, they're all yours to command." He kisses me again and then moves to the bed and promptly throws himself into the center, sprawled out, hard erection standing up straight as if goading me to approach and ride it like a wild stallion.

Raphael has remained in his defensive stance with his hands cupped over his crotch. I slide my hands down his rib cage to his hips and pry his hands free from his cock. I say as I look up at him, "There is nothing to be ashamed of when it's just all of us. I understand how Archangels are and how you are raised to believe you have to have control over everything. You're the first mate, so please dictate tonight's actions." I kiss him on his cheek and then turn to walk back to the bed.

Nimble fingers untie the sash at my waistline, and I drop my red robe behind me. As I get closer to the bed, I untie the sash around my waist again and drop my nightgown, leaving only a little red lace thong on me. Metatron's eyes widen as he takes in the bounce of my breasts as I move toward him. Climbing on the bed, I crawl on all fours to him and gently kiss his lips, trying to goad Raphael into joining us.

Metatron rolls me, pinning me beneath him. His thigh nudges between mine, spreading them wide as he moves his lower body over me. The heat from his cock presses against the top of my mound as he grinds himself against me, making me wet with anticipation. He grabs my wrists and pins my hands above my head. With a wicked grin on his face, he stares down at me. "Now, now, beautiful. It's not nice to tease Raphael," he says as he presses his lips against my cheek, working his way to my ear and nibbling on the lobe.

I realize Cyrus and he have been talking a lot lately, and this is a pure Cyrus move that he's pulling. I almost don't want to know what my dark knight has taught this behemoth above me. The bed shifts, and I turn my head to the side, looking over to see Raphael lying with his head on the pillow and staring at me.

"Be a good girl and do as Metatron says," he whispers as he moves up to the head of the bed. Kicking the pillow out of his way, he takes my wrists from Metatron and holds them tightly. Glancing between the two men, I let the gears turn in my head, thinking about where I've seen this before. Oh yes, it was one of the pornos Gage and Cyrus were watching several nights ago. They claimed they were conducting research to get inspiration for new things to try when we're all together.

Before I realize what's happening, Metatron slides quickly down my body, nipping at the soft flesh beneath him till he hooks my knees over the tops of his arms and lines himself up with my entrance. The gentle nudging of his cock against my core makes me squirm, trying to get him in me.

Raphael's grip on my wrists is tight, and I struggle against him. I want to grab Metatron and push him where I need him most. I whine and thrash slightly, trying to rock my hips to impale myself on his length. His large hands grip my hips and hold them still, practically pressing them into the bed, and he shakes his head slowly at me. "Bad girls don't get what they want," he says as he looks down at me and smiles.

This is not typical Metatron behavior. I glance over at Raphael, and he rolls his eyes at me. Apparently, Metatron's trying to take on the dominant role in this scene. Raphael is struggling to keep a straight face through this. I know these two must have talked to my Dark Nephilim mates to get this bold. I stare up at Raphael and try to grip his hands. The sudden forward thrust from Metatron has me careening forward from the intrusion. He stays still for several moments to allow me to adjust to his girth and length.

I feel the familiar stretch and sting of him inside me. He eventually releases his grip of my hips to allow me to work myself on his length as I adjust to him. With every slow rock and arch of my body, I feel the tingles building deep inside me. Nothing is hotter than having two of my angelic mates trying to emulate the Dark Nephilim side of the family. When Metatron feels the slick heat of my core gliding easily over his length, he grips my hips tightly again. He begins pistoning his cock in and out of me, rocking the bed with every thrust.

My head practically bangs into Raphael's inner thigh, and his cock ends up bouncing off my forehead with every thrust. I don't think they thought this out too well when they planned where each of us would be. Raphael's trying his best not to laugh, while I'm trying not to get my eye poked out. And Metatron is going to town, giving it his all.

With every thrust, my core wraps tightly, feeling the familiar tingle of my impending orgasm. I try to buck against his grip, but it's no use. He's holding on to me like a sex doll. He has full control of me, and when I'm least expecting it, he flips me over onto my hands and knees, withdrawing for a mere moment, only to line up and thrust back in again, sinking balls-deep in me. I rock forward and face-plant into Raphael's crotch. And I get the bright idea to take his length into my mouth.

I balance on my elbows, now that Raphael released my wrists, and grip his length at the base with my hand, guiding him to my mouth. The forward thrust from Metatron drives Rafael's cock down my throat, almost causing me to deep-throat him. I partially gag, and Metatron drags us back down the bed a little so his third thrust wouldn't choke me half to death. Not having done this very often, I lick and stroke at Raphael's length, trying to gain the confidence I need to do what needs to be done.

I can't exactly have him sit there stroking his own cock, watching his nest-mate have sex with me. We eventually find a rhythm between the thrust and the strokes, and everybody moans with every thrust, making the hair on the back of my neck stand on end and goose bumps run along my spine.

Having two Archangels in the bad-boy role is as hot as it is naughty. In a bold move, Raphael threads his fingers through my hair and starts rocking his hips in time with Metatron's thrusts. I now understand what Aurora means by being completely filled on both ends. Thank God, my girlfriend is more worldly than me and explained how these situations arise and what I can do to make it pleasurable for everybody. I tap Raphael's thigh as I feel my orgasm about to crash over me. Just as he releases my hair, I rise up on my hands and scream as my muscles crush down and milk Metatron's cock for all it's worth. My alpha-lock kicks in, and a blissful, full feeling washes over the two of us. Being mindful of what this means, I make sure there's no way for me to get pregnant at this time. There will be no egg released, and there will be no child from this union, especially not when we're at war.

Raphael moves forward to help support me as I tire out from the burning, pulsing throes of my orgasm. Poor Metatron follows me over the brink almost as quickly as the lock traps him in place. He grunts, groans, and moans through his stuttering thrusts with every pulse of my lock on his cock. Eventually, the big guy falls over and takes me with him. I lay with my head on Raphael's thigh, attempting to rest and regain my strength. Round two will definitely be a doozy.

I must have nodded off, during which time the guys took the time to clean me up after my time with Metatron. Slowly, I open my eyes and see Raphael lying next to me and Metatron curled tightly behind me, holding me to his chest. I reach out to Raphael and stroke his angelic face. His eyes slowly open, and he smiles. "Feel better, baby?" I simply nod at him.

Then, I look at the large arm over my rib cage. "I guess the big guy wasn't ready to let go of me yet, huh?" I know the answer to the question before I ask it. If Metatron can hold on to me always, he would.

But being the good guy he is, he tries to be mindful that the others need me too. The guys worked out a good rotation between them. And everyone gets their night alone with me in our bed. With him being the newest, I understand his need is driven to prove he's worthy to be in the bond. But to be perfectly honest, each of my mates brings their own uniqueness to the bond. Raphael brushes my hair away from my face, then leans forward to gently kiss me.

"We don't have to do anything if you don't want to. I understand, after that performance, you might be a little sore, especially after alpha-locking him." I nod along with his assessment, but I'm not as sore as I thought I'd be.

"I'm okay, Raph. Honestly." When he just smiles again, I know something's on his mind.

"What's bothering you?" I ask as I play with a rogue strand of hair that refuses to stay out of his eyes.

"We have three more rings to get through. I'm concerned that the bulk of the angelic side might not handle this invasion well. They might not be able to deal with what's to come." I consider what he's saying and get the hidden meaning behind it. For them to have to see their brethren who had previously fallen must be emotionally taxing on them. Those they've fought side by side with, possibly been roommates or bunkmates with over the centuries who have now fallen from grace and are unable to return to the Silver City.

"I get it," I whisper as I feel Metatron stir behind me.

"When it's time to go for Lucifer, if you guys feel you can't handle it, it'll be okay. I'll be at my strongest in the ninth ring, drawing on the full darkness there. I don't think Lucifer realizes the wheels he set in motion by killing my grandfather, Samael." I feel Metatron's fingers running through my hair, and he kisses my cheek from behind as he pulls himself out of the bed.

"You have our sword and shield, my love. Never forget that, but if you feel it's safer for the angelic side to not follow you into the viper's pit, then we'll understand and accept." His voice hesitates as he says the sentence, and I know full well he doesn't mean what he says. He'd rather die beside me than sit home, waiting to see if I return.

I roll over and rise onto my knees at the edge of the bed, kissing Metatron deeply, pushing all my love for him through the bond as our tongues intertwine. We kiss for several moments, and it feels like it's gone on for hours before we break apart. "I understand what you mean, and trust me, the decision won't be made lightly. I'd rather you stand with me than without me. But if it's safer for you guys to not be where I am, then that's what I'll ask of you." He nods, understanding where I'm coming from, even though I see the reluctance in his gaze as he stares at me. He'd rather not leave me and would take his chances of dying rather than to send me into the depths of Hell.

When it came to the mate lottery, I'm blessed beyond measure. Each one of my mates brings a unique skill set to the bond. Metatron is the utter definition of faithful and devoted. Raphael is the one who is constant. He keeps everyone and everything in order. Christian is security-minded and always concerned with keeping the family safe —not just physically safe, but mentally and emotionally safe as well. Gage is very aware of my emotions and how little I worry about myself. He knows I put others before myself and reminds me to take care of me. Cyrus fiercely guards my self-image and has worked hard to help me accept myself as a total person. For ages, the image of being perfect and trying to ascend was drilled into my head by my mother and Joscelyn's mom. They tried to force me to ignore my dark side and only feed the light.

The mood in the room has shifted, and Raphael declines being intimate at this point because of the head space we're in. They drag me into the shower and decide now is the time to get clean. Sighing, I close my eyes as I lean back against the countertop, listening to the sounds of the guys moving around in the bathroom.

Eventually, large warm hands caress my cheeks and pull me forward to the shower. A second set of hands covers my eyes as we move forward. I know who is where, so this is more of them trying to take care of me than keeping me on edge. The smaller of the two sets of hands disappears from my eyes and the larger set replaces it. I'm pulled flush against Metatron's broad chest as he bands an arm around me.

A kiss is pressed at the top of my mound, and I inhale sharply at how bold Raphael is being. Metatron moves behind me and uses his feet to spread my legs apart. A tentative lap of Raphael's tongue across my folds up to my sensitive nub almost has me bucking out of Metatron's grip. "Be a good girl, beautiful. Raphael wants to take care of you," Metatron says into my ear as he nibbles at the shell. My greedy core pulses with excitement that my two Archangels are playing well together.

Raphael hums as he presses his tongue against my clit. The sensations moving through me have me gripping Metatron's arm tighter and trying to grind myself on Raphael's face. My hips rock of their own volition with every lick and long slow suck he takes on my sensitive nub. Metatron suddenly reaches down and picks me up, hooking his arms under my thighs to spread me wide for Raphael.

Raphael slides up my body, inching his way up my stomach, kissing every inch of flesh he can put his lips on. Metatron holds me tightly, suspended in air and wide-open for his best friend's perusal. Before I know it, Metatron lowers me down slightly and Raphael sinks his length into me. It's kind of weird that, of all my mates, these two have decided today was the day they'd do things together.

Every stroke of Raphael's cock brings me closer to the edge. Tingles take over my entire body, spreading throughout my limbs and making my core burn. Finally, his last stroke, where he angles his hips differently than the time before, sends me crashing over the edge. Lights flash behind my eyelids. Screaming, I lean forward and wrap my arms around Raphael's shoulders, holding on for dear life. With stroke after stroke, he buries himself deeper and deeper within me. Metatron assists by bouncing me up and down in time with Raphael. I swear, these two are trying to kill me.

Finally, Raphael's movements become erratic, hitting harder than he has before, and then without warning, he groans into my shoulder, burying himself deep within me. The pulses of his cock inside me send me over the edge yet again. This time, my muscles lock down on him, trapping him in my alpha-lock and holding him in place. I concentrate on the lessons I've learned from my grandfather's memories to prevent myself from conceiving. Part of me feels bad for blocking the chance to have another child with either of my mates, but waging world war and being pregnant at the same time is not an option.

Raphael's legs quiver as his body jolts every time the lock

tightens and squeezes his length. He's essentially at my mercy at this point. There's no possible way for him to escape. Metatron laughs in my ear when he realizes what's happened. He reaches forward and wraps his arms around both Raphael and me, picking us both up and carrying us over to the bed. He plops us both down, pulls a blanket over us and then smiles and waves goodbye, laughing the entire time.

It's moments like this I envy him for the level of confidence he has. I can't help but lie here watching him as he disappears into the bathroom to go shower. Raphael gently strokes my rib cage as we both wait for my lock to release him. Slowly, I turn my gaze to him and smile, pleased with how our night has gone. "What's on your mind, beautiful?" Raphael asks.

I smile and reach out to run my fingers through his blonde hair, brushing it out of his eyes. "Not much, to be honest. Tomorrow we go after Leviathan." I keep focusing on the strands of hair sliding between my fingers as I nearly distract myself from the topic at hand. Tomorrow could be difficult, and it's not a day I'm looking forward to. One more ring closer to our target. One more ring deeper into the circles. I'm not sure how the Archangels outside of my mates will handle the descent. It's a thought that's been plaguing me since I agreed to bring them along.

Tomorrow we rip open the portal to the next realm, and I'm planning to drag the angels and Archangels who've agreed to help us through it. But I'm second-guessing whether this was a good idea. On the other hand, it would be absolutely brilliant if they hit the dark forces with their light before they get hit. We'd be victorious instantly. Raphael reaches out and runs his index finger between my eyebrows, then down the bridge of my nose and back up again.

"You're a horrible liar, Thana," he says in a joking tone. "Every time you're deep in thought," he continues rubbing between my brows, right above my nose, emphasizing the area he's talking about, "this particular area creases." He smiles as he stares at it and then lowers his gaze to my eyes.

"Until we were mated, I had a hard time reading your facial features. Now, your emotions sing to me through the bond," he says as his hand slides down my face to cup my cheek.

I glance down briefly before looking back up at him. "As much as I want to leave Michael with the children and Christian, I don't think it's a good idea. Michael needs to be at our side, but I'm also concerned that after Leviathan, it won't be safe for the angelic side of our forces to be with me," I state as bluntly as I can as the thoughts of what could occur plagues me. The turmoil of emotion whips up, and I see the change in Raphael's features as he senses what I'm no longer hiding from him. He moves forward and presses his lips to mine, fusing all the love he has for me into that one singular kiss.

When he pulls away, he smiles at me and lightly nods his head. "I completely understand what you're saying. I've been concerned from the start about bringing the angels and Archangels into the rings with us. There is only so much you can do to protect everyone, even though the Destroyer is powerful." He leans forward and kisses me once more. I mull over his words and consider what he's said.

"Then, let's do this. We'll bring only those in our bond with us because I can definitely protect you guys," I say as I tap my index finger on my bottom lip, pondering my next move.

"I'm going to need you to explain to the Archangels it's not wise to bring them any further. If they want to remain here in the castle, they can be safe within the walls of my fortress." I look around my room quickly, then back over to Raphael. "The fortress itself will protect them, move the walls, and put up traps to keep its inhabitants safe." I slowly slide away from Raphael as my lock releases him.

I lie flat on my back, staring at the ceiling and reach out to grab his hand and rest it on my rib cage as I hold on to it tightly. "We need to make it back in one piece, regardless of what the outcome of the next battle is. We have children to protect and raise. I don't want them to grow up without their parents." As I finish my statement, Metatron walks back into the bedroom, carrying a tray of refreshments and snacks. This big guy seems to have a sixth sense and knows what I need before I think of it. I smile and sit up, throwing my legs over the side of the bed and wait for him to sit the tray between Raphael and me. When he does this, we pass out the drinks and the snacks and have a simple meal together.

"So, what's the plan?" Metatron asks as he picks up a slice of fruit.

"Things have changed," I say flatly as I stare at him. "I'm sending the angels and most of the Archangels back to the Angelic Realm. Those who want to remain here can stay safe within the walls of the fortress." I lift a glass of juice to my lips and take a long sip. "Drink up, boys. Tomorrow we descend into Hell."

CHAPTER 81

CYRUS

Thana is truly the best mate any male could ever ask for. Not only does she understand the relationship I have with Gage, but she's accepting of it. Never in my lifetime have I ever known a female who wasn't threatened by my having another person in my life. Then again, with Thana, it's all about acceptance and love. Even though she's half Dark Nephilim like I am, her heart is still as light and pure as those light motherfuckers. I guess it works out to my benefit in the end. Leaving Gage still sleeping in the bed, I wander through the hallways and down the stairs into the main foyer of the castle.

Down the hall, I hear Thana's voice echoing. It sounds like she's already started the meeting about the assault today. I hustle down the hallway and make several turns before arriving at her war room. Thana stands at the head of the table like a brigadier general, barking out orders with that map with the characters moving on it of their own volition.

As I approach the table, the Archangels look up. Their eyes are glowing golden as they stare at me. It's still as eerie as fuck watching them do that. My own eyes blacken, and in response to how they're looking at me, shadows roll off me in waves almost as a defense mechanism. As much as Thana says we can trust these guys, after all the years of being tortured and having issues with them, I still don't feel that way at all.

The ones within our bond aren't bad, but it's the other assholes who have come into our ranks to battle beside us that I still have issues with. As much as I try not to hold past grievances against them, there are some scars that are still wide-open from all they've done to my mate and me.

Thana looks up and smiles at me, but then she realizes something is wrong. She vanishes from the head of the table, and the next thing I know, she manifests beside me and wraps her arms around me tightly.

Through the bond, I tell her what's bothering me, and she looks at the others. Within a matter of seconds, we're gone from the war room and are in the highest tower of the castle.

Looking out over the landscape, she turns and looks at me. "I know there are years of damage and torment you and I both have dealt with. Sadly, it was at the hands of those who are more of the light persuasion than us." She says this matter-of-factly as she wrings her hands in front of her, showing how uneasy she is with the subject.

Without hesitation, I move forward and wrap my arms around her. I unfurl my wings and encase her within my black feathers, providing her the comfort I know she needs right now. "They did far worse to you. Especially since you couldn't defend yourself since those assholes kept you from using your wings," I say venomously, trying not to sneer through my words. I feel my lip curl up, almost like I have canines wanting to descend just to show my level of agitation. It's hard to restrain my anger about how my mate was treated before she came to me.

Even though we weren't mated when we were in the hospital setting, I still watched out for her as best I could. It wasn't right, the things those lowlife light bastards constantly did to her. To add a little fun and mischief to her day, I used to swipe her cookies and her coffee. Little did I know, in some sense, she actually looked forward to the minor interaction we had. One day, I didn't do it, and she looked around as if missing me not messing with her.

Having gotten lost in that memory, I smile and reach out to run my fingers through her hair. I watch her golden locks slide between my fingers like liquid gold. "Everything will be fine, kitten. And I'm sure, no matter what we end up doing today, we'll definitely outdo everybody on the light side of the family," I say with no hesitance in my voice.

I know Gage and I are more than ready and willing to do what's necessary to keep Thana safe from what may come. The only ones on the side of the light who will protect her are those within our bond. As unfair as that may be, the others have never lifted a finger to protect me in the past. I was shunned and mistreated, merely because of the color of my wings and who my father is.

"Cyrus," Thana says softly as she looks up at me.

The most gentle smile crosses her red lips, and I swear I see the future within her eyes. She reaches out with both hands, gently cupping my cheeks and standing on her tiptoes to press her lips to mine. If this is what Heaven is like, then I wouldn't mind taking the chance of burning in its holy light. We stay lip-locked for several moments before she draws back and stares up at me again. Her eyes cycle from gray to silver and then to black as pitch. The black radiates with a power I've never seen behind them before. Smoky tendrils move out from her eyes, giving them the most demonic appearance I've seen in the entire time I've known her.

She taps me on the nose and then laughs. "Today's gonna be fun, Cyrus." She giggles that musical laugh of hers as she gently puts her hands on my wings and pushes them open.

"Think of it this way." She motions to the world around us. "You could unleash your full fury on the forces we're going to face, and there will be no repercussions." The way she says it makes me think she's been thinking about this for quite a while.

"In this place," she says, motioning out the windows of the

tower. "I'm in control. I'm the ultimate power. These are my lands, and those are my people." She articulates each statement with a force her voice has never held before. She's finally fully comfortable with who and what she is, and it's beautiful to watch her ascend into her full power. There's nothing sexier than a woman who's confident in herself.

"Today when we descend, you'll lead the armies of the north, the Balor," she says their name, and I know she's giving me one of the largest and strongest armies possible.

I bow my head gently to her. "Thank you, kitten. You honor me greatly by giving me a powerful army." This brings a smile to her lips, and she can't help but giggle.

"Nothing but the best for my dark knight." Her smile is so radiant, like a thousand suns bathing me in its light. She looks back out the window and rests her hands on the stone sill. "Gage will have the army that Eligos brings with him. The dark knights of the realm shall be at Gage's command," she says.

"What will Metatron, Raphael, and the other Archangels command?" I ask curiously because honestly, I'm not sure what they can do down here.

Thana shakes her head and starts laughing. "They can't command crap down here. They're going to do what they do best and be foot soldiers. Their biggest job is to defend my flank and make sure no one sneaks up behind me. The wolves and demons will be under my command. I'll blacken the sky with all the dark denizens I can summon to me." I watch her eyes pulse with power and then fade back to her human gray coloring. The dark promise that fell from her lips makes a chill run up my spine. She's going to war, and that's the end. Her sole purpose and drive at this point is to wipe the realms clean and start anew.

"I think we should get back down to the others to finish planning what we're doing today," I say as I offer her my hand with my palm upturned.

She looks at my hand, then back up at me, giving me a single nod before slipping her hand into mine. Gripping it tightly, I head down the stairs with her as she shakes her head, staring at me.

Within a matter of seconds, we're gone from the tower and back in the war room. It's almost unnerving how easily she moves between the shadows now that she's comfortable with everything.

"Gentlemen." Her voice reverberates around the interior of the castle, shaking things off of shelves and rattling loose stones from the walls.

"We leave in five, gather up all you need and be prepared. I'm only going to open this rift for a short period of time. We'll arrive on the outskirts of the Envy Ring." She makes this statement and then touches the pendant on her chest, donning her black-and-gold armor. She looks just as menacing as her grandfather did in the same armor.

Taking the hint, I touch the wolf on my chest. My armor moves like liquid silk over my body, encapsulating me in what's probably the strongest armor I've ever worn.

When Gage enters the room, finally catching up with everyone, he sees what's going on and without question, dons his armor as well. It's up to Thana when we'll depart. I, for one, am looking forward to the battle ahead of us.

Thana moves away from us and begins ripping open a portal in the middle of the war room. The black mass pulses is if it has a heartbeat of its own and slowly expands into existence. Thana unfurls her wings and armor moves like liquid over her wing bones, covering the primary structure of her wings and leaving only her feathers exposed.

When she has the portal open to the size she wants, she turns around to face us. "The Archangels in my bond are the only angels or Archangels who will follow us through the portal," she says with such finality, it makes the hair on the back of my neck stand up. "Everyone else is to remain here and protect the realm as well as my fortress," she states matter-of-factly.

I notice Metatron's about to say something, but Thana raises her hand, silencing him instantly. There is no room for argument in this. As I consider what we're about to do, it's painfully obvious it will be far too dangerous for those of angelic blood to travel the lower circles.

"You will remain here and act as sentinels. Those who can heal will be in charge of doing that if I send any of my wounded mates back to you." She sets her hands on her hips, one resting on the pommel of Daybreaker, and the other resting on the pommel of a sword I haven't yet seen her wield.

Metatron, Raphael, Gage, and I step forward, ready to follow her into the abyss. Before we do, I watch a much smaller version of Rex run into the room and leap at Gage. When the miniature dragon makes contact with him, he disappears almost instantly. I can only assume he's returning to a tattoo on his body like the rest of our familiars.

Looking through the portal Thana created, I see a dark, desolate landscape. The earth is scorched by thousands of years of fire, with no semblance of life to be found. Creatures appearing to be giant sand worms moving the earth are the only sign of life I can see. In the distance, it reminds me of seeing the Emerald City in that old movie about the girl and her dog.

Thana grins and looks over her shoulders at us. "Let's go!" She walks through the portal as if she's entering the grocery store. Glancing at my nest mates, I can't help but smile.

"Let's go!" I'd follow Thana to the end of the earth if she asked me to. Descending into Hell is just another adventure.

CHAPTER 82
GAGE

Watching Thana open a portal is nothing short of watching a miracle firsthand. She left the other angels and Archangels behind for their own safety because she's more concerned about them being destroyed by going further into Hell than anything else at this point. Her idea of preservation of life is far beyond that of any Dark Nephilim who's ever walked the earth.

Most still seek revenge against the angels and Archangels for the way they've been shunned for the past thousands of years since the great fall. I think because Thana is an almost perfect mix of human, darkness, and light, it gives her a perspective that none of us could ever understand.

Having spent most of my life in the light and then falling to save Thana, Cyrus, and the baby, I gained a new perspective on the life they both live. Until now, I didn't understand how badly shunned they were until revealing my wings at the last ball we went to. The degrading looks and the feelings of hatred emanating from the Light Nephilim and the angels was almost overwhelming for me.

These were people I'd once called brothers and sisters who I now can't trust. I now understand how the darkness will always be looked down on and mistreated and possibly ignored for any slight grievances against those with light feathers. And I now see why, at the Mated Ball, Thana became so defensive of Cyrus because of the man who tried to approach them and wanted to have Cyrus taken away. She could see the hatred in the man's eyes and how he was trying to drag her away from her mate.

Looking at her now as the Destroyer with her strength and self-confidence really does my heart good. Here is that once shy, quiet, reclusive female now gathering and leading armies across all the rings. I stand on the blackened sand, surrounded by the terrain of the Envy Realm, and take in the giant city ahead of us in the distance. Cyrus was right. It reminds me of the Emerald City and that old movie about the girl and her dog.

As I watch the cityscape in the distance, Thana expands her wings and begins flapping them until they vibrate. The rest of us stand back as the dust storm kicks up. After several moments, we hear the thundering of hooves across the sand as if something is racing toward us. I turn and look behind us, and in the distance, I see a giant dust cloud racing in our direction. It looks like the bottom part of the cloud is on fire.

Within a matter of moments, the dust cloud settles and dissipates as heavily armored warhorses stand before us. They rival the size of the horses used for plowing on earth. Clydesdales would look small compared to these black beasts. Their blood-red eyes glow as they stare down, judging each one of us. Upon their giant forms, heavy armor covers them, along with chain mail to protect their vitals. I'm not sure if it's part of the horse itself or if someone here, some stable unknown to me, had them settled and ready for Thana's arrival.

Thana's armor vanishes from her hand as she reaches out and runs her fingers through the mane of the largest horse in front of her. The horse lowers its giant armored head to Thana and watches the rest of us suspiciously. A musical giggle escapes from Thana as she turns to walk back to us. "This is how we're getting into the city of Envy across the great desert." She motions across the black sand.

"Giant worms live under the sand who will consume anyone and anything that walks across it." She motions back to the horses behind her.

"The Firemares' hooves ignite when they run over the sand, walking on a blanket of fire. The worms don't like the fire, so they don't surface to eat the horses," Thana says matter-of-factly as she looks back to the horses and then to us as if this is common knowledge.

"They'll carry us there and then wait for us to come back out to leave." She walks over to the lead horse. The horse bows down and allows her to use its front leg to climb on its back. Once seated on the horse's back, she takes the grip of its mane and holds on tightly.

"Put your hand out. The horses will choose their riders," she says with a smile as she lightly pats the armor on the neck of the horse she's astride.

We each stick our hands out and spread out so the horses can approach us, one at a time. Cyrus is the first one the horses approach, and one headbutts him, knocking him on his ass. Laughing, Cyrus stands up and dusts himself off, then walks over to the horse. Just as with Thana, the horse bows down and allows Cyrus to use its front leg to climb on. One by one, the horses approach each of us still standing. We mount up and ready ourselves to ride across the sands.

"Hold on tight, boys. Grab a chunk of the mane and give it a tug when you need to stop," Thana instructs before lightly nudging her horse and taking off, galloping across the black sands and leaving a trail of fire behind her. Without saying a word or even prodding my horse, it takes off, following the lead stallion Thana is on. We fly across the sand in a matter of moments versus what would've taken us hours walking. We ride in a circle around the outer edge of the city, trying to find a way in. Along the backside of the rampart we couldn't see before is a tree leaning against the wall, having toppled some bricks that were previously there.

Dismounting from her horse and walking to the fallen tree, Thana examines the wall. Once she stares at it a while and steps up on the tree, she turns and walks back over, patting her horse several times. "This looks like the best place to enter." She motions to the leaning tree.

"We can send the Firemares on their way, so they'll be safe." She pats the flank of her horse and looks at us.

"How are we supposed to leave if we send them away?" Raphael asks as he climbs down from his horse.

Thana shakes her head and laughs. "One of two ways, silly. Either I rip open a portal or I call the horses back." She shrugs her shoulders as if this should be common knowledge at this point.

Raphael rolls his eyes as the last of us dismount. With a wave of Thana's hand, the horses take off and disappear into the desert again.

I watch the horses and then turn to Thana. "I can't help but want some answers at this point."

She quirks a brow and tilts her head, looking at me. "What is it?" she asks as she leans against the trunk of the tree.

"You called them Firemares."

"Yeah, and?" Thana looks at the rest of our group, then back at me.

"Well, it's kind of obvious not all of them are female." I shrug my shoulders, bringing forward the faux pas she's made.

Rolling her eyes, she shakes her head. "I'll try to figure out a more suitable gender-neutral name for the horses later. It just so happens this herd is a mix of both genders. The majority of the time, only the females are ever seen. Hence the name Firemares." She paces, considering what I had brought up.

"Call them fire horses, desert horses, or desert-fire horses." She shrugs. "I'll figure out a suitable name for them later. Right now, let's go destroy this place. Take out Leviathan and then go home for a bit. Okay?" she asks just before she turns and climbs the tree.

We follow her up the tree and over the wall, entering the city of

Envy. Once inside the perimeter, each house is more appealing than the next. People are arguing and fighting in the streets over who has the best of whatever the current item is. Arguments and shouting matches and all sorts of chaos go on almost everywhere.

For the most part, the spirits here haven't given us the slightest bit of attention as we move through the city. With every step, a new argument is overheard. Thana just ignores it all, passing by it as if it's not happening around her. I watch how Raphael and Metatron are both put off by the level of sin occurring around us. I guess only having witnessed things on the angelic side makes it difficult for them to watch this kind of sin and suffering going on.

Even though these people brought this on themselves, I suspect it's difficult for them to handle it. They know one of their brethren is who sentenced these people here. I never understood how the darkness limited things until I had to watch Thana and Cyrus reap souls at the command of the Archangels. Cyrus was unaffected, but you can tell, in some ways, it still bothers Thana. As we move deeper into the city, more fights break out. These fights are over something different.

Apparently, there's a new mode of transportation within the city, newer than the one the day before. And obviously because of how sadistic Leviathan is, he only provided a handful of this new mode of transportation to cause more fighting within his realm. One person is more envious than the next and is willing to fight and kill to have the new best thing. It almost makes me sick, thinking about how petty they're being over physical property.

We follow Thana through the streets without comment, and that, by itself, raises the question for me. "Where are we going?" I ask her when I move to walk by her side.

She motions ahead of us. "That giant mansion on the hilltop. Out of all the buildings here, that's the only one with that color. My rationale is that it must be where Leviathan is. Every other house here is the exact shape, size, and color as the next one. The only differences with the houses is how they're decorated and what items they have inside. So, my guess is Leviathan controls the amount of envy the souls have by limiting the structures they live in," Thana deduces, then looks back over to Raphael. "Do you agree?" She tilts her head, looking at him, and he moves quickly to come up alongside her.

"Metatron and I were just discussing the same thing." He taps his chin, then looks back to Metatron, then to Cyrus, and then back to Thana and me.

"I believe your deduction is correct. If he's going to be anywhere, it would be the only building that's completely different from everyone else's. That way, the majority of the souls envy him for what he has," Raphael states in such a way, there's no other logical answer. Thana smiles at me and continues on her way, still maneuvering in and out of the crowds as we pass them. I'm almost afraid to see what we're running into when we reach our final destination.

CHAPTER 83
THANA

Stopping at the base of the hill, I stare at the large mansion and the surrounding grounds. Something doesn't feel right. I summon Eligos and the Balor chieftain to me. The sixty legions from the Duke of Hell line up. The Balor take to the sky, blotting out the blood-red sun. With a single move of my arm pointing forward, the troops descend upon the mansion on the hilltop.

Raising my taloned gauntlets, all manner of shadow creatures rise from the surrounding sand. Moving my hands forward again in a sweeping motion, my shadow creatures go on the offensive, attacking the mansion. Wave after wave of the creatures attack the incoming forces seeming to pour out of every opening in the mansion. I'm relieved my gut instinct warned me about approaching. I would almost liken them to Spider-Man's spidey-sense. I had that tingle at the base of my skull warning me of unforeseen dangers.

Taking full advantage of the confusion, I summon the fires of Hell to surround me, making me look like a blackened comet streaking across the sky, flying higher and higher. I look down at the mansion and find the weakest point in the roof. Drawing Daybreaker from its sheath at my side, I curl my wings in and plummet out of the sky.

I impact the roof of the mansion and burn my way through the levels and land in what appears to be the throne room. My blackened flames spread out across the floor, engulfing everything in its path. The screams of the dark denizens that live within the mansion echo just for brief seconds as the flames turn their bodies to ash before me. My mates show up shortly after my landing, and I extinguish the flames immediately.

Before I can react, a blackened arrow shoots from the wall and barely misses me, but it hits a target directly behind me. A loud thud and a groan sounds behind me, and I'm almost afraid to turn around to see what it was. Glancing over my shoulder, I see the arrow found a weak spot in Raphael's armor and is implanted in his shoulder. Panicking slightly, I look between him and Leviathan, who's emerging from the darkness.

My gaze shifts and locks on Metatron and Raphael, and I know exactly what I need to do. Raphael's being poisoned by the arrow, and if Metatron gets hit, he too will be poisoned. I quickly throw up a wall of flames that shield us for the brief moment I need to open the rift. I toss Daybreaker to Cyrus for him to defend me, just in case. Gage moves into a defensive stance before me, giving me the time I need to get Raphael and Metatron out of here.

Without hesitation, I open a smaller version of the normal portals that I open to my castle. I look at them as tears threaten to roll down my cheeks, fearing what's going to happen to my mate. "Get him out of here," I order, putting as much force behind my words as I can. Nodding, Metatron sticks his arms underneath Raphael to drag him through the portal back into my castle.

Shutting the portal quickly, I turn with a renewed sense of purpose. I think about the fact that my mate may die, and there's nothing I can do about it while I'm still here. The thudding of my heartbeat fills my ears as I feel something snap inside me. I feel a sense of anger and vengeance I've never allowed to surface before.

Lowering the flame wall, I notice Leviathan has three of his generals with him and his legion standing behind him. "What did you think you were going to accomplish, Destroyer?"

As I stare at him when the smoke dissolves around him, I notice he seems to be half-man and half-octopus. Looking at him closely, his lower half looks a little like that mythical creature the kraken. "It's simple," I say as I walk up beside Cyrus and take Daybreaker back from him. He draws his own sword and stands at the ready beside me.

Now, he notices the Duke of Hell, who's fighting alongside me, and part of his legion marches into the mansion with me. "What I wish to accomplish is putting your head on a pike, or I can actually grant you Elysium," I say in what sounds like a semi-haughty tone to me.

As I stare at him, his resolve flickers for several seconds before a hardened mask slips back over his beautiful face. "Elysium was lost to me a long time ago. How can one so young as you say I could be back there again?" He asks as more of his resolve flickers before me.

"I can't guarantee anything, but it never hurts to try." As I say this to him, I watch his generals becoming antsy. One makes the motion to move their troops forward more, as if trying to impress upon me we're outnumbered.

It really doesn't matter what physical number of troops he has here with him. He forgets I can manifest or turn his troops against him. Or he may not know I can do it.

"What will Satan and Lucifer say if I defect? What will they do to me? And will I survive the transition?" Arching a brow, I consider his questions. He's actually thinking about taking me up on my offer.

I want to laugh right now. This is far too easy. There's definitely something wrong. I can't put my fingers on it at the moment, but then it hits me. This is a setup. The walls of the mansion tremble and quake within a matter of seconds. Leviathan, his generals, and his army leave as the building caves in all around us. Grabbing my men, I pull them with me quickly through the shadows of the building to safety. The Duke of Hell and his men make it out easily since they're specters themselves.

Reassembling my legions is easy enough. I look over at the Duke of Hell, and he nods, getting his guys all back in line again. The Balor chief lands next to me, surveying the area. "Leviathan snuck out the back and started running toward the Field of Dreams," He tells me, pointing in the distance.

Arching a brow, I attempt to look in the direction he's pointing in. "What do you mean by 'the Field of Dreams'?" I follow him around the back of the building, and he points to a field filled with high wheatgrass, or at least what looks like wheatgrass to me.

Some force makes the wheatgrass sway from left to right like waves on the ocean. "It's called that because the minute you enter the field, some semblance of a dream traps you in there." This is quite concerning.

Motioning to the Duke of Hell, I point to the outskirts of the field. "Surround the field with your men. Do not allow them to enter the grass." He gives me a single nod and then barks out orders to his troops to surround the field.

Glancing back over the chief of the Balor, I look toward the field. "Those of us who can fly should, and if you spot Leviathan, call for me." He nods slowly and then barks out orders to his troops. All the Balor take flight, again blackening the sky.

It's now that I look back at Gage and raise my hand, stopping his forward motion. "Hang back and wait a few moments. I'm not sure I trust this situation enough for us to launch into it."

Cyrus strokes his chin. "You don't trust it enough for us to go in. Is that why you sent them first?"

"Yes," I state plainly.

"It's far easier for me to manifest more troops than it would be for me to handle either of you being killed because of a lack of judgment on my part. I prefer going into this cautiously rather than taking the chance of one or both of you dying because I didn't take this threat seriously enough." He nods and goes back to watching the fields.

Toward the middle of the field, we watch some of the grass moving in the opposite direction of the rest of the grass. My only assumption is that's where Leviathan is. Unleashing my familiars, they take a stance around me.

Looking back over to Gage, I smile. "Would you mind releasing the dragon?" I say in a singsongy voice.

A sadistic grin crosses over Gage's face slowly. His time around Cyrus is starting to show . . . With a gleam in his eyes, he tilts his head back and releases his familiar. Rex manifests and then assumes his full size. Staring up at the enormous skull dragon, I can't help but laugh. He gives a single nod of his head before he lumbers forward, shaking the earth beneath him.

When he reaches the edge of the field, you can hear the click of the ignitor in his chest as the green acid breath drips from his mouth before turning into a full-blown flamethrower. The acid moves along the field, and I watch troops from the Duke of Hell backing up and climbing trees to escape the acid fog. Everything the acid touches melts in its wake, turning into a puddle of goo on the ground.

Seeing movement in the center of the field, I motion for Rex to approach the field from the far side and unleash his breath again. Now, both sides of the field have melted toward the inner part. You can hear the frightened screams and cries from whoever and whatever is in the middle of the field. Several creatures I've never seen before take flight up and out of the grass and into the air.

Before they're able to get too far, the Balor strike their bony bodies down, decapitating them mid-flight. We hear still more shrieking and screaming as something tries to run frantically to the far side. Without our having to say a word, Rex moves and unleashes his breath on that side and then behind whoever is in the middle of the field.

The circle nearly closes in on whoever is thrashing around in the center, and with the wave of my hand, I stop the green acid from burning the field. There's a circle of about ten feet in diameter, and it's the only possible place Leviathan could be hiding. Rex returns to stand beside me, lowering his massive head. Using his sharp scales behind his horns as leverage, I climb up and stand on his shoulders. He lumbers into the field, and I ride atop him like a general running into battle.

As we get closer, I can clearly see it's Leviathan. His tentacles are thrashing around him frantically. The acid has burned almost half of them, and he's now malformed. I instruct Rex to lay down another ring of acid on the remaining grass. It shrinks the circle down to about a five-foot diameter. Yet again, I stop the flames. Leviathan launches himself out onto the blackened earth. The ash from the burned grass kicks up all around him, and as he emerges, the skeleton of his general that he had at his side falls.

"Well, look what we have here." My tone is about as condescending as I can make it.

Rex lowers his head, and I spread my wings wide to glide the rest of the way to the ground. "What should I do with you now?"

CHAPTER 84
GAGE

The change in my mate is incredible. The once unsure, kind, and slightly terrified female who I once knew is gone. Before me stands a woman who's grown into her confidence and has finally and completely accepted all aspects of herself. I've watched her grow and mature, loving herself for who she is and not the image others tried to press upon her. Not only is her self-confidence beautiful and sexy, it's about time that, as well as her intelligence, can shine bright as a diamond in the sky.

Whereas over a year ago, she'd never consider taking a position of power or instructing anyone to do anything because she was afraid of failure and ridicule. The woman who stands before us now has no problems taking control of the situation and doing everything possible to protect those she loves, as well as humanity. I'm guessing the big spark that occurred and changed with her was the death of her grandfather. He was the only family she had who ever encouraged her to be herself. It amazes me that after all these years of torment and torture the Light Nephilim have done to her, she's still able to love and accept everyone with her whole heart.

Now I stand here, completely amazed that, as one who wasn't

created for battle, she goes into it without fear. Watching her with her familiars as they encircle Leviathan, pride blooms within my chest as my love for her grows massively.

Using Rex was a stroke of genius on her part. Riding the dragon, she approaches and then glides to the ground of what's left of the wheatgrass. Rex's acid breath has melted parts of Leviathan's tentacles off and the other tentacles flailing around more than likely means they're injured. He's sputtering and cursing and throwing all kinds of profanities while Thana looks forward, staring at the claws on the ends of her gauntlets.

"Really, Levi. This is rather unbecoming for a once proud and strong Archangel who's now reduced to seafood." Her tone sounds bored and dismissive.

When did this mean and cruel streak develop within her? I'm slightly concerned, but I know deep down she needs to separate herself from the task at hand. She's not a fan of having to kill people, but unfortunately, holding the mantle of Destroyer, it's part of her job.

Levi raises his hand, and a sword manifests within seconds. Just as he lunges forward at Thana, she grabs the hilt of Daybreaker and swings it up quickly. The blade ignites the moment it leaves the sheath, and blackened flames follow it in its upward arc as it severs Leviathan's arm at the elbow. The severed arm with the blade land several yards away, hitting the ground. The stench of burned flesh fills the air. His left hand comes over and grips what's left of his arm as he falls back in shock.

"I would think one is old as yourself would be wiser than to strike out in anger," Thana says as Cyrus and I make it down the hill and flank her sides, watching Leviathan closely. Rex looms over the top of us as a dark sentinel, making sure no one can approach us. Thana and Cyrus's wolves surround us and also keep guard.

She holds the one sword that can destroy the divine and demonic. It doesn't differentiate between the two and is the only sword created to destroy Lucifer. Part of the curse of him is that his duality was split into Lucifer and Satan. Perhaps half of him can be saved, while the other half will have to be destroyed. Only time will tell, and it may depend on my mate's temperament at the time, whether we destroy one or both in the blink of an eye.

Walking up behind Thana, I gently rest my hand on her hip to let her know I'm standing right there with her. I stare down Leviathan, and it still hurts me deep in my soul to think this man was once an Archangel who fought with our bond brothers. Through the bond, I feel the same pain radiating from Metatron and Raphael as I catch them up to speed. Every time we watch one of the fallen be destroyed, it's like a piece of their soul is cut away. Because these men were once their brothers, and now because of Lucifer, they're all our enemies and must be dealt with accordingly.

"Gee, where is my brother, Raphael? How I've missed him," Leviathan sneers as he holds his stump and then waves it around. "What happened? Did he get an owie and have to be sent home? Poor baby." His words flow smoothly as silk in the same tone Lucifer used to convince the other Archangels to fall with him.

As he speaks, I no longer feel sorry for him and his fall. It's painfully apparent he's beyond being saved. As much as I wish to see him redeemed, I truly do not believe there's enough light left within him to even consider it. There's far too much damage that will be done to cleanse him of the darkness within. Part of his punishment for following Lucifer was his lower half becoming what appears to be an octopus. I think about the pain he and the others who have fallen have caused these poor souls well beyond their sins in life.

The utter cruelty on his lips and the way he talks about our mate only strengthens my resolve to complete the job that needs to be done here today. I glance up at Thana and give her a single nod, letting her know it's time. Without hesitation, she raises Daybreaker from her side and brings it down swiftly, embedding it into the center of Leviathan's chest. With a quick twist of the blade, it ignites, and the black flames burn him to ash instantly. The wisp of his soul slowly rises in a black, oozing ball. Thana reaches out and grips it from the air, turning it to ash as well. No soul means no resurrection. For all the atrocities he's done in the past several thousand years, he's finally paid for it with his life. Part of me should feel guilty, but the other part of me doesn't because of those he's mistreated in the past.

"There wasn't enough light left to allow him to ascend." Her words sound hollow, but her stony visage doesn't betray the pain she's feeling. In times of war, we all must wear a mask. I lean forward and press my lips against hers, pushing my love for her through the bond. Thana looks back at Cyrus and Azrael, and with a wave of her hand, she rips open a portal back to her castle. "Let's return and rest for tonight. Tomorrow, we go after Satan." Her tone is devoid of any emotion as she sends all her familiars through. Metatron extends his hand out to Thana through the portal back into her castle.

Returning to the castle is a bittersweet homecoming. I feel the weight of the loss of Leviathan through the bond. Even though he had not been a loyal brother to Metatron and Raphael in the past several thousand years, it's still a loss. Thana explains the Archangels feel the pain every time one of them is eviscerated. It's not a guilt that I wish for her to know at this point in her life. But it's a burden Metatron, Raphael, and the other Archangels will have to carry from now on.

Heading into the war room, we meet up with Uriel and Raziel. "These last two will be the hardest for us to go after," Azrael says as he approaches the table. We watch the chess piece that represents Satan moving around the mountain. He's nowhere near his fortress, and instead, he's out in the middle of a field.

"I wonder what he's doing?" I wonder aloud.

Thana comes in and stares at the maps as the pieces move around on them. Her eyes move over both chess pieces, but she keeps her eyes locked on Lucifer's the hardest. He seems to jump all over the map, never staying in one place for more than a brief period of time. At one point, we watch him bounce between all the rings and then back to his own in the end.

"What do you suppose he's doing?" Thana moves to my side the minute he stops moving.

"He's gathering an army from all the rings, scavenging whatever forces he can for himself. Even though he brings them to his inner-most ring, they won't be as powerful as they are in their own domains." Azrael sees me deep in thought, thinking about all this. He wraps his knuckles on the tabletop.

"Mind sharing with the rest of the class?" I guess he realized I was deep in conversation with Metatron and Raphael.

"That's easy." I brush my finger over the area where his castle is.

"Among those," I motion to the map of the rings. "I'm fairly certain he's taking what's left of the soldiers. Bringing them back to his ring." Drawing in a deep breath, I glance at Thana, and she motions for me to continue.

"The consensus is he will use them as cannon fodder just to ensure his own army lasts the longest." Thinking about this further, tactically, it's brilliant. But it just shows what lengths he'll go.

Thana stares at Lucifer, bouncing between the different rings, clearly avoiding the one Satan is in. "This is going to become rather interesting," she states plainly as she picks up Satan's piece. She laughs, staring at the piece, then places it back on the map.

"He honestly has no clue what he's unleashed upon himself," she states before kissing my cheek.

She grips both my cheeks in her hands as she stares into my eyes. An almost feral smile crosses her lips before she kisses me roughly. Releasing one hand, she extends it out to Cyrus, and he comes over quickly and kisses her cheek.

"He made the ultimate folly by attacking my family." She raises her eyebrows for a moment.

She releases Cyrus and me at the same time, then moves to stand before everyone as Metatron and a bandaged Raphael enter the room. "Lucifer made the mistake of killing my grandfather and forcing me to ascend. His second mistake was taking my daughter, intending to turn her into a succubus, just to be his own little plaything," she says, her voice devoid of all emotion. This on-off switch she seems to have developed concerns me greatly because this is not the woman I've known.

"And lastly, he brought this on himself. I won't allow others to suffer merely for his enjoyment." She crosses her arms under her chest and locks eyes with each of us, one at a time, turning her eyes to chrome serpentine slits.

"Hell hath no fury like a woman scorned," she says the words and then gazes down at the maps before her. Then she looks back up at us all again.

"I will avenge my grandfather. I will avenge my daughter for the precious time that was stolen from me. Lastly, I will avenge all those who have suffered because of his egomaniacal ways. He will pay for taking Elysium away from all of those Archangels and forcing me to have to kill them to cleanse the rings." The last words falling from her lips shock me. She's seeking revenge for the Archangels who had their futures stolen from them.

Perhaps maybe this is it. Unlike her grandfather before her, he would not have carried a vengeance for those who have been wronged. He would have done it just for the thrill of the battle. I only hope our future holds brighter days than those currently before us.

CHAPTER 85

THANA

I feel the fires burning in my chest as I stare down at the maps before me in my war room. Angels and archangels alike wander in and out of the room, each glancing cursorily at the map and keeping track of the pieces moving on it. The last two rings hold Satan and Lucifer. They're probably the most dangerous rings in existence. I'll have to pull a miracle from my back pocket to make it through these last rings unscathed, especially since half my mates with me are angelic and will burn in the hellfire.

My instinct tells me it would be better to leave Raphael and Metatron behind as we go into these final two rings. The strength of the evil that'll be found at these levels will be far greater than what we've exposed them to at this point. Lucifer and Satan will both be at their strongest when they're closest to the center ring. I know it won't phase me one bit, nor should it phase Cyrus and Gage. But I worry about the light side of my bond and how much damage they'll sustain if either of them is hit with a blast of Lucifer or Satan's powers.

Drumming my nails on the edge of the desk, I stare down at the map, watching Satan's piece move. I've been studying his particular ring for over an hour, and I've concluded there are only two viable ways in to hopefully not come out of it the worse for wear. The Firemares were extremely helpful in Leviathan's ring, but I'm not sure they can survive in Satan's realm. In the next ring, there be dragons. Technically, they're not dragons. They're more wyvern than anything else. But it would be a means to an end to take a creature living in that area and hide on it's back while flying in closer to my final destination.

A large hand wraps around my left shoulder, turning me. Azrael stands before me with a gentle smile on his lips but a worried look creasing his brow. Forcing a smile, I rip my eyes away from the map, trying to fake a jovial expression for his peace of mind.

"What's bothering you, daughter?" he asks, reaching forward and rubbing his thumb between my brows and down the bridge of my nose.

He's definitely learned to recognize the red flags indicating I'm in deep thought. I glance at the map again and then back up at him. I wink at him and grab his hand, moving us through the shadows to leave the war room and everyone else behind. I whisk us away to the balcony off the throne room on the second floor. When we arrive, small, winged creatures take flight from the railing and out across my lands.

"Many things currently plague my thoughts, Father," I say on a slow sighing exhale while I stare down at the land before me.

Azrael pulls me in for a side hug and holds me against him. "I'm here to help shoulder your burden. Whatever you want me to know or just need to talk through, I'll listen. If there's a way I can help, I'll tell you what I can do." His tone is so soft, and if I didn't know better, I'd never believe he was the head reaper—the Azrael feared in legends told by those who've been dragged to Hell by him personally.

I've spent hundreds of years terrified of him, thinking I was going to be dragged to Hell by him at any moment. And here he is, more of a father to me than Nyx ever was, and offering me more support than either of my birth parents did in my entire life. I nod slowly, getting lost in that minor memory, but then I finally turn my gaze to him and smile.

"I think it's best not to bring my angelic mates with me when I go into the last two rings. I know Raphael and Metatron will fight me tooth and nail on this. But I can't risk them being killed or wounded where I won't be able to get them out of there quickly." I grip the railing in front of me and crush some of the stones under my hands.

"It's very taxing to open a rift to the Angelic Realm from any of the rings. Doing it from here is hard enough. But down there, it depletes too much of my energy. I think it's too dangerous to risk it," I say, semi-defeated.

"I know my mates would rather leave me behind and take this task on themselves, but they can't travel through the rings without me. And I'd rather not go into this with the strategy of divide and conquer because if something happens to them when they're away from me . . ." Raising my hand, I run it down my face as I spill what's bothering me.

"The rings interfere with my ability to sense them, so I wouldn't know if something happened to them until it was too late. I'd probably feel something through the bond but not enough to react if I'm in the middle of battle at the time." Admitting to the crux of the problem lessens my stress level.

Laughing, Azrael pulls away from me and hops up to sit on the rail of the balcony. "I don't know what you're stressing over," he says as he unfurls his wings and flaps them several times.

"You are the Destroyer." He enunciates my title and makes the foundation of my fortress reverberate with its power.

"Your name alone is a killing word. Said with enough force by any aligned by you, it will stun or possibly kill a lesser creature," he tells me, beaming with so much pride I can't help but blush.

"I think you're confusing me with that desert movie, and what was it with the 80s and the giant worms?" I laugh and smile at him because it just so happens to be one of my favorite movies of all time.

Laughing to himself again, he sits where he is and shakes his head. "Well, I'm definitely no Atreides."

I grin conspiratorially at Azrael's reference to the ruling family in the movie. "And I'm definitely not the heroine in this story. I'm definitely not the dark knight either. That role goes to your son," I say, smiling broadly, thinking of Cyrus.

Briefly, I wonder how far and how long this love story has gone on. Whether it was known to either of us that it was written in the stars long ago. We've always been within reaching distance of each other, just not directly tangled in each other's lives until the Mate Trials. As my mind wanders, I feel a tap on the top of my hand and look up to see Azrael smiling at me. "Where did you go, Thana?" he asks with a knowing smile, and I can't help but laugh.

"I was thinking about that boy of yours." A soft sigh escapes me as I glance down and then out across the sandy fields.

"I know, little one. Life hasn't been easy for you, nor did I make it easy for the first three hundred something years," he says, his voice filled with regret.

"I know," I say softly and then lean over to give him a good hug. "But you taught me to be more self-reliant rather than to rely on those around me. By scaring me constantly, you kept me from doing a lot of the wicked things that crossed my mind." A sly grin crosses my lips as I tap my fingers on the rail.

"Oh? And what would that be?" Azrael turns to face me better.

"Well, for starters. I was going to lay a trap to set your son's ass on fire for constantly stealing my coffee. And stealing my chocolate. And for stealing my cookies *in front of me*." With each instance, I raise a finger with each item his son, at some point, stole from me, counting them off.

Azrael can't stop himself from laughing, and I laugh right along with him. Strong arms wrap around me from behind, and I lean back, knowing full well the devil himself has arrived. "You summoned me, kitten?" Cyrus leans down and kisses the shell of my ear. His wings fold down and rest on my shoulders like a cloak.

Shaking my head, I look back at his dad and laugh. "You see what I have to deal with?" I point at him over my shoulder, and he chuckles behind me.

"You? What *you* have to deal with? I have a tactical nuke in my arms. Who can literally decimate anything and everything she desires. How am I the troublemaker?" He tries to keep from laughing as he pokes fun at me.

Turning in his arms, I look up and tap him on the tip of the nose with my index finger. "I'm not the one who kept stealing my stuff. I'm not the one who played the part of the bully on the playground, pulling the girl's hair because he liked her." The love I have for him shines through my gaze as I smile broadly.

His head slowly descends, and his lips brush across mine, the silken caress doing funny things to my insides. My heart pounds a little harder, and my breath comes a little quicker. All I can feel in this moment is how much I mean to him and the depth of his love for me. As he leans further into me, I notice something else down in the southern region that's calling for my attention. By the time our kiss ends, I look over my shoulder to see Azrael is long gone and only Cyrus and I remain.

"What do you say, kitten? Want to hop in the shower before we go off and storm the next castle?" Tapping my bottom lip with my index finger, I still feel the ghost of his lips caressing mine.

The thrum from the blood coursing through my veins makes my core pulse with anticipation. Canting my head to the side, I give him a single nod, and then we're gone from the porch. We manifest back in his room, and I hear the shower running. Gage steps from the bathroom with only a towel wrapped around his hips. Water beads on his chest, rolling down into rivulets that trace every defined muscle of his abdomen.

"The guest of honor has arrived," Gage says. He takes two steps, and the towel falls from around his hips. "Let's get this party started," he says.

What have I walked into?

CHAPTER 86
CYRUS

With each passing day, I'm granted the privilege of watching my mate come into her full power. She, who was once resigned and had little to no faith in herself, now stands sure and powerful. Even as this little tryst Gage and I have set up catches her slightly off guard, she's walking into it like a queen with her head held high. Knowing full well what Gage and I have in store for her.

Before me are the two loves of my life in the same room together, both willing and able to share me with each other. Never in my wildest dreams did I ever expect to find a mate who would accept the fact that not only do I love women but also men as well. Be it a darknet film thing or anything else, I've never been one to hold to the gender norms of society.

Those on the light side beat into their children that a man must marry a woman, the woman must marry a man, blah, blah, blah. Well, I say fuck that. People should be allowed to marry whoever makes them happy, who will provide them with the love they deserve. Most times, a single gender doesn't have everything someone desires, especially someone like me. Yes, I crave the soft caresses and the curves of my mate. But I also enjoy the hard planes and powerful grip of Gage. In this union, I have the best of both worlds, from the soft caress of Thana to the strong brutality only Gage can give.

I love watching Thana's reaction to seeing Gage lose his towel as he's coming out of the bathroom. Her eyes caress every single inch of his exposed body, right down to the thickening of his cock between his legs. Thankfully for both of us, Gage is well-equipped. There is not one place that man is ever lacking. Thana quickly closes the distance between them and runs her hands over his body, caressing every visible inch.

I feel her hands on his body as if they're on my own, and then I notice it. Her eyes are black as pitch, darker than the dark of night. She smiles and looks back at me, then places her hands back on Gage.

"Interesting, love?" Thana asks as she looks between Gage and me.

That little minx has learned how to share experiences between mates. Wouldn't it be a kicker if the angelic side felt exactly what was going on tonight? With a wicked gleam in her eye, Thana laughs softly. I think she picked up on the hint I was dropping. She slides her hands down Gage's body, and I feel my cock thicken and start twitching, coming to life. I swear if I wasn't already a Dark Nephilim, I'd fall a thousand times just to be with her. She may not be the most experienced female I've ever been with, but she knows me and my dark desires. I watch her fingertips shift to claws as she stares at me. I wonder what my mate is up to next.

With the flick of her wrist, I fly across the room and hit the wall on the other side. Tendrils of leather fall free from the wall and wrap tightly around my wrists. Several more tendrils encapsulate my chest and separate my thighs, spreading them wide and then wrap around my ankles as well. Thana walks slowly toward me, her hips swaying with every step. And Gage walks behind her, sporting a massive hard-on.

I'm generally the predator in the stories, the one who usually starts our nights off. The one who directs how the scene plays out. This is an interesting turn of events to see Thana and Gage now calling the shots. With the slow tilt of her head, Thana smiles and then stares at the talons at the ends of her fingertips. "You know, Cy. I love our little games where we take turns bleeding, then licking the blood off each other's bodies," she says, enunciating each word, running her tongue over her lips, and exposing those now-lengthened canines of hers.

If the stories of vampires were true, I'd be concerned. But I know from experience it's one of the darker rights of the fallen. Gage and I can do the same as Thana does, just not to the same extent. She reaches out and touches my body, her hands gripping my ribcage and holding me in place momentarily. Then I feel her talons extend and slice through the fabric of my shirt, rending it from my flesh. An almost sadistic glee plays across her porcelain features as each shred of fabric falls to the floor. Gage looks a little concerned as he tries to process exactly what's going on.

It's not normal for Thana to be this dominant or this forthcoming. Usually it's Gage and me who have to encourage her to let loose and enjoy herself. I suppose accepting the mantle of Destroyer has actually come with her finally accepting who she is. We always encourage her to explore her darkest desires, that this is a safe place for her. I guess she's finally accepted that.

Tilting my head to the side, I look down at her. "What do you plan to do to me now?" I ask, hitting that low-honey tone that usually sends a chill down her spine and ramps up her desire.

She stares at what's left of the fabric as she shreds my pants off me. "Wouldn't you like to know?" she taunts with a smile that looks more devilish than innocent.

She bites her bottom lip and blood dribbles down her chin. I want to lick it off her. She leans over to Gage and offers him her blood and then stares over at me. "Gage, my love, remove Cyrus's boxers. They're in the way. If you happen a find anything interesting along the way, definitely turn it into a lollipop." She pops the "p" at the end of her word and then moves her hand again, calling forth the chair for herself, which she promptly sits down on.

Gage's eyes blacken almost immediately as he steps forward and reaches for the hem of my boxers, slowly inching them down my hips to just below my balls. Thana moves forward and just runs her finger along the edge of the elastic, then gently blows on it and the material disintegrates from my body. Shocked, Gage and I both stare at her, wondering what just happened. We're not sure whether this is a new power of hers or if this is something she recently learned how to do. Without further hesitation, Gage moves my pants down as far as they can go before the leather strap stops him.

Thana leans forward and simply touches what's left of my pants, and they turn to ash under her fingertips, falling to the floor. Gage's eyes practically bulge out of his head as he stares at what's left of the material. Thana moves to Gage and grips him by the back of the head. "Now, I'd like to see you take care of Cyrus," Thana says with a curious tone in her voice as she stares at Gage.

His jaw practically drops with what she's requesting of him. His eyes dart between Thana and me, and I simply nod, giving him permission. Thana moves to my side and leans her head against my rib cage to watch Gage.

He starts how he normally does and kisses his way up my inner thigh, heading straight to my groin. His hands grip and massage my thighs until he's eye level with my dick. Without hesitation, he grips the base tightly, cupping my balls in his other hand, and then he swallows me whole. A deep groan escapes my lips, feeling the wondrous warmth of his mouth wrapped around me. Thana's breath hitches as she watches Gage bobbing his head up and down my length. She nips at my side with her teeth, eventually drawing blood. Her tongue slowly sneaks out from between her ruby lips and laps at the droplets as they roll down my flesh.

A deep rumble escapes from her with every droplet she

consumes. I assume it's the rumble of the beast coiled within her chest, making the noise we hear now. Gage only falters for a moment before diving back in, almost making me see stars with how far my cock is down his throat. Thana steps out and walks behind Gage, then soundly smacks him on his ass—hard.

She watches him with rapt attention on every bob of his head as he sucks me deep into his throat. Her fingertips run the length of his spine up to the base of his skull. She intertwines her fingers into his hair and slowly starts taking control of the rhythm he's using on me. Occasionally, a slight strangled sound comes from the back of Gage's throat as she pushes me deeper into him. Every stroke, every bob of his head is now orchestrated by Thana's will. When did my kitten become such a dominant minx?

She speeds him up and watches the muscles of my abdomen tensing as I start feeling that slow rolling boil in the base of my stomach, feeling my conclusion coming upon me. Just as I'm about to tip over the edge, she stops him, pulling his head all the way back and his mouth off me. She gets down on her knees next to him, then kisses him deeply. Her left hand reaches up and grips my cock tightly and slowly strokes my length. Every nerve ending in my body is on fire. I don't know what's hotter right now, watching Thana control tonight or her kissing Gage in front of me while keeping me right on the edge, ready to explode at any moment.

Every time my cock twitches in her hand, she stops, releases Gage from the kiss, and looks up at me with those black, fathomless eyes. The new dark Thana is quite interesting indeed. Now, she completely releases me and leans over, pressing her lips to Gage's ear. As she whispers something to him, he looks between her and me, then back over to her, nodding. What does my kitten have in store for me?

With a wicked gleam in her eyes and her brow raised, she looks at me. I'm almost afraid to find out what my girl is about to do. With a fancy wave of her hand over the floor between us, a stone pillar rises to about hip level with her. She runs her hands down the sides of her body, and her clothes disappear. Gently, she lays herself down on the pillar, allowing her wings to unfurl as she spreads them wide. The minute she does, Gage moves behind her and runs his hand up her back reverently. He stretches out over her and spreads his arms over her wings, gently caressing every inch he can reach. Placing kisses down her spine, he slowly straightens back up again, then lines himself up and sinks balls-deep into our mate.

The slow roll of his head falling back in sheer pleasure and the look of ecstasy on her face are enough to make my cock twitch more than it was before. Thana's hand extends out, and she grips me hard at the base and begins pumping my length as Gage pounds relentlessly into her. I don't know what feels better at this moment, my mate's hand around my cock or having an unobstructed view of Gage fucking her.

Thana keeps working me, keeping me edged, just like Gage had done earlier. Her body moves and gyrates on the stone, signaling that she's close to her own release. Without warning, my own orgasm overtakes me, and I spill my seed on my mate's breasts and down the stone pillar in front of me. As soon as I become soft in Thana's hands, she releases her grip on me and frees me from the wall.

Once my feet hit the ground, I move in front of her and kiss her passionately. My hands reach up to grip her nipples, playing with the tips ever so gently with every twist and pinch, and her moans increase. Without warning, she flaps her wings once, and she stands upright, her back slamming into Gage's chest. Both of them cry out as her orgasm overtakes her. Beads of sweat run in rivulets down her chest. Stepping around the pillar, I reach around Thana to grab hold of Gage as they ride out their combined ecstasy.

Thana nuzzles my neck and my jaw line as she drapes her arms over my shoulder, holding onto me for dear life. Her breathing is rapid as she tries to calm herself down. Gage peeks over her shoulder at me, then smiles and gives me a wink. That smug bastard definitely got the best end of all of this. He eventually withdraws from Thana and walks back into the bathroom to grab towels. Carefully reaching down, I scoop her up in my arms and carry her across the room to the bed.

Gently, I lay her down and make sure she's comfortable. "Well, that didn't go according to plan," Thana says, laughing to herself as she stretches her wings out behind her before curling them back in.

"What do you mean?" Raising an eyebrow, I stare at her curiously because if that wasn't the plan, I really want to know what she had in mind for this evening.

She giggles softly to herself, and then, once her wings are folded in, she rolls slightly again to lie flat on her back. "Well, the plan to make our whole sexcapade last longer than it did." She holds her hands up in a placating manner. "Not that I'm blaming anyone," she says with a hesitant laugh.

"The plan for this to have taken all night." She fiddles with the sheets, biting her bottom lip. She looks up at me as Gage cleans her off.

"The plan that we would've finished clearing the rings already, and we'd have returned everything as it should've been. The plan for us being home with our children, snuggling them in tight, tucking them in bed, and planning for the next set of babies to be born." A sadness I've never noticed slowly moves over her face but then vanishes just as quickly.

"The plan that everything would be set back in order instead of wasting weeks battling here. By the time we get home, who knows how large or how grown our daughters will be? I've missed so much time with them." Her voice waivers as she says those words.

Suddenly, the crux of the problem becomes clear. The one thing she can't control in this realm is time. Time that was stolen from her with the children. Time that keeps moving, no matter what she does. Time itself cannot be controlled and dances to a beat of a different drummer. She forces a smile as Gage snuggles up behind her and throws an arm over her midsection.

"Let's get some rest, you two. Tomorrow's a big day," he says as he leans forward and kisses Thana on the temple. He missed seeing the wave of pain moving over our mate's face. And I guess, in some sense, ignorance is bliss.

CHAPTER 87

THANA

Morning comes easily after having one of the more blissful night's sleep I've had in a long time. When I finally awaken, both guys are already out of bed and gone. I don't bother with most of my morning routines, other than the ones that have to be done. I make my way downstairs, following the spiral staircase to my war room. My Archangel and Dark Nephilim mates are leaning on the table, looking down at the maps and the moving pieces.

"Staring at them will change nothing," I try to say in as light of a tone as I can muster this early in the morning. A demon comes scurrying in, carrying a cup on a tray, and then stops and kneels before me. I reach down and take the cup from him, giving him a single nod before he takes off and disappears again. Bringing the cup to my lips, I sip at it slowly and breathe a sigh of relief, realizing that the demon had brought me espresso.

"Even in Hell, we still have our coffee addictions. I suspect you consider coffee a sin, since it's rather addictive because of the caffeine boost it gives you." I stare back at my mates as they watch me sipping at my coffee and shrug my shoulders. The goal is still the same. Save those who can be saved, destroy everything else. There's no gray area when it comes to finishing this task. I move to the opposite side of the table from my mates and stare down at the pieces as they move.

With a wave of my hand, I move Lucifer's map and his chess piece off the table, out of my view, and onto a separate table on the other side of the room. I now focus all of my attention on Satan, the side of Lucifer that was split from him. The duality of the morningstar has always piqued my interest. Wrath and pride in one body until he fell. Upon falling, it ripped wrath from him and only pride remains. The other side of him assumed its own identity of Satan and separated itself fully from Lucifer to become autonomous.

"What's our plan of attack?" Raphael asks me with a grin, apparently proud of the leader I've become.

"To be perfectly honest, I'm not sure you're gonna like the answer I have for you." As the words slip from my lips, I unfurl my wings and flex them several times behind me before I allow them to hang half open. I touch the raven on my forearm and summon Azrael to my side. Upon his arrival, he moves to stand beside me and kisses my temple.

"Preparing to leave, daughter?" Azrael asks as he glances at the map and then over at my four mates who are present.

"Yes, I have my contingents of demons ready, as well as the creatures that live in the different realms, ready to go forth and dive deeper into Wrath." My answer is only related to the task at hand, not the elephant I still have to deal with.

"You know demon-like dragon creatures live down there, right?" His tone is slightly jovial as if he finds the situation funny. Shrugging, I finish the last of my coffee and make it vanish from my sight.

"I'm not concerned about the dragon demons. We've got one of our own." I raise my taloned hand and motion to Gage. He nods, acknowledging that he carries the dragon Rex. Raphael drums his fingers on the tabletop before Metatron rests his hand on his shoulder to get him to stop.

"I know and feel your agitation, Raphael." The words feel like velvet as they slip off my tongue, and he seems to soothe almost immediately. "Those last two rings are not safe for anyone with angelic blood." I lock eyes with him to get him to understand it's practically a death sentence for Metatron and him, as well as any of the other Archangels who want to fight at my side in the last two rings.

"If I need to, I won't be able to portal you or anyone else to the Angelic Realm if they strike you with a mortal blow." Enunciating every word and putting force behind each syllable is the only way I can get him to realize how dire the situation is.

"I can't lose you." The words come out with so much force, the walls shake along with everything else in the room. I don't mean to be so forceful, but he needs to understand what's happening. He looks down at the map briefly, then over at Metatron, then back at me again.

"I understand what you're saying, my love." His tone is soft and honeyed as he walks around the table to me, unfurling his opalescent white wings. He flexes them as he stands before me, offering me his hands. I take them without hesitation and try to force myself to smile, looking up into his eyes. He releases one hand and places it firmly on his chest. Then he cups my cheek and looks deeply into my eyes.

"I have waited a very long time for you." A soft sigh escapes his lips before he presses them gently to my forehead.

"All those years of being your guardian, I never once thought I'd ever be blessed with a mate. All those nights I stood watch over your apartment when the others were trying to torment you." He shakes his head and looks down briefly before turning his eyes to look at me again.

"I never once thought it was just my duty. And as my duty became more encompassing, and I watched how resilient you were to everything you were put through, I started falling in love with you." His admission rocks me to the core, and I stand there, almost in a state of shock.

"Please don't shut me out now when you need me the most." I've never heard Raphael beg for anything in the over three hundred years I've known him. Never once has he ever asked for anything of anyone else, especially not for himself.

My heart almost feels like it's breaking, knowing full well I have no choice but to refuse him. I free my other hand from him and raise both my hands to touch his cheeks. Through the mate bond and through my mind's eye, I show him exactly what Wrath looks like. Stones weep blood as if it's water leaking through a sandstone. Rivers of blood flow through the land like rivers of water flow through the Earth. Fire rains down from the sky, burning anything and everything it touches to ash. The leaves on the trees are like razor blades as they fly through the air, caught by the wind. They slice anything they come in contact with to ribbons.

Most of the creatures there are poisonous and lethal to anyone of angelic blood. I show this vision to everyone present, including Azrael, even though I'm pretty sure he knows what he's walking into. As I release Raphael's face, I stand up on tiptoes to press my lips gently against his. "I know what you mean when you say you can't lose me. For once, let me be your savior. Let me be your sword and shield," I say as passionately as possible, staring up into his eyes, allowing them to turn chrome, then back to my human gray.

"I can not lose you after only just getting you. We have a daughter to consider." My emotions almost get the better of me, and I sniffle briefly, trying to rein the tears back in.

"I need you to be here with Metatron, so I know you're safe." I kiss him again just as softly and close my eyes, hoping against hope he understands what I'm saying is the truth. That he understands this is all for his safety and Metatron's.

I suddenly feel warmth at my back and large hands resting on my hips. It can only be Metatron. "Brother, if what our mate says is true, then we must have faith and believe this is in our best interest." His tone is much softer than usual, lacking its normal firmness and reverberation when he's trying to get a point across.

"If she is trying to protect us, then for once we must lay down our swords and allow her to do what she was created for." I feel him press a kiss to the top of my head as he grips my hips firmly and gives them a slight squeeze, lending me his strength and support.

"I know this, brother, but it doesn't make it any easier." Raphael's tone is broken. As I open my eyes to look at him, emotions flicker over his visage.

"This is in no way, shape, or form a goodbye," I say firmly as I pull free of both of them.

Flexing my wings twice, I move about the room, trying to get my emotions under control. "We are literally descending into Hell," I say as I motion to the map before us. "This is the furthest into the rings anyone has gone since their creation just after the fall." I recant the history for Gage and Cyrus. I'm not sure how much they know about what happened before we were born. Not everyone is a history buff like me.

I know I struck a nerve with the Archangels because they simply nod along, knowing what I'm saying is 100 percent correct. "I promise you both this: neither Azrael nor my Dark Nephilim mates will leave my side the entire time we're down there."

Raphael and Metatron finally concede what's being done is in the best interest of all. I know it isn't an easy conclusion for them to come to, but it's one that's necessary. I smile as I walk over to Metatron and then motion for Gage to join me as well. "Between you two and Christian, the next time I'm ready to have children, hopefully one or two of you three will have a child of your own. But in good conscience, I can't bring another child into this world until I deal with this threat." Gage and Metatron exchange a glance with each other, then they both nod.

"I understand, sweet one," Metatron says as he looks down at me. "Still, it's difficult, nonetheless, to know you're walking into the lion's den without me. That I'm not able to offer you shelter or solace in any way." He bites his bottom lip, and it does funny things to me, even during this important conversation.

I know what he's trying to do. He's trying to derail my thought process, hoping to get me to reconsider what I've already decided. I pull away from Gage and Metatron and walk to the other side of the table to stand beside Cyrus. "Cyrus, Gage, Azrael, gather everything that you need. We're going in hot. I'll summon the Balor, the generals, and the wolves that can exist on that plane with me. We'll also summon Rex and all the other familiars that can survive there with us." I pace around as I list what and who we need.

"We'll take this next ring and then return. The last battle will be the worst of all of them, and I'm taking it the most seriously." I move forward and touch the table, making the map of the Wrath Ring raise up and become three-dimensional.

Every ridge, mountain, and valley becomes visible as does every river, stream, and fjord of blood. No secrets are left unturned. I stare at the area where Satan apparently lives. There appears to be a small fortress high up on a mountaintop, overlooking a valley of blood. "There's only one way to get up there, and it'll be on Rex or by our own wings." Having a large skull dragon at our disposal is helpful because we'll hide on his back and can avoid detection since our wings are black or mostly black.

I see the moment Azrael makes the same determination I have. He nods at me, then salutes and vanishes from sight. I know he's going to prepare for this last assault before we go after Lucifer. He may call forth others who owe him favors and bring them with us as well. Cyrus and Gage both nod and remain at my side. Raphael, Metatron, and the other Archangels who are here are now gathering in the far corner.

"We will be your eyes from here, watching the map to see if anything changes. If it does, we'll reach out to you through the bond and let you know." Strategically, this may give me an advantage, but on the downside, the map won't respond to him how it does for me.

Plucking a feather from close to my body, I turn it into another ring, this time a signet ring. I press the ring to the map. "The bearer of this ring is to be obeyed as if it's me. The wearer's wishes are my commands to do as he bids you to do," I say, taking in the imprint of the signet ring. The mark left behind looks like the scales of a snake. And not just any snake—a Basilisk. I move to Raphael and take his hand. I slide the signet ring on his ring finger.

"The map will do your bidding as long as you press the ring to this spot right here." I point to the spot where the mark is on the map. He nods, acknowledging what I'm telling him. He's reluctant to stay behind. But if he can at least be of service, he might not be so rough on himself while I'm gone.

"Make sure you come back in one piece," he says softly against my ear as he leans down and kisses the side of my cheek.

"I'll do my best. But for now, I need to gather the others. It's time to go." Without a backward glance, I leave my war room, heading down to the throne room where I usually open my portals. Now I have to wait for Azrael, Cyrus, and Gage to be ready to leave.

CHAPTER 88

THANA

Minutes tick away like hours as the heavy lub-dub of my heartbeat echoes in my ears. It reminds me of the story by that Poe guy I read years ago. He believed he heard the heartbeat of the man he'd murdered under the floorboards, and it haunted him.

My heartbeat seems to beat as loud as that heart right now, knowing every beat brings us closer to departure. I don't fear the mission before us. I'm more concerned with what we'll find on the other side. You can't go into these things being afraid because fear is the mind-killer which I learned from one of my other favorite movies.

First to arrive in the hall is Cyrus, who's smiling broadly and twirling his sword in his hand as if there's nothing wrong and we're not about to go to war. Sauntering in shortly after him is Gage. He's not as brash as Cyrus and seems to take this a little more seriously instead of acting like it's just a giant game. He has his sword and shield, and on his back is a bag containing who knows what.

Lastly, being dramatic, Azrael appears in a wisp of smoke, one sword on his hip and one in his hand, wearing a smirk to end all smirks. He looks like he's getting ready to fuck some shit up. And that's the winning attitude we're going to need for this battle ahead of us.

The Archangel side of the family moves forward, hugging and kissing me before I'm ready to leave. They shake hands with the Dark Nephilim side as well. They back away from where we're standing, and I turn my eyes to the obsidian wall before me. I've learned this wall seems to be the best for creating portals. I touch the wolf on my chest and manifest my Destroyer armor so I'm wrapped in its black-and-gold embrace. The movie I love the most has a character known as the Witch-king. More than anything else, it's fearsome and slightly terrifying, even to me, to stare into the king's abysmal eyes. The armor that I have manifested for myself since the beginning reminds me more of the witch-king than that of the armor my grandfather wore. It's more terrifying with additional sharp edges and a haunted quality to it. I hope channeling my favorite character from the books will strike fear in the hearts of my enemies. Refocusing on the task before me, my gauntleted hand extends out, and I move it in a full circle over and over until the portal rips open.

What we see on the other side is nothing short of the makings of a horror movie. I explained to the boys what they'd see, but it's far worse than even I expected. We see rivers of blood as well as bodies strung up and hanging off every available branch, alcove, rock, and structure. Whatever they can hang something off, they have. Bodies are strung up on pikes as if they're marionettes, lining the roads and leading us straight to the palace.

"I guess we know where Vlad the Impaler got his ideas." I try to sound jovial, attempting to crack a joke at the moment. Only Azrael and Cyrus laugh at what I'd said. The Archangels cringe, knowing my joke is more of a reality than anything else.

Stepping through the portal first, my boots hit the black sand and sink slightly into its depths. Nothing is what it seems here, and the stench of blood and decay hangs heavy in the air.

Glancing around slowly, I notice things moving under the surface of the sand. Eel-like creatures shoot up at me with their multi-fanged mouths open, ready to attack me and bite. With a quick twist of my gauntleted hand, my talons slice through the armored flesh of these creatures without an issue. The ones that make it past my talons hit my armor but are unable to gain purchase. They fall back to the sand again and then slither off, only to launch themselves at me for a second attempt.

When the last of the creatures are felled by my talons, Cyrus, Gage, and Azrael move through the portal. I make the mistake of turning around and looking back into the throne room on the other side of the portal. My Archangel mates, as well as their brothers, stand in a state of shock, seeing the world of Wrath. I shift my hand back to normal and raise my fingers to my lips, blowing a kiss to Raphael and Metatron. With a wave of my hand, I watch their reactions and then close the portal, keeping them safe from the creatures of Wrath.

I re-form my talon gauntlets and manifest my helm on my head. I slowly approach Gage and rest a hand on his shoulder, looking out across the horror-scape before us. "Time to unleash Rex," I say to him and then motion to the area before us.

He steps slightly away from everyone and removes his armor from the arm Rex rests on. He touches the great skull dragon's head and summons him. Being deeper within the circles adds to the power of the familiars we summon. Rex emerges initially as a large pulsing, viscous black mass. It pulses and throbs with a heartbeat of its own until it stretches out and becomes the wyrm dragon I know him to be. Being over thirty-five feet long and at least ten to twelve stories tall, he's massive.

The bone plates of his skull don't resemble any kind of scale that I ever remember seeing. Here, he can assume his true form, that of this wyrm dragon. He's essentially walking death with wings. When he lowers his massive head before us, we see his bone and his bone plate have replaced the scales that were there in his smaller form. Within his eye sockets are burning, bright-crimson embers.

I reach out and gently place my hand upon his great mull and give it a single pat. He lays down and extends a wing out for us to climb onto his back. I motion for my mates and my father-in-law to climb up his wing and sit between the plates on his back. Rex brings forth his large neck for me to climb on and raises me up so I can climb up to his head and sit behind his large curved horns. If I had to describe his horns to someone who hasn't seen him, I'd say they look like giant ram horns, except they're bony.

When I'm in place, he rises up on his legs and then takes a running start and spreads his wings wide, taking to the air. Once we're airborne, Azrael walks up his neck, holding onto the spines to stand alongside me. "We have wings of our own, daughter. Why do we need him to get us to where we're going?" Azrael asks the most obvious questions sometimes, and I can't help but laugh a little. Not long after the words leave his lips, large, winged creatures take to the air from a hidden alcove below us.

"Retract your wings. Get under the large scales, pit fiends are incoming," I scream and usher Azrael back down Rex's neck. The pit fiends descend on Rex like mosquitoes in the middle of summer. I hold on to the large horns on Rex's head as he takes evasive maneuvers to avoid the attacks by the fiends who wield fire weapons and electric whips. They could easily rip the wings from our bodies.

Thankfully, Rex's wings are not affected by their weapons, nor are his scales. Several of the fiends make the mistake of landing on Rex's back and meet the swords of my mates and my father-in-law. I remain on Rex's head to protect the back of his neck at the base of his skull, which is the only place that he has any vulnerability. Thankfully, it's not commonly known the soft spot exists, but I know because of my grandfather's knowledge. Two pit fiends land on his neck and start making their way toward me with fiery whips and enchanted maces in their hands. They start swinging as they get closer to me. But I can't unleash most of my weapons without causing harm.

Instead of unleashing the weapons at my disposal, I choose to channel part of the gift of the creature coiled within my chest. My eyes shift to serpentine slits and blaze to life as I make eye contact with the attacking pit fiends. The look of terror in their eyes as their bodies turn to stone is delicious. They try to escape and take flight, but it's already too late for them. Just as they gain lift-off from the dragon's back, their bodies transform to stone and fall to the ground below. I repeat this several times and then rush to my mates, who seem to be overwhelmed. I move quickly to shield Cyrus's eyes as I look at the pit fiends surrounding him. It just takes a few moments before they drop away as stone monuments to their own stupidity. I make my way through the remaining pit fiends, only occasionally having to use the stone gaze on them.

Several heartbeats pass quickly as I look around, maintaining vigilance over those under my watch. The attack was unexpected, but luckily, between Rex's armor and my newfound ability, we can keep them safe. Cyrus moves up beside me. Holding onto the dragon spine next to me, I unfurl my wings and flex them twice, stretching them in and back out again. The more I use my creature's gift, it seems to get closer to the surface, wanting to escape.

I know at some point I'll need to let him loose, but now is not the time. I look down and then back over at my father-in-law. "Father?" Arching a brow, I wait for his response. Azrael stares at me for several moments and then steps forward, moving his own child out of the way.

"Something is plaguing you, daughter. Speak plainly and tell me what it is." Biting my bottom lip, I search for the words I want to say versus the ones I need to say.

"I know I lose my spot in Elysium the minute I shift." I pause almost dramatically as I think further about what I'm saying.

"I'm not sure if I went in-depth with Cyrus and Gage about what would happen to me. So some of this may be a shock to them." I look at both my mates and know I missed telling them some of the severity of the situation. Turning slowly, I face both Gage and Cyrus and take a deep, slow breath, fortifying myself before the conversation I need to have with them.

"Grandfather told me before he passed to the other side that after I take the form of the beast within my chest, I will never be able to walk through the gates of the Silver City and live there." Biting my bottom lip, I stare down at my talons and exhale roughly.

Gage steps forward and gives me a hug, gripping me to his chest, and then he kisses my forehead. "Silver City or not, you're our mate, and whatever you decide is best for our family is what we'll follow."

I nod hesitantly as I think about what my shifting would do to the angelic side of the family. I'd never be able to enter the gates of the Silver City with them. I'd never be able to take my place there beside them. But if I did go there, I'd be leaving behind my two Dark Nephilim mates and one of my daughters, which also would not be fair. The castle is almost within our grasp, and I briefly kiss both of my mates before moving back to Rex's head to take control of our approach.

CHAPTER 89

GAGE

The ride on the dragon to this point has been nothing short of amazing. All Thana has to do is think about what she wants, and the dragon responds without a single word from her.

We battle those winged beasts tooth and nail. And then Thana comes forward, shielding our eyes, and she protects us from whatever magic she's wielding. Those demons fall from the sky like missiles plummeting faster and faster until they crash to the ground. Their destruction is utterly amazing. They shatter on impact and thus, will never be able to be resurrected.

After the battle, Thana moves back up to the dragon's head and rests her hands on his horns. He circles the castle several times as we watch the horde of demons and creatures within the castle walls. Rex rises high and then dive-bombs straight down, his green acid breath bathing all the creatures within the walls and melting their flesh instantly.

We continue circling the castle, and as more of the inhabitants pour out from the holes on the sides of the walls, Rex keeps unleashing his acid breath on them. Without warning, Thana dives off of his head, spreads her wings wide and takes on the largest of the demons that seem to be untouched by the acid breath.

I watch as she unsheathes Daybreaker, driving it directly into the monster's heart. He turns to ash almost immediately and falls away to nothing. Following Thana's lead, we dive off one at a time and do battle on the ground with the remaining demons.

It's unsettling how easy this appears to be. Every swipe of my sword and every hit with my shield seems to move much easier than it should. There must be something wrong.

Slicing through Satan's forces appears to be somewhat easier than I expected. Thana and Cyrus seem to be in their glory as they dodge and parry, almost dancing with each other as they battle Satan's minions. Azrael seems to be in his element, as well, as he rends the flesh from each of the demons crossing his path.

Wave after wave of demons come over the wall and through the tunnels at the base of the battlements. No matter how hard we fight or what weapons we use, for each one that falls, several more rise after it.

I wish we'd brought more than just ourselves with us since we're battling more demons than I expected. Thana breaks loose from the four demons she's been going toe to toe with and flies into the air.

At the last possible moment, I feel her calling to us through the bond to get out of her way. Cyrus rushes toward his father and grabs him as we both fly up and out of the castle walls.

Thana has turned herself into a blazing inferno, covered in blackened flames as she dive-bombs out of the sky. Upon impact, everything in her path is incinerated, leaving nothing but ash and molten rock around her. It's amazing to realize our beautiful angel, our delicate mate, has just obliterated several hundred demonic forces.

We fly down and land near her, checking her over and making sure she sustained no damage. A smile graces her lips as she laughs at herself. "Well, that was easier than I thought," she says, almost with sadistic glee.

Arching my brow, I stare at her, wondering where my innocent mate is and who this female is before me. Still laughing to herself, Thana comes over and caresses my cheeks. "Oh, come on, Gage. It wasn't that bad," she says as she ruffles my hair, sending it in all kinds of crazy directions.

"Thana, you just incinerated the entirety of the castle grounds." Running my hand down my face, I truly believe she doesn't get it.

"Okay?" she says as she moves over to check over Cyrus and Azrael. After she's sure there's nothing wrong with them at the moment, she walks back over to me and smiles, looking up.

"There's one of three ways this could've gone," she says, raising three fingers.

"The first way, I could've brought all of my legions here and exposed the forces I have." Her statements are very logical and, scarily enough, well-thought-out.

"The second way, I could've brought part of my forces here, still exposing some of the numbers I have, and then I'd have had casualties." She purses her lips as she looks at her index finger, which is the final one still standing.

"The third way, it was just easier for the four of us to get in here. I'm more than enough to handle everything that's happened. I'm hoping to draw Satan out of wherever he's hiding because with my not having the sheer force of numbers, I think he'll get overconfident and make a mistake." Shrugging, she continues to walk around the entire castle courtyard, examining everything.

For someone who's never been in the middle of a war, she has more knowledge than I'd have thought possible. But then again, her grandfather gave her all his knowledge of wars and warfare, and I keep forgetting to take that into account.

I can tell the moment she thinks about our next move by the way her brows furrow. Cyrus brought it up to me the other night, and I realized I'd never noticed it. I'm almost afraid to see the toll all this is taking on her. I know it can't be easy for someone who is normally a healer in her day job to now being a ruthless war general who's dispatching hundreds of lives almost daily.

I know, eventually, at the end of the war, we'll need to sit down and help her unpack this. But who will be the one to take on that burden? More than likely, she'll either go to Metatron or to Raphael about it. I don't really think Christian would be an option because he's just slightly more experienced than she is. Plus, he hasn't fought in as many wars as the archangels have.

The only other person who's had a lot more experience is Cyrus's father, but he wouldn't be as sympathetic as the two golden boys would be. Shit, now I'm referring to the angel side like Cyrus does. Maybe it is true what Cyrus complained about the night of the Mated Ball—that it seems like we're persecuted just because of the color of our wings.

In all honesty, I'm treated even worse because I chose to fall. I kick around skulls and bones as I wander around the interior of the castle until, that is, I feel a sharp blade at my back, and I halt. "Make a move and you die." Satan's voice is smooth as silk and warm as a summer's day.

It's the same tone Lucifer had when he enchanted the other angels to fall. But I know it's the other half of his personality standing behind me. "What do you want, Satan?" My voice is almost a growl as I feel him dig the tip of the blade between the pieces of metal of my armor.

"I want what every fallen one wants. Revenge." He practically growls the word "revenge" out, and you can taste the venom in his tone in the air.

I notice Thana has seen who's behind me, and she slowly makes her way over. "So, this is Satan." She flashes a million-dollar smile and then touches the wolf on her breast plate, making her armor vanish before us.

What is my mate thinking by making herself vulnerable? "The Destroyer. Forgive me if I don't bow before you." With a flourish of his free hand, Satan's arrogance is on full display.

The sanguine smile gracing Thana's lips sends a chill up my

spine. Her eyes are cold and calculating as they flicker between chrome and abyssal orbs.

"I see there's a disturbance in the force." Satan's honeyed tone makes Thana's right eye twitch.

"No disturbance," she says calmly and collectedly as she raises her hand up and runs her fingers through her hair.

He tilts his head to the side, still keeping the blade dug into my back as he backs us toward the wall so no one can sneak in behind him. "Is that so? Why did your eyes change?" He asks right next to my ear, and then he runs his tongue along the shell of it.

"I can smell the scent of Azrael's heir on this one. I guess I know how *you* fell." His sarcastic tone, laced with venom, almost makes my stomach turn.

"Well, at least I fell for someone I loved rather than being deceived," I say as he twists the blade again, this time going further into my skin and actually breaking through to grind against my ribs.

Gritting my teeth, I try not to wince from the pain of the blade pushing between two of my ribs and twisting, spreading them wider. I can hear a faint crack as one of my ribs breaks from the edge of the blade twisting.

Anger flares in Thana's eyes, and those abyssal orbs seem to ooze black viscous material down her pale visage. Her normal porcelain features start to contort slowly in rage. "I suggest you remove the blade from him," she says slowly, pausing between each word and trying to bite back the anger I know through the bond is welling up in her chest.

"And what will I get if I release him?" Satan asks as he slowly withdraws the blade from my side and brings the bloody tip to his lips to lick my blood off.

"Tastes like sin," he practically purrs as he stares at Thana. She steps forward just enough to be within touching distance of me.

In a matter of seconds, she presses her hand to me, and I'm gone. I end up back with the others in her castle fortress. Looking around in shock, I scream her name and head to the throne room, banging on the obsidian wall we used for the portal.

Raphael, Metatron, and the other angels come running the minute they hear me. "What happened? Why are you here?" Then they see the trail of blood leading to me as I start to suffer from blood loss. I begin to get woozy and drop to my knees before the obsidian wall.

"Thana sent me back, and now she's facing off with Satan," I utter before I pass out.

CHAPTER 90

THANA

That was the absolute and final straw. The fact that he drew Gage's blood and then licked it in front of me makes every fiber in my being want to obliterate him.

Without skipping a beat, I throw my hands out at him, bringing forth the waters of the River Styx to encapsulate him in it. Once he's fully restrained, I move forward quickly, donning my armor yet again. I prepare to rend the flesh from his bones in retribution for what he did to my mate and threatening his life.

"Wow, there's the Destroyer I was waiting for." A sick, twisted smile plays on his lips as he stares at me.

I have to admit, at one point in time, he must've been exquisite, but now all I see is the male that hurt my mate.

Reaching out, I touch his flesh, and a vision comes over me. Ash-gray wings adorn his back. His hair is no longer pitch black, but instead a dirty blonde. Several feathers along the arch of his wing are mottled black-and-white. And in his arms is a woman with snow-white hair and almost gray roots. As he opens his wings, I get a better look at who he's holding. It's my daughter.

My heart wants to stop in my chest as this revelation almost knocks the wind out of me. I wasn't careful, and I sent the vision throughout the entire bond.

Satan is to be the mate of one of my daughters. I stumble backward, and Cyrus catches me. Satan looks at me, just as puzzled as I am while I stare at him. Apparently, the contact shared the vision between the two of us, and both of us were completely shaken.

I look back over to Azrael and fumble, trying to get the words out for several moments before I finally spit them out. "How often do the Destroyer's visions come to fruition?" I ask him, not breaking eye contact with Satan.

"The Destroyer's visions occur 100 percent of the time. They are divine truth and justice, all in the same breath." I ponder exactly what my father-in-law is saying as I stare at the man before me.

There's only one way for me to find out if this is true. "We're taking him back with us."

"What the fuck do you mean 'we're taking him back with us'?" Cyrus roars as he runs forward with his blade drawn, preparing to impale Satan in the chest with it.

Reaching out, my hand becomes covered in my armor as I grip Cyrus's blade and stop him before he's able to harm Satan. "If what your father says is true, you cannot harm him." I finally break eye contact with Satan and beg with my eyes as I stare at Cyrus, trying to get him to understand.

He jabs his finger in Satan's direction. "He will not have my daughter." I bite my bottom lip as I look between the two of them.

"If he survives absolution, then whatever is written in the stars for him is what will happen." I make the motion with my hand to rip open the portal and slowly, it blazes to life before us.

Cyrus stomps through the portal first to go find Gage. Azrael and I walk side-by-side with the bound Satan into my castle fortress. I close the portal immediately behind us and keep him suspended in the waters from the River Styx.

Pacing the room, I try to figure out exactly what to do. Justice needs to be meted out, and yet with what I've seen, I can't do it. I will not bring intentional harm to my daughter by depriving her of one of her mates. Every mate is chosen for a reason. Why it's him is beyond me. But who am I to judge? I keep walking in circles around Satan, and he watches me silently, not attempting to utter a word and not putting up a fight.

I'd almost say it was suspect, but he saw the vision too. Drawing in a deep breath, I finally stop before him. Now my Archangel mates and the other Archangels finally come in from the throne room.

"We saw what you saw, Thana," Metatron says as he steps forward and then drops to one knee before me, taking both my hands into his. His sky-blue eyes gaze up at me in wonder as a calmness moves over his features. Utter peace and tranquility is what he's radiating at the moment, and I can't help but breathe easier, being in his presence.

"What do you think, Metatron?" I bend forward and kiss him on his forehead as I stare down at him, waiting to see what his divine wisdom imparts to me.

"The Destroyer's visions, like my own, have never been false. If you will permit me, I wish to hold your hand and touch him at the same time and see if I get a different understanding of the vision before you mete out justice." I glance briefly over at Satan, then back down to Metatron and nod my head.

He stands slowly and then walks over and places his hand on the back of Satan's neck. "It's been a long time, brother," he whispers to him, and a strange emotion moves over Satan's face.

All I've seen from him is anger and rage, but now I see sadness and regret. Perhaps he can be saved after all. My grip tightens on Metatron's hand, and I close my eyes, allowing myself to open up to him.

The vision plays like it did before. This time, we get a better line of sight on his inside feathers, the ones closest to his body on the underside of his wings. They're still pitch black.

As I pull Metatron out of the vision, the level of shock on his face is beyond measure. He glances quickly between Satan and me, and he shakes his head slowly. "How do you propose we cleanse him?"

I stare at Satan for several moments at the impact of Metatron's words. The knowledge is locked deep within me. And I know, just by instinct alone, that I'll be able to do it. He fortunately, and yet unfortunately, is pivotal in one of my daughters' futures.

As I approach Satan, concern crosses his visage as he fights against his bonds. "Stay away from me!" he screams as he begins to thrash, trying to escape.

"No!" I unleash the words with the full commanding force of the Destroyer. That one word reverberates around the interior of the house, echoing repeatedly.

Flexing my wings, I change the color of my feathers to match the wings he'll have. Satan screams in horror at what is happening before him.

Whatever I must look like to him scares the living daylights out of him. Smoke-gray wings with mottled black-and-white feathers adorn bits and pieces of me. The feathers underneath my wings, close to my body, are pitch black, whereas the long flight feathers range in colors from smoke gray to being tipped with white.

Pulling a stunt like I normally do when I'm a reaper, I hover several inches off the ground as I move toward him. "Remember who you were," I order him as I reach out and grip his face with both hands.

He struggles and strains, trying to break free of my grip as I stare down at him with chrome eyes. Leaning forward, I press my lips to his forehead and close my eyes. Using the lessons taught to me from my grandfather's knowledge, I purge all the negative energy and all the darkness within him. He is neither angel nor fallen, but instead somewhere in between.

He'll be in about the same class as Gage and Cyrus but slightly more on the dark side. I feel the burning in my veins as my body destroys the taint within him. When the pain slowly abates, I open my eyes and pull away from him.

His hair is dirty brown with blonde highlights. His dark charred skin is now a peachy color, almost bronze-gold in sections. "Open your eyes, Satan." I call his name as I release his cheeks, and he blinks his eyes twice. Staring up at me, his eyes are similar in color to mine. Their gray-green is as light as my steel-gray.

I remove the River Styx's waters from around him and allow him to stand on his own two feet again. I walk around him till I'm standing behind him after I've resumed my usual form. Touching the area by his shoulder blades where his wings would manifest, I make them rip free from his body.

His wings are pale smoke-gray, at least on the outside, with speckled black-and-white feathers along the wing bones. His flight feathers along the veins are pure obsidian, and the feather itself fades from gray to white. I move around to stand before him, and just like in my vision, the inside of his wings is black as night.

A soft smile graces my lips as I look up at him. "This is your second chance. Don't mess it up," I state plainly before moving out of the way to allow the Archangels to see their brother once again.

He's only half the man he used to be because the other half of him exists as Lucifer, hiding in the deepest depths of the rings of Hell. And I will eradicate the other half of him.

"How do I repay you?" he asks as he rushes over to take my hand in his. Dropping to his knees before me, he spreads his wings wide and presses his forehead to my knuckles in full submission.

Resting my free hand on the top of his head, I close my eyes and breathe deeply, seeing if a unique vision comes. Nothing's changed. The vision remains as it was before. In the future, he will be my daughter's mate.

"There is a lot to atone for, Satan." He slowly looks up at me as I speak to him, and a slow nod is given.

"I understand completely. What is it you wish for me to do?" That is the sixty-four million dollar question. What is it I wish for him to do?

I pace the room, flexing my wings before looking back at him again. "You're definitely not a Light Nephilim. You have all the powers and abilities of the Dark Nephilim, but you do still retain one power of the Light Nephilim."

He cants his head curiously as he looks up at me. "What would that be?"

Smiling broadly, I move to stand before him and grip both of his hands. "You can heal people. Devote your time to the hospital where Raphael and I work. Devote your time to taking care of the sick and the dying. Only then will you possibly atone for your sins. Only then, eventually, will you possibly be good enough to be trusted with my child." As the words fall from my lips, he drops his head low.

"Your wish is my command. You didn't have to save me, but you did. You could've destroyed me for all I've done." His words waiver slightly as his emotions overcome him.

When he looks up, tears roll down his high cheekbones. Blood vessels streak across the whites of his eyes, showing these are actual tears. Like a mother, I reach out and pull him to me. I rest his head against my shoulder, wrapping my arms and wings around him to comfort him. Gently, I thread my fingers through his hair, trying to soothe him. An angel who does not know love is no angel. And for him to be without love for the past few thousand years, he needs to learn it again to be a suitable mate and father in the future.

"I'm going to retire for the evening after we have dinner. Tomorrow, you will remain here with my angelic mates and the rest of the Archangels to relearn everything you've probably forgotten since you've been down there." Without a word, he bows his head again after he pulls away from me and stands up slowly.

Reaching back to my own feathers, I pluck one that's close to my body and turn it into a ring. Once the feather is a ring, I walk over and slide it onto Satan's finger. "Raphael will take you to the hallway where all the bedrooms are. All you need to do is touch my ring to a door, and it will open for you. That will be your room for as long as you're here."

I give Cyrus a simple nod, and he joins me where I'm standing.

"When we return to the Mortal Realm, I'll go with Cyrus and help him clean out his old apartment. You will live there since it's not too far from the hospital." Motioning once again to Raphael, he moves to me and bows his head slightly.

"On the first available Monday morning, you'll go to work with Raphael. He'll assign you tasks which you must complete day in and day out from now until the end of time. Each time we've been in a hospital too long, you'll move with us to the next one and start all over again. This is your penance." Satan drops his head again, accepting the task that's been given to him.

"If this is my penance, then what is it you did to receive the same penance?" It's an honest question, and sometimes I wonder about it myself.

A soft chuckle escapes my lips as I look at him. "I was born," is the only answer I have for him.

Once the answer escapes my lips, and the look of confusion crosses his face, I take my leave of the room and head off to mine to go shower.

CHAPTER 91

THANA

Last night differed from all the nights before it. Instead of rolling around in the throes of passion between one or more of my mates, all four of us slept curled up in my bed in the master chamber. The tension ebbs and flows from Raphael and Metatron, who are both concerned about me going after Lucifer without them.

I hear a knock at my chamber door, setting my familiars and me on edge. If it was an attack, they wouldn't be knocking. But to be disturbed right before going into the last battle definitely does not sit well with me.

Walking across the room, I touch the amulet around my neck and manifest my armor. With a wave of my hand, my chamber doors open, and I see my father-in-law, Azrael, standing there, smiling at me.

"When do we leave, Destroyer?" He phrases the question specifically that way, then bows deeply to me. I know it's all just for show because of the others who are in the castle with us.

I look back at my mates, who are still all clambered into bed together and then return my gaze back to my father-in-law. "Since it's just the four of us going, give me about twenty minutes."

619

With a simple bow of his head, he backs away and heads back downstairs. "Twenty minutes?" Raphael asks, and I hear the nervousness in his tone.

"You knew this day was coming," I say as I close the distance between him and me and caress his cheek gently.

"But why did it have to come so soon?" The words falling from his lips make my heart ache.

I know it's not that he questions my strength or ability. It's just that his life and Metatron's are tied directly to mine. If I fall in battle, the two of them will also cease to exist. I'm not sure how it will affect Christian, but I don't want to find out either.

Gently I kiss his lips, sipping on the bottom one and sucking it into my mouth, then give it a slight nip. "I will do everything within my power to come back to you in one piece. Have faith." Smiling, I throw his own words back at him.

They're the same words Archangels utter constantly in times of crises. He nods his head slowly before pulling me into a bone-crushing hug, then passing me off to Metatron. "I just got you," the big guy utters softly as he bows his head down with his lips next to my ear.

"I know," I say softly enough so only he hears me.

I wrap my arms around his neck and hold him as tightly to me as possible. A soft shudder moves through his body, and I hear his breathing stutter for a moment.

"I agree with Raph. I can't lose you." This time when Metatron says it, it hurts more. It hurts more because he's had next to no human interaction except for me and the job I do.

I force myself to nod and don't trust my voice as I feel the emotion bubble up in my chest. It's heartbreak. My heart is breaking over the fear that I may not make it back. I may be sentencing myself to death in order to put the world back into balance.

I kiss Metatron passionately as I hug him tightly to me, my fingers threading through his thick, golden locks. When I release my grip on him and back away just a little to look into his eyes, those golden orbs seem to glow with his power and might.

"I'll be back," I say against his lips, brushing mine against his. He presses our foreheads together and exhales roughly as I watch a single tear roll down his cheek.

Standing on my tiptoes, I kiss away Metatron's tear. Closing my eyes, I reach out through the bond to all five of my mates. I tell them how much I love them. I tell them how much each one of them means to me.

I reach out to my daughters and tell them Mommy loves them too. It's not that I'm saying goodbye. I'm being prepared just in case the worst happens. I'd be a fool to think, even though I've ascended to the mantle of Destroyer, that I'm omnipotent.

Only one being, from what I've been told, is to achieve that. And it's definitely not me. I feel everyone's love for me returned tenfold. It warms my heart and makes me realize what I'm doing absolutely has to be done. I have to provide a better world for my daughters.

I have to ensure the future is bright for any children I bring into this world. I have to set things back on course, even though they've been slowly derailing over the past thousand years. All I've suffered will be in vain if I fail this close to the finish line.

I pull back from Metatron and smile, then I look over at Raphael. "Wait for me," I whisper.

Both men nod, and I can see how much they're struggling with what's going on. Both of them are warriors of the highest order and are being asked to sit on the sidelines. This can't be easy for either of them, especially not Raphael, who was my guardian for most of my life.

Pulling away from Metatron, I reach out and take Gage and Cyrus's hands. "We'll be back as soon as we can," I say passionately as I squeeze both my Dark Nephilim mates' hands, trying more to assure myself of what I say than anyone else.

Reluctantly, both of them nod, and when they do, I pull Gage and

Cyrus through the shadows and down into the war room. Azrael is already waiting there for us.

That cold, hard mask I remember seeing for the past three hundred years barely slips when he sees us arrive. He motions toward the throne room, wanting us to get going. Without skipping a beat, we head there and prepare to engage in the toughest battle of our lives.

Like I've done many times before, I move my hands in a circular motion. As I pull and rip at the fabric of our existence, the blackened mist slowly ebbs and flows, twirling clockwise, almost like a tornado.

Looking down at the funnel, I see the opening at the bottom. The last ring will be the toughest battle any of us have ever faced. As the portal opens up, winged creatures fly in a concentric circle around what seems to be the city where we're heading in the distance.

These are creatures I've never seen before. They remind me of those flying monkeys in that old wizard movie. They're throwing spears down into the city. To what end, I have no idea.

Once the portal opens wide enough, Cyrus, Gage, Azrael, and I jump through, and I close it immediately behind us. Quickly, we move across the golden sand to a rock formation not far away.

"What do you think is going on?" Cyrus asks as he places a hand on my shoulder.

"I'm not sure. It's almost like they've been ordered to attack the citizens." We keep watching, and the attack continues for quite some time.

"I guess he's thought of a new way to torture the souls who've been entrusted to him," Azrael says as he moves to get a better view of the city.

"I was led to believe the Pride realm is a place where whatever you're most prideful of is the opposite of what you had when you were alive." The words tumble out of my mouth without a second thought as I try to figure out exactly what's happening.

"Once upon a time, daughter, that was correct. But the reason everything is off-balance is that each of the princes twisted the purpose of the rings to fit their own desires. From what I understand of the Pride ring now is that if the denizens who live here don't worship and pay homage to Lucifer, they are beaten, flogged, and have their flesh rended from their bodies. And since their torture is eternal, they heal, and it's done all over again." I raise both my eyebrows in a state of shock at this information.

I understood each person's personal hell is supposed to be different—to be tortured repeatedly over not having the thing that they were prideful over. But to literally and physically be tortured is an entirely different animal. I glance between both my mates, then back to Azrael. "Any suggestions?" He taps his finger on his bottom lip, staring down at the city below us.

"Call in all those favors you've garnered over the last four months." His tone leaves no room for argument. And sadly, I know what he says is truly the only option left for us.

The Balor, the wolves, and the generals I've made deals with—all their favors will have to be called in for this last assault. Not only do we have to wipe out Lucifer, but we also have to take out each of the denizens that have been working for him for the last millennium. There can be no survivors, other than the souls who are supposed to be punished here for their worst sin.

Drawing in a fortifying breath, I stand up and move us deeper into the mountainous region behind us. Once we're there, I summon everyone to me. I walk over to Cyrus and grip his cheeks, locking eyes with him. His eyes blacken immediately as I share with him the knowledge of how to rip open portals. I infuse his body with some of the power of the Destroyer so he can assist me with calling the others to me.

He double blinks, and a new understanding crosses his visage. When we break apart, we stand side-by-side while he mirrors my every move—right hand circling and left hand out, palm flat—as we both open portals at the same time.

I bring forth the wolves, and he calls forth the Balor. As each army arrives, we turn and open another portal, dragging the others through. Each one heeding the call of the Destroyer, ready and able to go to battle at my command.

This will take a while, but in the end, it's the only answer I have while in battle. One more fight, and it brings me closer to being able to go home. I just hope everyone's faith in me wasn't misplaced.

As we close the last portal, several thousand demons, denizens, animals, and corrupted souls stand at the ready to fight by my side. The leaders of each of the factions move forward and bow, taking a knee before me. As I look my army over, I can't help but feel I'm missing something.

Besides the fact that most of my mates are not here, something is still out of place. In my head, I hear the rattle and slide of scale upon scale. This may be the time I'll need to unleash the beast within me and doom myself to never cross the gates of the Silver City.

It will not be in vain. It would be what's needed to be done to set the world back within the sphere it's supposed to be. "Daughter, no one before has ever assembled an army of this magnitude," Azrael says, the wonder in his voice evident.

I force a smile, then move to stand before everyone gathered here. "Unleash your full power on this realm. Do not hold back."

The force behind my voice rattles the stone of the surrounding mountains. Fragments fall and rain down along the sides of the cavern. "Do not fear retribution, for I am here. I will protect all who serve me." I bring my fist down and a mighty staff manifests in my hand. The staff itself becomes a scythe, large and terrifying, with depictions of wars and skeletons etched along its blade.

"Bring them death eternal," I say as I point the scythe to my army and take on my reaper form, rising into the air. Below me a Firemare manifests—the stallion, the leader of the herd that I'd ridden before. He rears up and blows flames from his nostrils as the hairs on the backs of his legs ignite. We turn and head toward the city of Pride, ready to rain hell upon its battlements.

My army falls in step behind me as we head toward the city. Shadow creatures rise up around us, heeding my call. Every clop of my horse's hooves brings us one step closer to the final battle.

CHAPTER 92

THANA

Every step the stallion I ride takes feels like it thunders beneath me. As we move closer to the city of Pride, my heart pounds harder. It's not out of fear, but it's borne from the fact that I know I lead thousands into what may be the biggest battle in history.

We're in the lands where angels fear treading. We're literally in the land of nightmares. My mates Cyrus and Gage are mounted upon their own Firemares as we head toward the city. My father-in-law, Azrael, drifts beside us in his reaper form. He's just as terrifying as I remember seeing him so many years ago for the first time.

Thousands of soldiers march under my command, their steps rhythmically falling behind us, causing almost a mini-earthquake and announcing our arrival. Staring ahead, I watch the rising walls growing closer to us. There's only one thing I'm certain of at this moment, and that is we need to be victorious. There will be no survivors, nor will we allow anyone to surrender. They need a total cleansing of this ring, and I will deliver it.

In my dreams last night, a glowing gold orb came to me and showed me two different ways that this battle could play out. I don't know if it was Metatron's twin or the Creator himself showing me these possibilities. Both of them depicted victory. But in one, I lose Gage, and in the other, both mates survive without incident. The big difference between the two visions is that in one, I become the Basilisk. In the other, I do not. The Silver City was never something I thought I'd be able to ascend to. So the possibility of losing the ability to go there doesn't frighten me in the least. What bothers me is not being able to have all my mates in one place.

As we move closer to the walls, I motion with my scythe for my forces to spread out and surround the walls of the city. I thought the city of Pride would be much larger than it actually is. The big thing about the city is how ordinate everything appears to be. The flying monkey-like creatures are gone. In their wake are vulture-like creatures sitting on the peaks of the walls. I say vulture-like because they look like a vulture and a dragon had a baby. Where there should be feathers, there are scales, and where there should be leather, there are feathers. Without warning, the largest of them shrieks. Launching off the wall, they nearly blacken the sky as they fly toward us.

I raise my scythe up and then look over toward Cyrus. "Now is your time, my love. Unleash your full fury upon those winged beasts." I say with the most confidence I can infuse into my voice.

Cyrus glances at me for a mere second, then over to his father before assuming his reaper form. This is the first time I've seen him in his full reaper glory. Blackened tendrils extend from the robes he wears. He has a cloak hiding his wings. The scythe in his hand is large and menacing, and it makes me smile. The polished edge gleams in the light down here, adding to the foreboding nature of the weapon itself. He rises high above us and swings his scythe in a circle over his head. At the last moment, in a forward arc, he unleashes a wave of black flames out toward the creatures heading toward us. Upon impact, they incinerate, falling to ash before us. Nothing but bones and smoke is left. He advances, staying just before us, making sure nothing else is coming toward us. Glancing over at Azrael, I see a proud fatherly smile gracing his lips as he watches his son annihilate the targets ahead of us. Each time a foe rises, a swing of Cyrus's scythe fells our opponents within seconds. Gage looks awestruck, watching our mate unleash his full potential.

We finally arrive at the wall, and Cyrus resumes his seat on top of his mount. He returns to his normal self and smiles, proud of what he's done. I give him a single nod before swinging my scythe forward, sending the Balor to destroy the wall in front of us. They lower their great horned heads and repeatedly ram the stones in front of us. Eventually, they break through, and the wall crumbles. It starts a chain reaction, and the length of the wall on this side of the city of Pride falls in a wave. Sandstone falls every which way, all because of the Balor's show of force.

I jump down off my horse and pat it on its flank, sending it to run back to wherever it will go to be safe. Cyrus, Gage, and Azrael all mimic my action and then move to stand alongside me. I climb up on top of the pile of rocks before us and look out over my army. "Kill anything that gets in your way. Leave nothing alive. Cleanse this ring of all life that may turn against us," I enunciate each word, my voice reverberating like Metatron's.

I know the force I'm showing is almost unnecessary, but I need to set the precedent that they won't cross me, nor will they ignore me. We have a job to do here, and that's to cleanse the ring and restore balance to the world. When I drop my scythe, my armies take off with their orders clear. I know the demons and dark denizens I have summoned will more than meet the challenge ahead of them. With the utmost confidence, I stand for several minutes, watching my army go forth and do my dark bidding.

We wait several moments, listening to the destruction going on within the walls. Explosions, screams, and yelling seemed to echo in every direction. Only when I'm sure the area closest to where I'm standing is cleared do I proceed to walk through the hole in the wall and have my mates and father-in-law follow me. Once inside the walls of the city of Pride, I can feel the corruption blanketing my skin, making it want to crawl from the disgustingness in this place.

Even though my armor covers me, it feels is if a slime has embraced me. This is one of the most hideous feelings I've ever had in my life. And being a nurse, that says something.

We make our way further into the city, looking around and stepping over bodies as we head toward the center, remembering the map showed that's the location where Lucifer is holed up. Reaching out to Raphael, I use his eyes to look at the map on the table and study the positioning of Lucifer's chess piece. He's still within his castle, moving between the upstairs and downstairs, back and forth, and appearing to be quite anxious. At this point, I don't blame him. He's being hunted. Without warning, we're attacked from the right, but thankfully, Azrael was ready for it. He raises his hand, and black flames fly from his palm like a flamethrower. His fire smites the creature immediately, and what's left of it falls to the ground in a heap of bones and ash. I stare at the remnants for several seconds before moving to touch the wall of the castle before me.

I can feel Lucifer's fear. The life force of the castle almost rumbles with the power contained within it. But unfortunately, the person who wields the power is nervous. A volley of winged creatures breaches the walls of his castle. They dive, breathing fire down on us. Raising my scythe high, I create a dome to protect us. The creatures' fire bounces harmlessly off the dome and scorches the surrounding ground. The minute they regroup, Gage steps out and pulls a play from Cyrus's playbook. Raising his hands, he calls forth flames for the first time. The blackened mass whips out an uncontrolled lashing at its targets, destroying them instantly.

It takes Cyrus to help Gage get his flames under control and put them out. I'm guessing it was more of a gut reaction on Gage's part than an intentional action. "It's time to storm the castle, boys," I say to my mates and my father-in-law just as I touch the sandstone before me, melting it instantly. It falls away as if it's nothing more than sand before me. I create a hole wide enough that if I wanted to walk Rex through it, I could. Now is not the time for the dragon, nor is it the time for our familiars. It's better for them to remain safe at the moment. The thing I'm most concerned about is unleashing the beast within me. If the visions shown to me are correct, that will happen sooner rather than later.

Cyrus stares at me for several moments, and I know he and Gage can feel the battle waging within me. There is salvation for me if I don't shift, but if it's the only way I know both my mates are safe, then so be it. Walking through the hallowed halls, something feels off. There are no more attacks, and nothing jumps out at us. I don't want to say the "e" word, but it is definitely that—far too easy.

Rounding the corner, I stop dead in my tracks. A chimera stands in the middle of the hallway, its dragon-like tail swaying behind it. Tilting my head to the side, I stare at it, trying to study its body language. It's acting like a sentinel, blocking our forward progression. Raising my hand, everyone stops behind me, allowing me to move forward alone. The chimera's upper lip curls as a low growl rumbles from it. Its aggression awakens the beast inside me. A deep hiss escapes my lips as I bare my teeth at it. The chimera backs up two steps before turning to run.

I stare at it for several moments before turning to look back at everyone. "All clear." Making eye contact with my mates, I try to read their reactions. Gage is obviously concerned. Cyrus grins and shakes his head at me, nodding for me to move forward.

Turning around, I start back down the hallway, not noting anything out of the ordinary. Without warning, the doors in the hallway slam shut of their own volition. A grin crosses my lips as I assess the situation. This is all a scare tactic, and apparently we're heading in the right direction. Pushing forward, we arrive at the end of the hallway. We have two choices: go left or go right. Sending some of my forces to the left, I take my mates and father-in-law with me to the right.

At the end of the hallway, we come to what looks like a throne room. Stepping into the room, the lantern's light all at once.

"The castle recognizes its queen," a silky voice echoes in the room. The deep tone, combined with the smoothness in the way the words were delivered, catches my attention.

"Really, now? It knows its queen?" Shaking my head, I step away from my mates, keeping a safe distance from them.

"Yes, really." He steps from the shadows, dressed in a three-piece suit, cut in all the right places.

"Doubtful . . . And that tone you just used doesn't work on me." Dropping my armor, I try to make him overconfident that he has the upper hand.

His eyes rake over my body, and it makes my skin crawl. His gaze lingers on my chest, then travels up to meet my eyes. "I believe you'd look beautiful in scarlet." With a snap of his fingers, I'm wrapped in a scarlet gown.

I hear Cyrus laughing behind me. Both he and Gage are saying it's not my color. Winking at Lucifer, I touch the material and my reaper gown manifests. As I smirk, my gown moves of its own volition. "Nice try, Luci. I can dress myself."

"Enough!" he roars, and the walls shake. Stones and mortar fall all around us.

Turning, I look at my mates to make sure they're safe. Then it happens. The cold press of steel against my throat and the warm trickle of blood down my chest. Gage is beside himself, grabbing Cyrus. Cyrus looks alarmed, and Azrael gives me a single nod. That one nod snaps me out of the shock I'm in.

"You're mine, Thana. Say good bye to your little friends before I kill them." Lucifer presses the blade further into my skin. I feel it split more. Then it happens, heavily armored scales rise up under the blade's edge. The beast is angry and awake.

"Run . . . Go now! Get out of the castle!" I scream at them as blood tears stream down my face. My eyes shift to serpentine slits as I stare at them. Cyrus and Azrael take the hint, dragging Gage with them out the door.

It's now or never . . . This place is about to burn . . .

CHAPTER 93

AZRAEL

The toughest thing I've had to do in all of my existence is leave my son's mate in the hands of the madman. It took Cyrus and me to drag Gage out of the castle. The look in Thana's eyes was conflicted. The blood tears scream pain and sorrow, but the rising scales and the serpentine slits tell me she's going to end this once in for all.

"We have to go get her!" Gage screams as he struggles against Cyrus and me.

"No, we can't. Didn't you see the scales? She's going to unleash her beast. Its gaze can turn you to stone." I get in Gage's face and hold his shoulders, shaking him lightly.

His eyes slide to Cyrus, then back over to me. He lowers his gaze as the fight drains out of him. "We shouldn't have left her . . ." His tone is defeated. Cyrus nods at me, and we release Gage.

"Gage, love. We have to trust Thana knows what's best right now." My son's impassioned speech gets through to his lover, and he nods.

"I get that. I still feel like shit leaving her, even though she wanted us to go," Gage says as his eyes turn to face the retreating forces we brought with us.

"We all have a role to play, son . . ." I say to Gage as I turn to watch Cyrus take over, leading the army we lead here. They encircle the castle, killing anything that escapes.

Several species of demons escape the castle and barely make it into the air before we slaughter them. A deep rumbling comes from the center of the castle, and we watch part of the wall fall. Gage and Cyrus's wings unfurl in reaction to the cave-in. Part of me wants to rush back into the castle to find Thana myself. But I also know how deadly that creature within her is.

"Dad, we need to get to her." Cyrus motions to the collapsed area.

"That creature that's in her . . . the one she's reluctant to use . . . can obliterate this entire realm. You joke about the tactical nuke she is. Your joke isn't far from reality." As the words leave my lips, another section of the castle falls.

Dual screeches fill the air as a red-scaled tail whips up into the air. "What the fuck was that?" Cyrus stares at the building and at the whipping tail that's sticking up out of the rubble.

"When Lucifer took control of this realm, he gained a creature just like Thana did. He gained something similar to a red dragon. It's literally a flying flamethrower. I believe that's what Thana is battling against as we speak." I'm not saying anything negative against what Thana is capable of, just warning them about what she's facing.

They glance back and forth between the castle and me just as a cone of flames erupts from the center. The boys and I jump back several feet and keep a wary eye on the structure. A deep rattle sounds, and my eyes widen. I've heard that sound once before when Thana was napping in her chair. That's the sound of her beast moving through the castle.

The dragon bursts free of the castle's rubble, taking to the sky. Lucifer is trying to escape. Just before Cyrus can give the order for the Balor to attack, the Basilisk launches straight up out of the castle to catch him by the tail. The Basilisk drags him back within the castle walls.

Just when Lucifer thinks he has the upper hand, I send my mates and father-in-law out of the castle. "You can make this easy on yourself, beautiful," Lucifer says next to my ear.

As soon as I sense my mates are out of the building, I laugh. "I just made it easier on myself. The people I love are safe." As soon as the words leave my lips, Lucifer applies pressure on the blade and drags it across my throat.

I met his blade with the scales of my Basilisk. Pretending to crumple to the floor, I fall forward and land on my hands and knees. Lucifer makes a tsk-tsk sound as he kneels next to me. "You could have been my queen. It's sad the Destroyer was killed so easily. Your grandfather had the right idea—keep his head down and ignore me."

Lucifer mentioning my grandfather sets my scales on edge. The beast inside me awakens and calls for his blood. For once, I won't fight him about wanting to escape. I'll welcome him into this plane of existence with open arms. Laughing, I sit back and smile, looking at Lucifer, much to his dismay. "Time to pay the piper, Luci . . . Your time is up." Abject terror crosses his features as he stares at me, backing up quickly.

Deep within me, I feel the beast grin its toothy smile. Bone plates move in my face as I feel my body change for the first time. The burning pull and breaking of bones and tendons. *"Relax . . . Let me out . . ."* the voice in my head says. I feel my body stretching and the look of horror on Lucifer's face tells me he wasn't expecting this.

Rising up high above him, my beast roars, stretching its jaw wide open. It feels strange, like an out-of-body experience. I'm looking down on Lucifer with eyes that aren't my own. I'm not in the driver's seat. The beast is attacking and striking at him and playing with its food.

I hear its voice as if it's speaking to me. *"We are one. Accept me . . ."*

it says again, and then, I think I know what the problem is. The Basilisk is another side of me, not a separate entity, like I've been treating it.

The minute I decide to accept the Basilisk side of me, it's like there's a whoosh inside my head. And boom, I'm in the driver's seat. Just as I gain full control, Lucifer shifts as well. A red dragon, breathing fire, is left in his wake. He turns his flamethrower on me, but my scales resist the flames. The scaled ridge above his eyes arches up in what I suppose is shock. His wings spread wide, and he tries to escape through the hole in the roof. I guess he forgot just how big my serpent is. Coiling up, I launch up and bite onto his dragon's tail and drag him back into the castle.

Quickly, I launch up again and go for his throat, biting the dragon just under his head. Moving as fast as I can, my body coils around his dragon's body. His claws try to gain purchase on my scales, but to no avail. With every move he makes, I adjust my coils around his body, constricting tighter. *"We can poison him. Or turn him to stone,"* my beast tells me, teaching me more about this new form.

Both options sound wonderful, to be perfectly honest. My beast teaches me how to inject poison into Lucifer. The only thoughts crossing my mind are how much he hurt me and my grandfather. How he stole my daughter and my time spent with both my children away from me. The more rage I feel burning in my veins, the more venom I pump into him.

The nictating membrane over my eyes lifts slowly as Lucifer stops struggling in my coils. I look around and notice my mates and my father-in-law are in what remains of the throne room with me. When the last beats of Lucifer's heart sound, I lower his shifting body to the ground. Tilting my head to the side, I watch the dragon melt away to reveal the man he once was. Black wings are spread out beneath him, and the most peaceful smile graces his face.

I nudge his body several times with my maw, making sure that he's dead. Part of me cannot believe the horror that is Lucifer is over and gone. The other part of me is slightly sad that this once revered angel had to be put down because of insanity. Movement catches my attention on the other side of the throne room, and I whip my head around to face the challenge head-on. Several demons have entered, and they're armed and ready for battle. Without hesitating, I lower my head, and my eyes shift. Within seconds, the demons are nothing more than statues in the throne room.

I hear an audible gasp. Blinking quickly, I turn my head to see Gage standing there in shock. Laying my head down before him, I allow him to study my new form. His hand ghosts over my sandpaper-like armored scales. He points things out to Cyrus and Azrael concerning my new Basilisk form.

Eventually, my form melts away back to my normal human body. Breathing in a sigh of relief, I look down at Lucifer. "I can't believe it's finally over." On an exhale, I almost sigh again, looking down at the man who was the thorn in my side for the past year.

"It's been a long time coming, daughter. You understand you can never enter the gates of the Silver City, right?" Azrael looks almost sad to me.

"It's okay, Dad. And when Nikita is ready to take your place, I'll help you ascend if you wish it." I lower my voice as I step closer to him and place my hand on his cheek.

His blackened orbs flicker back to their human, warm chocolate-brown color. "I greatly appreciate the offer, daughter. Perhaps I may take you up on it after Nikita takes my place." Azrael leans forward and kisses my forehead, hugging me tightly to him.

We eventually break away, and my mates shove their way over to me to check me out from nose to toe. Once they're satisfied I'm in one piece, they back up and smile at me. "So what's next?" Cyrus asks curiously, looking down at Lucifer's body.

"Well, I need to decapitate him. Extinguish his light and destroy his soul, then we can head home." Smiling, I look between each mate and Azrael, shrugging.

Gage is slightly thrown off by what I've said. Cyrus is already looking at the blade of his scythe. Azrael really isn't shaken one way or the other about chopping off Lucifer's head. Extending my arm out, my scythe manifests in my hand. With a quick flick of my wrist, the blade swings around, then comes down, severing Lucifer's head in a second. Reaching down, I grip his hair and lift his head off the ground.

Staring into his eyes for a moment, I study the whites of his eyes before looking down at his body. Using the edge of the scythe, I ignite his body, turning it to ash. The orb of power drifting free of his corpse is lackluster at best. Reaching out, I take hold of the orb, then shove it into Cyrus's chest. The oof sound escapes his lips as he steps back, rubbing his chest.

"Seriously, kitten?" He rubs his sternum, looking at me.

Shrugging, I laugh, looking at the shocked look on his face. "What? I gave you a boost. Consider it an upgrade," I practically sing as I look at him and the now-laughing Gage.

Raising my scythe again, I spin it in front of me, opening a portal back to my fortress. "Let's go. I want to make it back to my children as quickly as possible." I look at Azrael, and he nods and steps into the portal first. My mates follow him, and I step through last. I close the portal the minute my boots hit the tile floor of my fortress.

"Dad, I'm leaving you as captain of the ship, so to speak." Smiling, I bow slightly to him out of respect.

"I'm honored, daughter. Let me know when you return to the Human Realm so I can visit my grandchildren." Azrael winks at me, and I can't help but nod at him.

Stepping a good distance away, I open a portal to the Angelic Realm to end up near the Tree of Life. Once in the Angelic Realm, I take flight, heading toward the house on the edge of the realm, just outside the gates to the Silver City. My heart breaks, thinking I cannot rush in there to hug my daughters and my mates. Instead, I'm sentenced to waiting on the outside, looking in on all I gave up.

CHAPTER 94

THANA

I honestly didn't think it would be this hard, standing on the outside, looking in. Watching all the high-ranking angels flying around on the other side of the wall makes my chest hurt. My daughters and my mates are there, safe within the walls, and I'm stuck here, waiting for them.

"Mommy!" Nikita's voice rings out.

Running on instinct alone, I turn and fly toward the gates. I slam into something hard and invisible that knocks me back several feet. Pain throbs through my shoulder and neck from hitting the barrier. Shaking my head, I realize my folly. I can never pass through the gates to the Silver City.

Nikita plows into me, and we're a mess of arms and wings as I encase my daughter in mine to protect her. Nikita breaks out into a giggle fit when we finally come to a complete stop. "I missed you, Mommy," Nikita says, perched on my rib cage, looking down on me.

She looks like an angel with her sun-kissed skin framed by snow-white hair. Her smile is the most radiant thing, rivaling the sun. "I missed you too, baby girl." Sitting up, I draw my daughter into a hug and kiss her cheek.

Nikita is now about the size of a seven- to eight-year-old child. We snuggle close and hold on to each other tightly. "Do you have to leave again?" Hearing those words brings tears to my eyes. Damn Lucifer for stealing time away. My poor baby only knows of her Mommy leaving. Blood tears threaten to break as I draw in a shuddering breath.

Looking up, I see Davina clinging to her father's leg, and I motion for her to join Nikita and me in our huddle. As I adjust the way I'm sitting, Davina sits with us, and I hug and kiss her too. "Mommy isn't leaving anymore. My work is done now, and I can finally rest." The words fall softly from my lips as I kiss both of my daughters' temples.

"Do you mean it?" Davina asks as she places her hands on my cheeks, making me face her. Nodding in response, she squeals, then puts me into a headlock, hugging me around my neck.

Laughing hysterically, Nikita joins in on trying to strangle me to death in a loving hug. "Kids? Can I get to see your mother?" Looking up, I see Christian for the first time in what feels like forever. My daughters get off my lap as if it was on fire to let me up.

Using my wings, I launch up and into Christian's arms and kiss him hard, wrapping him up in my wings and holding onto him as if he'll disappear on me. I know I'm being dramatic, but it feels like it's been forever since I've last held him in my arms. "Welcome home," he says reverently against my lips, barely breaking the kiss for more than a second at a time to allow us to breathe.

Someone clears their throat behind me, and my instinct is to react and protect Christian. My armor flows over my body without touching my pendant. As I spin, I notice it's Metatron and his twin, Sandalphon. "Congratulations on your success," he says, and I instantly calm, embarrassed by my reaction to the noise behind me. I've become rather jumpy in the past few months.

Breaking away from Christian, I walk over to Cyrus and retrieve the bag holding Lucifer's head from him. "Proof that it's truly over." I offer Sandalphon the bag, and he waves a hand, stopping me.

"No need, Thana. We felt the change in the universe the minute his flame was extinguished." A gentle smile graces his lips as my eyes drop to the bag in my hand.

A slight flex of my hand and the bag ignites, turning to ash in a matter of seconds. "From the Earth we came, to the Earth we return," I say as his ashes fall through the clouds.

"No truer words have ever been spoken," Sandalphon says and extends a hand out to me. "I owe you a debt of gratitude. You kept my brother and your family safe, making the most logical and the toughest decision for the greater good." His eyes lower as he looks at his hand.

Reaching out, I take his forearm and grip it firmly as we shake. I feel a wave of energy wash over me like a nice soft blanket. At this moment, I feel he'll be part of one of my daughters' nests. Double-blinking, I know my eye color has changed by how my vision has changed. Right now, I know my eye color is now pure chrome. Staring at Sandalphon, I can see his energy flow, and his wisps reaching towards my daughter Davina.

A slow smile creeps across my lips as I stare at the wisp reaching for her. Releasing his arm, I walk forward and extend a hand slowly to gently touch the fragile tendril. The smoke wisp reaches up and curls around my finger, extending back toward my daughter. It amazes me, watching how these fragile bonds form long before they're even slated for the Mate Trials to take place. The whole thing itself, the process, amazes me.

If you would have asked me fifty years ago what my thoughts were on the Mate Trials, and that everybody had someone, I'd have told you I thought it was all bullshit. But now that I've witnessed the tendrils twice with my own children, and once with my good friend, I take it as a true and honest event. I'm not sure what makes the higher powers determine who is placed with who. But in this case, I could not ask for a better, more honorable man than Sandalphon to be my daughter's mate.

The only one that I'd argue who might have a better mate is my daughter Nikita. I now know of two of her mates long before they even slated for the Mate Trials to take place for her. According to the rules set forth long before my birth, the female must be alive for a minimum of twenty-two years before she's able to attend her first Mate Trials. But that usually applies to the Nephilim. My daughters are more divine than those the rules were created for. I'll train them to not take any crap from anyone and make sure their Aunt Sigrun keeps up on their training. They need to be in top form and able to protect themselves in case they end up with one rotten mate. I will not have done to my daughters what was done to my best friend. Somehow, someway, she ended up with four bad mates who Cyrus and I had to put down.

Everything happens for a reason, and as I turn back to look in Sandalphon's eyes, I can see he realizes I know something beyond his knowledge. My other mates are also staring at me, trying to parse out exactly what I do and don't know. All I know is that the future is looking brighter, happier, and safer for both my little girls.

I can't help but smile broadly and then move to pull both my daughters against me and kiss them on the tops of their heads. As much as I wish to spend tonight with Christian and be wrapped up in his arms in the throes of passion, I know as a male who has a son, he'll understand my need to be with my children over him.

Michael steps forward and ushers us back toward his villa. Once inside, the girls head off to their room to play for the evening. The other adults and I sit around the table, trying to decompress from what feels like forever since we were all able to sit together peacefully. Looking up from the table, I see the chair my grandfather would sit in, and it makes me sad. I feel the pain of his loss far more than I felt when my mother died at the hands of my father and when my father died at my hands. Neither genetic donor meant half as much to me as my grandfather did. He accepted me for me and didn't expect me to change just to suit what everyone else thought I should be.

The guys carry on with their conversations, each one relaying their part of the mission in the rings back to the other Archangels who couldn't follow us. I laugh at the stance Cyrus and Gage take as they merely shake their heads, listening to the Archangels boast about what they did.

"Now, for guys who are supposedly so holy," Cyrus says as he grins, getting that sly look to him. "You all are quite prideful when it comes to your 'accomplishments.'" He makes air quotes around the word "accomplishments."

The Dark Nephilim side of my family and my father-in-law knew that Gage, Cyrus, and I did all the heavy lifting. Michael, Gabriel, Raziel, and Uriel all glance at each other quickly, trying to discern if they crossed the prideful line. Shaking my head and laughing, I raise a hand, silencing the room. "You guys are all good. Quit worrying. You're fine," I say, trying to settle everyone down as quickly as possible. "I have known angels to burn for less and sent to Hell for much worse."

It takes the guys several seconds before Michael forces himself to laugh and smile, looking down at me. Bringing two fingers to his forehead, he tips his fingers toward me, showing his gratitude. "Well, you'd be the expert on who should be burning," he says, and I can't help but laugh more before having a sip of my wine.

"Very true, boys. Nobody is burning on my watch tonight, so just behave yourselves." I smile and wave to them, setting their minds at ease.

We sit down to a nice quiet dinner and steer our conversation away from the war that was waged in Hell. It's nice to catch up with everyone and hear from Christian, Raphael, and Metatron what my daughters have been up to. Michael absolutely beams every time he mentions what Nikita's been doing. I can tell the old boy is quite smitten with her. This is his own personal purgatory, waiting for her to come of age. At this point in her life, she appears to be the size of a seven- to eight-year-old child. But chronologically, she's barely a year old. This whole being mostly divine, be it fallen or ethereal, is bullshit. Not only does the child grow and mature rapidly, they gain some of the knowledge from the parents who created them. That, in itself, is a wondrous thing. For the child, it's intelligence that far exceeds the physical appearance of its age. The child is full-grown at approximately two years of age and has most of the knowledge of, say, whichever father helped create her and me.

Listening to the boys talk about what they missed, I get lost in my own thoughts. I look forward to the next couple of years and watching my daughters grow. I don't know what the next ten, fifteen, twenty years, or the next millennium will bring, but one thing that I do know is having the best place possible for me and my children is of the utmost importance. Tomorrow, we'll return to our house on the hill and begin our life how it should have been almost a year ago.

It'll be nice for a while, not having to look over my shoulder, waiting for someone or something to try to harm me. But in a sense, I'll kind of miss the old days where Cyrus would come to my job to steal my cookies and coffee. Raphael will feign upset just to be able to dote on me in public. But if I look at it from the bigger picture, it's much nicer now that we don't have to hide our feelings for each other.

Sadly for myself, I won't be returning to work full-time. I might go in one or two nights a week and work a real shift. But other than that, I'll be on call, just like Cyrus is, to come over and take care of those who are ready to pass on. This will soon become my new norm as I think about counting down the months until I can try to have another set of babies with one or two of my other mates. Slowly, I glance down the table, looking at each of the boys in turn. I can't help but smile to myself. I'm finally happy, full of love and joy in my life. I always wanted a big family, and now's my chance to finally make my own dreams come true.

CHAPTER 95
EPILOGUE

Raphael - 10 years later

Raphael - 10 years later

Ten years and eight children later, my heart is full of love and happiness. Thana is back to doing what she loves most, working now in labor and delivery. Cyrus took up the job as security in the hospital to stay close to Thana.

I never in my life would have suspected he'd turn into a supportive and protective mate. I thought he was going to, as the kids say, yeet himself out of the picture to avoid the responsibility. All it took was for Nikita and Damien to be born, and boom, switch-up. It was hysterical, however, when his son was born without wings. He screamed expletives for several minutes in disbelief. When his son finally revealed his wings—they were light-gray with black over the wing bones—he passed out. Poor Cyrus . . . It took him several days to come to terms with the wing color.

Christian's reaction to being a dad was hysterical. He called his first-born son, Ben, to come meet his siblings each time. Christian's first baby was a daughter, and you'd think Thana hung the moon and stars for him. Around three months old, Thana got her to expose her wings. Wouldn't you know it? They were mostly white, with black veins and black primary feathers. Thana was honestly jealous of Selene's feathers.

Christian's son was born with his wings out, much to his dismay. Thana giggled, looking at the boy and naming him Samuel. It was an obvious nod to her grandfather, but not completely.

Metatron's daughter took us all by surprise and looked almost exactly like Nikita, with black wings and snow-white hair. Thana's best friend, Aurora, was present for that birth and offered the name of her twin, Seraphina, who died before birth. The two of them hugged it out in a big crying mess, and the name stuck. Metatron's son, that boy, was huge when he was born. He was the largest baby Thana had to date. Over twenty-two inches long and just shy of ten pounds. Thankfully, he was the only baby in that pregnancy. Trust me when I say Thana had Metatron jumping through hoops with how uncomfortable his son was making her. She ended up naming his son Gunnar, meaning warrior. Metatron was so honored by the name, tears threatened to break from his eyes.

Gage was anxious the entire time his and my babies were being carried. He was so wound up over it, he had a workshop built on the property. While I was at work, he had Thana in a recliner in the workshop with him. Cyrus and I had to talk him down off the literal edge of the roof of the house on more than one occasion through the pregnancy. When his daughter was born, he was mute all over again. The man didn't say a word until Thana asked him what to name his daughter. The most serene look crossed his face as his eyes blackened. Arielle was the name he chose for his wingless daughter. My son was also born without wings and, with Thana's permission, I named him Samael after her grandfather.

Having Gage's second baby took a while and trust that it was no significant burden for them to keep trying. On Thana's birthday of all days, she realized she was finally pregnant. Gage threw a party to end all parties to celebrate the impending birth of his child. I swear, this last pregnancy flew by like it was just yesterday. Shockingly enough, it was Davina who helped deliver her baby sister. Since it was just family, she unfurled her wings and spread them wide after the delivery. Her voice reverberated throughout the house, and I felt the impact of her voice all the way at the hospital. Davina announced the name of the baby was Freya. From what Thana told me, Davina imbued her name with power and kissed her forehead, blessing her. Thana and Gage didn't question it, nor did they argue with the baby's name.

Knocking on the door drags me out of my memories. Looking up, Nikita stands in the doorway with her brother Damien. "What brings you two in tonight? You don't start working till tomorrow."

Rolling her eyes, Nikita strolls into my office and sits on the arm of the chair. "Well, Da . . . Director. I was informed that tonight was going to be extra busy and my big boss needed assistance." Rolling her eyes, she quickly signals that Thana requested their help for something happening tonight.

I stare at Nikita for several moments too long, and Thana manifests in my office behind me. "Come with me." Thana reaches out and touches both children's clothing, transforming them into scrubs with medical ID badges. She glances back at me briefly, and her eyes blacken. Before I know it, all three of them vanish before my eyes. After their sudden departure, I'm reaching out with my senses to figure out what I'm missing.

Azrael and Cyrus walk in shortly after, looking around my office. "I felt a disturbance in the force," Cyrus says with a knowing half-smile.

"What do you two know that I don't?" My tone is clipped, just barely showing the level of agitation I'm feeling at the moment.

"It's not a question of what we know," Azrael says as he glances at his son briefly.

"Can we not talk in riddles? I swear, you two will be the death of me." Running my hand down my face, I attempt to calm myself.

"Like Dad said, it's not what we know, it's what Thana senses," Cyrus says as he looks between me and the hallway behind him.

The hospital dispatcher calls a code green, and the lights flash on the level my office is on. "Crap . . ." Looking around quickly, I do the only thing I can think of doing. I summon Davina, Selene, and Arielle to the hospital to assist.

Within a matter of moments, only Davina arrives in my office, and I look at her, puzzled. "Where are your sisters?"

Shaking her head, she changes her clothing to scrubs. "Mom sent them to the accident scene as EMTs to try to save as many lives as possible. She also called for Gunnar and Samael to help." Tilting her head to the side for a moment, she looks back to Cyrus and then Azrael before looking back at me again. "Freya, Seraphina, and Samuel are second-string to help Mom and Nikita if they get tired. I doubt it'll happen, but they're ready and waiting," Davina states like its gospel. Of all the children born to us, she's the closest to being an Archangel.

"Okay then, I guess we should all take our places in the hospital." My mate, my eternal love, in a matter of ten years, took over my job of director without the title. She's basically taken over everything involving the hospital. With whatever extra senses she's developed as the Destroyer, she knows hours before major events happen. She doesn't know the where, but she knows the when just moments before it happens. In one sense, it's a blessing and a curse.

Leaving my office in a hurry, I make it down to the emergency department to a mass of chaos. Thana is standing there, taking the role of charge nurse, directing every action that happens. Humans and angels respond to her power in the same way. The angels obey because of who she is. The humans respond because of the aura of authority radiating off her. I watch our children running around, doing what they can to help the victims of the accident.

Thana catches me staring and, placing Davina in charge of directing the action, walks over to me. "This was no accident."

Thana's voice is borderline feral as I see her pupils flicker into serpentine slits.

"What do you mean?" Glancing around quickly, I drag her into the charge nurse's office and close the door.

"One of the first survivors said they saw a mass of shadows before the bus flipped." Her eyes blacken immediately, as if she's searching the shadows for something.

Raising both eyebrows, I double-blink, trying to fathom what she's just told me. "Something's shifted?" I'm not sure what creatures exist in the Shadow Realm or in the Rings.

Shaking her head, her eyes return to human gray, and she draws in a deep breath. "I'm going to send Nikita and Damien to search the Shadow Realm for any disturbances. Davina is going to go see Sandalphon and seek his counsel."

Looking back out the window of the office door, I watch my daughter acting like a general in a war zone. Turning back to Thana slowly. "Are you sure that's wise? We know what he is to her." Biting my bottom lip, I'm hoping she has a plan for this.

"That's exactly the reason I'm sending her. A mate cannot deny their mate anything. If she seeks answers from him that he'd be hesitant to answer for me, he'll tell her because it pleases her." A quick raise of her eyebrows and a tilt of her head have me reeling. She's using the fragile connection between them to get the answers being hidden from her.

"That's three shades of wrong, Thana," I state, trying not to smile. It's absolutely brilliant on her part. But on the angelic side of it all, using the bond to serve one's own purpose isn't right.

"I know. But if it saves lives . . . Isn't it worth skirting the edge of being proper? I mean, the Mate Trials are this summer, and I know I said I'd make them wait till they were older." Biting her bottom lip, she moves to look out the office window.

"They're ready . . . Sigrun helped shape them into the powerful warriors they are. To top it off, they're wise beyond their years. Being more divine sped everything up." She rests her hand against the glass.

"If you feel they're ready, I'll have Uriel add Davina and Nikita to the list for this summer." Laughing, I lean my back against the wall near Thana, looking at her. "You know Nikita is going to be pissed."

A sadistic grin crosses her blood-red lips. It's borderline feral the way she looks at me. "I know. She also needs to take the mantle of Death sooner rather than later. I need Azrael to take the rank of Duke of Hell and rule from my castle as my proxy." Pushing off the door, she prowls the office.

"Something is coming, and I'm not sure what it is. Davina will ascend and take the rank of Speaker for the divine, taking Metatron's place. Nikita will become Death eternal." As if summoning the big guy, Metatron arrives in the office.

"Davina is ascending and taking my place?" His blue eyes bore into her, searching for answers.

"Yes. One above, one below. That's how we'll maintain balance. It all makes sense to me now. It's why Nikita and Davina were born together." She glances out the window, then back at us again.

"Look at the big picture. Nikita was born with white-blonde hair and black wings. Davina was born with black hair and white wings. All my other children were born with a blending of colors, except Seraphina, who looks somewhat like Nikita." Everything happens for a reason.

I'll be damned, Thana is right. Metatron and I look at each other, and it's shocking we never saw it before Thana pointed it out. "We'll alert the others in the nest, and Metatron and I will talk with the other Archangels about your revelation." Before I ask Metatron to go, he's already left.

"Back to work, Raphael. Something big is brewing, and we have to be ready for it," Thana says as she opens the door, jumping back into the fray.

Not once in the thousands of years I've lived did I ever think something like this would be possible. A new evil is rising from the depths to do who knows what. The only thing we know is our children are old enough and strong enough to fight alongside us now. I know, for a fact, no matter how much I beg, Davina and Nikita will not sit on the sidelines, watching their mother fight to save the world again. To make matters worse, the Mate Trials are in less than three months, and my baby girl is going to be there. My chest hurts, thinking about it. I'm not ready, not by a long shot.

~Up next - The Daughters of the Destroyer - Expansion~
- Nikita
- Davina {Possible late 2022 / Early 2023}
- Seraphina {2023}

BONUS CONTENT
HAPPENS BEFORE KLAUS CHRISTMAS AND BEFORE DISCOVERED

My morning starts like any other morning: coffee, a shower, and then head out the door. I plan to walk to the bakery for a muffin and a snack before I head to the park to read. As I stroll towards the center of town, it gives me time to reflect on the past week's events.

I still don't know who is stealing my shit at work. Raphael is ridiculously handsome, and it's distracting when he's in my wing. Having drinks with Christian and his squad was a riot, especially because of the karaoke. He told me there are bars like that all over China and Japan. Apparently, it's a common after work activity to go bust out a song.

My phone buzzes, and I pull it out of my pocket to see who it is. Mark's sent me yet another meme about coffee and books. He likes to make fun of the reverse harem books I read, but he doesn't know why I enjoy them. Most Nephilim end up in a polyamorous relationship, so I figured I needed to do some research.

When I get to the bakery, I see Jayce rushing around and Klaus trying desperately to calm him. The bell rings and the scent of baked bread assaults my senses as I watch the two love birds fuss at one another. Jayce is talking to someone on the phone, his tone frantic. Klaus looks like he's going to pull his hair out strand by strand.

I have to help.

Striding over to Klaus, I take his hands and hold them, so he stops yanking at his hair. "What happened?"

His gaze is full of fear. "Aurora is in labor, and we're three hours away."

I flick my eyes over to Jayce, hating the tears that run down his cheeks. "Theres more than that happening. Tell me, maybe I can help?"

At my offer, he stops pacing. His eyes open wide when he remembers I'm a nurse, and he abruptly hangs up on the person he was speaking to. Facing me, he gives me a pleading look. "The baby is stuck."

His admission makes my chest constrict. Lycans frequently have difficulty with carrying babies to term and, even worse, issues giving birth. Aurora may not be a pureblood Lycan, but even a drop of their blood increases her chance of birthing issues. I weigh my options as I pace across the bakery floor. If I shadow walk to her, it means I have to embrace my darker nature. I've suppressed it for so long, but this is an emergency. "Where are they?"

"They are in Dominik's pack. It's an hour past my pack lands." Klaus sounds defeated, and his acceptance that either Aurora or the baby could die decides for me.

"Lock up. I will get us there as fast as possible. Take me to the darkest part of the store." My nerves get the better of me as I watch them get their business shut down. I feel jittery, but my best friend and her baby need me to be strong right now.

"Are you sure, Thana? We don't want you to get in trouble." Jayce bites his bottom lip, clearly worried about what Azrael will do to me.

Taking a deep breath, I nod. "Let's go before I chicken out." Klaus takes me to the storage room and turns out the lights. The shadows whisper, and I feel them seep into me. "What you see today cannot ever be shared with anyone else."

My friends nod their heads as I unfurl my wings. Flexing them several times, I extend my hands to draw them to me. I wrap my wings around us all to help lessen the effect of the shadows. Luckily, I went to Dominik's house for the Easter hunt this year, so I know where I'm going.

"Close your eyes and hold on tight. It will feel like the initial drop of a roller coaster." After warning the guys, I focus on my intended location. Sifting through the shadows is the quickest way to get anywhere without being seen.

In a matter of seconds, we manifest in a closet in Dominik's home. I open my wings to see Klaus stabilizing an unsteady Jayce. "We're here."

As the words leave my lips, they rip the door open and a furious Dimitri stands in front of us with his bear damn close to breaking free.

"Thana..." Dimitri growls. His bear settles when he sees Klaus and Jayce with me. "What have you done?"

Pushing my shoulders back, I stare up at the mountain of a man. "Aurora needs me, and I'm here. Consequences be damned." I allow my eyes to blacken as I stare up at him, unwillingly to budge on the topic.

Sighing, Dimitri grabs my hand and drags me through the hall-ways to the bedroom where Aurora is struggling. I watch her, my heart in my throat, and allow myself one moment of fear before I turn coldly clinical. "I need hot water, clean towels, and a coffee."

My last demand makes Alaric do a double take, but he and Arnulf take off to gather the supplies, regardless.

"How's my bitch doing?" I joke as I look at my best friend.

Aurora grunts and forces a grin. "Peachy keen, fluffy. How the fuck did you get here so fast?" A contraction hits her, and she lets out a long, low growl. Dominik is holding her hand as she crushes it, wincing from his place by her bed.

"You needed me; fuck the consequences. I shifted us through the shadows." I point to Jayce and Klaus with a grin.

Aurora relaxes a little once she sees her two wayward mates, giving me a nod. She screams again as another contraction hits her. Arnulf returns and offers me my coffee and Alaric has everything I asked for and sets it up on the side table. Chugging my coffee, I finish it quickly, then head into the bathroom and wash my hands before heading over to Aurora.

I pull back the sheets and look the situation over, assessing what I need to do next. "Let's move her to the edge of the bed so I can get this baby out."

This is going to be much tougher than I originally expected because I can see the baby's heels.

The guys jump into action and maneuver Aurora into place, chuckling as I joke with her about getting all up in her business. Turning to one of her mates, I point to the several areas of stretched skin. "Alaric, I need to you chill this area right here."

Alaric touches where I asked, numbing the skin so I can continue to get Aurora ready. I smile when Arnulf offers me sterile gloves, sliding them on with a snap. Once I'm prepared, I inch my fingers in along the legs of the baby.

My eyes shift to the chrome color of my powers, and I can see the life force of the baby. It gives me a faint outline of how it's positioned inside, so I know how to adjust. With gentle turns and twists, I get the baby lined up, and it progresses more easily. Reaching into the birth canal, I position the baby's arms, making minor adjustments with every contraction.

After a few agonizing moments, the baby slides free. Lifting it up, I clear the airway and we hear her first cries. Smiling with relief, I cut the cord before offering her to Aurora. I pass my hand over the child, using my healing light to make sure that she's completely healthy. "You have a beautiful daughter."

Dominik stares at his little girl in wonder, then looks up at me with a grateful smile. "I don't know what we would have done without you. Klaus's grandmother is at the castle of wolves. She won't be here for at least another hour, even if she flies."

When he describes what happened before I arrived, I realize with my intervention, the baby would not have made it. It makes the risky decision to come here seem worth it. I couldn't have lived with myself if my friend had lost her child because I wasn't brave enough to defy the edicts.

After Aurora passes the placenta, I heal the damage from childbirth, smiling as I watch her feed her new daughter. I wash my hands in the basin after I remove my gloves, whispering to my friend. "What are you going to name her?"

"I'm not sure. Do you have a suggestion?" Aurora kisses her daughter's cheek as she replies, not taking her eyes off the nursing infant.

I look at the babe in her arms, considering as I see how enamored Dominik is with her. "How about Isabella? You can call her Isi or Bella or Bells for short?"

"That's perfect. Isabella, you shall be, little one." Aurora burps her, grinning broadly before offering her to me.

Cradling the baby in my arms, I unfurl my wings and rock her. Kissing her temple, I whisper her name to imbue it with power. Either at birth or later, I bless each every child I help bring into this world. "You're going to do great things, little one."

I flex my wings once more before putting them away. Aurora's house is one of the few places I can expose my wings without breaking angelic law. With these males already mated, I am not breaking protocol at all. I will miss that freedom when I leave. "I should get going."

Greeting Aurora's other children as they come running in, I walk around the room to give my friends their hug good-bye. I watch the large family with a pang of jealousy—I don't know when or if I'll ever have something like this myself. Once I've said farewell to everyone, I head back towards the hall closet I manifested in when we arrived.

"Thana, wait!" Dominik shouts over the pounding of his boots behind me.

I stop with my hand on the doorknob, spinning to face him. His tone has me prepared to rush back into the room where my friend is. "Did something happen to the baby? Am I still needed?"

He laughs as he holds his hands up in supplication. "They're fine. I didn't mean to scare you."

It takes a moment to catch my breath—fear had almost closed my windpipe. Tilting my head to the side, I study him, wondering why he came rushing out.

"I want to give you a gift. I appreciate all you do for our family." His fist is closed around something small, and he's looking at me with an earnest expression.

"You don't have to give me anything; you guys are like family to me." I step towards the closet, but something tells me he won't let this go.

"I get that, but I wouldn't feel right. Take this as my token of my gratitude." Dominik places something small and warm in my hand. When I open it, tears well up in my eyes. The key to the red SRT Hellcat sits in my hand.

"Dom, you can't be serious! This is your baby! It's your favorite possession." I offer him the key back, unable to fathom such a generous present.

Aurora wobbles over, wrapping her hands around mine. "She's yours. I've been wanting to give her to you for a long time, Thana."

I lunge forward and hug them both, unable to find the words to express how I feel. This is the kindest thing anyone has ever done for me. I've delivered a majority of their children, but I didn't expect anything in return, much less something so valuable.

"Come on. Let's go introduce you to your new ride," Dominik says as he takes my hand. He leads me down the hall, not commenting on my stunned silence.

Just outside the front door is Aurora's lifted black diesel—nick-named Black Beauty aka the Beast. The sleek jet black SRT Challenger—aka the Harlot—is right next to it. They named the Challenger after the song "The Beast and the Harlot" from A7X, which is one of Aurora's favorite bands. Approaching it reverently, I run my fingers over the curves of the car.

Dominik watches me with a big grin. "I can tell you're gonna love her like I do." He steps over and opens the driver's door to show me a perfect interior I couldn't see because of the blacked-out windows.

Sliding into the driver's seat, I press the brake and clutch pedals and the roar of the engine makes my heart race. The rumbling purr rattles my very soul and I can't help the manic smile that crosses my lips. Wiggling the shifter left to right, I look up at Dominik. "Anytime you're in the area, please come visit your car. I know she'll miss you."

He nods, laughing as he shows me the spare fob in his hand. "I intend to. Thank you again for all of your help, Thana. I don't know what we would do without you."

Turning to face him, I beam. "I love you guys. If you need me, I'll always be there." My word is my bond, and Dominik knows I'm serious.

"Enjoy the rest of your day off. I'm sure Aurora will video call you later."

Saying goodbye is never easy, but I know I have friends for life in Aurora and her mates.

I flip through the channels until I find the Black Veil Bride's 'Fallen Angels'. It's the anthem of my life, and I sigh in happiness.

Dominik closes the driver's door as I drop into first gear. Mashing down on the pedal, I launch onto the road.

The roar of the engine rivals my loud singing. The song I love so much is about not being accepted for who you are, and it feels like they wrote it for me. All four of the band members are Dark Nephilim, so they know how I feel.

According to GPS, I have an almost four-hour drive back to reality. Grinning, I look at the screen, accepting the challenge—I'll beat that time in minutes to spare.

ALSO BY SERENITY RAYNE

The Aurora Marelup Saga the complete series (RH)

Klaus Christmas (RH + extended family)

Tiamat - My Bloody Valentine (Aurora and Tia go on an adventure)

Hybrid Royals (Ménage)

Elemental Mates Steamy wolf fated mate romance (RH)

Children of the Moon - New Moon (RH Dual Harems)

Blood Moon Pack - Omegaverse (RH Novella)

Daughters of the Destroyer - Nikita (RH)

Once upon a Raven - MF Horror

Heart Shaped Box (An Edgar Allan Poe Retelling)